W9-AUR-423

KIMBERLY PAULEY

CaT GiRL'S
DaY OFF

Tu Books
an imprint of Lee & Low Books, Inc.
New York

To cat lovers everywhere
(especially the ones who have always wondered
what little Fluffy was *really* thinking)

♥

Copyright © 2012 by Kimberly Pauley
All rights reserved. No part of this book may be reproduced,
transmitted, or stored in an information retrieval system in any form or by any
means, electronic, mechanical, photocopying, recording, or otherwise, without
written permission from the publisher.
TU BOOKS, an imprint of LEE & LOW BOOKS Inc.,
95 Madison Avenue, New York, NY 10016
www.leeandlow.com
Manufactured in the United States of America by
Worzalla Publishing Company, April 2012
Book design by Einav Aviram
Book production by The Kids at Our House
The text is set in Cochin

10 9 8 7 6 5 4 3 2 1
First Edition

Library of Congress Cataloging-in-Publication Data
Pauley, Kimberly, 1973-
Cat Girl's day off / Kimberly Pauley. — 1st ed. p. cm.
Summary: High schooler Natalie Ng has always kept secret her talent for talking
with cats, but when she learns--from a cat—that a celebrity has been replaced by an
imposter, she and her friends investigate, becoming movie extras to get the scoop.
ISBN 978-1-60060-883-4 (hardcover : alk. paper) —
ISBN 978-1-60060-884-1 (e-book)
[1. Human-animal communication--Fiction. 2. Cats — Fiction. 3. Motion
pictures — Production and direction — Fiction. 4. High schools — Fiction. 5.
Schools — Fiction. 6. Family life — Illinois — Chicago — Fiction. 7. Chicago
(Ill.) — Fiction. 8. Mystery and detective stories.] I. Title.
PZ7.P278385Cat 2012
[Fic]--dc23
2011042997

EASTON WEST'S BLOG

Wednesday, September 2, 6:02 A.M.: La, la! You read that right, little poppets! Six frickin' o'clock in the morning! What, you ask, could you possibly be doing up at such a god-awful hour, O Easton love?

There's only one thing that could get me up this early, poppets! And, no, that's not it! Get your minds out of the gutter! I am headed to LAX to wing my way out to the Windy City (that's Chicago, little ones . . . really, you should get out more) to watch a movie being born!

And not just any movie, but THE movie. Or, THE movie of next year (these things take time—think an elephant's gestation cycle, 'kay?) . . . *Freddy's Day Off*! Starring the one and only Ty McKenzie and good-girl-turned-diva Victoria Welling! (Is she really going to be the next big Hollywood starlet to melt down? I'll tell you here first!)

This promises to be a fun movie, since it's a takeoff on one of my personal faves, the classic teen movie *Ferris Bueller's Day*

Off, which was written and directed by the amazing John Hughes! Total homage to the great man, may he rest in peace. Ty's character is a loser nerd (ha, that'll be a stretch for him to pull off! Hey, makeup lady!) who decides to spice up his life by re-creating a day in the life of ultimate slacker Ferris Bueller.

I'm sure you'd like to know how I got an all-access pass to the set, but a girl's got to have her secrets. More soon! ♥

ONE

SUNDAY, SEPTEMBER 6, 5:46 P.M.

"Never listen to a cat."
—Natalie Ng

I opened the front door to my house and gagged. The smell of something burnt beyond recognition enveloped me like a toxic cloud. Meep, my cat, was sitting by the door as if she had been waiting on me, which she probably had, since no one else paid any attention to her.

Someday, she yowled, *your mom is going to burn the entire house down.* Like I could do anything about it. Then she took off down the hall toward my room without bothering to see if I was going to reply. That's a cat for you—sometimes they just need to complain.

Though Meep had a point. My mom may be one of the ten smartest and Talented people on the planet, but she can't cook. At all. Actually, she can't do anything remotely domestic. I've been washing my own clothes since the time she turned my entire wardrobe pink back in the seventh grade.

I held my nose and went inside, almost running right into

3

my older sister, Viv, as she carried out a charred, smoking pot full of something vile and vaguely orange. Our would-be dinner, I supposed. Mom had been ambitious today.

"I've got it, Mom! Why don't you go work on your research paper? I'll take care of this," Viv yelled over her shoulder toward the kitchen. "Hey, Natalie." She nodded at me. "I didn't make it home in time to stop her. Can you boil some water for noodles? I'm going to throw away the risotto. And the pot."

"Is that what that was?" I tried to avoid looking at the wreckage—it would only make me lose my appetite.

"Yeah. Pumpkin risotto. She didn't stir it. Or cut up the pumpkin."

I let Viv by and went into the kitchen to start a pot of water. Mom had already disappeared into her office. The only days we ever ate a decent meal were when Viv came home from Northwestern and did the cooking. Sunday was supposed to be her day, but Mom often seemed to inconveniently forget and start her own disaster, fueled by weekend ambition or a badly timed cooking show.

Dad was almost as bad a cook as Mom, but at least he had the sense to order out when it was his turn. Mom didn't believe that there was anything she couldn't do and she ignored all failures—at least, her own. Hence the pumpkin risotto. If there were any way to cancel only the Food Network, we could probably save ourselves a fortune in spoiled cookware.

Emmy, my younger sister, came in and opened the window and the back door to air out the house. "It doesn't take a genius, you know," she said with a smirk.

"Ha ha." Not funny at all, considering Emmy has the current highest recorded IQ in the Western Hemisphere. And is twelve. And is two years ahead of me at Shermer High. She'd actually already be in college except Dad wanted to make sure she experienced "normal life." Like there's anything normal about being a twelve-year-old senior in high school, but whatever.

At least Emmy had only one officially recognized Talent (since supergeniusness didn't count), unlike Viv and her trifecta of superness: truth divination, levitation, and X-ray vision. All Class A Talents. It was no wonder Viv had followed in Dad's footsteps and was already working for the Bureau of Extrasensory Regulation and Management (or BERM) part time even though she was just a freshman in college. All Emmy could do was blend into her surroundings like a chameleon. It was Class B, but definitely a cool enough Talent that she'd probably get BERM attention as a covert-ops analyst or something someday, especially when you added in her smarts. She was a shoo-in, so long as they didn't expect a good personality.

Though, that chameleon thing was nearly as annoying as her supergeniusness. Let's face it: a know-it-all, bratty little sister who always won at hide-and-seek was a huge pain in the butt.

Of course, all of that completely trumped me and my Class D—as in totally dumb—Talent. I've even met cats that didn't want to talk to other cats. I was ranked right down there with the rest of the idiots with "party trick" Talents. BERM wouldn't want someone like me for anything more than hired entertainment at their annual Christmas celebration, telling the director how much his widdle Buddy-cat loved him.

Viv entered the kitchen like the super-efficient whirlwind she was, and spaghetti sauce was bubbling away in no time at all. Dad wandered in from work a few minutes before dinner was served. Weekends meant nothing to him—he usually worked Saturdays *and* Sundays. And given that he always came in right before dinner, no matter what time it was served, you'd think impeccable timing was his Talent, rather than hypersensitive olfactory perception with a side of chemical conductivity, which sounds really complex . . . and is. I think he was classified as an A Talent since even BERM didn't know what to call him. He worked for them now, so apparently they'd figured out a use for whatever it was he was good at other than sniffing out the chemical components in things.

Viv finally pried Mom out of her office by levitating her laptop into the dining room.

"You could have called me," Mom said as she kissed Dad on his bald spot on her way to her end of the table. He was still standing, but being that Mom's family was Nordic and he was Chinese, she had him by half a head at least. Pity I'd inherited Dad's height instead of hers.

Viv smiled sweetly and didn't mention the three times she had called Mom. Our mother was incredibly focused, but only on "important" things such as her research and Emmy's grades. Maybe it was her laser vision or maybe the fact that the rest of the world (other than Emmy) couldn't keep up with her brain, I don't know. But she simply couldn't seem to retain "extraneous" information. You know, stuff like birthdays and grocery lists.

"Everything smells good," said Dad. Given his olfactory prowess, he was obviously trying to be nice to Mom, since even I could still smell the lingering odor of burned pumpkin. Come to think of it, maybe that's why he always got home right before a meal — so he could miss the full brunt of Mom's disasters. He had an olfactory inhibitor, which he had invented when he was only six (naturally), but he didn't usually wear it at home. He said it made his nose itch. I think he didn't want to insult Mom.

We started eating. All you could hear for a good ten minutes was the clink of silverware and Emmy slurping noodles. It doesn't matter how smart you are when you're twelve. You're still twelve.

"So," said Mom, "what's the plan for school this week after the holiday break?" If Mom had her way, we wouldn't even get Labor Day off. Seriously. If she ruled the world, she probably wouldn't even give us weekends off.

That was our cue. Suck-up Emmy gave her report first, as always, then me, then Viv. Youngest to oldest. It wasn't like I had anything in particular to report anyway, but this was the one area of our lives that Mom meddled in. Constantly. You'd think she was the overachieving Asian parent instead of Dad.

"I've got a trig test this week. Should be a piece of cake," I said. That was a safe topic, since it's my best subject. I'm no supergenius like Emmy, but I could hold my own in trig.

"How about biology?" Mom asked.

"Fine," I said, stabbing a meatball. "Nothing to report." She would ask. I've had issues with Mr. Tollfinger since I refused to dissect a cat. I wasn't about to explain to him why, so I spent a week in detention. Mom told me to suck it up, basically. She didn't even go to bat for me with Principal Johnson. I mean, like I could disembowel someone I could have had a conversation with the day before? I don't think so. Personally, I think she was too ashamed to admit in public that any daughter of hers could have such a lame Talent.

"Are you sure about that?" asked Viv, all sweetness and light.

"Yes." I glared at her. She could just keep her little lie detector Talent to herself, thank you very much.

"I liked Mr. Tollfinger," Viv continued. "He was a great teacher. I don't know why you have such problems with him."

"Are you having issues with your teacher, Natalie?" Mom

turned her steely gaze back to me. I bet she wished she had Viv's Talent. Laser vision was great in a lab, but it didn't help you weasel the truth out of your kids.

"*No,*" I said again, ignoring Viv smirking around a mouthful of pasta. "Everything is *fine*. No problems at all. We're practically best friends."

"Hmmm. Let's keep it that way, shall we?" she said, and then turned her focus to Viv, who had apparently decided she'd tortured me enough for now. Or maybe she'd figured out that I was about two seconds away from kicking her under the table with my combat boots. Steel toed. So much more than a fashion statement.

It was like I wasn't even at the table anymore. You'd think being invisible was actually my Talent. Actually, that would be cool. That's got to be a Class A or B at least. Though with my luck, I'd probably get, like, half invisibility or it would only work every other Tuesday or something and I'd just be a Class C.

"Genevieve," continued Mom, "how is your job at the BERM treating you? Not interfering with your school work, is it?"

"Everything's good. I heard I might be getting a promotion to field agent, and they'd like me to go full time during summer." Viv took a dainty sip of her water. If I had a water-based Talent like one girl I knew from school, I could have made Viv choke on her drink or given her a wicked case of the burps. Maybe not useful, but definitely satisfying. "And my social psych professor asked if I would be willing to do an in-class demonstration of my lie detection."

Well, isn't that nice. My Talent makes my biology teacher detest me. Viv's gets her the star treatment. I rolled my eyes as Viv shot me another smarmy grin when Mom wasn't looking. My friends were so lucky they didn't have any siblings, especially ones with annoying Talents.

I grabbed two breadsticks from the basket and considered holding them out from my head like antennae, but decided not to bother. No one would notice anyway. Dad was deep into a discussion with Viv about some top secret BERM stuff. They were even whispering. Mom and Emmy were talking quarks or string theory or I don't know what.

If Emmy was Mom's favorite, Viv was Dad's. They spoke the same language. The only one in our family that speaks my language is Meep.

Speaking of the furry little devil in disguise, Meep sauntered into the room, licking her lips. *Nice sauce*, she said. *A little heavy on the garlic, though.* Like most cats, she was never one to let an opportunity pass. Viv must have left the lid off the pot.

"You better not have left a mess," I whispered down to her as she jumped in my lap.

Me? she said. *Of course not.* She grinned a wicked cat grin up at me. I knew what that meant. She'd marked her territory. Somewhere in the pot was at least one cat hair, not to mention cat saliva. Why did cats have to do that? I made a mental note to skip the leftovers.

I stuck one breadstick upright in my spaghetti and took a big bite out of the other one as Meep settled into my lap. *Did you bother telling your mom you got an A+ on your English paper?* I shrugged and kept on chewing. *Or that your art teacher picked your project to display in the case during Parents' Night last week?*

I swallowed my bite and hissed at Meep, "Give it a rest, would you?" She's always on me to be more "involved," like that's something a cat knows anything about. I swear sometimes that she's half dog. She's the only cat I know who's more interested in people (i.e., me) than in other cats.

Besides, Mom and Dad had both gone to Parents' Night, but neither of them had noticed my artwork. They had, of course, been all over Emmy's science project. Well, them and a reporter from the Chicago Tribune. I guess isolating some kind of isotope in a high-school lab is bigger news than an interpretation of some of Leonardo da Vinci's mathematical concepts using a vector-based fractal program. But whatever.

"Dennis," said Mom, "did you know that the school is allowing a movie to be filmed during school hours?" Both of her eyebrows went up and she set down her fork. Bad news. "Emmaline told me that they actually moved her calculus quiz to next week because they are being forced to vacate their classroom and work in the library!"

Ooooooo, said Meep. *What a crisis for poor widdle Emmy! Call the papers! Alert the police! Something must be done!*

I totally snorked the sip of water I was drinking. See,

Meep gets me even if no one else does. I scratched her in her favorite spot by her left ear.

"No," said Dad, barely looking up from his tête-à-tête with Viv. "I wasn't aware of —"

"Well, we'll just see about it," said Mom. "It's absolutely scandalous that they're even considering interfering with our child's education for something so frivolous! Besides, couldn't they have just filmed during Labor Day?"

Great. Mom was on a crusade, though it was obvious that she was worried about only one of our educations. I didn't bother mentioning to her that they already were filming this weekend, or the possibility that Melly, one of my best friends, was probably going to sign up as an extra and there was a good chance I'd be dragged along. That counted as extraneous information anyway, right?

I volunteered for dish duty so I could make a faster exit and check for any telltale Meep mess in the kitchen. Viv actually cleans as she cooks, so it's super easy on her nights. (Have I mentioned how totally flawless she is? I swear she never even gets pimples.) And Emmy thinks she's the smart one. Now it would be her turn when Mom cooked, and she'd be scrubbing for hours.

TWO

"THE CAT IS ABOVE ALL THINGS,
A DRAMATIST."—MARGARET BENSON

I headed over to my friend Oscar's house as soon as I finished washing the dishes, leaving the rest of the family to a rousing game of extreme science trivia. Melly was already camped out in Oscar's bedroom. It was our unofficial headquarters since Oscar's parents didn't mind a little mess and noise. They were both artists. My house was supergeek central (literally) and Melly's dad liked everything to be perfect, as in *perfectly* clean and quiet. He'd been like that since Melly's mom died back in fifth grade, like he had to be both a dad and an übermom too. We came to Oscar's so we could let loose a little.

"Nat! You're finally here! Let the drooling commence!" Oscar hugged me and then spun around in circles with his arms spread wide. "I cannot believe Ty McKenzie and Victoria Welling are going to be at our school this week. *Filming.* I swear, I'm going to faint as soon as I see them." Oscar collapsed theatrically onto his bed, his Hello Kitty pillow

13

clutched to his chest. "Preferably, right into Ty's arms."

I laughed. "I'm pretty sure Ty doesn't swing that way."

Melly, my slightly saner best friend, threw a teddy bear at Oscar. "You better not make a scene," she said. "This is totally my chance to be discovered. You think, Nat?"

I snorted, but she was right. With her light brown hair strategically streaked honey blonde, delicate porcelain complexion, practically anime-sized eyes, and curves in all the right places, Melly was nearly fairy-tale beautiful. If I didn't love her, I'd have to hate her. She was way prettier than that Victoria Welling actress. Not to mention, Melly could actually act. As far as I could tell from Victoria's last movie, she ought to be playing Pinocchio. As in, someone made of wood.

"We *have* to be extras. You guys are going to sign up with me, right?" Melly looked from me to Oscar and back again.

"Of course!" I said, trying to sound enthusiastic. Not that I remotely wanted to be involved with the whole movie thing. Even though my best friends were complete and total attention hogs, I wasn't. My invisibility "talent" worked for me in school just like at home. I was perfectly happy that almost no one at Shermer High even knew my name.

But I wasn't too worried. The chance of me actually getting picked as an extra was pretty slim. Short, flat-chested, half-Chinese chicks with purple streaks in their hair? I've yet to see one of those in a movie that wasn't animated. And come to think of it, even the animated characters usually weren't all that flat chested. Melly, on the other hand, was a shoo-in, and

Oscar could probably talk his way into anything, even with his crazy Asian-dude-with-attitude hair and non-mainstream fashion sense. I was perfectly happy to cheer them on from the sidelines.

Though usually where I found myself was right in the middle of whatever scheme Oscar had cooked up. Some of the kids at school called us the Vienna Finger, with Melly being the cream-colored filling to our Asian yellowness. I never have figured out whether they mean it nicely or not. Of course, they might also be referring to the Halloween that Oscar had made us come to school dressed as a three-part cookie. The theory had been good, but he'd neglected to consider the fact that we wouldn't be attached at the hip. I'd wandered around school all day looking like a piece of cardboard.

Oscar flipped open his laptop and began clicking like a madman. I groaned, but Melly clapped her hands. It was time for the Oscar Report, whether I wanted to listen to it or not. He was more reliable (and sensationalistic) than CNN.

"Quit your bellyaching," said Oscar. "You know you wanna know."

"Not so much," I said, and went to sit down on his desk chair, even though it was covered in clothes. Melly climbed on the bed and leaned over his shoulder. Oscar was certifiably addicted to celebrity dirt and she was his all-too-willing audience. She claimed it would help her with her acting, but I couldn't see how. What would knowing which teen actress was getting drunk or what the stars were wearing on the red carpet do for her career?

"So, who do you want to hear about first?" asked Oscar. He wiggled his eyebrows suggestively. "Victoria or Ty?"

"Can't we talk about something else tonight?" I said, not completely managing to keep the whine out of my voice. "We could complain about our families." Or maybe we could talk about a certain somebody in my trig class. I could use some advice, but definitely just from Melly. She was much luckier in the love department than either Oscar or me. Okay, technically Oscar had had more boyfriends than me too, but his last breakup had been pretty rough.

Oscar looked at me like I was insane. "Victoria and Ty are going to physically be in our high school tomorrow. *Tomorrow.*" He paused for a moment to take a deep breath. "In our school. We have to prepare!"

"But—"

"Come on, Nat, this is really important," Melly said. "I need to know *everything*. You never know what will give you a foot in the door in this business." She was practically batting her eyelashes at me. Oh, for heaven's sake.

"Yeah, you can moan about your mom any time," said Oscar. "She's always good for it. How often do famous people come to *our* school?"

"Oh, all right," I said. They were too worked up about the movie thing anyway, even though they hadn't talked about anything else for weeks. I would be glad when it was all over. Maybe I could figure something out about Ian on my own anyway. At least I was able to talk to him without stammering now. I'd barely been able to look in his direction the first week of trig class, and I sat right next to him. I hadn't been able to take notes on anything Mr. Beck had written on the left side of the white board that whole week.

"Woot! Okay, where was I?" said Oscar.

"Ty," Melly said, grabbing my hand and pulling me over onto the bed.

"Uh-uh," said Oscar, and gave us his evil grin. "Let's save the beefcake for last, shall we? Let's talk Victoria Welling!" He pushed the laptop screen back a little so we could both see it. "According to this article, Victoria has turned into a diva with a capital D, just like Easton West was saying on her site last week. Victoria actually had a five-page list of demands that the directors had to agree to before she signed on to *Freddy's Day Off*. Total prima donna." He pointed at the screen. "I mean, look at this. She actually insisted on having an entire house rented for her in the suburbs so she could 'really feel what it was like to live near Chicago' and prepare for her role. But not just any house. One with"—he peered at the screen—"at least two floors and a finished basement, plus a home security system and minimum seven-foot-tall privacy fence. Oh, and a pool. Who even has a pool here? It's *Chicago*. We have *winter*. It's September and it's already, like, 50 degrees."

Melly pointed to something farther down the screen.

17

"Not to mention getting some special brand of Japanese spring water flown in."

Oscar batted her hand away. "I was getting to that!"

"Maybe she bathes in it," I said. Oscar and Melly both looked at me. "What?" Why did they even care about this stuff? She could drink rainwater from Argentina for all I cared.

"Anyway," said Oscar, "I think Easton came out here to chronicle Victoria's meltdown. That's what she's best at, being there when an actor goes down. She was there when Rory Barnes bit the dust. Remember that? Victoria's probably, like, one step away from shaving her head." He rubbed his hands together. "I cannot wait for school. We're going to have front row seats! This movie is the best thing to happen to us in, like, *ever*."

That was probably the first I'd ever heard Oscar looking forward to school since the eighth grade, when he wanted to show off his first pair of combat boots. "I still don't see why they want to film at Shermer High," I said. "It's such a lame school. Why aren't they filming at one of the schools in the city?" It wasn't like Shermer even had a cool building. It was mostly prison-issue concrete block all the way. Usually, the high schools shown in movies were all brick or some kind of imposing historical building. Not that I'd ever seen one like that in real life, but presumably they existed somewhere. Maybe downtown.

"D'oh!" said Oscar and flipped a big *L* for "loser" at me.

"Haven't you been paying any attention? They have to film it here for authenticity. The story totally wouldn't work if they didn't film it here."

"Authenticity?" We'd watched *Ferris Bueller's Day Off* a few times over the years and I liked it okay, but I didn't see what the connection was.

Oscar looked at Melly. "One of the best teen movies of ALL TIME," he said to her, "and the girl doesn't pay any attention at all."

"What?" Yeesh, it's just a movie. Sometimes, I really didn't get them. It had been a lot easier back in elementary school when Melly had first moved here and Oscar and I had adopted her. We had been united in our hatred of *High School Musical* back then.

"Shermer High is where John Hughes filmed parts of *Ferris Bueller's Day Off*! Didn't you ever notice while you were watching it with us that parts of the school looked really, really familiar?"

"*The Breakfast Club* too!" chimed in Melly. I assumed that was another movie I hadn't paid enough attention to. Was it too much to ask to just watch a movie for entertainment, rather than dissect it for career advancement?

"Sorry I asked," I mumbled.

"Hey, what's this about Easton?" asked Melly, looking at a *News of the Weird* headline. Praise poodles. At least we could get off of my shortcomings in movie knowledge now.

"Omigod! Did I not show you that yet? It's awesome!

Just watch. Funniest thing I've seen in forever!" Oscar launched the video and waved his hand at the screen like a magician. He was in full-on Oscar mode.

I recognized the hotel from walking past it whenever we go to Millennium Park downtown. The York? Something like that. It had these huge marble columns and they always rolled out an actual red carpet on the sidewalk so that visiting famous people wouldn't get their feet dirty or something.

Some tourist must have been taking the video while on an architecture tour of the city because at first, all you could hear was some boring tour guide droning on about the stonework and Grecian columns. Then someone said, "There's a limo! Who is that? Is it someone famous?" and the picture swerved way too fast to finally focus on a limousine at the curb. The doorman stepped forward and opened the car door, and the first thing that came out was a pair of hot-pink stilettos attached to some really long legs. Like, legs for days.

"Easton West," whispered Oscar reverently. Like we couldn't tell from her signature shoes. She was known for three things: her pink shoes (actually, pink everything, but especially the shoes), her ability to out-scoop major newspapers on her blog, and her lavish, jet-setting lifestyle. She'd been heiress-rich even before she became famous.

Easton climbed out of the limo with a fluffy yapper dog tucked under one arm. It was barking its head off. I couldn't blame it. It had been dyed the same shade of bright pink as

Easton's hair and shoes. She should be arrested for animal cruelty.

Then she leaned in the car, giving the videographer a gratuitous shot of her butt, and came back out pulling a leash. On the other end of the leash was a really, really pissed off cat, also dyed bright pink. As soon as Easton yanked it out of the car, it went totally mental. If the cat hadn't had little pink plastic things on every claw, Easton's entire body would have been bloody. She juggled the dog and the cat while everyone stood by and shouted out not so helpful advice. She finally threw both of her pets at the chauffeur and went shrieking into the York. The crowd applauded and the video ended.

"Is that not to die for? I mean, I love Easton, but that's pure awesome," said Oscar. "It's totally going viral."

"Wait," I said, "can you play it again? And turn up the volume?"

"Sure, I could watch that over and over." Oscar hit play again and cranked up the sound. When it got to the part with the cat, I leaned forward.

Help me! screamed the cat. *Hellllllppp me! Kill the imposter!*

"Crapola," I said.

"What is it?" asked Melly. "What's the cat saying?"

Melly and Oscar were some of the very few people outside my family who knew my secret. Basically, the only people who knew I could talk to cats were my two best friends, my family, and some poor schmo who filed the registry paperwork over

21

in Washington at the BERM. What a waste of paperwork. What good is being able to talk to cats? I'd really rather we all pretended my Talent didn't exist. After all, the rest of my family had Talent to spare.

"Play it again," I said, and then repeated back for them the rest of what the cat had said.

What's wrong with you people? This isn't Easton West. This is not my person! Save us! Stop barking and bite her, Fergie! Do I have to do everything myself? Stop laughing, you cretins! You there, fat man, drop the camera! Help us! She'll kill us all!

"Not so funny now, huh, Oscar?"

Oscar dropped his laptop and dived off the bed and halfway into his book bag. He came up with his cell phone and punched three numbers. I don't think I'd ever seen him move that fast.

"What are you doing?" I asked.

"What do you think? Calling 911! We have to tell the authorities! Easton West has been murdered!"

"Are you crazy?" I tackled him and grabbed the phone as a voice came on saying, "9-1-1. What is your emergency?"

"So sorry," I said into the phone. "Wrong number." I hung up the phone and glared at Oscar. He glared back at me.

"Hold on, you guys," said Melly, holding one palm out to each of us. Always the mediator. "Nat, are you sure that's what the cat said?" I just looked at her. Why would I make that up? "Okay," she continued. "Then why shouldn't we call the police?"

22

I took a deep breath. "Okay, for one thing, how do we even know the cat is telling the truth? It's a cat. Cats lie. That's what they do." Sometimes it seemed like every other thing out of Meep's mouth was a lie . . . or a thinly veiled attempt at scoring some tuna. "Two, what are you going to say to the police? That you think some famous blogger has been murdered or abducted because a cat said so?"

"Yeah, but your Talent—" said Oscar.

"Is not something I want broadcasted around." We all knew what had happened to Jonas Smith, the kid who could kiss frogs and turn them different colors. Word about his Talent got out and no one has talked to him since—except to call him Frog Boy. I have no desire to lower my social rank even further into Cat Girl territory.

"But we have to do something!" Oscar grabbed his phone back but held it without dialing. Then it rang. Oscar looked at the caller ID and dropped the phone like it was on fire. "It's the police," he whispered, like they could hear him even though he hadn't answered the phone.

I grabbed the phone and answered it. "Hello?" I said as calmly as I could while motioning at Oscar to shut up and stop whimpering. Melly clamped a hand over his mouth.

A woman's voice came on the line. "Someone dialed 911 from this number and we're calling to confirm that no emergency is in progress. Is everything okay?"

"Sorry, that was us. I mean, me. I, uh, butt dialed by accident. I'm really sorry. It won't happen again."

"Please see that it doesn't." *Click.*

I threw the phone back at Oscar. "Great," I said. "Now the police have your number. If you ever really need 911, you're screwed."

"Whatever," he said, and shook off Melly's hand. She wiped it on his furry purple bedspread. "We're talking about Easton West!" He flopped back on his bed and nearly landed on his laptop. "And you know what? She hasn't put up a new blog post in days, since that one about coming here to Chicago. That's not like her at all! She usually posts at least once a day. I think the cat is right. Something has happened to her."

"Cats are known to exaggerate," I said. "Just like you, Oscar, only they're furrier, and with worse breath. Besides, what're we supposed to do about it? We're teenagers. Even if we did tell someone, they wouldn't believe us."

"What about your parents?" asked Melly.

"What about them?" My Class A Talented, supergenius, overachieving parents with their two super-Talented daughters: Genevieve and Emmaline. My Talent was not something we ever talked about, either in or out of the family. I'd met one of Mom's coworkers once and she hadn't even known there was a third daughter in our family because all Mom talked about were the cool things Emmy and Viv were always doing.

"Couldn't you . . ." Melly trailed off and then smiled apologetically at me. She's met my mom. At least her dad supports her. He even schlepped her around to acting classes in the city. She'd been to every Broadway play that ever opened in town. I sometimes wondered if my parents even remembered my middle name—and they'd given it to me.

"We have to do *something*." Oscar looked about as distraught as I'd ever seen him. Even more than the time his favorite dancer got kicked off of that celebrity dancing show, and he'd lost his TV privileges for a month then because of how crazy he'd driven his parents over the whole thing.

"We'll submit an anonymous tip. How about that?" Melly asked. "Then they can at least check it out, right?" Melly looked so pleased with herself at coming up with a solution that I didn't argue, even though it sounded like a stupid idea to me. Not that I'm an expert on Easton West or anything, but the person in the video looked exactly like her. Either the cat was lying or something weird was going on. I didn't see how the cops could possibly tell.

Melly used her cell phone since she had a blocked number because her dad was both anal and overprotective. She called the main police number instead of 911 and used her best adult voice, the same one that she'd used for the part of the weirdo mother in *The Glass Menagerie* last year. "Yes, I'd like to report some foul play," she said.

Oscar, back in good humor again now that someone was doing something, clucked and flapped his arms like a chicken. "*Fowl* play, get it?" he whispered. Melly and I ignored him.

"I believe that Easton West, the celebrity blogger, has

been"—she faltered a minute and then recovered—"is in danger or has been hurt. I—um—am concerned for her safety." She answered a few more questions, and then it seemed like the police officer was getting a little suspicious. The officer wanted to know how Melly knew Easton, why the blogger was in town, what their relationship was, and all kinds of other things that Melly, of course, didn't know how to answer. The police probably thought it was some kind of weird prank call. Not that I blamed them. I mean, "Hello, police, someone I don't know anything about might possibly be in danger. Can you please go check on it?" How much more vague and stalkery can you get?

Finally, Melly faked a bad connection and hung up the phone.

"I think they bought it," she said.

"Awesome sauce!" said Oscar. "Now that we've got that out of the way, how about we talk Ty?" I didn't have the heart to tell Oscar the possibility of the police believing Melly was worse than my chances of winning an Academy Award.

 26

E A S T O N   W E S T ' S   B L O G

Sunday, September 6, 10:35 P.M.: To whoever it was out there in crazy Internet land who apparently cannot live for a few days without the stellar wisdom of Easton West, I AM FINE. If, in the future, I ever happen to not post something for a few days, how about we restrain ourselves a little and NOT CALL THE POLICE?

I am in Chicago and busy hanging with the ultrafab Victoria Welling. She's my new bestie, and all those rumors about her being a total diva are a complete exaggeration. More soon. I've got all kinds of plans for the city — Millennium Park and that famous Bean sculpture, a Chicago-style hot dog, and drinks at the John Hancock. ❤

THree

🐈

"NO ONE OWNS A CAT. HUMANS
MERELY BORROW OUR TIME."—MEEP

I woke up to the sound of my cell phone screeching "Born this Way" by Lady Gaga. Oscar had custom selected that ringtone for himself on my phone. I glanced at the clock and fumbled around for my cell, nearly knocking it off my bedside table into a pile of dirty clothes. What in the world was he doing calling me so early on a holiday?

"This better be good," I said as I answered the phone.

"Get dressed. You have five minutes." He hung up.

What? Did somebody die? Did tickets to something go on sale? I considered going back to sleep, but I was awake now anyway. I pulled on a pair of comfortable jeans, a red and white plaid shirt, and a hoodie and went downstairs.

Dad nodded at me as he slowly chewed a bite of his standard breakfast: plain oatmeal with butter and salt. I think he liked it because it was so bland, though he was always saying that nothing's bland, not when you can really smell it. I nodded back at him, grabbed three store-bought (and therefore safe) blueberry muffins and stuck them in my backpack along with a few bottles of water. If I was doomed to wait in line for tickets to some show, I was going to be prepared.

"I'm going out with Oscar and Melly," I said to him. He nodded again and kept reading the paper. "Be back, oh, tomorrow or the next day. Maybe Friday."

"Have fun," Dad said with a little smile, and turned the page.

Yep, Invisible Girl, that's me. Who said I had only one Talent?

I went outside and sat down on the front porch to wait for Oscar and Melly. I didn't have to wait long. Melly's Volvo (her dad picked it out—highest safety rating for its class, whatever that means) came roaring around the corner in a manner I'm sure her dad never intended. Why Melly ever let Oscar drive is a mystery to me, but maybe she was hoping he'd get in a fender bender so she could get a new car. She really wanted a Prius, like all the conspicuously eco-conscious Hollywood people were driving now.

"Get in!" Oscar yelled out the window as he slammed on the brakes.

I hopped in the back. "Where're we off to? I brought muffins."

"We're going downtown to the York," said Oscar as he sped off. "We're going to save Easton West, if she's still alive to be saved."

"Are you insane?" I looked from him to Melly. "Melly, you're not seriously going to let Oscar drive your car downtown. That's just suicide."

"Don't be silly," said Oscar. "I'm not that crazy. We're going to take the train."

I was still arguing with him when he pulled into the Metra station. He parked the car, got out, and opened the door to the back seat. For once, his timing was perfect. The train was pulling into the station. He must have actually looked at a schedule.

". . . And it's a stupid idea," I finished. Oscar sighed and shook his head, then picked me up and slung me over his shoulder. I tried poking him in the ribs as he carried me to the train, but his jacket was so covered in the patches that he'd collected while traveling that he didn't even feel it. I wasn't even close to being able to fight my way to the ground. Unlike me, he'd lucked out in the half-Asian birth lottery and was tall like his standard-issue white-bread dad. It was completely unfair. His Japanese mom was even shorter than I was.

"Melly," I said, "do something!" I glared at her from my upside-down vantage point.

"I am," she said, and grabbed my book bag and her purse. Traitor. She's usually much saner than Oscar, but if she had one weakness, it was for anything related to Hollywood.

Oscar dumped me into a seat in the back of a mostly

empty train car. "Here's the deal," he said, pulling out his train pass and sticking it in the ticket holder on the back of the seat. "Easton posted last night that the police came and checked on her and that she's peachy keen and everybody should get a grip."

"Okay, good." I couldn't see why that necessitated a trip into the city.

"No, *not* good. If you read Easton like I do—"

"Religiously," interrupted Melly. I snickered, but Oscar ignored us.

"—then you'd know that this latest post had to have been written by an impostor. It doesn't sound anything like her at all! The impostor may have fooled the police, but she hasn't fooled me!"

"Oscar, maybe she was just stressed or something . . . or pissed. Wouldn't you be pissed if the police came knocking on your door?" I knocked lightly on Oscar's head, but he just shook me off.

"But that's not all," he said. "She wrote that she was going to go eat a hot dog. Chicago style." He looked at me triumphantly.

"Um, so? Lots of people do that when they come to visit Chicago. It's one of the things the city is known for—hot dogs, Italian beefs, and those gross tamales."

"Yeah, but she's been an ovo-lacto vegetarian since July. There's no way she'd eat a *hot dog*. She's morally opposed."

"What, she'll dye her dog and cat bright pink but she won't eat a hot dog?" We were pulling into Morton Grove station. I wondered if I should make a run for it.

"She dyed them pink in support of breast cancer aware-ness," said Oscar. "For serious."

"Tickets?" asked a train conductor.

"All the way to Union Station," said Melly. She and I handed over some money while Oscar waved impatiently at his pass. The conductor pulled out two tickets for us and handed them over, humming a little tune as he went on to the next passenger.

The interruption gave me a moment to think. I didn't really believe the breast cancer thing. I've read Easton's blog a few times and she seemed like your standard airhead gossipmonger to me. But Oscar never failed to amaze me. He really and truly buys into the whole celebrity thing. It's like his religion.

"Well, maybe she couldn't hack being a vegetarian," I said. "It's been, what, two months since she switched? She probably started craving meat and you missed the big announcement. What does it matter anyway? We can't do anything about it." The train pulled out again. I rested my forehead against the window and watched the station dis-appear. I really should have gotten off.

"I do remember reading about the vegetarian thing," said Melly. "The whole thing seems pretty suspicious, Nat. I read the post and she even talked up Victoria like they're best friends. When does she ever do that? About a girl, anyway."

"Maybe she's realized what a snot she is and decided she

needs more women friends."

Oscar snorted but then turned serious. "You have to do something," he said. "It's your duty."

"It's *my* duty? What are you talking about?" I turned away from the window to look at him.

Oscar tapped the seat in front of him for emphasis. "You've seen *Spider-Man*," he said. "'With great power comes great responsibility.' It's your *duty* to do something about Easton. You're the only one on the planet who could've seen that video and known something was wrong. That's kismet."

He had to be freaking kidding me. "Oh, come on, Oscar. This is real life, not a movie. And I am so not a superhero. It was just a stupid video. I'm sure Easton's fine. Maybe she even staged the whole attack as some weird kind of publicity stunt."

I had to admit that evidence to the contrary had piled up a bit, but still. What am I supposed to do about it? And why should I care about some stupid celebrity blogger? If I passed her on the street, she probably wouldn't even notice me unless she had something snarky to say about my hair.

Oscar stared at me, his brown eyes wide and unblinking. Melly cleared her throat and said, "Nat," like she was disappointed in me. She hated it when we fought. Not that it was really a fight. It was just Oscar being typical crazy Oscar. I was surprised, honestly, that he was still going on about the whole Easton thing. Normally, he'd have moved on to whatever the news of the day was.

I turned away and sat there staring out the window as

the suburbs turned into city, Oscar letting out a not so quiet *humph* every five minutes or so. He was going to be insufferable, I could tell. Maybe if I humored him for a while, he'd lose interest and Melly could stop acting like me being the sane one was a bad thing.

"Okay, okay," I finally said as we were pulling into Union Station. "What's the plan?"

"Um . . . ," said Oscar. Great. That meant there was no plan. Normal Oscar operating procedure.

"Fine," I said. "Let's get to the York and see what we can find out." At least it wasn't far from Union Station, probably about halfway between the station and Grant Park. The chances of us actually running into Easton seemed pretty slim to me. She was probably living it up on the town right now, if she wasn't sleeping in after partying last night. I figured we'd go, hang out in the lobby for a while, and go home. Then Oscar'd have to get off my back about it because at least we'd have tried.

I'd never been in the lobby of the York before, but it looked pretty much exactly how I imagined it would: fancy. Like, living-room-of-the-rich-and-famous kind of fancy. The only way the three of us would have stood out more is if we had walked in on our hands. My ratty hoodie made me look like a homeless person comparatively, and Oscar looked more like a street performer than a guest. At least Melly looked as beautiful as always. Maybe people would think she belonged. We sat down on one of the posh leather sofas and

34

tried to look inconspicuous.

Oscar picked up a magazine from a side table and held it up in front of his face. Upside down. "See anything?" he stage whispered as his eyes panned back and forth across the room.

"No," I answered back in a normal tone of voice, though I did see the concierge, an older guy with dark gray hair and the tiniest mustache I'd ever seen, staring at us suspiciously. Yes! We were going to get kicked out of here in no time at all. I restrained myself from cheering.

"I'll watch the elevators," said Melly. She picked up a fashion magazine too, right-side up, and pretended to read.

Oscar flipped magazine pages abnormally fast as his head swiveled back and forth from the front door to the entrance to the hotel's bar, The Sax. He looked like he could take flight at any minute. I watched the concierge, who watched Oscar. A few minutes later, Oscar's craziness got to be too much for the poor guy. He walked our way with that look that adults get when they're about to do something unpleasant. We'd been kicked out of places before, but never quite as fast. It had to be a record. Goes to show what a fancy place it was.

I smiled helpfully at the concierge as he strode purposefully in our direction. Oscar hadn't even noticed him yet.

Then Melly let out a little gasp. "It's her!" she said and nearly dropped her magazine. I turned to look at the elevator and she was right. Of all the dumb luck. There was Easton — or whoever it was who looked and sounded exactly like Easton — click clacking out of the elevator in some neon-pink Jimmy Choos.

"Oh, Richie!" Easton sat down on the edge of the concierge desk, crossed her legs, and started jiggling her toe up and down. "Where do you think you're going? I have a problem here!" She snapped her fingers.

The concierge had stopped short as soon as she'd called out his name. The look on his face went from slightly displeased to absolute horror. Then he straightened his shoulders, wiped the terror-stricken look off of his face, put on a smarmy smile, and turned around to face Easton. "On my way, Ms. West," he said brightly and headed over to her.

Easton frowned at him. "There are only five towels in my room. We talked about this."

"My apologies, Ms. West, I'll—"

"And the tulips are *wilted*."

"So sorry, I'll—"

"Not to mention the lack of bubble bath."

"I'll have—"

"And where's my dog walker? She should have been here five minutes ago! Do I have to do everything myself? What am I paying you people for anyway?"

The concierge snapped his fingers at a uniformed hotel guy who was standing by the front desk. "You!" he said. "Bring some towels, fresh flowers, bubble bath, and chocolates up to room 2930 right away." He turned back to Easton. "I'm sure the dog walker will be here momentarily, Ms. West. I'll call to check. Is there anything else I can do for you?"

"No," she said icily. She hopped off the desk and walked to the elevator, clearing her throat and looking pointedly at the concierge. He leaped forward and pushed the elevator button for her. Easton didn't bother to say thank you or anything else to him; she just tapped her toe until the bell dinged. Then she got in and left.

Wow. What a total witch.

"That can't be the real *Easton*," Oscar hissed, his eyebrows drawn down to a point between his eyes. "I know Easton and she's nowhere near that cranky."

I don't know about that. He'd been reading her blog to us for a while and she always sounded kind of snarky to me, but maybe not quite so evil-rude. Her brand of snark usually seemed more clever than mean. Maybe Oscar was right.

What was I *thinking*? Oscar was *not* right.

The concierge was still standing there staring at the elevator door, just breathing and standing, probably trying not to slam his fist into the wall. I hoped he wouldn't remember us right away. I wanted to be thrown out, but not by anyone in that frame of mind.

Oscar dropped the magazine and turned to me. "We have to find out what happened to Easton. We have to save her if she's not dead. We can't let that impostor take over her life."

"Maybe she's possessed," I said. "Or maybe she's got a concrete wedgie."

Melly snorted.

Oscar ignored me. "Okay," he said. "I've got a plan. The only way to find out the truth is to talk to Easton's cat. So we have to get Nat up to her room."

"How are we going to do that?" asked Melly.

"Yeah, I'm not about to go knocking on her door," I said.

"Oh yes, you are," said Oscar. "You're going to be the dog walker."

Four

"THE CAT WHO FRIGHTENS THE MICE AWAY IS
AS GOOD AS THE CAT WHO EATS THEM."
—GERMAN PROVERB

"The dog walker?" I shook my head at Oscar, but he just blinked innocently at me, batting those long eyelashes of his. There had to be a way out of this mess. "In case you hadn't noticed, the concierge was about to kick us out. There's no way he's letting us in the elevator." I nodded at the concierge, who had wandered over to the front desk. He looked like he was retelling the horror story that was Easton to a desk clerk, but he kept glancing over in our direction. He was probably spoiling for a fight after his run-in.

"I'll take care of him," said Melly. "Just let me turn on my Marilyn Monroe. Or maybe more Hannah Montana gone bad. He looks like he might be more into slutty than sexy. You guys just go do your thing." She stood up, tossed her hair a few times, and strutted toward the concierge. A group of businessmen came in at the same time and approached the front desk to check in. All of the desk clerks became suddenly

39

busy helping them. Was the world conspiring against me?

"Okay," said Oscar. "Let's go."

"Wait," I said. "What if he's not into jailbait?" I mean, Melly is beautiful, but she doesn't look a day over sixteen.

Oscar snorted and grabbed my hand. He pulled me to the elevator and pushed the button.

I looked back. Amazingly, Melly already had Richie practically eating out of her hand. He was smiling and laughing as she leaned in toward him and twirled some of her hair around her finger. Dirty old man.

The bell dinged and the elevator doors opened. Oscar pushed me in before I could say another word, and then he hit the button for the twenty-ninth floor. The doors opened again on the right floor before I could even finish protesting.

"I'll keep watch and hold the elevator. You go and talk to the cat." Oscar pushed me out in the direction of the suite.

I followed the signs and stopped in front of room 2930. No one was around. I could not believe I was about to do this. Taking a step back, I looked at the elevators. Oscar waved and gave me a thumbs-up.

The things I do for my friends. I knocked on the door.

Nothing happened.

Did I have the wrong room number? I knocked again and this time the door flew open. Easton, cell phone glued to her ear, stared at me blankly. Her pink hair was standing on end like she'd just pulled on it. "What?" she demanded. "What do you want?"

"Uh, dog walker?" I said.

She waved me in the room. It was more like a mini apartment than a normal hotel room. At least, not like any hotel room that I'd ever been in. The front part was a living room, complete with leather couches and a fancy marble-topped coffee table. Off to one side was a kitchenette with marble counters. A door to the left was open and I could see an unmade bed with pink clothes heaped on top of it and a trail of pink shoes leading to it. The rumors were true. She really did wear nothing but pink.

The dog was sitting on the couch, looking at me expectantly. She looked like a furry pink cupcake, lime-green leash already attached. A plastic pink cat carrier was sitting on the floor by the couch. Easton walked by it and the cat let out a bloodcurdling screech that made both of us jump. Easton kicked at the carrier. The cat hissed.

Just wait until I get out of here. You are going down, human!

I had no idea how I was going to talk to the cat with Easton in the room. Even if she went into the bedroom, she would still be able to hear me. It's not like I could communicate with them telepathically or anything. I walked slowly over to the dog and made a show of petting it and calling it silly dog names while I looked at the cat out of the corner of my eye. The cat hadn't bothered to even look at me yet; he was keeping a baleful glare focused on Easton. Considering how bugged-out his eyes were, I wondered how she could ignore him at all. He had to be one of those fancy breed cats that always win at cat shows.

"I don't care what time you do it, just do it," she spat into the phone. "I want it done yesterday. And stay out of the upstairs!" She paced near the carrier again and the cat let out another howl and tried in vain to swipe at her ankle. "Freaking cat!" screamed Easton. "Watch it, you mangy bag of fur! I'm going to toss you out that window!"

"Um," I said.

Easton whirled on me and pulled the phone slightly away from her ear. "What?" she said. "You got a problem?" She took a step toward me like she was ready to throw me out the window too.

"No. Just—would you like me to walk the cat too? I can take them both if you want." That's when the cat finally noticed me. He crammed his face up against the door of his carrier and stopped hissing.

Easton looked at me a minute. "Sure, yeah, whatever. Get him out of my face." She began pacing again, giving one more kick to the side of the carrier. A rhinestone glued to the side went flying off. Someone had gone a little nuts bedazzling it.

I picked up the carrier and the dog's leash and walked to the door. Was I actually going to get away with it?

She hung up on whoever she was talking to. "Wait," she said. "Dog walker."

Crap. I should have walked faster. I turned to look at her. She had one hand on her hip and her toe was tapping.

"I've got to leave for filming—I mean, the set. We famous people don't get a day off." She attempted a smile, but it came across more like a grimace. "You can drop the cat and dog off with the concierge. I'll make sure he knows what to do with them."

Yeah, I bet she would. I managed a nod and went out the door. I ran all the way to the elevator, the dog yipping excitedly. Oscar punched the button as soon as I was in.

"You did it! You did it!" he said and jumped up and down. The dog yapped louder.

Shut up, Fergie, the cat said. The dog immediately stopped barking and sat down on top of Oscar's foot. The cat peered up at me through the bars. *So, you want to tell me what's going on? Who are you? Are you with her?*

Oscar looked from me to the cat. "Is it talking to you? What did it say?"

"He," I said really quickly. Never call a cat an "it" if you want to keep your skin intact. "Nothing yet. Give me a second." I bent down to look in the carrier. "I'm Natalie," I said. "We're not with Easton." I caught a whiff of some strong perfume and something else.

That's not Easton, said the cat firmly. *I'm asking if you're with her.*

"Um, no," I said. "We're not with her. In fact, that's why we came to find you. That's why we're here."

The elevator dinged and the door opened on the lobby. Oscar stuck his head out and looked to the left and right and back again.

"Melly still has the perv talking to her up at the desk.

And hey, perfect! There's a group of tourists coming in. Get ready to go in one . . . two . . . three!" He sprinted out of the elevator and headed straight out the front door, nearly taking out one of the tourists on the way.

I poked my head out and followed more slowly. Why in the world did everything of Easton's have to be so pink? I mean, how much more noticeable could I be, with a pink dog and a pink cat in a pink cat carrier studded with rhinestones? Maybe I shouldn't have worn the lime-green hoodie today. We looked like sherbet on parade. I matched Fergie's leash.

"Don't make a sound," I whispered to the cat, who passed it on to the dog. I kept my head held high and walked as fast as I could without going too fast. A bellman by the door gave me a curious look, but I held up the leash and shrugged, and he didn't say anything. I made it through the door, looked back to make sure no one was looking, and then ran down the block. The cat carrier banged into my knee with every step, with the cat letting out a small growl each time.

"This way!" yelled Oscar, pinwheeling his arms in the air. Someone should seriously explain spy stuff to him. Attracting attention like that was the last thing we needed. I sighed and followed him around the corner. "We did it!" he yelled again and pumped his fist. A guy in a suit stared at him and moved to the edge of the sidewalk to get around us. Wouldn't be the first time.

The cat hissed softly. *Your friend sounds like something ran over his tail,* he said.

I grabbed Oscar's arm and pulled it down. "Oscar, shut up! Half the city's heard you by now."

"Oops, sorry," he said. "I just can't believe it worked!"

"Why don't you go get Melly?" I looked around for some place less conspicuous than the street corner. "I'll be over there at that sidewalk café."

Oscar took off and I lugged the carrier over to the café. I picked an outside table in the far corner underneath the awning and behind a large potted palm tree. I stuck the cat carrier in a chair and put my backpack over the top of it to try to hide the pinkness of it all.

Let me out of here, said the cat. *I've been in here for two days.*

"I can't," I said. "Look, here comes a waitress now. I'm probably not even supposed to have pets here."

I am not your pet, hissed the cat. I shushed him and pushed my backpack more toward the front of the carrier so it hung over the door a little.

The waitress came up to the table and sniffed at me suspiciously. She looked pointedly at the cat carrier and then down at Fergie, who wagged her little pink tail.

"Um, there's a performance artist doing something in Millennium Park today. Have you seen her stuff? I'm giving the—um—props a break." I held my breath.

She sighed but handed a menu to me. "Just keep them contained, okay? And if anyone complains, you've got to go."

"Thanks," I said. "Sure." I glanced down at the menu. I had only about ten dollars on me and I was going to need money for the train ride back. Melly probably had some cash, but Oscar was perennially broke. At least he had a Metra pass. The waitress turned to walk away. "Um, hey," I said. "Could I get three lemonades?"

She sighed, turned around, and took the menu back.

"Art doesn't really pay much," I said lamely. She nodded and left.

So who are you again? the cat asked.

"I'm Natalie," I said. "Nat. My friend —"

The loud one?

"Yeah. Oscar. He showed me this video of you attacking Easton —"

The cat hissed.

"Sorry, the person who's impersonating Easton. And I heard what you were saying. Oscar's a big fan of hers and dragged me down here to see what was going on." I looked around to make sure no one was watching me talk to a cat. "So, what is going on?"

We got here a few days ago. Easton left us in the hotel to go meet up with one of the actors from that film she's here to cover. When she came back, she wasn't Easton anymore.

"How can you tell?"

The cat hissed again. Talk about pitching a hissy fit.

"She looks just like Easton to me," I said. Even if human cloning were legal, who'd want to clone some celebrity blogger anyway?

Cats are obviously better suited at detection than humans. I

46

can tell. That . . . person . . . is not my human. She doesn't smell the same. She may look the same, but she's not. She didn't even know what our names were. She had to look them up on the computer.

Oh. Yeah, that would be a pretty good clue. "What is your name? The dog's Fergie, right?"

I'm Rufus Brutus the Third. Easton calls me Tiddlywinks. Fergie's the dog's real name and human name. She doesn't have much imagination. She's just a dog.

Fergie sat up at her name and wagged her poofy pink tail. Yeah, she didn't look like the sharpest tool in the shed, that's for sure. But maybe it was the pink fur.

"Tiddlywinks?"

Rufus pushed his face up against the carrier door again and glared at me malevolently, his yellow-green eyes practically glowing. *I said* Easton *calls me that. You may call me Rufus Brutus the Third.*

"Right," I said. "Okay, Rufus Brutus the Third." Delusions of grandeur, anyone? "Any ideas on who this Easton impostor is? And whether or not the real Easton is okay? And why someone is impersonating Easton to begin with?"

Before Rufus could say anything else, Oscar and Melly came running across the street and joined us at the table.

"That was pure awesome!" said Oscar. He high-fived Melly. "We are rockin' the casbah!" I rolled my eyes, but didn't say anything because the waitress was coming back with our drinks. She set the lemonades and the bill on the table and left without bothering to ask if we wanted to order

47

anything else. She must have served broke teenagers before.

"So what have you found out so far?" asked Melly, taking a sip of her lemonade.

I introduced Rufus Brutus the Third/Tiddlywinks and Fergie and summed it up. Not like I'd learned a lot so far anyway. Rufus was more of a hisser than a sharer.

Oscar leaned over so his head was directly in front of Rufus. "Who would do this to Easton?" he asked, loudly and deliberately like he was talking to a five-year-old who didn't speak English. It was a good thing Rufus was contained. I saw his eyes narrow.

"You can talk normally," I said before Rufus came unglued. "He's not deaf or dumb. He's just a cat."

Your friend is an idiot, Rufus said. *But tell him I don't know who did this. All I know is that she keeps disappearing and leaving us in the hotel room. She calls someone named Alan a lot and complains. But it's very strange. She sticks her hand in a bag of hair before she makes the call and she uses a different voice. Before you ask, no, I don't recognize the hair or the voice.*

I relayed all of that weirdness to Oscar and Melly. "Do you think your Easton is still okay?" I asked Rufus.

Rufus was silent for a minute. Then he extended his claws again and didn't bother to draw them back. *I think so,* he said. *Because the impostor keeps threatening to kill her whenever I get a scratch in.*

FIVE

MONDAY, SEPTEMBER 7, 11:46 A.M.

"OF COURSE CATS ARE SMARTER THAN DOGS.
DO I LOOK LIKE I FETCH?"
—RUFUS BRUTUS THE THIRD

Fergie began barking and jumping around like she'd sudden-ly been possessed. She looked like some kind of demented fluffy pink tennis ball.

"What's she saying?" Melly asked me.

"I don't know," I said. "I don't speak Dog. Just Cat." Every now and then I could get a word out of what a dog said, but usually it sounded like barking to me. Dogs and cats could talk to each other, apparently, though mostly they didn't like to. Meep said most dogs were slow and it wasn't worth bothering to talk to them. I was pretty sure dogs probably said the same thing about cats. Of course, Meep could be pretty stupid sometimes.

She says the dog walker is across the street, said Rufus. *Be quiet, Fergie, she might hear you.*

Fergie quieted down, not a moment too soon. Some girl with four dogs in tow was on the other side of the street,

49

headed toward the York. They were pulling her along, and at the rate the collie was going, they were going to be at the hotel soon. Very soon.

"Oh crap," I said. "We've got to get you guys back before the dog walker figures out you're gone."

I am NOT going back.

"What do you mean?" I asked.

I think I was pretty clear. I am not setting foot in that room again. I've been in this prison for days. I've even soiled myself. I am NOT going back.

I leaned over to look at him more carefully. I didn't smell cat pee, but I did smell perfume. A lot of it. It was really floraly, and not in a good way. And what? Was that hairspray? Close up, I could see that his fur was sticking out in every direction.

"What happened to you?" I asked, rubbing at my nose.

He was quiet for just a second. *She got me back into this cage by emptying a can of hairspray on me. And she sprayed me with perfume a few times.*

A few times? Smelled more like an entire bottle. I guess whoever the impostor was, she was pro animal testing. "Well, we still need to get you back," I said. "We can't take you with us."

"What's going on?" asked Melly.

"Rufus says he won't go back." I looked across the street. The dog walker was picking up some poop, but she was still dangerously close to the corner. I stood up and grabbed the carrier and Fergie's leash. "We've got to go!"

I will scream like you have never heard a cat scream, said Rufus. *Everyone within the block will hear. You don't want that, do you?*

I stopped. His eyes were boring holes into my soul. I didn't doubt he would do exactly what he said. For a not very large cat with a weird round head and funky, tiny folded ears, he was pretty intimidating.

"But—"

Besides, you may be useful. You can help me find Easton.

I sighed and looked from Melly to Oscar to Rufus. "What do you guys think?" I asked.

"No idea," said Oscar. "I've only heard half the conversation. But I'm all for whatever the cat says. Whoever that is up there is evil. Eeeev-viiiillll."

"What about Fergie?" I asked. Did I have to think of everything? "How are we supposed to smuggle a pink dog and a pink cat all the way back to the suburbs? What're we supposed to do with them when we get home? And what about the dog walker?" She'd finished picking up the poop and was untangling the leashes of a really overweight bulldog and a poodle. But she was getting closer to the corner.

Fergie will be fine with the impostor, won't you, Fergie? She can be our eyes and ears on the inside.

Fergie let out one quick yip and panted. Rufus had her trained well. He was obviously the brains in the operation, which left Fergie as the not very muscular muscle.

"I don't think—"

Melly cleared her throat and jerked her head in the

direction of the dog walker. She and Oscar looked at me like they were waiting for instructions.

Frick on a stick. I closed my eyes for a moment. "Okay, okay. Let's do this."

I dumped the water bottles and muffins out of my backpack and opened the door to the cat carrier. Rufus immediately poked his head out but paused when I held up my hand. At least he was listening to me — a little. That was more than I got out of Meep. Or my human friends, for that matter.

"I'm not lugging that smelly cat carrier. It's too noticeable." I mean, really. Hot pink with rhinestones? And the Eau du Cat plus whatever nasty perfume she'd sprayed him down with wasn't helping. "And we're riding on Metra. I don't think they even allow animals. So you have to go in here." I held open the top of my backpack. Rufus sniffed loudly once, but climbed in.

Oy. Out of the carrier, he smelled even worse. I was going to have to fumigate my backpack after this. Some perfumes should be outlawed as chemical warfare.

"Oscar, Melly, you guys get going to Union Station. I'll meet you on the 12:35 train, okay? Last car. Can you get me a ticket?"

Oscar saluted. "What're you going to do?" he asked.

"I'm not sure yet," I said. I just knew it would probably be easier to do whatever it was without Oscar's help. He and Melly took off after one last sip of lemonade. I threw down the money for the bill and an extra dollar tip for the waitress. It probably wouldn't make up for ditching the cat carrier there, but it was the best I could do. I looked across the street, where the dog walker was stopped at the corner waiting for the light.

I slung the backpack over my shoulder and caught up with the dog walker. "Hey," I called out when I was close enough. She turned and saw Fergie and came to meet me.

"What's up?" she asked. "Did She-Who-Shouldn't-Be-Named finally decide to replace me?" She bent down to pet Fergie, who went into a total paroxysm of glee. I will never understand dogs.

"Um, no," I said. "She was running late and Fergie had to . . . you know, go, so I said I'd walk the dog and meet you. You can give Fergie to the concierge when you're done." I held out the leash and the dog walker took it.

"Huh. I'm surprised she didn't just let poor little Fergs go in the room again." She pulled the poodle back from his in-depth sniff of my backpack and rear end. I shuffled a few steps backward before the poodle could get any closer to Rufus.

"Yeah, me too," I said and let out the breath I'd been holding. It looked like she'd bought the story. "Well, have fun!" I turned to go. That was easy.

Nice job, said Rufus. He poked his head out of the top of the pack. *You're a pretty good liar.*

"Um, thanks," I said. Coming from a cat, that was actually a compliment.

"Hey, wait!" yelled the dog walker. "Is that Tiddlywinks? Hey, where are you going? Stop!"

I didn't bother to turn around. I just ran.

 53

SIX

MONDAY, SEPTEMBER 7, 12:25 P.M.

"ANYBODY CAN EXERCISE . . . BUT THIS KIND OF LETHARGY
TAKES REAL DISCIPLINE."
—GARFIELD THE CAT (JIM DAVIS)

I found Oscar and Melly on the last train car. I flopped down next to Oscar, completely out of breath, and dropped the backpack on the facing seat opposite, right next to Melly. Let her deal with the smell for a while.

"What happened?" asked Melly. "Are you okay?"

"She saw Rufus as I was leaving. I had to make a run for it." Stupid cat.

Rufus poked his head out. *It doesn't matter. They would have discovered my absence soon enough.*

"Yeah, well, I could have done without the exercise."

Well, I could have done without feeling like a milkshake. You really ought to work on your pacing and stride.

Nice. Exercise advice from a cat who probably sleeps more than he walks. The train took off and I let out a sigh of relief. The dog walker had really followed me for only about a block, and had given up when the bulldog had got-

54

ten tangled up with Fergie. Or maybe Fergie had done that on purpose. I don't know. Rufus had been yelling something at her. But I couldn't shake the feeling that everyone was staring at me, looking for the catnapper. I put my feet up on the seat opposite me and sank down as far as I could.

"So, what now?" asked Oscar. "Whose butt do we kick next?"

"First things first," I said. "Where are we going to stash Rufus?"

Oscar looked at me like I was nuts. "He goes home with you, of course. You're the only one who can talk to him."

"My mom is allergic to cats."

"But you've got a cat," said Melly, while Oscar said, "D'oh!"

"I know *that*," I said. "Meep's a designer cat. She's hypoallergenic. Mom's really allergic to cats, but they figured the only way to support my Talent was to get a cat, so they found Meep for me. Paid the big bucks for her too." Probably a good thing. Otherwise, I'd have no one to talk to at home.

"Oh," said Oscar. "Well, *I* can't take him. Fluff would chew him into little bitty pieces. He hates cats." That was true. Oscar's dog was a huge Doberman and had a serious chip on his shoulder about cats. I'd tried to have Meep talk to him once to find out why, and Fluff had nearly gone through Oscar's screen door trying to eat poor Meep. That had cost me some serious tuna.

"I can't take him," said Melly. "My dad would freak. He's

got some big meetings set up at his home office this week with some investor people. I'm not even supposed to be home if I can help it. I've even got blanket permission to sleep over at Oscar's house or your place."

Monkey snot. Monkey snot on a stick. "Okay, okay. I'll take him tonight, but we've got to figure out something better."

"So," said Melly. "I think we should be logical about this." She pulled out a notebook and a pen from her bag. "What do we know so far?"

That I should never listen to my friends. Or cats. And, apparently, I was never going to make it as a cross-country runner.

"Not much," said Oscar. For once, I agreed with him completely.

"Well," said Melly, scribbling, "that's not entirely true. We know that someone is impersonating Easton West."

"For reasons unknown," I said.

"And that the real Easton is alive," she continued.

"Presumably," I said. Rufus hissed at me.

"And the impostor has a bag of hair that isn't Easton's." Melly wrinkled her nose as she wrote that part down.

"Which is pretty high on the grossness scale," said Oscar. "I mean, even if it was Ty's hair? Still gross."

"And the impostor talks to someone on the phone named Alan." Melly stopped writing.

"And has a seriously bad attitude," I added.

And I am going to scratch her eyeballs out, said Rufus.

I didn't bother to relay that information on. This cat was a serious handful. I opened the top of my bag so I could give him the evil eye. "You are not to leave my room when we get to my house. At all. You got it?"

I'll be requiring some decent food and a litter box, he said. *If you have that in your room, then we are agreed.*

It was going to be a long night.

♥

Oscar and Melly dropped me off at home and left to do some Internet research at Oscar's house to see if they could figure out who Alan might be and what else they could dig up. Oscar was the king of the Internet, after all. I went in the back-door, hoping to avoid everyone. No luck. Emmy was in the kitchen.

"What're you up to?" she asked.

"Nothing. What are *you* up to?" I walked around her and grabbed a couple of bowls, some cat food, and a glass of water. Meep wasn't big on sharing her food. Or her house, probably. I grabbed a can of tuna too. A bribe was in order.

"I'm getting a snack. Why'd you come in the back door?"

Geez. Suspicious much? "No reason. Why're you so annoying?"

"Why're you so grouchy?"

I grunted at her and left the kitchen, juggling all the stuff. The best policy to take with Emmy was to ignore everything, deny everything, and stay out of her sight. She was nosy squared. Mom should have never given her those *Harriet the Spy* books when she was younger. Of course, she'd been, like, three when she read them. Overachiever.

Meep woke up from her midafternoon windowsill nap when I shut my bedroom door and locked it. She stretched and yawned, then came to attention as she caught a whiff of Rufus—or, rather, the perfume-plus-hairspray explosion. It was giving me a headache.

What's up? asked Meep. *Who's in the bag?*

I set the backpack on the floor and opened the top flap. Rufus shot out on full alert. When he saw Meep, he sat down all prim and proper and started cleaning his shoulder—or tried to. There was so much hairspray on him that his shoulder fur was kind of flared out in solid wings. Cat politics. I guess I could have warned him that Meep's not big on protocol.

"Meep," I said, "meet Rufus Brutus the Third. Rufus, meet Meep."

Meep stretched again and then ambled over to sniff Rufus's butt. She was a lot like a dog that way, though I'd never tell her that. I like my bed not peed in.

Where'd you find this one? asked Meep. *He smells.* She cocked an eye at the tuna I was carrying. *I hope that's for me?*

Rufus flattened his ears and sat up straighter. *I'll have you know I was being held against my will. I am perfectly capable of bathing myself in normal circumstances.* He bared his teeth slightly.

Time for some distraction before they got in a literal or

figurative pissing fight. I divvied up the tuna and set both bowls down. "Snack time," I said. "Play nice, Meep. It's not Rufus's fault he stinks—or that he's pink."

Pink? Meep looked up from her tuna. *What are you talking about?*

Oh yeah. I always forget that cats can't see shades of red. I guess it's a good thing Easton hadn't dyed Rufus lime green. *That* he would have noticed and he probably wouldn't have been pleased.

"Nothing," I said, and flopped down on my bed. As soon as I did, my cell phone went off. Lady Gaga again. I stuck it under my pillow. Oscar could wait.

Rufus finished his tuna first, which I wasn't surprised at. The Easton impostor probably hadn't been feeding him. He went back to trying to clean himself, keeping one eye on Meep. Meep gulped the last bite, looked pointedly at me and wrinkled her nose.

I sighed. "Rufus, we've got to get you a real bath. I think you could sit there all day doing that and you'd still reek." Besides, who knew if that stuff was okay for cat consumption? If they didn't even want to test it on animals, they probably wouldn't recommend they ingest it either.

He looked offended, but he didn't argue. His tongue probably felt shellacked.

"Meep, can you check and see if anyone's between my room and the bathroom? I know Emmy's home, but I'm not sure about Mom and Dad."

Fine, said Meep. *But I want more tuna later.*

I held open the door just enough for her to get through and closed it again after her. Meep came back a minute later and scratched at the door.

All clear, she said. *I don't see anyone.*

I opened the door and motioned for Rufus to follow me. We were almost at the bathroom when Emmy's face materialized in front of me with an evil grin. She stepped away from the wall and shook off the stripes of the wallpaper.

"Emmy!" I yelped. "Meep, you said you didn't see anyone!"

I didn't, said Meep. *You didn't say anything about smell. Besides, her stink is all over the house. How was I supposed to know?*

"I knew you were up to something!" Emmy said. "Where'd that cat come from? Why's it pink? What's going on?"

I heard a door shut somewhere in the house. "Gah!" I said. "Everybody, in the bathroom! Now!" I pushed Emmy ahead of me and Rufus and Meep ran between our legs. I shut the door and locked it.

"Mom's gonna kill you," said Emmy. "You know she's allergic."

"I know that!" I put my hand over my eyes and counted silently to ten. "Look, Emmy, it's a secret, okay?"

"Why?"

I removed my hand and looked at her. Maybe I could try the truth? She did have a soft spot for animals in distress. Whenever we ran into cats wandering around outside she'd make me ask them if they were lost. "Oscar and Melly and

I are trying to find this cat's person. She's been kidnapped. The owner, that is, not Rufus."

Emmy looked at me doubtfully and put her hands on her hips.

"Fine," I said. "I'll owe you one, okay? Anything you want. Just help me hide the cat from Mom."

Emmy smiled her evil smile again. I was doomed, but at least Rufus was going to get a bath.

EASTON WEST'S BLOG

Monday, September 7, 9:35 P.M.: I was planning on posting today about the incredible time I'm having on set watching Victoria do her thing. But instead, I have some terrible news.

For the second time in two days, I've had to deal with the Chicago police. This time, apparently some crazy fan has stolen my beloved Tiddlywinks. Be on the lookout for a short girl with dark hair and a pink cat.

I am, of course, completely inconsolable. Victoria has so kindly offered to put me up at her house in the suburbs so I can be alone in my grief. ❤

seven

TUESDAY, SEPTEMBER 8, 7:35 A.M.

"A MAN HAS TO WORK SO HARD SO THAT SOMETHING OF HIS PERSONALITY
STAYS ALIVE. A TOMCAT HAS IT SO EASY. HE HAS ONLY
TO SPRAY AND HIS PRESENCE IS THERE FOR YEARS ON RAINY DAYS."
—ANONYMOUS INTERNET QUOTE, OFTEN INCORRECTLY ATTRIBUTED TO ALBERT
EINSTEIN, WHO WAS PROBABLY TOO SMART TO MESS AROUND WITH CATS

Oscar and Melly were waiting for me on the right side of
the concrete front steps in our standard meeting spot outside
school. It was a little chilly out, so everyone else was hurrying inside, making Oscar and his pitch-black hair and green-
streaked bangs even easier to spot than normal. He's nearly
six feet tall, which really isn't fair. We're both half Asian, and
I barely crack five feet. Even worse, Emmy inherited Mom's
height. She's already taller than me.

"Nat!" Oscar yelled as soon as he saw me. "Why didn't
you call me back last night? Get over here right now, girl!
You have to see this!" He waved his open laptop around in
the air and nearly took off some guy's head. The stream of
people around him eddied even farther out. By the time I
fought my way through to join my friends, it was like we
were a little island of freakishness.

"So what did you guys figure out?" I asked.

Melly shrugged and gestured to Oscar, who swung his laptop around and stuck it right in my face. Easton's blog was on the screen. I pushed the laptop back a few inches away from my nose. "Can you break it down for me, Oscar? The bell's gonna ring anytime now."

"Basically, she says you kidnapped her cat and that she's going to be recovering from the trauma at Victoria's house." He closed his laptop and stuck it in his messenger bag.

"Great."

"She notified the police too, and they're on the lookout for a short girl with a pink cat." Oscar sounded way too happy about the news.

"Lovely."

"Something wrong?" asked Melly.

I yawned. "I owe Emmy big time, my backpack still kinda smells even after I washed it, and I got no sleep with all the arguing Meep and Rufus were doing last night." I had the bad feeling I was going to come home to a room completely shredded. I'd threatened Meep and Rufus both, but some territorial urges can't be denied. "Not to mention there's probably a wanted poster with my name on it somewhere. What could be wrong?" The only luck I'd had so far was that Mom had been out until late working on something, so no huge allergy attacks. Yet.

"We did find out a couple of possibles named Alan. I made a list." Oscar handed me a sheet of paper folded into a tiny triangle. "I thought we could run them by Rufus after school and see if anything jogs his memory."

"Okay," I said. "Sounds good." Not really, but if it helped get my life back to normal, I was for it.

Oscar gave me his thousand-watt smile. "I knew you were on board," he said. "Come on, Cat Girl, what are we standing out here for? It's cold!"

He looped his arm through mine and reached back to pull Melly along for the ride too. I looked around, but at least no one seemed to have caught his Cat Girl comment.

Not that anyone generally paid any attention to us anyway.

♥

For once, I was glad that the first half of my school day didn't include Oscar or Melly so I could put the whole Easton fiasco out of mind. I had trig first period, which is plain evil as far as scheduling goes. No one should be expected to do math first thing in the morning. There were only two good things about the situation: it was my best subject (even if it was way too early and I was the only sophomore in the class) and Ian Abbott sat right next to me.

Not that I'd ever admit it, but I was glad Melly wasn't as good at math as I was. She and Oscar were both in geometry, along with the rest of the tenth graders. Most boys had a way of completely forgetting I was in a room when Melly was around. Even the juniors and seniors. Ian seemed different, but you never knew about testosterone. It addled the brain.

He wasn't her type anyway. She had a thing for tortured

artists who also happened to work out a lot. Ian was tall and lanky, but there wasn't anything tortured about him. He always seemed to have a sly grin on his face, like he'd just thought of this hilarious joke that he was about to tell you and it would be so funny you would pee your pants. And he knew you would, which was why he was smiling to begin with.

The only remotely tortured thing about him was his dark wavy brown hair. It always looked like he'd woken up, combed it through once with his fingers, and then said the heck with it. Some days it was all I could do not to reach over and fix his hair while we were in class.

I slid into my seat a few minutes before the bell rang and smiled at Ian. He grinned back and wrinkled his nose at me. His nose was a little too big for his face, just like his grin, but instead of making him look clownish, it gave him a devilish air. Or maybe that was his eyebrows. They had a natural arch to them.

"Hey, Natalie," he said. "What did you get for the last problem? I swear I did it five times and got five different answers."

Mr. Beck was not afraid of ruining a student's holiday weekend. In fact, I think that's what he aimed for. I shuffled through my backpack and came up with last Friday's homework, which thankfully hadn't absorbed the lingering odor of cat and perfume. I handed it over to Ian and he compared it to his.

"Great. Not one of my answers matches up with yours."

"I could be wrong," I said. Doubtful, but possible. Let's be honest: I rock trig.

"No, I'm sure you're right. After all, super-geniusness runs in the family, doesn't it?" He wiggled one of those perfect eyebrows at me.

I took my paper back. "That's just my little sister." And my mom, but who's counting?

"She's a senior, right? How old is she?"

I nodded once, held my breath, and went back to digging in my backpack. "Twelve." I dug out some pencils, but when I came up for air, he was still looking at me expectantly.

"I saw her do her chameleon thing in the hall once. It was totally cool. Your whole family has Talent, right?"

I nodded again and braced myself for The Question. I guessed I should be glad it had taken this long to come up between us, since I'd been in geometry with him all last year, though it had only been since trig that I'd worked up the courage to actually sit next to him. Usually, the Talent thing is the first thing people ask me when they find out what my last name is. Viv hadn't been shy about her Talents. Her levitation skill had figured prominently in the senior prank last year. People were still talking about it.

He didn't disappoint. "So, what's your Talent?"

"Sorry," I said, looking down into my backpack again instead of at him. "Classified." That's a complete lie, but one that always worked with the non-Talented. People always believed anything that sounded like a conspiracy theory. Besides, it made my Talent sound much cooler than it was.

"Oh, yeah," he said. "Sorry."

"No problem!" I said as cheerfully as I could manage. "Emmy's really not supposed to show hers off in public, but she's twelve, so whaddaya do, right?"

"Yeah, my little brother is ten. I know exactly what you mean. He still picks his nose in public." He looked a little uncomfortable after I'd blown him off, but that was still better than what I'm sure his reaction would have been if I'd actually told him I could talk to cats. Not that I ever told anyone.

At least, not since kindergarten. I'd learned *that* lesson quickly. Luckily, the kid I'd told had moved away soon after and I hadn't had to live with the taunts for long. A month of being meowed at was enough for me. I didn't tell Oscar or Melly until we'd been good friends for half a year—and I'd made them pinky swear first.

I decided to change the subject. The last thing I wanted was for Ian to feel awkward around me. I felt inept enough for both of us. "So, are you ready for the test this week?"

He leaned back in his chair and groaned. "No! Not even close. And knowing the Beck-Man, he'll load us up with more homework tonight. The man is evil."

That was probably true. Mr. Beck was notorious for his homework. The bigger the test, the more he'd pile on us right before it. He called it practice. Right now, I'd call it an opportunity.

"I could help if you want. I mean, I'm not doing anything after school today." At least, nothing that I wanted to be doing. I hoped he didn't notice me swallow the sudden flood of saliva that had hit my mouth.

"Really? That would be great! You always kick my butt on the tests. You really don't mind?"

"It's Tuesday. I don't have anything more exciting going on, and I've gotta do the homework anyway." And I'd do an entire book full of problems to hang out with Ian outside of school.

"My house or yours?"

"Yours, if that's okay. My house is a little crazy." Like an insane asylum crazy, plus one stuck-up pink cat. The last thing I wanted to do was bring Ian into that mess. That would've been about as bad as telling him I talk to cats. Maybe worse.

He scribbled his address and phone number on my notebook, which was convenient since I wasn't about to sound like a stalker and admit that I already knew where he lived.

EIGHT

"WAY DOWN DEEP, WE'RE ALL MOTIVATED BY THE SAME URGES.
CATS HAVE THE COURAGE TO LIVE BY THEM."
—JIM DAVIS

The day was definitely looking up. Melly could now officially get off my back about making a move on Ian. (She just didn't get it. It was easy for her. She never had to make the first move. Guys came to her.) I'd even snuck a quick nap in my third period art class during a video about pointillism.

"Guess what?" I said as soon as I joined Melly and Oscar at our usual lunch table.

"You've come up with a plan to help Easton?" mumbled Oscar around a bite of his tuna fish sandwich. Half of it was already gone. He was always the first of us to arrive at lunch, being both incredibly food motivated and having a class two doors down from the cafeteria. How he managed to stay stick thin, I'll never know.

"No, much better." Easton was the last thing on my mind. "I've got a homework date with Ian Abbott!"

"Woot!" said Melly, and gave me a high five. Oscar stood

70

up and did his crazy dance, waving his arms in the air. A teacher gave him a warning look from across the cafeteria and he sat back down, thankfully. At least he wasn't wearing his kilt today.

"Melly, you'll give me a ride after school, right?" I didn't have a car. Though even if I had one, I wouldn't be able drive it. My mom was requiring me to complete seventy-five hours of supervised driving time on my learner's permit on top of the time I'd already spent in driving school this past summer. Since neither she nor dad ever actually wanted to set foot in a car with me, I'd probably be eighteen before I got my full license.

"Wait," said Oscar. "You mean today? You can't go today."

I took a deep breath and counted to three silently while Oscar wagged his finger in my face. "*What* are you talking about?"

"You promised you'd talk to Rufus!"

I pushed his hand away and opened my yogurt. "Look, I want to find Easton and get rid of that cat as much as you do, but it can wait for two hours."

"The clock is ticking," said Oscar. "There's no telling what that impostor is doing to Easton West. Right. Now."

I looked at Melly for help. There was no way I was canceling my homework date with Ian to talk with an annoying cat about his equally annoying owner.

Melly cleared her throat. "I've got news too," she said. "I signed us all up as extras in the movie!" She passed out

71

sheets of paper to me and Oscar. "These are the releases. You have to have a parent sign it and be sure to bring it back tomorrow. There's a cafeteria scene, so technically we're rehearsing right now!"

"Awesome sauce!" said Oscar, the prospect of his big acting debut enough to divert him for a moment at least.

When he was done fist pumping, she continued. "I'm a little bummed, though. They're only going to be shooting a few scenes here at the school with background extras — that's what we'd be. The rest of the shoots are going to be on location around the city."

"Don't worry," said Oscar. "You come to school tomorrow looking hotter than hot, and I know you'll have the director drooling all over you. They'll probably hire you on the spot, if Ty doesn't propose first." He ate the rest of his tuna sandwich in one bite. I threw a napkin at him. He took the hint and wiped his chin.

Melly winked at me. "You never know," she said. "Maybe you're Ty's type after all."

That launched Oscar into a discussion of Ty's soulful brown eyes and whether or not he looked better blond like in his last movie or his usual dark brown. I smiled at Melly. She had my back.

But I'd be on my own with Ian tonight.

 72

NINE

"THOU ART THE GREAT CAT, THE AVENGER OF THE GODS, AND THE JUDGE OF
WORDS, AND THE PRESIDENT OF THE SOVEREIGN CHIEFS, AND THE GOVERNOR OF
THE HOLY CIRCLE; THOU ART INDEED . . . THE GREAT CAT."
— A HYMN TO THE EGYPTIAN GOD RA

Melly dropped me off at Ian's house with a promise to pick
me up at 5:30. I took a couple of deep breaths, swallowed the
last of the breath mint Melly had pushed on me, and knocked
on the door.

A little kid answered and just stood there staring at me.
He must be the nose picker Ian had told me about earlier.

"Um, hi? I'm Nat. I'm here to study with Ian?"

"Ian!" The kid yelled at the top of his lungs, nearly blowing my eardrums. "There's a girl for you at the door!"

"I'll be right there!" Ian yelled back.

The kid didn't budge an inch, just stayed right in the
middle of the doorway staring at me. Nice. I stared back at
him. I knew how to play the game. I've got a little sister.

Then an orange and white tabby cat strolled up to the
door, looked up at me, and blinked in surprise. I don't know
how or why it works, but cats all immediately know that they

can talk to me as soon as they see me. I've asked Meep about it before, but Meep's got the attention span of a gnat and I've never gotten anything more out of her than "we just know," which is her answer to lots of things.

Hello, the cat mewed at me. *I didn't know Ian knew anyone interesting. This one is Jasper. If you take one step toward him, he'll scatter. He's like a rat that way.*

I was getting tired of standing on the stoop, so I did what the cat suggested and took a quick step toward Jasper. His eyes opened wide and he disappeared somewhere into the house.

"Thanks," I said, and went inside and closed the door. "I'm Nat." I'd learned long ago that cats are really particular about introductions. They find it unutterably rude if you don't introduce yourself.

I'm Purr Daddy. You can call me PD. The humans here call me Pebbles. He let a delicate shudder ruffle the fur across his back as he said it, though I personally thought "Purr Daddy" sounded stupider than Pebbles. But I'm not a cat.

"Nice to meet you," I said.

What are you doing here?

"I'm here to study trig with Ian." Another lesson I learned a long time ago: cats are nosy and will give you no peace until you tell them what's up. It's best to get it over with up front unless you have a reason to lie, but then you'd better have a really good poker face, since they could usually tell when you were lying. Not quite as reliable as Viv's built-in lie detector, but most cats could spot a lie a mile away.

Oh, he said, and studied me intently for a moment. *He always feeds me on time, not like the little rat. I like Ian. He's okay.* He wound between my legs and rubbed his head on my shin, then looked up at me from between my purple Converse All Stars.

He sings in the shower, you know. Mostly reggae. Won't do it in front of people, though.

"Um, okay," I said. I was saved from saying anything else by Ian clumping down the stairs. PD sat on my foot.

"What're you doing at the door? Where'd Jasper go? Didn't he invite you in?" He noticed PD sitting on my foot. "Oh, I hope you're not allergic to cats or anything."

"I'm okay with cats," I said, and lightly shook my foot. PD stretched and stood up. "Your brother took off somewhere."

"Sorry," he said. "I was just, uh, upstairs."

Bathroom, said PD. *Combing his hair, by the looks of it.* He looked up at me and purred. I could swear he winked.

Ian's hair was remarkably tamed. It still stuck up in back, but the front looked like he'd actually won the battle for once. It made me want to mess it up.

"Well," he said. "I set everything up in the dining room. Mom said we need to be done by six because of dinner. Is that okay?"

"Sure, my friends Melly and Oscar are picking me up before then." I shouldered my bag and followed him into the dining room. It was nice and comfortable with cushiony seats and flowers on the table, completely unlike mine at home, which was often covered in research paper stuff in between (and sometimes during) meals. Ian's stuff was spread out at one end of the table along with a pitcher of lemonade and some crackers, cheese, and chocolate chip cookies.

"Wow," I said, sitting down in the chair next to his. "Nice! I don't have it this good at home. I need to study at your house more often!" Oops. I hoped he didn't think that was too forward, but seriously. Cookies?

He ducked his head and blushed a little. "My mom always says that you think better on a full stomach than an empty one." Oh, too cute. But I decided then and there that he should never ever meet my mom, not until some far off day after we'd fallen in love and were about to get married. Maybe not even then.

We got to work on the trig. The test was likely to be of epic proportions based on the amount of homework Mr. Beck had given us. Ian actually was doing pretty well on the problems, though he had a tendency to mix up the reciprocal of a function with its inverse.

Ian's mom came by after about an hour to refill the lemonade and the plate of cookies. It was easy to see where Ian got his looks from. He had her eyelashes and the same dimple in his chin, though her hair was a lot neater and blonde-ish. She patted him on the head and then went back to the kitchen, probably to make some more cookies. I should be so lucky.

"Your mom is really nice," I said.

"She's okay. Mom works part time as an office manager and my dad works at Wrigley Field. Just back office stuff, nothing interesting. It must be a lot cooler to be in your family, with everyone having a superpower."

"Talent," I said automatically, then winced. Mom had ingrained that in my head. She always said that superpowers were for comic books. "It's not really all that cool, trust me. I'd rather my mom could bake cookies as good as your mom." The last time my mom had made cookies, I could have donated them to the field hockey team to use as pucks.

Ian didn't look convinced, but he went back to work. I was really flubbing up this not-date homework date royally. I sounded so stuck up, correcting him like that. I doodled in my notebook while I tried to think of some way to get things back on track.

Then Ian's mom yelled at him from the kitchen. "Ian, I need you to give Pebbles his pill now."

"Aw, Mom, can't I do that later? We're right in the middle of trig!" He shot a dirty look at Pebbles, a.k.a. Purr Daddy, who had wandered in a while ago and was sunning himself on a windowsill. Ian whispered to me, "I hate giving him his stupid pills. He always freaks out. It's like trying to wrestle a chainsaw."

PD licked a paw and winked at me. Such a cat.

"No, I need you to do it now. We're supposed to give him the pill at the same time every day."

"Can't Jasper do it? We're busy!"

"You want to trade, you trade. But that means you're back on litter box duty. Besides, it will take you all of two seconds."

"All right already!" Ian got up. "Crap. I'll be right back. Can you keep an eye on him for me so he doesn't get away? Last time I had to dig him out from behind the couch. I don't know how he always seems to know what's coming."

"Sure," I said. Maybe this was my chance to impress Ian. After all, if there was any Talent that I could be said to have, it was with cats. I waited until I thought Ian was out of hearing range.

"PD, how about you let me give you the pill and you take it nicely?"

He blinked at me. *Why?* he purred. *I like to play with Ian. It's the only exercise I get these days. And besides, the pills taste awful.*

They taste awful? I could point out that he'd spent the better part of the last twenty minutes licking his hind end, but I figured that wouldn't get me anywhere. Cats aren't much for logic.

"Because it's good for you."

Like I believe that. That's what they said before they took the boys.

The boys? "What're you talking about?"

You know, the boys. The furry dice. My balls. He rolled over flat onto his back and flicked his tail at the nether region he'd been so assiduously cleaning.

Oh. The boys. Who knew? Male cats were more like teenage boys than I'd ever thought.

"Well, this isn't like that. These pills actually do help you. And, you know, I just —"

PD stopped licking himself to really stare at me. *Hmm-mmm, you're in heat for him, aren't you? How cute!*

I blushed. Called out by the cat. My life was hitting a new low. "I'm not in *heat*," I whispered at him. "I just *like* him, that's all." PD rolled around on the floor, chuckling, which sounded a bit like he was going to cough up some-thing nasty. "Look, what do you want? How about some tuna?" That always works with Meep. I think she'd sell her soul for tuna.

PD stopped rolling and perked up his ears. Ha ha, I got him! But then he surprised me.

Not tuna . . . but I'll think of something. It's a deal.

Now that worried me. PD was obviously smarter than Meep. But how bad could it be? Either way, before I could change my mind, Ian was back with a pill bottle, a box of bandages, and a stoic look on his face.

"Can you cover the door for me, Nat? He's bound to make a run for it."

Now was my chance. "Hey, Ian, why don't you let me try? I'm pretty good with cats."

"Oh no, I couldn't let you do that. He'll rip you to shreds.

I know he looks cute and everything, but he's like a little demon in a fur coat."

I took the bottle from him and got a pill out. It was now or never. "I bet I can get him to take it on the first try. And if I can't, you can take over and I'll do the next ten problems. How's that?"

Ian looked doubtful, which, I had to say, was a really adorable look for him. "He's never taken it on a first try."

"Well, I bet I can get him to. You in?"

"Sure, but be careful." He grinned at me. "Number 18 looks like a real headache of a problem."

I smiled and turned to PD. He'd better not back out on me now. "Come here, Pebbles," I cooed and wiggled my fingers at him. He stretched and yawned, but then jumped up on the table and ambled over to me, to Ian's amazement. I scratched him a few times behind the ears and tapped him on the nose lightly. Might as well put on a good show.

"I've got a treat for you," I said and held up the pill. PD meowed, playing along, but gave me the evil eye from the side Ian couldn't see. I held the pill out to him and he knocked it back like it was a piece of sushi. I gave him a few more pats on the head as Ian stared at me, openmouthed.

"I can't believe it! How did you do that? He's like demon spawn normally, I swear!"

PD purred and jumped down to twine his way back and forth around my ankles. Geez, what a ham. I am so not ever introducing him to my cat. He might give Meep some bad

80

ideas she would be too stupid to think up on her own.

"I told you, I'm good with cats."

"Well, I guess the next ten problems are mine, huh? You won that one fair and square." Ian sat back down next to me and picked up his pencil.

"Actually," I said, as PD jumped in my lap, "I was thinking maybe something else."

"Oh?"

"How about a movie? Maybe this Friday night? I've been wanting to see that new alien invasion movie." I held my breath. Would it work? I'd thrown in the most guy-sounding movie that was out.

"Sure," said Ian with a smile. "You earned it, between the homework help and getting Pebbles to take his pill."

PD poked his head up and headbutted my arm. *You're pretty crafty for a human. I like that.* Then he settled back down and started kneading a hole in my jeans.

Yeah. And he was pretty crafty for a cat. That was two favors I owed now and I wasn't sure whose was going to be worse to pay back: Emmy or PD.

TEN

"ANYONE WHO CONSIDERS PROTOCOL UNIMPORTANT
HAS NEVER DEALT WITH A CAT."
—ROBERT A. HEINLEIN

I walked in the door at home and the first thing I heard was "Aaaaachooo!"

"Bless you," I yelled out, not thinking anything about it. I was halfway down the hallway to my room when Emmy grabbed my arm and pulled me into her room. Rufus was lounging on her bed, licking himself. He didn't even bother to nod at me.

"Where have you been?" she demanded.

"Not that it's any of your business, but I was doing trig homework at somebody's house." I shrugged off her hand. "What's your problem?"

"AaaaaaaaaaCHOO!" Sounded like Mom, probably in her office.

"That's the problem," said Emmy. "But it's yours, not mine." She pointed at Rufus. "Your little buddy there is giving Mom a serious allergy attack."

"Oh, crap," I said, finally remembering. I poked my head out into the hallway. Mom was standing in the doorway of her office, holding a handful of wadded up tissues. Her nose was stoplight red and her eyes looked bloodshot even from down the hall.

"AAAaaaaaaa . . . AAAAAAAaaaa . . . AAAAA-CHOO!" The force of her sneeze made her lose balance and she sagged against the doorframe of her office.

"Um, bless you," I said. She blurrily focused on me. Kind of.

"Oh, Nat," she said. "I didn't hear you come in. Can you get dinner tonight? I just need to rest my eyes for a minute. I don't know what I'm coming down with, but I don't want you girls to get it. I don't want you to miss any school. I felt fine when I came home, but it hit me after that. I think I'm going to have to stay home from work tomorrow."

Oh, man. That was huge. Mom never missed work. Ever. She missed birthday parties and award ceremonies, but she never ever missed work. I'd forgotten just how bad her allergies were. No wonder they'd shelled out the big bucks for Meep. Designer cats weren't cheap.

"Sure, Mom," I said to her back as she turned around and shuffled into her office. I stepped back into Emmy's room and closed the door.

Emmy poked me in the arm. "He's gotta go," she said. "Mom'll figure out she doesn't have the flu soon enough."

"What's he doing out of my room anyway? Rufus, I told you to stay in there and not leave."

Rufus stopped his licking just long enough to glare at me. *I was bored*, he said.

"Emmy—" I said.

"What? He kept meowing at your door. It was annoying." She shrugged.

I sighed and picked up Rufus and tucked him in my backpack, then poked my head back in the hallway. I heard another sneeze and a small, sad little moan come from behind Mom's closed door. I hurried across the hall to my room.

"If you don't fix this by tomorrow, I'm telling," Emmy called after me. I slammed my door. Frick on a stick. I had to get Rufus out of the house. Sooner or later Mom would figure it out—or wind up in the hospital.

Where in the world was I going to hide a pink cat?

♥

I managed to keep Rufus contained in my room all night, though Meep was no help. They both complained constantly about having to be in the same room together. By the time morning came around, I felt like I got about two hours of sleep. Rufus flat out refused to stay outside while I was at school or actually go outside at all. Apparently, the suburbs just didn't cut it for him.

These paws have not touched grass in years, he said. *And they aren't going to start now.*

Melly pulled up outside and honked her horn. Poodle farts. I grabbed Rufus, stuffed him in my backpack again, and ran for the door. I passed Mom in the hallway and she let out a giant sneeze as I went by.

"Hab a good day at schoolb," she said. "Pay attention to your teaschers."

Well, at least she'd have a better day now that I was getting Rufus out of the house. My day? Somehow, I didn't think it was going to be very good.

I tossed my backpack onto the backseat of Melly's car as I climbed in. It slipped across the leather and banged against the door on the opposite side.

Hey, said Rufus. *Watch it! I'm delicate!*

"Is that the cat?" asked Oscar from the front. "You're taking him to school?"

"I had to. It was either that or Mom was going to sneeze a hole through a wall." I opened the bag so Rufus could stick his head out. "I couldn't think of anything else to do with him."

"Cool," said Oscar. "This'll be fun."

Sometimes I don't know what planet Oscar is on. "So, did you figure anything else out last night?" The last I'd heard, Oscar and Melly were doing more research on guys named Alan that were connected with Easton in any way.

"Not much," said Melly. "She dated a guy named Alan Partridge once, but that was, like, five years ago. He was her tennis instructor when she was a teenager."

"Pretty hot," said Oscar. "I'd return his volleys!"

Like he really would. Oscar was mostly all talk. His last boyfriend had burned him bad. I whacked him in the back of the head. "Get your hormones under control, would you? Have we got anything else to go on?"

"Did you get anything else out of Rufus?" asked Melly.

I glared at the cat. He bared his teeth and gave me his version of a cat smile. "No. Just attitude. He said she talks on the phone a lot, disappears for hours at a time, and smells like makeup." Which describes just about any socialite, as far as I know—and at least half the girls at my school, if not all of them.

Your backpack still smells, said Rufus.

"Just don't pee in it and make it worse," I said. I'd washed it again last night, but there was still a slight lingering odor about it if you put your nose right on it.

"What?" said Melly. She turned around in her seat and the car swerved. "Rufus isn't peeing in my car, is he?"

"Eyes! Road!" I said. "No, he's not peeing in your car. Just drive!"

"Okay, okay," said Melly. "Did you guys get your permission forms signed?"

"You better believe it," said Oscar.

I was drawing a blank. "What form?"

Melly groaned. "To be an extra? Nat, how could you forget?"

"Oh," I said. "Well, I was a little busy trying to keep my wheezing, sneezing mom from discovering that it was my fault she couldn't breathe. Not to mention making dinner and keeping Emmy from telling on me." I dug down into my backpack past Rufus and finally came up with the form. He had put a claw or two through it, but other than that it was okay.

Getting a little fresh, aren't you? asked Rufus. *You could have asked first.*

I ignored him and spread the form out on my lap. I'd learned how to do Mom's signature back in middle school when she was always forgetting to sign permission slips for things. I scribbled a messy "Allison Ng" across the bottom and held it up so Melly could see it in the rearview mirror.

"Okay? All better?"

"Yes," she smiled at me in the mirror. "I couldn't do it without you!"

"Five more miles and I can see Ty," said Oscar. "Drive faster, would you, Melly?"

I sighed. "What about the whole Easton-Rufus thing? How about some focus, you guys?" I really wanted this cat out of my house — and my life. Meep may be stupid, but she's not half as annoying as Rufus. He's classic cat, whereas she's practically part dog.

Oscar made a face at me. "I am a child of the times," he said. "I can totally multitask. Besides, Easton is supposed to be here covering the movie, so maybe she'll be on set while they're filming." He stuck his tongue out at me. "And seriously, girl, it's Ty McKenzie. He's hotter than . . ." He paused. "I don't even know how hot he is, he's so hot."

You people are strange, said Rufus.

Yeah, and that coming from a pink cat with a weird round head and an attitude the size of Texas. This day could not end fast enough for me. But at least I'd get to see Ian first thing. God bless trigonometry.

Now there's something I never thought I'd say.

♥

I stuck my Rufus-filled backpack between my feet as I sat down in trig. I'd warned him—repeatedly—that he was not to even let a whisker show, but I didn't trust him. I figured I'd be able to feel him move if I kept the bag there. I set all my books and notebooks down under the desk, except for my trig stuff. With Rufus in my pack, I was carrying almost everything else. Pity my locker was on the other side of the campus.

Ian came in right after me. "Hey, Nat," he said. "Sleep good?" He sat down and smiled at me, a corner of his mouth higher than the other and one eyebrow raised. Wow, that was entirely too shmexy for this early in the morning. My day was looking much better already.

I smiled back. "Okay," I said. "You?"

"Visions of functions dancing in my head," he said and laughed. "Thanks to you."

"Oh, so you were dreaming about me then, huh?" Ha, look at me. Taking a flirting page out of the book of Melly. I put my hand on my face and leaned on my elbow to hide the blush I could feel threatening to come out.

He winked at me. "Yeah, you must have done a 'number' on me yesterday."

Oh, we were just made of cheese. I was trying to think of some funny but flirty comeback when Rufus poked a claw all the way through my book bag and into my leg. I jumped and knocked my notebook onto the floor. Why had I let that stupid cat talk me into removing the claw protectors on his paws? Maybe that Easton lookalike had the right idea. If I didn't know I'd lose a finger or even a hand in the attempt, I'd try to trim those claws. But if Rufus was anything like Meep, clipping his toenails was completely out of the question. She hated it worse than bath time. I'd yet to meet a cat that didn't, though there were rumors they existed.

"You okay?" Ian asked. He picked up my notebook and handed it to me.

"Um, yeah," I said. "Peachy. My leg just fell asleep, I guess." I kicked like I was trying to wake my leg up, but it didn't dislodge Rufus' claw. He let out a little yelp and dug in harder. I coughed to cover up the noise. I reached down and shifted my bag to unhook him, all the while smiling at Ian like a clown on drugs. He just looked at me with that one eyebrow climbing higher and higher.

"Frog in my throat," I said. I wished once again that my cat talking was telepathic. If it were, I'd be giving Rufus a piece of my mind—a big piece. I shoved the bag back under the chair, not caring if I ruffled the fur of his precious highness.

"Oo-kay," said Ian. "Do you need some water?"

"No, I'm fine," I said. Stupid cat. Mr. Beck saved me by coming in the room waving a handful of papers.

"Okay, people," Mr. Beck said. "Are you ready? What do you say we take a test today?"

I loved how he made it a question, as if we had any choice at all in the matter. He handed the stack of tests to a guy named Shackerman and told him to pass it out. Ian looked at me a little nervously and I gave him a thumbs-up. Hopefully the tutoring yesterday helped him and he'd want to do it again. Melly always said the way to a guy's heart was through his stomach (she could make a mean cupcake), but I hoped you could get there through homework too.

The test was pretty easy. I hoped Ian was doing as well on it as I was. I peeked his way a few times and saw him chewing on his pencil, but he wasn't obviously sweating bullets or anything. If my tutoring had helped, that had to be a good thing, right?

I was almost done with the test when I felt Rufus moving around. I poked him with my toe. He stopped for a second and then started shifting around again. I looked around, but no one seemed to have noticed. Mr. Beck was staring at the clock and humming. I dropped my pencil on the floor and leaned down to get it.

"Stop it," I whispered. "Someone is going to see you."

I have to use the facilities, Rufus whispered back.

"What?"

I have to pee!

I faked another coughing fit to cover up Rufus' outburst. Ian looked over at me and raised his eyebrow again. Mr. Beck did too, but it wasn't nearly so cute on him.

"Problem, Miss Ng?" he asked.

"Just a little cough," I said. Now half the class was looking at me. I felt my face turn red. I hoped Ian couldn't tell . . . much. "Um, could I go to the bathroom?" I coughed again, doing my best to sound like I was hacking up a fur ball. "I think maybe I just need some water."

Mr. Beck sighed. "All right, Miss Ng, but no loitering in the hallways. You've only got another ten minutes to finish your test."

I nodded and coughed again. I leaned over to get my backpack and stood up to leave. I was two steps away from the door when Mr. Beck cleared his throat.

"You can leave the backpack," he said. "We are in the middle of a test here, Miss Ng."

I wished he'd quit with the "Miss Ng" thing. It was really annoying, especially since he could barely pronounce it. He drew it out too long. How hard was it to just say "ing"?

"I, um, need it," I said.

Now everyone in the class was looking at me. My face felt like it was on fire.

"You 'need' it?" asked Mr. Beck. He raised his eyebrow again. Someone should really tell him that's not attractive on an old guy. At least, not one with a double chin and really bushy eyebrows.

"Yeah . . . ," I said and stopped. I couldn't think of a good reason to give that didn't involve a cat about to pee on my homework.

Shackerman giggled. "Lady troubles," he said loud enough for everyone to hear. Oh, God. My face went from fire to molten lava.

Mr. Beck's face did too. "Just go, Miss Ng. But hurry back."

I rushed out the door. Hurry back? I might never return. This stupid cat was ruining my life.

 92

eleven

WEDNESDAY, SEPTEMBER 9, 9:03 a.m.

"CATS, FLIES, AND WOMEN ARE EVER AT THEIR TOILETS."
—FRENCH PROVERB

I hurried down the hall to the bathroom and pushed through
the door. No one was in there, for once. At least one of my
prayers had been answered. I went in the stall farthest from
the door and opened the bag so Rufus could get out.

"Don't even talk to me," I said. "Just go."

Go where, exactly? Rufus looked around the stall. It was
standard school issue: chipped green paint, dingy gray tile,
and a toilet with water stains around the base.

"Oh, for . . . here." I picked him up and held him over the
toilet. He immediately tried to climb up my arms toward my
head. "Ow! What are you doing?"

What are you doing? There's water in there!

"Duh! It's the toilet! Hold still. I won't let you fall in.
It's the only place I've got for you to go!" I grabbed him
firmly around the middle and tried to force him back down
to the seat. He went whirling dervish on me and wound up

93

clinging to my shoulder with all four paws — and his claws.

"Agh! Let go! I told you, I'm not going to let you fall in! You have to have seen a toilet before. I mean, *come on*! You're not a kitten!"

Rufus finally released my shoulder and I dropped him onto the ground. He landed on a stray piece of (hopefully unused) toilet paper that was lying on the floor. I tried to get a look at my shoulder. It felt like a bad acupuncturist had gone crazy on me.

This place, he said, *is absolutely disgusting.*

Like a litter box isn't pure nasty? "It's a public high-school bathroom. What did you expect? It's all we've got." He gave me a wicked look. "Look, there's a seat, okay? I'm just going to hold you up on it so you can go. I promise I will not drop you. You will not get wet. So do you have to go or not? I've got to get back to class."

If I must. But if one drop of water lands on this fur, I will carve you into little pieces.

Yeah, like he hadn't already. I could see at least one pin-prick of blood coming through my T-shirt already and there were bound to be more. I picked him up again and held him over the toilet. Just as he was getting his feet firmly planted on the seat, I heard the door open.

Frick. "Just do your thing and don't say anything," I whispered. It was a good thing I'd closed the stall door out of habit.

"Oh, wow, I haven't been in a bathroom this gross since

94

high school," said a voice that sounded strangely familiar.

"Well, Victoria's camped out in the teacher's lounge bathroom, so this is it. Alan seriously needs to have a talk with her. She's a total—"

"Shhhh, Claire! Someone might hear you."

"Oh, I don't care, Candace. Everyone knows she's turned into a huge diva. It's ridiculous. I don't care if she is the love interest. This is Ty's movie, not hers." A toilet flushed.

Claire? Candace? It must be Claire Ryan and Candace Grace! They were B-level teen starlets. I vaguely remembered Oscar mentioning they were in the film too. But Alan? Who was he? I tried to take a peek through the crack between the door and the wall, but I couldn't move far enough to see without dropping Rufus. He hissed. Quietly, thankfully.

"Sorry," I whispered.

"I worked with her on her first movie, you know," said Candace. "I thought she was pretty nice."

"Yeah, well, fame does some funny things to people. She could act back then too." A stall door banged open.

"Seriously. Hey, have you seen Easton? I told her I'd do an exclusive, but I haven't seen her on the set since the day she got here."

Rufus finally started to pee. He obviously really had to go. He must have drunk a gallon of water this morning, from the sound of it.

"No, I haven't seen her," said Claire. "Did you hear about her cat being kidnapped? It even made *The Daily*

Show. Supposedly, Easton's staying at Victoria's place to recuperate."

"Total weirdness. I swear I saw them about to throw down the first day Easton showed up on set, and then I haven't seen her since. I thought she was here to write about how bad Victoria sucks now."

Someone turned the water on for a few seconds and then turned it back off. There was a moment of silence, and a small horrified gasp. Claire said, "Do you smell *that*?"

Two words: cat pee. Actually, five words. Prodigious amounts of cat pee.

"Shhhh," said Candace. "Let's just go, okay? Don't be rude."

I heard the door swing shut behind them. A few moments later, Rufus finally stopped peeing. *You can put me down now,* he said.

I put him directly back in my backpack. I wasn't going to take any chances and besides, I had only, like, three minutes to get back to class and finish my test. Good thing I had only one more problem to do.

Honestly, if I didn't have to turn my test in and pick up my books, I'd skip going back entirely. At least Candace and Claire hadn't actually seen me. Even though I didn't know them, I still didn't want them to think my pee smelled like cat pee. That was just wrong.

TWeLVe

"THe CaT PreTenDS TO SLeeP, THe BeTTer TO See."
—Francois-auguste rene De CHaTeauBrianD

I met Melly and Oscar outside the cafeteria after dumping all of my books and notebooks in my locker. Rufus wasn't as fat as Meep, but he was heavy enough. And when you added his weight to all the books I normally had to cart around, the result was nothing short of a big backache. Dropping off my books didn't seem to make a difference, though. I was starting to think he must have smuggled some cans of tuna in there or something.

"I've got news," I said. "I heard Claire Ryan and Candace Grace talking in the bathroom. They said they haven't seen Easton on set since the day she got here."

"You saw Claire Ryan and Candace Grace?" Oscar jumped up, his eyes as round as bowling balls and his hands flapping. "What were they wearing? How did they look?"

"I don't know," I said. "I only heard them pee. I didn't actually see them. Rufus had a bathroom emergency."

"Oh," said Oscar, momentarily deflated. "Well, how did they sound?"

"Gross!" said Melly before I had a chance to say it.

"I meant their voices, you goons! Get your minds out of the toilet!"

Oscar and Melly followed me into the cafeteria. "You're missing the point, Oscar," I said. "They said they haven't seen Easton on the set at all since the first day. So there's no way we're going to run into the lookalike here."

We got in the sandwich line and I ordered two tuna sandwiches.

"Hungry?" asked Oscar.

"One's for Rufus," I said. "Duh."

"Oh yeah! I forgot all about that. How's that going?"

"Don't ask." I should have made Oscar carry the stupid cat around all day. At least Rufus had kept his head down for second period, but in my art class, he'd started sneezing like crazy. He'd said it was the smell of paint, but whatever it was, I'd had to fake sneeze all through class to cover it up. By the end of the day, the entire school was going to think I was some allergy-prone weirdo with "lady troubles."

We sat down and I opened the backpack enough to stick the tuna sandwich in. Rufus didn't even complain for once, he just tore into it. I was seriously going to have to throw away my backpack after this craziness was over. He wasn't exactly a delicate eater.

"Are you guys as excited as I am?" asked Melly. "Only

a few hours to go until we get to be extras in a real movie!"

"You know it," sang out Oscar. "I am R-E-A-D-Y ready!"

"So, how's it work?" I asked. I'd given Melly my permission form in the car after faking my mom's signature, but I hadn't actually read it, so I really had no clue.

"We're just going to be background extras. That means that we may or may not even be in the movie. Like, they're going to have a bunch of kids around for 'color,' but there's no guarantee we'll actually be in the shot." Melly sighed.

"And they'll feed us!" said Oscar the bottomless pit. "Craft services, here I come!"

"No, I meant, like where are we supposed to go and stuff like that?" Not like I was ever going to be doing this again. I didn't care about the really technical details.

"Oh! We're supposed to meet at the auditorium for a costume check right when school lets out and then come back here to the cafeteria. They're shooting a lunchroom scene. That's why they need all the extras."

"Costume check?"

"Yeah, they make sure no one is wearing any kind of logo on their T-shirts and stuff like that. Maybe give out some clothes if someone shows up in something really inappropriate."

"Like that freshman girl who's always being sent home for the tiny skirts," said Oscar. "You think she'd learn. I mean, seriously, no one wants to see your thong."

"How long is this going to take?" I was hoping to have some new place to dump Rufus at tonight. There was no way

I could bring him home again, and so far, I had absolutely no idea what I was going to do with him. He'd suggested a kitty hotel, but I'd looked them up and they were super expensive, especially the one he said he wanted to go to after I read him the descriptions. Like he needed catnip brought to him on a pillow.

"We should be done by six o'clock. Maybe seven. The cafeteria scene is pretty short." She lowered her voice and pulled some papers from her bag. "I snitched some of the pages for today's shoot from the guy I turned the forms in to. Ty is Freddy and Victoria is Molly."

"Rock on!" said Oscar. He grabbed the pages from Melly and started to pore over them. "You wait and see, Melly. You're going to wind up starring in this movie. I just know it."

I'd bet ten bucks that Oscar already knew the pages by heart. It always amazed me how his brain worked. Stuff that would take me hours to commit to memory he could get in seconds. But ask him to do a math problem? It wasn't pretty.

Sometimes it amazed me that the three of us had become such good friends. Oscar and Melly had the whole starstruck thing in common, but I was honestly not all that interested in any of it. Who wore what when and why and all of that just didn't excite me. Of course, when we'd first started hanging out, Oscar's celebrity addiction really hadn't started yet and Melly had been a scrawny tomboy with semipermanent scabs on her knees from daredevil stunts on the playground. A lot had changed over the years. Yet here we were, still together even if we did drive each other a little nuts. In a good way.

"Make sure you read the pages, Nat," said Melly as we were getting up to go. "We should all be prepared. It could give us an edge."

"Yeah, sure," I said. She gave me an I-don't-believe-you look, so I took the pages from Oscar and started reading on my way out of the cafeteria. It was okay. Kinda normal teen movie stuff. I knew what they were talking about only because Melly had made us watch the Ferris Bueller movie twice this past weekend in preparation.

I wondered if Ian was into old movies. Melly had a collection of, like, every teen movie ever made, and her dad had built a theater room down in their basement so she could study up on them. That could work as a second date, couldn't it? Assuming we actually made it through the first one okay. Also assuming it was safe to bring Ian around Melly and Oscar in their natural habitat. People thought Oscar was crazy at school, but it was nothing like as weird as he could get out of school. It might take some warm-up time for Ian to appreciate the jaw-dropping awesomeness that the full-on Oscar experience brought to your life.

I was folding the pages up to stick them in the front pouch of my backpack when Emmy appeared out of nowhere and grabbed my arm. I nearly dropped the backpack and Rufus let out a grumpy growl.

"Watch it!" I said. "What're you doing?"

"Was that the cat?" asked Emmy, her eyes wide.

"Shhh! Yeah, I couldn't leave him at home, not with mom there."

"Well, she's not there now. She's *here*. I just saw her heading to the principal's office."

"What? Why?" Surely Mr. Beck hadn't called about the whole trig thing? He'd seemed okay when I got back to class. He just wouldn't look at me, unlike stupid Shackerman, who'd given me a huge wink. The jerk. I hated that guy.

"She said she was feeling better. I guess because Rufus was gone, so that makes sense now. And since she wasn't at work, she thought she'd come in to complain about the movie thing. You know, because of my test being moved and all that? Oh my God, Nat, what am I going to do? If she really gets the movie shoot canceled and people find out it was my fault, I'm dead!"

Holy hairy llamas. She wasn't the only one. I'd be guilty by association.

"You've got to do something!" Emmy had a death grip on my arm, but that was second to my own realization that there was actually something one of my sisters couldn't handle. Imagine that. A chink in her armor.

Inspiration, though sketchy, finally came to me. "You go find Principal Johnson and delay him. I saw him in the cafeteria a few minutes ago." He'd made me nervous too, what with Rufus in my bag. He had a knack for figuring out when you were up to something. "I'll deal with Mom."

"Okay," said Emmy. "I'll try." She paled even more and turned to go.

"And Emmy?"

She looked at me.

"If this works out, we're even. Got it?"

She nodded and scampered off like a scared rabbit. Heh. Depending on how painful the next ten minutes were, maybe I should have said that *she* would owe *me*.

THIrTeen

WeDNeSDaY, SepTeMBer 9, 11:44 a.M.

"exercise Is For DOGS."
—rUFUS BrUTUS THe THIrD

I ran down the hall toward the principal's office. Mom would've had to come in through the main door, since it was the only one accessible during the day for visitors. I had a chance of getting to her before she got to the office if I cut through the library.

I almost ran over a freshman carrying a stack of books, but I saw Mom ahead of me walking in that stiff I'm-going-to-kick-butt way she did whenever she was about to go medieval on someone. I slowed down.

If you do that again, I'm going to use your back as a pin cushion. I told you before, I don't enjoy the sensation of becoming a milkshake, said Rufus.

"Shhh!" I whispered over my shoulder. "I'm sorry, but if you say another word, I'm totally going to dunk you in the toilet." He let out a low hiss, but didn't say anything else. "And I'm sorry for this too, but you're just going to

104

have to suck it up." I let the bag slip down my left arm and I stuck my right hand in the top and rubbed it all over Rufus, making sure I came in contact with his skin. That's where the dander was. Then I shut the top up tight again before he could bite me.

"Mom!" I said as I caught up to her. "What're you doing here? Are you feeling better?"

"Oh hi, Natalie. Yes, I suppose it must have been one of those twenty-four hour things. I'm feeling fine now." She stopped walking as I stepped in front of her. "Shouldn't you be in class?"

"I just got out of lunch. I've got a few minutes. It's, um, good to see you!" Would she buy that? I patted her on the shoulder for good measure, hoping some of Rufus's hair would stick to her cardigan.

"Well, thank you. It's good to see you too." She looked at me quizzically, like she was trying to determine if I was up to something—which I was. Good thing Viv wasn't here to rat me out.

"I just don't get to see you during the day usually, you know. So it's good to see you." I smiled big and hoped she hadn't noticed the sweat popping out on my forehead. I really sucked at lying.

"Right," said Mom, ever the literal one. "I'm usually at work while you're at school."

This wasn't going exactly well. How was I supposed to get Rufus's dander on her? If I kept up this inane conversation,

I could bet the next step would be for her to frog-march me to the school nurse and have me checked for mind-altering substances.

"So, um, what are you doing in school?" That would be the obvious next question, right?

"I'm here to talk to your principal about the movie being filmed here. It's just unacceptable!"

Uh-oh, maybe I shouldn't have gone there. She looked fired up.

"I don't know what he was thinking when he okayed it, but he certainly didn't ask the PTA!" Did a principal need to get permission from the PTA to hold an event at his school? I didn't know, but Mom sure thought he did.

Was it possible to reason with her? That wasn't the route I normally chose, but it was apparent that just proximity to Rufus's dander wasn't doing the trick.

"It's really not a big deal," I said. "They've kept the disruptions to a minimum, you know. And most of the filming stuff is taking place after hours and on weekends."

"Anything that interrupts the school day is a big deal, Natalie." She raised her eyebrows at me like she couldn't believe I would suggest otherwise.

"But it's a good extracurricular activity, don't you think? It's, um, allowing us to experience firsthand what the movie business is like. And some of the students are really excited about being able to act as extras. That's an opportunity they wouldn't normally get, especially not in a safe environment like school, don't you think?" I'd thrown in every buzzword I could think of.

Mom looked at me closely, her blue eyes blinking rapidly like she was trying to process what I'd said. It obviously wasn't computing for her. "Are Melly and Oscar caught up in this movie-making thing?"

Busted. But maybe I could keep her talking long enough for Rufus to have an effect on her. "Yes, but you know how much it would mean to Melly to be discovered. This could be her chance."

"Natalie," said Mom gently, "I've told you before what I think of Melly's dream. That's all it is—a dream. You both would be better off concentrating on your schoolwork and real life."

I shuffled my feet. The halls were starting to thin out. In about one minute I was going to be late for my biology class. Emmy had B lunch, so hopefully she was still on Principal Johnson's case, but I wasn't sure if I could trust her to keep him occupied. She was such a suck-up. She never did anything she wasn't supposed to.

"Dreams aren't necessarily a bad thing," I said. Though in my mom's world, I guessed they were. If you couldn't put some kind of quantitative value on it, it wasn't real.

"Of course not, but school is not the time or place for—" Mom stopped and sighed. I think even she was realizing what a stick she sounded like. "Natalie, I'm sure you'll understand when you're older."

Like I hadn't heard that before. Apparently, once I hit twenty-one, I was going to have some kind of epiphany and the world would suddenly make sense. Or maybe it wouldn't be until I was thirty. Mom had never been too clear on that point.

"But you really ought to be getting to class. I'll see you at home and we can talk about it some more then, okay?" She stepped around me and sneezed.

"Wait!" Oh man, just when Rufus was finally starting to get to her!

"What now, Natalie?"

I had to do something. I reached up and put a hand on either side of her face, trying to position my right hand as close to her nose as I could without actually covering it up. It wasn't too hard to do that, since I could barely reach her face anyway, she was so tall. I pulled her face down to mine and kissed her on the cheek.

"I just want you to know that I, um, really appreciate what you're doing for me and Emmy. I know you're only doing it for our own good, even if I don't agree with you." I let her go and stepped back. Now there's something I never thought I'd say. Would she buy it or would she drag me off to the nearest research lab to conduct tests on the alien that had obviously taken over her daughter's body?

Mom touched her cheek and came away with a cat hair, but I don't think she noticed. "Why, Natalie. That's so sweet of you!" Were her eyes actually tearing up? Wow. I think I just seriously bought myself some brownie points. She wiped at her eye and blinked. Was it my imagination or did her eye start swelling immediately?

"You okay, Mom?" The guilt started welling up just a little, looking at that eye. It was *definitely* swollen. Maybe even a little red.

"Fine," she said, and sneezed again, then sniffled.

"Maybe you're still sick? You really ought to go back home." I stepped back. "I don't want to get sick."

"Maybe you're right." Mom sneezed again. That Rufus. Boy, he's got some powerful dander. I felt a little bad about infecting Mom again, but not too much. I knew she was going to feel better as soon as she got away from Rufus. Well, and washed her face.

"Maybe you should go take a nice hot bath and have some soup." I grabbed her arm and started leading her down the hall back to the front door. At first she pulled back, but then she sneezed three more times and let me lead her along. "And tonight is Dad's night for dinner. You should take it easy."

"Well, I—" She sneezed again and stopped resisting completely. "Hmph. If this doesn't clear up by tomorrow, I'm going to have to call the doctor. Okay, Natalie. If you start feeling sick too, call your father, okay? We don't want to infect anyone else."

"No problem," I said. "I mean, I feel fine, but I'll call Dad if I need to." I gave her back one final pat and watched as she went off down the hall. Then I made a run for biology.

 109

FOUrTeen

🐈

"HONEST AS THE CAT WHEN THE MEAT'S OUT OF reACH."
—OLD ENGLISH ProverB

The wardrobe lady deemed my jeans acceptable, but made me change shirts because of the little blood specks that had seeped through. I told her they were ketchup so she wouldn't be totally grossed out, though I had no idea how I would have gotten ketchup on my shoulder. She gave me a sleeveless black and white striped shirt with a really weird collar and lace fringe and told me to keep the collar up. I'm not sure what look she was going for. I looked like I had neck wings.

Then she sent me to the makeup lady for some extra eyeliner. She seriously layered it on, so I looked like Cleopatra after a crying jag. Very cringeworthy. I hoped I was one of the extras who didn't make it into the movie. The good news was that even if, by some miracle, the Easton impostor actually did show up, the chances of her recognizing me were pretty slim.

Melly and Oscar were accepted as is, which completely

astonished me—about Oscar, anyway. Melly looked kind of on the preppy-pretty side today, but Oscar was his typical slightly grunge, slightly punk self. I guess with his hair being what it was, he was going to be typecast anyway. Maybe that was why they'd stuck me in a strange shirt, to go with my kinda funky dip dyed purple hair.

When we got to the cafeteria, there were already a bunch of kids in line. It looked like half the school had shown up. I even saw Ian over in a corner with a bunch of other juniors. I was debating about heading over that way, even after the whole trig debacle from the morning (not to mention the hideous shirt and eyeliner), when a guy with a clipboard came up to us.

"Okay," he said. "What do we have here? Did you already turn in your slips?"

Melly gave him our names and he checked us off a list. Then he looked us up and down, spending an extra long time on Melly. "You," he said, pointing to her. "Let's put you on table three. That's over there." He pointed to a table right next to the one that was obviously the actors' table, based on all the lights focused on it. Melly squealed and took off without even waiting for us.

Oscar and I started to follow. "Wait a minute," said the guy. "You two, you're on table five. That one." He pointed to another table a few tables down from Melly's, kind of close to the cash register. There were already a few kids sitting there, including two junior girls who were either really emo or had also had a run-in with the makeup lady, and a senior guy with a nose ring, an eyebrow ring, and probably a few other metallic embellishments in places I didn't even want to think about. Clearly, we had been relegated to the freak table while Melly was all set to enjoy herself in the land of the "cool" kids.

Oscar and I looked at each other and then trudged over to the table and sat down. "Hey," said the guy with all the piercings. We nodded at him. I'd seen him around before, but I didn't know anything about him other than that he was a senior. The two depressed-looking girls just ignored us. I sat my book bag with Rufus in it on the seat between me and Oscar. Luckily, Rufus was still in a tuna coma from lunch. I hoped it was going to last through the shoot.

"Isn't this movie about a guy who *isn't* cool?" I asked Oscar. "Isn't that why he wants to re-live Ferris Bueller's day?"

"Yeah," said Oscar. "But there's regular uncool and movie uncool. We're real-life cool. You can't bottle that."

Apparently, we were uncool to these people in any situation. Melly had been deemed worthy, and Ian too. He was seated at her table. She finally noticed that we weren't sitting with her at the unpierced kids table. We waved to her. She made a face like she was going to get up and move, but then Ty McKenzie came in and she sat her butt back down. Betrayed by my best friend for a teen star! But I can't lie. Ian was at that table. I'd probably have stayed too.

Ty took his place at the table by Melly's. Oscar started

hyperventilating, as did pretty much every girl in the cafeteria. I noticed that Melly was mostly keeping it together, trying to act cool. But I could tell she was freaking out because she kept almost picking at her nails and then stopping. She'd broken herself from the habit by sheer willpower when she was in middle school, but it still popped up every now and then when she got stressed out.

"Okay, kids!" said the same guy who'd relegated us to the freak table. "Listen up! My name is Jason and I'm the AD."

"Ah," said Oscar. "The assistant director." He nodded like he knew what he was talking about, and the pierced guy looked at him with new respect.

"We've got a tight schedule today, so I need you to listen up. Everyone needs to take his or her assigned positions. If I didn't give you one when you came in, come see me. Now, in all of the shots we're going to be taking today, we need you to be as quiet as possible unless I say otherwise. But we want you to act natural, like you're eating or talking with your friends. Do not look directly at the cameras. I know most of you have never acted before, so I've got Candace Grace and Claire Ryan here to show you how it's done."

The two girls I'd heard in the bathroom stepped forward. If I remembered right, they were actually both twenty-two, but they looked like sixteen-year-olds, if sixteen-year-olds commonly had boob jobs. They smiled at all of us and waved to a couple of guys who were wolf whistling in the back of the cafeteria. Then the girls started chatting with each other without making a sound.

"So cool," said Oscar. "I can totally do that."

I snorted. It would be a miracle if Oscar made it through five minutes without making a sound. But maybe the excitement of being on a movie set would hold him in check. I kind of doubted it.

The girls finished, gave another wave, and we all politely applauded. It didn't actually look that hard.

"Okay," said Jason. "That's how it's done. We'll also be doing a short panning shot as Ty and Victoria walk to their table. They're going to be doing lines while this is going on, so I want to stress again how important it is for you to be as quiet as possible. That also goes for applause at the end of a scene. Even if the director has said, 'Cut,' I expect all of you to sit quietly. There are no exceptions." He looked around the room with a stern glare. I elbowed Oscar and he studiously ignored me. The safe bet would be that we were going to get kicked out by the end of filming.

"Okay then. Alan will be out in a second and then we're all getting started. Now would be a good time for a bathroom break if you need one."

"He said Alan!" I said to Oscar. "Did you hear that? Who's Alan?"

"A. F. Leonard, the director," said the pierced guy. "Alan Francis. He's why I'm here. He directed *Rough Diamonds*. Incredible movie. I'm not much of a Ty McKenzie fan."

"D'oh!" said Oscar, and whacked himself in the fore-head. "I should have realized that! Thanks, man!"

"No problem. It's Garrett, by the way."

I noticed how Garrett was only looking at Oscar and not at all at me or the two emo chicks, who were huddled as far away from us as they could get. Hmmm. I wondered if Oscar had noticed. It didn't seem like it. He just dived right into movie talk instead of flirting. Maybe that was his way of flirting? I didn't often get to see him do his thing.

"*Rough Diamonds* was awesome. But you have to give Ty credit for *Cyber Runner*. He totally pulled that one off."

"Um, not to interrupt, Oscar, but can we get back to our little Rufus problem?" I smiled at Garrett so he wouldn't think I was totally ignoring him. He didn't even look at me.

"Who's Rufus?" he asked Oscar.

"Oh, Rufus? He's—"

I kicked Oscar under the table. "Nobody," I said. I smiled at Garrett again. "Hey, isn't that the director over there?" He turned to look where I was pointing. Some longhaired guy had just walked in, but I had no idea if it was really the direc-tor or not. I pulled Oscar's head down next to mine. "We're back at zero," I whispered. "We already knew Easton knew the director guy. That's probably how she wound up on the set, right? So it tells us nothing."

"I don't know about that," said Oscar. "Didn't Rufus say something about her always changing her voice when she talked to him on the phone? And demanding stuff? Easton's super famous and rich as all sin, but what's she going to demand from him? He's the director!"

"Hey," said Garrett, "that is Alan! And there's Victoria Welling too."

Even the emo twins turned to look. Victoria was in the lead and she looked like she was reading Alan the riot act about something. I couldn't hear her from here, but neither of them looked happy. Actually, Alan looked unhappy. Victoria just looked constipated.

Then she turned and looked right at me and froze. Her face broke into something I could only describe as a snarl. Geez. The shirt wasn't *that* bad.

FIFTEEN

"THE PROBLEM WITH CATS IS THAT THEY GET THE SAME EXACT LOOK
WHETHER THEY SEE A MOTH OR AN AX-MURDERER."
—PAULA POUNDSTONE

Jason, the AD (as he liked to remind us constantly), walked
us through a test shot as practice. Ty, Victoria, Claire, and
Candace were all on their marks or whatever. Ty and Victoria
had lunch trays in front of them with sandwiches and fruit.
I couldn't tell from here if it was fake or not, but it looked
way better than the sandwich I'd eaten at lunch. Claire and
Candace were apparently supposed to have brought their
meals. Claire only had a yogurt but Candace had the full sushi setup with chopsticks and everything. If she had been a
real teenager at our school, she'd have been laughed out of the
lunchroom. Not to mention, where would she have kept
raw fish refrigerated all morning? In her locker? Whoever
was in charge of props had obviously never gone to a public
high school.

Melly's table was right next to theirs and the camera
was pointed right at her. Well, at the actors, with Melly

right behind them. I could tell by the way she was practically vibrating in her seat that she was totally flipping out, but she was holding it together pretty well. Ian's back was to the camera, which meant he was more or less facing me. He looked really cute in the blue shirt the costume lady must have given him. He hadn't been wearing it this morning. It looked like they'd made him brush his hair too.

Alan, the director guy, was sitting behind a big monitor on one of those classic director's chairs. I didn't know they actually used those in real life. His name wasn't written on the back, though.

I had to admit this was kind of cool. It felt like we were in the middle of one of those behind the scenes things on a DVD. I would never ever, however, admit this to Oscar.

"Okay, kids, when it's time for you do your thing, I'll yell out 'Background!' and I expect you to shut up immediately. Remember, don't look at any of the cameras." Jason pointed to the biggest camera, which was trained directly on Ty. "Just act natural."

Yeah, natural. I doubted if he really wanted that. He wanted movie natural, not regular high-school natural.

Jason walked back over near the director. "Then Alan will say 'Rolling!' or 'Roll film.' Sometimes he'll jump right to 'Action,' but either way, it means things are underway."

He walked over to the actors and nodded to Ty. "Let's go ahead and walk through a few lines and then I'll turn everyone over to Alan."

Ty nodded. Then, without even stopping to mentally prepare himself or whatever it is that actors do, he turned to Victoria and started his lines.

"I'm going to do it," he said.

Victoria looked blankly at him and picked up her sandwich. "Do what?"

Claire and Candace slowly walked by the table and crossed behind Ty. From the angle of the camera, I guessed they were kind of in the background of the shot.

Ty leaned over and looked intently into Victoria's eyes. "Do something about my life, that's what!" He glanced over his shoulder at Claire. She was dressed as a typical queen bee movie hottie: short plaid skirt, tight-fitting white Oxford shirt halfway unbuttoned, and some low red heels. Basically, hot girl a la Britney Spears in the early days. I doubted Principal Johnson would actually allow that outfit on a real student.

"Trina is never going to notice me. No one is ever going to notice me unless I do something—something big."

Victoria glanced from Claire (who, apparently, was playing the character named Trina) to Ty and made an exaggeratedly sad face. If I had to guess the plot, I'd say she was the always-a-bridesmaid best friend, but the eventual love interest of Ty's character. They'd stuck some clunky glasses on her and pulled her hair back into an unflattering messy ponytail, the hallmarks of the "ugly" girl who always gets a makeover by the end.

"Like what?"

"Remember that old movie we watched last weekend? The one about Ferris Bueller?"

"Yeah?"

"*That's* what I'm going to do."

"Cut!" yelled Jason, making everyone except the actors jump. They were probably used to it. "Okay, kids, you did good with the keeping quiet, but I need you to not watch the actors and hang on their every word. Remember, this is supposed to be an average school day for you. Ty isn't Ty McKenzie, he's Freddy Barnes, okay?"

"That was awesome," whispered Oscar. "Just like in the script."

Garrett immediately perked up. "You have a copy of the script?"

I pulled the slightly crumpled pages out of my backpack and held them out. Oscar grabbed them from me and passed them to Garrett like I wasn't capable of doing it myself. Or maybe he wanted to be the one to give them to Garrett.

"Just this scene. My friend Melly got them," said Oscar. "She's over at the good table." He nodded in Melly's direction.

"Cool," said Garrett, reading the pages under the table.

"All right, Jason, it's my turn," said Alan. "Let's take it from the top, shall we?"

What happened next was the most boring hour or so of my life, ever. Alan had the actors do the scene a bunch of times using different inflection in their voices, sometimes changing a line or two or just changing how Claire walked by. He gave them some pep talks, even sat at the table once and showed Ty how he wanted him to look. Between takes, Victoria was constantly hounding the director for some perceived slight in shooting her, or alternately, she complained when he corrected her acting and asked her to act more natural. I saw Candace and Claire roll their eyes more than once.

The actors eventually got through more dialog than the first run-through, though it took longer because of Victoria's interruptions. But after listening to it five or six times, I was already sure I didn't need to see the movie to know what was going to happen. Ty (a.k.a. Freddy) was the so-called loser at school with a crush on a hot girl. Victoria (Molly) was his best friend with a crush on him. He decides to go all Ferris Bueller, goes on crazy adventures with Victoria, and attracts the admiration of Claire (Trina). But in the end he realizes that Victoria's the girl for him. Classic ugly duckling teen story. In real life, Freddy's antics would make him a laughingstock, his "ugly" best friend would ditch him as soon as she got the makeover, and the crazy stunts he pulled would get him expelled. And the hot girl? She was probably dating the captain of the football team.

That wasn't entirely true. The captain of our cheerleading squad was actually dating the captain of the basketball team.

I was bored out of my skull, but Melly still seemed perky as ever and Oscar was even behaving himself. Between takes, he and Garrett chatted about Alan's other movies, and which movies Ty had sucked in. Rufus snored a little, but luckily it happened between takes and no one noticed. I was just thankful he was still asleep.

They finally set up for the next take, which was apparently the scene before the one we'd just watched them film a bazillion times. In this one, Victoria and Ty were walking to their lunch table. They were actually going to pass right by ours. Oscar nearly hyperventilated when he heard that, but quickly controlled himself. That was probably Garrett's influence. If it was just me at the table, he probably would have done his happy dance.

They did a practice run first, with the camera tracking them along the way. While they were setting up the camera, I noticed Victoria staring at me again. Even Garrett noticed.

"Did you, like, send her bad fan mail or something?" he asked. "With naked pictures?"

"*No*," I said. "I barely even watch her movies, except the ones Oscar makes me go to." She was kind of creeping me out. Of course, she'd been arguing off and on with Alan the whole time, so maybe she just didn't like anyone. Well, other than Ty. She could barely get through her lines half the time, she was making such goggle eyes at him. Way more than the part called for.

"Okay," barked the Director. "I'm not liking the dynamic here. Victoria, let's have you on the other side of Ty. And pause here to do your lines instead of walking through them." He put down some masking tape in an X pattern only a foot away from our table, right behind my back. Oscar started primping his hair. Great. Now I really was going to be in the movie. Like, visible. Stupid neck wings.

"Let's walk through one more time. On your marks, please, everyone."

Jason gave all of us the evil eye again and we all settled down quickly. He'd already kicked Shackerman off the set for not shutting up fast enough. Served him right.

Ty and Victoria walked from their starting mark to the new spot Alan had put on the floor. They ran their lines and then continued on to their table. Then Victoria came unglued all over Alan.

"I should be standing on the other side. It's closer to the camera. He's blocking me." Ty stood back, looking supremely bored, as she got in Alan's face for yet another diva attack. Easton had been totally right about her.

That's when my good luck with Rufus apparently ran out. He woke up. I could tell because my backpack wiggled and thumped as he struggled to poke his head through. Luckily, everyone's eyes were on Victoria and Ty.

I hunched over the bag. "Stop it! What are you doing? Do you have to pee again?" I poked Oscar in the side. He looked confused for a minute and then leaned over too to help me cover things up.

No, hissed Rufus. *I smell the impostor! Let me out!*

What? "Who do you smell?" I looked around. I didn't see the Easton lookalike anywhere. There was a crowd of people near the door, but it looked like the same crowd that had been milling around the whole shoot. Maybe the lookalike was over there?

Rufus successfully poked part of his head out of the top of the bag and turned his practically rabid-looking eyes on me. *I know what I smell! Just a moment ago I smelled her! Where is she?*

I looked at Oscar and whispered. "He says he smells the lookalike."

"Hey, what's in the bag?" asked Garrett. He half stood up on the other side of the table to see if he could get a look. I leaned over farther.

"Nothing," I said, at the same time that Oscar said, "Oh, that's Rufus." I punched him in the arm and nearly fell on the floor.

"Rufus?" asked Garrett.

He looked really confused, but I couldn't blame him. He probably thought we had the world's smallest little person in my backpack or that we were totally insane. Maybe both.

"Background!" yelled Jason. Garrett sat back down.

I put my hand over Rufus's head and pushed him back into the bag. "Stay," I whispered as threateningly as I could.

"Rolling!"

Victoria must have lost the argument with Alan. She was on the side closest to our table. She and Ty walked, stopped, and started their lines.

Then Rufus exploded out of my bag. *Banzai!* he howled.

Die, impostor, die! He landed on top of Victoria's head and did his best impersonation of a blender.

She screamed. Not that I could blame her, seeing as how I'd removed the claw protectors. She windmilled her arms and tried to bat him off her head. For just a moment, the whole room was dead silent except for Victoria and Rufus. Then absolute epic pandemonium broke out.

Ty reached out to attempt to help Victoria, but then Jason jumped on him and pulled him back. "No, you're the lead!" he screamed. Meanwhile, some of the equipment guys came running over, but then they just kind of stood there shouting out not so helpful advice like "Throw it off!" and "On your left!" No one wanted to grab the whirling pink dervish that Rufus had turned into. All of the extras were yelling, except for a few kids who had broken into hysterical laughter. The director was just screaming incoherently. Some people were running for the door.

Oscar was looking at me, totally aghast. "Do something," he yelled. He grabbed me by the shoulders and started shaking me. So much for staying cool in front of Garrett.

I pushed him back and stood up. What was I supposed to do? Everyone knew not to grab a fighting cat. You'd just get clobbered.

"Rufus," I yelled ineffectually. "Stop it! What are you doing? Get off of Victoria!" I picked up my backpack and tossed it halfheartedly in the direction of Rufus. There was no way I was getting him back in it, not right now. Probably ever.

This is the impostor, Rufus snarled back at me in between yowls. *I don't know whom she's trying to fool, but this is her and I'm taking her down!*

"How are we supposed to find out what's happened to Easton if you take her down?" I yelled back at him. He just kept up the attack. There was no reasoning with him normally, and with him in bloodlust mode, I had no chance.

As soon as I said the name Easton, Victoria turned to me. She somehow managed to focus on me through the wall of fur and claws. She took a step in my direction, still screaming.

I picked up a drink from the cafeteria table and threw it at Rufus, mostly missing him but drenching the front of Victoria's now blood-speckled shirt. "Oscar, everybody," I yelled. "Throw liquids! As much as you can!" I grabbed one of those little chocolate milk cartons that had been sitting in front of Garrett and opened it all the way. Everyone around us grabbed their drinks too. "On the count of three," I screamed. "One, two, THREE!"

A multicolored wave of every kind of drink imaginable hit Victoria and Rufus. Milk, soda, water, you name it. One of the equipment guys grabbed a full cooler of tea from the refreshment table and came charging in. He dumped it directly over Victoria's head. Rufus shrieked like he was on fire and went down in the puddle of liquid ooze that was spreading out from the epicenter of the blast area.

I jumped on top of Rufus before he could go on the attack again. Someone cheered as I wrestled with him, both

126

of us skidding across the slippery cafeteria floor. My back hit something solid. I rolled over and saw the cooler that the guy had dropped. It had fallen on its side and the top was open. I shoved Rufus inside, then slammed the lid shut.

I got up on my knees and looked up. Everyone who hadn't fled the cafeteria when the melee broke out was staring at me. Victoria was down on her knees with her hands on her head about three feet from me. Her face, hands, and arms were covered in bloody scratches. Her eyes focused on me, and then she pulled a Rufus.

"You! I knew it was you!" she shrieked, and dived at me with her fingers held out like claws.

She hit me like a battering ram. I fell over backward and my head knocked into the floor. Liquid goo splashed up around us like a geyser. I tried to hold her off, but she was determined. I had about given up on getting out of this with my vision intact when someone pulled her off me.

I wiped a combination of milk and orange juice out of my eyes and looked up. Jason and Ian each had one of Victoria's arms. Jason looked mad, but it was Ian's face that made my heart skip. He was looking at me like he didn't know who I was. Alan came running up.

"What the hell is going on here?" he yelled. He looked from me to Victoria and back again. Rufus picked that moment to let out a howl and throw himself at the lid of the cooler. One of the gaffers sat down on it. "And what," continued Alan, "was that pink monstrosity that attacked my actors?"

I decided not to point out that Rufus had attacked only Victoria. But before I could even say anything, Victoria spoke up. "This is the girl who stole Easton's cat." She pulled her arm away from Ian and pointed at the cooler. "And *that's* Tiddlywinks in there."

Rufus let out another howl, but luckily, I was the only one who understood what he actually said because it wasn't repeatable. I didn't even know cats knew words like that or that they'd use them. Cats tended to be more poetic and cryptic about cussing you out. And I was pretty sure Victoria's mom wasn't physically capable of what he was saying.

"Is this true?" asked Alan.

I opened my mouth and then shut it. Ian was still standing right there looking at me with those eyes. Everyone was looking at me, but his gaze was the one that hurt the most.

"Nat, tell him what's really going on!" Oscar stepped forward and pulled me to my feet. I skidded a little in the puddle of goo.

Victoria narrowed her eyes at him and pulled her other arm free. She took a step forward and Oscar and I took a step back. "*I'll* tell you what's going on," she said. "We've got a stalker here, that's what. Alan, you need to call the police."

"They've already been called," he said. "But I still want to know what's going on. Young lady, do you realize how much money you've wasted by delaying our shoot today? Not to mention the mess? And just look at Victoria! She's a bloody mess!"

"I'm sorry," I said. "I didn't know the cat was going to do that."

"Ha!" said Victoria. "She admits she brought the cat!"

Not like I could deny it. Everyone saw Rufus catapult out of my backpack like a furry angel of death.

Oscar leaned over to whisper urgently in my ear, "Nat, *tell* them. Just tell them about your Talent. Have Rufus tell you something only he would know. They'll have to believe you!"

I thought about it and opened my mouth. I looked at Melly. She stood up and held her hand out to me, though I wasn't sure what she was trying to say. I looked at Ian. He looked confused and upset. Well, so was I.

"I'm not a stalker," I finally said. I couldn't bring myself to say anything about my Talent, not in front of all these people. There had to be another way. It was time for some damage control. Just living down what had happened so far was going to be bad enough. Maybe too much. Adding "Cat Girl" on top of that? Social suicide.

Not to mention dating suicide.

Speaking of death, I noticed the guy was still sitting on the cooler. "Hey," I called out. "Get the cat some air, okay?" If he suffocated in there, I'd have no chance of anyone believing my story. As if anyone would believe it anyway. Why in the world would Victoria Welling impersonate Easton West?

For a minute, I didn't think the guy was going to do anything, but then he got up and cracked the lid. Rufus let out a yowl and the guy dropped the lid shut again. Jason gave him a stern look and the poor guy found a book to wedge in between the lid and the side, then sat down again to keep Rufus from escaping. A steady stream of cat cursing issued forth from the cooler.

I was trying to think of anything else at all to say or do when the police arrived, along with Principal Johnson. Alan gave a brief summary of things to the policemen, with Victoria interjecting comments. Melly and Oscar both tried to get me to talk again, but I stared them down. The police finally mercifully said it was time to go somewhere less public. The female officer tentatively grabbed my multicolored, liquid-soaked arm and frog-marched me to the door.

I kept my head down as I walked past Ian and everyone else. Who was I kidding? There was no way I was ever going to live this down.

SIXTEEN

"ONE OF THE MOST STRIKING DIFFERENCES BETWEEN A CAT
AND A LIE IS THAT A CAT HAS ONLY NINE LIVES."
—MARK TWAIN

"Okay, Natalie, give me one good reason why I should bail you out of this mess and not tell Mom and Dad." Viv widened her eyes at me, making her look even more like a living, breathing manga character than normal. "And you know I can tell if you're lying."

She didn't have to remind me. Her built-in lie detector Talent was her most annoying feature. And even when I didn't need to lie, I would normally never ask my perfect sister for help. But when the cops had gotten the answering machine at home (and I'd lied and said my parents didn't have cell phones), the police hadn't known who else to call. Honestly, I wasn't really sure if having Viv here was better or worse for me.

Actually, that wasn't true. I had a chance of survival with Viv. If Mom found out I'd been suspended from school, she would kill me. Sure, she'd be mad about the whole police

131

thing, but messing with my education? I was so dead if Mom found out.

At least, for once, the true story was on my side. Mostly.

So I told Viv the whole story. Everything. She sat there the whole time looking at me like I was insane. When I was finally done, she shook her head and stared at me.

"That's crazy," she said.

"But true."

"Yeah, I know. I got that." Her chair creaked as she slumped down and focused her eyes on the table. We were in a room at the police station. It looked just like in the TV shows: two wooden chairs, a plain table, and an institutional paint job. A fluorescent light above us flickered on and off. I felt oppressed just sitting there. At least I didn't have hand-cuffs on.

There was even one of those one-way window things. I wondered if anyone was on the other side shaking their head in disbelief. The police had said we'd have our privacy, but I wasn't sure if I believed them or not. They'd also told me they'd let me clean up, but all they'd done was give me a couple of paper towels.

Viv seemed to come to some sort of decision. She glanced at the window, then sat up straight and leaned forward, look-ing me right in the eye. "Are you positive that the cat said that actress Victoria was the impostor?"

"Positive," I said. Hello. He went completely Animal Planet on Victoria's head. Cats are many things, including crazy, but they don't do go completely kung fu unless they mean it. And Rufus definitely meant it when he went after Victoria.

Viv nodded. "Okay, but why? Why would a fairly successful teenage actress want to impersonate a celebrity blogger?"

I'd been thinking about that ever since Rufus had come flying out of my book bag. "Oscar said Easton was probably in town to write about Victoria and how she was in the middle of a starlet meltdown, which he said could sink her down to D-list status. I bet she kidnapped Easton and impersonated her to get her to stop. Remember when that Rory actress had her meltdown and Easton wrote about it and posted those pictures of her?" Rory had literally been committed for a while, and when she'd gotten out, she'd sued Easton. She hadn't won, but the fight had gone on for a year. Oscar had kept us up to date on everything that had happened. Rory's last movie role had been as a talking squirrel in an animated feature that went straight to DVD.

"I guess that sort of makes sense," said Viv. "Stupid, but I guess if she's trying to save her career and she had the means to do it, it's possible."

I'd never heard that Victoria had a Talent, but maybe she kept it hidden like I did. Of course, hers was kind of cool. If I had a Talent like that, I probably wouldn't be quiet about it.

Well, unless I was all evil and everything. That could explain a lot. I'd seen the look on Victoria's face when she went for my eyes. If that wasn't evil, I didn't know what was.

"So, here's what we're going to do." Viv tapped her fingers on the tabletop. "First, I'm going to talk to the police and get you out of this mess. Then I'm going to check the registry database to confirm Victoria's Talent. I'll talk to my superiors at the BERM and we'll come up with a plan."

"What do you want me to do?"

"Stay out of trouble. Let the professionals handle it."

Well, wasn't that all big sister of her. "What about Mom and Dad? And school? I got suspended, you know."

"Yeah, I know." Viv looked deep into my eyes again. What was she trying to see? Was this part of her truth divining stuff? Blech. And she wondered why no guys ever asked her out after they found out what her Talents were.

She finally blinked. "Let's leave Mom out of it for now. I want to see what I can find out first. I think we'll have to leave your school situation as is for now. Since they're still filming there, we don't want to tip Victoria off that anything's up. If you go back to school with no consequences, she'll know something is going on." She stared at me again. "You're positive Oscar didn't say anything about your Talent where she could hear?"

"Yes. I'd have killed him. He knows that."

"Perfect. So as far as we know, she really does just think you're some kind of crazy stalker."

Yeah, great. Her and my entire school.

Viv dropped me off at home after grabbing me some dinner at McDonald's. The police had been suitably impressed by her BERM credentials, though one of them made me demonstrate my Talent by calling her husband and having him put their cat on the phone. She wanted to know what the cat's favorite toy was. According to Whiskers, it was the cop's toothbrush, but he told me to tell her it was a polka-dotted mouse stuffed with catnip. *Otherwise*, he'd said, *she'll probably lock me out of the bathroom.* She totally bought the mouse.

Mom and Dad were both in the living room typing away on their laptops with the TV going. This was their normal Wednesday night routine. There was some History channel thing about ancient scientists or something that they liked to "watch" together. It was also the reason why they hadn't answered the phone. After all, it *was* their date night.

I waved at them as I went by and they both nodded, but didn't look away from the show. I'd been counting on that. I'd cleaned up as much as I could at the police station, going through an entire roll of paper towels. I'd finally mostly dried off, but if you looked close, I was pretty sticky.

Dad sniffed. "What's that smell?"

Figures. The supersniffer strikes again, which was weird since I could see he actually had his olfactory inhibitor on for once. He must have forgotten to take it off when he'd gotten home. "I spilled something on myself," I said, and kept walking along the edge of the room. Hopefully, I was in the shadows enough they couldn't see exactly how goopy I was.

If you really looked, it was obvious it would have taken, like, thirty cups of stuff, not just one. Or, you know, a cafeteria full.

He wrinkled his nose. "New flavor? Doesn't smell very good." I did reek. It was a good thing he had the inhibitor on or else he probably wouldn't have bought my story at all. I could only imagine what I'd smell like to him then. But it also meant that I smelled so bad he could tell *something* was up even with the inhibitor on. I needed a shower, bad.

"Yeah," I said. "I wouldn't recommend it."

Mom cleared her throat. "Do you have any homework? You're home rather late."

"No homework tonight," I said. Or for the next two weeks while I was suspended, but I definitely didn't mention that. Hopefully, Viv could clear everything up soon and I could try and put all of this mess behind me. As if I could ever live down a multibeverage wrestling match.

"You sound better, Mom."

"Yes, thanks. I think you were right about the bath. I felt much better after a long soak."

"Big Mac and a large fry?" asked Dad.

"Yeah," I said, waving the McDonald's bag and inching closer to the hallway.

He sniffed again. "And an apple pie?"

"Yep," I said. "You're good!" He liked to play the guessing game. He said it helped keep his nose sharp. Maybe he was wearing the inhibitor to test it again. He did that from time to time.

"A little challenging tonight, with whatever it was you spilled. I really would avoid it in the future, if I were you. Or whatever situation you were in that caused you to spill it in the first place. You should be careful out there." He peered at me and wrinkled his nose.

"Trust me," I said, "I will." That was about the longest parental advice speech I'd ever gotten from Dad. Usually all mandates came from Mom.

I ducked out of the room and let out the breath I'd been holding. Then I snuck into Mom's office to check the answering machine. She forgot to listen to them half the time anyway, but better safe than sorry. Strangely, there were no messages. The police must not have left one after all.

I shut the office door quietly behind me.

Holy spoiled milk, Batman, screeched Meep, who was coming down the hall. *I thought I smelled something rank, but . . . phew! What happened to you?*

"Shhh!" I said. "Be quiet! I'll tell you everything later."

Meep backed away from me, wrinkling her nose. *After a bath,* she said. *I'll smell you later.* She ran off in the opposite direction.

At least I could eat in peace for once without her begging for food. The one crimp in my plan was Emmy, but apparently she hadn't said anything to either of them. Then again, maybe she hadn't heard about it. She hadn't signed on to be an extra (the only extracurricular things she did were the chess club and some future business leaders thing, both activities that Mom approved of as "appropriate" for school) and the whole fiasco hadn't gone down until after school hours, so maybe the story hadn't made the rounds yet.

That hope was dashed as soon as I got to my room. Emmy flew through the door, shut it, and put her hands on her hips.

"Why aren't you in jail?" she demanded.

"Thanks," I said. "Didn't know you cared."

"Well? It's all over the school's online forum."

That made me pause. "We have an online forum?" I didn't even know we had a website.

"Quit changing the subject! Everyone is talking about it. They said you were arrested! Does this have anything to do with that pink cat? Tell me the truth!"

I sat down at my desk and took out my sandwich and fries. I needed a shower, but I was hungry. First things first. "Viv sprung me. And yes, of course it has to do with the pink cat. I told you somebody was in big trouble, didn't I?"

Emmy sat down with a thump on my bed. "Oh man, oh man. I *knew* I shouldn't have helped you with that cat. Mom is going to kill us. We're in *so* much trouble."

"*We're* in trouble? Hello? Who was the one who got hauled off by the police?" I took a bite of my burger. I guess this explained why Emmy hadn't told Mom and Dad. It wasn't my skin she was worried about, just her own. "Don't worry about it, though. Viv is on the case now with her BERM buddies and she said she wasn't going to tell Mom and Dad until she sorted something out with BERM." I ate a couple of french fries while Emmy digested the news. "Oh, but when you go to school tomorrow, don't tell anyone. Viv said to pretend I was guilty." That won't be hard for her. She's been doing that all her life.

"Oh," said Emmy. "Where's the cat? And what happened to you? What's all over you?" She scooted a little farther down the bed from me, like I could contaminate her with goo from my desk chair.

I ignored the question about the sticky glop, though I did smell. It was the milk, I think, or maybe the combination of milk and orange juice. A shower was definitely next on my agenda, right after I finished eating. "I don't know where the cat is," I said. "Did they say anything about him on the forum?"

"No. Mostly it was just all stuff about you and how you got into a throw down with Victoria Welling. And something about JELL-O wrestling."

You'd think someone would have mentioned that a crazed pink cat had attacked her first. Or that I'd saved her from possible dismemberment by orchestrating a liquid deluge.

"There was no JELL-O," I said. "Trust me. And where's my thank you for saving your butt this afternoon?"

"Oh, yeah," said Emmy. "Thanks. Now stop changing the subject."

Nice. See if I do her any more favors. In retrospect, maybe I should have let Mom do her thing at school. If she'd managed to get the shoot canceled, I wouldn't be suspended and I wouldn't have gotten arrested. I'd still be stuck with Rufus, but I wouldn't be coated in goo, going through the third degree with my little sister.

Emmy made me tell her the whole sordid story, but I finally got rid of her so I could get clean. It took me three shampoos and a lot of unsolicited advice from Meep (who always has to go in the bathroom with me, no matter how many times I tell her it's kind of creepy—apparently, it's a "cat thing"), but I finally got all of the residual stickiness out. But there was a good chance I was never going to drink milk or orange juice again.

 140

EASTON WEST'S BLOG

Wednesday, September 9, 7:05 P.M.: The good news is that my beloved Tiddlywinks has been returned to me, and my stalker, a teenage girl who I'm not allowed to name, has been caught red-handed. The bad news is that the wonderfully brave Victoria was injured when she attempted to rescue Tiddlywinks. And yes, this all took place on set!

Victoria's prognosis is good, and like the true professional she is, she'll be back at work tomorrow.

However, I'm very worried about poor Tiddlywinks. I think the ordeal may have been too much for him. I've brought him to a vet and they are keeping an eye on him. I'll be making the big decision about him later today. My only goal is to make sure that he doesn't suffer.

I hope you will understand, dear readers, if I go into seclusion for a while. I am just absolutely devastated by everything that has happened since I came to Chicago. If it weren't for Victoria, I don't know what I would do. ♥

seventeen

"THOSE WHO WILL PLAY WITH CATS MUST EXPECT TO BE SCRATCHED."
—CERVANTES

After my shower, I called Melly first, since she was the least likely one to scream my ear off.

"Nat! Are you okay? Where are you? I'm at Oscar's. He's practically ready to bake a file in a cake. Wait, let me —"

"NATALIE!" shrieked Oscar. "Are you okay? Don't let anyone make you their bitch! We'll get you out of there!"

I held the phone away from my ear a little. "Guys, calm down. I'm fine. I'm at home."

There was the sound of struggle and a pause that I could only imagine was Oscar and Melly fighting over the phone. Oscar, of course, won. He fights dirty. Melly is too nice. She never sees it coming.

"You're home? Are you on the lam? Did you bust out?"

"Don't be silly. I called Viv. She got me out. And even better, she's going to take care of everything and she's not

142

going to tell Mom and Dad. We can relax now. The professionals are going to take care of it."

"What do you mean?"

"The BERM, goofus! We're off the hook! Our lives can get back to normal now. That psycho cat is out of my house, the authorities are on the job, and as soon as they've cleared things up, I can go back to school." I felt like spinning around in celebration, but I was too tired, so I settled for a nice big flop backward onto my fringed chartreuse bedspread.

There was silence on the other end of the phone for at least half a minute, which was a record with Oscar. "I think Victoria's going to put Rufus down."

"What? What are you talking about?" I sat up.

Melly took the phone back from Oscar. "After the police took you away, Victoria made this huge production out of finding a proper carrier for Rufus and everything. Kept going on and on about how she had to get the poor cat back to her dear friend Easton."

"Such a faker!" Oscar yelled in the background. Poor Melly. Her ears were probably shot.

"And then she did a blog post as Easton tonight, and it doesn't sound good for Rufus. She's got him at a vet, where it sounds like she's going to do something drastic."

Oscar took control again. "She's getting rid of evidence, that's what she's doing! And I bet Easton herself is next. Go read the blog, you'll see what I mean."

I went to my desk and opened up my laptop. Oscar had bookmarked Easton's blog for me before, so I went right to it and read the post. Victoria was tricky and obviously up to no good. How far would she go to shore up her sucky acting career?

"Okay," I agreed, "it doesn't sound good. But the BERM is on it now."

"Rufus will be dead by the time they get around to doing something," said Oscar. "Trust me. My uncle works for the government."

"I don't—"

"And probably Easton's a goner too. What do you bet Victoria's writing up a suicide blog post right now and scheduling it to run after she has the vet give Rufus his lethal injection?"

I closed my laptop. "Look, Oscar, I'll call Viv, okay? That's all I can do. She told me to stay out of it."

"*Humph.*" I couldn't believe he actually humphed me.

I sighed. "Oscar, there's nothing I can do."

"Well, *we'll* do what we can. *We'll* be on set again tomorrow and *we'll* watch her like hawks. Won't we, Melly?"

I didn't hear whatever Melly responded since Oscar hung up on me.

Meep headbutted me. *You're not going to let them kill that cat, are you?* She'd been listening in on my entire conversation, as usual.

"I didn't think you even liked Rufus," I said.

He was okay. He's just a cat, said Meep. Ha. Truer words

were never spoken. *He was annoying, but that doesn't mean he deserves to die.*

True enough. If you killed cats for being annoying, there wouldn't be any cats left on the planet. But would Victoria really kill Rufus? Or Easton, for that matter?

eighteen

"THE CAT, HAVING SAT UPON A HOT STOVE LID, WILL NOT SIT
UPON A HOT STOVE LID AGAIN.
BUT HE WON'T SIT UPON A COLD STOVE LID, EITHER."
—MARK TWAIN

I lay awake half the night thinking about what Oscar and
Meep had said. Rufus was definitely the most annoying cat
I'd ever met, but he really didn't deserve to be put down because of it. I hated that phrase, actually. "Put down," like
there was anything nice and gentle about it. Maybe if you
couldn't talk to cats and truly thought they were just emo-
tionless, mindless furry critters, you could justify it. Maybe.
But I knew better. I mean, not that there weren't an awful
lot of stupid cats, but they weren't stuffed animals. They had
feelings and they felt pain.

Morning finally rolled around. I shoved Meep off my
head (she likes to sleep up there like some kind of furry,
purring hat). I got dressed like I was going to school and
went to the kitchen to grab some breakfast. Mom was sitting
at the counter with Emmy, both of them eating cereal. The
kitchen TV was on the local morning show, and thankfully

not the Food Network. But I guess even Mom couldn't mess up cereal.

"It seems that even the northern suburbs have starstruck teenagers," said a chirpy anchorwoman.

"I think you mean stalkers, don't you?" laughed a guy with teeth that were far too big and way too white.

"Geez, Mom," I said. "How about we watch some real news?"

Emmy sat up straight and shot me a look. She reached for the remote, but Mom stopped her. "Hold on, I'm watching that. Besides, it sounds like a cautionary tale. You should both listen." Yeah. Mom was big on "learning experiences," which generally meant listening to stories where some teenagers ruined their lives by not paying attention to their parents. I just looked at Emmy and shrugged. The police had assured us that my name would not be released.

"Yes," said the anchorwoman. "It seems that Easton West, a celebrity blogger, is in town to cover the filming of *Freddy's Day Off,* which is being filmed at our local Shermer High and in locations throughout the city."

"See," said Mom. "I told you girls that no good would come of letting a movie be filmed at your school. I really need to call your principal. I should have just toughed it out yesterday."

Oh, crap. I made a mental note to call Viv and make sure she'd called Principal Johnson. She said she would straighten things out and just swear him to secrecy. Wait, did that involve telling him about my Talent? If so, he needed to be sworn to top-level classified secrecy. I was hoping he'd let me at least have Melly pick up my homework so I wouldn't get too behind. If I kept up on schoolwork, maybe Mom wouldn't be as pissed when she found out what happened.

"Are you sure you're feeling okay today, Mom?" I asked. Maybe I should have brushed Rufus and kept some of his fur around for emergencies. I put some cereal in my bowl and got out the milk, trying to act nonchalant.

"So, this teenage girl was so enamored with Easton that she allegedly kidnapped Easton's cat!" continued the woman with a snarky grin. The segment went to a picture of Easton (apparently an old picture with the real Easton, since Rufus wasn't trying to dismember her) holding Rufus. "And yes, that *is* a pink cat! Tiddlywinks is quite famous in his own right and has his own fan club." No wonder Rufus had such a big head.

"But not only did this local girl kidnap the cat, she's a student at Shermer High! She brought the cat with her to school and was caught red-handed when the kitty escaped from her book bag during the film shoot."

The anchorman laughed. Smarmy talking head. "I guess no one told her not to let the cat out of the bag!"

Emmy groaned and put her hand over her eyes. I felt like doing the same, but I tried to keep my cool so Mom wouldn't suspect anything.

"That's right, Cory! And what makes this story even

crazier is now the cat is being held at the Happy Paws veterinarian clinic in Northbrook under a 'death watch,' and animal activists from the Chicago area have descended on the place to protest!" They cut to a small mob scene outside a vet. People were chanting and holding up signs that read Free Tiddlywinks! A lot of the protestors were waving stuffed pink cats in the air. In other words, utter chaos.

They cut to another shot of Easton (or rather, Victoria looking like Easton) surrounded by news reporters. She was wearing some huge dark sunglasses, probably to hide the fact that she had no tears. I mean, seriously, after watching her yesterday, I didn't know why she was an actress. She couldn't act, not even like a spoiled celebrity blogger, and it's not like that was a stretch.

"You just would not believe the pressure I'm under. The pain!" Easton-Victoria moaned. "Tiddlywinks is my life!"

I rolled my eyes at Emmy, but she had her head buried in her hands. Mom was staring intently at the screen. Maybe if she watched the cooking shows like that, she'd actually be able to cook.

"After his ordeal at the hands of that . . . that *wicked* girl . . . it was obvious that Tiddlywinks is not the same. He's been irrep—irreper . . . deeply wounded. I've agonized over this decision, but it's for the best." She fake sobbed. Emmy raised her head and shot me yet another pointed look.

"Teenagers today," Mom said. She picked up the remote and shut off the TV. "You girls can take a lesson from that."

"What lesson?" I asked. Don't be a sucky actress? Don't watch crappy morning TV?

"Not to get caught up in the celebrity culture. It makes you do crazy things. You know, Natalie, I should really have a word with your friend Oscar's parents."

"Oh no," I said. "I mean, his parents talk to him about it, Mom. It's under control." Not really, but having her talk to them about it? That was a bad idea on so many levels, especially the fact that Oscar might never forgive me. His parents were finally sort of comfortable with him being gay. There was no need to add the doubtful appellation of potential celebrity stalker to the list. Besides, I'm pretty sure they were aware of his celebrity news addiction. It's not like he tried to hide it.

"Nat," said Emmy, "don't *you* think it's a shame what they're doing to that cat?" She stared at me and pointed her spoon, which was dripping with milk, in my direction. "How they're probably going to *kill* him through no fault of his own?"

This from the girl who once tried to flush poor Meep down the toilet. *"Yes,"* I said. "Of course I do." I pushed my half-eaten bowl of cereal away. Like I could eat when I was thinking about what they might do to Rufus. Stupid Victoria. What an ego! It's not like Easton would have been lying about her acting talent—she didn't have any. And she *is* a total diva. What good did her ruse do anyone?

"Well," said Emmy, hopping down from her stool. "Time

for *me* to go to school!" She looked meaningfully at me again.

Sometimes I wondered if all super-geniuses were as annoying as Emmy, or if it was just the fact that she was my little sister.

♥

A few hours later, I was standing across the street from Happy Paws watching the crowd of Tiddlywinks (a.k.a. Rufus) supporters. There were even more now than they'd shown on the TV earlier, maybe a hundred or so. Some of them had chained themselves together and were sitting in a big circle in the parking lot. The building itself was small and brick, with a fenced-in area in the back. There was a happy little dog caricature on the Happy Paws sign. It looked pretty cheerful—you know, for a house of death.

I really didn't know what I was going to do or why I was there. I'd left my house around the same time as Emmy since I had to at least pretend to go to school. Then I'd taken the bus to the mall to kill time, and then felt like an idiot when I'd finally gotten there because it didn't open until ten. I'd tried calling Viv to see if she had any news, but I kept getting her voice mail. I'd even thought about going back home, but somehow, I'd found myself walking to Happy Paws instead. It wasn't that far from the mall.

I walked over to the edge of the crowd and stood next to a woman carrying a stuffed pink lion and a sign that read *Save Tiddlywinks!* She even had a pink stripe in her hair. I wondered if she'd still be protesting if she knew Rufus like I knew him.

"What's up?" I asked her. I tried to look inconspicuous. Maybe I should have borrowed something pink to wear.

She dropped her sign and grabbed me in a huge hug. That was when I noticed she had tears running down her face. "Someone just announced they're gonna do it!" she cried.

"What?" I asked, even though I had the sinking feeling I knew what she meant.

"They're going to give Tiddlywinks a *lethal injection*!" She sobbed louder, and some other people around her began crying and wailing too.

What kind of quack vet worked at Happy Paws? How had Victoria convinced them to do it? There hadn't been anything wrong with Rufus other than general pissed offedness the last time I saw him, unless they'd left him in the cooler for too long. But then they wouldn't even be talking about killing him, he'd already be dead.

I disentangled myself from the woman and walked off a few feet. A policeman was standing in front of the door, probably because of all the crazies out front. I tried Viv again on my cell phone. The BERM should be able to stop this. After all, wouldn't they need Rufus to prove their case?

It rang through to her voice mail again. Crapola.

"If I ever get my hands on the girl who did this to poor Tiddlywinks . . ." The woman who had been sobbing on my shoulder just a minute ago had stopped crying. She punched her right hand into her left, which was still holding the stuffed lion. It squeaked, and she looked at it guiltily. She patted it and put it in her bag, then punched her hand again. I backed away a little farther.

I probably didn't have anything to worry about. The newscasters really hadn't described me in any detail. They'd just said I was a local high-school student, probably because I was a minor. Not to mention I wasn't actually arrested, but that wasn't public knowledge.

And not to mention they really *ought* to be mad at Victoria-pretending-to-be-Easton anyway. What kind of person decides to kill their cat off for no reason? But I guess celebrity saves you from a lot of criticism. If I had any pull with the press, I'd be pointing the finger at the cat killer.

I looked around the crowd. Almost everyone there was older, which made sense since it was school hours. But there was another girl on the other side of the parking lot who looked like she could be in high school. Even better, she was carrying, like, five stuffed pink cats, which would normally make her look really weird. In this crowd, she stood out only a little.

I sidled over to the weeper with the violent streak. "Hey," I said. "Didn't they say the girl who stole Tiddlywinks was blonde?" I motioned in the general direction of the girl across the way, and the woman turned to look. Then I tapped another woman next to her. "And didn't they say she, um, was kind of tall and skinny?" Both total lies, but hey, it was for a good cause. I silently apologized to the girl, who I'd never seen before. But if this worked and I saved Rufus, we were all working toward the same goal, right?

"Yeah," said the first woman, narrowing her eyes. "I think they did."

"I bet that's her!" said the other one. "She looks kind of shifty to me. Check out how she keeps petting her stuffed cats."

"Get her!" yelled the first one and took off. "That's the girl who did this to Tiddlywinks!"

That was all it took. The whole crowd started surging at the poor blonde girl, who looked up in surprise, shrieked, and hugged her stuffed animals to her. She didn't even try to run. I think she was too confused by the sudden turn of events.

It might have been the first time in history it ever sucked to be tall, thin, and blonde.

 154

NINETEEN

"CURIOSITY KILLED THE CAT, BUT SATISFACTION BROUGHT IT BACK."
—ANONYMOUS INTERNET MISQUOTE OF A FAMOUS PLAYWRIGHT

The policeman stepped into the fray, but I could still see a couple of employees inside gathered around the door and the picture window in front. They were all staring at the carnage and shaking their heads. Well, at least they were distracted. I felt a little guilty about the blonde girl, but only a little. All the protestors looked kind of crazy to me. It's not like they were protesting outside of a puppy mill or something. This was all about celebrity.

I jogged around the side of the building to see if I could find another way in. I peeked through the side of the wooden gate and didn't see anyone, so I tried the gate. Locked, of course. But I guess it'd be idiotic not to have it locked with the mob out front. I took a deep breath, looked over my shoulder to make sure no one was watching, and climbed the fence. It was fairly high but kind of decorative, so it had plenty of places to grab onto, which was good for me since

155

I hadn't climbed anything since I was younger than Emmy.

I'd taken only about three steps toward the building when a really huge Doberman came charging straight for me out of a pet door cut into the back door. He was even bigger than Oscar's dog, Fluff, and that was saying something. This dog was like the Mack truck of Dobermans.

WOOF! Woof! Woof! Dude. I could practically feel the ground buckling under his charge.

I held up my hands and immediately stopped walking. "Hey," I said. "I'm just here to rescue someone that's about to be put to sleep, okay?" I held my breath. Would he understand me? Some animals did pretty well with just regular human speech, but there were some that would just look at you like you were speaking Swahili. And only some dogs seemed to understand Cat. I didn't have much experience with large dogs other than Oscar's, and Fluff definitely wasn't much of a conversationalist.

He skidded to a stop about a foot away and lowered his head. *Grroowwwf?* he said.

Hmm. Maybe he did understand me? I spoke slowly. "There's a cat in there and they're going to put him down. I'm here to save him. There's nothing wrong with him. Can you let me by? Please?"

He gave me a long look and then gave me a doggy smile, his tongue lolling out. *GRrrruuuuffffuuuu*, he said.

Oh, wow. "Yeah, that's right. Rufus. Can you show me where he is?" The dog turned around and loped to the back door and went in through the doggy door. I tried the doorknob, but it was locked. I tried the window, but it was locked too.

The dog stuck his head through the doggy door and looked at me. *Wrrooof?* He backed up and his head disappeared.

It was worth a shot. I got down on my hands and knees and stuck my head through the doggy door. Good thing he was a Doberman, and a huge one at that. If they'd had a doggy door for a Chihuahua, I'd have been completely out of luck. I pushed myself through and got a face full of doggy saliva before I could stand up. Gross. That was one thing that I preferred about cats—they mostly kept their tongues to themselves.

"Um, thanks," I said, and patted his head. We were in a room with a bunch of vet supplies and stainless steel tables, and cages along one wall. Some of the cages had pets, including cats, but none of them were pink. "Now, can you show me where Rufus is?"

They took him to the death chamber, piped up a scrawny orange and white cat in a cage close to the door. *Two doors down on the left. They don't come back from there, you know. At least, not alive.*

"Oh, thanks." I went to the door and opened it a crack to take a look. I was at the end of a hallway. The front waiting room was directly down the white tile hall. I let the door swing softly shut. If any of the employees turned around, they'd see me as soon as I opened the door.

I'm probably next, the scrawny cat continued. *Ain't what I used to be. At least, that's what my human keeps saying.* He let out a strangled sounding cough.

You're just in here for a teeth cleaning, said a white cat in the next cage. *Stop being such a baby.*

You never know, the first cat said darkly. *You never know. Look what they're doin' to that hoity-toity cat the girl's looking for. He's a lot younger than I am.*

"That's why I'm here," I said. "I'm trying to save him. There's nothing wrong with him."

The white cat snorted. *Oh, I wouldn't say that.*

"What do you mean?" I asked. Maybe Victoria had done something to him after all. Maybe he was brain-dead after being locked in the cooler. Oh, no. Had I killed Rufus? Was it really my fault after all?

Even drugged up, that one's got an attitude.

"Oh," I said. "Uh, yeah. That would be Rufus." I cracked the door and peeked out again. I counted three employees at the front window and another behind a check-in counter. They all had on colorful hospital-style scrubs with pictures of happy-looking little kittens and puppies frolicking around. Killers. How did they sleep at night?

They were all still staring out the front window, but the room the cat had said Rufus was in was only one door down from them. There was no way I could get in there without being seen, even with the diversion going on out front. I needed them out of the room.

Sneaking him out, eh? asked the white cat.

"Well," I said, "I was going to try to. I'm not technically his person, so I can't just go up front and get him."

I figured that, said the white cat. *I saw her when they brought him in. I understand where he gets his attitude from, though he didn't seem to like her much.*

"She's not actually his human either. That's part of the problem. She wants him gone."

The dog interrupted. *Woof! Woof?*

What's that again? asked the orange and white cat. *My dog ain't what it used to be either.*

He says we could help, said a black cat in the corner cage. *I've got a dog at home, though I'm better at ferret.*

"How?" I asked.

My person has two ferrets too, the black cat continued. *Smelly little things, but they're pretty nice. Really preoccupied with chewing, but friendly.*

"No, I mean, what does the dog mean about helping?"

They ignored me and conferred with each other. I peeked out the door again. I could hear some shouting from outside, and one of the employees was shaking her head. I felt a little bad for the blonde, but hey, sometimes you hit the birth lottery and sometimes you don't. Besides, if she really was a fan of Tiddlywinks, she'd probably be glad to have had a hand in helping save him.

Okay, said the white cat. *You there, girl. Let us all out except for Daisy over there on the end. We'll take care of it. Just open the door and give us a few minutes, then go get Attitude Boy and get out of here.*

It was worth a shot. I didn't have any other ideas. I started opening cages. "Why not Daisy?" I asked as I opened the white cat's cage.

The white cat jumped nimbly down to the floor. *Pregnant as a bowling ball*, she said. *We take care of our own. No use endangering the kittens.*

"Oh," I said. I guessed that's why they were helping me free Rufus anyway. Who knew? Meep always seemed pretty aloof when it came to other cats, and I'd taken my cat cues from her. But then, Meep was kind of weird even by cat standards. I figured it was all the weird genetic inbreeding or whatever they did to make her hypoallergenic. Other cats tended to make fun of her. They said she smelled funny.

I finished letting everyone out of their cages and opened the door enough for them all to go through one by one. All told, there were three dogs and five cats. I kept the door cracked open and watched as the white cat and the Doberman led the way.

They all quietly crept to the end of the hallway. None of the employees noticed them. Then as if on cue (apparently, reports of an animal sixth sense are true), they rushed the front door with the Doberman leading the way, barking his head off. He crashed right into the door and it popped open with a bang and a tinkle from the bell they had looped on the door handle. It looked like he'd done it before. The cats and other dogs followed him out, howling and yowling all the way. For just a second, no one moved. Then everyone up front said their curse word of choice and went barreling out the door after the escapees.

I gave it a second to make sure no one else was around and went in Rufus's room. He was in a cage lying on a faded blue towel. He lifted his head as I entered the room and looked at me. Or rather, he tried to look at me. Literally, one eye was going in one direction and the other eye was going in another. With his smooshed-in ears and big round eyes, he looked a lot like an owl—a drunk owl.

"What happened to you?" I asked as I opened the door of the cage.

That evil imposter gave me a double dose of my travel medicine, said Rufus. *But she told the vet it was from being abused while I was kidnapped. Personally, I think she paid off the vet.*

I hesitated before reaching in the cage. "Are you sure you're okay to be moved?"

He focused his left eye on me. *I'll be a lot worse if you don't move me. Where have you been? I've been waiting!*

"Good point." I picked him up.

Crap. I should have brought my book bag. But the last time I'd seen it, it was floating in a pile of assorted liquids in the cafeteria. I hadn't been planning on a rescue attempt when I left the house and I hadn't brought anything useful with me, just my purse, and there was no way Rufus was going to fit in that. And there was no way I could just carry him out. I mean, not only was he pink, but he was probably the most recognizable cat on the planet, especially to the mob of freaks outside the door.

Frick on a stick. I looked around, but there wasn't much in the room, mostly just medical-looking stuff. But there was a stack of folded blankets and towels on a table. I grabbed one and tried to conceal Rufus in it. Not unsurprisingly, he freaked.

What do you think you're doing? Trying to send me parcel post? I can't breathe!

"No, but I've got to hide you in something. Dude, you're pink!" I stopped struggling with him. We probably had only a few minutes left before the employees started coming back.

Rufus took a swipe in the general direction of the blanket and almost managed to snag it out of my hand. I pulled it back and held it out of his reach. It was light blue with little stars on it, kind of like a baby blanket. That gave me an idea. Last year in health class, they'd made us practice swaddling fake babies. I think it was supposed to be a preventative measure or something, along with talks about STDs and carrying around bags of flour and pretending they were kids. (It made no sense to me. I mean, who would ever mistake a bag of flour for a kid?) But I remembered how to swaddle, kind of.

"I'm going to swaddle you like a human baby," I said. "Just hold still. You'll be able to breathe, okay?"

He humphed, but lay there and let me swaddle him. When I was done, he looked like one seriously ugly, furry baby, with only the front of his face sticking out. I hoped that as long as I held him close to my chest, no one would notice. Or maybe they'd just think I was babysitting a really ugly kid. With a lot of pink facial hair. And a lazy eye.

This is ridiculous, said Rufus.

"Tell me about it," I said. I cradled him in my arms like I'd practiced with the baby doll and flour bag, and peeked my head out the door. The front door was still wide open. I walked out the door, went down the steps, edged around the crowd, and kept going. I couldn't tell if the blonde girl was still standing or if the protestors had completely taken her out. The cats and the Doberman were nowhere to be seen either.

A bus was pulling up to the stop at the corner. I didn't know where it was going, but I climbed on anyway, paid, and sat down in the back.

As it was pulling away, I heard some shouting. Then the whole crowd took up the chant. "Tiddlywinks escaped! Tiddlywinks escaped! Hooray!"

TWENTY

"ANYONE WHO CLAIMS THAT A CAT CANNOT GIVE A DIRTY LOOK EITHER HAS NEVER KEPT A CAT OR IS SINGULARLY UNOBSERVANT."
—MAURICE BURTON

I transferred to another bus that was going back toward home after I got off the first one somewhere in Glenview. It was more crowded than the first bus had been, but I still managed to find a seat in the back next to an older woman in a tweedy-looking pantsuit. She sniffed at me as I sat down.

"You're awfully young to have a baby," she said.

"I'm just babysitting," I said. Like it was any of her business anyway.

She sniffed again like she didn't believe me. "In my day, they had a name for girls like you."

"Um, babysitters?" I said it with as much innocence as I could muster, but I couldn't help letting a little snark slip through.

She looked at me over the top of her glasses and sniffed one more time. "I think you know the word I'm thinking of," she said.

Rufus let out a hissy kind of cat laugh. *She thinks you're a —*

"Shhhh!" I said to Rufus. The lady looked at me suspiciously. I started to hum the "Hush, Hush" song to cover up his cat giggling. You'd think he'd be a little nicer, considering I'd just saved his butt from lethal injection.

"Is there something wrong with your baby?" She reached out a hand and pulled on a corner of the blanket. "He doesn't sound right. Maybe he has a cold. You young mothers don't know what you're doing."

"I told you," I said through gritted teeth, "he's not my kid. And he's fine. Maybe just some allergies or something." Rufus kept sniggering, which actually sounded a lot like phlegmy coughing, now that I thought about it.

The nosy woman leaned over and then pulled on the blanket again. "Let me see," she said. "I'm a grandmother. I know what *I'm* doing —" She stopped as the flap of blanket I'd put over Rufus's face came loose and his crossed, bulging eyes and pink fur peeked out. "Aaaaah!" She shrieked and shrank back in her seat.

Some of the other passengers were looking at us now. "It's okay," I told her as I flipped the blanket back down. "I can explain."

She stood up and looked down at me. "Honey," she said, "I'm sorry, but that is the ugliest baby I have ever seen in my life. It's just not right." She lurched a bit as the bus came to a stop, shook her head at me one more time, and then got off the bus.

A few people were still looking at me with undisguised interest. "He, um, takes after his dad," I said lamely. Rufus just kept laughing.

♥

I finally made it home and went straight to my room, even though no one else was around, not even Meep. I set Rufus on the bed and unswaddled him.

You should have seen your face! He was still laughing.

"Well, you should see yours. Your eyes are still crossed. Besides, you're the ugly baby, not me."

He stopped to consider that. *All of your hairless human babies are ugly, if you ask me. But I want a mirror. What do you mean my eyes are crossed?*

"You can't tell?" I got him a mirror and held it up in front of him. He peered at it, but only his right eye seemed remotely focused on it.

He was silent for a moment. *If my eyes stick like this, that woman is going to pay.* He raised his head and looked at me. At least, with one eye. *Why did you pull me off her? I had her!*

"Rufus, you're insane. We were in a room full of witnesses. You got me arrested!"

He ignored that. *And then you let her take me away! She was going to have me killed!* He swiped a paw at me and I jumped back, but I didn't really need to. His aim was way off. *And she threatened to kill Easton!* He stood up on wobbly legs. *We've got to find my person before it's too late!*

166

"Wait," I said. "Tell me exactly what she said. Tell me everything, from the beginning."

He sat back down after he nearly fell off the bed. *Fine*, he said. *After we left your school, she brought me to a house. Easton was there somewhere; I could smell her. The evil woman —*

"Victoria."

Victoria, then. She had all of our things. She went digging into our stuff, just flinging it everywhere, and found my travel pills. The whole time she was doing this, she was yelling so my person could hear her. She said this was all more trouble than it was worth and that we were both expendable. She said she was going to take care of it all this Saturday when she had a break from shooting. Then she shoved the pills in my mouth and made me swallow them.

I sat down on the bed next to Rufus and stroked his back. His hackles were up. "I'm sorry, Rufus," I said.

I would have taken her out if I hadn't been restrained.

"Of course you would have." I petted him a few more times and then got my phone. "Just hang on, okay? My sister works for the BERM. It's . . . um . . ." How to explain a governmental agency to a cat? "Well, it's kind of like the police . . ." Well, it was, *kind of*. Maybe more like the Secret Service, but would a cat even know what that was? "But they just monitor people with Talents. Anyway, I've told her everything. She's taking care of things. I just need to let her know I rescued you." I called Viv and got her stupid voice mail again. I left another message. Where was she? And why wasn't she returning my phone calls?

Now all we could do was wait.

Oscar and Melly arrived as soon as school was out. I'd sent a text to Oscar and he'd texted back, even though texting wasn't allowed in school. He was such a pro he could actually text with his hand in his pocket. Mad skills.

I gave them the whole story as soon as they came in, with Rufus interrupting me every now and then to make himself look better. Like they could even understand him.

"Wow," said Oscar. "This is a new low for Hollywood. Killing a blogger because they're gonna out you as a sucky actress? Sounds like a B-grade movie plot."

"What did Viv say?" asked Melly.

"Nothing. I've left her three messages so far." I gave Rufus another pat on the head. "So, what's the word at school?" I almost didn't want to ask. I'd been trying really hard not to remember the look on Ian's face as I'd been dragged out of the cafeteria.

"Well," said Oscar, "you're totally famous!"

He held up his hand to high-five me, but I didn't take the bait. That was his dream, not mine. "What are they saying?" I looked at Melly. Surely she at least understood the whole cafeteria scene was not good for my reputation. Not that I'd really *had* a reputation before, but whatever I'd had before was completely shot now.

"Mostly, no one can believe it. And they're wondering why you did it."

Yeah, I was kind of wondering the same thing myself. "Anything from Ian?" I couldn't believe the words had come out of my mouth. I was obviously a glutton for punishment.

"I didn't see him today," said Melly, playing with the fringe on my bedspread instead of looking at me. "Sorry."

I wasn't sure if I believed that or not. Maybe she was just being nice. How was I ever going to face Ian again?

"What are we going to do if Viv doesn't call back?" asked Oscar. "They're filming in the city tomorrow at Wrigley Field. And then it's Saturday, and *then* it's lights out for Easton." He drew his finger across his throat.

Rufus coughed pathetically as he tried to growl. *I must do something*, he said.

"Dude," I said. "Just settle down. You're in no condition to do anything." I wondered how long it would take for the drugs to wear off. The vet had given Meep something once, but it certainly hadn't made her eyes cross. I tried Viv again on the phone, just in case. No answer. What good were the professionals if you could never get in touch with them?

"What do you think we should do?" asked Melly.

"I'm sure Viv will call back," I said, though I really wasn't sure at all. Other than her weekly night at home, I didn't really talk to Viv regularly, especially since she had moved out for college. We weren't like those sisters in the Hallmark commercials. Honestly, I had no idea what her schedule looked like.

Though you'd think she'd call me back after bailing me out and promising to fix everything.

"But what if she doesn't?" asked Oscar again. He attempted to pet Rufus, who responded by trying to bite his hand.

I was about to reassure everyone again that Viv would take care of it, when Melly spoke up. "We'll have to do something," she said. "We have to. If you know something bad is going to happen and you can prevent it, then you have to do something. It's our responsibility as human beings." She stood up, put her hands on her hips, and looked right at me.

I snapped my mouth shut. Ouch. There was the responsibility thing again.

Rufus purred and wiggled in Melly's direction. She scratched him behind his ear but kept her eyes on me. Then Rufus opened his still-crossed eyes wide at me and blinked.

"Oh, all right already!" I sighed. "If Viv doesn't call back tonight, we'll figure something out. I guess we need to find out where Victoria is hiding Easton. Maybe see if we can get some incriminating evidence or something."

"Yay!" Oscar cheered like we weren't talking about taking on a homicidal maniac on purpose. "Skip day!" He pulled out some sheets of paper and handed them to me. "Here's all the notes I took when I was listening to the filmmakers talk about their shoot tomorrow. And some pages from the script that I, um, borrowed."

Wow, Oscar took notes on something. That truly was amazing. Of course, it wasn't school related, but still. I read through as much as I could decipher while Melly intently studied the script pages. His handwriting needed work. I peeked over Melly's shoulder at the script. They didn't really say much either. Maybe I didn't know how to read them. There were only a few pages and it seemed like there had to be more. Who knew what they were going to be filming tomorrow?

"I'm guessing that most of the shooting will be around the press box? Or the ticket booth? And I guess the stands," I said. I didn't remember Ferris ever going in the press rooms, but I supposed the script called for at least doing a few original things in this new movie. "We should definitely be able to catch them filming outside the ticket windows since you don't need to be inside the stadium for that."

"Maybe we can sign up as extras," said Oscar.

"That won't work," said Melly. "The call went out over a week ago. They've already signed everybody up that they need."

Oscar looked at her. "Oh?"

She had the decency to blush. "Yeah. I tried to sign up, but Dad wouldn't let me skip school for it since we have that test in English."

"You've still got the test," I said. "Maybe you guys shouldn't skip tomorrow after all." Not that I wanted to tackle any of this on my own.

"Pfffft," said Oscar, waving his hands. "English shminglish. We're taking the day off with you."

"That was before someone's life was on the line," said Melly. "Besides, I'm not going to tell my dad. Oscar and I can make the test up later or something. And you're still suspended."

Thanks for reminding me. "Well, okay," I said. "So, we don't know what they're shooting tomorrow. If they aren't doing the ticket window scene, they're probably doing one of these other bits." I pointed to the script pages that Melly was still clutching in her hand. "And that means we've got to get inside the stadium."

"Didn't you say Ian's dad works for the Cubbies?" Melly said sweetly. Darn her for paying attention.

"I don't think—"

Oscar grabbed me by both shoulders and put his nose right up against mine. "Girl, this is life or death! Don't think! Do!"

Frick on a stick. For once, he actually wasn't exaggerating.

Wrigley Stadium - Day

FADE IN:
Outside of Wrigley Stadium. Freddy and Molly
walk up to a ticket window . . .

>   **TICKET VENDOR**
> Can I help you?
>   **FREDDY**
> Yeah, two tickets to today's game,
> please. (Pause.) Hey, can we get the
> Ferris Bueller seats?
>   **TICKET VENDOR**
> The what?
>   **MOLLY**
> Freddy, give it a rest.
>   **FREDDY**

Freddy turns to Molly and then back
to the window. The ticket vendor is
peering through the window, clueless.

> Hey, if I'm going to do it, I want
> to go all the way.

> (To ticket vendor): You know, the
> seats Ferris Bueller sat in for the
> movie?

> **TICKET VENDOR #2**
> Sam, he wants Section 104, row
> three, seat 9.

> **TICKET VENDOR**
> Oh, sorry. I'm new. Let me see what we've
> got available there.

> **FREDDY**
> Great, thanks!

Freddy bounces on the balls of his feet
while Molly looks annoyed.

> **TICKET VENDOR**
> I'm sorry, I've got row two, but row three
> is all sold out.

> **FREDDY**
> Oh no! Are you sure?

> **MOLLY**
> Freddy, just get the tickets. It's close
> enough.

> **TICKET VENDOR**
> So do you want them or not?

> **FREDDY**
> Yeah, I guess so.

> **TICKET VENDOR**
> They're $50 each.

> **FREDDY**
> Ouch. Um, Molly?

Molly rolls her eyes and opens up her purse
to pull out a credit card. She hands it to
the ticket vendor.

FREDDY
Thanks, Molly, I owe you.
MOLLY
Technically, you'll owe my dad.
TICKET VENDOR
Okay, here you go. Enjoy the game.

Cut to Freddy and Molly walking down the
steps to their seats. Freddy is holding
the tickets in his hand. He pauses at row
three.

FREDDY
Nobody's here yet . . .
MOLLY
Just sit where we're supposed to.
It doesn't matter.
FREDDY
I just want to do this right. All my life
I've been close enough. I want to be there.
MOLLY
Freddy, how many times do I have to tell
you? Real life isn't like the movies. We
couldn't get in to visit the stock market
like Ferris did, there's no such restau-
rant as Chez Quiz so we couldn't eat lunch

where Ferris ate, and the parade isn't until
tomorrow. Life's all about compromise.

Molly passes by row three to sit in row
two. After a moment, Freddy follows her. A
teenage girl is seated next to Freddy.

> **FREDDY**
> Maybe you're right. I don't know. Today
> isn't working out like I thought it would.
> **MOLLY**
> Like I said, that's life.

They watch the game in silence. It's approxi-
mately the fourth inning. The Cubs are up at
bat.

> **MOLLY**
> It's like the Cubs, you know? They haven't
> won the series for over a hundred years,
> but they don't give up. They keep on trying.

A player hits a grand slam and the stands
erupt. You can hear the announcer (Pat Hughes)
screaming, "Get out the tape measure, LONG
gone!"

> **FREDDY**
> Whoooooo!

Freddy stands up and cheers. The girl next
to him is standing and cheering too.
They high-five each other, then Freddy
suddenly grabs her in a hug and kisses her.
Molly stands, stunned. He hugs her too.
The girl laughs and high-fives him again.

> FREDDY
> You know what, Molly? Life doesn't have
> to be like that. Life can be anything you
> want. I'm going to prove it to you.

Freddy runs up the stairs and disappears
into the stadium. Molly stares after him.

FADE IN:
Freddy outside the press box area
Freddy is knocking on the door leading to the
press box area. People are passing by on the
concourse. The door finally opens.

> WRIGLEY EMPLOYEE
> What's going on, kid? This is a restricted
> area. Quit banging on the door. We've got
> people working in here.

> FREDDY
> Yeah, I know. I need to talk to Pat or Ron.

WRIGLEY EMPLOYEE

And who are you?

FREDDY

I'm Freddy and I'm the guy who's going to sing during the seventh inning stretch.

TWENTY-ONE

"WHEN MY CATS AREN'T HAPPY, I'M NOT HAPPY.
NOT BECAUSE I CARE ABOUT THEIR MOOD, BUT BECAUSE I KNOW
THEY'RE JUST SITTING THERE THINKING UP WAYS TO GET EVEN."
—PERCY BYSSHE SHELLEY

Melly and Oscar left only after I swore up and down that I'd call Ian after dinner if Viv hadn't called back. And, of course, Viv didn't call. After Mom's dinner interrogation was over, I asked Mom and Dad if they knew what Viv was up to, but they didn't have any idea either.

Dad was curious as to why I wanted to know, so I told him a friend of mine wanted to go to Northwestern and had questions. Then he said I could ask *him* since he'd gone there too, and I had to think up some college-related questions off the top of my head. Thankfully, he never asked which idiot friend of mine wanted to know which dorms had the best rooms or where the best fast food was on campus, since that was all I could think of to ask him.

"Any other questions?" he asked when I stopped babbling about how the quality of pizza could seriously impact a person's study habits. "Or maybe something else you'd like to talk about? Something bothering you?"

"Nope," I said. "I'm good. I'll, uh, ask my friend if they have any other questions tomorrow." I took a final bite of dinner and put my fork down. At least it was Emmy's turn to do the dishes.

But just as I was about to ask to be excused, Dad asked me another question. "How is Meep feeling?"

"Meep?" He *never* asked about Meep.

"I noticed there's a different kind of cat smell in the house and I haven't seen her today. She usually begs at dinner. Maybe she's sick?"

Emmy's eyes bugged out of her head and she started coughing like she was choking on something. She had actually been trying to help keep Mom away from my room, but the strain of lying to Mom was killing her. I had the feeling she was going to crack at any time. I shot her a look and leaned over so I could pound her on the back.

"I'm fine, I'm fine," she finally spit out, her face flushed.

Normally, Mom would have freaked out about Emmy hacking up a lung, but she was distracted with her own health issues. The Rufus Effect had already hit her, even though I'd brushed him, given him two baths in a row (much to his displeasure), and hidden him in my room. She'd been sneezing all through dinner.

Meep hadn't come out for dinner because she was keeping Rufus company. I think she felt sorry for him, since his eyes were still crossed and he couldn't walk in a straight line. It was the nicest I had ever seen her treat anyone. She'd even tried to give him some of her tuna. I'd think it was love if they weren't both fixed.

"Well," I said brightly to Dad, "now that Emmy's stabilized, I'm just going to go check up on Meep. She seemed okay before dinner, but I'll ask. I'll tell her you were thinking of her!"

"Okay," said Dad, grinning a little. "If you need anything else, I'm here."

I nodded and made my way to my bedroom as fast as I could, trying not to look any more suspicious than I already did.

Any word from your sister? asked Rufus as soon as I got in the door.

"No," I said. "I guess I'm going to have to call Ian."

Well, get to it then. If Rufus were able, I think he'd have his paws on his hips. Patience was definitely not his thing. But he was right. I had promised.

I picked up my phone and took a deep breath. I dialed Ian's number without even using my contact list. Even though this was my first time calling, I already had committed his number to memory from when he'd written it on my notebook in class. I could pretend that I was that good with numbers, but let's face it, I memorized anything that had to do with Ian.

"Hello?" It was Ian. I almost dropped the phone.

"Um, hi," I managed to get out. "This is Nat." You know, the girl who got arrested in front of the entire school.

"Nat!" He sounded surprised, but I didn't blame him. I

couldn't believe I was calling him either. "Are you okay? Is everything all right?"

At least he hadn't asked if I was certifiably insane. Yet. "Yeah, I'm okay. I know all that stuff at school yesterday seemed pretty . . . crazy."

"A little," he said.

"A little?"

He laughed. I shouldn't have prompted him. He must really think I was nuts. "Okay, a lot. Do you want to tell me what was going on?"

Did I? Yes and no. "I really can't."

"Oh," he said. Did he sound disappointed? Mad? I wasn't sure.

"I really want to, but I can't. I'm sorry." I took another deep breath and then stopped mid inhale. Adding "heavy breather" to my list of attributes was probably not a good idea. "Really sorry."

"Okay," he said. He definitely didn't sound happy. "I get it."

No, he totally didn't. How could he? But what was I supposed to say? Viv had told me to keep it quiet. But if I was honest with myself, I had no desire to tell him about the whole talking to cats thing anyway. It would be better if he thought I were some celebrity stalker rather than the weird girl who talks to cats. Right? To steel my resolve, I kept picturing Frog Boy in my head, sitting alone at his lunch table like he had the plague or something.

"I need to ask you a huge favor," I said.

"Okay . . ."

Maybe I should have had this conversation in person. I couldn't tell from his tone what he was thinking. No, wait, that would have sucked even more.

"You know how your dad works for the Cubs?" Well, that sounded stupid. Of course he knew. I could just picture him rolling his eyes.

"Um, yeah?"

"I really need to get into Wrigley Field tomorrow. Is there any way you could get, like, some backstage passes or something from him? Like, three?"

Long pause. "Would this have anything to do with the film crew being at Wrigley Field tomorrow?"

"Yes, but it's not what you think. I promise."

"Nat . . ."

"I swear on my trigonometry book that I am not a celebrity stalker." Please, please believe me.

Another long pause.

"I *really* wish I could tell you everything. And I will, I promise! As soon as I can. But this is really, really important. Like, literally someone's life is at stake."

"Someone's life is at stake?" He sounded really doubtful.

"Yes." I could feel my eyes tearing up a little. Poodle farts. I blinked to hold the tears back. Thank frick he couldn't see me. "Please, Ian, trust me."

"You can't tell me anything?"

"Just that someone's in really bad trouble and this is the

only way I know of to try and save them. If there were any other way, trust me, I wouldn't be asking." Seriously. I'd rather pull my toenails off with a pair of pliers.

"Come on, Nat. Give me something. Anything."

What could I say that wouldn't sound stupid and wouldn't make Viv mad? And most important, wouldn't out me as the cat whisperer? "I can't tell you how I know or why, but Victoria isn't . . . nice."

"That's pretty obvious," he said. "Remember, I was there yesterday and I heard her after you left."

"I am definitely *not* stalking her or Easton West," I said. "Really. Victoria's involved in something bad and I'm trying to help fix it." Oh, man. He wasn't going to buy it, was he?

He sighed. "Okay, Nat. I'll talk to my dad and see if he can leave you passes at the Will Call window. I can't promise anything, though."

"Thank you so much, Ian. Really. You have no idea. I owe you — big time." I slumped down on my bed, completely drained.

"Yeah," he said.

I told him thank you a few more times and then finally hung up. There were fingernail marks in my palm from where I had been clenching my hand. That was by far the most painful phone call I'd ever made. He was pretty nice about it all in all, considering. But I realized a few minutes later that neither one of us had brought up our Friday night date.

The chances of me seeing that alien invasion movie with Ian tomorrow night were right down there with my social status.

 184

TWENTY-TWO

FRIDAY, SEPTEMBER 11, 11:30 A.M.

"TO SOME CATS, PATIENCE IS A VIRTUE.
TO OTHERS, SOMETHING TO LAUGH AT."
—NATALIE NG

Oscar and Melly skipped out on school right before lunch and picked me up, and we drove to the train station. I'd spent the morning packing and unpacking an old backpack of Viv's with supplies, like I even knew what spies—or whatever it was you called BERM agents (which we weren't)—should carry.

We were so doomed.

I actually hadn't even pretended to leave for school. I just stayed in my room, but Mom was so preoccupied with her sneezing that she hadn't noticed I wasn't gone when she left for work. I'd been really worried that she was going to stay home again, but her workaholic side had prevailed. That was the first time *that* had worked in my favor.

The hardest thing had been leaving Rufus behind. He had really wanted to go and finish what he'd started with Victoria, but after what had happened the last time I'd taken him with me, there would've been no way I was going to chance it. Besides which, whatever pills Victoria had given him had been potent. His eyes had finally straightened out, but he was still walking like he was a drunken sailor. Meep had promised to keep him company, but ultimately, I'd had to duck out while he was using the litter box so I wouldn't have to deal with him screeching at me.

I'd put on a Cubs baseball cap and a Cubs T-shirt of Dad's. The shirt was huge on me, but at least I wouldn't stick out like a sore thumb. Oscar hadn't quite grasped the concept of blending in. He was wearing black jeans with silver studs down the side and a black shirt with a shredded Cubs T-shirt over the top of it.

"You do know we're going to a baseball stadium, right?" I asked him. At least Melly had worn something normal looking. It wasn't a Cubs shirt, but at least it was red. She looked perfect, as usual.

"What do you mean?" He looked down at his outfit and pointed at the Cubs logo on the front, which was slashed completely in half. "This is very sporty."

Yeah, in some parallel universe. We were lucky there weren't going to be any real Cubs fans at the stadium that day who might take offense to the defacement of their logo or something. I pulled my Cubs hat down lower over my forehead and tucked a few stray hairs back up underneath. It was not a good look for me, but if the movie security people were on the lookout for the crazy celebrity stalker girl, hopefully they wouldn't notice crazy Cubs fan girl in clothes that were too big for her.

We finally made it to Wrigley Field after a Metra train ride, a transfer to the El, and a short walk. There were a few people out front taking pictures of the famous red and white sign that read Wrigley Field: Home of Chicago Cubs, which was pretty normal. There were always tourists checking it out.

We checked all of the ticket windows, but there were no film crew people anywhere to be seen. They must have either already filmed the ticket window part or were going to do it another time, so we were going to have to get into the stadium.

We went up to the will call window. Had Ian been able to talk his dad into leaving some passes? The lady at the window waved us forward.

"Um, hi," I said. "I'm Natalie Ng. Do you have some passes for me by any chance? From, um, Mr. Abbott?"

"Hmmmm." she said, flipping through a box. "Let me see . . ." She kept flipping. My heart sank. Either Ian's dad hadn't come through, or Ian hadn't even asked. Not that I could blame him. But what were we going to do? Maybe we could sneak in somehow?

"It's Ng, spelled N-G," said Oscar. Ah, good point. Maybe she was looking under I. Oscar was lucky it was his mom who was Asian. His last name was Green. You couldn't mangle that.

"Ah, here you go!" She pulled out three lanyards with a

plastic card attached to them and handed all of them to me through the little window. "Remember to leave the passes on where they can be seen. And watch out for the film crew today!"

"Thank you," I said. I couldn't believe it. Oscar let out a cheer behind me. I passed around the lanyards and we walked over to the nearest gate.

"See!" Oscar said. "Ian *wuuuvvvvsss* you! I told you so!"

"Let's just get inside, okay?" I honestly didn't think Ian would do it. Not that I had a backup plan in case of disaster, but I was still amazed. PD was right: Ian was awesome.

There was a huge line of extras at the gate, all wearing Cubs clothes and carrying slips of paper. We finally got to a security guy. He waved Melly in when she held up her pass, but stopped me. "I've got one, too," I said. I held up the lanyard.

"I see it," he said. "But I need to check your backpack."

"Oh, okay," I said, and held it out to him. He put it on a table and started digging around inside. He pulled out my dad's video camera.

"You've got a stadium pass and I'm assuming you're not an extra, but you do know you can't use this to record any of the filming, right?"

"Right," I said. "We're, um, here to, um . . ."

"We're filming a short promotional spot for a local charity," Oscar said smoothly. "We won't be near the film crew at all, just in the offices."

"Okay, but if you're caught filming around the movie

crew, they will ask you to leave," said the guy. He set the camera aside, then peered into the bottom of the bag.

"What's this?" he asked.

"What?" I wasn't sure what he meant. I'd packed some dark sunglasses (more potential disguise), my cell phone, my keys, a regular digital camera, a notepad and pen, and an extra (non-Cubs) shirt that actually fit me so I could change later.

He pulled out two black wooden sticks hooked together with a chain. "Nunchucks? Seriously?" He looked at me like I was crazy. Oscar started whistling.

"Uh . . . ," I said.

"Miss, you can't bring weapons into the park. I'm going to have to confiscate them." Oscar stopped whistling.

"Wait," he said, "Can we, like, coat check them or something? They're my dad's."

"Sorry, we don't have a coat check for weapons." The guy stuck the nunchucks in a box under the table. He put everything else back in my bag and handed it to me. "No foolishness from you three, okay?"

"No, sir," I said. "Sorry about that." I whacked Oscar in the back as we went through the gate and joined Melly, who'd been standing there waiting.

"What were you thinking?" I asked him when we were out of earshot of the security guy.

"Victoria totally attacked you last time. I thought she was gonna claw your eyes out. I figured we could use a weapon, you know, just in case."

I really didn't even know what to say to that. His heart was in the right place. Sort of. But *nunchucks*?

"Why does your dad even own nunchucks?" asked Melly, which was exactly the same thing I had been thinking. I mean, his dad was complete white bread. Not that I could imagine my dad with nunchuks. He may work for the BERM, but he wasn't a field agent by any stretch of the imagination.

"I dunno." Oscar shrugged. "He has a secret desire to be a ninja? He's got some throwing stars too, but I didn't bring those."

"Good thing," I said. The security guy probably wouldn't have let us in. The nunchuks had been bad enough. And what would I have done with throwing stars? I wasn't Batman.

We wandered around the lower stands, the doors to the locker room, and the concession areas, but saw no sign of a film crew or any of the stars. There were a lot of people wandering around in Cubs stuff, but I couldn't tell if they were extras who'd answered the casting call or what. It looked like it was time for us to go up to the press area and see if they were filming there.

We found the entrance to the press boxes and showed our passes to a guy who happened to be walking out at the same time. He just glanced at the passes and waved us through without really looking at them. I let out a sigh of relief. Maybe everything would work out after all. Things seemed to be going so well, other than the nunchuks. I imagined how we'd find them filming, conceal ourselves, and get a video of Victoria saying something damaging or giving a clue as to where her rental house was. I already knew it had to be near Northbrook or Glenview somewhere. After all, why would she have brought Rufus to a vet far away from her house? It wouldn't make sense. And then I could get in touch with Viv and give her all the details and that would be it. Case closed.

Of course, I knew I was dreaming.

 191

TWENTY-THREE

FriDAY, SepTeMBer 11, 1:45 P.M.

"Beware OF PeOPLe WHO DISLIKe caTS."
—IrISH PrOVerB

Just like I'd hoped, we found the film crew without much trouble. There was a narrow hallway with a few offices and a small break room/cafeteria-looking area leading up to the actual press boxes. It wasn't really a very big area. That meant there were a lot of people and equipment crowded into a tiny spot, which was mostly good for us. Everything was so harried and packed, and we were just three more bodies in the way.

They were running a scene where, apparently, Ty's character was talking the announcer guys into letting him sing during the seventh-inning stretch. I'd been to only a few Cubs games in my life, but even I knew the seventh-inning stretch was a big deal at Wrigley Field. It was a huge tradition.

They had big name (and no name) celebrities come perform. Basically, some famous person would sing "Take Me Out to the Ball Game" and the crowd would sing along. And, you know, stretch after sitting for so long, I guess. Baseball games always seemed interminable to me, but the hot dogs were good. Dad wasn't very sporty, so I was spared having to watch them on television, at least.

It soon became apparent that watching them film the same scene over and over wasn't getting us anywhere. Victoria wasn't even in this scene. We needed to be somewhere where we could catch her off guard. Off movie camera and less public. With all the movie security people around, we couldn't even take our own camera out without risking getting thrown out. We moved back along the hallway to talk it over.

"I vote for the dressing room," Melly said.

"What about the craft services table?" asked Oscar. It was set up in the break room behind us.

"You're just hungry," I said, and punched him in the shoulder.

"True," he said. "But everyone winds up by the craft services table sooner or later."

They both looked at me like I should be the one making the decision. Like I had a clue. Finally I told Oscar to go over by the craft services table, and Melly and I would try to find Victoria's dressing room. After all, they might have the girls' and guys' areas separated, so Oscar wouldn't be able to get close anyway.

Not to mention he looked pretty conspicuous in his punk Cubs outfit, even around the movie people.

We split up, and our luck still looked good. We watched

as Oscar slipped into the break room and took up station by the food. He busied himself with straightening stacks of sandwiches and lining up bottles of water. No one questioned him at all.

Melly and I mingled with the people nearest the filming. When a lady I recognized as the costume designer walked by us, I poked Melly. She nodded and we followed the woman around the corner and down the hall to a section of offices, making sure to stay way back. Hopefully, she wouldn't recognize us. I'd even tucked the purple-streaked portions of my hair well up into the hat so I'd stand out less. She might not have recognized me without my neck wings anyway. The woman flipped through a rack of clothing in the hall, grabbed a Cubs shirt, and went back to the filming, not even glancing in our direction.

It really seemed like our good fortune was holding. A few of the office doors had paper signs taped on them. One had Victoria's name right on it. We'd actually found the dressing rooms, and even better, no one was hanging around in the hallway. They were all back where the action was.

Melly and I looked at each other. I knocked on the door, ready to run if it actually opened. Nothing happened and we didn't hear any noise from inside, so Melly opened the door and I followed her in. It looked like some poor guy's windowless office had been commandeered for Victoria. The desk (really, a glorified table) had a large three-part lighted mirror set up on it, and it was covered in makeup and curlers and hairbrushes. Another clothing rack had been shoved up against one wall, and a bookcase had been pushed out of the way near it. It wasn't a huge office to begin with, and with so much of Victoria's stuff sprawled on the desk, it looked like people from that TV show about hoarders had come through and made themselves at home.

"What do you think?" I asked.

"Not a whole lot of options," said Melly.

We looked at each other and then the clothing rack. I rearranged the clothes on it so all the longer pieces were on the side closest to the bookcase, and we shoved ourselves behind the rack. As long as no one pulled out a piece of clothing directly in front of us, we'd hopefully be okay. I pulled out Dad's video camera and made a space to stick it through and aimed it at the desk.

Then we waited.

"This is pretty cool," whispered Melly. "Though I really thought the dressing rooms would be nicer than this."

"I imagine you've got to make do with what you can when you're on location," I said, almost sounding like I knew what I was talking about.

Then the door burst open. Melly and I froze. I turned the camera on as quietly as I could and looked through the viewfinder. It was Victoria and the crazy eyeliner makeup lady. The door slammed behind them and Victoria sat down in the chair. Perfect. She was right in my sights. Amazingly, all of her wounds from the day before were completely gone.

She looked good as new. Either her Talent had taken care of them or the film crew used some seriously good makeup for moviemaking. What kind of Talent could she have, though, that both healed and allowed her to impersonate someone? It had to be Class A. At the very least, she was probably multi-Talented like Viv.

She leaned in toward the mirror and made a face as she looked closely at her eyebrows. She whirled on the makeup lady. "You're useless. You missed two hairs right here." She stabbed a finger at her left eyebrow. The poor makeup woman backed up and held up a brush like a shield.

"I can —" she started to say.

"Forget it! Just get out of here! I'll take care of it myself! It's no wonder Alan didn't want to give me a close-up!" She spun back around and makeup flew off the table as she started digging around in the pile, presumably looking for tweezers. The makeup lady left without another word.

I tilted my head slightly and widened my eyes at Melly. She looked back at me and wrinkled her nose. Seriously, Victoria was a starlet needing a serious come down. Hopefully, we'd be the ones to do it. I zoomed the camera in on her face. After we send a copy to the BERM, I was so going to stick it up on YouTube.

"Stupid people," she mumbled to herself. "I have to do everything myself." She leaned in so close to the mirror that her eyeball was practically touching it. She plucked out the two hairs, letting out a shriek with each one. Drama queen.

Finished, she sank back in her chair and stared at herself in the mirror. "What a freaking mess," she said to herself. "The stupid cat is missing again. I've got to take care of that idiot blogger today. At least it gives me an excuse." She sat up straight and said in a whiny voice, "I just can't go on without my beloved Tiddlywinks!" She slumped back down and was quiet for a minute, not taking her eyes off herself in the mirror. Homicidal freak. How could someone talk so casually about killing someone else? I guessed if you could do it to a cat, a human being was the next step up.

Then she leaned forward and breathed deeply, staring intently at herself. "I can do it. I am successful, rich, healthy, and happy. I am powerful. I am in charge. No one can stop me from getting what I want. People fear me."

I managed to hold back my laughter. For a classic villain, she was a total dork. I zoomed the camera back out as she kept repeating her mantra over and over again. Melly let out a small snort, but Victoria was too wrapped up in herself to notice.

Then my cell phone went off with "I Am Woman." Holy flying pancakes. Of all the times for Viv to finally call me back. Why hadn't I turned my ringer off? I fumbled with the camera and passed it to Melly, then plunged my hand in my backpack. Where was the damn phone?

It didn't matter. By the time the phone stopped ringing as it went to voice mail, Victoria was in front of us ripping clothes off their hangers and throwing them on the floor.

"You again," she practically snarled, peering at my face under the brim of my hat. She reached through the few remaining shirts hanging up and grabbed each of us around a wrist, yanking us both out. I went sprawling on the floor, but Melly managed to stay standing, barely. Victoria let go of me as I went tumbling, but she had Melly's wrist firmly in her grasp. "What do you want?" Victoria demanded.

I scrambled to my feet and backed toward the door with my book bag in my hand. "We're on to you!" I said. "We know you're planning to kill Easton West!"

Victoria stopped. "I don't know what you're talking about. You don't have any proof of anything. In fact"—she snatched my dad's camera from Melly's hand—"I'll take this."

"That's what—" I started to say, but Melly shook her head at me. She was right. Why tell her what we know from Rufus?

"Fine," I said. "You're right. Whatever you say. Why don't you let Melly go and we'll get out of here."

For a moment, it looked like Victoria was going to do just that. Then her eyes narrowed at me and she tightened her grip on Melly's wrist. "Why aren't you in jail? Why did the police let you go?" she asked. "I told them I wanted to press charges." She took a step in my direction, dragging Melly with her.

"Um, I've got a good lawyer?" I must not have sounded too sure, since her eyes narrowed even further. Craptastic.

"I don't believe you," she said.

"Maybe they just thought I was a better actress than you," I said, and leaped forward to try and grab the camera.

I almost got my hand on the strap, but then she shoved forward and hit me in the chest with the camera. I heard something crack and hoped it was the camera instead of one of my ribs. It hurt bad enough that I wasn't sure. She pulled her hand with the camera back up over her head like she was going to bash me in the head next. Melly jumped, trying to grab her arm, and Victoria gave her wrist a vicious pull. From the way she was able to keep hold of Melly, who yelped as I backed up, Victoria was stronger than she appeared.

Then I almost fell into both of them as the door slammed into my back.

"Oh! Sorry!" said Alan, the director. "Didn't know anyone else was in here. We're ready for you, Victoria."

Victoria dropped the hand with the camera behind her back. "Of course, Alan. I was just getting ready when these fans showed up," she said. She looked from me to him to Melly and then smiled. Uh-oh. I ducked my head so he couldn't see my face. "Hey, Alan, don't you think Melly here would be perfect for that little scene you were planning with Ty and a Cubs fan in the stands? I heard that the girl you wanted to do it didn't show."

She turned to me. "You wouldn't mind, would you?" she said, and grinned an absolutely evil grin. "I'd really love to get to know Melly here better, and I could keep an eye on her during shooting so you wouldn't have to worry about *anything* happening to her."

It was the way she said the last part that seriously worried me. I rubbed the sore spot on my chest.

"I don't—" I started to say, but Alan interrupted.

"You're right! She'd be perfect." He stepped forward without even looking at me and took Melly's chin in his hand, moving her face from side to side. "Just the right look. What do you think, Melly? Are you up for it? I'd just need to get a permission form from your parents. How old are you anyway?"

"You've already got one," squeaked out Melly. "I go to Shermer High."

"Melly!" I said. She looked at me, her eyes big and round, and shrugged. Oh my God. I couldn't believe it. She was going along with Victoria's ploy because she had a chance at being in the movie! Was she nuts? Who knew what Victoria was going to do to her when the cameras stopped rolling!

"Sorry," said Alan, barely registering that I was in the room. "I only need one. But maybe next time!" He put an arm around Melly's shoulder, apparently not noticing that Victoria still held her by the wrist. "Let's go talk about it out on the bleachers, okay? The second unit is getting ready to shoot now."

"Sure!" said Melly. She smiled excitedly at me and gave a little finger wave from the side Victoria didn't have a death grip on as the three of them swept out the door.

Holy cheese on a cracker. What was I supposed to do now? Melly was certifiable. She'd just willingly turned herself over to the enemy. Did she want to be an actress bad enough to *die* for it?

TWENTY-FOUR

🐈

FRIDAY, SEPTEMBER 11, 2:35 P.M.

"NEVER TRUST A HUMAN."
—RUFUS BRUTUS THE THIRD

I found Oscar eating some chips by the craft services table and told him what had happened. At first, he was excited for Melly, until I whacked him on the forehead.

"Ouch!" he said. "Okay, okay, I get it. Victoria's evil, blah, blah, blah. Still, what's she going to do while they've got the cameras rolling? And we'll keep an eye on her too. You'll see, it'll be fine. Melly's gonna be in the movie!" He did his happy dance, whacking his hip into the table and knocking over a small tower of soda cans. I pulled him away from the table before he could do any more damage.

We found Alan, Melly, and Victoria as they went out into the stands. We were stopped at some caution tape by a security guard who gave Victoria a thumbs-up sign as he stepped in front of us.

"Sorry, no can do, kids," he said. "You'll have to watch your friend from here." He crossed his arms over his chest,

202

which was wholly unnecessary seeing as how his chest alone was as big around as the two of us together. Probably bigger.

Oscar looked ready to argue, but I pulled him away. The dude was seriously beefy. Oscar looked like a toothpick next to him. We stood off to the side and watched as Alan walked Melly (and the ever-present Victoria) over to Ty McKenzie.

"Oh. My. God," said Oscar. "He's introducing her to Ty!" He was so excited he didn't even jump up and down, just sort of vibrated in place.

Melly looked like she was holding it together pretty well, though I could tell even from where I was that she was nervous. Like, two seconds away from squealing. Ty held out his hand to shake hers and Victoria was forced to let go of Melly's wrist or look like a real freak.

"Run, Melly, run," I whispered under my breath, but she just shook Ty's hand and giggled. Victoria looked my way, grinned, and waved. She knew she had me. Or rather, she had Melly—hook, line, and sinker.

"Like she'd run," snorted Oscar. "This is the kind of thing she's been dreaming about all her life!"

"Being held hostage by a homicidal maniac?"

"No, Nat." Oscar patted me on the head. "Being on a *real* movie set with *real* actors with a *real* chance to be in a movie. We were talking about it on the phone last night. She was hoping we could wrap the Victoria business up quick so she could really get a close look at the shoot and maybe even drop off some headshots with someone. But this is way beyond that!" Oscar did another happy dance and threw in a twirl for good measure. "Melly is *so* lucky!"

Both of my best friends were crazy.

Oscar and I watched as they sat Melly down right next to Ty, with Victoria on his other side. A bunch of extras were directed to sit around them. Then some of the movie people passed around drinks and hot dogs as well as various Cubs paraphernalia. Basically, one section of the stands was filled in, while the rest of the stadium was pretty much empty.

Then Alan talked to everyone, but especially to Melly. With all of the noise from the extras, I couldn't hear anything he was saying, but I saw Melly first go completely red and then completely pale.

"Can you hear anything?" I asked Oscar.

"No," he said. "But it's either really good or really bad. Did you see Melly's face? Wait. Oh. My. God. Did you say it was for Ty's scene with a Cub's fan?"

"Yeah," I said. "Why?"

Oscar didn't reply. He squeaked out "Just watch!" and leaned as far forward over the caution tape as he could without falling over.

They finally set up for the first take. After Alan gave the word, Ty, Melly, and some of the other extras stood up and cheered like the Cubs had just hit a home run. Since there was actually nothing happening on the field, it looked rather odd. Then Ty turned and high-fived Melly, grabbed her in a giant bear hug, and laid a huge kiss right on her lips. After that, he turned to Victoria and squished her in another big hug.

Oh. Wow. This was part of the scene from the script that Oscar had stolen. Melly was the "attractive teenage girl." I felt a little weak in the knees myself. Ty McKenzie had just kissed my best friend.

Oscar let out a strangled sound next to me. "It *was* . . . he did . . . oh my . . ." He gulped and sat down right there in the middle of the aisle. Finally, he recovered enough to speak. "Nat," he said, looking up at me, "next time I want to stake out the craft services table instead of going with you, just hit me, okay?"

All told, Ty kissed Melly no fewer than ten times as Alan filmed Victoria's reaction to it from different angles. Each time, Oscar practically fainted. I was actually really impressed with Melly because she *hadn't* fainted. It looked like she really had the makings of an actress, if we could just get her away from Victoria in one piece. I'd seen Melly in a bunch of school plays and even community theater stuff, but this was so different from that. She was a natural.

Then they filmed Ty running up the stairs. It was weird how everything was all out of order. The kissing scene had come before the press box stuff, and they'd filmed that first. How did the actors keep everything straight? And it was no wonder Ty was so built. Alan had him run up the stairs at least half a dozen times. It was actually kind of mesmerizing. How did his hair manage to flop so perfectly?

205

I shook my head and scanned the stands. I grabbed Oscar's arm. "Oscar! Where's Melly? Where's Victoria? Do you see them?" I didn't see either one of them anywhere. What were we doing watching Ty?

Stupid question. I knew exactly why we were watching Ty—the same reason Jason had been reminding all of the extras to look at the field between each take. There was a reason he was the star of the show.

Oscar looked too and shook his head. "Nope. I don't see them. Maybe they went back inside?"

We ran back to where they had been filming earlier. A few extras were hitting the craft services table, but I didn't see Victoria or Melly. Her dressing room was empty too.

I finally grabbed someone wandering around with a clipboard. "Hey, have you seen the girl they used in the stands? The one Ty kissed? Or Victoria?"

The lady checked her clipboard. "Don't know about the girl, but it looks like Victoria's not scheduled for anything else for a while. She probably left. She usually doesn't stick around any longer than she has to."

Oscar and I looked at each other. Holy bat fingers. Victoria was on a kidnapping spree and now she had Melly.

TWENTY-FIVE

Friday, September 11th, 4:44 p.m.

"There is nothing a cat doesn't know,
especially the things you don't want us to know."
—Meep

Oscar and I sat staring at each other in my room, Rufus and Meep in standard cat bread loaf poses between us. We'd immediately run outside the stadium, but with no idea what direction Victoria had gone with Melly, there was nothing we could do. Oscar had managed to locate his dad's nunchuks and steal them back from the box without the security guy noticing, but that was the only thing we could remotely call a success for the day. We hadn't gained any real information and we'd lost Melly, not to mention my dad's camera. Well, at least that wasn't a big loss. He didn't use it much. I'd checked the card and the last thing he'd recorded had been Emmy's tenth birthday party. We hadn't really captured anything hugely incriminating to use against Victoria, either, even if we could have found the camera again.

I dialed Viv's number but, of course, she didn't answer. It was ridiculous. No wonder the newspapers were always filled with stories about terrorist threats. You couldn't reach the authorities even when they were your own sister!

That's when I remembered that I probably had a voice mail. It was Viv: "Nat, just a quick message. I've got a couple of classes and then a department meeting downtown and an interrogation they want me to sit in on. My battery's about dead, but I'll get back to you as soon as I can. I checked the registration database and there's no record for Victoria Welling. I thought at first she might be an unregistered, but we both know how unlikely that is since the BERM started infant testing over twenty-five years ago. So, just for kicks I did a search on the database for Talents matching what you'd told me. And bingo! There it was! There are only two people registered who have any kind of Talent similar to what you mentioned. And one of them I happened to notice was from the same town as Victoria. Remember how we watched that behind the scenes thing on one of her movies and she talked about being from Gun Barrel City, Texas? I remembered it because it was such a weird name. Anyway, some girl named Regina Fedorka was registered, and she had a record a mile long with all kinds of petty theft and even an assault and battery charge. What do you bet she changed her name when she left home to become an actress?"

There was some noise like she was interrupted, and then she came back.

"Oh, I forgot, the registry mentioned that the subject she's impersonating has to be alive and she's got to touch them on a regular basis, otherwise she turns back into herself. It's only a Class B Talent. Anyway, that means that Easton is alive and well. I'll talk to you later. And stop freaking out! You left me, like, a billion voice mails. I haven't even had time to listen to them all! Everything's going to be fine. We're on the case."

Whoa. I had Oscar listen to the message too so I wouldn't have to repeat it all. Then Rufus made me play it for him too.

So, Rufus said, *your sister, who was supposed to save the day, is unreachable and probably hasn't even listened to half the messages you left her. Am I getting that right?*

"Yeah," I said. "And Victoria's real name is Regina Fedorka." I could see why she'd changed her name, even without the criminal record. You'd never get a starring role with a name like "Fedorka." My head was reeling, trying to take it all in. "I wonder if Easton had discovered something about her past?"

"I know you don't think so," said Oscar, "but Easton really is a good investigative reporter."

I snorted. How many crack investigative reporters wear six-inch pink heels?

"Seriously," he said. "I bet she figured it out. She came out here to break a story on Victoria's acting. If she stumbled onto a story about a stuck-up actress with a Talent for shape-shifting who also happened to have a lengthy criminal record, it'd be like hitting the jackpot. She'd have been all over that."

Absolutely, said Rufus. *My person is very talented*. He glared at me.

"Okay, okay," I said. "Easton is amazing. But what are we supposed to do now?"

Oscar pulled out his cell phone. "It is time," he said theatrically, "to call the cops." He dialed 911 then handed the phone to me. "You talk," he said. "They make me nervous. Besides, you've already met them."

Yeah, if that's what you want to call being arrested.

"911, what's your emergency?"

"Um, hi," I said. "I'm calling about a kidnapping. Actually, I guess, *two* kidnappings."

"Two kidnappings?" the lady asked. There was a pause. "Okay, please provide me with all of the details."

"Okay." I took a deep breath and tried to organize my thoughts. "First off, that blogger Easton West was kidnapped by Victoria Welling. You know, the actress? Well, it turns out Victoria's real name is actually Regina Fedorka and she's got a criminal record. Easton probably figured that out and that's why she was kidnapped. You know, to shut her up. We were, like, gathering evidence and then she—Regina—also kidnapped my best friend Melly. Are you following this?"

There was a pause. "Let me get this straight," she said. "You're calling to report the kidnapping of a blogger and your best friend . . . by an actress?"

"Yeah, Vic—sorry, *Regina* kidnapped Melly a couple of hours ago from Wrigley Field. We think she's holding everybody at a rental house somewhere in the Northbrook area or maybe around Glenview. Oh, and she can shape-shift."

I heard some typing on the other end of the line. "I see that this number was recently input into our system as having made a false 911 call. You do realize that fake emergency calls are against the law, don't you, young lady?"

"I explained that one! It was a butt dial. But this is for real—"

"I'm going to be lenient this time, but I've flagged this number. If you make any more false reports, you *will* be criminally charged. Do you understand?"

"Wait!" I said. "There are some officers who know what I'm talking about! When they arrested me and my sister came—she works for the BERM—to bail me out—"

Click.

That didn't go entirely well, I take it, said Rufus.

I handed the phone back to Oscar. "I wouldn't use your phone to call 911 again," I told him. "Ever."

"What now?" asked Oscar.

"I have no idea," I said.

"You could tell your parents."

"They won't even be home for a few more hours. They almost always work late on Fridays. They're workaholic freaks. Besides which, they're useless." And I also had less than no desire to tell them. They probably wouldn't believe me, not without Viv to back me up, wherever she was.

"Call the BERM directly?"

"I guess I can give it a shot." It was worth a try.

Oscar looked up the number on the Internet and I dialed the phone. After going through about half a dozen automated voice prompts, I finally got a real person on the phone. I started out by explaining that my sister worked there in the hope that would lend some legitimacy to my story.

"Genevieve Ng?" the woman repeated for about the fourth time.

"Yes, that's my sister. Sometimes she goes by Viv? Anyway, we need to get in touch with her or her supervisor."

"Let me see," she said. "Okay, I'm connecting you now." *Click.* Three rings later and I was in Viv's work voice mail. I left a message and then called the main number back again. Five minutes later, I was finally back on with the same woman who'd transferred me.

"Hi," I said. "I just spoke with you a few minutes ago. You connected me to my sister Viv's voice mail . . ."

"Please hold," she said.

Some elevator music came on. I rolled my eyes at Oscar and he shrugged. Then click.

"She hung up on me!" I tried again, but this time I went right to being on hold. Then another click. I hung up the phone. "Aaaagggggggghhhhhh!"

Oscar patted me on the shoulder. "Do you want me to try?"

"Fine," I said. "You try." I left my room to get a glass of water and cool off. When I came back, I got there just in time to see Oscar throw the phone on the bed.

You people obviously have no clout.

"Okay, you were right. That was useless. But we have to do something! That crazy Regina woman has Melly, and there's no telling what she'll do! If she can look like anyone at all in the world, she could just kill everyone and disappear and start over!" Finally, Oscar was getting it.

"Well, what are we supposed to do? We can't just go door to door looking for kidnap victims. Even if we found the right house by some miracle, Regina could disguise herself as someone else and we'd never know." I rolled Meep over and scratched her on her tummy. Sometimes that helped me think and it had the added benefit of keeping her happy too. "Do you even know how many houses there are between Northbrook and Glenview?"

Why don't you ask? purred Meep, looking up at me.

"Ask who? I don't think 411 has that kind of information. Besides, who really cares how many houses there are?"

No, stupid. She means, why don't you ask the cats? said Rufus.

"What are you talking about?" I really had no idea, but Rufus and Meep were looking at each other like they'd revealed some incredible pearl of obvious wisdom.

Cats know everything, said Rufus sagely.

Whatever. "Fine." I made an exaggerated bow to my cat. "Meep, where is Regina holding Melly?"

Oscar, Rufus, and Meep all gave me a look like I was insane.

Not me, said Meep. *You know I don't talk to cats.*

213

Rufus rolled over to get some tummy love too. *You need a savvy cat*, he said. *Someone more like me, but who knows other cats around here. Someone who gets around.*

Where was I going to find a cat like that?

TWENTY-SIX

"THERE IS, INCIDENTALLY, NO WAY OF TALKING ABOUT CATS
THAT ENABLES ONE TO COME OFF AS A SANE PERSON."
—DAN GREENBURG

"I cannot believe I'm doing this," I said for probably the
fiftieth time as I opened the passenger's side door. I looked
back at Oscar, who had commandeered Melly's car. It's
not like she was using it. He gave me a thumbs-up from
the driver's seat. Rufus and Meep, in the back, peered at
me through the side window from up on their hind legs.

I rang Ian's doorbell. In what felt like hours later, he
answered it.

"Nat," he said. "Um, hi. Did you get the passes this
afternoon okay? Everything work out with your life or
death thing?" He looked a little confused to see me. Or
maybe just confused that I had the guts to show up on his
doorstep.

"Oh, um, yeah, thanks for the passes. We got them fine.
The other thing, though . . . it didn't go as planned. We could
really use your help."

"I don't think my dad's got any more access than what he gave you," said Ian.

"It's not about the ballpark," I said. "It's about PD."

"PD? What's that?"

Oh, yeah. Crap. What was it they called Purr Daddy? "Oh, sorry! Pebbles. I need to, um, see Pebbles."

The confused look changed to completely baffled. "You need to see my cat?" he said slowly and deliberately. He stepped back from the door a little like whatever I had might be catching.

"Yeah," I said miserably. "Can I please see Pebbles?" At least Dad would be happy about me killing all my chances of ever having a date in high school. Maybe I could find one once I went off to college.

"I don't know if that's a good idea. Maybe . . . maybe you should go." He moved to close the door, but I held out my hand to stop him.

"Okay," I said quickly without giving myself time to think about what I was about to do. "Do you really want to know what's going on? I'll tell you." I had no choice, not with Melly's life on the line. And maybe I could just go to college somewhere far away where they had no idea who I was. Like in another state. Or maybe another country.

"Sure," he said, though he didn't invite me in. So I stood on his stoop and told him an abbreviated version of the whole story, starting with the video and ending with us driving over to his house to enlist the help of PD.

He listened to the whole convoluted mess without interrupting, but his eyebrows kept climbing higher and higher until I feared they would disappear into his unruly mop of hair and never be seen again. There was complete silence for a minute.

"So," he said finally, running a hand through his hair. "You talk to cats. And there's a crazy shape-shifting kidnapper actress out there somewhere who's holding Melly and Easton West hostage. Does that about sum it up?"

"Yes," I said. "And Meep and Rufus suggested that we use the cat network to find out where Regina is hiding them." I felt stupid for even saying the words "cat network," but I didn't know what else to call it. I shoved my hands in my pockets and kicked my toe at the edge of their cheerful little flowery doormat.

"Natalie," he said, "you know you sound totally insane, right?" The door creaked a little as he shifted his weight. Was he going to shut it in my face?

And yes, *of course* I knew all of this sounded crazy. There was no part of any of it that sounded remotely like normal life. Like a normal person's life. But that wasn't my life. It never had been. I mean, my little sister was doing calculus when she was three. My first good friend was a cat. My older sister was a human lie detector, and my mom had more patents than most people had cookbooks. My dad could smell what you had for dinner two days ago if you didn't brush your teeth well enough. I was a freak from a family of freaks.

Tell him he's wearing his SpongeBob boxer shorts, the ones with the holes. His mom keeps trying to throw them away.

I looked past Ian to see PD saunter into the front hall. "I can't say that," I said.

"What?" asked Ian. He turned to look at PD. "Are you saying that Pebbles just said something to you?"

Okay, fine. Tell him he had Fruit Loops for breakfast.

"PD says you had Fruit Loops for breakfast."

Ian looked momentarily surprised. "Lots of people eat that for breakfast," he said, but he was keeping one eye on PD and one on me.

But not everyone pours orange juice over them, said PD. *Milk I understand, but orange juice I really don't get. The smell is unbelievable.*

"In orange juice," I told Ian. "Fruit Loops with orange juice." Gross.

He stared at me with eyes as big as baseballs. "What did he tell you a minute ago?"

"I'd rather not say," I said. Underwear is just so personal.

"No," he said. "Tell me."

I was already in dateless territory. Might as well go whole hog. "Um, SpongeBob," I said, covering my eyes for a moment. "SpongeBob underpants."

Ian's face went to immediate lobster red, but so did mine. I should have made something else up. He'd never have known the difference.

"He told me before you like reggae. When I was here

218

to do homework." That's what I should have said. It would have been much safer.

"Wait," he said. "You talked to him last time you were here?"

I looked down at the doormat again. It actually said Have a Nice Day under the sunflowers. *That* wasn't going to happen. "Yeah. A little."

I could practically hear the wheels turning around in Ian's head. "Is *that* why he took his medicine from you so easily? Because you told him to?"

"Um . . ."

He's got you on that one. Just tell him you're in heat for him, said PD. *It can't hurt.*

This was rapidly becoming the most painful conversation I had ever had, even worse than the phone call when I asked him for the passes. "Yeah," I finally said. "I asked PD if he'd take the pill for me so I could trick you into a date with me." I forced myself to look Ian in the eye. "Because I really like you."

He looked at me for a beat, his brown eyes wide. "Why didn't you just ask me?"

I just raised my eyebrows at him. Was he kidding me?

This is charming and all, said PD, *but didn't I hear you say something about someone's life being on the line?* PD walked over to Ian and headbutted his ankle, then looked up at me.

"Right," I said. "Um, Ian, can we talk about that later? Right now, I really need PD's help."

"I'm coming too," said Ian. He grabbed a jacket from

219

the hooks by the door. He bent down to pick up PD, but PD gave him a look that you didn't need to understand Cat to get. Then PD stuck his tail straight in the air and led the way to Melly's car. I scrambled after him and opened the back door. PD jumped in. Ian, a bemused look on his face, followed after him. I climbed in the front passenger's side without a word. As soon as we were in and our seat belts were on, Oscar gunned it. All three cats went flying.

"Hey, Ian, welcome to the party," said Oscar.

"Um, hi, Oscar. Do you know where you're going?" asked Ian, holding on to the back of my seat with both hands.

"No," I said, and whacked Oscar in the shoulder. "Slow down, Oscar. I need to talk to PD!"

"Oh, okay," said Oscar. He barely let off the gas.

"This is so weird," said Ian. He was staring down at the cats, who had all climbed back on the seat and were looking right back at him.

This is the boy you talk about in your sleep? asked Meep. *Hmmmm.*

PD let out a cat giggle. *She's in heat for him*, he said to Meep. All three of the cats laughed.

"What are they saying?" asked Ian.

"Nothing," I said. "Just . . . you know, cat stuff."

Liar, said Rufus.

I ignored him. "Okay," I said to PD, "here's the deal. We need to locate a particular house. It's probably pretty close to here." I gave as full a description of Regina, Easton, and

220

Melly as I could, using as many cat terms as I could. Like pink hair meant nothing to them, but the fact that Melly always wore vanilla-scented perfume might help. I wished I knew more about Regina. Rufus added in as much as he could too. He said Regina smelled like stale pretzels, acne medicine, and some Cat word I didn't know. Ian watched the whole conversation with great interest while Oscar drove in really fast circles around the block.

Okay, said PD. *I know exactly where to start. Take me to the park that's by my house. That's where Queenie hangs out.*

"Where's the park?" I asked Ian. It was pretty useless asking a cat for street directions, since they told you how to get places by telling you how things smelled or how the light looked. Street signs meant nothing to them. Neither did streets or stop signs, for that matter, but I'd finally taught Meep to pay attention to those by appealing to her instincts of self-preservation.

Ian gave directions to Oscar and we arrived just a few minutes later. We all got out of the car and followed PD over to some picnic tables. It was a small park, but there was a BBQ grill, a slide, some swings, and a sandbox (i.e., a litter box, if you were a cat — I'd learned early on to never, ever play in one of those).

Hey, Queenie, said PD. *Got somebody for you to meet!*

An incredibly fat black cat with a tuft of white fur under her chin came waddling out of some bushes. *Purr Daddy! Been awhile. Where've you been, fishbreath?*

Queenie and PD brushed noses and sniffed butts. *I'd love to chat*, said PD, *but I'm here on business today.*

And I see you brought some friends, said Queenie. She sniffed Rufus and Meep, and then took a good look at me. *Well*, she said wonderingly. *What do we have here?*

"Hi," I said. "I'm Natalie. And this is Ian and Oscar."

Ian's mine, said PD, *so don't go getting any ideas, Queenie.*

Sure, sure, she said. *I remember him from when he used to come to the park when he was a little kitten. Still smells the same. Earthy and sweet. And don't get your tail in knots. I'm happier when I'm free.*

I'd never thought about it, but that is kind of what Ian smelled like. I wasn't sure if Queenie had meant it as a compliment or not, though. Meep's favorite smells were my gym shoes and three-week-old tuna cans. She was always squirreling them away under my bed.

PD and Rufus explained the situation to Queenie. I was glad to let them do it. I was honestly getting tired of telling the same depressing story over and over again. Each time I told it, I couldn't help but wonder if Melly was still okay. How desperate was Regina? What was she capable of doing? Would she really kill someone? I mean, she was psyching herself up with a cheesy mantra. Did she have the guts to actually do anything? I hoped she didn't.

Of course, she *had* nearly scratched my eyes out. And she hadn't even known then that I knew anything. She'd just known that I was the one who took Rufus. Would Melly tell her anything? I shook my head. I didn't want to think about it anymore. I joined Oscar and Ian, who were apparently discussing what they imagined cats talked about.

"I still can't believe it," said Ian. "Sorry, Nat. It's just really unreal. If you'd asked me, I wouldn't even have thought cats were intelligent enough to have a conversation with."

I leaned forward and whispered so our feline companions couldn't hear me. "Some of them really aren't. But then again, some of them are about as smart as your average middle schooler. It depends." At least he hadn't started calling me Cat Girl. That was something.

I'll put the word out. Just give me fifteen minutes, said Queenie. *I'll find out which house you need.* She darted off into the bushes, far faster than I would have thought she was capable of moving.

Quite a cat, that one, said Rufus. He sounded grudgingly impressed.

You know it, said PD. Then he went into a story that I wasn't about to repeat and most certainly didn't want to hear about Queenie and some dead animal they'd once found in the park. I grabbed Oscar and Ian by the hand and led them over to a picnic table so we could sit down and wait.

"Meep," I called, "why don't you come over here too?" Really, I didn't think she needed to hear stuff like that. I know I sure didn't.

Are you kidding? she called back. *I don't think so! I need to hang out with these cats more often!*

Great. There was no telling what kind of trouble she'd be getting into now. I probably wouldn't be able to keep her in the house. Who knew what she was going to be rolling herself around in?

"You really think that cat will be able to do it?" asked Oscar. He looked worried. It was about time. I felt like I'd been doing the worrying for both of us.

"Maybe," I said. "Cats are everywhere, you know. And they get around. Meep doesn't leave the house much, but she's gone over a mile away before without me even knowing about it until later. They're sneaky like that."

"Pebbles is — wait. Sorry, what did you say his name was again?"

"Um, Purr Daddy, or PD for short." I blushed a little, though I didn't know why. It's not like it was my idea to call him that.

"Right. PD is mostly an indoor cat, but my little brother lets him out sometimes. But I don't think he ever goes out of our yard."

PD was obviously paying attention to what we were talking about, since he started cat laughing.

Ian looked at him. "So, I'm guessing he doesn't agree with that assessment?"

"Not so much," I said. "Seriously, cats are pretty devious. I bet he gets out more than you know." After all, he knew right where to find Queenie.

Speaking of the devil, Queenie came sauntering back into view. *I've got some good news and some bad news, she said. What do you want first?*

224

TWENTY-SEVEN

"NEVER UNDERESTIMATE A CAT. ACTUALLY, I TAKE THAT BACK.
PLEASE, UNDERESTIMATE US ALL YOU WANT."
—QUEENIE

"The good news first, I guess," I said. Maybe it would have been better to start off with the bad, but I felt like I'd already had enough bad news to last me a lifetime. Ian and Oscar just looked back and forth from me to the cat.

Well, honey, I found the house you want. It actually isn't that far from here as the cat walks. You can get there in less than ten minutes in your car.

"That's great!" I turned to Oscar and Ian and hugged them both. "She found the house!" Oscar let out a huge cheer. Rufus started sharpening his claws on a picnic table.

"Did she say something about bad news too?" asked Ian. "I heard you say you wanted the good news."

Well, said Queenie, *I had Tom-Tom look in the windows — he's the one that reported in first with the location — and he said it doesn't look like there's anyone there. But he did smell a dog.*

Oh, that'll just be Fergie, said Rufus. *Totally harmless.*

"Just that it doesn't look like anyone's there. But that might be good. Maybe we can get in and scope things out before she gets home." I smiled, but I was worried. Where would she have taken Melly other than the house? Did she have more than one hiding spot?

Queenie gave me detailed directions—or rather, cat-level detailed directions. Ian and I deciphered them and we were off. Ten minutes later, just like Queenie promised, we pulled up outside a standard-issue North Shore suburban house in a nondescript subdivision. It could have been anyone's house: white siding with a red brick façade, bland front yard with close-cut grass, and evergreen bushes.

"You sure this is it?" asked Oscar after he turned off the car.

"That's what Queenie said." I shrugged.

"I just pictured it being more, I dunno, evil looking or something." Oscar looked disappointed.

"Well, she got it because she demanded it as part of her movie contract, right? That whole wanting-to-see-what-living-in-the-suburbs-was-like thing. So wouldn't it stand to reason that it'd look like an everyday house?"

"I guess so," said Oscar doubtfully. "It's just so *normal*."

It really was an exceptionally normal-looking place. There weren't even any flowers to give it personality. The backyard did have a tall privacy fence, though, which jibed with what that article had said. Not all houses had privacy fences around here. Quite a few people opted for the white picket fence thing or no fence at all.

Let me out, said Rufus. *I'll take a sniff.*

Me too, said PD. *I want in on the action.*

Me three! said Meep. Total follower.

"Okay," I said. "But don't go crazy. Come right back and tell me if you smell Fergie. That way we'll know it's really the right place. Then we need to plan our attack." I got out and opened the back door. The three cats all streaked out and made a beeline for the house. Meep went for the front door, while Rufus and PD each took a side.

Rufus came racing back mere moments later. He ran halfway across the yard and stopped. *It's the house*, he called. *I smell Fergie*. Then he was gone, back around the corner of the house.

"Rufus! Come back!" I half shouted. I didn't want to yell in case anyone was actually inside. Rufus, of course, didn't even respond. "Crap," I said to Oscar and Ian. "The kamikaze cat strikes again. What should we do?"

"Well, if no one is in there, maybe we should just, you know, break in?" Oscar made a motion like he was throwing a rock through a window or something. We all looked at each other and then at the house.

It looked quiet. Maybe too quiet?

"Okay," I said. "Let me think a minute." I put my hand over my eyes so I could concentrate, not that it really seemed to help. "How about this: Oscar, why don't you move the car down the street a bit? That way, if Regina comes back, hopefully, she won't notice it. And I'm going to call Viv one more time, you know, just in case." Just in case some crazy maniac kidnapper killed us all and our families needed to find the bodies. "Then I guess we should do it—break in."

I left Viv yet another message with all the details, including the address, while Oscar moved the car. Ian was kind of standing there watching everything. He looked lost. Why had I dragged him into this mess? If we survived, there was no way he was ever going to talk to me again. I just hoped the Cat Girl thing didn't get out. Maybe I could blackmail him with the SpongeBob underpants thing.

Oscar came back and the three of us joined Meep at the front door. There was no sign of either Rufus or PD anywhere.

I've been listening, said Meep, *but I haven't heard anything much. There are a couple of mice under those bushes. Other than that . . .* She looked hungrily in that direction, though I seriously doubted she'd ever caught a mouse in her life. She was all talk.

I tried the doorknob. Locked, of course. Ian cleared his throat. "Maybe we should try the back or the side? This is kind of exposed, don't you think?" He was looking up and down the street. Someone a few doors down was getting their mail.

"Good point." We went around the side of the house that Rufus had disappeared around. There were some windows and a gate to the backyard. We tried each window as we walked by, but none of them were open and the curtains were all closed. Happily, the gate actually was open. It didn't look like it had a lock at all. We opened it and quickly went in, shutting it behind us.

There was a patio and a small in-ground pool, but no sign of Rufus or PD or anyone else. Oscar went to a set of French doors and peeked inside. "The coast is clear," he said. Ian and I took a peek. It looked like a layout from a Pottery Barn catalog. You know the ones I mean, those perfectly arranged rooms that look like a human being has never set foot in them. Off to the left there was a kitchen and some signs of life: a bag of cheap dog food on the counter, an open box of cereal, and an empty milk jug.

I tried the door, but our luck had ended with the gate being unlocked. "What should we do?" I whispered.

Oscar didn't say anything. He just reached into my backpack and pulled out his dad's nunchucks. I'd forgotten he'd even stuck them in there. Before Ian and I even had time to get out of the way, he slammed the wooden ends into a pane of glass by the doorknob. *Crash.* One hit was all it took.

"Oscar!" I said.

"What? We had to get in, right?" He pulled his sleeve over his hand and brushed the glass away. If I didn't know better, I'd think he'd done that before.

"What if someone heard that?" I looked around, but nothing had changed anywhere.

"Who?" asked Oscar. "There's nobody here." He reached in, unlocked the door, and turned the knob. The door opened and he went in.

Two seconds later, Fergie came charging around the corner right at us, yapping her head off. Her pink fur was matted and had bits of gunk stuck in it, like she'd been used as a doggy mop.

"Shhhh! Fergie, shut up!" I said. The house seemed quiet other than Fergie, but I didn't want to take any chances. I picked her up and smoothed down the fur around her face. Poor thing, she smelled terrible. Regina definitely wasn't good with pets. And that says a lot about a person.

Fergie kept barking, but with less volume. She was looking at me like she desperately wanted me to understand something. Or maybe she just wanted to be fed. "Can you tell what she's saying?" I asked Meep.

I'm not very good at Dog, said Meep. *All I can get is that she's hungry and freaked out about someone seeing you? Being you? Smelling you? Sorry.*

"You don't speak Dog?" asked Ian. "Just Cat?"

"Yeah," I said. "Dogs just sound like dogs to me. Meep doesn't really get what she's saying either. Rufus can talk to her, but I don't know where he is, stupid cat." I put Fergie down and picked up the bag of dog food. The only bowl I found was one in the sink with old Cheerios stuck to it, so I just poured some food on the tile floor. Fergie dived right in. Ian rinsed out the Cheerios bowl and filled it with water for her too. See, *he* was good with pets.

"Well, I guess we should search the house," I said. If no one had come running after the breaking of the glass and

Fergie's loud welcome, then probably no one was here.

"Righty-o," said Oscar. "How about I take the upstairs?"

"Maybe we should stick together," I said. In movies, the characters always get picked off one by one when they separate. The house was actually kind of creepy, but maybe that was my mind playing tricks. If I weren't here looking for kidnap victims, it might seem like a nice place, even if everything was in shades of beige.

"Suit yourself," said Oscar. "We might as well start down here, then."

We left Fergie chowing down in the kitchen and walked the rest of the first floor. Besides the stuff we'd already seen, there was a dining room, an entry hall, a small office, and a bathroom. Everything was tastefully but blandly decorated. The only thing out of place was a ficus tree that had obviously died a slow, withering death.

Hey, said Meep. *I hear something upstairs.*

"Shhhh!" I told Oscar and Ian. "Meep hears something upstairs."

"Probably Rufus," said Oscar. "Or Ian's cat."

"Yeah, where is Pebbles?" asked Ian. "I haven't seen either one of them since they got out of the car."

"Is it Rufus or PD?" I asked Meep.

I'm not Talented, in case you've forgotten, said Meep. *I just hear something. I don't know what it is.*

I led the way to the stairs and we slowly climbed them. Oscar still had the nunchucks in his hand, and I was wishing

I'd brought something more useful than a cell phone. Maybe even the throwing stars. At the top of the landing, there were three closed doors. The hallway was carpeted in more beige and the walls were painted off white. The owners had left off the decorating up here. The walls were empty. It reminded me of a hospital.

"I don't think it could be Rufus," I whispered, "unless he's figured out how to open and close doors."

Ian opened the first door. It was a bedroom with piles of pink clothes and pink suitcases everywhere. We'd found Easton's stuff, but no Easton. The closet was empty except for a couple of pairs of shoes—non-pink and obviously larger than the ones Easton wore, so maybe they were Regina's.

We went to the next door and Oscar tried that one, leaping in with his nunchucks held in front of him after Ian opened the door. It was a bathroom. Makeup was spread out all over the counter, just like it had been in the dressing room at Wrigley. Regina was a total slob wherever she settled in, apparently.

We went back out into the hall and stood in front of the last door. We looked at each other. Then I grabbed the door handle and turned the knob.

TWENTY-EIGHT

*"YOU WILL ALWAYS BE LUCKY IF YOU KNOW
HOW TO MAKE FRIENDS WITH STRANGE CATS."
—COLONIAL AMERICAN PROVERB*

There were piles of non-pink clothes, an armoire, a chair, a random chain snaking across the floor, and a solitary mattress with a sheet crumpled on top of it. Meep must have been hearing things.

I took a step inside and was immediately knocked off my feet by someone or something shoving the door into me. I fell back against Ian, who had been right behind me, and we both toppled into Oscar. We all landed in a heap in the doorway, blocking whoever or whatever had knocked us over from escaping. Oscar's nunchucks whacked me in the head.

"Mmmrpphhmff!"

You should have listened to me, said Meep. *I told you I heard something up here.*

I quickly crawled to my feet and backed up so I could get a look at what we were up against. It wasn't Melly or Easton. Someone who looked like a sickly imitation of Victoria Welling stood there with her eyes wide open and her hands tied behind her back. She had duct tape over her mouth, her hair had been chopped off in big, uneven lumps, and a dog chain around her ankle tied her to the leg of the solid wood armoire. And she was skinny. Like, anorexic skinny, not just movie star skinny. Well, even beyond normal anorexic movie star skinny. But her cheekbones and eyes were unmistakable.

"Victoria?" I said, totally confused. If this was Victoria, who was the other Victoria? Or Regina? Whoever.

"Oh my God!" shouted Oscar. "It is Victoria!" He obviously came to the same conclusion I did about this Victoria because he scrambled up, putting a foot in Ian's stomach on the way. "I'm your biggest fan!" he babbled to her, which was really a total lie, since I knew he'd have said the same thing to Ty in different circumstances. He grabbed her in a big hug. After just a moment too long, he dropped his arms from around her and stepped back to give her a good look. Or maybe it was to get farther away from the smell. I could smell her from the doorway. Regina obviously didn't consider hygiene or food to be important for her kidnap victims.

We had to find Melly. Soon.

"Victoria," he said, looking her up and down, "what on earth is going on?"

Smells pretty obvious to me, said Meep. *She had an accident. Or three.*

I motioned to Meep to shut up. At least no one else knew what she was saying. Victoria had definitely seen better days. She was wearing a pair of ragged gray sweatpants and a stained T-shirt. No shoes. She looked down at herself and then back up at him, her eyes still open as wide as they could go. "Mrrmmpphff!" she said.

"Oh!" said Oscar. He reached out and pulled the duct tape off in one quick motion before I could warn him to take it easy.

"Aaaaggh!" yelped Victoria, doubtless from losing a couple of layers of skin off her lips.

"There you go," he said. "Better?"

"Who *are* you?"

"I'm Oscar!" Before Oscar could hug her again, Ian stepped forward and ducked under Oscar's outstretched arms to go behind Victoria.

"Let's get her untied first, okay, Oscar?"

"Oh! Right! Sorry," said Oscar. "I'm just so excited to meet you. I mean, I was excited to meet you before, but apparently that wasn't even really you, so it doesn't count. And she was totally evil anyway, so it wasn't really all that exciting to meet *her*, if you know what I mean."

Victoria processed that. "You know about Regina?" she asked, rubbing her wrists once Ian had removed her bonds.

"Yes!" said Oscar before I could say anything at all. "We're here to rescue you!" Not exactly, but close enough, I guessed. I was even more worried about Melly now. Victoria looked scary. Like, you could knock her over with a feather. It was amazing she had managed to knock us over, which she'd probably accomplished only because we weren't expecting an attack. We'd make terrible BERM agents.

"I'm Nat," I said. "And you've met Oscar. This is Ian. Not to rush you or anything, but do you know where Regina is? And did she come by here with a girl named Melly? She kidnapped our friend today because we were on to her. Oh, and do you know where Easton West is?"

Victoria looked dazed. She sat down on the mattress, still rubbing her wrists. Her ankle was still chained, but it reached far enough for her to lie down on the mattress. I wondered how long she'd been tied up. How long had Regina been holding her? It had to have taken her a while to lose so much weight. Not that she was fat before or anything, but she had been one of the few starlets I'd have considered healthy. Or, at least, Regina as Victoria was healthy looking. I'm assuming that's how Victoria looked at one point. Most starlets looked like they were on the I-eat-only-one-meal-a-day plan. And why didn't Regina look like skin and bones when she looked like Victoria? She looked like Victoria was *supposed* to look. My head was seriously hurting. Personally, I think the BERM had it wrong. They'd classified Regina's Talent a B level? Seriously? She was obviously Talented enough to have been getting away with whatever she had been doing for ages.

"I don't know where Regina is. I thought you were her."

"That's why you jumped us?" asked Ian.

"Yes. Sorry about that. I was worried. When she left this

morning, she just sounded . . . well, desperate. I thought she was going to do something drastic. I thought . . . I thought she was finally going to kill me." Victoria rubbed at her ankle, which was raw and red where the chain was attached to her leg.

"Do you know where the key is to that?" Ian asked.

"Yeah, it's on the wall behind you." The key was hanging on a picture hanger in the far corner of the room, just out of Victoria's reach. That was evil. So close, but so far. Oscar grabbed the key.

"Oh, Victoria," said Oscar, unlocking the manacle around her ankle. He sat down by her and didn't even wrinkle his nose at the smell or the dirty clothes he had to push out of the way, which was more than I could say for myself. It was all I could do not to hold my nose. He put an arm around her and hugged her to his side. "We're here now. Everything is going to be okay."

"Oscar," I said. "We've got to find Melly. Regina had a reason to keep Victoria alive. If she's willing to get rid of a famous actress, what's stopping her from getting rid of Melly?" I couldn't think of a single thing other than maybe using her against me, and that worried me. She didn't even know how much I knew.

"Wait," said Victoria, "who is Melly again?"

I gave her the thousand-foot overview of the last week as quickly as possible, how it had all started with that video of Regina pretending to be Easton and ending with her kidnapping Melly. "So," I finished up, "do you have any idea at all where Regina could be keeping Easton or Melly? We thought she had Easton here."

"As far as I know, Easton is still here. I haven't heard her since Regina got mad that we were talking through the walls and moved her. I figured she was downstairs somewhere. Regina hasn't let me out of this room except to go to the bathroom since we got here." She picked up the chain and tossed it away from herself. "And not even much for that." Well, that explained the smell. Apparently, the bucket in the corner had been doing double duty.

"You poor, poor thing," said Oscar. "Everything is going to be okay. We're here now." He'd kept one arm around Victoria throughout the whole conversation, petting her arm. She leaned against him and started crying. For all his craziness, Oscar did know when to turn on the comfort when it was necessary. He'd been through tough stuff himself and knew how it was. I mean, coming out to your parents? Had to be one of the toughest things ever, and Oscar had made it look easy. I always wished I had the same level of confidence he had. Of course, I wasn't really good at the touchy-feely thing in general. I stood there, feeling like an unempathetic idiot.

Ian cleared his throat. "So, what next?" he asked me, like I had any clue at all.

Just then, I heard the pitter-patter of little cat feet coming up the stairs. A lot of little cat feet. PD and Rufus flew through the door, followed by an entire herd of cats I'd never seen before. Victoria screamed and even Ian backed up against a wall. It was like Revenge of the Cats or something.

"Where have you been?" I demanded. "And what's up with the cat army?"

I found some reinforcements, said PD.

Where is Easton? asked Rufus. He went up to Victoria and sniffed her. She shrank back against Oscar. What, was she afraid of cats?

The chatter of the cats was practically deafening.

"Everybody, shut up!" I yelled. They quieted down, and Victoria looked at me like I was the new messiah.

"Okay," I said, taking a deep breath. "Rufus, I don't know where Easton is. We haven't found her. PD . . ." I stopped. I didn't even know what to say about all of the cats. How had he found so many in such a short amount of time? There had to be, like, thirty of them. Maybe even more. The room was crawling with cats. What was I supposed to do with all of them?

Fergie said Easton isn't here, Rufus said. Fergie barked in agreement. She had followed the cats into the room. *She said she hasn't seen Easton since this morning. I'm very concerned.*

So was I, but I didn't want to freak him out more than he already was — or everyone else, since they were all looking at me like I knew what I was doing. "We just need to figure out our next move," I said.

You might want to figure that out elsewhere, said a black and white cat I didn't know. *You do know this house has an alarm system, right?*

Holy pants on fire. "Crap!" I yelled. "Everyone, out! We've got to get out of here! The police are probably on their way right now!" How long had we been standing here chatting? How long did it take for the police to respond to an alarm? I had too many questions and not enough answers. We didn't have time for the police and their inevitable questions.

"What?" said Oscar, jumping up and pulling Victoria to her feet. "What are you talking about?"

"Alarm system!" Now I remembered. We should have known. Oscar had said the house Victoria was staying in had an alarm system. It had been one of her demands. I really should have paid more attention to the Oscar Report. His addiction was useful—or would have been if I'd paid attention.

Ian was already halfway down the stairs. I followed him, along with a stream of cats. Oscar and Victoria brought up the rear. She stumbled into the wall a few times.

"Out the back," said Ian. "It'll be safer. We can cut through the neighbor's yard just in case." I followed him as he went out the back door, skidding a little on the broken glass. I looked back as Oscar slung Victoria over his shoulder so her bare feet wouldn't get cut. The cats poured out around us and Fergie brought up the rear.

"To the left," Oscar said. "I parked the car a few houses down in that direction!"

We exited out the gate and took off through a neighbor's backyard. Luckily, most of the houses didn't have monster privacy fences. We ran through three backyards, seriously surprising a guy taking out the trash, and ducked between some houses. Who knows what he thought was weirder, the herd of cats or Oscar carrying a barefoot Victoria over his shoulder. Probably the cats. There were just so many of them.

Ian crept to the corner and peered out. "The coast is clear," he said. I choked back some hysterical laughter. Had he really said that? Should I respond with "The crow flies at midnight" or something? Ian looked at me and grinned, like he knew what I was thinking. "Always wanted to say that," he said.

Oscar set Victoria down and pushed the button on Melly's key chain to unlock the car. "Let's make it quick," he said. "Who knows how long we've got."

He led the way and opened the passenger side door for Victoria to help her in. Ian and I climbed in the back seat and the cats started cramming in with us.

"Hold on a minute," I said. "Are all of you guys coming?"

Why not? asked PD. *Who knows how much help we'll need?*

I was going to argue when Oscar said, "Hurry up! It's the police!" I looked out the window and saw a car pulling up in front of Regina's house. The last of the cats pushed in and I shut the door. There were cats *everywhere*. About ten or fifteen of them had oozed into the front seat and were draped on Victoria's lap and at her feet. There were even two fighting for space on Oscar's lap in the driver's seat. I had to tell one to get out from under Oscar's legs or we weren't going anywhere. Meep, Rufus, and PD were all perched on my lap, and I heard Fergie yip somewhere under the pile. I couldn't even see my feet for the cats covering them. If my mom and her allergies had been with us, she probably would have exploded.

"Slowly!" I said as Oscar started the car. "Don't make them suspicious." He nodded and pulled away from the curb at a reasonable speed, especially for Oscar.

I watched out of the corner of my eye as we drove past the police car. It was a cul-de-sac and we had no choice but to go by them. One officer was in the car and the other was walking up the front path. He didn't seem to be in a hurry. Oscar drove to the corner and came to a full and complete stop at the stop sign, another rarity for him.

I was about to breathe a sigh of relief when Ian yelled, "Go, go, go!" I looked out the back window at where he was looking. The guy who'd been taking out the trash had come out of his house and was jogging toward the police car and pointing in our direction.

Oscar floored it, and cats went flying in every direction.

TWENTY-NINE

"CATS DON'T ALWAYS LAND ON THEIR FEET.
SOMETIMES, THEY LAND ON THEIR CLAWS."
—NATALIE NG

For once, Oscar's crazy driving came in handy. That, and the fact that the police car was facing in the opposite direction. We were blocks away in no time with no sirens on our tail. My thighs, however, were not so lucky. Meep, Rufus, and PD had all instinctively dug in when Oscar took off.

"Whooo!" yelled Oscar. "Where to?"

"Just keep driving. Go toward the city, I guess," I said.

"Where in the city?" asked Ian, strapping on his seat belt while pushing cats out of the way. "Do you have any idea where we should go?"

"No," I said. "I have absolutely no idea."

"How about wherever they're filming?"

That seemed about as good of an idea as any I'd had. "Victoria," I asked, "Do you know if they'd still be filming at Wrigley this late? Or would they be done for the day? Or, hey, can you call Alan?"

"I don't know Alan's number," she said, "but he's got a reputation for working late."

"Wait," said Oscar. "But you worked with him on your last movie!"

"No," she said, "I met him when I auditioned for *Cheerleaders Don't Cry*. But Regina kidnapped me before I got a chance to work on it."

Holy crap. I was doing the math in my head, but Oscar beat me to it. "Regina took over your life that long ago? That, what, had to be, like, two years ago!"

"Over two and a half," said Victoria grimly.

Wow. I couldn't imagine. Two and a half *years*? How had Regina gotten away with it? It did explain why her acting sucked so bad in the last movie. She wasn't even in it. I wasn't going to go there, but Oscar couldn't resist.

"It's no wonder you were so terrible in *Cheerleaders*," he said. "It wasn't even you! How did Regina even talk herself into being in *Freddy's Day Off*?"

"Blackmail," said Victoria. "She's got something big on one of the producers."

Hollywood. Figures. "Well, Oscar," I said, "you're the movie expert, I guess. Do you think they're still at Wrigley or what?"

"I'm not sure," said Oscar, "but I know who to call." He dug around in his pocket for his phone. The car swerved back and forth in the lane and two people honked at us.

"Dude!" said Ian. "Case in point as to why Chicago is a hands-free cell-phone city."

"Fine, fine," said Oscar. "I'll do the Bluetooth thing through Melly's car." He turned for a moment and looked at me. "But no smart aleck comments from you, Nat, okay?"

"What? What about?" What'd I do? I hadn't said a word. "Who are you calling?"

He didn't answer me. He turned back around and got his phone connected with Melly's car about the same time that he pulled onto the highway headed toward the city. Then he dialed a number and we all listened to the phone ring.

I think I'm getting carsick, said a small gray cat near my feet. I didn't relay the information to anyone else. I just prayed the cat was wrong.

Someone answered Oscar's call. "Garrett. You may speak."

Garrett? Oh, yeah. The really pierced guy from our table at the cafeteria. The one who'd seemed interested in Oscar. Obviously, they'd both been attracted enough to exchange phone numbers. That was big. Oscar had sworn off dating after he'd broken up with he-who-shall-not-be-named, otherwise known as Darren. He was the guy who'd moved on to a pretty blond kid who didn't have even a quarter of the personality of Oscar, and who liked to flaunt said new boy in front of Oscar.

I didn't know why Oscar thought I'd have anything bad to say about it. Garrett had seemed nice enough, plus he was totally built and seriously pierced. Exactly the kind of guy Oscar ought to go parade in front of Darren, who was on the scrawny side. I'd never liked him. Not because he was scrawny or anything, but because he really hadn't been that nice to Oscar. And he had bad breath.

"Hey, Garrett. This is Oscar—"

"Oscar!" Garrett's voice warmed right up. Definitely attracted. "I'm glad you called! I wasn't sure if you would. Is everything okay with your crazy friend?"

"Um, yeah," said Oscar. "Actually, Nat's here. In the car. With me. Right now."

"Hey, Garrett," I said, for lack of anything better to say.

There was a pause. "Oh hi, Nat. I didn't mean—"

"Don't worry about it," said Oscar. "I mean, there's not time right now. It's an emergency. Do you know what the filming schedule is today? Are they still at Wrigley or what?"

"Yeah, actually, I'm here! I came out as soon as school let out. I signed up weeks ago. Right now I'm working my way through the craft services table. They opened it up for the extras after our part of the shoot was done." Wow. Oscar and Garrett were totally made for each other.

"Oh, so they're done shooting for the day?"

"Nah. They're just done with the outside stuff and the crowd scenes with the extras. They've moved inside."

"Great! That's perfect!" said Oscar. "Have you seen Victoria? Or Easton? Or Melly?"

"I saw Victoria a little while ago. Maybe about twenty minutes ago? The director was completely pissed because she showed up late or something. I heard some of the gaffers talking about it. She sounds like a total diva." He paused, and the only sound for a moment was the steady purring of a cat. I wasn't sure which one. It seemed really out of place, what with everything going on, but some cats purr when they're nervous. Garrett started talking again. "It's funny you should ask about Easton, though. I'm surprised you haven't heard."

"Heard what?" asked Oscar at the same time as Rufus. Fergie was even paying attention. She dug herself out from under the pile of cats by Ian's feet so she could hear better.

"She's in the hospital. They found her in her room at the York about half an hour ago. There was a suicide note and everything. Looks like she tried to OD. They haven't released any more details than that, but the blogs are all saying she did it because of the thing with her cat. I've been following the story online. Everyone's talking about it. And they still have no idea where the cat disappeared to yesterday morning."

I could hear the unspoken question in his voice. He obviously thought it was my fault.

"Wow, I can't believe she did it," said Oscar.

"Oscar!" I said.

"I don't mean Easton," said Oscar. "I mean Regina."

"Who's Regina?" asked Garrett.

"You'll find out soon enough," said Oscar grimly. "We're on our way to stop her now. Just start spreading the word, would you? Nat's the one who's going to save the day. None of this is her fault. It's going to stop tonight at Wrigley." He looked at me in the rearview mirror and nodded once decisively. "Thanks, Garrett. Talk to you soon. Call me if you see Victoria anywhere." Then he hung up and stepped on the gas.

I heard a whimper and looked down to see that Fergie had managed to climb up on my lap and was huddled into a miserable looking ball as close to Rufus as she could get. Rufus was licking her on the head. That said a lot about Easton, that her pets loved her so much. She must not be anything like Regina had pretended to be while she was her.

"I'm sure she'll be fine," I told them. "They'll take care of her at the hospital and we'll get you guys to her as soon as possible."

Ian reached over and scratched Fergie behind her ear. He looked at me and squeezed my hand and then went back to scratching the dog.

Oscar stomped on the gas and the car sped off even faster toward the city. If Regina had snuck off to drug Easton, what had she done with Melly?

 248

THIRTY

FRIDAY, SEPTEMBER 11, 8:11 P.M.

"NO MATTER HOW MUCH CATS FIGHT,
THERE ALWAYS SEEMS TO BE PLENTY OF KITTENS."
—ANONYMOUS QUOTE, OFTEN ATTRIBUTED TO ABRAHAM LINCOLN
(BUT THE INTERNET THINKS ABRAHAM LINCOLN SAID EVERYTHING)

We made it into the city and all the way to Wrigleyville with the help of Melly's GPS. Someday, I was going to have to thank her dad for being anal and overprotective—if we got Melly out of this alive. The last couple of miles were the worst, after we got off the highway and things slowed to a crawl. When we got there, Oscar didn't even bother looking for a parking spot. He just drove right up onto the brick sidewalk off of Seminary Avenue and Clark Street and stopped the car by a statue of some guy with a baseball bat.

"Oscar," I said, "you can't just leave the car here! You'll get towed!"

He opened the door to get out. "Nat, it's now or never. There's no time. Go!"

I couldn't argue with that. The last thirty minutes driving and waiting had been miserable. If Regina was obviously willing to attempt to kill a famous blogger, what would she be willing to do to an unknown high-school student?

Victoria had told us everything that had happened to her on the ride in. I think she was happy to have a chance to talk to someone at all. Regina had kept her on a really tight leash. She'd been moved among basements and closets and everything in between. She'd even been stuck in the trunk of a car at one point. Regina had driven her everywhere, since she couldn't chance taking her on an airplane and going through security.

It had all started when Regina called her up out of the blue and pulled the whole "Hey, remember me?" thing and talked her into meeting for lunch. Victoria had only done it because she felt kind of guilty for how people, including her, had treated Regina back in high school, though she found out later Regina got her number not through her parents, like she'd claimed, but by calling her agent while impersonating a big time reporter.

Apparently, high school Regina had been seriously unpopular due to a combination of her crappy personality, an unfortunate bladder accident in the ninth grade, and bad hygiene. She'd kept her talent hidden well. Rumors of her criminal activities hadn't helped either. She had been caught stealing stuff from the locker rooms during games, and people had suspected her of some nasty pranks but could never prove it.

Oscar finally asked Victoria why she looked like hell and why Regina didn't. It turned out that Regina's Talent literally sucked some of the health out of you. She'd actually been feeding Victoria fattening fast food the whole time, but then stole the nutrients right back out of her. So Regina looked how Victoria *should* look, and Victoria looked like some kind of concentration camp victim. Her hands kept shaking and she gobbled down a granola bar I found in Melly's emergency stash like she hadn't seen food in a year.

She'd only recently butchered Victoria's hair. Regina had needed to change her voice when talking to Alan on the phone (while looking like Easton) and the hair in the bag had retained enough Victoria-ness for her to do that. It didn't last long, though, which was why Victoria's hair was so choppy. A few more days of it and she'd probably have wound up bald.

Even so, Victoria was ready to fight. She was out of the car and heading toward the stadium before Ian and I had even opened our doors. We, and a carload of cats, followed behind her. Two guys walking down the street stopped to stare at all of us.

"Cool," called one. "You guys got a trained cat show or something?"

"Um, yeah," I called back. "Jump, Meep, jump!" Meep shot me a look, but took a hop in the air and leapfrogged over PD.

"Awesome!" said the second guy. They both started to follow us. Well, it couldn't hurt. Maybe more witnesses would make things better. Regina would be less likely to do something desperate if people were watching. You'd think, anyway.

"This way," called out Oscar. "I think we can get in through this side." He led us over to a loading dock area off Seminary Avenue. There was a small moving truck there and someone had propped open a door with a crate.

"The back door is a good idea," I whispered to Ian. "I don't have a pass for you or Victoria, and there's no way we could sneak all these cats in past a guard anyway." I was still wearing my pass. For a moment I considered taking it off—why had I worn it all day?—but then I figured it might come in handy now that we were back at Wrigley. Not to go in the front door, though—that security guy from this afternoon certainly wouldn't buy our trained cat show story, and he probably remembered us anyway.

"Do we have any weapons?" Ian asked.

"I've got my nunchucks," said Oscar, waving them around. I saw the guys behind us pause and look at each other.

"Just part of the show," I called and smiled reassuringly. They nodded back and gave each other a high five. Who knows what they thought we were going to do with them.

You don't need any weapons, said Rufus. *Not when I've got these.* He stood on his hind legs and batted both his front paws in the air with his claws out. The two guys cheered as the other cats imitated him. We did look like a trained cat show.

"I think we're good," I said, gesturing to the cats. "Besides, the only other thing I've got in my bag is my phone."

"Okay," said Ian doubtfully, and followed Oscar and Victoria through the door and into a stark concrete block tunnel that was painted white. I brought up the rear.

"This way," said Oscar. "I bet they're by the locker room. I added Alan's Twitter to my feed." He held up his phone. "And he just posted something about how the room smells like Cheetos and funk."

Yeah, sounded like a locker room to me. We followed Oscar as he wound his way around. It was kind of amazing, actually. He had a great sense of direction, which was not something I was born with, especially not indoors. I had no idea where we were and then suddenly we were in the main concourse. Oscar ducked down behind a beer stand.

We heard the noise on the set before we saw it. Or rather, we heard the AD yelling at someone. Oscar peered around a corner of the beer stand. "Okay," he whispered. "They're here. I can see Ty and Alan, but I don't see Regina-Victoria or Melly anywhere." He turned around. "What should we do? Just run in kamikaze style and demand to see them?"

"Hey," said one of the guys, coming up behind me, "What gives? Is there a show or not?" I'd forgotten they were there. Apparently, they were pretty hard up for entertainment. Close up, though, I could smell the beer on them, so maybe that was why they'd been so willing to follow us. I mean, what, did they think random trained cat shows performed at Wrigley all the time?

"Shhh," I said to them. "They're shooting that Ty McKenzie–Victoria Welling movie up ahead."

"Cool!" said the brown haired one a little too loudly.

253

I shushed him again, and he put his index finger up to his mouth and swayed just a tiny bit. "Victoria's hot," he whispered back. "You guys know her? Can you hook me up?"

I glanced at the real Victoria. She turned around to face the guy directly with a somewhat hopeful look. He looked right at her with no sign of recognition. Ouch. That was rough.

"Dude," said Ian, "I heard that Victoria loves it when guys mob her. If you see her, you totally should."

I poked him. "What are you doing?" I asked. I smiled apologetically at Victoria. Way to rub it in.

Ian leaned over to whisper in my ear. "If they see someone that looks like Victoria, it'll be Regina, right?"

"Oh!" I turned to the guys. "Yeah, she loves it. Like, full-on hugging and everything! She totally gets off on it."

"Really?" said the one with the glasses. "That rocks!" He wobbled, then turned around back the way we'd come. "I'm gonna go get the rest of the guys over at the Cubby Bear. They gotta get in on this!"

"Good idea!" said the hard up one with the brown hair. They both ran back the way we'd come, glasses guy bouncing off the wall a few times. I'd be amazed if we saw them again, but maybe they had a better sense of direction than I did.

"Anyway," said Oscar, "what should we do now? Nat?"

I avoided answering the question by creeping to the edge of the beer stand and taking a look at the set. A small crowd of movie people was standing outside two open white metal doors, along with a bunch of equipment.

"That's the locker room?" I would never have guessed it.

"Yeah, that's the entrance to it, anyway," said Oscar.

"How do you even know that? I don't see a sign," I said. And it was right in the middle of the first floor concourse. Near a condiment station. I mean, ketchup and Cubs?

"Hey, just because I'm gay doesn't mean I can't watch baseball," said Oscar. Then he grinned. "It's bonding time with my dad. We've done the ballpark tour a couple of times and everything. I just made him promise not to expect me to remember a player's RBI and he made me promise not to tell him which players had cute butts."

"Huh," said Ian.

"For the record," said Oscar, "the first baseman is kinda hot. And the locker room really does smell like Cheetos."

It looked like they were getting ready to film inside the locker room. Everyone's attention outside the locker room was focused inward, and while I was watching, I saw Ty and Alan step inside.

"Well, I don't think we should storm the castle or anything." I said, deciding as I said it. "Not when we don't know where Regina is. Besides, if they recognize me, they probably won't even listen before they call the cops. I'm not exactly their favorite person. I'm just lucky Alan didn't pay any attention to me earlier today. He had eyes only for Melly." I looked back at everyone to see if they agreed. Ian and Oscar were nodding. "Do you think Victoria—sorry, Regina—would be in a scene in the locker room?"

"*I'd* like to be in that scene," said Oscar.

Ian snorted. "Focus, Oscar," he said. He was learning fast. Oscar just grinned.

"I've read the script," said Victoria. "Regina made me run lines with her. She's not in the locker room scene, just the stuff in the stands and the buying tickets and things like that."

"So, she's probably not in there." I said. "Which means she's hopefully maybe in her dressing room?"

"Or hiding out in the stands or something," said Ian. "Maybe we should spread out and look. Meet back here in, like, ten minutes? Or raise the alarm if we see her?"

I couldn't think of anything better, so I nodded. "I'll check out the dressing room, since I know where it is and it's more private."

"I'll take Victoria," said Oscar. He grabbed Victoria by the hand. "The real Victoria. We'll do the stands. I'll find Garrett too, and he can help."

"Ian, they don't know what you look like, unless they remember you from the cafeteria scene. So you're probably still on their good side. You want to try and see if you can get a peek into the locker room, just in case?"

Ian saluted me. "Aye, aye, Captain," he said.

"What about the cats?" asked Victoria.

Oh. Good question. A whole herd of cats was kind of noticeable. "Um," I looked down at Rufus and Meep, who were sitting on my feet. "Why don't you guys park it right here and try and stay out of sight?"

I don't like it, said Rufus.

Me either, said Meep. *What if you need us?* She held up a paw and stuck her claws out.

"Well, if someone needs you, we'll just yell 'Cats!' okay?" I looked at Oscar and Ian. They nodded. Meep still looked doubtful, so I figured I'd try and butter them up a little. "Since you all have such excellent hearing and sense of direction, I'm sure you'll be able to find whoever has called for you. So it'll be like you're on call, okay?"

Acceptable, said Rufus. *But whoever finds her had better save her for me.* He let out a small growl from the back of his throat.

♥

I managed to get to the area where I'd found the storage closet/dressing room without running into anyone other than a blue-shirted Wrigley employee with a broom. She took a glance at my lanyard and pass and didn't say anything. Good thing I'd left it on.

I didn't see anyone around, but I thought I heard footsteps. I ducked behind a bunch of equipment and some racks of clothing. I went to peek around the corner, managed to trip over an electrical cord, and fell into one of the racks. The whole thing fell on top of me with a huge crash.

"Crapola!" I said, batting away a shirt. I heard some more footsteps and a door being slammed. I flung clothes off left and right, stood up, and looked down the hall.

"Nat! Oh my God, get me out of here!" Melly was

running to me, her eyes wide and her hair completely disheveled.

"Melly!" I threw off the last shirt and ran to meet her. I swallowed her up in a huge hug. "I was so worried about you! Are you okay? Did she do anything to you?"

"No, I'm fine. I just want to get out of here. Let's go!"

"Okay," I said. "This way. Oscar and the cats are over this way." I grabbed her hand and tried to pull her down the tunnel back the way I had come.

"The cats? Tiddlywinks is here?"

I laughed. "Don't let Rufus hear you call him that!" I pulled her a few more steps. She seemed so sluggish and confused. I wondered if Regina had slipped her something. Maybe one of Rufus's pills. Would cat medicine work on a person? "I'll explain later. It's total craziness. You won't believe what we've been through. Just follow me. Ian's even here, if you can believe it!"

Melly finally showed some life. "We don't have time to mess around with all that," she said firmly. "We've got to get out of here! Victoria will be back any minute. Just follow me!" Melly tried to pull me in the opposite direction.

"Oh, yeah," I said, not budging. "I forgot you don't know the latest! Victoria's not the problem. It's Regina we need to watch out for."

Melly dropped my hand and stepped back, her nose wrinkled in confusion. "What are you talking about?"

"It's a *really* long story and I'll tell you all about it, I promise. But let's get back to everyone else first." I reached for her hand, but she stepped even farther back down the hall. I don't know why she wanted to go that way. She didn't know her way around Wrigley any better than I did. "You can even meet Victoria. The *real* Victoria. She's with Oscar. And Easton's okay too. She's just in the hospital. Now that you're safe, it's all good. We can let the BERM take care of Regina."

Melly stopped retreating and put her hands on her hips. "I did not come this far for you to screw everything up for me." She stepped forward and shoved me. I fell back against a wall and cracked my head on the concrete.

Frick on a stick. It wasn't Melly. Couldn't be. Melly would have known about Rufus. And Melly would never leave Oscar behind or slam me into a wall, for that matter. It had to be Regina.

"Regina—" was all I managed to choke out before she had her hands on my throat and pushed me back against the wall.

"I heard you coming," she said. "I thought I could get you out of the way once and for all, but here you are telling me you've brought the BERM into this." Flecks of spittle hit me in the face, she was leaning so close to me.

I pushed, but she wasn't moving. I couldn't get a sound out because I couldn't breathe. I was starting to see sparkly flashes of light when I heard Meep say, *What do you think you're doing to my Natalie?*

I had never been so glad to have Meep completely disregard my instructions before in my entire life. She let out a throat-rattling battle cry. I caught a glimpse from the corner of my eye of her launching herself at Regina with the obvious intention of doing great bodily harm. Regina screamed and her grip on my neck loosened. I pushed at her as hard as I could and she fell back.

"Go, Meep," I yelled. "Get help! Cats!" Meep took one last swipe at Regina's leg and darted off down the hall faster than I had ever seen her move, still yowling.

Regina punched me right in the face and pulled back her hand to do it again, but I caught it, barely. She sneered at me, which was a look I'd never seen on Melly's face before. Then I felt something almost like a pull deep down inside me, kind of around the general vicinity of my stomach. A warm burning feeling spread upward through my torso.

"This won't hurt a bit," she snarled. That was a total lie. I felt like someone was twisting my insides into knots and squeezing parts of me that weren't meant to be squeezed. I blinked back tears as I watched her face transform into mine. The clothes she was wearing seemed to shimmer for a moment and then —*blink*—they matched mine.

I stumbled. She took advantage of my momentary weakness by grabbing me around the throat again and pushing me against the wall. I managed to get my hands around her throat at the last minute and did my best to push her off. We struggled back and forth, but she definitely had the upper hand. I felt really weak, like she'd sucked a year of my life away.

That's when the brigade arrived with Meep in the lead. They must have already been on their way after hearing Meep's battle cry. Oscar had even managed to find Garrett, apparently.

"Nat!" yelled Ian. "Wait . . . Nat?"

I grunted, but Regina copied me and grunted too. I couldn't get a word out. Oscar and Ian looked at each other, then Oscar grabbed Regina and Ian grabbed me and they pulled, but Regina wasn't letting go, so I didn't let go either.

For the love of kittens, said Rufus. *You humans can't do anything right.* He squirmed between Oscar's legs and sunk his teeth into Regina's leg. Meep, PD, and the rest of the cats followed him and swarmed Regina. Oscar was pushed out of the way by the furry tide. Regina was forced to let go of me when a couple of calicos and a Maine Coon jumped on her arms and held on with their claws. I fell back against Ian.

The hall wasn't that big, and now it was completely packed full of people and cats yowling their heads off. Cat war cries were echoing around us. You could barely see Regina for the cats, though you could hear her cussing up a storm — in my voice. Oscar was on the opposite side of her, watching the mayhem and holding Victoria back with one hand. She looked like she wanted to join in. She'd grabbed a baseball bat from somewhere and was holding it over her head like a war club, though she looked like she would keel over from the effort.

"Are you okay?" asked Ian. That was when I noticed I was leaning back against his chest. We were both breathing hard.

"Yeah," I said, wondering how long I could stay there before it got weird. There was no telling if I'd ever be in this spot again. Well, hopefully never again in exactly this spot, not in these circumstances. "I'm okay now. She was pretending to be Melly and she caught me by surprise." That's when it hit me. "Oh no, where is Melly?" I took a step toward the cat pileup. "Guys, hey guys!" I yelled. "Back off! I need to ask Regina a question."

The cats reluctantly pulled back to reveal a very scratched and bloody Regina kneeling on the floor, who still looked like me. It was surreal. They surrounded her, practically piled up on top of each other. She dragged herself onto all fours and stared up at me with utter hate in her eyes.

Told you, said one calico to another. *Tastes like chicken*.

Looking at Regina, I realized I needed to get a haircut, and that I should never ever sneer. It was definitely not a good look for me. Of course, neither was the ripped shirt with my raggedy old bra showing. I hoped Ian wasn't looking.

Even completely torn up and surrounded by cats, Regina wasn't ready to give up. Rufus parked himself directly in front of her, no more than an inch away from her face.

"Regina, where is Melly?" I asked.

She just bared her teeth at me. I made another mental note to never do that in public. It was beyond creepy looking at her looking like me and yet so evil.

I was about to question her again, maybe this time with some prodding from Rufus, when Jason, the AD, came running up behind Oscar, followed by Alan and a bunch of other people from the set. One guy had a handheld camera and it looked like he was still recording.

"What in hell is going on?" asked Alan. He looked first at me, then down at Regina, then back at me again. Both of our hats had been knocked off. "You again?" he said, but slowly, like he was confused. "There are two of you? Did you come here to attack Victoria again?" He turned to Jason. "Call the police, would you?"

"Wait a minute," said the real Victoria and pointed at Regina with the bat. "That's who you need to have arrested."

Alan stepped forward to get a good look at Victoria. Her butchered hair was standing up all over the place, she had no makeup on, and she'd probably lost at least twenty-five pounds, but she was definitely and unmistakably Victoria Welling. That is, unless you were an inebriated horndog fan. "Victoria?" he said. "What happened to you? Just what is going on here?"

Regina must have realized at that point that the jig was up. She shrieked and dived at Victoria. "You ruined my life!" she howled. Even the cats were taken by surprise.

Regina didn't so much grab Victoria as land on her. They fell into the pile of clothing and a few of the cats, who screeched and fled. I watched as Regina transformed into Victoria—or how Victoria would look, if she didn't look like death warmed over—and the real Victoria passed out. All of the wounds Regina had gotten from the cats were gone, but she was still in my clothing. Apparently, she could control her wardrobe. Class B Talent my skinny butt. Those BERM paper pushers were idiots.

"What the—" said Alan and Jason together. Then Alan turned to the camera guy. "Are you getting this?"

"You bet I am," said the guy. Movie people. Not even remotely fazed by the craziness. I mean, did they think this was all special effects or something?

Regina stood up. Oscar and I each took a step toward her and she held up a hand. "One step closer and I'll kill her," she said. She reached down and pulled Victoria up by her armpits.

"With what?" I asked. She didn't have anything other than her hands, and even though she was strong, I didn't think she was that strong. And she definitely wasn't hiding anything in her shirt other than a too-exact copy of my ratty bra.

"She's already weak," said Regina. "If I pull from her one more time, it'll kill her." She started backing up, dragging Victoria along with her.

"Wait a minute here," said Alan. He turned to me. "Would someone mind telling me what's going on?"

"You've been working with a fake Victoria," I said. "That's really Regina Fedorka. Her Talent is to be able to transform into anyone she touches. And she's got the real Victoria right there." I left out the part about her being about to kill the real Victoria, since he hopefully got that from Regina. But maybe not. He took a step toward Regina like he was planning on being the hero of this story.

"I wouldn't do that," I said. "She did it once to me—that pulling thing—and I think she's telling the truth. I think she could kill Victoria." Anyone looking at Victoria could see it was possible. She looked practically translucent, she was so pale. She hadn't even come to yet.

"And you can bet I will," said Regina. She kept backing up, and Oscar had to step out of her way. "She's outlived her usefulness anyway. And this acting thing isn't as much fun as I'd imagined it would be."

"Explains a lot," I heard one of the movie guys say to another one. "Her acting sucks."

Regina heard him too. She sneered in his direction, but kept dragging Victoria along the hall with her.

"What should we do?" asked Oscar. "The cats?"

Rufus and PD began following Regina. "Call off the cats," she told me. "I mean it, Cat Girl. I don't know what kind of control you've got over them, but call them off now."

"Stand down, guys," I said.

I can be very, very fast, said Meep.

"I know you can," I said, "but I don't think it would take her long to kill Victoria. We can't chance it."

"Are you talking to the *cat*?" asked Alan, master of the obvious.

I ignored him. Regina was dragging Victoria backward. If Victoria had been a healthy weight and conscious, maybe that would have slowed Regina down more. As it was, Regina was progressing pretty steadily. If I remembered

265

right, that way was one of the main concourse areas that led to a big ramp and then the gates. If we let her get away, I had no idea how we'd ever find her again. She'd probably ditch Victoria, but then she could just grab anyone on the street and change her face. She could be anyone and we'd never know.

That was not a comforting thought.

"Rufus," I whispered as softly as I could and trying not to move my lips, since I knew with his cat hearing, he'd pick up on it anyway, "You all get ready. I'm going to see if I can get her talking to delay her."

Okay, he said, *but I still think I could have her by the throat before she knew what hit her.*

"Regina," I called out, "I just want to know one thing."

She laughed a brittle dry laugh. "Find your friend on your own time," she said.

"No, that's not it," I said, though Melly's location was topmost in my mind. I took a couple of slow steps in her direction. She kept walking and dragging, but didn't say anything. Some of the cats crept forward a little too.

"Why'd you do it? I mean Easton. Why'd you kidnap her too? Didn't you have enough on your plate keeping Victoria locked up?"

Regina laughed again, but it was about the most humorless sound I'd ever heard. "That stupid blogger. She was going to ruin the whole thing with her big mouth. Would you believe she actually found my house? She broke in with her credit card, of all things. I caught her talking to Victoria. I wasn't about to let her ruin everything, just like I'm not going to let you ruin everything either. You can stop right where you are."

I stopped midstep and put my foot back down. Frick on a stick. She'd figured me out.

Hey, said PD, *I smell beer.*

"It's a ballpark," I whispered back. Beer smell came with the territory.

Yeah, continued PD, *but I also smell unwashed guys.*

Ah. The drunk dudes who'd gone to find their friends. They'd actually made it back into Wrigley. I cleared my throat and cupped my hands around my mouth. "And next up, we have an AMAZING, death-defying trick featuring not one, not two, but five cats and a ring of fire! With our special guest star, Victoria Welling! Everyone give a nice round of applause to welcome our special guest!" I motioned to everyone standing behind me and started clapping.

Ian picked up on it first and started clapping like crazy and wolf whistling. Then Oscar joined in, elbowing Garrett so he'd start clapping too. After a moment, even Alan and Jason and the movie guys were clapping and stomping their feet. Regina stopped and stared at us.

"I don't know what—" she started to say when a crowd of guys rounded the corner behind her and shouted when they saw us. There were at least ten of them.

"We made it!" shouted the blond guy.

"Welcome to the show!" I shouted back. "Why don't you give our special guest a big Chicago welcome!"

They whooped, took one look at Regina-Victoria, and descended on her with open arms.

THIRTY-ONE

"IN A FIGHT, ALWAYS BET ON THE CAT."
—PD

The guys didn't even notice the real Victoria, whom Regina was separated from in the first two seconds after they mobbed her. Oscar ran to Victoria and caught her as she slumped to the floor.

"Okay," I said to anyone who was listening. "We've got to grab her, like a bunch of us at once, I think. So if she weakens one person by pulling from them, everyone else will still be okay. Are you ready?" I caught a nod from Ian and one from Alan, who still looked very confused, but I didn't wait for any more. I didn't want to give Regina a chance to get over her surprise.

I ran forward and spotted Regina's flailing arm in the middle of the guys. I grabbed her hand and pulled. Ian came up beside me and grabbed her wrist. Alan and Garrett wiggled through and shouldered their way between two guys in Cubs baseball caps to grab her other arm and her shoulder. We all pulled and extracted her from her fans.

"Guys, guys! Great job! A Chicago welcome I'm sure she'll never forget!" I shouted. "Next show in ten minutes! And free refreshments! Go wait in the bleacher section!"

They ran off in the direction of the field, cheering and completely oblivious. As soon as they were gone, a ring of cats surrounded Regina.

If she makes a single move, said Rufus, *we're taking her out.*

"Agreed," I told him. Then I leaned over to stare Regina in the face. "You try anything," I said, "anything at all, and I'll let Tiddlywinks eat your liver for dinner. And trust me, he really wants to."

She glared at me. Alan waved a few more movie guys over and told them to get something to tie her up with so we wouldn't have to hold her any longer. They came back with some rope (where they found it, I really don't know, but I guess that's why they were on staff) and tied up Regina. She still hadn't said a word.

"Well," said Alan, looking at me. "I guess I owe you an apology."

"I'm not worried about that right now," I said. "I just really want to know where my friend Melly is."

"Nat?"

I nearly fell over, I turned around so fast. Melly—the real Melly—stood in the door of a supply closet with her hand to her head. I whooped and ran to her to grab her up in a hug. Oscar managed to clap his hands without dropping Victoria.

"Don't you ever do that again," I said.

"Do what?" she asked. She looked like she didn't even know which way was up.

"Go off with the bad guy. Your life is much more important than your acting career. Seriously, woman, dead girls can't act."

"Okay, okay," she said. "You can yell at me later. Right now, can I just get something to eat?"

I was with her on that one. After what Regina had done, that pulling thing or whatever she called it, I was starving. I also couldn't remember the last time I'd eaten today in between the running around, breaking into houses, and saving people.

"Excuse me," said Alan, "but what are we supposed to do with her?" He pointed to Regina, who looked like she wanted to bite his finger off.

Honestly, I really didn't care what he did with her. but he was looking at me like I should have the answers.

You could let me have her, said Rufus.

That was actually pretty tempting. I was seriously considering it when my phone rang. I answered it. "Nat!" screamed Viv in my ear. "Where are you? I'm at the house you told me about and there's broken glass, but nothing else. Where are you?"

"Here," I said, and handed my phone to Alan. "This is Viv. She's my sister and she's with the BERM. Why don't you guys talk about it? We're going to go eat." Let someone else deal with the drama for a while. Stick a fork in me. I was done.

And we left, a stream of cats following us. Rufus, of course, stayed behind to guard Regina, who still looked like Victoria. I wondered if we'd ever know what she really looked like.

♥

Meep led us to the craft services table. Apparently, tuna sandwiches were on the menu, so she had no trouble finding it. Melly had wanted to go get real food at a restaurant, but there was no way we could get into any place with all of the cats. Ian called his dad to tell him what was going on, and his dad told him how to get into his office (after some moments of stunned silence) so we could have somewhere private to recuperate in.

Oscar woke Victoria up by waving some fruit juice under her nose. She grabbed it and drank it down before her eyes even opened. The boys just kept passing food to Melly, Victoria, and me. I had no idea how Victoria had done it for so long. After just one touch from Regina, I was absolutely starving. I'd never been so hungry in my life.

Melly was ultra-relieved to find out that Easton had survived. While we had been zooming around the suburbs breaking into a house and herding cats, Melly had been living her own nightmare. Her first clue that a walk-on role in the movie may not have been worth it was when Regina pulled a knife on her to get her out of Wrigley. Then seeing

Easton West out cold and trussed up in the trunk of a rental car had *really* brought it home.

Regina forced Melly to drive her to the York, where they got Easton upstairs after Regina-as-Victoria made some kind of excuse about Easton suffering from a massive hangover from partying too hard. Since Easton (a.k.a. Regina) wasn't on the hotel staff's good side anyway, they'd taken that at face value. Melly had even tried to give the concierge a clue, but Regina had given her a sharp poke in the side that shut her up. Upstairs, Melly had been absolutely horrified and helpless to see Regina pump Easton full of some kind of drug and write out a suicide note.

The only good thing about Melly being there was that Easton would probably be dead otherwise. She'd pretended she had to go to the bathroom while Regina was writing the note, plugged the sink, and turned the water on. It had taken a little while, but water had seeped out into the hall and down through the floor into the room below. That was how the hotel had found Easton. I had to give it to Melly. I don't think I would have thought of doing something like that. Or I'd have tried the bathtub and it would have taken so long to overflow it would have been too late, or so loud that Regina would have caught me.

Garrett followed us to craft services and listened to the whole story with wide eyes as he sat right next to Oscar. He even asked if he could hold the nunchuks, but what I think he really wanted to hold was Oscar's hand.

Alan found us after a while and said Viv was on her way with a whole contingent of BERM guys. Too little too late, if you asked me, but at least I didn't have to worry about it anymore. He had us tell him everything that had happened, starting from the beginning. He kept shaking his head like he didn't believe us, and he made me demonstrate the whole cat thing.

So I had PD sniff him, and he told me Alan had eaten an Italian beef for lunch and that he had a smelly foot fungus, but I left that last part out. I figured Alan probably already knew that and if he didn't, I didn't want to be the one to tell him.

After we'd eaten pretty much everything left on the craft services table that was edible (seriously, tofu dogs?), we went looking for Melly's phone and my dad's video camera. Regina had pocketed both of them, but Alan's guys had patted her down and she didn't have either one on her. We finally found my dad's camera smashed up in a trash can. Melly's phone wound up being really easy to find because it started ringing while we were searching the dressing room.

It was her dad and it was apparently his fourth attempt at reaching her. He was not pleased. Melly tried to explain to him what was going on, but she only got as far as "kidnapped," and he told her to stay put because he was on his way, and hung up.

"I guess I ought to call my parents too, huh?" asked Oscar. They probably weren't freaked like Melly's dad since they were used to Oscar wandering in late on Friday nights, but still. This was pretty big. "Are you going to call your parents, Nat?"

I thought about it. Really, I did. For about two seconds. "Viv's already on her way. I'll wait and see what she says." Delay the inevitable as long as possible.

Mr. Zinsz, Melly's dad, arrived in record time. He must have floored it the entire way. Viv or the BERM people had contacted the cops, and they were swarming all over the place, interviewing extras and the drunk guys and whatnot, so we didn't even know Mr. Z had arrived until there was a huge commotion at one of the entrances. We were on our way to get Oscar's phone out of Melly's car when we heard Mr. Z shouting and ran the rest of the way down to check it out. We had left all the animals hanging out in the office except Meep, who'd decided I wasn't to be trusted on my own anymore and was trotting along beside me. It was kind of sweet, for Meep.

"Melly!" That was Mr. Z. "That's my daughter!" He looked like he was about to haul off and hit the cop who was trying to stop him. "You let me in right now or I'm going to sue the department for everything they've got!" Even thirty yards away, we could see that his face was bright red.

"Whoa," said Oscar, slowing down. "Mr. Z's gone postal."

"Yeah," said Garrett. "He's gonna get tased."

"Dad!" yelled Melly and ran on. Oscar, Ian, Garrett, and I hung back a little. Good thing Victoria had stayed in the office with Alan to recuperate. Mr. Z was okay, but he was pretty overprotective and it often seemed like he thought we were a bad influence on Melly. Maybe it was the way he unfailingly said something about the purple streaks in my hair or the green in Oscar's. It was kinda like he was joking, but kind of not at the same time. And really, going, "Hey, what's that in your hair, mold?" every time he saw us wasn't all that funny anyway.

The police saw Melly coming and let her dad in. He grabbed her in a huge hug. He was still crushing her ribs when Oscar and I walked up.

"Hey, Mr. Z," I said.

He let Melly go, but kept a hand on her shoulder. "Whose fault is this?" His glare was clearly focused on both me and Oscar equally. Ian kind of ducked behind us. I didn't blame him. Mr. Z is a big guy with a round head and he always wore a perfectly tailored suit. He's kind of imposing. Like a villain in a James Bond movie.

"I don't know that it's anybody's fault, exactly," I said. "Things just kind of got out of hand."

"Things always get out of hand with you two, don't they?" He pulled Melly to him.

That wasn't fair. It's not like we'd ever gotten Melly kidnapped before. And it's not like any of this was *my* idea. She was the one talking about responsibility and all of that, and it wasn't my fault she went along with Regina in the beginning, though she still redeemed herself in the end by, hey, *saving*

Easton's life. I raised my eyebrows at Melly a little, hoping she would notice but Mr. Z wouldn't. Wasn't she going to say anything to defend us?

"Dad," she finally said, "it's not their fault. We were all —"

But that was as far as she got before Viv and her brigade arrived. Viv swept in and crushed me in a huge hug. Then she hugged Oscar too. She was going to hug Melly, but Mr. Z still had his arm wrapped tight around Melly's shoulder. He didn't look like he was ever going to let go.

"I'm so glad you guys are okay!" Viv's normally perfect hair was messy and even her shirt was untucked. "You were supposed to wait to hear back from me!"

"We couldn't get in touch with you," I said.

"And the clock was ticking," said Oscar.

"Yeah, Dad," said Melly. "If they'd waited any longer, who knows what would have happened to me. Regina tried to kill Easton West. I know. I was with her. She made me watch."

"Who is Easton West? Wait," said her dad. "I don't care. We're going home. You can tell me the rest of the story there."

"Wait a minute, sir," said Viv. "I'm afraid we've got to take a statement from your daughter first. As you're obviously aware, some serious crimes have been committed."

"And who the hell are you?" asked Mr. Z, taking a step toward Viv and dragging Melly along with him like a rag doll.

Wow. Mr. Z was seriously off the deep end. One of Viv's coworkers, a largish guy in a dark blue suit and serious sideburns, stepped forward warningly. I mean, hello. Other than Viv, they all exuded "secret government agency." Not that they were secret, exactly. Most people knew the BERM existed, but hardly anyone knew exactly what they did. Other than what Viv had let slip during dinner conversations, I didn't really know what they did either. What was Mr. Z thinking?

Viv held up a hand. "I'm Natalie's sister. But I'm also an agent with the Bureau of Extrasensory Regulation and Management. And I think maybe you need to calm down a little." She didn't flinch.

Woof. Go, Viv!

Mr. Z went from red to purple.

That was when Mr. Sideburns intervened. He swept forward, murmured some words to Mr. Z and then led him and Melly off somewhere into the stadium. Four more agents split off from the pack and each one took one of us by the arm. Before I knew it, I was settled into someone's Wrigley office being officially debriefed. Meep was there and Viv popped in every now and then, but I had no idea where anyone else was. I felt kind of like a criminal or like I was in a bad spy movie. All that was missing was a bright overhead light shining in my face. I got the feeling they'd have used one if one were available, but the lights at Wrigley were normal ballpark fare.

I was pretty fed up. I felt like I had explained everything at least three times by the time Viv finally came back in. "I am so done here," I said to her, ignoring the agent who had been annoying me with all the questions. His name was Frank and he had the personality of a sponge. "Where is everyone else?"

"Oscar and Melly are just about done," she said. "And all those cats are waiting for you. Where in the world did you find them all anyway?"

I ignored the question about the cats. I'd already gone over that with Frank. Repeatedly. "And Victoria? Regina? What's going on with them?"

"They've taken Victoria to the hospital for observation." She looked sidelong at Frank. "And Regina has been taken to the BERM headquarters for her interrogation."

Interrogation? They should be taking her there for a beating. But that probably wasn't legal.

When they finally let me out of the room, I ran into Ian in the hallway. He was leaning against the wall, looking about as worn out as I felt.

"Hey," he said. "They let me out a little early since I didn't really have much to say. Oscar and Melly are still talking and Oscar's parents got here a little while ago. How are you holding up?"

I'm fine, said Meep sarcastically. *Thanks for asking*. I ignored her. She was just miffed because the goons hadn't asked her any questions.

"I feel like Jason Bourne," I said, "but without all the muscles—or the mad skills."

He laughed. "My dad got here a little while ago too. He can't wait to meet you."

I didn't know what to say to that. Was that a good thing? Or a "he can't wait to meet you because he's heard you're such a sideshow freak" kind of thing? Instead of replying, I started off to where the craft services table was.

"Hold on. You don't want to go that way."

"Why not? I need to check on the cats." I was worried they were going to start using the outfield as a litter box or that Rufus might have led them in a rebellion.

"Pebbles helped me move the cats. They're all waiting down by my dad's car. If you go that way, there's a bunch of TV and newspaper reporters. I think Alan called them."

"Oh!" I stopped. "Thanks. That's the last place I want to be. I just want to go home." That wasn't entirely true. Viv had told me she'd called home and explained everything, but I wasn't exactly anxious to face the music. After all, I was the suspended-got-arrested-caused-total-chaos child. I couldn't even imagine the talking-to I was going to get when I got home. They'd finally notice me all right — but not the kind of notice I was necessarily hoping for.

"Your chariot awaits." He took my arm and led me off down the hall. "You know," he said, "it's really weird, actually talking to Pebbles and having him listen."

"You have no idea," I said. Thank heavens he couldn't hear what PD was probably saying back.

 280

THIRTY-TWO

FRIDAY, SEPTEMBER 11, 9:59 P.M.

"HOW YOU BEHAVE TOWARDS CATS HERE BELOW
DETERMINES YOUR STATUS IN HEAVEN."
—ROBERT A. HEINLEIN

The plan was for Ian and me to take all the cats home in his
dad's car since that way, they could tell me where to drop
them off in the neighborhood. Ian's dad was going to take the
train home. He was on the phone when Ian brought me by
for introductions, so I got off easy with a wave and a smile.

I climbed into the car, and Meep, Rufus, Fergie, and PD
climbed in to sit on my feet. The rest of the cats were piled in
the back, wedging themselves into a space that should have
been much too small to fit them all. That was a cat Talent I
wish I had sometimes. Since Easton was still in the hospital, Rufus and Fergie were coming home with me—mostly
because Rufus had refused to go off with any of the BERM
guys, saying they hadn't proven their trustworthiness yet. I
took that as a compliment, though I had the sneaking suspicion that they'd refused to let him guard Regina and he was
just pissed at them.

Ian pulled out of the parking lot and started home. "Well," he said after a few minutes, "that was crazy."

He always has been a master of understatement, said PD.

I laughed.

Ian looked at me sideways out of the corner of his eye. "Did Pebbles say something?"

PD laughed his cat laugh. *He's always going to wonder now, isn't he? This could be fun.*

"He just said you had a talent for understatement, that's all." I winked at PD. "PD likes you a lot," I said. "You don't have to worry about anything. You might want to stop calling him Pebbles, though."

"Yeah," said Ian. "PD. Sorry, man."

No problem, said PD. *Pebbles was your mom's fault anyway.*

Huh. Now that my secret was out, was I going to have to translate for people all the time? That could get annoying.

"You know," I said, "you really don't have to tell anybody at school. About the whole talking to cats thing."

"You don't want anybody to know? Why not? It's cool." He sounded surprised.

Cool? In what universe? "Yeah . . . I mean, like what about Jonas Smith?"

"Frog Boy?"

"Exactly," I said. I couldn't help but wince a little.

"Well, you're not Jonas Smith. He doesn't bathe, you know. And he, like, *sniffs* people's hair. He'd be weird even if he didn't kiss frogs or whatever it is he does."

I've been telling you, said Meep. *It won't be that bad. And cats are way better than frogs. Frogs are dinner.*

That reminded me, once again, of why I was not one of those people who kissed their cats on the nose.

♥

We dropped off all the neighborhood cats back on various streets surrounding Regina's house. A few people walking their dogs gave us strange looks as we stopped and let a cat out, but no one said anything. Of course, that could have been because we just drove off as fast as we could. Then Ian drove over to my house. All the lights were on, so Mom and Dad were definitely home and awake. Ian parked and turned off the car.

"Do you want me to come in with you?"

"No!" I opened the door. "I mean, no, thanks. I probably need to, um, explain a few things to them." It would be best if he didn't meet my mom seconds before she was about to tear into me. Actually, it would be best if he never met my mom at all.

I climbed out, and Meep, Fergie, and Rufus followed me. "Thanks for the ride. And . . . you know, everything." Like not telling me I was a freak. And trying to save me from a crazy lunatic. All that stuff.

"Sure." He leaned over the passenger seat and smiled up at me. "You know," said Ian, "that was one heck of a first date. Maybe next time we can try it without the psycho killer, you think?"

Yeah, PD yelled from somewhere around Ian's ankles. *And maybe next time there'll be kissing!*

Meep and Rufus snickered as I turned red. I waved at Ian as he drove off, glad once again that no one else could understand cats.

But did he say "next time"?

I opened the door and was immediately assaulted by Emmy. She must have been waiting right there, probably watching through the window.

"Look at your eye!" She shrieked, right in my ear. "It's purple!" Then she grabbed me in a huge hug and practically crushed my ribs. She was getting strong, but then again, she hadn't given me a hug since she was about six. She wasn't much of a hugger and neither was I. She pulled back, looked at me again, and then hauled off and hit me in the arm. "Don't you ever do that again!" she said.

"Do what?" I shut the door behind me after all the animals had made it in. I wished she hadn't mentioned my eye. I had been able to ignore the throbbing until she reminded me. Regina had a mean right hook.

Emmy gaped at me. "You could have *died*," she wailed. Then she burst into tears and ran off down the hall. What the hell?

"Natalie? Is that you?" my mother called from her office.

Who else would it be? "Yeah," I said. Viv said she had already explained, so I just dived in. "It's me. And Rufus—the other cat—is here, just to warn you. And a dog. You ought to stay clear unless you have a mask." Was it too much to hope that she wouldn't leave her office?

No such luck. Mom and Dad both arrived at the same time. They stopped in the entryway. They were backlit by the light from the hall and I couldn't tell whether they were sad or mad or furious or what. Rufus and Meep sat down in front of me and we all stared back. Fergie had already passed out asleep in a corner. She was snoring little doggy snores.

"See, it all started with Oscar and this video—" I began. Then they both ran at me. I flinched. Not that they'd ever been into corporal punishment or anything, but I'd never been in so much trouble before. I imagined if they ever wanted to take it up, now would be the time.

Then they both grabbed me and squeezed, just like Emmy had, except without the tears. Rufus and Meep scattered to keep from getting stepped on. Then Mom stood back, took me by the shoulders, and took a good look at me.

"Look at your eye! Dennis, look at her eye!"

I needed a mirror. Just how bad exactly did my eye look? Ian hadn't said anything about it. Neither had Viv. Maybe it was getting worse, the way bruises do sometimes. I'd gotten a glimpse of it in the car window and it hadn't looked *that* bad.

"I'm sorry," I started again.

"Natalie," said Dad, "just stop." Even though he had on his striped pajamas, he looked serious.

I shut up.

Mom pointed to the couch. I sat. Meep and Rufus joined

me, but Meep especially looked ready to run. She knew how Mom could be. I had the feeling I was going to be grounded for the next few years. Maybe until I was out of college. Could they do that? Knowing Mom, if she could, she would.

"First off," said Mom, "you should have come to us right away."

I opened my mouth to say something, but she wasn't done yet.

"Sneaking around like that—smuggling a cat into the house, getting suspended—getting arrested!" Rufus sank down a little and hid his head behind my ankle. *Finally* something scared him. "What were you thinking?"

"I—"

"*Allison*," said Dad. He gave Mom a let-me-do-the-talking look, which was very rare. He put a hand on my shoulder. "Natalie, your mom is just worried about you. I've been worried too. I wondered what you were up to when I first smelled the new cat in the house."

"You knew about Rufus?"

"He was kind of hard to miss," said Dad. "Especially at first."

Rufus raised his head. He looked a little put out, but Dad was right. I couldn't believe he hadn't said anything. What had I been thinking, trying to sneak Rufus past the supersniffer?

"But why—"

"Because I trust you," said Dad. He looked at Mom, who had her lips pursed like she'd just sucked on a lime. "We *both* do."

He elbowed mom and she very pointedly did not look at him but she did allow herself a small nod. "Of course we do," she said. Someone should tell her she's not a very good liar. I didn't need to be Viv to see right through her.

"And I knew you and Genevieve had everything under control when I heard you at the police station."

"Wait. What? What are you talking about?" I looked from Dad to Mom and back again. Mom looked a little peeved, but she held her tongue. "You were there?"

Holy tuna cakes, said Meep to Rufus. *Dad's been holding out on us. I knew he was sneakier than he looked. He's got the sniffer of a bloodhound, you know.*

"I got there late," he said, "but I was there on the other side of the window. I heard the whole story. I thought it was a great opportunity for both you and your sister to prove yourselves to the BERM."

"What?" It was a good thing I was already sitting down. My head swam a little.

"Especially you, Natalie," he continued. "I've been telling the bureau chief for years that we need to re-examine our priorities. The BERM has always seen the potential in Talents like Genevieve's and in people like Regina, but they've completely disregarded the potential of Talents like yours."

"Stupid ones," I said automatically.

Hey, said Meep, *I told you to stop that.*

"Never say that, Natalie," said Mom. "Your Talent isn't stupid."

I looked at her. Who was she kidding?

"Granted," she said, "it doesn't seem as useful as some at first glance."

Dad held up a hand at her and she stopped talking. He truly was wearing the pants in the family tonight. "*All* Talents have a purpose," he said. "And I'd say that you proved that to the BERM with your actions over the last week."

"We just hope that next time, you'll think about letting me in on what's going on so I don't have to hear about it secondhand," said Mom. She gave Dad the elbow this time, and it was his turn to nod.

Let's hope there's not a next time, said Meep.

You said it, said Rufus. *I really don't think my fur can stand it.*

I couldn't help it. I laughed. Hysterically. "Sorry," I spit out between giggles, "I just . . . I don't even know what to think about this. You guys trust me? And Dad thinks I'm the new BERM poster child for the Talented? But I'm your screwup daughter!" I started hiccupping.

"Language!" said Mom. "What do you mean our 'screw-up daughter'?"

"Emmy . . . ," I said. "Viv . . . you're always going on and on about them." *Hiccup*. Horny toads on a stick. Of course I'd be hiccupping now.

Mom actually put her arm around my shoulder. "Natalie, if I don't spend as much time haranguing you as your sisters, it's because you don't need to be coddled and encouraged like they do. You've always been comfortable doing your own thing and succeeding on your own."

Meep snorted. So did Rufus. Comfortable? Me? Succeeding? I hiccupped again. I didn't know what to say.

They both hugged me again. "Why don't you go get cleaned up and get some sleep," said Dad. "It's getting late. We can talk more tomorrow. I'll get some ice for your eye, okay?"

Mom sneezed. "Just take the pink cat along with you, would you?"

I wandered off in the direction of the bathroom, Meep and Rufus trailing behind me. Apparently, I was in a parallel universe and no one had thought to tell me.

THIRTY-THREE

SATURDAY, SEPTEMBER 12, 7:32 A.M.

"NEVER TRY TO OUT-STUBBORN A CAT."
—ROBERT A. HEINLEIN

I woke up to Emmy screaming in my ear. "You're in the paper!" She dropped a section of the *Chicago Tribune* right on top of my face. I pulled it off and wiped the sleep out of my eyes, wincing when I touched my black eye. Considering how it had looked before I went to bed, it was probably deep purple by now. Meep, still asleep, rolled off my pillow and fell into Rufus.

Cretin, mumbled Rufus, and swished his tail right into my nose. Note to self: never have more than one cat at a time.

"Just look!" Emmy shouted right in my ear again. "You're on the front page!"

"What are you screaming about?" I shoved both cats off the bed and sat up. The paper fell onto the floor. Emmy huffed, picked it up, and stuck it in my face again. I took it.

She was right. There was last year's school picture (with the unfortunately large pimple right next to my nose, making

290

me look like I had three nostrils) front and center. "'Cat Girl' saves celebrities" was the headline.

Oh no.

I read the article. Everything was there. *Everything.*

"Oh my God," I said. I threw the paper on the floor where Meep pounced on it and shredded a couple of pages before Emmy could get it from her. Good kitty.

"Isn't it awesome?" Emmy was dancing around my room, dangling strips of the shredded newspaper in front of Meep and Rufus. They batted at it and flip-flopped themselves end over end all over the room. Cats may sleep a lot, but they can wake up awfully fast when they want to.

"Awesome? Are you kidding? I'm going to have to move." There was no way I could go back to school. School? Heck, I needed to move out of state! I wondered if Auntie Esther would take me in? She lived in California. Maybe that would be far enough away.

"It's on the Internet too," said Emmy with a wicked glint in her eye, completely ignoring my misery. "And I heard Viv say something about the story being nationally syndicated or something. She's here, you know. Downstairs."

Oy. Maybe California wasn't far enough away. Well, there was always the family we had in China, even though I only knew, like, four words in Chinese.

"Mom said to come out when you're ready." She smiled sweetly at me and twirled out the door. Evil, evil girl. She'd gotten over her upset over my near-death experience pretty quickly.

Poodle farts on a stick. I flopped back on my bed and pulled my pillow down over my face. Maybe I could just stay in my room. Mom was a supergenius. She could home school me.

Oh, get up, said Meep. *Go face the tuna. So your secret's out. You're a hero. Get over it.*

"You wouldn't understand," I said. Not that the article had been bad, exactly, but my life was over. I was Cat Girl now. There was no going back. I wondered if Frog Boy had room at his lunch table.

I pulled on a pair of jeans and a T-shirt from the floor, giving them the sniff test. I needed clean laundry bad, but I'd worry about it after breakfast. I stumbled out the door and down the hall to the living room.

Viv was on the couch, but so were a bunch of guys. Mostly all in suits. One of them was Alan. They all stood up as I came into the room, except for Viv. Mom and Dad came in from the kitchen. Mom looked at my hair and cleared her throat, but didn't say anything. Maybe I should have brushed it—and maybe Emmy could have *told* me we had visitors. I put up my hand to comb my fingers through it but then decided that was a little too obvious, so I stopped. Then I figured that looked spastic and I was going to turn it into a greeting, but I wound up just kind of standing in the doorway with my hand in the air.

"Um," I said.

"Natalie," said Dad, "you've met Alan Leonard already, I believe."

I wanted to say, "Yeah, Dad, he's the guy who got me arrested," but I resisted. Instead, I gave Alan a little wave, which gave me an excuse to lower my hand.

"And this is Mr. Whaley, the *mayor* of Chicago," said Mom, motioning at a stocky older guy with slicked-back black hair and gray sideburns. Crap. I *really* should have brushed my hair. And my teeth. No wonder Emmy had been smiling her evil smile. I bet she was doing her chameleon thing right now and hiding out somewhere in the room. First she goes all huggy on me last night, and now this. At least things were back to normal . . . I guess.

"Nice to meet you," I said. I didn't wave this time.

Dad introduced the rest of them. There was a guy from the *Tribune*, another from the *Daily Herald*, a BERM dude who worked with Viv (not Frank the sponge, but the one who had talked to Mr. Z), and a guy from the *Jerry King Show*. Holy mother of TV shows. No amount of hair brushing would have made a difference, not for this crowd. Maybe a makeover.

"Young lady," said the mayor, "I just want to shake your hand. You've really done Chicagoland proud." He stepped forward and held out his hand. I took it. He pumped my hand up and down a few times while Mom beamed at me.

Alan stood up. "Everyone in the crew would like to invite you and your friends onto the set today while we're filming the big parade sequence. We've cleared it with your parents."

He patted me on the back. "And I personally wanted to thank you, but also apologize."

"Um, sure," I said. I had the nagging feeling I was still asleep and dreaming. Mom said it was okay to go on set? Though I guess it wasn't a school day, so maybe that was why.

He should be apologizing to me too, said Rufus. *Tell him I want tuna.*

"Oooh! Did he say something?" asked Jerry King.

"Yeah, he, um, wants some tuna."

"That's just amazing!"

A cat wanting tuna? That wasn't amazing. That was *normal*.

Each of the guys in turn came over and either shook my hand or patted me on the back and told me how incredible I was. The TV show guy actually wanted me to come on his show, along with Rufus, Easton, and Victoria. Easton, apparently, was okay, just weak. They'd pumped her stomach in time to prevent any permanent damage, though she still needed time to recover. The doctors had thought her ravings about being kidnapped were side effects of the drugs she'd almost overdosed on. They'd actually bought the whole "I'm going to kill myself because of my cat" thing.

"What about Regina?" I asked the BERM guy when everyone finally sat down again. He looked pretty much exactly what I expected an agent to look like: close-cropped hair, button-down shirt, and kind of a square jaw. Thankfully, I'd lucked into Frank last night. He had been annoying, but not as scary as this guy would have been.

"Don't worry about her," he said. "We have things under control. The BERM is evaluating her status right now."

Rufus snorted. *You should have let us finish her off. Then you really wouldn't need to worry about her. I watch the news. She'll be out in no time, just you wait and see.*

Everyone looked at me like they wanted me to translate what Rufus had said. "He said . . . thanks. And he's sure she's in good hands."

Rufus rolled his eyes at me, but didn't say anything else. He wasn't stupid.

But what he said worried me. They were evaluating her status? What did that mean? Were they evaluating her as in they were going to deport her butt to Siberia? Or were they evaluating her as having a Talent they could exploit? They were a governmental agency. I wasn't sure I trusted them. But maybe I just watched too much TV. Besides, Dad and Viv were very pro BERM and I did trust them. Well, Dad, anyway.

♥

The mayor had arranged for us to have a police escort and everything, which was good since a lot of streets were closed. I'd actually never been to the Von Steuben German Day Parade, but from the size of the crowd, it was a pretty big deal. Either that, or people had gotten wind that the movie was going to be filming. Maybe both. Emmy had been waving to people as we drove by, which had driven Viv absolutely nuts. They had argued about it the whole time. Maybe Mom had been right. I was definitely less annoying than they were sometimes. Dad had finally told them both to calm down.

"Cat Girl!" yelled Oscar. He and Melly had converged on me as soon as I had exited our car. I cringed and looked around to see if anyone had heard him. I couldn't help it. He grabbed me in a huge full-body Oscar hug and nearly squashed Rufus against my chest. I hadn't wanted to take Rufus with me (thank goodness Meep had decided she'd had enough adventure to last her a lifetime), but he'd insisted that he wanted to experience one of our "quaint cultural ceremonies" and then he'd guilted me with the fact that Easton always took him to everything. Cats could lay on the guilt like you wouldn't believe. The only person I knew who was better at it was my grandmother. My *nai nai* could even get my dad to eat his broccoli, and he hated it. He said it smelled like farts.

"Oops, sorry, little furry dude," Oscar said. "Didn't see you there."

I am going to ignore that, said Rufus. *This time. But tell him not to call me that again or the claws are coming out.*

"Your eye!" said Melly. "It's—"

"Yeah, I know," I said. "Purple." At least the throbbing had died down to a dull ache overnight, but ibuprofen was my best friend today.

"And blue!" said Oscar. "I think I see some green in there too. You're in Technicolor!"

Melly reached out a finger to touch the edge of my eye.

It was pretty spectacular, if I said so myself. Regina packed quite a wallop. But it was the bump on the back of my head that hurt the worst.

"Your dad let you come?" I asked. The last time I'd seen Mr. Z, he'd seemed like he wasn't going to let Melly out of his sight until she was eighteen.

"Yeah," said Melly. "Sorry about that last night. He's over in the stands, along with Oscar's parents. Everybody's here. Dad was okay, mostly, after he calmed down. But I'm grounded."

"Grounded?" That's nice. Get kidnapped, get grounded. "Then why did he let you come?"

"We can talk about that later," said Oscar. "Right now, we've got to get you to makeup!"

Emmy made as if she was going to follow us, but Viv held her back. Viv was definitely getting a better than normal Christmas present from me this year. And another battery charger for her phone.

I held on tight to Rufus with one arm as Melly pulled me with the other. Oscar followed behind. We passed some floats, including one that looked like a boat. Lots of people were lining up in groups, most of them in some kind of weird German outfit. Lederhosen? Or is that a Swiss thing? Maybe I should have worn something more festive. I'd changed out of my smelly T-shirt into a nicer, cleaner one (and brushed both my hair and my teeth), but I still had on my jeans.

Melly led us to a white trailer down an alley and opened

the door without even knocking. Claire Ryan was sitting in a chair with a makeup lady fussing over her. Another chair was open and Melly pushed me down into it.

"Hey, Hannah, I've got another one for you. Hi, Claire, how are you doing?" said Melly, like hobnobbing with actresses and makeup artists was something she did every day.

Claire nodded. "I'm good." Then she stood up and fluffed her hair after peering at herself in the mirror. "Looks nice, Hannah, thanks," she said to the makeup lady. "Break a leg today," she said to Melly, and left the trailer.

"What was that about?" I set Rufus down on the makeup table. "Break a leg? And why do I need makeup?"

"You haven't heard yet?" Oscar plopped himself down and lounged in the chair Claire had left. It was a normal-sized chair, but somehow he found a way to stretch out and curl up at the same time. Nobody could get comfortable like Oscar.

"Heard what? I haven't heard anything. But I did meet the mayor this morning. And Jerry King." The news didn't have the reaction I expected. They both just nodded. Geez, how much had I missed last night?

"Alan's letting me audition for the movie! Victoria isn't going to be able to do it because of, you know. . . ."

"Because she looks like hell on a cracker," said Oscar. "Regina should sign up as a Weight Watchers counselor — or maybe that would be dictator."

"They're going to have to reshoot all of the scenes Regina was in. Claire's going to be auditioning for the Molly part too, so even if I don't get it, I've got a chance at Claire's current part!" Melly was literally jumping up and down. "Even my dad is psyched! He said maybe all those acting lessons are paying off after all. Alan totally schmoozed him too."

"Wow," I said. Just, wow. I guess she is getting used to hobnobbing with famous people. I bet her "grounding" wouldn't last long. Her dad may be anal, but he totally dotes on Melly and spoils her rotten.

"Hold still," said Hannah. She globbed a bunch of concealer around my eye. "That's quite a shiner you've got."

You should see the other guy, said Rufus. *Oh, wait, you barely even touched her. . . .*

"Shut up," I said.

"Excuse me?" asked Hannah. She raised her eyebrows at me, causing them to disappear beneath her shaggy bangs.

"Sorry, I was talking to Rufus," I said.

"I heard about that cat thing you do," she said. She bent down to stare into Rufus's face. He held his ground and stared right back at her. "Can you have him tell me something?"

Oh, this was going to get real old. Fast.

Rufus curled his lip up on one side so his canine tooth showed. *You can tell her I have nothing to say to someone who stinks of grease. That woman eats entirely too many french fries.*

"Um," I said, "he's not feeling real talkative right now."

And she should lay off of the hairspray. I know about the ozone layer. She's probably responsible for the hole over the Antarctic. He cat laughed.

"He's just thirsty," I said. "Probably a fur ball coming along. I'll get him some water in a minute."

Rufus totally humphed at me, but he sat down and shut up. Hannah kept working on my face while Melly and Oscar told me everything that I'd missed. Mostly, I realized that they were the ones who had spilled everything to whoever would listen, which included a bunch of reporters (Alan had been the one to call them last night; probably figured it would be good for his movie), not just the Trib. The story was *everywhere*, as was my last year's school picture.

"Yeah," said Oscar, "sorry about that. I tried to give them a better picture, but they were in a hurry. They got it from the paper's archive from when you won that math competition last year."

I took back all the good things I've ever said about math.

The picture was only the icing on the cake, though. Oscar and Melly had told *everything*. Alan, I understood — he had a business to promote and he didn't know me. But my friends? So much for pinkie swears. So much for trust. "How could you guys do this to me?"

"What?" asked Oscar. He raised his eyebrows and looked at Melly like they were completely innocent.

"You totally outed me!" I batted Hannah's hand away and swiveled the chair to face the two people who were always supposed to have my back.

"What do you mean?" asked Melly.

I just silently looked from one to the other with my

eyebrows raised. They were both doing their best to look blameless. Finally, Melly had the decency to look down.

"What's the one thing that I've always kept hidden? That I asked you both to never tell anyone, ever? The one thing you *swore* you'd never reveal?"

"Yeah, but —" said Oscar.

"But what?" I stood up and Oscar straightened in his chair. "Oscar, I would never have done this to you."

"That's not fair," he said. "This is completely different."

"Nat," said Melly, "it was going to come out anyway. I mean, Alan saw everything. He even got part of it on camera. Even Ian knows."

"Ian isn't going to say anything. He promised me last night. Like you guys promised me." I picked up Rufus around the middle and he hung from my arm like a furry pink purse. "I gotta go," I said. I opened the door and then stopped to turn back to Melly. "Just because you want to be famous," I said, "doesn't mean I want to." I let the door slam shut behind me. Hopefully Hannah had mostly finished before I'd waved her off. An eye that was half covered up would be worse than one that wasn't covered at all.

Well, said Rufus, *that was enjoyable. How do you treat your enemies?*

"Shut up," I said. "They had no right to talk to anyone about it. They're my *friends*. And Viv could have made Alan keep it quiet."

Sure, sure, said Rufus. *Certainly the BERM would have bribed dozens and dozens of media hungry movie people to keep them quiet.*

"Whatever." I knew he was right, but that didn't make it okay that they'd told.

By the way, in case you hadn't noticed, I am not a fashion accessory. Perhaps you could carry me with a little more dignity?

I ignored him and kept walking. I finally found my family chatting with Alan by a parade float.

"Can we go?" I asked my dad.

"Go?"

"Home," I said. Duh. Why was I here anyway? So Alan could show me off to the media?

"Oh, you can't go!" said Alan. He put an arm around my shoulders and started walking. I shifted Rufus so he wouldn't get squished. "I've got a special spot for you in the reviewing stands! Right next to the mayor! It'll be the perfect spot — you'll be able to see your friend Melly as she auditions. I'm going to be taping the whole route and the parade master has kindly allowed us to put our float in the parade so I can get some good shots. We're even having a whole 'Twist and Shout' moment! Of course, we'll be doing the real close-up shots later on with extras as the crowd, but this will allow us to get some usable footage of the whole parade, just like John Hughes did! Except we have permission."

He's a talker, isn't he? I shifted Rufus so that his butt fit into my elbow and he wasn't dangling quite so much. He did look pretty silly being carried like a purse. People were staring at us.

"Did he say something?"

"No," I said. I refused to translate anything else. I wished Rufus would shut up so people would stop asking.

"Well, you can tell him that Easton is going to be in the stands as well! She insisted that the hospital let her out in time for the parade so she could meet you."

You are not going home, said Rufus firmly. He poked me with a claw. *You'll just have to stick it out. I want my person.*

My whole family was following along behind us. "We'll all be there, Natalie," said Mom. Emmy squinted at me like she was daring me to ruin Rufus's day. Even Dad looked like he wanted to stay. So much for being on my side.

"Fine," I told Rufus. "Whatever." At least I'd be getting rid of the root of all furry evil. But as soon as this parade was over? I was out of here, even if I had to take the train home by myself. Nothing good could come of this.

"Great, great," said Alan. "And here we go!" He stopped in front of a set of bleachers. It was filling up with people. As promised, the mayor was right in the center and Easton was sitting in front of him. And so was Victoria. She'd been cleaned up, but she still looked like something had run her over. Her hair had been clipped short all the way around to get rid of the spots where Regina had cut chunks away.

As soon as Rufus caught sight of Easton, he used me as a springboard and flung himself into the bleachers. He narrowly missed some guy's head, but then squirreled his way up the rest of the rows to throw himself in Easton's lap.

"Tiddlywinks!" she shrieked, making everyone who hadn't already freaked out jump. "My baby!" She gathered him up and gave him a huge hug and then started making kissy faces with him. Gross. Maybe I should tell her what he does with that mouth.

"You must be Natalie!" Easton called out to me after she finished kissing on Rufus. "Get up here, my little poppet!"

Everyone who'd been staring at her turned to stare at me. Then the whispering and pointing started. I thought about turning around and leaving, but Alan and my family were right behind me, so I kept climbing instead. I sat down between Easton and Victoria, where Easton was patting the bleachers. Well, now I knew how a fish in a fishbowl felt.

"Good to see you again," said Victoria. "Easton, meet my savior."

Savior? Sheesh. "Hey, Victoria," I said. "You look, um, better. I didn't expect to see you here. And hi, Easton. As you can tell, Ru—um, Tiddlywinks is glad to see you."

Rufus had mentioned before he didn't want to tell her about the name thing. He didn't want her to think he didn't like the name she'd given him. It was kind of sweet, for Rufus.

It felt really weird to be sitting there between two celebrities and down one row from the mayor and chatting like it was normal. Not to mention all the people staring at me. You'd think they'd be staring at Victoria instead. Or at Easton.

"The doctors didn't want to let me out but I made them," said Victoria. "I've been cooped up for two and a half years.

304

It's just so good to be outside. Besides, I wanted to say thank you again." She gave me a shoulder squeeze. I nodded, not really sure what to say.

Easton looked a little pale herself, but that could have been all the pink she had on. She even had on her trademark high heels, which I would never have attempted in bleachers. Or after being in the hospital. Actually, never at all. I was purely a Converse or combat boots kind of girl.

"There was no way I was going to miss this chance to meet you either. Tell me *everything*," said Easton. She put Rufus on her lap, grabbed my face in her hands, and kissed both of my cheeks. I had the distinct feeling that I was now covered in pink lipstick.

"I'm sure you've already heard pretty much everything," I said. "It was all in the paper." I looked out at the crowd, glad to have something to focus on besides my weird situation. The people around me had gone back to doing whatever they were doing, but I still felt like someone was watching me. Maybe Rufus did too. His hackles were up. Or maybe that was because Easton apparently liked to pet him the wrong way. Strangely enough, he didn't seem to mind.

"No," said Easton. "*Not that.*" She turned to Rufus. "Tiddlywinkums, tell Momma everything!"

Great. There went my rule about not translating any-more today.

THIRTY-FOUR

"IF YOU WANT TO KNOW THE CHaraCTer OF a MaN,
FIND OUT WHaT HIS CaT THINKS OF HIM."
—aNONYMOUS

Awhile later, I was saved from Rufus rehashing his early days (apparently, he had a lot to say on Easton's choice of men during those years) by the arrival of Ian. Victoria welcomed him with a hug and invited him to sit between us. I think she was as happy to see him as I was. We'd both had enough of Rufus and Easton.

There were really no limits to what Rufus wanted to tell Easton and no limits to what Easton wanted to know about. One thing I could say about her: she really, really loved her cat. It was kind of disturbing. Maybe that whole suicide scheme that Regina had dreamed up wasn't as far-fetched as I'd thought it was. The only fly in her day was that we hadn't brought Fergie with us too. Poor dog, she was still at home sleeping. Those little fluffy mutts didn't have much stamina.

"Hey, Ian," I said, wishing I'd given him a hug like Victoria had. But it would have been kind of weird with my family sitting on the next row up near the mayor. And I wasn't completely sure we were in the okay-to-hug stage. Honestly, I had no idea what stage we were in at all. Yesterday had been one heck of a first date. More like a first disaster.

"Hi, Nat." He smiled at me and then gave Rufus a pat.

"Oooohhh, cute," said Easton. "And who are you?" She looked like she wanted to eat him up. Geez, back off, cougar woman!

"This is Ian," I said. "My—" I sputtered to a stop. "My, um, friend." Frick on a stick. That was lame.

"Ian helped Nat and Oscar save me from Regina. They all go to the same high school," said Victoria. At least Victoria hadn't manhandled him when she hugged him. Easton was looking at him like she wanted to take a bite out of him.

"Yeah," said Ian. "Nat's my trig partner in crime." He leaned into me and bumped shoulders.

Trig partner? Was I back to that? Had I ever been beyond that?

Easton quizzed Ian while I sat there like an idiot trying to think of something to say. Trig partner? *Really?*

Then the parade finally got going. I hadn't been so excited to see a parade start since I was a kid, though it was more like relief. Had Ian been staring at Easton's cleavage? I couldn't tell for sure. But then, probably everyone was staring at her cleavage. Her shirt was cut practically to her belly button. At least she wasn't rocking one of those split-down-the-middle hospital gowns. I got the distinct feeling it

307

wouldn't bother her at all to have all her bits on display.

The first part of the parade was a bunch of official-looking people walking. I clapped along with everyone else in the stands. They had a big banner, but other than that, nothing interesting unless, I guess, you were German American. The next bit was better, with some floats and some people in funny German outfits dancing. I didn't see Melly or Ty or any of the other actors yet, though there was a camera stationed at the far right corner of the stands filming the whole thing.

Then I heard the unmistakable Wonder Woman theme song. That could only be Viv's phone. Who else on this planet would have that as their ringtone? I couldn't believe she'd forgotten to turn her phone to vibrate. I twisted around to glare at her. She looked embarrassed, but she still took the call. From the look on Mom's face, it was obvious Viv was going to be hearing about this faux pas later.

Viv went pale and pocketed her phone. She whispered something to Mom and Dad, then they all got up and started clambering down the bleachers, stopping to gather up Oscar's parents and Melly's dad (who hadn't even bothered to say hello to me earlier). Viv stopped at our row and stepped over a few people—and on one of them. She bent down and whispered in my ear, with her elbow in Ian's face.

"Regina's escaped. They think she's after you and probably Victoria too. There's a good chance she's heading this way or maybe even already here, since she knew the shooting schedule. We all need to go. *Right now.*"

"What? Escaped? How?" What good were the professionals if they let the bad guy escape?

"What's going on?" asked Victoria. She looked like she was on full alert.

Viv sighed. Quietly, so that Victoria could hear too, she said, "Regina's escaped custody. Based on the record of her initial testing in the system, we believed her power was restricted to mimicking only females. So she was being guarded by all male guards. But apparently her Talent isn't limited in the way we thought. She managed to knock out her guard during a shift change by touching him and then she basically walked out of the building using his ID. They believe she's headed this way. They found a day trader from the Chicago Mercantile Exchange passed out on the street, and a jogger as well, not too far from here. We don't currently know who she looks like for sure, but she's got a gun."

"Great," I said. Total frick on a stick.

"I'm sure everything will be fine. There are tons of agents out looking for her and the police have been notified as well. But my superiors think it would be best if I got all of you somewhere safe."

Fine my foot. I should have listened to that feeling of impending doom I'd passed off as paranoia. "And where would that be?" I asked. "She could be anyone, anywhere, anytime." I looked down at the street. Suddenly, everyone looked threatening. Even the women dressed in the old-fashioned German dresses that were dancing by in the parade. Was the one with the red hair staring at me with an evil glint in her eye?

"I'm sure they'll catch her," said Viv. "It's just a matter of time."

"Yeah, right," said Victoria. "I kept thinking someone would stop her and save me. If it hadn't been for Nat, I'd still be trapped. Or dead." She was glancing up and down the street frantically and all around us like Regina could pop out of anywhere—which was true.

Easton finally caught on completely to what we were talking about. "Ack!" She fumbled in her little pink clutch, nearly dropping Rufus. She pulled out a taser, which was practically too big to even fit in her tiny purse to begin with, and started waving it around. It was, of course, bright pink. With sparkles. Ian grabbed it before she could shock one of us or some random unsuspecting person in the bleachers below us.

"Let's go," said Viv. She grabbed my arm. "We can talk about all of this later when we're in a secure location, okay?"

Poodle farts. On a stick. I could only imagine one of two scenarios here: (a) they would try to catch Regina and fail miserably (because, seriously, how are they going to catch someone who can look like someone else and knows that they are looking for her?), and we would have to go into hiding or protective custody or whatever for the rest of our lives, or (b) they would try to catch her and fail miserably, and we would refuse to go into hiding and wake up one morning to

Regina standing over our beds with a waffle iron in her hand. Not that she even needed a weapon when she could touch you, steal your identity, and drain your life away.

Neither of those options sounded good to me at all. There was only one way to recapture Regina. There was only one person who could pick her out of a crowd no matter what she looked like.

Me. With the help of Rufus's nose.

THIRTY-FIVE

🐈

SATURDAY, SEPTEMBER 12, 2:32 P.M.

"WHEN TROUBLE STRIKES, YOU WANT A CAT AT YOUR BACK.
BARRING THAT, A HUMAN WILL DO."
—RUFUS BRUTUS THE THIRD

Viv was herding Easton and Victoria down the bleachers when she noticed I wasn't following behind her.

"Come on, Nat," she said, looking up at me in the bleachers. "Let's go." She looked at me intently, like she was afraid I was going to do exactly what I was planning to do. I'd have to be careful with what I said. If I lied, she'd know.

I looked her square in the eye. "I'll be right behind you." She paused a moment, then nodded and kept going.

"Hey, Easton," I said. "I'll take Ruf—Tiddlywinks for you." I held out my hands and put on an innocent face. "You ought to be careful in those heels, especially what with recovering from your ordeal and everything."

"Oh, you're too sweet," she said. She handed Rufus over to me. "I wouldn't trust Tiddlywinks to just anyone, you know."

"I'll take good care of him," I said. Rufus looked at me curiously, but I waved Easton on ahead of me. She followed

312

behind Viv. I stayed a few steps back and followed behind as well, like I'd said I would, but when I got to the bottom of the bleachers and they went left, I headed right instead and ducked behind a group of parade watchers. I found a big-bellied guy who was paying close attention to the parade (the current float had some pretty blonde girls dressed in some kind of native German folk costumes that had low, square-cut necklines) and made sure he was between me and Viv. If I was lucky, she wouldn't notice I was gone for a while.

So, what's up? I'm sure you didn't bring me down here to get a closer look at the parade.

"Nope," I said. "I need your help, Rufus. Do you remember what Regina smells like?"

Remember? Her stench is burned into my brain. Why? What are you thinking?

"We can get Regina if you help me. It's the only way. You know it and I know it."

"And I know it, too," said Ian.

I jumped about a foot in the air and almost elbowed the big guy in the gut. "What are you doing here?"

"I saw you give your sister the slip and figured you were up to something. Which you obviously are."

"Well, go back," I said. "It's too dangerous. She's got a gun and who knows what else she's picked up on the way here?"

"Exactly," he said. "You can't do this by yourself."

She won't be by herself, stupid. I'll be with her, said Rufus.

Maybe Ian was starting to pick up a little Cat. "*And* you need someone with you who's taller than knee height. I don't care if he does have claws. Besides, I've got this." He held up Easton's pink taser.

A little old woman with overly permed hair gave us a slightly terrified look. I put my hand on Ian's and brought it down. I took the taser from him and jammed it in my pocket.

"Thanks," I said. "I hadn't thought about a weapon. Do you know how to use it?"

"Not sure. I think you point and shoot it like a gun. I've only seen one on some reality TV show when they shocked some celebrities for fun."

Just leave it to me, said Rufus. *You'll probably hurt yourselves. I'll take care of her.*

"You know," said Ian, "we *could* enlist the help of one of the agents." He motioned back toward the bleachers where a sunglass-wearing, solidly built guy in a suit had appeared and was monitoring the crowd. He had BERM written all over him. Not literally, but it might as well have been. He couldn't be any more obvious unless he was wearing a T-shirt with the BERM logo on it.

"Are you kidding me? If Regina sees him with us, she'll know something's up for sure."

"True enough. But that's another reason why I'm perfect to help you out," said Ian. "Regina won't think it's suspicious at all if I'm with you."

Why? Because she's seen us together before? Because he's my age? Because . . . ?

"Okay," I said. "But whatever we do, we should hurry. Once Viv figures out we're gone, she'll be back and she'll probably have reinforcements."

Ian grabbed the hand that wasn't hanging on to Rufus and pulled me past the big guy. We slipped through the crowd along the parade route in the opposite direction Viv and everyone else had gone. I hoped he couldn't tell that my hand was all sweaty. And I hoped no one was paying any attention to the huge bulge in my right pocket. Easton's taser felt big enough to take out an elephant.

"If Regina's already here and paying attention, we'll just look like boyfriend and girlfriend getting away from the family," he whispered.

Oh. "Right. Very not suspicious." Except for the fact that, as love-struck teens, we apparently needed a cat chaperone. But maybe she wouldn't notice Rufus.

What was I thinking? Of course she'd notice Rufus. He was *pink*. I'd boosted him up and he was draped around my shoulders like some kind of living scarf now, but he was still bright pink.

"And we won't get separated this way." He squeezed my hand.

Was it just me, or was he justifying the hand holding a little too much?

"I noticed something yesterday," I said. "I think she can't

change when she's touching more than one person. Or being touched. Whatever. Like when all the guys grabbed her? She just stayed as Victoria and didn't try to turn."

"Interesting," he said.

Who cares? said Rufus. *Just use that stun gun thing on her and make her beg. Then let me at her when she's down.*

"Hey," said Ian. "Isn't that Melly and Oscar on that float?"

It was the float I'd seen Alan standing by earlier. Strangely enough for a German Day parade float, it had American flags on it. It paused in front of the stands, and the camera crew looked like they were on full alert. Oscar was dressed in some odd lederhosen kind of thing and a Peter Pan-style hat with a feather and everything. He was in the back of the float, along with a bunch of other similarly dressed people. But Melly was center stage, right next to Ty. Or rather, center float.

Ty grabbed a microphone and started lip-syncing to "Twist and Shout." He grabbed Melly around the waist and danced with her. She sang along with him, or at least mouthed the words. It was hard to tell. All of the other people on the float, including Oscar, were clapping and swaying. About halfway through the song, Alan made a motion with his hand and Melly jumped down from the float. Some of the movie crew helped Claire up and she took Melly's place. I guessed it must be part of the audition thing Melly had told me about. Maybe they were filming the audition and would decide between the two later? It wasn't like they could reschedule German Day for a filming delay, so they seemed to be making the best of it.

The crowd was singing and dancing along with the people on the float, pretty much just like I remembered from the *Ferris Bueller* movie, except not so choreographed. It was like a giant party.

I think I smell her, yowled Rufus over the noise, right into my ear.

I squeezed Ian's hand. He looked at me and I nodded and motioned with my chin toward Rufus. Ian raised an eyebrow, then nodded back.

"Where?" I asked Rufus. He had his claws firmly embedded in my shoulders. With the number of times I'd been clawed this week, I was probably going to be scarred for life.

I don't know yet, he growled. *There are a lot of people here, in case you hadn't noticed, and many of them smell decidedly unwashed. I'll let you know.*

I put my right hand in my pocket on the taser and scanned the crowd. Melly had moved off to the side and was holding her hands up and swaying with the music. She looked absolutely ecstatic. I saw Alan nudge one camera guy and point to her. The camera guy swiveled his camera away from the center of the float and pointed it at Melly. I bet Claire wouldn't like that.

Someone else didn't seem to like it either. A skinny girl with dishwater blonde hair was staring at Melly with this look on her face like she'd eaten something foul. There wasn't anything particularly ugly about her, but she just looked *mean*. Her mouth was curled in a familiar snarl. It *had* to be Regina. No matter what body she was in, she had the same evil look.

"Is that her?" I asked Rufus. "Can you tell?"

He took a look and sniffed the air. *I can't tell for sure. The smell is coming from that way, definitely, but there are a lot of smells coming from that way. And the horse that passed by earlier had some bad grain.*

"It has to be her," I said to Ian. "Who else would be looking at Melly like that?"

"Maybe she's just jealous?"

I groaned. What a guy thing to say. "Sorry," he said. "You're probably right. But are you sure enough about it to stun her with the taser before she does anything?"

Well, when he put it that way. I watched the girl for a few minutes. She hadn't made a move on Melly or anything. She was just glaring at her. It's not like it was a crime to glower at someone.

"Rufus?"

Still can't tell, he said. *You'll have to get me closer.*

"Closer," I said to Ian. He nodded and stepped forward to squeeze between two older women dancing to "Twist and Shout." I followed behind him as he pulled on my hand. I got an elbow in my ear from one overly enthusiastic dancer. Rufus swiped at her. Luckily she didn't notice.

"Keep it together, Rufus," I said.

You try picking out one person's smell in this mess, said Rufus. *And I'm going to have a headache for days. It's loud.*

"Sorry," I said.

We snaked between gyrating dancers and old people with walkers and some parade security people until we were about five feet away from Melly and the mystery girl. She still hadn't done anything, and Melly was still dancing and singing, oblivious to everything but the camera. Good thing the camera guy was positioned kind of behind and to the left of the mystery girl, or else she'd be ruining the shot with the sour expression on her face.

"Okay, Rufus," I whispered. "I think this is as close as we can get. What do you think?"

Before he could take a good sniff, the girl looked up and saw us. Her lip pulled back even further. She was practically baring her teeth at us. It had to be Regina. Who else would hate me on sight? Other than old people who just hate teenagers. She glanced at Melly, then back at me, and gave me the most wicked grin I've ever seen. She put her hand in her pocket and stepped toward Melly.

I fumbled getting the taser out of my pocket, but managed to point it at her. I dropped Ian's hand so I could put both hands on the taser to aim it. Rufus dug his claws into my shoulder, steadying himself.

"Gun!" yelled a woman next to me, and at first I thought she was talking about the taser. It was vaguely gun shaped, though I'd never seen a gun that was anywhere near so pink.

But it was Regina she was pointing at. She'd pulled a real gun out of her pocket. I couldn't tell who she was bringing it up to point at. Was she trying to shoot Melly? Me? Rufus?

People screamed and panicked, but with the crowd plus camera crew everywhere, there wasn't anywhere to go. Melly stopped dancing and looked around, confused. One guy shoved in between me and Regina, screaming his head off, leaving a hole in the crowd.

Shoot her! Rufus howled.

I pulled the trigger.

Nothing happened.

"It must have a safety!" Ian shouted at me, but there was no time to look for one. I had no idea what a safety looked like. I barely knew what a *trigger* looked like.

I took Rufus, still yowling, from around my neck and pitched him as hard as I could in the general direction of Regina. "I'm sorry, Rufus!" I shouted, and followed behind him. He landed on her forearm as the gun went off, but Regina stayed standing, barely. I couldn't tell where the bullet had gone, but no one dropped, so that was a good sign. People scattered in every direction, except for Melly, who froze where she was.

Ian had leaped at the same time I did, but I reached Regina first. I didn't see Rufus. Had she shot him? Oh, no. Maybe I should have thrown the stupid taser instead. What was I thinking? Well, I guess I'd been thinking "ticking furry time bomb with claws." It had worked once before, after all.

Then Rufus shrieked and I saw him climbing up the back of her leg. *The gun*, he yowled. *Get the gun!*

Regina raised the gun and pointed it at me. Before she could pull the trigger, I whacked her square across the face with the taser so hard that I heard it crack. The taser, that is. I wouldn't have minded if it were her face. She stumbled, but she didn't drop the gun. I threw the taser down and grabbed for her gun instead. I pushed so that it was pointed straight up in the air. We danced around like that as Ian tried to help and Rufus kept climbing until he was up to the back of her neck. He hauled himself over her shoulder and bit her right on the nose.

If she hadn't hated cats before, I was pretty sure she did now.

"I'm going to kill you and then your stupid cat," she yelled at me from behind the wall of wailing fur that was Rufus. She shook her head and his grip on her nose loosened, but he was still firmly attached with his claws to her shoulder. A crow bar couldn't pry him off this time.

"Not if I have anything to do about it," I said grimly, and kept working at wrestling the gun away from her.

Then she surprised me by just letting it go. I stumbled back, juggling the gun, and almost lost it. She grabbed Rufus by the neck and pulled him off, losing some skin and strips of her shirt in the process. She threw him on the ground and kicked him toward the sidewalk. People were still stampeding by, except for the camera guy, who seemed completely blasé about the whole thing and was still filming.

I didn't have time to see if Rufus was okay, though, because she grabbed my arm, and at first I thought she was going for the gun again. But then I felt that familiar pull. She was trying to drain me of energy! Or maybe she was just trying to change her look long enough to confuse things. Either way, I could feel my knees starting to buckle.

"Ian," I yelled, "Touch me! Or grab her! Or both!" I hoped he remembered what I'd said. I wasn't sure if it was better for him to be touching her or me. Or if it would work at all. Maybe she'd just been surprised by the guys at the ballpark and my bright idea was going to get us both killed.

Regina was kind of swinging me around, making it hard to stay on my feet and probably harder for Ian to grab us. He finally wrapped us both in a huge bear hug. The feeling I was being pulled apart from the inside out immediately stopped.

"Don't let go!" I yelled and dropped the gun to grab her myself.

That was when Oscar took a running leap from atop the float and landed on top of all of us.

THIrTY-SIX

🐈

"I'Ve HearD IT SaID THaT CaTS are DeVIOUS, eVIL, aND MeaN. WHY arGUe?
We aLSO HaVe MaNY OTHer GOOD QUaLITIeS."
—rUFUS BrUTUS THe THIrD

I kept insisting it was Oscar who had saved the day with
his flying leap, but that didn't stop everyone from wanting
to talk to me. Mom and Dad hadn't let me out of their sight
on Sunday as we made the rounds of the BERM offices
and the mayor's office, and we were even interviewed on
one of the local news channels. I really hadn't wanted to
do the interview, but so many reporters were hounding us
and surrounding our house that Dad finally agreed to one
interview to get them off our backs. Principal Johnson had
even given us a call after the interview had aired. He had
actually apologized for doubting me in the whole cafeteria
fiasco, not to mention the ancient-history dustup with my
biology teacher. Mom, of course, had grabbed the phone
from me and had given him a talking to about ever allowing
crazy movie people around the students of Shermer High
again.

She'd also given a piece of her mind to Viv, not to mention the BERM higher-ups, including Dad. The pants in the family had definitely gone back on Mom.

Regina was in BERM custody again under constant watch by no fewer than three agents at a time in a maximum-security facility. She was in a cell by herself with no body contact allowed. If she somehow managed to escape again, I didn't want to be the guy in charge. Mom was ready to seriously go medieval on the BERM if they let Regina break out again.

When I arrived at school on Monday, it was surreal. Oscar and Melly were waiting for me in our usual spot. But this time, it wasn't like we were an island of freakishness that everyone else just flowed around on their way into the building. It was more like we were the main stage at Lollapalooza.

There was a lot of "Hey, Cat Girl" going on, but also a bunch of "Tase her, dude!" and high fives for all of us. A couple of seniors tried to get Oscar to duplicate his flying tackle, but Garrett came along at exactly the right time and managed to talk him out of it. Finally, Principal Johnson himself came out and told us to get to class so that everyone would disperse. We went inside to one last round of applause.

"Well," I said. "I gotta go to trig. I guess I'll see you later?"

"Sure!" said Oscar. Melly gave me a hug and nodded, then they both left. Things were still a little weird among the three of us. We hadn't had a chance to really talk since I'd blown up at them in the makeup trailer. They'd been interviewed all over the place on Sunday too, but I'd seen them and their families only in passing in the BERM building.

Or since Alan had turned over the camera guy's tape of the parade to the local CBS station, as if the newspaper article and interview hadn't been bad enough. The clip was even on YouTube (and somehow, I kind of suspected Oscar might have put it up there himself). I was officially famous. We all were. It kind of made Oscar and Melly talking to the press on Friday a bit less important. I was still mad about it, but Emmy had summed it up. "The cat's out of the bag now," she'd said last night. "You might as well get used to it."

At least no one had meowed at me so far.

I pushed open the door to trigonometry and the room went silent. Then Shackerman from his spot in the back of the room called out, "Hey, Ian. Here's your girlfriend! *Meee-yoooow-ow!*"

I froze.

Ian stood up. "Hey, Shackerman, you just wish you *had* a girlfriend. Or that she was half as kick-ass as Nat."

"Yeah, watch out, Shack," said Sarah Yung from the front row. "Or maybe Cat Girl will scratch your eyes out." She laughed and then meowed at Shackerman. He hissed back and clawed in her direction like a cat.

I ran.

♥

The thing about school is, there's really nowhere to run to. The hallways were still pretty full of kids making their way to class, the classrooms were obviously full, and even the bathrooms were busy. Shoot, girls' bathrooms were pretty much always busy. That left the cafeteria or the library, and I really didn't want to set foot on the site of my last huge school humiliation, so I headed straight to the library.

It was empty, thankfully. Half the lights hadn't even been turned on yet. I sat down in one of the study cubicles in a dark corner and put my head down on my crossed arms. I had to admit that I'd had hope this morning that maybe it wouldn't be so bad. Then all the kids outside had been all "you go, girl" and slapping me on the back. But I should have known better. After all, this was high school. Let the nightmare and the meowing begin.

"Hey," said Ian.

I didn't lift my head. "How did you find me?" I said into my sleeve.

"I was right behind you. Didn't you hear me calling you?"

"No." Great. I bet that was a nice scene going down the hallway. Yet another thing to live down. "Sorry."

I heard the scrape of a chair as he pulled one over from the next cube and sat down. I could just make out the toe of his right shoe. He'd drawn a smiley face with X's for eyes on it.

"So, what're you doing?"

"Nothing," I said. Which was true. This was pretty much as nothing as it gets.

"This isn't the Nat I know," he said. "The Nat I know totally kicks butt. She takes out body-stealing kidnappers and

326

breaks into houses." He put his hand on my shoulder. It felt warm even though my shirt.

"I knew this was going to happen," I said. I felt like I was back in kindergarten with that kid getting everyone to meow at me and the teachers just standing by not doing anything.

"What?"

"The whole Cat Girl thing. The meowing." I hitched my shoulders up and let them fall again, but his hand stayed where it was. I was *not* going to cry. Not in front of Ian.

"Shackerman? Shackerman is a douche biscuit with a brain the size of a peanut. He's only scraping by in trig because he cheats like a madman."

"You know it won't be just Shackerman." And even if he was an idiot, he was a popular one. Parties at his house always wound up with half the school there and the cops being called. They were legendary. Last year, he'd been voted most likely to take over a small Caribbean island nation.

"Nat. Look at me." He squeezed my shoulder.

I squished my eyes shut tight for a second, then picked up my head and looked at Ian. He had his head cocked to the side like a curious puppy.

"Do you really care what people like Shackerman think of you? I mean, *Shackerman*? Does anyone even know what his first name is?"

I couldn't help it. I laughed. Then I hiccupped. So much for being cool. But cool really wasn't me. And I really and truly had no clue what Shackerman's first name was.

"That's better." He took his hand from my shoulder and put it under my chin instead. "Do you think Shackerman would have the balls to throw a cat at someone who'd pulled a gun?"

I laughed again. "He'd probably pee himself."

He smiled, then turned serious on me. "Nat, there will always be people out there who'll have something crappy to say. You know, not everyone appreciates my stellar sense of humor—or my style." He ran his free hand through his hair, giving it even more of an I-just-woke-up look. "I figure, why let someone else ruin my day? That's what I've got parents for."

"Does Shackerman by any chance have a cat?"

"I believe he does." He gave me a wicked grin. "Now *that* is the Nat I know and love." He went red as he realized what he'd said, and so did I.

I cleared my throat. "Well, I guess we'd better get back to class before Mr. Beck sends out a search squad." We both stood up, but neither of us took a step toward the door.

"You know, if we count Saturday, we've been on two dates now." Ian was still a little red.

"Both with a psycho killer," I said. "Sorry about that. Though I don't know that I'd count the parade as a date. More like a train wreck."

"Still . . ." He cupped my chin again. "*If* we count that and, you know, you grant me a little leeway with the definition of a date and we count *this* . . ."

"The library?" Did my voice actually squeak? And how

had I never noticed before that the library was actually kind of romantic, in a dusty kind of way? Or maybe it was that only half of the lights were on.

"Sure," he said. "Isn't there some kind of rule about third dates and kissing?"

I didn't know if there was one or not, but I nodded. I didn't think I could actually say anything coherent.

He lowered his head to mine until his lips were only an inch away. "So," he said, "what do you think? Is this a date?"

I could feel his breath tickling my lips. To heck with being timid. I reached up with both hands and pulled his face down that final inch. His lips were softer than I expected and he tasted like cinnamon and orange juice. My knees went a little liquid as his tongue just barely touched my lower lip.

"Wow," he whispered, pulling back. "Cat Girl can kiss."

EASTON WEST'S BLOG

Tuesday, September 15, 3:45 P.M.: Hellooooo poppets! Am I glad to be back! And the real me too! If you weren't following the news, I apologize for the purely uninspired and blatantly FALSE blog posts (which I've deleted now) you've found here . . . but it wasn't me! It was just someone who looked like me, not that all of you lovelies out there in cyberspace can see me as I sit here typing diligently away. (Or can you? I forget how my webcam works. . . .)

Yes, dear readers, I was a victim of Regina Fedorka, along with the lovely Victoria Welling (who isn't actually looking so lovely right now, but you can't blame her for that—she's been a kidnappee for over two YEARS).

And if it weren't for one plucky young lady named Natalie "Cat Girl" Ng and her intrepid band of friends, there's a very good chance I'd be a ghost right now! And not just me! My beloved Tiddlywinks too!

Besides saving my life (with the help of my Tiddlywinks, I might add—my brave furry boy!), Cat Girl has done the impossible!

I always knew that my furry baby was special. With Cat Girl's help, I've been able to really sit down and talk with him, and he's got a lot to say! So stay tuned. I might be having an extended stay here in Chicagoland so I can get to know Tiddlywinks even better.

And you, dear readers, will of course be the first to find out! ♥

author's note

Ferris Bueller's Day Off, written and directed by John Hughes, was released in 1986. Starring Matthew Broderick as Ferris, as well as Alan Ruck, Mia Sara, and Jennifer Grey, it has been called one of the best 100 films of all time by *Total Film* magazine and the number one teen film of all time by *Empire* magazine.

Hughes, who died in 2009, went to high school in Northbrook, Illinois, and he often returned to that locale in his films, though he either left the actual town name unreferenced or called it "Shermer." (Shermerville was the original name of Northbrook.) I don't think he would mind that I borrowed the name for Natalie's high school.

The movie was filmed in 1985 primarily in the Chicago area, including scenes at two local high schools (New Trier High School and Glenbrook North High School) and many of Chicago's most famous landmarks. Many students served as extras on the film and it has a huge following even today, so many years later.

Hughes once said, "Chicago is what I am. A lot of *Ferris* is sort of my love letter to the city."

While I lived in the Chicago area for only a few years, I enjoyed my time there and I really loved exploring Ferris

Bueller's Chicago, from Wrigley Field to Sears Tower (now Willis Tower, though it will always be Sears Tower to me). I suppose you could consider this book my love letter to Chicago, John Hughes, and to teens everywhere who don't realize how special they are.

acKNOWLeDGeMeNTS

Big thanks to the Ready Writers critique group in the northern suburbs of Chicago (Lorijo Metz, Shawn Wickersheim, Timnah Gretencord, Jeff Moore, Kellie Cozza, Allan Woodrow, Suzanne Slade, Kathy Bostrom, and Roger Peck). You guys are awesome and talented. Not to mention Saundra Mitchell, for her always sound advice.

Also, much thanks to all my nieces and nephews, since I borrowed so many of your names for this book. I hope you don't mind.

Much appreciation also to my editor, Stacy, for believing in *Cat Girl* and laughing at some of my stupidest cat jokes.

And I can't forget the tour guide at Wrigley, who answered all of my questions, even the really silly ones (once he figured out I wasn't an insane stalker casing the joint).

And, lastly, to all the cats I've had in my life: Thomas Sawyer, the sweetest; Sebastian, who always had a mind of his own and could beat up any dog; Momma Cat and all her kittens; Harley, with his silent meow and ability to insert himself into the exact middle of any bed; and Gracie, a true diva in every sense of the word.

TO KILL A
Mockingbird

To Kill a Mockingbird

Harper Lee

HARPER

An Imprint of HarperCollins*Publishers*

HarperCollins books may be purchased for educational, business, or sales promotional use. For information, please e-mail the Special Markets Department at SPsales@harpercollins.com.

Originally published in 1960 by J. B. Lippincott Company.

FIRST EDITION

Library of Congress Cataloging-in-Publication Data has been applied for.

ISBN: 978-0-06-242333-7

15   16   17   18   19   OFF/RRD   10   9   8   7   6   5   4   3   2   1

for Mr. Lee and Alice
in consideration of Love & Affection

Lawyers, I suppose, were children once.
—*Charles Lamb*

PART ONE

1

When he was nearly thirteen, my brother Jem got his arm badly broken at the elbow. When it healed, and Jem's fears of never being able to play football were assuaged, he was seldom self-conscious about his injury. His left arm was somewhat shorter than his right; when he stood or walked, the back of his hand was at right angles to his body, his thumb parallel to his thigh. He couldn't have cared less, so long as he could pass and punt.

When enough years had gone by to enable us to look back on them, we sometimes discussed the events leading to his accident. I maintain that the Ewells started it all, but Jem, who was four years my senior, said it started long before that. He said it began the summer Dill came to us, when Dill first gave us the idea of making Boo Radley come out.

I said if he wanted to take a broad view of the thing, it really began with Andrew Jackson. If General Jackson hadn't run the Creeks up the creek, Simon Finch would never have paddled up the Alabama, and where would we be if he hadn't? We were far too old to settle an argument with a fist-fight, so we consulted Atticus. Our father said we were both right.

Being Southerners, it was a source of shame to some members of the family that we had no recorded ancestors on either side of the Battle of Hastings. All we had was Simon Finch, a fur-trapping apothecary from Cornwall whose piety was exceeded only by his stinginess. In England, Simon was irritated by the persecution of those who called themselves Methodists at the hands of their more liberal brethren, and as

Simon called himself a Methodist, he worked his way across the Atlantic to Philadelphia, thence to Jamaica, thence to Mobile, and up the Saint Stephens. Mindful of John Wesley's strictures on the use of many words in buying and selling, Simon made a pile practicing medicine, but in this pursuit he was unhappy lest he be tempted into doing what he knew was not for the glory of God, as the putting on of gold and costly apparel. So Simon, having forgotten his teacher's dictum on the possession of human chattels, bought three slaves and with their aid established a homestead on the banks of the Alabama River some forty miles above Saint Stephens. He returned to Saint Stephens only once, to find a wife, and with her established a line that ran high to daughters. Simon lived to an impressive age and died rich.

It was customary for the men in the family to remain on Simon's homestead, Finch's Landing, and make their living from cotton. The place was self-sufficient: modest in comparison with the empires around it, the Landing nevertheless produced everything required to sustain life except ice, wheat flour, and articles of clothing, supplied by river-boats from Mobile.

Simon would have regarded with impotent fury the disturbance between the North and the South, as it left his descendants stripped of everything but their land, yet the tradition of living on the land remained unbroken until well into the twentieth century, when my father, Atticus Finch, went to Montgomery to read law, and his younger brother went to Boston to study medicine. Their sister Alexandra was the Finch who remained at the Landing: she married a taciturn man who spent most of his time lying in a hammock by the river wondering if his trot-lines were full.

When my father was admitted to the bar, he returned to Maycomb and began his practice. Maycomb, some twenty miles east of Finch's Landing, was the county seat of Maycomb County. Atticus's office in the courthouse contained little more than a hat rack, a spittoon, a checkerboard

4

and an unsullied Code of Alabama. His first two clients were the last two persons hanged in the Maycomb County jail. Atticus had urged them to accept the state's generosity in allowing them to plead Guilty to second-degree murder and escape with their lives, but they were Haverfords, in Maycomb County a name synonymous with jackass. The Haverfords had dispatched Maycomb's leading blacksmith in a misunderstanding arising from the alleged wrongful detention of a mare, were imprudent enough to do it in the presence of three witnesses, and insisted that the-son-of-a-bitch-had-it-coming-to-him was a good enough defense for anybody. They persisted in pleading Not Guilty to first-degree murder, so there was nothing much Atticus could do for his clients except be present at their departure, an occasion that was probably the beginning of my father's profound distaste for the practice of criminal law.

During his first five years in Maycomb, Atticus practiced economy more than anything; for several years thereafter he invested his earnings in his brother's education. John Hale Finch was ten years younger than my father, and chose to study medicine at a time when cotton was not worth growing; but after getting Uncle Jack started, Atticus derived a reasonable income from the law. He liked Maycomb, he was Maycomb County born and bred; he knew his people, they knew him, and because of Simon Finch's industry, Atticus was related by blood or marriage to nearly every family in the town.

Maycomb was an old town, but it was a tired old town when I first knew it. In rainy weather the streets turned to red slop; grass grew on the sidewalks, the courthouse sagged in the square. Somehow, it was hotter then: a black dog suffered on a summer's day; bony mules hitched to Hoover carts flicked flies in the sweltering shade of the live oaks on the square. Men's stiff collars wilted by nine in the morning. Ladies bathed before noon, after their three-o'clock naps, and by nightfall were like soft teacakes with frostings of sweat and sweet talcum.

People moved slowly then. They ambled across the square, shuffled in and out of the stores around it, took their time about everything. A day was twenty-four hours long but seemed longer. There was no hurry, for there was nowhere to go, nothing to buy and no money to buy it with, nothing to see outside the boundaries of Maycomb County. But it was a time of vague optimism for some of the people: Maycomb County had recently been told that it had nothing to fear but fear itself.

We lived on the main residential street in town—Atticus, Jem and I, plus Calpurnia our cook. Jem and I found our father satisfactory: he played with us, read to us, and treated us with courteous detachment.

Calpurnia was something else again. She was all angles and bones; she was nearsighted; she squinted; her hand was wide as a bed slat and twice as hard. She was always ordering me out of the kitchen, asking me why I couldn't behave as well as Jem when she knew he was older, and calling me home when I wasn't ready to come. Our battles were epic and one-sided. Calpurnia always won, mainly because Atticus always took her side. She had been with us ever since Jem was born, and I had felt her tyrannical presence as long as I could remember.

Our mother died when I was two, so I never felt her absence. She was a Graham from Montgomery; Atticus met her when he was first elected to the state legislature. He was middle-aged then, she was fifteen years his junior. Jem was the product of their first year of marriage; four years later I was born, and two years later our mother died from a sudden heart attack. They said it ran in her family. I did not miss her, but I think Jem did. He remembered her clearly, and sometimes in the middle of a game he would sigh at length, then go off and play by himself behind the car-house. When he was like that, I knew better than to bother him.

When I was almost six and Jem was nearly ten, our sum-

6

mertime boundaries (within calling distance of Calpurnia) were Mrs. Henry Lafayette Dubose's house two doors to the north of us, and the Radley Place three doors to the south. We were never tempted to break them. The Radley Place was inhabited by an unknown entity the mere description of whom was enough to make us behave for days on end; Mrs. Dubose was plain hell.

That was the summer Dill came to us.

Early one morning as we were beginning our day's play in the back yard, Jem and I heard something next door in Miss Rachel Haverford's collard patch. We went to the wire fence to see if there was a puppy—Miss Rachel's rat terrier was expecting—instead we found someone sitting looking at us. Sitting down, he wasn't much higher than the collards. We stared at him until he spoke:

"Hey."

"Hey yourself," said Jem pleasantly.

"I'm Charles Baker Harris," he said. "I can read."

"So what?" I said.

"I just thought you'd like to know I can read. You got anything needs readin' I can do it. . . ."

"How old are you," asked Jem, "four-and-a-half?"

"Goin' on seven."

"Shoot no wonder, then," said Jem, jerking his thumb at me. "Scout yonder's been readin' ever since she was born, and she ain't even started to school yet. You look right puny for goin' on seven."

"I'm little but I'm old," he said.

Jem brushed his hair back to get a better look. "Why don't you come over, Charles Baker Harris?" he said. "Lord, what a name."

"'s not any funnier'n yours. Aunt Rachel says your name's Jeremy Atticus Finch."

Jem scowled. "I'm big enough to fit mine," he said. "Your name's longer'n you are. Bet it's a foot longer."

"Folks call me Dill," said Dill, struggling under the fence.

"Do better if you go over it instead of under it," I said. "Where'd you come from?"

Dill was from Meridian, Mississippi, was spending the summer with his aunt, Miss Rachel, and would be spending every summer in Maycomb from now on. His family was from Maycomb County originally, his mother worked for a photographer in Meridian, had entered his picture in a Beautiful Child contest and won five dollars. She gave the money to Dill, who went to the picture show twenty times on it.

"Don't have any picture shows here, except Jesus ones in the courthouse sometimes," said Jem. "Ever see anything good?"

Dill had seen *Dracula*, a revelation that moved Jem to eye him with the beginning of respect. "Tell it to us," he said.

Dill was a curiosity. He wore blue linen shorts that buttoned to his shirt, his hair was snow white and stuck to his head like duck-fluff; he was a year my senior but I towered over him. As he told us the old tale his blue eyes would lighten and darken; his laugh was sudden and happy; he habitually pulled at a cowlick in the center of his forehead.

When Dill reduced Dracula to dust, and Jem said the show sounded better than the book, I asked Dill where his father was: "You ain't said anything about him."

"I haven't got one."

"Is he dead?"

"No . . ."

"Then if he's not dead you've got one, haven't you?"

Dill blushed and Jem told me to hush, a sure sign that Dill had been studied and found acceptable. Thereafter the summer passed in routine contentment. Routine contentment was: improving our treehouse that rested between giant twin chinaberry trees in the back yard, fussing, running through our list of dramas based on the works of Oliver Optic, Victor Appleton, and Edgar Rice Burroughs. In this matter we were lucky to have Dill. He played the character parts formerly thrust upon me—the ape in *Tarzan*, Mr. Crabtree in *The Rover Boys*, Mr.

Damon in *Tom Swift*. Thus we came to know Dill as a pocket Merlin, whose head teemed with eccentric plans, strange longings, and quaint fancies.

But by the end of August our repertoire was vapid from countless reproductions, and it was then that Dill gave us the idea of making Boo Radley come out.

The Radley Place fascinated Dill. In spite of our warnings and explanations it drew him as the moon draws water, but drew him no nearer than the light-pole on the corner, a safe distance from the Radley gate. There he would stand, his arm around the fat pole, staring and wondering.

The Radley Place jutted into a sharp curve beyond our house. Walking south, one faced its porch; the sidewalk turned and ran beside the lot. The house was low, was once white with a deep front porch and green shutters, but had long ago darkened to the color of the slate-gray yard around it. Rain-rotted shingles drooped over the eaves of the veranda; oak trees kept the sun away. The remains of a picket drunkenly guarded the front yard—a "swept" yard that was never swept—where johnson grass and rabbit-tobacco grew in abundance.

Inside the house lived a malevolent phantom. People said he existed, but Jem and I had never seen him. People said he went out at night when the moon was down, and peeped in windows. When people's azaleas froze in a cold snap, it was because he had breathed on them. Any stealthy small crimes committed in Maycomb were his work. Once the town was terrorized by a series of morbid nocturnal events: people's chickens and household pets were found mutilated; although the culprit was Crazy Addie, who eventually drowned himself in Barker's Eddy, people still looked at the Radley Place, unwilling to discard their initial suspicions. A Negro would not pass the Radley Place at night, he would cut across to the sidewalk opposite and whistle as he walked. The Maycomb school grounds adjoined the back of the Radley lot; from the Radley chickenyard tall pecan trees shook their fruit into the schoolyard, but the nuts lay untouched by the children: Radley pecans would kill you. A baseball hit into the Radley yard was a lost ball and no questions asked.

The misery of that house began many years before Jem and I were born. The Radleys, welcome anywhere in town, kept to themselves, a predilection unforgivable in Maycomb. They did not go to church, Maycomb's principal recreation, but worshiped at home; Mrs. Radley seldom if ever crossed the street for a mid-morning coffee break with her neighbors, and certainly never joined a missionary circle. Mr. Radley walked to town at eleven-thirty every morning and came back promptly at twelve, sometimes carrying a brown paper bag that the neighborhood assumed contained the family groceries. I never knew how old Mr. Radley made his living—Jem said he "bought cotton," a polite term for doing nothing—but Mr. Radley and his wife had lived there with their two sons as long as anybody could remember.

The shutters and doors of the Radley house were closed on Sundays, another thing alien to Maycomb's ways: closed doors meant illness and cold weather only. Of all days Sunday was the day for formal afternoon visiting: ladies wore corsets, men wore coats, children wore shoes. But to climb the Radley front steps and call, "He-y," of a Sunday afternoon was something their neighbors never did. The Radley house had no screen doors. I once asked Atticus if it ever had any; Atticus said yes, but before I was born.

According to neighborhood legend, when the younger Radley boy was in his teens he became acquainted with some of the Cunninghams from Old Sarum, an enormous and confusing tribe domiciled in the northern part of the county, and they formed the nearest thing to a gang ever seen in Maycomb. They did little, but enough to be discussed by the town and publicly warned from three pulpits: they hung around the barbershop; they rode the bus to Abbottsville on Sundays and went to the picture show; they attended dances at the county's riverside gambling hall, the Dew-Drop Inn &

Fishing Camp; they experimented with stumphole whiskey. Nobody in Maycomb had nerve enough to tell Mr. Radley that his boy was in with the wrong crowd.

One night, in an excessive spurt of high spirits, the boys backed around the square in a borrowed flivver, resisted arrest by Maycomb's ancient beadle, Mr. Conner, and locked him in the courthouse outhouse. The town decided something had to be done; Mr. Conner said he knew who each and every one of them was, and he was bound and determined they wouldn't get away with it, so the boys came before the probate judge on charges of disorderly conduct, disturbing the peace, assault and battery, and using abusive and profane language in the presence and hearing of a female. The judge asked Mr. Conner why he included the last charge; Mr. Conner said they cussed so loud he was sure every lady in Maycomb heard them. The judge decided to send the boys to the state industrial school, where boys were sometimes sent for no other reason than to provide them with food and decent shelter: it was no prison and it was no disgrace. Mr. Radley thought it was. If the judge released Arthur, Mr. Radley would see to it that Arthur gave no further trouble. Knowing that Mr. Radley's word was his bond, the judge was glad to do so.

The other boys attended the industrial school and received the best secondary education to be had in the state; one of them eventually worked his way through engineering school at Auburn. The doors of the Radley house were closed on weekdays as well as Sundays, and Mr. Radley's boy was not seen again for fifteen years.

But there came a day, barely within Jem's memory, when Boo Radley was heard from and was seen by several people, but not by Jem. He said Atticus never talked much about the Radleys: when Jem would question him Atticus's only answer was for him to mind his own business and let the Radleys mind theirs, they had a right to; but when it happened Jem said Atticus shook his head and said, "Mm, mm, mm."

So Jem received most of his information from Miss

Stephanie Crawford, a neighborhood scold, who said she knew the whole thing. According to Miss Stephanie, Boo was sitting in the livingroom cutting some items from *The Maycomb Tribune* to paste in his scrapbook. His father entered the room. As Mr. Radley passed by, Boo drove the scissors into his parent's leg, pulled them out, wiped them on his pants, and resumed his activities.

Mrs. Radley ran screaming into the street that Arthur was killing them all, but when the sheriff arrived he found Boo still sitting in the livingroom, cutting up the *Tribune*. He was thirty-three years old then.

Miss Stephanie said old Mr. Radley said no Radley was going to any asylum, when it was suggested that a season in Tuscaloosa might be helpful to Boo. Boo wasn't crazy, he was high-strung at times. It was all right to shut him up, Mr. Radley conceded, but insisted that Boo not be charged with anything: he was not a criminal. The sheriff hadn't the heart to put him in jail alongside Negroes, so Boo was locked in the courthouse basement.

Boo's transition from the basement to back home was nebulous in Jem's memory. Miss Stephanie Crawford said some of the town council told Mr. Radley that if he didn't take Boo back, Boo would die of mold from the damp. Besides, Boo could not live forever on the bounty of the county.

Nobody knew what form of intimidation Mr. Radley employed to keep Boo out of sight, but Jem figured that Mr. Radley kept him chained to the bed most of the time. Atticus said no, it wasn't that sort of thing, that there were other ways of making people into ghosts.

My memory came alive to see Mrs. Radley occasionally open the front door, walk to the edge of the porch, and pour water on her cannas. But every day Jem and I would see Mr. Radley walking to and from town. He was a thin leathery man with colorless eyes, so colorless they did not reflect light. His cheekbones were sharp and his mouth was wide, with a thin upper lip and a full lower lip. Miss Stephanie Crawford

12

said he was so upright he took the word of God as his only law, and we believed her, because Mr. Radley's posture was ramrod straight.

He never spoke to us. When he passed we would look at the ground and say, "Good morning, sir," and he would cough in reply. Mr. Radley's elder son lived in Pensacola; he came home at Christmas, and he was one of the few persons we ever saw enter or leave the place. From the day Mr. Radley took Arthur home, people said the house died.

But there came a day when Atticus told us he'd wear us out if we made any noise in the yard and commissioned Calpurnia to serve in his absence if she heard a sound out of us. Mr. Radley was dying.

He took his time about it. Wooden sawhorses blocked the road at each end of the Radley lot, straw was put down on the sidewalk, traffic was diverted to the back street. Dr. Reynolds parked his car in front of our house and walked to the Radleys' every time he called. Jem and I crept around the yard for days. At last the sawhorses were taken away, and we stood watching from the front porch when Mr. Radley made his final journey past our house.

"There goes the meanest man ever God blew breath into," murmured Calpurnia, and she spat meditatively into the yard. We looked at her in surprise, for Calpurnia rarely commented on the ways of white people.

The neighborhood thought when Mr. Radley went under Boo would come out, but it had another think coming: Boo's elder brother returned from Pensacola and took Mr. Radley's place. The only difference between him and his father was their ages. Jem said Mr. Nathan Radley "bought cotton," too. Mr. Nathan would speak to us, however, when we said good morning, and sometimes we saw him coming from town with a magazine in his hand.

The more we told Dill about the Radleys, the more he wanted to know, the longer he would stand hugging the light-pole on the corner, the more he would wonder.

"Wonder what he does in there," he would murmur. "Looks like he'd just stick his head out the door."

Jem said, "He goes out, all right, when it's pitch dark. Miss Stephanie Crawford said she woke up in the middle of the night one time and saw him looking straight through the window at her . . . said his head was like a skull lookin' at her. Ain't you ever waked up at night and heard him, Dill? He walks like this—" Jem slid his feet through the gravel. "Why do you think Miss Rachel locks up so tight at night? I've seen his tracks in our back yard many a mornin', and one night I heard him scratching on the back screen, but he was gone time Atticus got there."

"Wonder what he looks like?" said Dill.

Jem gave a reasonable description of Boo: Boo was about six-and-a-half feet tall, judging from his tracks; he dined on raw squirrels and any cats he could catch, that's why his hands were bloodstained—if you ate an animal raw, you could never wash the blood off. There was a long jagged scar that ran across his face; what teeth he had were yellow and rotten; his eyes popped, and he drooled most of the time.

"Let's try to make him come out," said Dill. "I'd like to see what he looks like."

Jem said if Dill wanted to get himself killed, all he had to do was go up and knock on the front door.

Our first raid came to pass only because Dill bet Jem *The Gray Ghost* against two Tom Swifts that Jem wouldn't get any farther than the Radley gate. In all his life, Jem had never declined a dare.

Jem thought about it for three days. I suppose he loved honor more than his head, for Dill wore him down easily: "You're scared," Dill said, the first day. "Ain't scared, just respectful," Jem said. The next day Dill said, "You're too scared even to put your big toe in the front yard." Jem said he reckoned he wasn't, he'd passed the Radley Place every school day of his life.

"Always runnin'," I said.

But Dill got him the third day, when he told Jem that folks

in Meridian certainly weren't as afraid as the folks in Maycomb, that he'd never seen such scary folks as the ones in Maycomb.

This was enough to make Jem march to the corner, where he stopped and leaned against the light-pole, watching the gate hanging crazily on its homemade hinge.

"I hope you've got it through your head that he'll kill us each and every one, Dill Harris," said Jem, when we joined him. "Don't blame me when he gouges your eyes out. You started it, remember."

"You're still scared," murmured Dill patiently.

Jem wanted Dill to know once and for all that he wasn't scared of anything: "It's just that I can't think of a way to make him come out without him gettin' us." Besides, Jem had his little sister to think of.

When he said that, I knew he was afraid. Jem had his little sister to think of the time I dared him to jump off the top of the house: "If I got killed, what'd become of you?" he asked. Then he jumped, landed unhurt, and his sense of responsibility left him until confronted by the Radley Place.

"You gonna run out on a dare?" asked Dill. "If you are, then—"

"Dill, you have to think about these things," Jem said. "Lemme think a minute . . . it's sort of like making a turtle come out . . ."

"How's that?" asked Dill.

"Strike a match under him."

I told Jem if he set fire to the Radley house I was going to tell Atticus on him.

Dill said striking a match under a turtle was hateful.

"Ain't hateful, just persuades him—'s not like you'd chunk him in the fire," Jem growled.

"How do you know a match don't hurt him?"

"Turtles can't feel, stupid," said Jem.

"Were you ever a turtle, huh?"

"My stars, Dill! Now lemme think . . . reckon we can rock him. . . ."

Jem stood in thought so long that Dill made a mild concession: "I won't say you ran out on a dare an' I'll swap you *The Grey Ghost* if you just go up and touch the house."

Jem brightened. "Touch the house, that all?"

Dill nodded.

"Sure that's all, now? I don't want you hollerin' something different the minute I get back."

"Yeah, that's all," said Dill. "He'll probably come out after you when he sees you in the yard, then Scout'n'me'll jump on him and hold him down till we can tell him we ain't gonna hurt him."

We left the corner, crossed the side street that ran in front of the Radley house, and stopped at the gate.

"Well go on," said Dill, "Scout and me's right behind you."

"I'm going," said Jem, "don't hurry me."

He walked to the corner of the lot, then back again, studying the simple terrain as if deciding how best to effect an entry, frowning and scratching his head.

Then I sneered at him.

Jem threw open the gate and sped to the side of the house, slapped it with his palm and ran back past us, not waiting to see if his foray was successful. Dill and I followed on his heels. Safely on our porch, panting and out of breath, we looked back.

The old house was the same, droopy and sick, but as we stared down the street we thought we saw an inside shutter move. Flick. A tiny, almost invisible movement, and the house was still.

2

Dill left us early in September, to return to Meridian. We saw him off on the five o'clock bus and I was miserable without him until it occurred to me that I would be starting to school in a week. I never looked forward more to anything in my life. Hours of wintertime had found me in the treehouse, looking over at the schoolyard, spying on multitudes of children through a two-power telescope Jem had given me, learning their games, following Jem's red jacket through wriggling circles of blind man's buff, secretly sharing their misfortunes and minor victories. I longed to join them.

Jem condescended to take me to school the first day, a job usually done by one's parents, but Atticus had said Jem would be delighted to show me where my room was. I think some money changed hands in this transaction, for as we trotted around the corner past the Radley Place I heard an unfamiliar jingle in Jem's pockets. When we slowed to a walk at the edge of the schoolyard, Jem was careful to explain that during school hours I was not to bother him, I was not to approach him with requests to enact a chapter of *Tarzan and the Ant Men*, to embarrass him with references to his private life, or tag along behind him at recess and noon. I was to stick with the first grade and he would stick with the fifth. In short, I was to leave him alone.

"You mean we can't play any more?" I asked.

"We'll do like we always do at home," he said, "but you'll see—school's different."

It certainly was. Before the first morning was over, Miss

Caroline Fisher, our teacher, hauled me up to the front of the room and patted the palm of my hand with a ruler, then made me stand in the corner until noon.

Miss Caroline was no more than twenty-one. She had bright auburn hair, pink cheeks, and wore crimson fingernail polish. She also wore high-heeled pumps and a red-and-white-striped dress. She looked and smelled like a peppermint drop. She boarded across the street one door down from us in Miss Maudie Atkinson's upstairs front room, and when Miss Maudie introduced us to her, Jem was in a haze for days.

Miss Caroline printed her name on the blackboard and said, "This says I am Miss Caroline Fisher. I am from North Alabama, from Winston County." The class murmured apprehensively, should she prove to harbor her share of the peculiarities indigenous to that region. (When Alabama seceded from the Union on January 11, 1861, Winston County seceded from Alabama, and every child in Maycomb County knew it.) North Alabama was full of Liquor Interests, Big Mules, steel companies, Republicans, professors, and other persons of no background.

Miss Caroline began the day by reading us a story about cats. The cats had long conversations with one another, they wore cunning little clothes and lived in a warm house beneath a kitchen stove. By the time Mrs. Cat called the drugstore for an order of chocolate malted mice the class was wriggling like a bucketful of catawba worms. Miss Caroline seemed unaware that the ragged, denim-shirted and floursack-skirted first grade, most of whom had chopped cotton and fed hogs from the time they were able to walk, were immune to imaginative literature. Miss Caroline came to the end of the story and said, "*Oh*, my, wasn't that nice?"

Then she went to the blackboard and printed the alphabet in enormous square capitals, turned to the class and asked, "Does anybody know what these are?"

Everybody did; most of the first grade had failed it last year.

I suppose she chose me because she knew my name; as I

read the alphabet a faint line appeared between her eyebrows, and after making me read most of *My First Reader* and the stock-market quotations from *The Mobile Register* aloud, she discovered that I was literate and looked at me with more than faint distaste. Miss Caroline told me to tell my father not to teach me any more, it would interfere with my reading.

"Teach me?" I said in surprise. "He hasn't taught me anything, Miss Caroline. Atticus ain't got time to teach me anything," I added, when Miss Caroline smiled and shook her head. "Why, he's so tired at night he just sits in the living-room and reads."

"If he didn't teach you, who did?" Miss Caroline asked good-naturedly. "Somebody did. You weren't born reading *The Mobile Register.*"

"Jem says I was. He read in a book where I was a Bullfinch instead of a Finch. Jem says my name's really Jean Louise Bullfinch, that I got swapped when I was born and I'm really a—"

Miss Caroline apparently thought I was lying. "Let's not let our imaginations run away with us, dear," she said. "Now you tell your father not to teach you any more. It's best to begin reading with a fresh mind. You tell him I'll take over from here and try to undo the damage—"

"Ma'am?"

"Your father does not know how to teach. You can have a seat now."

I mumbled that I was sorry and retired meditating upon my crime. I never deliberately learned to read, but somehow I had been wallowing illicitly in the daily papers. In the long hours of church—was it then I learned? I could not remember not being able to read hymns. Now that I was compelled to think about it, reading was something that just came to me, as learning to fasten the seat of my union suit without looking around, or achieving two bows from a snarl of shoelaces. I could not remember when the lines above Atticus's moving finger separated into words, but I had stared at them all the evenings in my memory, listening to the news of the day, Bills To Be Enacted into Laws, the diaries of Lorenzo Dow—anything Atticus happened to be reading when I crawled into his lap every night. Until I feared I would lose it, I never loved to read. One does not love breathing.

I knew I had annoyed Miss Caroline, so I let well enough alone and stared out the window until recess when Jem cut me from the covey of first-graders in the schoolyard. He asked how I was getting along. I told him.

"If I didn't have to stay I'd leave. Jem, that damn lady says Atticus's been teaching me to read and for him to stop it—"

"Don't worry, Scout," Jem comforted me. "Our teacher says Miss Caroline's introducing a new way of teaching. She learned about it in college. It'll be in all the grades soon. You don't have to learn much out of books that way—it's like if you wanta learn about cows, you go milk one, see?"

"Yeah Jem, but I don't wanta study cows, I—"

"Sure you do. You hafta know about cows, they're a big part of life in Maycomb County."

I contented myself with asking Jem if he'd lost his mind.

"I'm just trying to tell you the new way they're teachin' the first grade, stubborn. It's the Dewey Decimal System."

Having never questioned Jem's pronouncements, I saw no reason to begin now. The Dewey Decimal System consisted, in part, of Miss Caroline waving cards at us on which were printed "the," "cat," "rat," "man," and "you." No comment seemed to be expected of us, and the class received these impressionistic revelations in silence. I was bored, so I began a letter to Dill. Miss Caroline caught me writing and told me to tell my father to stop teaching me. "Besides," she said. "We don't write in the first grade, we print. You won't learn to write until you're in the third grade."

Calpurnia was to blame for this. It kept me from driving her crazy on rainy days, I guess. She would set me a writing task by scrawling the alphabet firmly across the top of a tablet, then copying out a chapter of the Bible beneath. If I reproduced her penmanship satisfactorily, she rewarded me with an open-faced sandwich of bread and butter and sugar. In Calpurnia's teaching, there was no sentimentality: I seldom pleased her and she seldom rewarded me.

"Everybody who goes home to lunch hold up your hands," said Miss Caroline, breaking into my new grudge against Calpurnia.

The town children did so, and she looked us over.

"Everybody who brings his lunch put it on top of his desk."

Molasses buckets appeared from nowhere, and the ceiling danced with metallic light. Miss Caroline walked up and down the rows peering and poking into lunch containers, nodding if the contents pleased her, frowning a little at others. She stopped at Walter Cunningham's desk. "Where's yours?" she asked.

Walter Cunningham's face told everybody in the first grade he had hookworms. His absence of shoes told us how he got them. People caught hookworms going barefooted in barnyards and hog wallows. If Walter had owned any shoes he would have worn them the first day of school and then discarded them until mid-winter. He did have on a clean shirt and neatly mended overalls.

"Did you forget your lunch this morning?" asked Miss Caroline.

Walter looked straight ahead. I saw a muscle jump in his skinny jaw.

"Did you forget it this morning?" asked Miss Caroline. Walter's jaw twitched again.

"Yeb'm," he finally mumbled.

Miss Caroline went to her desk and opened her purse. "Here's a quarter," she said to Walter. "Go and eat downtown today. You can pay me back tomorrow."

Walter shook his head. "Nome thank you ma'am," he drawled softly.

Impatience crept into Miss Caroline's voice: "Here Walter, come get it."

Walter shook his head again.

When Walter shook his head a third time someone whispered, "Go on and tell her, Scout."

I turned around and saw most of the town people and the entire bus delegation looking at me. Miss Caroline and I had conferred twice already, and they were looking at me in the innocent assurance that familiarity breeds understanding.

I rose graciously on Walter's behalf: "Ah—Miss Caroline?"

"What is it, Jean Louise?"

"Miss Caroline, he's a Cunningham."

I sat back down.

"What, Jean Louise?"

I thought I had made things sufficiently clear. It was clear enough to the rest of us: Walter Cunningham was sitting there lying his head off. He didn't forget his lunch, he didn't have any. He had none today nor would he have any tomorrow or the next day. He had probably never seen three quarters together at the same time in his life.

I tried again: "Walter's one of the Cunninghams, Miss Caroline."

"I beg your pardon, Jean Louise?"

"That's okay, ma'am, you'll get to know all the county folks after a while. The Cunninghams never took anything they can't pay back—no church baskets and no scrip stamps. They never took anything off of anybody, they get along on what they have. They don't have much, but they get along on it."

My special knowledge of the Cunningham tribe—one branch, that is—was gained from events of last winter. Walter's father was one of Atticus's clients. After a dreary conversation in our livingroom one night about his entailment, before Mr. Cunningham left he said, "Mr. Finch, I don't know when I'll ever be able to pay you."

"Let that be the least of your worries, Walter," Atticus said.

When I asked Jem what entailment was, and Jem described

it as a condition of having your tail in a crack, I asked Atticus if Mr. Cunningham would ever pay us.

"Not in money," Atticus said, "but before the year's out I'll have been paid. You watch."

We watched. One morning Jem and I found a load of stovewood in the back yard. Later, a sack of hickory nuts appeared on the back steps. With Christmas came a crate of smilax and holly. That spring when we found a croker-sack full of turnip greens, Atticus said Mr. Cunningham had more than paid him.

"Why does he pay you like that?" I asked.

"Because that's the only way he can pay me. He has no money."

"Are we poor, Atticus?"

Atticus nodded. "We are indeed."

Jem's nose wrinkled. "Are we as poor as the Cunninghams?"

"Not exactly. The Cunninghams are country folks, farmers, and the crash hit them hardest."

Atticus said professional people were poor because the farmers were poor. As Maycomb County was farm country, nickels and dimes were hard to come by for doctors and dentists and lawyers. Entailment was only a part of Mr. Cunningham's vexations. The acres not entailed were mortgaged to the hilt, and the little cash he made went to interest. If he held his mouth right, Mr. Cunningham could get a WPA job, but his land would go to ruin if he left it, and he was willing to go hungry to keep his land and vote as he pleased. Mr. Cunningham, said Atticus, came from a set breed of men.

As the Cunninghams had no money to pay a lawyer, they simply paid us with what they had. "Did you know," said Atticus, "that Dr. Reynolds works the same way? He charges some folks a bushel of potatoes for delivery of a baby. Miss Scout, if you give me your attention I'll tell you what entailment is. Jem's definitions are very nearly accurate sometimes."

If I could have explained these things to Miss Caroline, I

would have saved myself some inconvenience and Miss Caroline subsequent mortification, but it was beyond my ability to explain things as well as Atticus, so I said, "You're shamin' him, Miss Caroline. Walter hasn't got a quarter at home to bring you, and you can't use any stovewood."

Miss Caroline stood stock still, then grabbed me by the collar and hauled me back to her desk. "Jean Louise, I've had about enough of you this morning," she said. "You're starting off on the wrong foot in every way, my dear. Hold out your hand."

I thought she was going to spit in it, which was the only reason anybody in Maycomb held out his hand: it was a time-honored method of sealing oral contracts. Wondering what bargain we had made, I turned to the class for an answer, but the class looked back at me in puzzlement. Miss Caroline picked up her ruler, gave me half a dozen quick little pats, then told me to stand in the corner. A storm of laughter broke loose when it finally occurred to the class that Miss Caroline had whipped me.

When Miss Caroline threatened it with a similar fate the first grade exploded again, becoming cold sober only when the shadow of Miss Blount fell over them. Miss Blount, a native Maycombian as yet uninitiated in the mysteries of the Decimal System, appeared at the door hands on hips and announced: "If I hear another sound from this room I'll burn up everybody in it. Miss Caroline, the sixth grade cannot concentrate on the pyramids for all this racket!"

My sojourn in the corner was a short one. Saved by the bell, Miss Caroline watched the class file out for lunch. As I was the last to leave, I saw her sink down into her chair and bury her head in her arms. Had her conduct been more friendly toward me, I would have felt sorry for her. She was a pretty little thing.

24

3

Catching Walter Cunningham in the schoolyard gave me some pleasure, but when I was rubbing his nose in the dirt Jem came by and told me to stop. "You're bigger'n he is," he said.

"He's as old as you, nearly," I said. "He made me start off on the wrong foot."

"Let him go, Scout. Why?"

"He didn't have any lunch," I said, and explained my involvement in Walter's dietary affairs.

Walter had picked himself up and was standing quietly listening to Jem and me. His fists were half cocked, as if expecting an onslaught from both of us. I stomped at him to chase him away, but Jem put out his hand and stopped me. He examined Walter with an air of speculation. "Your daddy Mr. Walter Cunningham from Old Sarum?" he asked, and Walter nodded.

Walter looked as if he had been raised on fish food: his eyes, as blue as Dill Harris's, were red-rimmed and watery. There was no color in his face except at the tip of his nose, which was moistly pink. He fingered the straps of his overalls, nervously picking at the metal hooks.

Jem suddenly grinned at him. "Come on home to dinner with us, Walter," he said. "We'd be glad to have you."

Walter's face brightened, then darkened.

Jem said, "Our daddy's a friend of your daddy's. Scout here, she's crazy—she won't fight you any more."

"I wouldn't be too certain of that," I said. Jem's free dispensation of my pledge irked me, but precious noontime minutes were ticking away. "Yeah Walter, I won't jump on you again. Don't you like butterbeans? Our Cal's a real good cook."

Walter stood where he was, biting his lip. Jem and I gave up, and we were nearly to the Radley Place when Walter called, "Hey, I'm comin'!"

When Walter caught up with us, Jem made pleasant conversation with him. "A hain't lives there," he said cordially, pointing to the Radley house. "Ever hear about him, Walter?"

"Reckon I have," said Walter. "Almost died first year I come to school and et them pecans—folks say he pizened 'em and put 'em over on the school side of the fence."

Jem seemed to have little fear of Boo Radley now that Walter and I walked beside him. Indeed, Jem grew boastful: "I went all the way up to the house once," he said to Walter.

"Anybody who went up to the house once oughta not to still run every time he passes it," I said to the clouds above.

"And who's runnin', Miss Priss?"

"You are, when ain't anybody with you."

By the time we reached our front steps Walter had forgotten he was a Cunningham. Jem ran to the kitchen and asked Calpurnia to set an extra plate, we had company. Atticus greeted Walter and began a discussion about crops neither Jem nor I could follow.

"Reason I can't pass the first grade, Mr. Finch, is I've had to stay out ever' spring an' help Papa with the choppin', but there's another'n at the house now that's field size."

"Did you pay a bushel of potatoes for him?" I asked, but Atticus shook his head at me.

While Walter piled food on his plate, he and Atticus talked together like two men, to the wonderment of Jem and me. Atticus was expounding upon farm problems when Walter interrupted to ask if there was any molasses in the house. Atticus summoned Calpurnia, who returned bearing the syrup pitcher. She stood waiting for Walter to help himself. Walter poured syrup on his vegetables and meat with a generous hand. He would probably have poured it into his milk glass had I not asked what the sam hill he was doing.

The silver saucer clattered when he replaced the pitcher, and he quickly put his hands in his lap. Then he ducked his head.

Atticus shook his head at me again. "But he's gone and drowned his dinner in syrup," I protested. "He's poured it all over—"

It was then that Calpurnia requested my presence in the kitchen.

She was furious, and when she was furious Calpurnia's grammar became erratic. When in tranquility, her grammar was as good as anybody's in Maycomb. Atticus said Calpurnia had more education than most colored folks.

When she squinted down at me the tiny lines around her eyes deepened. "There's some folks who don't eat like us," she whispered fiercely, "but you ain't called on to contradict 'em at the table when they don't. That boy's yo' comp'ny and if he wants to eat up the table cloth you let him, you hear?"

"He ain't company, Cal, he's just a Cunningham—"

"Hush your mouth! Don't matter who they are, anybody sets foot in this house's yo' comp'ny, and don't you let me catch you remarkin' on their ways like you was so high and mighty! Yo' folks might be better'n the Cunninghams but it don't count for nothin' the way you're disgracin' 'em—if you can't act fit to eat at the table you can just set here and eat in the kitchen!"

Calpurnia sent me through the swinging door to the dining-room with a stinging smack. I retrieved my plate and finished dinner in the kitchen, thankful, though, that I was spared the humiliation of facing them again. I told Calpurnia to just wait, I'd fix her: one of these days when she wasn't looking I'd go off and drown myself in Barker's Eddy and then she'd be sorry. Besides, I added, she'd already gotten me in trouble once today: she had taught me to write and it was all her fault. "Hush you fussin'," she said.

Jem and Walter returned to school ahead of me: staying

behind to advise Atticus of Calpurnia's iniquities was worth a solitary sprint past the Radley Place. "She likes Jem better'n she likes me, anyway," I concluded, and suggested that Atticus lose no time in packing her off.

"Have you ever considered that Jem doesn't worry her half as much?" Atticus's voice was flinty. "I've no intention of getting rid of her, now or ever. We couldn't operate a single day without Cal, have you ever thought of that? You think about how much Cal does for you, and you mind her, you hear?"

I returned to school and hated Calpurnia steadily until a sudden shriek shattered my resentments. I looked up to see Miss Caroline standing in the middle of the room, sheer horror flooding her face. Apparently she had revived enough to persevere in her profession.

"It's alive!" she screamed.

The male population of the class rushed as one to her assistance. Lord, I thought, she's scared of a mouse. Little Chuck Little, whose patience with all living things was phenomenal, said, "Which way did he go, Miss Caroline? Tell us where he went, quick! D.C.—" he turned to a boy behind him—"D.C., shut the door and we'll catch him. Quick, ma'am, where'd he go?"

Miss Caroline pointed a shaking finger not at the floor nor at a desk, but to a hulking individual unknown to me. Little Chuck's face contracted and he said gently, "You mean him, ma'am? Yessum, he's alive. Did he scare you some way?"

Miss Caroline said desperately, "I was just walking by when it crawled out of his hair . . . just crawled out of his hair—"

Little Chuck grinned broadly. "There ain't no need to fear a cootie, ma'am. Ain't you ever seen one? Now don't you be afraid, you just go back to your desk and teach us some more."

Little Chuck Little was another member of the population who didn't know where his next meal was coming from, but he was a born gentleman. He put his hand under her elbow and led Miss Caroline to the front of the room. "Now don't you fret, ma'am," he said. "There ain't no need to fear a cootie. I'll just fetch you some cool water."

The cootie's host showed not the faintest interest in the furor he had wrought. He searched the scalp above his forehead, located his guest and pinched it between his thumb and forefinger.

Miss Caroline watched the process in horrid fascination. Little Chuck brought water in a paper cup, and she drank it gratefully. Finally she found her voice. "What is your name, son?" she asked softly.

The boy blinked. "Who, me?" Miss Caroline nodded.

"Burris Ewell."

Miss Caroline inspected her roll-book. "I have a Ewell here, but I don't have a first name . . . would you spell your first name for me?"

"Don't know how. They call me Burris't home."

"Well, Burris," said Miss Caroline, "I think we'd better excuse you for the rest of the afternoon. I want you to go home and wash your hair."

From her desk she produced a thick volume, leafed through its pages and read for a moment. "A good home remedy for— Burris, I want you to go home and wash your hair with lye soap. When you've done that, treat your scalp with kerosene."

"What fer, missus?"

"To get rid of the—er, cooties. You see, Burris, the other children might catch them, and you wouldn't want that, would you?"

The boy stood up. He was the filthiest human I had ever seen. His neck was dark gray, the backs of his hands were rusty, and his fingernails were black deep into the quick. He peered at Miss Caroline from a fist-sized clean space on his face. No one had noticed him, probably, because Miss Caroline and I had entertained the class most of the morning.

"And Burris," said Miss Caroline, "please bathe yourself before you come back tomorrow."

The boy laughed rudely. "You ain't sendin' me home, missus. I was on the verge of leavin'—I done done my time for this year."

Miss Caroline looked puzzled. "What do you mean by that?"

The boy did not answer. He gave a short contemptuous snort.

One of the elderly members of the class answered her: "He's one of the Ewells, ma'am," and I wondered if this explanation would be as unsuccessful as my attempt. But Miss Caroline seemed willing to listen. "Whole school's full of 'em. They come first day every year and then leave. The truant lady gets 'em here 'cause she threatens 'em with the sheriff, but she's give up tryin' to hold 'em. She reckons she's carried out the law just gettin' their names on the roll and runnin' 'em here the first day. You're supposed to mark 'em absent the rest of the year . . ."

"But what about their parents?" asked Miss Caroline, in genuine concern.

"Ain't got no mother," was the answer, "and their paw's right contentious."

Burris Ewell was flattered by the recital. "Been comin' to the first day o' the first grade fer three year now," he said expansively. "Reckon if I'm smart this year they'll promote me to the second. . . ."

Miss Caroline said, "Sit back down, please, Burris," and the moment she said it I knew she had made a serious mistake. The boy's condescension flashed to anger.

"You try and make me, missus."

Little Chuck Little got to his feet. "Let him go, ma'am," he said. "He's a mean one, a hard-down mean one. He's liable to start somethin', and there's some little folks here."

He was among the most diminutive of men, but when Burris Ewell turned toward him, Little Chuck's right hand went to his pocket. "Watch your step, Burris," he said. "I'd soon's kill you as look at you. Now go home."

Burris seemed to be afraid of a child half his height, and Miss Caroline took advantage of his indecision: "Burris, go home. If you don't I'll call the principal," she said. "I'll have to report this, anyway."

The boy snorted and slouched leisurely to the door.

Safely out of range, he turned and shouted: "Report and be damned to ye! Ain't no snot-nosed slut of a schoolteacher ever born c'n make me do nothin'! You ain't makin' me go nowhere, missus. You just remember that, you ain't makin' me go nowhere!"

He waited until he was sure she was crying, then he shuffled out of the building.

Soon we were clustered around her desk, trying in our various ways to comfort her. He was a real mean one . . . below the belt . . . you ain't called on to teach folks like that . . . them ain't Maycomb's ways, Miss Caroline, not really . . . now don't you fret, ma'am. Miss Caroline, why don't you read us a story? That cat thing was real fine this mornin'. . . .

Miss Caroline smiled, blew her nose, said, "Thank you, darlings," dispersed us, opened a book and mystified the first grade with a long narrative about a toadfrog that lived in a hall.

When I passed the Radley Place for the fourth time that day—twice at a full gallop—my gloom had deepened to match the house. If the remainder of the school year were as fraught with drama as the first day, perhaps it would be mildly entertaining, but the prospect of spending nine months refraining from reading and writing made me think of running away.

By late afternoon most of my traveling plans were complete; when Jem and I raced each other up the sidewalk to meet Atticus coming home from work, I didn't give him much of a race. It was our habit to run meet Atticus the moment we saw him round the post office corner in the distance. Atticus seemed to have forgotten my noontime fall from grace; he was full of questions about school. My replies were monosyllabic and he did not press me.

Perhaps Calpurnia sensed that my day had been a grim

one: she let me watch her fix supper. "Shut your eyes and open your mouth and I'll give you a surprise," she said.

It was not often that she made crackling bread, she said she never had time, but with both of us at school today had been an easy one for her. She knew I loved crackling bread.

"I missed you today," she said. "The house got so lonesome 'long about two o'clock I had to turn on the radio."

"Why? Jem'n me ain't ever in the house unless it's rainin'."

"I know," she said, "but one of you's always in callin' distance. I wonder how much of the day I spend just callin' after you. Well," she said, getting up from the kitchen chair, "it's enough time to make a pan of cracklin' bread, I reckon. You run along now and let me get supper on the table."

Calpurnia bent down and kissed me. I ran along, wondering what had come over her. She had wanted to make up with me, that was it. She had always been too hard on me, she had at last seen the error of her fractious ways, she was sorry and too stubborn to say so. I was weary from the day's crimes.

After supper, Atticus sat down with the paper and called, "Scout, ready to read?" The Lord sent me more than I could bear, and I went to the front porch. Atticus followed me.

"Something wrong, Scout?"

I told Atticus I didn't feel very well and didn't think I'd go to school any more if it was all right with him.

Atticus sat down in the swing and crossed his legs. His fingers wandered to his watchpocket; he said that was the only way he could think. He waited in amiable silence, and I sought to reinforce my position: "You never went to school and you do all right, so I'll just stay home too. You can teach me like Granddaddy taught you 'n' Uncle Jack."

"No I can't," said Atticus. "I have to make a living. Besides, they'd put me in jail if I kept you at home—dose of magnesia for you tonight and school tomorrow."

"I'm feeling all right, really."

"Thought so. Now what's the matter?"

Bit by bit, I told him the day's misfortunes. "—and she

said you taught me all wrong, so we can't ever read any more, ever. Please don't send me back, please sir."

Atticus stood up and walked to the end of the porch. When he completed his examination of the wisteria vine he strolled back to me.

"First of all," he said, "if you can learn a simple trick, Scout, you'll get along a lot better with all kinds of folks. You never really understand a person until you consider things from his point of view—"

"Sir?"

"—until you climb into his skin and walk around in it."

Atticus said I had learned many things today, and Miss Caroline had learned several things herself. She had learned not to hand something to a Cunningham, for one thing, but if Walter and I had put ourselves in her shoes we'd have seen it was an honest mistake on her part. We could not expect her to learn all Maycomb's ways in one day, and we could not hold her responsible when she knew no better.

"I'll be dogged," I said. "I didn't know no better than not to read to her, and she held me responsible—listen Atticus, I don't have to go to school!" I was bursting with a sudden thought. "Burris Ewell, remember? He just goes to school the first day. The truant lady reckons she's carried out the law when she gets his name on the roll—"

"You can't do that, Scout," Atticus said. "Sometimes it's better to bend the law a little in special cases. In your case, the law remains rigid. So to school you must go."

"I don't see why I have to when he doesn't."

"Then listen."

Atticus said the Ewells had been the disgrace of Maycomb for three generations. None of them had done an honest day's work in his recollection. He said that some Christmas, when he was getting rid of the tree, he would take me with him and show me where and how they lived. They were people, but they lived like animals. "They can go to school any time they want to, when they show the faintest symptom of wanting an education," said Atticus. "There are ways of keeping them in school by force, but it's silly to force people like the Ewells into a new environment—"

"If I didn't go to school tomorrow, you'd force me to."

"Let us leave it at this," said Atticus dryly. "You, Miss Scout Finch, are the common folk. You must obey the law." He said that the Ewells were members of an exclusive society made up of Ewells. In certain circumstances the common folk judiciously allowed them certain privileges by the simple method of becoming blind to some of the Ewells' activities. They didn't have to go to school, for one thing. Another thing, Mr. Bob Ewell, Burris's father, was permitted to hunt and trap out of season.

"Atticus, that's bad," I said. In Maycomb County, hunting out of season was a misdemeanor at law, a capital felony in the eyes of the populace.

"It's against the law, all right," said my father, "and it's certainly bad, but when a man spends his relief checks on green whiskey his children have a way of crying from hunger pains. I don't know of any landowner around here who begrudges those children any game their father can hit."

"Mr. Ewell shouldn't do that—"

"Of course he shouldn't, but he'll never change his ways. Are you going to take out your disapproval on his children?"

"No sir," I murmured, and made a final stand: "But if I keep on goin' to school, we can't ever read any more. . . ."

"That's really bothering you, isn't it?"

"Yes sir."

When Atticus looked down at me I saw the expression on his face that always made me expect something. "Do you know what a compromise is?" he asked.

"Bending the law?"

"No, an agreement reached by mutual concessions. It works this way," he said. "If you'll concede the necessity of going to school, we'll go on reading every night just as we always have. Is it a bargain?"

34

"Yes sir!"

"We'll consider it sealed without the usual formality," Atticus said, when he saw me preparing to spit.

As I opened the front screen door Atticus said, "By the way, Scout, you'd better not say anything at school about our agreement."

"Why not?"

"I'm afraid our activities would be received with considerable disapprobation by the more learned authorities."

Jem and I were accustomed to our father's last-will-and-testament diction, and we were at all times free to interrupt Atticus for a translation when it was beyond our understanding.

"Huh, sir?"

"I never went to school," he said, "but I have a feeling that if you tell Miss Caroline we read every night she'll get after me, and I wouldn't want her after *me*."

Atticus kept us in fits that evening, gravely reading columns of print about a man who sat on a flagpole for no discernible reason, which was reason enough for Jem to spend the following Saturday aloft in the treehouse. Jem sat from after breakfast until sunset and would have remained overnight had not Atticus severed his supply lines. I had spent most of the day climbing up and down, running errands for him, providing him with literature, nourishment and water, and was carrying him blankets for the night when Atticus said if I paid no attention to him, Jem would come down. Atticus was right.

4

The remainder of my schooldays were no more auspicious than the first. Indeed, they were an endless Project that slowly evolved into a Unit, in which miles of construction paper and wax crayon were expended by the State of Alabama in its well-meaning but fruitless efforts to teach me Group Dynamics. What Jem called the Dewey Decimal System was school-wide by the end of my first year, so I had no chance to compare it with other teaching techniques. I could only look around me: Atticus and my uncle, who went to school at home, knew everything—at least, what one didn't know the other did. Furthermore, I couldn't help noticing that my father had served for years in the state legislature, elected each time without opposition, innocent of the adjustments my teachers thought essential to the development of Good Citizenship. Jem, educated on a half-Decimal half-Duncecap basis, seemed to function effectively alone or in a group, but Jem was a poor example: no tutorial system devised by man could have stopped him from getting at books. As for me, I knew nothing except what I gathered from *Time* magazine and reading everything I could lay hands on at home, but as I inched sluggishly along the treadmill of the Maycomb County school system, I could not help receiving the impression that I was being cheated out of something. Out of what I knew not, yet I did not believe that twelve years of unrelieved boredom was exactly what the state had in mind for me.

As the year passed, released from school thirty minutes before Jem, who had to stay until three o'clock, I ran by the

Radley Place as fast as I could, not stopping until I reached the safety of our front porch. One afternoon as I raced by, something caught my eye and caught it in such a way that I took a deep breath, a long look around, and went back.

Two live oaks stood at the edge of the Radley lot; their roots reached out into the side-road and made it bumpy. Something about one of the trees attracted my attention.

Some tinfoil was sticking in a knot-hole just above my eye level, winking at me in the afternoon sun. I stood on tiptoe, hastily looked around once more, reached into the hole, and withdrew two pieces of chewing gum minus their outer wrappers.

My first impulse was to get it into my mouth as quickly as possible, but I remembered where I was. I ran home, and on our front porch I examined my loot. The gum looked fresh. I sniffed it and it smelled all right. I licked it and waited for a while. When I did not die I crammed it into my mouth: Wrigley's Double-Mint.

When Jem came home he asked me where I got such a wad. I told him I found it.

"Don't eat things you find, Scout."

"This wasn't on the ground, it was in a tree."

Jem growled.

"Well it was," I said. "It was sticking in that tree yonder, the one comin' from school."

"Spit it out right now!"

I spat it out. The tang was fading, anyway. "I've been chewin' it all afternoon and I ain't dead yet, not even sick."

Jem stamped his foot. "Don't you know you're not supposed to even touch the trees over there? You'll get killed if you do!"

"You touched the house once!"

"That was different! You go gargle—right now, you hear me?"

"Ain't neither, it'll take the taste outa my mouth."

"You don't 'n' I'll tell Calpurnia on you!"

Rather than risk a tangle with Calpurnia, I did as Jem told me. For some reason, my first year of school had wrought a great change in our relationship: Calpurnia's tyranny, unfairness, and meddling in my business had faded to gentle grumblings of general disapproval. On my part, I went to much trouble, sometimes, not to provoke her.

Summer was on the way; Jem and I awaited it with impatience. Summer was our best season: it was sleeping on the back screened porch in cots, or trying to sleep in the treehouse; summer was everything good to eat; it was a thousand colors in a parched landscape; but most of all, summer was Dill.

The authorities released us early the last day of school, and Jem and I walked home together. "Reckon old Dill'll be coming home tomorrow," I said.

"Probably day after," said Jem. "Mis'sippi turns 'em loose a day later."

As we came to the live oaks at the Radley Place I raised my finger to point for the hundredth time to the knot-hole where I had found the chewing gum, trying to make Jem believe I had found it there, and found myself pointing at another piece of tinfoil.

"I see it, Scout! I see it—"

Jem looked around, reached up, and gingerly pocketed a tiny shiny package. We ran home, and on the front porch we looked at a small box patchworked with bits of tinfoil collected from chewing-gum wrappers. It was the kind of box wedding rings came in, purple velvet with a minute catch. Jem flicked open the tiny catch. Inside were two scrubbed and polished pennies, one on top of the other. Jem examined them.

"Indian-heads," he said. "Nineteen-six and Scout, one of 'em's nineteen-hundred. These are real old."

"Nineteen-hundred," I echoed. "Say—"

"Hush a minute, I'm thinkin'."

"Jem, you reckon that's somebody's hidin' place?"

"Naw, don't anybody much but us pass by there, unless it's some grown person's—"

"Grown folks don't have hidin' places. You reckon we ought to keep 'em, Jem?"

"I don't know what we could do, Scout. Who'd we give 'em back to? I know for a fact don't anybody go by there—Cecil goes by the back street an' all the way around by town to get home."

Cecil Jacobs, who lived at the far end of our street next door to the post office, walked a total of one mile per school day to avoid the Radley Place and old Mrs. Henry Lafayette Dubose. Mrs. Dubose lived two doors up the street from us; neighborhood opinion was unanimous that Mrs. Dubose was the meanest old woman who ever lived. Jem wouldn't go by her place without Atticus beside him.

"What you reckon we oughta do, Jem?"

Finders were keepers unless title was proven. Plucking an occasional camellia, getting a squirt of hot milk from Miss Maudie Atkinson's cow on a summer day, helping ourselves to someone's scuppernongs was part of our ethical culture, but money was different.

"Tell you what," said Jem. "We'll keep 'em till school starts, then go around and ask everybody if they're theirs. They're some bus child's, maybe—he was too taken up with gettin' outa school today an' forgot 'em. These are somebody's, I know that. See how they've been slicked up? They've been saved."

"Yeah, but why should somebody wanta put away chewing gum like that? You know it doesn't last."

"I don't know, Scout. But these are important to some-body. . . ."

"How's that, Jem . . . ?"

"Well, Indian-heads—well, they come from the Indians. They're real strong magic, they make you have good luck. Not like fried chicken when you're not lookin' for it, but things like long life 'n' good health, 'n' passin' six-weeks tests . . . these are real valuable to somebody. I'm gonna put 'em in my trunk."

Before Jem went to his room, he looked for a long time at the Radley Place. He seemed to be thinking again.

Two days later Dill arrived in a blaze of glory: he had ridden the train by himself from Meridian to Maycomb Junction (a courtesy title—Maycomb Junction was in Abbott County) where he had been met by Miss Rachel in Maycomb's one taxi; he had eaten dinner in the diner, he had seen two twins hitched together get off the train in Bay St. Louis and stuck to his story regardless of threats. He had discarded the abominable blue shorts that were buttoned to his shirts and wore real short pants with a belt; he was somewhat heavier, no taller, and said he had seen his father. Dill's father was taller than ours, he had a black beard (pointed), and he was president of the L & N Railroad.

"I helped the engineer for a while," said Dill, yawning.

"In a pig's ear you did, Dill. Hush," said Jem. "What'll we play today?"

"Tom and Sam and Dick," said Dill. "Let's go in the front yard." Dill wanted the Rover Boys because there were three respectable parts. He was clearly tired of being our character man.

"I'm tired of those," I said. I was tired of playing Tom Rover, who suddenly lost his memory in the middle of the picture show and was out of the script until the end, when he was found in Alaska.

"Make us up one, Jem," I said.

"I'm tired of makin' 'em up."

Our first days of freedom, and we were tired. I wondered what the summer would bring.

We had strolled to the front yard, where Dill stood looking down the street at the dreary face of the Radley Place. "I—smell—death," he said. "I do, I mean it," he said, when I told him to shut up.

"You mean when somebody's dyin' you can smell it?"

"No, I mean I can smell somebody an' tell if they're gonna die. An old lady taught me how." Dill leaned over and sniffed me. "Jean—Louise—Finch, you are going to die in three days."

"Dill if you don't hush I'll knock you bowlegged. I mean it, now—"

"Yawl hush," growled Jem, "you act like you believe in Hot Steams."

"You act like you don't," I said.

"What's a Hot Steam?" asked Dill.

"Haven't you ever walked along a lonesome road at night and passed by a hot place?" Jem asked Dill. "A Hot Steam's somebody who can't get to heaven, just wallows around on lonesome roads an' if you walk through him, when you die you'll be one too, an' you'll go around at night suckin' people's breath—"

"How can you keep from passing through one?"

"You can't," said Jem. "Sometimes they stretch all the way across the road, but if you hafta go through one you say, 'Angel-bright, life-in-death; get off the road, don't suck my breath.' That keeps 'em from wrapping around you—"

"Don't you believe a word he says, Dill," I said. "Calpurnia says that's nigger-talk."

Jem scowled darkly at me, but said, "Well, are we gonna play anything or not?"

"Let's roll in the tire," I suggested.

Jem sighed. "You know I'm too big."

"You c'n push."

I ran to the back yard and pulled an old car tire from under the house. I slapped it up to the front yard. "I'm first," I said.

Dill said he ought to be first, he just got here.

Jem arbitrated, awarded me first push with an extra time for Dill, and I folded myself inside the tire.

Until it happened I did not realize that Jem was offended by my contradicting him on Hot Steams, and that he was patiently awaiting an opportunity to reward me. He did, by pushing the tire down the sidewalk with all the force in his body. Ground, sky and houses melted into a mad palette, my ears throbbed, I was suffocating. I could not put out my hands to stop, they were wedged between my chest and knees. I could only hope that Jem would outrun the tire and me, or that I would be stopped by a bump in the sidewalk. I heard him behind me, chasing and shouting.

The tire bumped on gravel, skeetered across the road, crashed into a barrier and popped me like a cork onto pavement. Dizzy and nauseated, I lay on the cement and shook my head still, pounded my ears to silence, and heard Jem's voice: "Scout, get away from there, come on!"

I raised my head and stared at the Radley Place steps in front of me. I froze.

"Come on, Scout, don't just lie there!" Jem was screaming. "Get up, can'tcha?"

I got to my feet, trembling as I thawed.

"Get the tire!" Jem hollered. "Bring it with you! Ain't you got any sense at all?"

When I was able to navigate, I ran back to them as fast as my shaking knees would carry me.

"Why didn't you bring it?" Jem yelled.

"Why don't *you* get it?" I screamed.

Jem was silent.

"Go on, it ain't far inside the gate. Why, you even touched the house once, remember?"

Jem looked at me furiously, could not decline, ran down the sidewalk, treaded water at the gate, then dashed in and retrieved the tire.

"See there?" Jem was scowling triumphantly. "Nothin' to it. I swear, Scout, sometimes you act so much like a girl it's mortifyin'."

There was more to it than he knew, but I decided not to tell him.

Calpurnia appeared in the front door and yelled, "Lemonade time! You all get in outa that hot sun 'fore you fry alive!" Lemonade in the middle of the morning was a summertime ritual. Calpurnia set a pitcher and three glasses on the porch, then went about her business. Being out of Jem's good graces did not worry me especially. Lemonade would restore his good humor.

Jem gulped down his second glassful and slapped his chest. "I know what we are going to play," he announced. "Something new, something different."

"What?" asked Dill.

"Boo Radley."

Jem's head at times was transparent: he had thought that up to make me understand he wasn't afraid of Radleys in any shape or form, to contrast his own fearless heroism with my cowardice.

"Boo Radley? How?" asked Dill.

Jem said, "Scout, you can be Mrs. Radley—"

"I declare if I will. I don't think—"

"'Smatter?" said Dill. "Still scared?"

"He can get out at night when we're all asleep. . . ." I said.

Jem hissed. "Scout, how's he gonna know what we're doin'? Besides, I don't think he's still there. He died years ago and they stuffed him up the chimney."

Dill said, "Jem, you and me can play and Scout can watch if she's scared."

I was fairly sure Boo Radley was inside that house, but I couldn't prove it, and felt it best to keep my mouth shut or I would be accused of believing in Hot Steams, phenomena I was immune to in the daytime.

Jem parceled out our roles: I was Mrs. Radley, and all I had to do was come out and sweep the porch. Dill was old Mr. Radley: he walked up and down the sidewalk and coughed when Jem spoke to him. Jem, naturally, was Boo: he went under the front steps and shrieked and howled from time to time.

As the summer progressed, so did our game. We polished and perfected it, added dialogue and plot until we had manufactured a small play upon which we rang changes every day.

Dill was a villain's villain: he could get into any character part assigned him, and appear tall if height was part of the devilry required. He was as good as his worst performance; his worst performance was Gothic. I reluctantly played assorted ladies who entered the script. I never thought it as much fun as Tarzan, and I played that summer with more than vague anxiety despite Jem's assurances that Boo Radley was dead and nothing would get me, with him and Calpurnia there in the daytime and Atticus home at night.

Jem was a born hero.

It was a melancholy little drama, woven from bits and scraps of gossip and neighborhood legend: Mrs. Radley had been beautiful until she married Mr. Radley and lost all her money. She also lost most of her teeth, her hair, and her right forefinger (Dill's contribution. Boo bit it off one night when he couldn't find any cats and squirrels to eat.); she sat in the livingroom and cried most of the time, while Boo slowly whittled away all the furniture in the house.

The three of us were the boys who got into trouble; I was the probate judge, for a change; Dill led Jem away and crammed him beneath the steps, poking him with the brush-broom. Jem would reappear as needed in the shapes of the sheriff, assorted townsfolk, and Miss Stephanie Crawford, who had more to say about the Radleys than anybody in Maycomb.

When it was time to play Boo's big scene, Jem would sneak into the house, steal the scissors from the sewing-machine drawer when Calpurnia's back was turned, then sit in the swing and cut up newspapers. Dill would walk by, cough at Jem, and Jem would fake a plunge into Dill's thigh. From where I stood it looked real.

When Mr. Nathan Radley passed us on his daily trip to town, we would stand still and silent until he was out of sight, then wonder what he would do to us if he suspected. Our activities halted when any of the neighbors appeared, and once I saw Miss Maudie Atkinson staring across the street at us, her hedge clippers poised in midair.

One day we were so busily playing Chapter XXV, Book II of One Man's Family, we did not see Atticus standing on the sidewalk looking at us, slapping a rolled magazine against his knee. The sun said twelve noon.

"What are you all playing?" he asked.

"Nothing," said Jem.

Jem's evasion told me our game was a secret, so I kept quiet.

"What are you doing with those scissors, then? Why are you tearing up that newspaper? If it's today's I'll tan you."

"Nothing."

"Nothing what?" said Atticus.

"Nothing, sir."

"Give me those scissors," Atticus said. "They're no things to play with. Does this by any chance have anything to do with the Radleys?"

"No sir," said Jem, reddening.

"I hope it doesn't," he said shortly, and went inside the house.

"Je-m . . ."

"Shut up! He's gone in the livingroom, he can hear us in there."

Safely in the yard, Dill asked Jem if we could play any more.

"I don't know. Atticus didn't say we couldn't—"

"Jem," I said, "I think Atticus knows it anyway."

"No he don't. If he did he'd say he did."

I was not so sure, but Jem told me I was being a girl, that girls always imagined things, that's why other people hated them so, and if I started behaving like one I could just go off and find some to play with.

"All right, you just keep it up then," I said. "You'll find out."

Atticus's arrival was the second reason I wanted to quit the game. The first reason happened the day I rolled into the Radley front yard. Through all the head-shaking, quelling of nausea and Jem-yelling, I had heard another sound, so low I could not have heard it from the sidewalk. Someone inside the house was laughing.

5

My nagging got the better of Jem eventually, as I knew it would, and to my relief we slowed down the game for a while. He still maintained, however, that Atticus hadn't said we couldn't, therefore we could; and if Atticus ever said we couldn't, Jem had thought of a way around it: he would simply change the names of the characters and then we couldn't be accused of playing anything.

Dill was in hearty agreement with this plan of action. Dill was becoming something of a trial anyway, following Jem about. He had asked me earlier in the summer to marry him, then he promptly forgot about it. He staked me out, marked as his property, said I was the only girl he would ever love, then he neglected me. I beat him up twice but it did no good, he only grew closer to Jem. They spent days together in the treehouse plotting and planning, calling me only when they needed a third party. But I kept aloof from their more foolhardy schemes for a while, and on pain of being called a g-irl, I spent most of the remaining twilights that summer sitting with Miss Maudie Atkinson on her front porch.

Jem and I had always enjoyed the free run of Miss Maudie's yard if we kept out of her azaleas, but our contact with her was not clearly defined. Until Jem and Dill excluded me from their plans, she was only another lady in the neighborhood, but a relatively benign presence.

Our tacit treaty with Miss Maudie was that we could play on her lawn, eat her scuppernongs if we didn't jump on the arbor, and explore her vast back lot, terms so generous we seldom spoke to her, so careful were we to preserve the delicate balance of our relationship, but Jem and Dill drove me closer to her with their behavior.

Miss Maudie hated her house: time spent indoors was time wasted. She was a widow, a chameleon lady who worked in her flower beds in an old straw hat and men's coveralls, but after her five o'clock bath she would appear on the porch and reign over the street in magisterial beauty.

She loved everything that grew in God's earth, even the weeds. With one exception. If she found a blade of nut-grass in her yard it was like the Second Battle of the Marne: she swooped down upon it with a tin tub and subjected it to blasts from beneath with a poisonous substance she said was so powerful it'd kill us all if we didn't stand out of the way.

"Why can't you just pull it up?" I asked, after witnessing a prolonged campaign against a blade not three inches high.

"Pull it up, child, pull it up?" She picked up the limp sprout and squeezed her thumb up its tiny stalk. Microscopic grains oozed out. "Why, one sprig of nut-grass can ruin a whole yard. Look here. When it comes fall this dries up and the wind blows it all over Maycomb County!" Miss Maudie's face likened such an occurrence unto an Old Testament pestilence.

Her speech was crisp for a Maycomb County inhabitant. She called us by all our names, and when she grinned she revealed two minute gold prongs clipped to her eye-teeth. When I admired them and hoped I would have some eventually, she said, "Look here." With a click of her tongue she thrust out her bridgework, a gesture of cordiality that cemented our friendship.

Miss Maudie's benevolence extended to Jem and Dill, whenever they paused in their pursuits: we reaped the benefits of a talent Miss Maudie had hitherto kept hidden from us. She made the best cakes in the neighborhood. When she was admitted into our confidence, every time she baked she made a big cake and three little ones, and she would call across the street: "Jem Finch, Scout Finch, Charles Baker Harris, come here!" Our promptness was always rewarded.

In summertime, twilights are long and peaceful. Often as not, Miss Maudie and I would sit silently on her porch, watching the sky go from yellow to pink as the sun went down, watching flights of martins sweep low over the neighborhood and disappear behind the schoolhouse rooftops.

"Miss Maudie," I said one evening, "do you think Boo Radley's still alive?"

"His name's Arthur and he's alive," she said. She was rocking slowly in her big oak chair. "Do you smell my mimosa? It's like angels' breath this evening."

"Yessum. How do you know?"

"Know what, child?"

"That B—Mr. Arthur's still alive?"

"What a morbid question. But I suppose it's a morbid subject. I know he's alive, Jean Louise, because I haven't seen him carried out yet."

"Maybe he died and they stuffed him up the chimney."

"Where did you get such a notion?"

"That's what Jem said he thought they did."

"S-ss-ss. He gets more like Jack Finch every day."

Miss Maudie had known Uncle Jack Finch, Atticus's brother, since they were children. Nearly the same age, they had grown up together at Finch's Landing. Miss Maudie was the daughter of a neighboring landowner, Dr. Frank Buford. Dr. Buford's profession was medicine and his obsession was anything that grew in the ground, so he stayed poor. Uncle Jack Finch confined his passion for digging to his window boxes in Nashville and stayed rich. We saw Uncle Jack every Christmas, and every Christmas he yelled across the street for Miss Maudie to come marry him. Miss Maudie would yell back, "Call a little louder, Jack Finch, and they'll hear you at the post office, I haven't heard you yet!" Jem and I thought this a strange way to ask for a lady's hand in marriage, but then Uncle Jack was rather strange. He said he was trying to

48

get Miss Maudie's goat, that he had been trying unsuccessfully for forty years, that he was the last person in the world Miss Maudie would think about marrying but the first person she thought about teasing, and the best defense to her was spirited offense, all of which we understood clearly.

"Arthur Radley just stays in the house, that's all," said Miss Maudie. "Wouldn't you stay in the house if you didn't want to come out?"

"Yessum, but I'd wanta come out. Why doesn't he?"

Miss Maudie's eyes narrowed. "You know that story as well as I do."

"I never heard why, though. Nobody ever told me why."

Miss Maudie settled her bridgework. "You know old Mr. Radley was a foot-washing Baptist—"

"That's what you are, ain't it?"

"My shell's not that hard, child. I'm just a Baptist."

"Don't you all believe in foot-washing?"

"We do. At home in the bathtub."

"But we can't have communion with you all—"

Apparently deciding that it was easier to define primitive baptistry than closed communion, Miss Maudie said: "Foot-washers believe anything that's pleasure is a sin. Did you know some of 'em came out of the woods one Saturday and passed by this place and told me me and my flowers were going to hell?"

"Your flowers, too?"

"Yes ma'am. They'd burn right with me. They thought I spent too much time in God's outdoors and not enough time inside the house reading the Bible."

My confidence in pulpit Gospel lessened at the vision of Miss Maudie stewing forever in various Protestant hells. True enough, she had an acid tongue in her head, and she did not go about the neighborhood doing good, as did Miss Stephanie Crawford. But while no one with a grain of sense trusted Miss Stephanie, Jem and I had considerable faith in Miss Maudie. She had never told on us, had never played cat-and-mouse with us, she was not at all interested in our private lives. She was our friend. How so reasonable a creature could live in peril of everlasting torment was incomprehensible.

"That ain't right, Miss Maudie. You're the best lady I know."

Miss Maudie grinned. "Thank you ma'am. Thing is, foot-washers think women are a sin by definition. They take the Bible literally, you know."

"Is that why Mr. Arthur stays in the house, to keep away from women?"

"I've no idea."

"It doesn't make sense to me. Looks like if Mr. Arthur was hankerin' after heaven he'd come out on the porch at least. Atticus says God's loving folks like you love yourself—"

Miss Maudie stopped rocking, and her voice hardened. "You are too young to understand it," she said, "but some-times the Bible in the hand of one man is worse than a whiskey bottle in the hand of—oh, of your father."

I was shocked. "Atticus doesn't drink whiskey," I said. "He never drunk a drop in his life—nome, yes he did. He said he drank some one time and didn't like it."

Miss Maudie laughed. "Wasn't talking about your father," she said. "What I meant was, if Atticus Finch drank until he was drunk he wouldn't be as hard as some men are at their best. There are just some kind of men who—who're so busy worrying about the next world they've never learned to live in this one, and you can look down the street and see the results."

"Do you think they're true, all those things they say about B—Mr. Arthur?"

"What things?"

I told her.

"That is three-fourths colored folks and one-fourth Stephanie Crawford," said Miss Maudie grimly. "Stephanie Crawford even told me once she woke up in the middle of the night and found him looking in the window at her. I said what did you do, Stephanie, move over in the bed and make room for him? That shut her up a while."

50

I was sure it did. Miss Maudie's voice was enough to shut anybody up.

"No, child," she said, "that is a sad house. I remember Arthur Radley when he was a boy. He always spoke nicely to me, no matter what folks said he did. Spoke as nicely as he knew how."

"You reckon he's crazy?"

Miss Maudie shook her head. "If he's not he should be by now. The things that happen to people we never really know. What happens in houses behind closed doors, what secrets—"

"Atticus don't ever do anything to Jem and me in the house that he don't do in the yard," I said, feeling it my duty to defend my parent.

"Gracious child, I was raveling a thread, wasn't even thinking about your father, but now that I am I'll say this: Atticus Finch is the same in his house as he is on the public streets. How'd you like some fresh poundcake to take home?"

I liked it very much.

Next morning when I awakened I found Jem and Dill in the back yard deep in conversation. When I joined them, as usual they said go away.

"Will not. This yard's as much mine as it is yours, Jem Finch. I got just as much right to play in it as you have."

Dill and Jem emerged from a brief huddle: "If you stay you've got to do what we tell you," Dill warned.

"We-ll," I said, "who's so high and mighty all of a sudden?"

"If you don't say you'll do what we tell you, we ain't gonna tell you anything," Dill continued.

"You act like you grew ten inches in the night! All right, what is it?"

Jem said placidly, "We are going to give a note to Boo Radley."

"Just how?" I was trying to fight down the automatic terror rising in me. It was all right for Miss Maudie to talk—she was old and snug on her porch. It was different for us.

Jem was merely going to put the note on the end of a fishing pole and stick it through the shutters. If anyone came along, Dill would ring the bell.

Dill raised his right hand. In it was my mother's silver dinner-bell.

"I'm goin' around to the side of the house," said Jem. "We looked yesterday from across the street, and there's a shutter loose. Think maybe I can make it stick on the window sill, at least."

"Jem—"

"Now you're in it and you can't get out of it, you'll just stay in it, Miss Priss!"

"Okay, okay, but I don't wanta watch. Jem, somebody was—"

"Yes you will, you'll watch the back end of the lot and Dill's gonna watch the front of the house an' up the street, an' if anybody comes he'll ring the bell. That clear?"

"All right then. What'd you write him?"

Dill said, "We're askin' him real politely to come out sometimes, and tell us what he does in there—we said we wouldn't hurt him and we'd buy him an ice cream."

"You all've gone crazy, he'll kill us!"

Dill said, "It's my idea. I figure if he'd come out and sit a spell with us he might feel better."

"How do you know he don't feel good?"

"Well how'd you feel if you'd been shut up for a hundred years with nothin' but cats to eat? I bet he's got a beard down to here—"

"Like your daddy's?"

"He ain't got a beard, he—" Dill stopped, as if trying to remember.

"Uh huh, caughtcha," I said. "You said 'fore you were off the train good your daddy had a black beard—"

"If it's all the same to you he shaved it off last summer! Yeah, an' I've got the letter to prove it—he sent me two dollars, too!"

"Keep on—I reckon he even sent you a mounted police uniform! That'n never showed up, did it? You just keep on tellin' 'em, son—"

Dill Harris could tell the biggest ones I ever heard. Among other things, he had been up in a mail plane seventeen times, he had been to Nova Scotia, he had seen an elephant, and his granddaddy was Brigadier General Joe Wheeler and left him his sword.

"You all hush," said Jem. He scuttled beneath the house and came out with a yellow bamboo pole. "Reckon this is long enough to reach from the sidewalk?"

"Anybody who's brave enough to go up and touch the house hadn't oughta use a fishin' pole," I said. "Why don't you just knock the front door down?"

"This—is—different," said Jem, "how many times do I have to tell you that?"

Dill took a piece of paper from his pocket and gave it to Jem. The three of us walked cautiously toward the old house. Dill remained at the light-pole on the front corner of the lot, and Jem and I edged down the sidewalk parallel to the side of the house. I walked beyond Jem and stood where I could see around the curve.

"All clear," I said. "Not a soul in sight."

Jem looked up the sidewalk to Dill, who nodded.

Jem attached the note to the end of the fishing pole, let the pole out across the yard and pushed it toward the window he had selected. The pole lacked several inches of being long enough, and Jem leaned over as far as he could. I watched him making jabbing motions for so long, I abandoned my post and went to him.

"Can't get it off the pole," he muttered, "or if I get it off I can't make it stay. G'on back down the street, Scout."

I returned and gazed around the curve at the empty road. Occasionally I looked back at Jem, who was patiently trying to place the note on the window sill. It would flutter to the ground and Jem would jab it up, until I thought if Boo

Radley ever received it he wouldn't be able to read it. I was looking down the street when the dinner-bell rang.

Shoulder up, I reeled around to face Boo Radley and his bloody fangs; instead, I saw Dill ringing the bell with all his might in Atticus's face.

Jem looked so awful I didn't have the heart to tell him I told him so. He trudged along, dragging the pole behind him on the sidewalk.

Atticus said, "Stop ringing that bell."

Dill grabbed the clapper; in the silence that followed, I wished he'd start ringing it again. Atticus pushed his hat to the back of his head and put his hands on his hips. "Jem," he said, "what were you doing?"

"Nothin', sir."

"I don't want any of that. Tell me."

"I was—we were just tryin' to give somethin' to Mr. Radley."

"What were you trying to give him?"

"Just a letter."

"Let me see it."

Jem held out a filthy piece of paper. Atticus took it and tried to read it. "Why do you want Mr. Radley to come out?"

Dill said, "We thought he might enjoy us . . ." and dried up when Atticus looked at him.

"Son," he said to Jem, "I'm going to tell you something and tell you one time: stop tormenting that man. That goes for the other two of you."

What Mr. Radley did was his own business. If he wanted to come out, he would. If he wanted to stay inside his own house he had the right to stay inside free from the attentions of inquisitive children, which was a mild term for the likes of us. How would we like it if Atticus barged in on us without knocking, when we were in our rooms at night? We were, in effect, doing the same thing to Mr. Radley. What Mr. Radley did might seem peculiar to us, but it did not seem peculiar to him. Furthermore, had it never occurred to us that the civil way to communicate with another being was by the front door instead of a side window? Lastly, we were to stay away from that house until we were invited there, we were not to play an asinine game he had seen us playing or make fun of anybody on this street or in this town—

"We weren't makin' fun of him, we weren't laughin' at him," said Jem, "we were just—"

"So that was what you were doing, wasn't it?"

"Makin' fun of him?"

"No," said Atticus, "putting his life's history on display for the edification of the neighborhood."

Jem seemed to swell a little. "I didn't say we were doin' that, I didn't say it!"

Atticus grinned dryly. "You just told me," he said. "You stop this nonsense right now, every one of you."

Jem gaped at him.

"You want to be a lawyer, don't you?" Our father's mouth was suspiciously firm, as if he were trying to hold it in line.

Jem decided there was no point in quibbling, and was silent. When Atticus went inside the house to retrieve a file he had forgotten to take to work that morning, Jem finally realized that he had been done in by the oldest lawyer's trick on record. He waited a respectful distance from the front steps, watched Atticus leave the house and walk toward town. When Atticus was out of earshot Jem yelled after him: "I thought I wanted to be a lawyer but I ain't so sure now!"

6

Yes," said our father, when Jem asked him if we could go over and sit by Miss Rachel's fishpool with Dill, as this was his last night in Maycomb. "Tell him so long for me, and we'll see him next summer."

We leaped over the low wall that separated Miss Rachel's yard from our driveway. Jem whistled bob-white and Dill answered in the darkness.

"Not a breath blowing," said Jem. "Looka yonder."

He pointed to the east. A gigantic moon was rising behind Miss Maudie's pecan trees. "That makes it seem hotter," he said.

"Cross in it tonight?" asked Dill, not looking up. He was constructing a cigarette from newspaper and string.

"No, just the lady. Don't light that thing, Dill, you'll stink up this whole end of town."

There was a lady in the moon in Maycomb. She sat at a dresser combing her hair.

"We're gonna miss you, boy," I said. "Reckon we better watch for Mr. Avery?"

Mr. Avery boarded across the street from Mrs. Henry Lafayette Dubose's house. Besides making change in the collection plate every Sunday, Mr. Avery sat on the porch every night until nine o'clock and sneezed. One evening we were privileged to witness a performance by him which seemed to have been his positively last, for he never did it again so long as we watched. Jem and I were leaving Miss Rachel's front steps one night when Dill stopped us: "Golly, looka yonder."

He pointed across the street. At first we saw nothing but a kudzu-covered front porch, but a closer inspection revealed an arc of water descending from the leaves and splashing in the yellow circle of the street light, some ten feet from source to earth, it seemed to us. Jem said Mr. Avery misfigured, Dill said he must drink a gallon a day, and the ensuing contest to determine relative distances and respective prowess only made me feel left out again, as I was untalented in this area.

Dill stretched, yawned, and said altogether too casually, "I know what, let's go for a walk."

He sounded fishy to me. Nobody in Maycomb just went for a walk. "Where to, Dill?"

Dill jerked his head in a southerly direction.

Jem said, "Okay." When I protested, he said sweetly, "You don't have to come along, Angel May."

"You don't have to go. Remember—"

Jem was not one to dwell on past defeats: it seemed the only message he got from Atticus was insight into the art of cross examination. "Scout, we ain't gonna do anything, we're just goin' to the street light and back."

We strolled silently down the sidewalk, listening to porch swings creaking with the weight of the neighborhood, listening to the soft night-murmurs of the grown people on our street. Occasionally we heard Miss Stephanie Crawford laugh.

"Well?" said Dill.

"Okay," said Jem. "Why don't you go on home, Scout?"

"What are you gonna do?"

Dill and Jem were simply going to peep in the window with the loose shutter to see if they could get a look at Boo Radley, and if I didn't want to go with them I could go straight home and keep my fat flopping mouth shut, that was all.

"But why in the sam holy hill did you wait till tonight?"

Because nobody could see them at night, because Atticus would be so deep in a book he wouldn't hear the Kingdom coming, because if Boo Radley killed them they'd miss school instead of vacation, and because it was easier to see inside a dark house in the dark than in the daytime, did I understand?

"Jem, *please*—"

"Scout, I'm tellin' you for the last time, shut your trap or go home—I declare to the Lord you're gettin' more like a girl every day!"

With that, I had no option but to join them. We thought it was better to go under the high wire fence at the rear of the Radley lot, we stood less chance of being seen. The fence enclosed a large garden and a narrow wooden outhouse.

Jem held up the bottom wire and motioned Dill under it. I followed, and held up the wire for Jem. It was a tight squeeze for him. "Don't make a sound," he whispered. "Don't get in a row of collards whatever you do, they'll wake the dead."

With this thought in mind, I made perhaps one step per minute. I moved faster when I saw Jem far ahead beckoning in the moonlight. We came to the gate that divided the garden from the back yard. Jem touched it. The gate squeaked.

"Spit on it," whispered Dill.

"You've got us in a box, Jem," I muttered. "We can't get out of here so easy."

"Sh-h. Spit on it, Scout."

We spat ourselves dry, and Jem opened the gate slowly, lifting it aside and resting it on the fence. We were in the back yard.

The back of the Radley house was less inviting than the front: a ramshackle porch ran the width of the house; there were two doors and two dark windows between the doors. Instead of a column, a rough two-by-four supported one end of the roof. An old Franklin stove sat in a corner of the porch; above it a hat-rack mirror caught the moon and shone eerily.

"Ar-r," said Jem softly, lifting his foot.

"'Smatter?"

"Chickens," he breathed.

That we would be obliged to dodge the unseen from all

directions was confirmed when Dill ahead of us spelled G-o-d in a whisper. We crept to the side of the house, around to the window with the hanging shutter. The sill was several inches taller than Jem.

"Give you a hand up," he muttered to Dill. "Wait, though." Jem grabbed his left wrist and my right wrist, I grabbed my left wrist and Jem's right wrist, we crouched, and Dill sat on our saddle. We raised him and he caught the window sill.

"Hurry," Jem whispered, "we can't last much longer."

Dill punched my shoulder, and we lowered him to the ground.

"What'd you see?"

"Nothing. Curtains. There's a little teeny light way off somewhere, though."

"Let's get away from here," breathed Jem. "Let's go 'round in back again. Sh-h," he warned me, as I was about to protest.

"Let's try the back window."

"Dill, *no*," I said.

Dill stopped and let Jem go ahead. When Jem put his foot on the bottom step, the step squeaked. He stood still, then tried his weight by degrees. The step was silent. Jem skipped two steps, put his foot on the porch, heaved himself to it, and teetered a long moment. He regained his balance and dropped to his knees. He crawled to the window, raised his head and looked in.

Then I saw the shadow. It was the shadow of a man with a hat on. At first I thought it was a tree, but there was no wind blowing, and tree-trunks never walked. The back porch was bathed in moonlight, and the shadow, crisp as toast, moved across the porch toward Jem.

Dill saw it next. He put his hands to his face.

When it crossed Jem, Jem saw it. He put his arms over his head and went rigid.

The shadow stopped about a foot beyond Jem. Its arm came out from its side, dropped, and was still. Then it turned and moved back across Jem, walked along the porch and off the side of the house, returning as it had come.

Jem leaped off the porch and galloped toward us. He flung open the gate, danced Dill and me through, and shooed us between two rows of swishing collards. Halfway through the collards I tripped; as I tripped the roar of a shotgun shattered the neighborhood.

Dill and Jem dived beside me. Jem's breath came in sobs: "Fence by the schoolyard!—hurry, Scout!"

Jem held the bottom wire; Dill and I rolled through and were halfway to the shelter of the schoolyard's solitary oak when we sensed that Jem was not with us. We ran back and found him struggling in the fence, kicking his pants off to get loose. He ran to the oak tree in his shorts.

Safely behind it, we gave way to numbness, but Jem's mind was racing: "We gotta get home, they'll miss us."

We ran across the schoolyard, crawled under the fence to Deer's Pasture behind our house, climbed our back fence and were at the back steps before Jem would let us pause to rest.

Respiration normal, the three of us strolled as casually as we could to the front yard. We looked down the street and saw a circle of neighbors at the Radley front gate.

"We better go down there," said Jem. "They'll think it's funny if we don't show up."

Mr. Nathan Radley was standing inside his gate, a shotgun broken across his arm. Atticus was standing beside Miss Maudie and Miss Stephanie Crawford. Miss Rachel and Mr. Avery were near by. None of them saw us come up.

We eased in beside Miss Maudie, who looked around. "Where were you all, didn't you hear the commotion?"

"What happened?" asked Jem.

"Mr. Radley shot at a Negro in his collard patch."

"Oh. Did he hit him?"

"No," said Miss Stephanie. "Shot in the air. Scared him pale, though. Says if anybody sees a white nigger around, that's the one. Says he's got the other barrel waitin' for the next sound he hears in that patch, an' next time he won't aim high, be it dog, nigger, or—Jem *Finch!*"

"Ma'am?" asked Jem.

Atticus spoke. "Where're your pants, son?"

"Pants, sir?"

"Pants."

It was no use. In his shorts before God and everybody. I sighed.

"Ah—Mr. Finch?"

In the glare from the streetlight, I could see Dill hatching one: his eyes widened, his fat cherub face grew rounder.

"What is it, Dill?" asked Atticus.

"Ah—I won 'em from him," he said vaguely.

"Won them? How?"

Dill's hand sought the back of his head. He brought it forward and across his forehead. "We were playin' strip poker up yonder by the fishpool," he said.

Jem and I relaxed. The neighbors seemed satisfied: they all stiffened. But what was strip poker?

We had no chance to find out: Miss Rachel went off like the town fire siren: "Do-o-o Jee-sus, Dill Harris! Gamblin' by my fishpool? I'll strip-poker you, sir!"

Atticus saved Dill from immediate dismemberment. "Just a minute, Miss Rachel," he said. "I've never heard of 'em doing that before. Were you all playing cards?"

Jem fielded Dill's fly with his eyes shut: "No sir, just with matches."

I admired my brother. Matches were dangerous, but cards were fatal.

"Jem, Scout," said Atticus, "I don't want to hear of poker in any form again. Go by Dill's and get your pants, Jem. Settle it yourselves."

"Don't worry, Dill," said Jem, as we trotted up the sidewalk, "she ain't gonna get you. He'll talk her out of it. That was fast thinkin', son. Listen . . . you hear?"

We stopped, and heard Atticus's voice: ". . . not serious . . . they all go through it, Miss Rachel. . . ."

Dill was comforted, but Jem and I weren't. There was the problem of Jem showing up some pants in the morning.

" 'd give you some of mine," said Dill, as we came to Miss Rachel's steps. Jem said he couldn't get in them, but thanks anyway. We said good-bye, and Dill went inside the house. He evidently remembered he was engaged to me, for he ran back out and kissed me swiftly in front of Jem. "Yawl write, hear?" he bawled after us.

Had Jem's pants been safely on him, we would not have slept much anyway. Every night-sound I heard from my cot on the back porch was magnified three-fold; every scratch of feet on gravel was Boo Radley seeking revenge, every passing Negro laughing in the night was Boo Radley loose and after us; insects splashing against the screen were Boo Radley's insane fingers picking the wire to pieces; the chinaberry trees were malignant, hovering, alive. I lingered between sleep and wakefulness until I heard Jem murmur.

"Sleep, Little Three-Eyes?"

"Are you crazy?"

"Sh-h. Atticus's light's out."

In the waning moonlight I saw Jem swing his feet to the floor.

"I'm goin' after 'em," he said.

I sat upright. "You can't. I won't let you."

He was struggling into his shirt. "I've got to."

"You do an' I'll wake up Atticus."

"You do and I'll kill you."

I pulled him down beside me on the cot. I tried to reason with him. "Mr. Nathan's gonna find 'em in the morning, Jem. He knows you lost 'em. When he shows 'em to Atticus it'll be pretty bad, that's all there is to it. Go'n back to bed."

"That's what I know," said Jem. "That's why I'm goin' after 'em."

I began to feel sick. Going back to that place by himself—I remembered Miss Stephanie: Mr. Nathan had the other barrel waiting for the next sound he heard, be it nigger, dog . . . Jem knew that better than I.

I was desperate: "Look, it ain't worth it, Jem. A lickin' hurts but it doesn't last. You'll get your head shot off, Jem. Please . . ."

He blew out his breath patiently. "I—it's like this, Scout," he muttered. "Atticus ain't ever whipped me since I can remember. I wanta keep it that way."

This was a thought. It seemed that Atticus threatened us every other day. "You mean he's never caught you at anything."

"Maybe so, but—I just wanta keep it that way, Scout. We shouldn'a done that tonight, Scout."

It was then, I suppose, that Jem and I first began to part company. Sometimes I did not understand him, but my periods of bewilderment were short-lived. This was beyond me. "Please," I pleaded, "can'tcha just think about it for a minute—by yourself on that place—"

"Shut up!"

"It's not like he'd never speak to you again or somethin' . . . I'm gonna wake him up, Jem, I swear I am—"

Jem grabbed my pajama collar and wrenched it tight. "Then I'm goin' with you—" I choked.

"No you ain't, you'll just make noise."

It was no use. I unlatched the back door and held it while he crept down the steps. It must have been two o'clock. The moon was setting and the lattice-work shadows were fading into fuzzy nothingness. Jem's white shirt-tail dipped and bobbed like a small ghost dancing away to escape the coming morning. A faint breeze stirred and cooled the sweat running down my sides.

He went the back way, through Deer's Pasture, across the schoolyard and around to the fence, I thought—at least that was the way he was headed. It would take longer, so it was not time to worry yet. I waited until it was time to worry and listened for Mr. Radley's shotgun. Then I thought I heard the back fence squeak. It was wishful thinking.

Then I heard Atticus cough. I held my breath. Sometimes when we made a midnight pilgrimage to the bathroom we would find him reading. He said he often woke up during the night, checked on us, and read himself back to sleep. I waited for his light to go on, straining my eyes to see it flood the hall. It stayed off, and I breathed again.

The night-crawlers had retired, but ripe chinaberries drummed on the roof when the wind stirred, and the darkness was desolate with the barking of distant dogs.

There he was, returning to me. His white shirt bobbed over the back fence and slowly grew larger. He came up the back steps, latched the door behind him, and sat on his cot. Wordlessly, he held up his pants. He lay down, and for a while I heard his cot trembling. Soon he was still. I did not hear him stir again.

7

Jem stayed moody and silent for a week. As Atticus had once advised me to do, I tried to climb into Jem's skin and walk around in it: if I had gone alone to the Radley Place at two in the morning, my funeral would have been held the next afternoon. So I left Jem alone and tried not to bother him.

School started. The second grade was as bad as the first, only worse—they still flashed cards at you and wouldn't let you read or write. Miss Caroline's progress next door could be estimated by the frequency of laughter; however, the usual crew had flunked the first grade again, and were helpful in keeping order. The only thing good about the second grade was that this year I had to stay as late as Jem, and we usually walked home together at three o'clock.

One afternoon when we were crossing the schoolyard toward home, Jem suddenly said: "There's something I didn't tell you."

As this was his first complete sentence in several days, I encouraged him: "About what?"

"About that night."

"You've never told me anything about that night," I said.

Jem waved my words away as if fanning gnats. He was silent for a while, then he said, "When I went back for my breeches—they were all in a tangle when I was gettin' out of 'em, I couldn't get 'em loose. When I went back—" Jem took a deep breath. "When I went back, they were folded across the fence . . . like they were expectin' me."

"Across—"

"And something else—" Jem's voice was flat. "Show you when we get home. They'd been sewed up. Not like a lady sewed 'em, like somethin' I'd try to do. All crooked. It's almost like—"

"—somebody knew you were comin' back for 'em."

Jem shuddered. "Like somebody was readin' my mind . . . like somebody could tell what I was gonna do. Can't anybody tell what I'm gonna do lest they know me, can they, Scout?"

Jem's question was an appeal. I reassured him: "Can't anybody tell what you're gonna do lest they live in the house with you, and even I can't tell sometimes."

We were walking past our tree. In its knot-hole rested a ball of gray twine.

"Don't take it, Jem," I said. "This is somebody's hidin' place."

"I don't think so, Scout."

"Yes it is. Somebody like Walter Cunningham comes down here every recess and hides his things—and we come along and take 'em away from him. Listen, let's leave it and wait a couple of days. If it ain't gone then, we'll take it, okay?"

"Okay, you might be right," said Jem. "It must be some little kid's place—hides his things from the bigger folks. You know it's only when school's in that we've found things."

"Yeah," I said, "but we never go by here in the summertime."

We went home. Next morning the twine was where we had left it. When it was still there on the third day, Jem pocketed it. From then on, we considered everything we found in the knot-hole our property.

The second grade was grim, but Jem assured me that the older I got the better school would be, that he started off the same way, and it was not until one reached the sixth grade that one learned anything of value. The sixth grade seemed to please him from the beginning: he went through a brief Egyptian Period that baffled me—he tried to walk flat a great deal, sticking one arm in front of him and one in back of him, putting one foot behind the other. He declared Egyptians walked that way; I said if they did I didn't see how they got anything done, but Jem said they accomplished more than the Americans ever did, they invented toilet paper and perpetual embalming, and asked where would we be today if they hadn't? Atticus told me to delete the adjectives and I'd have the facts.

There are no clearly defined seasons in South Alabama; summer drifts into autumn, and autumn is sometimes never followed by winter, but turns to a days-old spring that melts into summer again. That fall was a long one, hardly cool enough for a light jacket. Jem and I were trotting in our orbit one mild October afternoon when our knot-hole stopped us again. Something white was inside this time.

Jem let me do the honors: I pulled out two small images carved in soap. One was the figure of a boy, the other wore a crude dress.

Before I remembered that there was no such thing as hoo-dooing, I shrieked and threw them down.

Jem snatched them up. "What's the matter with you?" he yelled. He rubbed the figures free of red dust. "These are good," he said. "I've never seen any these good."

He held them down to me. They were almost perfect miniatures of two children. The boy had on shorts, and a shock of soapy hair fell to his eyebrows. I looked up at Jem. A point of straight brown hair kicked downwards from his part. I had never noticed it before.

Jem looked from the girl-doll to me. The girl-doll wore bangs. So did I.

"These are us," he said.

"Who did 'em, you reckon?"

"Who do we know around here who whittles?" he asked.

"Mr. Avery."

"Mr. Avery just does like this. I mean carves."

Mr. Avery averaged a stick of stovewood per week; he honed it down to a toothpick and chewed it.

"There's old Miss Stephanie Crawford's sweetheart," I said.

"He carves all right, but he lives down the country. When would he ever pay any attention to us?"

"Maybe he sits on the porch and looks at us instead of Miss Stephanie. If I was him, I would."

Jem stared at me so long I asked what was the matter, but got Nothing, Scout for an answer. When we went home, Jem put the dolls in his trunk.

Less than two weeks later we found a whole package of chewing gum, which we enjoyed, the fact that everything on the Radley Place was poison having slipped Jem's memory.

The following week the knot-hole yielded a tarnished medal. Jem showed it to Atticus, who said it was a spelling medal, that before we were born the Maycomb County schools had spelling contests and awarded medals to the winners. Atticus said someone must have lost it, and had we asked around? Jem camel-kicked me when I tried to say where we had found it. Jem asked Atticus if he remembered anybody who ever won one, and Atticus said no.

Our biggest prize appeared four days later. It was a pocket watch that wouldn't run, on a chain with an aluminum knife.

"You reckon it's white gold, Jem?"

"Don't know. I'll show it to Atticus."

Atticus said it would probably be worth ten dollars, knife, chain and all, if it were new. "Did you swap with somebody at school?" he asked.

"Oh, no sir!" Jem pulled out his grandfather's watch that Atticus let him carry once a week if Jem were careful with it. On the days he carried the watch, Jem walked on eggs. "Atticus, if it's all right with you, I'd rather have this one instead. Maybe I can fix it."

When the new wore off his grandfather's watch, and carrying it became a day's burdensome task, Jem no longer felt the necessity of ascertaining the hour every five minutes.

He did a fair job, only one spring and two tiny pieces left over, but the watch would not run. "Oh-h," he sighed, "it'll never go. Scout—?"

"Huh?"

"You reckon we oughta write a letter to whoever's leaving us these things?"

"That'd be right nice, Jem, we can thank 'em—what's wrong?"

Jem was holding his ears, shaking his head from side to side. "I don't get it, I just don't get it—I don't know why, Scout . . ." He looked toward the livingroom. "I've gotta good mind to tell Atticus—no, I reckon not."

"I'll tell him for you."

"No, don't do that, Scout. Scout?"

"Wha-t?"

He had been on the verge of telling me something all evening; his face would brighten and he would lean toward me, then he would change his mind. He changed it again. "Oh, nothin'."

"Here, let's write a letter." I pushed a tablet and pencil under his nose.

"Okay. Dear Mister . . ."

"How do you know it's a man? I bet it's Miss Maudie—been bettin' that for a long time."

"Ar-r, Miss Maudie can't chew gum—" Jem broke into a grin. "You know, she can talk real pretty sometimes. One time I asked her to have a chew and she said no thanks, that—chewing gum cleaved to her palate and rendered her speechless," said Jem carefully. "Doesn't that sound nice?"

"Yeah, she can say nice things sometimes. She wouldn't have a watch and chain anyway."

"Dear sir," said Jem. "We appreciate the—no, we appreciate everything which you have put into the tree for us. Yours very truly, Jeremy Atticus Finch."

"He won't know who you are if you sign it like that, Jem."

Jem erased his name and wrote, "Jem Finch." I signed, "Jean Louise Finch (Scout)," beneath it. Jem put the note in an envelope.

Next morning on the way to school he ran ahead of me

and stopped at the tree. Jem was facing me when he looked up, and I saw him go stark white.

"Scout!"

I ran to him.

Someone had filled our knot-hole with cement.

"Don't you cry, now, Scout ... don't cry now, don't you worry—" he muttered at me all the way to school.

When we went home for dinner Jem bolted his food, ran to the porch and stood on the steps. I followed him. "Hasn't passed by yet," he said.

Next day Jem repeated his vigil and was rewarded.

"Hidy do, Mr. Nathan," he said.

"Morning Jem, Scout," said Mr. Radley, as he went by.

"Mr. Radley," said Jem.

Mr. Radley turned around.

"Mr. Radley, ah—did you put cement in that hole in that tree down yonder?"

"Yes," he said. "I filled it up."

"Why'd you do it, sir?"

"Tree's dying. You plug 'em with cement when they're sick. You ought to know that, Jem."

Jem said nothing more about it until late afternoon. When we passed our tree he gave it a meditative pat on its cement, and remained deep in thought. He seemed to be working himself into a bad humor, so I kept my distance.

As usual, we met Atticus coming home from work that evening. When we were at our steps Jem said, "Atticus, look down yonder at that tree, please sir."

"What tree, son?"

"The one on the corner of the Radley lot comin' from school."

"Yes?"

"Is that tree dyin'?"

"Why no, son, I don't think so. Look at the leaves, they're all green and full, no brown patches anywhere—"

"It ain't even sick?"

"That tree's as healthy as you are, Jem. Why?"

"Mr. Nathan Radley said it was dyin'."

"Well maybe it is. I'm sure Mr. Radley knows more about his trees than we do."

Atticus left us on the porch. Jem leaned on a pillar, rubbing his shoulders against it.

"Do you itch, Jem?" I asked as politely as I could. He did not answer. "Come on in, Jem," I said.

"After while."

He stood there until nightfall, and I waited for him. When we went in the house I saw he had been crying; his face was dirty in the right places, but I thought it odd that I had not heard him.

8

For reasons unfathomable to the most experienced prophets in Maycomb County, autumn turned to winter that year. We had two weeks of the coldest weather since 1885, Atticus said. Mr. Avery said it was written on the Rosetta Stone that when children disobeyed their parents, smoked cigarettes and made war on each other, the seasons would change: Jem and I were burdened with the guilt of contributing to the aberrations of nature, thereby causing unhappiness to our neighbors and discomfort to ourselves.

Old Mrs. Radley died that winter, but her death caused hardly a ripple—the neighborhood seldom saw her, except when she watered her cannas. Jem and I decided that Boo had got her at last, but when Atticus returned from the Radley house he said she died of natural causes, to our disappointment.

"Ask him," Jem whispered.

"You ask him, you're the oldest."

"That's why you oughta ask him."

"Atticus," I said, "did you see Mr. Arthur?"

Atticus looked sternly around his newspaper at me: "I did not."

Jem restrained me from further questions. He said Atticus was still touchous about us and the Radleys and it wouldn't do to push him any. Jem had a notion that Atticus thought our activities that night last summer were not solely confined to strip poker. Jem had no firm basis for his idea, he said it was merely a twitch.

Next morning I awoke, looked out the window and nearly died of fright. My screams brought Atticus from his bathroom half-shaven.

"The *world's* endin', Atticus! Please do something—!" I dragged him to the window and pointed.

"No it's not," he said. "It's snowing."

Jem asked Atticus would it keep up. Jem had never seen snow either, but he knew what it was. Atticus said he didn't know any more about snow than Jem did. "I think, though, if it's watery like that, it'll turn to rain."

The telephone rang and Atticus left the breakfast table to answer it. "That was Eula May," he said when he returned. "I quote—'As it has not snowed in Maycomb County since 1885, there will be no school today.'"

Eula May was Maycomb's leading telephone operator. She was entrusted with issuing public announcements, wedding invitations, setting off the fire siren, and giving first-aid instructions when Dr. Reynolds was away.

When Atticus finally called us to order and bade us look at our plates instead of out the windows, Jem asked, "How do you make a snowman?"

"I haven't the slightest idea," said Atticus. "I don't want you all to be disappointed, but I doubt if there'll be enough snow for a snowball, even."

Calpurnia came in and said she thought it was sticking. When we ran to the back yard, it was covered with a feeble layer of soggy snow.

"We shouldn't walk about in it," said Jem. "Look, every step you take's wasting it."

I looked back at my mushy footprints. Jem said if we waited until it snowed some more we could scrape it all up for a snowman. I stuck out my tongue and caught a fat flake. It burned.

"Jem, it's hot!"

"No it ain't, it's so cold it burns. Now don't eat it, Scout, you're wasting it. Let it come down."

"But I want to walk in it."

"I know what, we can go walk over at Miss Maudie's."

Jem hopped across the front yard. I followed in his tracks. When we were on the sidewalk in front of Miss Maudie's, Mr. Avery accosted us. He had a pink face and a big stomach below his belt.

"See what you've done?" he said. "Hasn't snowed in Maycomb since Appomattox. It's bad children like you makes the seasons change."

I wondered if Mr. Avery knew how hopefully we had watched last summer for him to repeat his performance, and reflected that if this was our reward, there was something to say for sin. I did not wonder where Mr. Avery gathered his meteorological statistics: they came straight from the Rosetta Stone.

"Jem Finch, you Jem Finch!"

"Miss Maudie's callin' you, Jem."

"You all stay in the middle of the yard. There's some thrift buried under the snow near the porch. Don't step on it!"

"Yessum!" called Jem. "It's beautiful, ain't it, Miss Maudie?"

"Beautiful my hind foot! If it freezes tonight it'll carry off all my azaleas!"

Miss Maudie's old sunhat glistened with snow crystals. She was bending over some small bushes, wrapping them in burlap bags. Jem asked her what she was doing that for.

"Keep 'em warm," she said.

"How can flowers keep warm? They don't circulate."

"I cannot answer that question, Jem Finch. All I know is if it freezes tonight these plants'll freeze, so you cover 'em up. Is that clear?"

"Yessum. Miss Maudie?"

"What, sir?"

"Could Scout and me borrow some of your snow?"

"Heavens alive, take it all! There's an old peach basket under the house, haul it off in that." Miss Maudie's eyes narrowed. "Jem Finch, what are you going to do with my snow?"

"You'll see," said Jem, and we transferred as much snow as we could from Miss Maudie's yard to ours, a slushy operation.

"What are we gonna do, Jem?" I asked.

"You'll see," he said. "Now get the basket and haul all the snow you can rake up from the back yard to the front. Walk back in your tracks, though," he cautioned.

"Are we gonna have a snow baby, Jem?"

"No, a real snowman. Gotta work hard, now."

Jem ran to the back yard, produced the garden hoe and began digging quickly behind the woodpile, placing any worms he found to one side. He went in the house, returned with the laundry hamper, filled it with earth and carried it to the front yard.

When we had five baskets of earth and two baskets of snow, Jem said we were ready to begin.

"Don't you think this is kind of a mess?" I asked.

"Looks messy now, but it won't later," he said.

Jem scooped up an armful of dirt, patted it into a mound on which he added another load, and another until he had constructed a torso.

"Jem, I ain't ever heard of a nigger snowman," I said.

"He won't be black long," he grunted.

Jem procured some peachtree switches from the back yard, plaited them, and bent them into bones to be covered with dirt.

"He looks like Miss Stephanie Crawford with her hands on her hips," I said. "Fat in the middle and little-bitty arms."

"I'll make 'em bigger." Jem sloshed water over the mud man and added more dirt. He looked thoughtfully at it for a moment, then he molded a big stomach below the figure's waistline. Jem glanced at me, his eyes twinkling: "Mr. Avery's sort of shaped like a snow man, ain't he?"

Jem scooped up some snow and began plastering it on. He permitted me to cover only the back, saving the public parts for himself. Gradually Mr. Avery turned white.

Using bits of wood for eyes, nose, mouth, and buttons,

Jem succeeded in making Mr. Avery look cross. A stick of stovewood completed the picture. Jem stepped back and viewed his creation.

"It's lovely, Jem," I said. "Looks almost like he'd talk to you."

"It is, ain't it?" he said shyly.

We could not wait for Atticus to come home for dinner, but called and said we had a big surprise for him. He seemed surprised when he saw most of the back yard in the front yard, but he said we had done a jim-dandy job. "I didn't know how you were going to do it," he said to Jem, "but from now on I'll never worry about what'll become of you, son, you'll always have an idea."

Jem's ears reddened from Atticus's compliment, but he looked up sharply when he saw Atticus stepping back. Atticus squinted at the snowman a while. He grinned, then laughed. "Son, I can't tell what you're going to be—an engineer, a lawyer, or a portrait painter. You've perpetrated a near libel here in the front yard. We've got to disguise this fellow."

Atticus suggested that Jem hone down his creation's front a little, swap a broom for the stovewood, and put an apron on him.

Jem explained that if he did, the snowman would become muddy and cease to be a snowman.

"I don't care what you do, so long as you do something," said Atticus. "You can't go around making caricatures of the neighbors."

"Ain't a characterture," said Jem. "It looks just like him."

"Mr. Avery might not think so."

"I know what!" said Jem. He raced across the street, disappeared into Miss Maudie's back yard and returned triumphant. He stuck her sunhat on the snowman's head and jammed her hedge-clippers into the crook of his arm. Atticus said that would be fine.

Miss Maudie opened her front door and came out on the porch. She looked across the street at us. Suddenly she grinned. "Jem Finch," she called. "You devil, bring me back my hat, sir!"

Jem looked up at Atticus, who shook his head. "She's just fussing," he said. "She's really impressed with your—accomplishments."

Atticus strolled over to Miss Maudie's sidewalk, where they engaged in an arm-waving conversation, the only phrase of which I caught was ". . . erected an absolute morphodite in that yard! Atticus, you'll never raise 'em!"

The snow stopped in the afternoon, the temperature dropped, and by nightfall Mr. Avery's direst predictions came true: Calpurnia kept every fireplace in the house blazing, but we were cold. When Atticus came home that evening he said we were in for it, and asked Calpurnia if she wanted to stay with us for the night. Calpurnia glanced up at the high ceilings and long windows and said she thought she'd be warmer at her house. Atticus drove her home in the car.

Before I went to sleep Atticus put more coal on the fire in my room. He said the thermometer registered sixteen, that it was the coldest night in his memory, and that our snowman outside was frozen solid.

Minutes later, it seemed, I was awakened by someone shaking me. Atticus's overcoat was spread across me. "Is it morning already?"

"Baby, get up."

Atticus was holding out my bathrobe and coat. "Put your robe on first," he said.

Jem was standing beside Atticus, groggy and tousled. He was holding his overcoat closed at the neck, his other hand was jammed into his pocket. He looked strangely overweight.

"Hurry, hon," said Atticus. "Here're your shoes and socks."

Stupidly, I put them on. "Is it morning?"

"No, it's a little after one. Hurry now."

That something was wrong finally got through to me. "What's the matter?"

By then he did not have to tell me. Just as the birds know

where to go when it rains, I knew when there was trouble in our street. Soft taffeta-like sounds and muffled scurrying sounds filled me with helpless dread.

"Whose is it?"

"Miss Maudie's, hon," said Atticus gently.

At the front door, we saw fire spewing from Miss Maudie's dining-room windows. As if to confirm what we saw, the town fire siren wailed up the scale to a treble pitch and remained there, screaming.

"It's gone, ain't it?" moaned Jem.

"I expect so," said Atticus. "Now listen, both of you. Go down and stand in front of the Radley Place. Keep out of the way, do you hear? See which way the wind's blowing?"

"Oh," said Jem. "Atticus, reckon we oughta start moving the furniture out?"

"Not yet, son. Do as I tell you. Run now. Take care of Scout, you hear? Don't let her out of your sight."

With a push, Atticus started us toward the Radley front gate. We stood watching the street fill with men and cars while fire silently devoured Miss Maudie's house. "Why don't they hurry, why don't they hurry . . ." muttered Jem.

We saw why. The old fire truck, killed by the cold, was being pushed from town by a crowd of men. When the men attached its hose to a hydrant, the hose burst and water shot up, tinkling down on the pavement.

"Oh-h Lord, Jem . . ."

Jem put his arm around me. "Hush, Scout," he said. "It ain't time to worry yet. I'll let you know when."

The men of Maycomb, in all degrees of dress and undress, took furniture from Miss Maudie's house to a yard across the street. I saw Atticus carrying Miss Maudie's heavy oak rocking chair, and thought it sensible of him to save what she valued most.

Sometimes we heard shouts. Then Mr. Avery's face appeared in an upstairs window. He pushed a mattress out the window into the street and threw down furniture until men shouted, "Come down from there, Dick! The stairs are going! Get outta there, Mr. Avery!"

Mr. Avery began climbing through the window.

"Scout, he's stuck . . ." breathed Jem. "Oh God . . ."

Mr. Avery was wedged tightly. I buried my head under Jem's arm and didn't look again until Jem cried, "He's got loose, Scout! He's all right!"

I looked up to see Mr. Avery cross the upstairs porch. He swung his legs over the railing and was sliding down a pillar when he slipped. He fell, yelled, and hit Miss Maudie's shrubbery.

Suddenly I noticed that the men were backing away from Miss Maudie's house, moving down the street toward us. They were no longer carrying furniture. The fire was well into the second floor and had eaten its way to the roof: window frames were black against a vivid orange center.

"Jem, it looks like a pumpkin—"

"Scout, look!"

Smoke was rolling off our house and Miss Rachel's house like fog off a riverbank, and men were pulling hoses toward them. Behind us, the fire truck from Abbottsville screamed around the curve and stopped in front of our house.

"That book . . ." I said.

"What?" said Jem.

"That Tom Swift book, it ain't mine, it's Dill's . . ."

"Don't worry, Scout, it ain't time to worry yet," said Jem. He pointed. "Looka yonder."

In a group of neighbors, Atticus was standing with his hands in his overcoat pockets. He might have been watching a football game. Miss Maudie was beside him.

"See there, he's not worried yet," said Jem.

"Why ain't he on top of one of the houses?"

"He's too old, he'd break his neck."

"You think we oughta make him get our stuff out?"

"Let's don't pester him, he'll know when it's time," said Jem.

The Abbottsville fire truck began pumping water on our house; a man on the roof pointed to places that needed it most. I watched our Absolute Morphodite go black and crumble; Miss Maudie's sunhat settled on top of the heap. I could not see her hedge-clippers. In the heat between our house, Miss Rachel's and Miss Maudie's, the men had long ago shed coats and bathrobes. They worked in pajama tops and nightshirts stuffed into their pants, but I became aware that I was slowly freezing where I stood. Jem tried to keep me warm, but his arm was not enough. I pulled free of it and clutched my shoulders. By dancing a little, I could feel my feet.

Another fire truck appeared and stopped in front of Miss Stephanie Crawford's. There was no hydrant for another hose, and the men tried to soak her house with hand extinguishers.

Miss Maudie's tin roof quelled the flames. Roaring, the house collapsed; fire gushed everywhere, followed by a flurry of blankets from men on top of the adjacent houses, beating out sparks and burning chunks of wood.

It was dawn before the men began to leave, first one by one, then in groups. They pushed the Maycomb fire truck back to town, the Abbottsville truck departed, the third one remained. We found out next day it had come from Clark's Ferry, sixty miles away.

Jem and I slid across the street. Miss Maudie was staring at the smoking black hole in her yard, and Atticus shook his head to tell us she did not want to talk. He led us home, holding onto our shoulders to cross the icy street. He said Miss Maudie would stay with Miss Stephanie for the time being.

"Anybody want some hot chocolate?" he asked. I shuddered when Atticus started a fire in the kitchen stove.

As we drank our cocoa I noticed Atticus looking at me, first with curiosity, then with sternness. "I thought I told you and Jem to stay put," he said.

"Why, we did. We stayed—"

"Then whose blanket is that?"

"Blanket?"

"Yes ma'am, blanket. It isn't ours."

I looked down and found myself clutching a brown woolen blanket I was wearing around my shoulders, squaw-fashion.

"Atticus, I don't know, sir . . . I—"

I turned to Jem for an answer, but Jem was even more bewildered than I. He said he didn't know how it got there, we did exactly as Atticus had told us, we stood down by the Radley gate away from everybody, we didn't move an inch— Jem stopped.

"Mr. Nathan was at the fire," he babbled, "I saw him, I saw him, he was tuggin' that mattress—Atticus, I swear . . ."

"That's all right, son." Atticus grinned slowly. "Looks like all of Maycomb was out tonight, in one way or another. Jem, there's some wrapping paper in the pantry, I think. Go get it and we'll—"

"Atticus, no sir!"

Jem seemed to have lost his mind. He began pouring out our secrets right and left in total disregard for my safety if not for his own, omitting nothing, knot-hole, pants and all.

". . . Mr. Nathan put cement in that tree, Atticus, an' he did it to stop us findin' things—he's crazy, I reckon, like they say, but Atticus, I swear to God he ain't ever harmed us, he ain't ever hurt us, he coulda cut my throat from ear to ear that night but he tried to mend my pants instead . . . he ain't ever hurt us, Atticus—"

Atticus said, "Whoa, son," so gently that I was greatly heartened. It was obvious that he had not followed a word Jem said, for all Atticus said was, "You're right. We'd better keep this and the blanket to ourselves. Someday, maybe, Scout can thank him for covering her up."

"Thank who?" I asked.

"Boo Radley. You were so busy looking at the fire you didn't know it when he put the blanket around you."

My stomach turned to water and I nearly threw up when Jem held out the blanket and crept toward me. "He sneaked out of the house—turn 'round—sneaked up, an' went like this!"

Atticus said dryly, "Do not let this inspire you to further glory, Jeremy."

Jem scowled, "I ain't gonna do anything to him," but I watched the spark of fresh adventure leave his eyes. "Just think, Scout," he said, "if you'd just turned around, you'da seen him."

Calpurnia woke us at noon. Atticus had said we need not go to school that day, we'd learn nothing after no sleep. Calpurnia said for us to try and clean up the front yard.

Miss Maudie's sunhat was suspended in a thin layer of ice, like a fly in amber, and we had to dig under the dirt for her hedge-clippers. We found her in her back yard, gazing at her frozen charred azaleas.

"We're bringing back your things, Miss Maudie," said Jem. "We're awful sorry."

Miss Maudie looked around, and the shadow of her old grin crossed her face. "Always wanted a smaller house, Jem Finch. Gives me more yard. Just think, I'll have more room for my azaleas now!"

"You ain't grievin', Miss Maudie?" I asked, surprised. Atticus said her house was nearly all she had.

"Grieving, child? Why, I hated that old cow barn. Thought of settin' fire to it a hundred times myself, except they'd lock me up."

"But—"

"Don't you worry about me, Jean Louise Finch. There are ways of doing things you don't know about. Why, I'll build me a little house and take me a couple of roomers and—gracious, I'll have the finest yard in Alabama. Those Bellingraths'll look plain puny when I get started!"

Jem and I looked at each other. "How'd it catch, Miss Maudie?" he asked.

"I don't know, Jem. Probably the flue in the kitchen. I kept a fire in there last night for my potted plants. Hear you had some unexpected company last night, Miss Jean Louise."

"How'd you know?"

"Atticus told me on his way to town this morning. Tell you the truth, I'd like to've been with you. And I'd've had sense enough to turn around, too."

Miss Maudie puzzled me. With most of her possessions gone and her beloved yard a shambles, she still took a lively and cordial interest in Jem's and my affairs.

She must have seen my perplexity. She said, "Only thing I worried about last night was all the danger and commotion it caused. This whole neighborhood could have gone up. Mr. Avery'll be in bed for a week—he's right stove up. He's too old to do things like that and I told him so. Soon as I can get my hands clean and when Stephanie Crawford's not looking, I'll make him a Lane cake. That Stephanie's been after my recipe for thirty years, and if she thinks I'll give it to her just because I'm staying with her she's got another think coming."

I reflected that if Miss Maudie broke down and gave it to her, Miss Stephanie couldn't follow it anyway. Miss Maudie had once let me see it: among other things, the recipe called for one large cup of sugar.

It was a still day. The air was so cold and clear we heard the courthouse clock clank, rattle and strain before it struck the hour. Miss Maudie's nose was a color I had never seen before, and I inquired about it.

"I've been out here since six o'clock," she said. "Should be frozen by now." She held up her hands. A network of tiny lines criss-crossed her palms, brown with dirt and dried blood.

"You've ruined 'em," said Jem. "Why don't you get a colored man?" There was no note of sacrifice in his voice when he added, "Or Scout'n'me, we can help you."

Miss Maudie said, "Thank you sir, but you've got a job of your own over there." She pointed to our yard.

"You mean the Morphodite?" I asked. "Shoot, we can rake him up in a jiffy."

Miss Maudie stared down at me, her lips moving silently. Suddenly she put her hands to her head and whooped. When we left her, she was still chuckling.

Jem said he didn't know what was the matter with her—that was just Miss Maudie.

9

You can just take that back, boy!"

This order, given by me to Cecil Jacobs, was the beginning of a rather thin time for Jem and me. My fists were clenched and I was ready to let fly. Atticus had promised me he would wear me out if he ever heard of me fighting any more; I was far too old and too big for such childish things, and the sooner I learned to hold in, the better off everybody would be. I soon forgot.

Cecil Jacobs made me forget. He had announced in the schoolyard the day before that Scout Finch's daddy defended niggers. I denied it, but told Jem.

"What'd he mean sayin' that?" I asked.

"Nothing," Jem said. "Ask Atticus, he'll tell you."

"Do you defend niggers, Atticus?" I asked him that evening.

"Of course I do. Don't say nigger, Scout. That's common."

" 's what everybody at school says."

"From now on it'll be everybody less one—"

"Well if you don't want me to grow up talkin' that way, why do you send me to school?"

My father looked at me mildly, amusement in his eyes. Despite our compromise, my campaign to avoid school had continued in one form or another since my first day's dose of it: the beginning of last September had brought on sinking spells, dizziness, and mild gastric complaints. I went so far as to pay a nickel for the privilege of rubbing my head against the head of Miss Rachel's cook's son, who was afflicted with a tremendous ringworm. It didn't take.

But I was worrying another bone. "Do all lawyers defend n–Negroes, Atticus?"

"Of course they do, Scout."

"Then why did Cecil say you defended niggers? He made it sound like you were runnin' a still."

Atticus sighed. "I'm simply defending a Negro—his name's Tom Robinson. He lives in that little settlement beyond the town dump. He's a member of Calpurnia's church, and Cal knows his family well. She says they're clean-living folks. Scout, you aren't old enough to understand some things yet, but there's been some high talk around town to the effect that I shouldn't do much about defending this man. It's a peculiar case—it won't come to trial until summer session. John Taylor was kind enough to give us a postponement . . ."

"If you shouldn't be defendin' him, then why are you doin' it?"

"For a number of reasons," said Atticus. "The main one is, if I didn't I couldn't hold up my head in town, I couldn't represent this county in the legislature, I couldn't even tell you or Jem not to do something again."

"You mean if you didn't defend that man, Jem and me wouldn't have to mind you any more?"

"That's about right."

"Why?"

"Because I could never ask you to mind me again. Scout, simply by the nature of the work, every lawyer gets at least one case in his lifetime that affects him personally. This one's mine, I guess. You might hear some ugly talk about it at school, but do one thing for me if you will: you just hold your head high and keep those fists down. No matter what anybody says to you, don't you let 'em get your goat. Try fighting with your head for a change . . . it's a good one, even if it does resist learning."

"Atticus, are we going to win it?"

"No, honey."

"Then why—"

"Simply because we were licked a hundred years before we started is no reason for us not to try to win," Atticus said.

"You sound like Cousin Ike Finch," I said. Cousin Ike Finch was Maycomb County's sole surviving Confederate veteran. He wore a General Hood type beard of which he was inordinately vain. At least once a year Atticus, Jem and I called on him, and I would have to kiss him. It was horrible. Jem and I would listen respectfully to Atticus and Cousin Ike rehash the war. "Tell you, Atticus," Cousin Ike would say, "the Missouri Compromise was what licked us, but if I had to go through it agin I'd walk every step of the way there an' every step back jist like I did before an' furthermore we'd whip 'em this time . . . now in 1864, when Stonewall Jackson came around by—I beg your pardon, young folks. Ol' Blue Light was in heaven then, God rest his saintly brow. . . ."

"Come here, Scout," said Atticus. I crawled into his lap and tucked my head under his chin. He put his arms around me and rocked me gently. "It's different this time," he said. "This time we aren't fighting the Yankees, we're fighting our friends. But remember this, no matter how bitter things get, they're still our friends and this is still our home."

With this in mind, I faced Cecil Jacobs in the schoolyard next day: "You gonna take that back, boy?"

"You gotta make me first!" he yelled. "My folks said your daddy was a disgrace an' that nigger oughta hang from the water-tank!"

I drew a bead on him, remembered what Atticus had said, then dropped my fists and walked away, "Scout's a cow—ward!" ringing in my ears. It was the first time I ever walked away from a fight.

Somehow, if I fought Cecil I would let Atticus down. Atticus so rarely asked Jem and me to do something for him, I could take being called a coward for him. I felt extremely noble for having remembered, and remained noble for three weeks. Then Christmas came and disaster struck.

*   *   *

Jem and I viewed Christmas with mixed feelings. The good side was the tree and Uncle Jack Finch. Every Christmas Eve day we met Uncle Jack at Maycomb Junction, and he would spend a week with us.

A flip of the coin revealed the uncompromising lineaments of Aunt Alexandra and Francis.

I suppose I should include Uncle Jimmy, Aunt Alexandra's husband, but as he never spoke a word to me in my life except to say, "Get off the fence," once, I never saw any reason to take notice of him. Neither did Aunt Alexandra. Long ago, in a burst of friendliness, Aunty and Uncle Jimmy produced a son named Henry, who left home as soon as was humanly possible, married, and produced Francis. Henry and his wife deposited Francis at his grandparents' every Christmas, then pursued their own pleasures.

No amount of sighing could induce Atticus to let us spend Christmas day at home. We went to Finch's Landing every Christmas in my memory. The fact that Aunty was a good cook was some compensation for being forced to spend a religious holiday with Francis Hancock. He was a year older than I, and I avoided him on principle: he enjoyed everything I disapproved of, and disliked my ingenuous diversions.

Aunt Alexandra was Atticus's sister, but when Jem told me about changelings and siblings, I decided that she had been swapped at birth, that my grandparents had perhaps received a Crawford instead of a Finch. Had I ever harbored the mystical notions about mountains that seem to obsess lawyers and judges, Aunt Alexandra would have been analogous to Mount Everest: throughout my early life, she was cold and there.

When Uncle Jack jumped down from the train Christmas Eve day, we had to wait for the porter to hand him two long packages. Jem and I always thought it funny when Uncle Jack pecked Atticus on the cheek; they were the only two men we ever saw kiss each other. Uncle Jack shook hands with Jem and swung me high, but not high enough: Uncle Jack was a head shorter than Atticus; the baby of the family, he was younger than Aunt Alexandra. He and Aunty looked alike, but Uncle Jack made better use of his face: we were never wary of his sharp nose and chin.

He was one of the few men of science who never terrified me, probably because he never behaved like a doctor. Whenever he performed a minor service for Jem and me, as removing a splinter from a foot, he would tell us exactly what he was going to do, give us an estimation of how much it would hurt, and explain the use of any tongs he employed. One Christmas I lurked in corners nursing a twisted splinter in my foot, permitting no one to come near me. When Uncle Jack caught me, he kept me laughing about a preacher who hated going to church so much that every day he stood at his gate in his dressing-gown, smoking a hookah and delivering five-minute sermons to any passers-by who desired spiritual comfort. I interrupted to make Uncle Jack let me know when he would pull it out, but he held up a bloody splinter in a pair of tweezers and said he yanked it while I was laughing, that was what was known as relativity.

"What's in those packages?" I asked him, pointing to the long thin parcels the porter had given him.

"None of your business," he said.

Jem said, "How's Rose Aylmer?"

Rose Aylmer was Uncle Jack's cat. She was a beautiful yellow female Uncle Jack said was one of the few women he could stand permanently. He reached into his coat pocket and brought out some snapshots. We admired them.

"She's gettin' fat," I said.

"I should think so. She eats all the leftover fingers and ears from the hospital."

"Aw, that's a damn story," I said.

"I beg your pardon?"

Atticus said, "Don't pay any attention to her, Jack. She's trying you out. Cal says she's been cussing fluently for a week, now."

Uncle Jack raised his eyebrows and said nothing. I was

proceeding on the dim theory, aside from the innate attractiveness of such words, that if Atticus discovered I had picked them up at school he wouldn't make me go.

But at supper that evening when I asked him to pass the damn ham, please, Uncle Jack pointed at me. "See me afterwards, young lady," he said.

When supper was over, Uncle Jack went to the livingroom and sat down. He slapped his thighs for me to come sit on his lap. I liked to smell him: he was like a bottle of alcohol and something pleasantly sweet. He pushed back my bangs and looked at me. "You're more like Atticus than your mother," he said. "You're also growing out of your pants a little."

"I reckon they fit all right."

"You like words like damn and hell now, don't you?"

I said I reckoned so.

"Well I don't," said Uncle Jack, "not unless there's extreme provocation connected with 'em. I'll be here a week, and I don't want to hear any words like that while I'm here. Scout, you'll get in trouble if you go around saying things like that. You want to grow up to be a lady, don't you?"

I said not particularly.

"Of course you do. Now let's get to the tree."

We decorated the tree until bedtime, and that night I dreamed of the two long packages for Jem and me. Next morning Jem and I dived for them: they were from Atticus, who had written Uncle Jack to get them for us, and they were what we had asked for.

"Don't point them in the house," said Atticus, when Jem aimed at a picture on the wall.

"You'll have to teach 'em to shoot," said Uncle Jack.

"That's your job," said Atticus. "I merely bowed to the inevitable."

It took Atticus's courtroom voice to drag us away from the tree. He declined to let us take our air rifles to the Landing (I had already begun to think of shooting Francis) and said if we made one false move he'd take them away from us for good.

Finch's Landing consisted of three hundred and sixty-six steps down a high bluff and ending in a jetty. Farther down stream, beyond the bluff, were traces of an old cotton landing, where Finch Negroes had loaded bales and produce, unloaded blocks of ice, flour and sugar, farm equipment, and feminine apparel. A two-rut road ran from the riverside and vanished among dark trees. At the end of the road was a two-storied white house with porches circling it upstairs and downstairs. In his old age, our ancestor Simon Finch had built it to please his nagging wife; but with the porches all resemblance to ordinary houses of its era ended. The internal arrangements of the Finch house were indicative of Simon's guilelessness and the absolute trust with which he regarded his offspring.

There were six bedrooms upstairs, four for the eight female children, one for Welcome Finch, the sole son, and one for visiting relatives. Simple enough; but the daughters' rooms could be reached only by one staircase, Welcome's room and the guestroom only by another. The Daughters' Staircase was in the ground-floor bedroom of their parents, so Simon always knew the hours of his daughters' nocturnal comings and goings.

There was a kitchen separate from the rest of the house, tacked onto it by a wooden catwalk; in the back yard was a rusty bell on a pole, used to summon field hands or as a distress signal; a widow's walk was on the roof, but no widows walked there—from it, Simon oversaw his overseer, watched the river-boats, and gazed into the lives of surrounding landholders.

There went with the house the usual legend about the Yankees: one Finch female, recently engaged, donned her complete trousseau to save it from raiders in the neighborhood; she became stuck in the door to the Daughters' Staircase but was doused with water and finally pushed through. When we arrived at the Landing, Aunt Alexandra kissed Uncle Jack, Francis kissed Uncle Jack, Uncle Jimmy shook hands silently with Uncle Jack, Jem and I gave our presents to Francis, who gave us a present. Jem felt his age and gravitated to the adults, leaving me to entertain our cousin. Francis was eight and slicked back his hair.

"What'd you get for Christmas?" I asked politely.

"Just what I asked for," he said. Francis had requested a pair of knee-pants, a red leather booksack, five shirts and an untied bow tie.

"That's nice," I lied. "Jem and me got air-rifles, and Jem got a chemistry set—"

"A toy one, I reckon."

"No, a real one. He's gonna make me some invisible ink, and I'm gonna write to Dill in it."

Francis asked what was the use of that.

"Well, can't you just see his face when he gets a letter from me with nothing in it? It'll drive him nuts."

Talking to Francis gave me the sensation of settling slowly to the bottom of the ocean. He was the most boring child I ever met. As he lived in Mobile, he could not inform on me to school authorities, but he managed to tell everything he knew to Aunt Alexandra, who in turn unburdened herself to Atticus, who either forgot it or gave me hell, whichever struck his fancy. But the only time I ever heard Atticus speak sharply to anyone was when I once heard him say, "Sister, I do the best I can with them!" It had something to do with my going around in overalls.

Aunt Alexandra was fanatical on the subject of my attire. I could not possibly hope to be a lady if I wore breeches; when I said I could do nothing in a dress, she said I wasn't supposed to be doing things that required pants. Aunt Alexandra's vision of my deportment involved playing with small stoves, tea sets, and wearing the Add-A-Pearl necklace she gave me when I was born; furthermore, I should be a ray of sunshine in my father's lonely life. I suggested that one could be a ray of sunshine in pants just as well, but Aunty said that one had to behave like a sunbeam, that I was born good but had grown progressively worse every year. She hurt my feelings and set my teeth permanently on edge, but when I asked Atticus about it, he said there were already enough sunbeams in the family and to go on about my business, he didn't mind me much the way I was.

At Christmas dinner, I sat at the little table in the diningroom; Jem and Francis sat with the adults at the dining table. Aunty had continued to isolate me long after Jem and Francis graduated to the big table. I often wondered what she thought I'd do, get up and throw something? I sometimes thought of asking her if she would let me sit at the big table with the rest of them just once, I would prove to her how civilized I could be; after all, I ate at home every day with no major mishaps. When I begged Atticus to use his influence, he said he had none—we were guests, and we sat where she told us to sit. He also said Aunt Alexandra didn't understand girls much, she'd never had one.

But her cooking made up for everything: three kinds of meat, summer vegetables from her pantry shelves; peach pickles, two kinds of cake and ambrosia constituted a modest Christmas dinner. Afterwards, the adults made for the livingroom and sat around in a dazed condition. Jem lay on the floor, and I went to the back yard. "Put on your coat," said Atticus dreamily, so I didn't hear him.

Francis sat beside me on the back steps. "That was the best yet," I said.

"Grandma's a wonderful cook," said Francis. "She's gonna teach me how."

"Boys don't cook." I giggled at the thought of Jem in an apron.

"Grandma says all men should learn to cook, that men oughta be careful with their wives and wait on 'em when they don't feel good," said my cousin.

"I don't want Dill waitin' on me," I said. "I'd rather wait on him."

"Dill?"

"Yeah. Don't say anything about it yet, but we're gonna get married as soon as we're big enough. He asked me last summer."

Francis hooted.

"What's the matter with him?" I asked. "Ain't anything the matter with him."

"You mean that little runt Grandma says stays with Miss Rachel every summer?"

"That's exactly who I mean."

"I know all about him," said Francis.

"What about him?"

"Grandma says he hasn't got a home—"

"Has too, he lives in Meridian."

"—he just gets passed around from relative to relative, and Miss Rachel keeps him every summer."

"Francis, that's not so!"

Francis grinned at me. "You're mighty dumb sometimes, Jean Louise. Guess you don't know any better, though."

"What do you mean?"

"If Uncle Atticus lets you run around with stray dogs, that's his own business, like Grandma says, so it ain't your fault. I guess it ain't your fault if Uncle Atticus is a nigger-lover besides, but I'm here to tell you it certainly does mortify the rest of the family—"

"Francis, what the hell do you mean?"

"Just what I said. Grandma says it's bad enough he lets you all run wild, but now he's turned out a nigger-lover we'll never be able to walk the streets of Maycomb again. He's ruinin' the family, that's what he's doin'."

Francis rose and sprinted down the catwalk to the old kitchen. At a safe distance he called, "He's nothin' but a nigger-lover!"

"He is not!" I roared. "I don't know what you're talkin' about, but you better cut it out this red hot minute!"

I leaped off the steps and ran down the catwalk. It was easy to collar Francis. I said take it back quick.

94

Francis jerked loose and sped into the old kitchen. "Nigger-lover!" he yelled.

When stalking one's prey, it is best to take one's time. Say nothing, and as sure as eggs he will become curious and emerge. Francis appeared at the kitchen door. "You still mad, Jean Louise?" he asked tentatively.

"Nothing to speak of," I said.

Francis came out on the catwalk.

"You gonna take it back, Fra—ancis?" But I was too quick on the draw. Francis shot back into the kitchen, so I retired to the steps. I could wait patiently. I had sat there perhaps five minutes when I heard Aunt Alexandra speak: "Where's Francis?"

"He's out yonder in the kitchen."

"He knows he's not supposed to play in there."

Francis came to the door and yelled, "Grandma, she's got me in here and she won't let me out!"

"What is all this, Jean Louise?"

I looked up at Aunt Alexandra. "I haven't got him in there, Aunty, I ain't holdin' him."

"Yes she is," shouted Francis, "she won't let me out!"

"Have you all been fussing?"

"Jean Louise got mad at me, Grandma," called Francis.

"Francis, come out of there! Jean Louise, if I hear another word out of you I'll tell your father. Did I hear you say hell a while ago?"

"Nome."

"I thought I did. I'd better not hear it again."

Aunt Alexandra was a back-porch listener. The moment she was out of sight Francis came out head up and grinning. "Don't you fool with me," he said.

He jumped into the yard and kept his distance, kicking tufts of grass, turning around occasionally to smile at me. Jem appeared on the porch, looked at us, and went away. Francis climbed the mimosa tree, came down, put his hands in his pockets and strolled around the yard. "Hah!" he said. I asked

him who he thought he was, Uncle Jack? Francis said he reckoned I got told, for me to just sit there and leave him alone.

"I ain't botherin' you," I said.

Francis looked at me carefully, concluded that I had been
sufficiently subdued, and crooned softly, "Nigger-lover . . ."

This time, I split my knuckle to the bone on his front
teeth. My left impaired, I sailed in with my right, but not for
long. Uncle Jack pinned my arms to my sides and said, "Stand
still!"

Aunt Alexandra ministered to Francis, wiping his tears
away with her handkerchief, rubbing his hair, patting his
cheek. Atticus, Jem, and Uncle Jimmy had come to the back
porch when Francis started yelling.

"Who started this?" said Uncle Jack.

Francis and I pointed at each other. "Grandma," he
bawled, "she called me a whore-lady and jumped on me!"

"Is that true, Scout?" said Uncle Jack.

"I reckon so."

When Uncle Jack looked down at me, his features were
like Aunt Alexandra's. "You know I told you you'd get in trouble if you used words like that? I told you, didn't I?"

"Yes sir, but—"

"Well, you're in trouble now. Stay there."

I was debating whether to stand there or run, and tarried
in indecision a moment too long: I turned to flee but Uncle
Jack was quicker. I found myself suddenly looking at a tiny
ant struggling with a bread crumb in the grass.

"I'll never speak to you again as long as I live! I hate you
an' despise you an' hope you die tomorrow!" A statement that
seemed to encourage Uncle Jack, more than anything. I ran to
Atticus for comfort, but he said I had it coming and it was
high time we went home. I climbed into the back seat of the
car without saying good-bye to anyone, and at home I ran to
my room and slammed the door. Jem tried to say something
nice, but I wouldn't let him.

When I surveyed the damage there were only seven or

eight red marks, and I was reflecting upon relativity when someone knocked on the door. I asked who it was; Uncle Jack answered.

"Go away!"

Uncle Jack said if I talked like that he'd lick me again, so I was quiet. When he entered the room I retreated to a corner and turned my back on him. "Scout," he said, "do you still hate me?"

"Go on, please sir."

"Why, I didn't think you'd hold it against me," he said. "I'm disappointed in you—you had that coming and you know it."

"Didn't either."

"Honey, you can't go around calling people—"

"You ain't fair," I said, "you ain't fair."

Uncle Jack's eyebrows went up. "Not fair? How not?"

"You're real nice, Uncle Jack, an' I reckon I love you even after what you did, but you don't understand children much."

Uncle Jack put his hands on his hips and looked down at me. "And why do I not understand children, Miss Jean Louise? Such conduct as yours required little understanding. It was obstreperous, disorderly, and abusive—"

"You gonna give me a chance to tell you? I don't mean to sass you, I'm just tryin' to tell you."

Uncle Jack sat down on the bed. His eyebrows came together, and he peered up at me from under them. "Proceed," he said.

I took a deep breath. "Well, in the first place you never stopped to gimme a chance to tell you my side of it—you just lit right into me. When Jem an' I fuss Atticus doesn't ever just listen to Jem's side of it, he hears mine too, an' in the second place you told me never to use words like that except in ex-extreme provocation, and Francis provocated me enough to knock his block off—"

Uncle Jack scratched his head. "What was your side of it, Scout?"

"Francis called Atticus somethin', an' I wasn't about to take it off him."

"What did Francis call him?"

"A nigger-lover. I ain't very sure what it means, but the way Francis said it—tell you one thing right now, Uncle Jack, I'll be—I swear before God if I'll sit there and let him say somethin' about Atticus."

"He called Atticus that?"

"Yes sir, he did, an' a lot more. Said Atticus'd be the ruination of the family an' he let Jem an' me run wild. . . ."

From the look on Uncle Jack's face, I thought I was in for it again. When he said, "We'll see about this," I knew Francis was in for it. "I've a good mind to go out there tonight."

"Please sir, just let it go. Please."

"I've no intention of letting it go," he said. "Alexandra should know about this. The idea of—wait'll I get my hands on that boy. . . ."

"Uncle Jack, please promise me somethin', please sir. Promise you won't tell Atticus about this. He—he asked me one time not to let anything I heard about him make me mad, an' I'd ruther him think we were fightin' about somethin' else instead. Please promise . . ."

"But I don't like Francis getting away with something like that—"

"He didn't. You reckon you could tie up my hand? It's still bleedin' some."

"Of course I will, baby. I know of no hand I would be more delighted to tie up. Will you come this way?"

Uncle Jack gallantly bowed me to the bathroom. While he cleaned and bandaged my knuckles, he entertained me with a tale about a funny nearsighted old gentleman who had a cat named Hodge, and who counted all the cracks in the sidewalk when he went to town. "There now," he said. "You'll have a very unladylike scar on your wedding-ring finger."

"Thank you sir. Uncle Jack?"

"Ma'am?"

98

"What's a whore-lady?"

Uncle Jack plunged into another long tale about an old Prime Minister who sat in the House of Commons and blew feathers in the air and tried to keep them there when all about him men were losing their heads. I guess he was trying to answer my question, but he made no sense whatsoever.

Later, when I was supposed to be in bed, I went down the hall for a drink of water and heard Atticus and Uncle Jack in the livingroom:

"I shall never marry, Atticus."

"Why?"

"I might have children."

Atticus said, "You've a lot to learn, Jack."

"I know. Your daughter gave me my first lesson this afternoon. She said I didn't understand children much and told me why. She was quite right. Atticus, she told me how I should have treated her—oh dear, I'm so sorry I romped on her."

Atticus chuckled. "She earned it, so don't feel too remorseful."

I waited, on tenterhooks, for Uncle Jack to tell Atticus my side of it. But he didn't. He simply murmured, "Her use of bathroom invective leaves nothing to the imagination. But she doesn't know the meaning of half she says—she asked me what a whore-lady was . . ."

"Did you tell her?"

"No, I told her about Lord Melbourne."

"Jack! When a child asks you something, answer him, for goodness' sake. But don't make a production of it. Children are children, but they can spot an evasion quicker than adults, and evasion simply muddles 'em. No," my father mused, "you had the right answer this afternoon, but the wrong reasons. Bad language is a stage all children go through, and it dies with time when they learn they're not attracting attention with it. Hotheadedness isn't. Scout's got to learn to keep her head and learn soon, with what's in store for her these next few months. She's coming along, though. Jem's getting older and she follows his example a good bit now. All she needs is assistance sometimes."

"Atticus, you've never laid a hand on her."

"I admit that. So far I've been able to get by with threats. Jack, she minds me as well as she can. Doesn't come up to scratch half the time, but she tries."

"That's not the answer," said Uncle Jack.

"No, the answer is she knows I know she tries. That's what makes the difference. What bothers me is that she and Jem will have to absorb some ugly things pretty soon. I'm not worried about Jem keeping his head, but Scout'd just as soon jump on someone as look at him if her pride's at stake. . . ."

I waited for Uncle Jack to break his promise. He still didn't.

"Atticus, how bad is this going to be? You haven't had too much chance to discuss it."

"It couldn't be worse, Jack. The only thing we've got is a black man's word against the Ewells'. The evidence boils down to you-did—I-didn't. The jury couldn't possibly be expected to take Tom Robinson's word against the Ewells'— are you acquainted with the Ewells?"

Uncle Jack said yes, he remembered them. He described them to Atticus, but Atticus said, "You're a generation off. The present ones are the same, though."

"What are you going to do, then?"

"Before I'm through, I intend to jar the jury a bit—I think we'll have a reasonable chance on appeal, though. I really can't tell at this stage, Jack. You know, I'd hoped to get through life without a case of this kind, but John Taylor pointed at me and said, 'You're It.'"

"Let this cup pass from you, eh?"

"Right. But do you think I could face my children otherwise? You know what's going to happen as well as I do, Jack, and I hope and pray I can get Jem and Scout through it without bitterness, and most of all, without catching Maycomb's usual disease. Why reasonable people go stark raving mad when anything involving a Negro comes up, is something I don't pretend to understand . . . I just hope that Jem and Scout come to me for their answers instead of listening to the town. I hope they trust me enough. . . . Jean Louise?"

My scalp jumped. I stuck my head around the corner. "Sir?"

"Go to bed."

I scurried to my room and went to bed. Uncle Jack was a prince of a fellow not to let me down. But I never figured out how Atticus knew I was listening, and it was not until many years later that I realized he wanted me to hear every word he said.

10

Atticus was feeble: he was nearly fifty. When Jem and I asked him why he was so old, he said he got started late, which we felt reflected upon his abilities and manliness. He was much older than the parents of our school contemporaries, and there was nothing Jem or I could say about him when our classmates said, "*My* father—"

Jem was football crazy. Atticus was never too tired to play keep-away, but when Jem wanted to tackle him Atticus would say, "I'm too old for that, son."

Our father didn't do anything. He worked in an office, not in a drugstore. Atticus did not drive a dump-truck for the county, he was not the sheriff, he did not farm, work in a garage, or do anything that could possibly arouse the admiration of anyone.

Besides that, he wore glasses. He was nearly blind in his left eye, and said left eyes were the tribal curse of the Finches. Whenever he wanted to see something well, he turned his head and looked from his right eye.

He did not do the things our schoolmates' fathers did: he never went hunting, he did not play poker or fish or drink or smoke. He sat in the livingroom and read.

With these attributes, however, he would not remain as inconspicuous as we wished him to: that year, the school buzzed with talk about him defending Tom Robinson, none of which was complimentary. After my bout with Cecil Jacobs when I committed myself to a policy of cowardice, word got around that Scout Finch wouldn't fight any more, her daddy wouldn't let her. This was not entirely correct: I wouldn't fight publicly for Atticus, but the family was private ground. I would fight anyone from a third cousin upwards tooth and nail. Francis Hancock, for example, knew that.

When he gave us our air-rifles Atticus wouldn't teach us to shoot. Uncle Jack instructed us in the rudiments thereof; he said Atticus wasn't interested in guns. Atticus said to Jem one day, "I'd rather you shot at tin cans in the back yard, but I know you'll go after birds. Shoot all the bluejays you want, if you can hit 'em, but remember it's a sin to kill a mockingbird."

That was the only time I ever heard Atticus say it was a sin to do something, and I asked Miss Maudie about it.

"Your father's right," she said. "Mockingbirds don't do one thing but make music for us to enjoy. They don't eat up people's gardens, don't nest in corncribs, they don't do one thing but sing their hearts out for us. That's why it's a sin to kill a mockingbird."

"Miss Maudie, this is an old neighborhood, ain't it?"

"Been here longer than the town."

"Nome, I mean the folks on our street are all old. Jem and me's the only children around here. Mrs. Dubose is close on to a hundred and Miss Rachel's old and so are you and Atticus."

"I don't call fifty very old," said Miss Maudie tartly. "Not being wheeled around yet, am I? Neither's your father. But I must say Providence was kind enough to burn down that old mausoleum of mine, I'm too old to keep it up—maybe you're right, Jean Louise, this is a settled neighborhood. You've never been around young folks much, have you?"

"Yessum, at school."

"I mean young grown-ups. You're lucky, you know. You and Jem have the benefit of your father's age. If your father was thirty you'd find life quite different."

"I sure would. Atticus can't do anything. . . ."

"You'd be surprised," said Miss Maudie. "There's life in him yet."

"What can he do?"

"Well, he can make somebody's will so airtight can't anybody meddle with it."

"Shoot . . ."

"Well, did you know he's the best checker-player in this town? Why, down at the Landing when we were coming up, Atticus Finch could beat everybody on both sides of the river."

"Good Lord, Miss Maudie, Jem and me beat him all the time."

"It's about time you found out it's because he lets you. Did you know he can play a Jew's Harp?"

This modest accomplishment served to make me even more ashamed of him.

"*Well* . . ." she said.

"Well what, Miss Maudie?"

"Well nothing. Nothing—it seems with all that you'd be proud of him. Can't everybody play a Jew's Harp. Now keep out of the way of the carpenters. You'd better go home, I'll be in my azaleas and can't watch you. Plank might hit you."

I went to the back yard and found Jem plugging away at a tin can, which seemed stupid with all the bluejays around. I returned to the front yard and busied myself for two hours erecting a complicated breastworks at the side of the porch, consisting of a tire, an orange crate, the laundry hamper, the porch chairs, and a small U.S. flag Jem gave me from a popcorn box.

When Atticus came home to dinner he found me crouched down aiming across the street. "What are you shooting at?"

"Miss Maudie's rear end."

Atticus turned and saw my generous target bending over her bushes. He pushed his hat to the back of his head and crossed the street. "Maudie," he called, "I thought I'd better warn you. You're in considerable peril."

Miss Maudie straightened up and looked toward me. She said, "Atticus, you are a devil from hell."

When Atticus returned he told me to break camp. "Don't

you ever let me catch you pointing that gun at anybody again," he said.

I wished my father was a devil from hell. I sounded out Calpurnia on the subject. "Mr. Finch? Why, he can do lots of things."

"Like what?" I asked.

Calpurnia scratched her head. "Well, I don't rightly know," she said.

Jem underlined it when he asked Atticus if he was going out for the Methodists and Atticus said he'd break his neck if he did, he was just too old for that sort of thing. The Methodists were trying to pay off their church mortgage, and had challenged the Baptists to a game of touch football. Everybody in town's father was playing, it seemed, except Atticus. Jem said he didn't even want to go, but he was unable to resist football in any form, and he stood gloomily on the sidelines with Atticus and me watching Cecil Jacobs's father make touchdowns for the Baptists.

One Saturday Jem and I decided to go exploring with our air-rifles to see if we could find a rabbit or a squirrel. We had gone about five hundred yards beyond the Radley Place when I noticed Jem squinting at something down the street. He had turned his head to one side and was looking out of the corners of his eyes.

"Whatcha looking at?"

"That old dog down yonder," he said.

"That's old Tim Johnson, ain't it?"

"Yeah."

Tim Johnson was the property of Mr. Harry Johnson who drove the Mobile bus and lived on the southern edge of town. Tim was a liver-colored bird dog, the pet of Maycomb.

"What's he doing?"

"I don't know, Scout. We better go home."

"Aw Jem, it's February."

"I don't care, I'm gonna tell Cal."

We raced home and ran to the kitchen.

"Cal," said Jem, "can you come down the sidewalk a minute?"

"What for, Jem? I can't come down the sidewalk every time you want me."

"There's somethin' wrong with an old dog down yonder."

Calpurnia sighed. "I can't wrap up any dog's foot now. There's some gauze in the bathroom, go get it and do it yourself."

Jem shook his head. "He's sick, Cal. Something's wrong with him."

"What's he doin', trying to catch his tail?"

"No, he's doin' like this."

Jem gulped like a goldfish, hunched his shoulders and twitched his torso. "He's goin' like that, only not like he means to."

"Are you telling me a story, Jem Finch?" Calpurnia's voice hardened.

"No Cal, I swear I'm not."

"Was he runnin'?"

"No, he's just moseyin' along, so slow you can't hardly tell it. He's comin' this way."

Calpurnia rinsed her hands and followed Jem into the yard. "I don't see any dog," she said.

She followed us beyond the Radley Place and looked where Jem pointed. Tim Johnson was not much more than a speck in the distance, but he was closer to us. He walked erratically, as if his right legs were shorter than his left legs. He reminded me of a car stuck in a sand-bed.

"He's gone lopsided," said Jem.

Calpurnia stared, then grabbed us by the shoulders and ran us home. She shut the wood door behind us, went to the telephone and shouted, "Gimme Mr. Finch's office!"

"Mr. Finch!" she shouted. "This is Cal. I swear to God there's a mad dog down the street a piece—he's comin' this way, yes sir, he's—Mr. Finch, I declare he is—old Tim Johnson, yes sir . . . yessir . . . yes—"

She hung up and shook her head when we tried to ask her what Atticus had said. She rattled the telephone hook and said, "Miss Eula May—now ma'am, I'm through talkin' to Mr. Finch, please don't connect me no more—listen, Miss Eula May, can you call Miss Rachel and Miss Stephanie Crawford and whoever's got a phone on this street and tell 'em a mad dog's comin'? Please ma'am!"

Calpurnia listened. "I know it's February, Miss Eula May, but I know a mad dog when I see one. Please ma'am hurry!"

Calpurnia asked Jem, "Radleys got a phone?"

Jem looked in the book and said no. "They won't come out anyway, Cal."

"I don't care, I'm gonna tell 'em."

She ran to the front porch, Jem and I at her heels. "You stay in that house!" she yelled.

Calpurnia's message had been received by the neighborhood. Every wood door within our range of vision was closed tight. We saw no trace of Tim Johnson. We watched Calpurnia running toward the Radley Place, holding her skirt and apron above her knees. She went up to the front steps and banged on the door. She got no answer, and she shouted, "Mr. Nathan, Mr. Arthur, mad dog's comin'! Mad dog's comin'!"

"She's supposed to go around in back," I said.

Jem shook his head. "Don't make any difference now," he said.

Calpurnia pounded on the door in vain. No one acknowledged her warning; no one seemed to have heard it.

As Calpurnia sprinted to the back porch a black Ford swung into the driveway. Atticus and Mr. Heck Tate got out.

Mr. Heck Tate was the sheriff of Maycomb County. He was as tall as Atticus, but thinner. He was long-nosed, wore boots with shiny metal eye-holes, boot pants and a lumber jacket. His belt had a row of bullets sticking in it. He carried a heavy rifle. When he and Atticus reached the porch, Jem opened the door.

"Stay inside, son," said Atticus. "Where is he, Cal?"

"He oughta be here by now," said Calpurnia, pointing down the street.

"Not runnin', is he?" asked Mr. Tate.

"Naw sir, he's in the twitchin' stage, Mr. Heck."

"Should we go after him, Heck?" asked Atticus.

"We better wait, Mr. Finch. They usually go in a straight line, but you never can tell. He might follow the curve—hope he does or he'll go straight in the Radley back yard. Let's wait a minute."

"Don't think he'll get in the Radley yard," said Atticus. "Fence'll stop him. He'll probably follow the road. . . ."

I thought mad dogs foamed at the mouth, galloped, leaped and lunged at throats, and I thought they did it in August. Had Tim Johnson behaved thus, I would have been less frightened.

Nothing is more deadly than a deserted, waiting street. The trees were still, the mockingbirds were silent, the carpenters at Miss Maudie's house had vanished. I heard Mr. Tate sniff, then blow his nose. I saw him shift his gun to the crook of his arm. I saw Miss Stephanie Crawford's face framed in the glass window of her front door. Miss Maudie appeared and stood beside her. Atticus put his foot on the rung of a chair and rubbed his hand slowly down the side of his thigh.

"There he is," he said softly.

Tim Johnson came into sight, walking dazedly in the inner rim of the curve parallel to the Radley house.

"Look at him," whispered Jem. "Mr. Heck said they walked in a straight line. He can't even stay in the road."

"He looks more sick than anything," I said.

"Let anything get in front of him and he'll come straight at it."

Mr. Tate put his hand to his forehead and leaned forward. "He's got it all right, Mr. Finch."

Tim Johnson was advancing at a snail's pace, but he was not playing or sniffing at foliage: he seemed dedicated to one course and motivated by an invisible force that was inching him toward us. We could see him shiver like a horse shedding flies; his jaw opened and shut; he was alist, but he was being pulled gradually toward us.

"He's lookin' for a place to die," said Jem.

Mr. Tate turned around. "He's far from dead, Jem, he hasn't got started yet."

Tim Johnson reached the side street that ran in front of the Radley Place, and what remained of his poor mind made him pause and seem to consider which road he would take. He made a few hesitant steps and stopped in front of the Radley gate; then he tried to turn around, but was having difficulty.

Atticus said, "He's within range, Heck. You better get him now before he goes down the side street—Lord knows who's around the corner. Go inside, Cal."

Calpurnia opened the screen door, latched it behind her, then unlatched it and held onto the hook. She tried to block Jem and me with her body, but we looked out from beneath her arms.

"Take him, Mr. Finch." Mr. Tate handed the rifle to Atticus; Jem and I nearly fainted.

"Don't waste time, Heck," said Atticus. "Go on."

"Mr. Finch, this is a one-shot job."

Atticus shook his head vehemently: "Don't just stand there, Heck! He won't wait all day for you—"

"For God's sake, Mr. Finch, look where he is! Miss and you'll go straight into the Radley house! I can't shoot that well and you know it!"

"I haven't shot a gun in thirty years—"

Mr. Tate almost threw the rifle at Atticus. "I'd feel mighty comfortable if you did now," he said.

In a fog, Jem and I watched our father take the gun and walk out into the middle of the street. He walked quickly, but I thought he moved like an underwater swimmer: time had slowed to a nauseating crawl.

When Atticus raised his glasses Calpurnia murmured, "Sweet Jesus help him," and put her hands to her cheeks.

Atticus pushed his glasses to his forehead; they slipped down, and he dropped them in the street. In the silence, I heard them crack. Atticus rubbed his eyes and chin; we saw him blink hard.

In front of the Radley gate, Tim Johnson had made up what was left of his mind. He had finally turned himself around, to pursue his original course up our street. He made two steps forward, then stopped and raised his head. We saw his body go rigid.

With movements so swift they seemed simultaneous, Atticus's hand yanked a ball-tipped lever as he brought the gun to his shoulder.

The rifle cracked. Tim Johnson leaped, flopped over and crumpled on the sidewalk in a brown-and-white heap. He didn't know what hit him.

Mr. Tate jumped off the porch and ran to the Radley Place. He stopped in front of the dog, squatted, turned around and tapped his finger on his forehead above his left eye. "You were a little to the right, Mr. Finch," he called.

"Always was," answered Atticus. "If I had my 'druthers I'd take a shotgun."

He stooped and picked up his glasses, ground the broken lenses to powder under his heel, and went to Mr. Tate and stood looking down at Tim Johnson.

Doors opened one by one, and the neighborhood slowly came alive. Miss Maudie walked down the steps with Miss Stephanie Crawford.

Jem was paralyzed. I pinched him to get him moving, but when Atticus saw us coming he called, "Stay where you are."

When Mr. Tate and Atticus returned to the yard, Mr. Tate was smiling. "I'll have Zeebo collect him," he said. "You haven't forgot much, Mr. Finch. They say it never leaves you."

Atticus was silent.

"Atticus?" said Jem.

110

"Yes?"

"Nothin'."

"I saw that, One-Shot Finch!"

Atticus wheeled around and faced Miss Maudie. They looked at one another without saying anything, and Atticus got into the sheriff's car. "Come here," he said to Jem. "Don't you go near that dog, you understand? Don't go near him, he's just as dangerous dead as alive."

"Yes sir," said Jem. "Atticus—"

"What, son?"

"Nothing."

"What's the matter with you, boy, can't you talk?" said Mr. Tate, grinning at Jem. "Didn't you know your daddy's—"

"Hush, Heck," said Atticus, "let's go back to town."

When they drove away, Jem and I went to Miss Stephanie's front steps. We sat waiting for Zeebo to arrive in the garbage truck.

Jem sat in numb confusion, and Miss Stephanie said, "Uh, uh, uh, who'da thought of a mad dog in February? Maybe he wasn't mad, maybe he was just crazy. I'd hate to see Harry Johnson's face when he gets in from the Mobile run and finds Atticus Finch's shot his dog. Bet he was just full of fleas from somewhere—"

Miss Maudie said Miss Stephanie'd be singing a different tune if Tim Johnson was still coming up the street, that they'd find out soon enough, they'd send his head to Montgomery.

Jem became vaguely articulate: "'d you see him, Scout? 'd you see him just standin' there? . . . 'n' all of a sudden he just relaxed all over, an' it looked like that gun was a part of him . . . an' he did it so quick, like . . . I hafta aim for ten minutes 'fore I can hit somethin'. . . . "

Miss Maudie grinned wickedly. "Well now, Miss Jean Louise," she said, "still think your father can't do anything? Still ashamed of him?"

"Nome," I said meekly.

"Forgot to tell you the other day that besides playing the

Jew's Harp, Atticus Finch was the deadest shot in Maycomb County in his time."

"Dead shot . . ." echoed Jem.

"That's what I said, Jem Finch. Guess you'll change *your* tune now. The very idea, didn't you know his nickname was Ol' One-Shot when he was a boy? Why, down at the Landing when he was coming up, if he shot fifteen times and hit fourteen doves he'd complain about wasting ammunition."

"He never said anything about that," Jem muttered.

"Never said anything about it, did he?"

"No ma'am."

"Wonder why he never goes huntin' now," I said.

"Maybe I can tell you," said Miss Maudie. "If your father's anything, he's civilized in his heart. Marksmanship's a gift of God, a talent—oh, you have to practice to make it perfect, but shootin's different from playing the piano or the like. I think maybe he put his gun down when he realized that God had given him an unfair advantage over most living things. I guess he decided he wouldn't shoot till he had to, and he had to today."

"Looks like he'd be proud of it," I said.

"People in their right minds never take pride in their talents," said Miss Maudie.

We saw Zeebo drive up. He took a pitchfork from the back of the garbage truck and gingerly lifted Tim Johnson. He pitched the dog onto the truck, then poured something from a gallon jug on and around the spot where Tim fell. "Don't yawl come over here for a while," he called.

When we went home I told Jem we'd really have something to talk about at school on Monday. Jem turned on me.

"Don't say anything about it, Scout," he said.

"What? I certainly am. Ain't everybody's daddy the deadest shot in Maycomb County."

Jem said, "I reckon if he'd wanted us to know it, he'da told us. If he was proud of it, he'da told us."

"Maybe it just slipped his mind," I said.

"Naw, Scout, it's something you wouldn't understand. Atticus is real old, but I wouldn't care if he couldn't do anything—I wouldn't care if he couldn't do a blessed thing."

Jem picked up a rock and threw it jubilantly at the carhouse. Running after it, he called back: "Atticus is a gentleman, just like me!"

11

When we were small, Jem and I confined our activities to the southern neighborhood, but when I was well into the second grade at school and tormenting Boo Radley became passé, the business section of Maycomb drew us frequently up the street past the real property of Mrs. Henry Lafayette Dubose. It was impossible to go to town without passing her house unless we wished to walk a mile out of the way. Previous minor encounters with her left me with no desire for more, but Jem said I had to grow up some time.

Mrs. Dubose lived alone except for a Negro girl in constant attendance, two doors up the street from us in a house with steep front steps and a dog-trot hall. She was very old; she spent most of each day in bed and the rest of it in a wheelchair. It was rumored that she kept a CSA pistol concealed among her numerous shawls and wraps.

Jem and I hated her. If she was on the porch when we passed, we would be raked by her wrathful gaze, subjected to ruthless interrogation regarding our behavior, and given a melancholy prediction on what we would amount to when we grew up, which was always nothing. We had long ago given up the idea of walking past her house on the opposite side of the street; that only made her raise her voice and let the whole neighborhood in on it.

We could do nothing to please her. If I said as sunnily as I could, "Hey, Mrs. Dubose," I would receive for an answer, "Don't you say hey to me, you ugly girl! You say good afternoon, Mrs. Dubose!"

She was vicious. Once she heard Jem refer to our father as "Atticus" and her reaction was apoplectic. Besides being the sassiest, most disrespectful mutts whoever passed her way, we were told that it was quite a pity our father had not remarried after our mother's death. A lovelier lady than our mother never lived, she said, and it was heartbreaking the way Atticus Finch let her children run wild. I did not remember our mother, but Jem did—he would tell me about her sometimes—and he went livid when Mrs. Dubose shot us this message.

Jem, having survived Boo Radley, a mad dog and other terrors, had concluded that it was cowardly to stop at Miss Rachel's front steps and wait, and had decreed that we must run as far as the post office corner each evening to meet Atticus coming from work. Countless evenings Atticus would find Jem furious at something Mrs. Dubose had said when we went by.

"Easy does it, son," Atticus would say. "She's an old lady and she's ill. You just hold your head high and be a gentleman. Whatever she says to you, it's your job not to let her make you mad."

Jem would say she must not be very sick, she hollered so. When the three of us came to her house, Atticus would sweep off his hat, wave gallantly to her and say, "Good evening, Mrs. Dubose! You look like a picture this evening."

I never heard Atticus say like a picture of what. He would tell her the courthouse news, and would say he hoped with all his heart she'd have a good day tomorrow. He would return his hat to his head, swing me to his shoulders in her very presence, and we would go home in the twilight. It was times like these when I thought my father, who hated guns and had never been to any wars, was the bravest man who ever lived.

The day after Jem's twelfth birthday his money was burning up his pockets, so we headed for town in the early afternoon. Jem thought he had enough to buy a miniature steam engine for himself and a twirling baton for me.

I had long had my eye on that baton: it was at V. J.

Elmore's, it was bedecked with sequins and tinsel, it cost seventeen cents. It was then my burning ambition to grow up and twirl with the Maycomb County High School band. Having developed my talent to where I could throw up a stick and almost catch it coming down, I had caused Calpurnia to deny me entrance to the house every time she saw me with a stick in my hand. I felt that I could overcome this defect with a real baton, and I thought it generous of Jem to buy one for me.

Mrs. Dubose was stationed on her porch when we went by.

"Where are you two going at this time of day?" she shouted. "Playing hooky, I suppose. I'll just call up the principal and tell him!" She put her hands on the wheels of her chair and executed a perfect right face.

"Aw, it's Saturday, Mrs. Dubose," said Jem.

"Makes no difference if it's Saturday," she said obscurely. "I wonder if your father knows where you are?"

"Mrs. Dubose, we've been goin' to town by ourselves since we were this high." Jem placed his hand palm down about two feet above the sidewalk.

"Don't you lie to me!" she yelled. "Jeremy Finch, Maudie Atkinson told me you broke down her scuppernong arbor this morning. She's going to tell your father and then you'll wish you never saw the light of day! If you aren't sent to the reform school before next week, my name's not Dubose!"

Jem, who hadn't been near Miss Maudie's scuppernong arbor since last summer, and who knew Miss Maudie wouldn't tell Atticus if he had, issued a general denial.

"Don't you contradict me!" Mrs. Dubose bawled. "And *you*—" she pointed an arthritic finger at me—"what are you doing in those overalls? You should be in a dress and camisole, young lady! You'll grow up waiting on tables if somebody doesn't change your ways—a Finch waiting on tables at the O.K. Café—hah!"

I was terrified. The O.K. Café was a dim organization on the north side of the square. I grabbed Jem's hand but he shook me loose.

"Come on, Scout," he whispered. "Don't pay any attention to her, just hold your head high and be a gentleman."

But Mrs. Dubose held us: "Not only a Finch waiting on tables but one in the courthouse lawing for niggers!"

Jem stiffened. Mrs. Dubose's shot had gone home and she knew it:

"Yes indeed, what has this world come to when a Finch goes against his raising? I'll tell you!" She put her hand to her mouth. When she drew it away, it trailed a long silver thread of saliva. "Your father's no better than the niggers and trash he works for!"

Jem was scarlet. I pulled at his sleeve, and we were followed up the sidewalk by a philippic on our family's moral degeneration, the major premise of which was that half the Finches were in the asylum anyway, but if our mother were living we would not have come to such a state.

I wasn't sure what Jem resented most, but I took umbrage at Mrs. Dubose's assessment of the family's mental hygiene. I had become almost accustomed to hearing insults aimed at Atticus. But this was the first one coming from an adult. Except for her remarks about Atticus, Mrs. Dubose's attack was only routine. There was a hint of summer in the air—in the shadows it was cool, but the sun was warm, which meant good times coming: no school and Dill.

Jem bought his steam engine and we went by Elmore's for my baton. Jem took no pleasure in his acquisition; he jammed it in his pocket and walked silently beside me toward home. On the way home I nearly hit Mr. Link Deas, who said, "Look out now, Scout!" when I missed a toss, and when we approached Mrs. Dubose's house my baton was grimy from having picked it up out of the dirt so many times.

She was not on the porch.

In later years, I sometimes wondered exactly what made Jem do it, what made him break the bonds of "You just be a gentleman, son," and the phase of self-conscious rectitude he had recently entered. Jem had probably stood as much guff about Atticus lawing for niggers as had I, and I took it for granted that he kept his temper—he had a naturally tranquil disposition and a slow fuse. At the time, however, I thought the only explanation for what he did was that for a few minutes he simply went mad.

What Jem did was something I'd do as a matter of course had I not been under Atticus's interdict, which I assumed included not fighting horrible old ladies. We had just come to her gate when Jem snatched my baton and ran flailing wildly up the steps into Mrs. Dubose's front yard, forgetting everything Atticus had said, forgetting that she packed a pistol under her shawls, forgetting that if Mrs. Dubose missed, her girl Jessie probably wouldn't.

He did not begin to calm down until he had cut the tops off every camellia bush Mrs. Dubose owned, until the ground was littered with green buds and leaves. He bent my baton against his knee, snapped it in two and threw it down.

By that time I was shrieking. Jem yanked my hair, said he didn't care, he'd do it again if he got a chance, and if I didn't shut up he'd pull every hair out of my head. I didn't shut up and he kicked me. I lost my balance and fell on my face. Jem picked me up roughly but looked like he was sorry. There was nothing to say.

We did not choose to meet Atticus coming home that evening. We skulked around the kitchen until Calpurnia threw us out. By some voo-doo system Calpurnia seemed to know all about it. She was a less than satisfactory source of palliation, but she did give Jem a hot biscuit-and-butter which he tore in half and shared with me. It tasted like cotton.

We went to the livingroom. I picked up a football magazine, found a picture of Dixie Howell, showed it to Jem and said, "This looks like you." That was the nicest thing I could think to say to him, but it was no help. He sat by the windows, hunched down in a rocking chair, scowling, waiting. Daylight faded.

Two geological ages later, we heard the soles of Atticus's shoes scrape the front steps. The screen door slammed, there was a pause—Atticus was at the hat rack in the hall—and we heard him call, "Jem!" His voice was like the winter wind.

Atticus switched on the ceiling light in the livingroom and found us there, frozen still. He carried my baton in one hand; its filthy yellow tassel trailed on the rug. He held out his other hand; it contained fat camellia buds.

"Jem," he said, "are you responsible for this?"

"Yes sir."

"Why'd you do it?"

Jem said softly, "She said you lawed for niggers and trash."

"You did this because she said that?"

Jem's lips moved, but his "Yes sir" was inaudible.

"Son, I have no doubt that you've been annoyed by your contemporaries about me lawing for niggers, as you say, but to do something like this to a sick old lady is inexcusable. I strongly advise you to go down and have a talk with Mrs. Dubose," said Atticus. "Come straight home afterward."

Jem did not move.

"Go on, I said."

I followed Jem out of the livingroom. "Come back here," Atticus said to me. I came back.

Atticus picked up *The Mobile Press* and sat down in the rocking chair Jem had vacated. For the life of me, I did not understand how he could sit there in cold blood and read a newspaper when his only son stood an excellent chance of being murdered with a Confederate Army relic. Of course Jem antagonized me sometimes until I could kill him, but when it came down to it he was all I had. Atticus did not seem to realize this, or if he did he didn't care.

I hated him for that, but when you are in trouble you become easily tired: soon I was hiding in his lap and his arms were around me.

"You're mighty big to be rocked," he said.

"You don't care what happens to him," I said. "You just

send him on to get shot at when all he was doin' was standin' up for you."

Atticus pushed my head under his chin. "It's not time to worry yet," he said. "I never thought Jem'd be the one to lose his head over this—thought I'd have more trouble with you."

I said I didn't see why we had to keep our heads anyway, that nobody I knew at school had to keep his head about anything.

"Scout," said Atticus, "when summer comes you'll have to keep your head about far worse things . . . it's not fair for you and Jem, I know that, but sometimes we have to make the best of things, and the way we conduct ourselves when the chips are down—well, all I can say is, when you and Jem are grown, maybe you'll look back on this with some compassion and some feeling that I didn't let you down. This case, Tom Robinson's case, is something that goes to the essence of a man's conscience—Scout, I couldn't go to church and worship God if I didn't try to help that man."

"Atticus, you must be wrong. . . ."

"How's that?"

"Well, most folks seem to think they're right and you're wrong. . . ."

"They're certainly entitled to think that, and they're entitled to full respect for their opinions," said Atticus, "but before I can live with other folks I've got to live with myself. The one thing that doesn't abide by majority rule is a person's conscience."

When Jem returned, he found me still in Atticus's lap. "Well, son?" said Atticus. He set me on my feet, and I made a secret reconnaissance of Jem. He seemed to be all in one piece, but he had a queer look on his face. Perhaps she had given him a dose of calomel.

"I cleaned it up for her and said I was sorry, but I ain't, and that I'd work on 'em ever Saturday and try to make 'em grow back out."

"There was no point in saying you were sorry if you

aren't," said Atticus. "Jem, she's old and ill. You can't hold her responsible for what she says and does. Of course, I'd rather she'd have said it to me than to either of you, but we can't always have our 'druthers."

Jem seemed fascinated by a rose in the carpet. "Atticus," he said, "she wants me to read to her."

"Read to her?"

"Yes sir. She wants me to come every afternoon after school and Saturdays and read to her out loud for two hours. Atticus, do I have to?"

"Certainly."

"But she wants me to do it for a month."

"Then you'll do it for a month."

Jem planted his big toe delicately in the center of the rose and pressed it in. Finally he said, "Atticus, it's all right on the sidewalk but inside it's—it's all dark and creepy. There's shadows and things on the ceiling. . . ."

Atticus smiled grimly. "That should appeal to your imagination. Just pretend you're inside the Radley house."

The following Monday afternoon Jem and I climbed the steep front steps to Mrs. Dubose's house and padded down the open hallway. Jem, armed with *Ivanhoe* and full of superior knowledge, knocked at the second door on the left.

"Mrs. Dubose?" he called.

Jessie opened the wood door and unlatched the screen door.

"Is that you, Jem Finch?" she said. "You got your sister with you. I don't know—"

"Let 'em both in, Jessie," said Mrs. Dubose. Jessie admitted us and went off to the kitchen.

An oppressive odor met us when we crossed the threshold, an odor I had met many times in rain-rotted gray houses where there are coal-oil lamps, water dippers, and unbleached domestic sheets. It always made me afraid, expectant, watchful.

In the corner of the room was a brass bed, and in the bed was Mrs. Dubose. I wondered if Jem's activities had put her there, and for a moment I felt sorry for her. She was lying under a pile of quilts and looked almost friendly.

There was a marble-topped washstand by her bed; on it were a glass with a teaspoon in it, a red ear syringe, a box of absorbent cotton, and a steel alarm clock standing on three tiny legs.

"So you brought that dirty little sister of yours, did you?" was her greeting.

Jem said quietly, "My sister ain't dirty and I ain't scared of you," although I noticed his knees shaking.

I was expecting a tirade, but all she said was, "You may commence reading, Jeremy."

Jem sat down in a cane-bottom chair and opened *Ivanhoe*. I pulled up another one and sat beside him.

"Come closer," said Mrs. Dubose. "Come to the side of the bed."

We moved our chairs forward. This was the nearest I had ever been to her, and the thing I wanted most to do was move my chair back again.

She was horrible. Her face was the color of a dirty pillow-case, and the corners of her mouth glistened with wet, which inched like a glacier down the deep grooves enclosing her chin. Old-age liver spots dotted her cheeks, and her pale eyes had black pinpoint pupils. Her hands were knobby, and the cuticles were grown up over her fingernails. Her bottom plate was not in, and her upper lip protruded; from time to time she would draw her nether lip to her upper plate and carry her chin with it. This made the wet move faster.

I didn't look any more than I had to. Jem reopened *Ivanhoe* and began reading. I tried to keep up with him, but he read too fast. When Jem came to a word he didn't know, he skipped it, but Mrs. Dubose would catch him and make him spell it out. Jem read for perhaps twenty minutes, during which time I looked at the soot-stained mantelpiece, out the window, anywhere to keep from looking at her. As he read along, I noticed that Mrs. Dubose's corrections grew fewer and farther between, that Jem had even left one sentence dangling in mid-air. She was not listening.

I looked toward the bed.

Something had happened to her. She lay on her back, with the quilts up to her chin. Only her head and shoulders were visible. Her head moved slowly from side to side. From time to time she would open her mouth wide, and I could see her tongue undulate faintly. Cords of saliva would collect on her lips; she would draw them in, then open her mouth again. Her mouth seemed to have a private existence of its own. It worked separate and apart from the rest of her, out and in, like a clam hole at low tide. Occasionally it would say, "Pt," like some viscous substance coming to a boil.

I pulled Jem's sleeve.

He looked at me, then at the bed. Her head made its regular sweep toward us, and Jem said, "Mrs. Dubose, are you all right?" She did not hear him.

The alarm clock went off and scared us stiff. A minute later, nerves still tingling, Jem and I were on the sidewalk headed for home. We did not run away, Jessie sent us: before the clock wound down she was in the room pushing Jem and me out of it.

"Shoo," she said, "you all go home."

Jem hesitated at the door.

"It's time for her medicine," Jessie said. As the door swung shut behind us I saw Jessie walking quickly toward Mrs. Dubose's bed.

It was only three forty-five when we got home, so Jem and I drop-kicked in the back yard until it was time to meet Atticus. Atticus had two yellow pencils for me and a football magazine for Jem, which I suppose was a silent reward for our first day's session with Mrs. Dubose. Jem told him what happened.

"Did she frighten you?" asked Atticus.

"No sir," said Jem, "but she's so nasty. She has fits or some-thin'. She spits a lot."

"She can't help that. When people are sick they don't look nice sometimes."

"She scared me," I said.

Atticus looked at me over his glasses. "You don't have to go with Jem, you know."

The next afternoon at Mrs. Dubose's was the same as the first, and so was the next, until gradually a pattern emerged: everything would begin normally—that is, Mrs. Dubose would hound Jem for a while on her favorite subjects, her camellias and our father's nigger-loving propensities; she would grow increasingly silent, then go away from us. The alarm clock would ring, Jessie would shoo us out, and the rest of the day was ours.

"Atticus," I said one evening, "what exactly is a nigger-lover?"

Atticus's face was grave. "Has somebody been calling you that?"

"No sir, Mrs. Dubose calls you that. She warms up every afternoon calling you that. Francis called me that last Christmas, that's where I first heard it."

"Is that the reason you jumped on him?" asked Atticus.

"Yes sir . . ."

"Then why are you asking me what it means?"

I tried to explain to Atticus that it wasn't so much what Francis said that had infuriated me as the way he had said it. "It was like he'd said snot-nose or somethin'."

"Scout," said Atticus, "nigger-lover is just one of those terms that don't mean anything—like snot-nose. It's hard to explain—ignorant, trashy people use it when they think somebody's favoring Negroes over and above themselves. It's slipped into usage with some people like ourselves, when they want a common, ugly term to label somebody."

"You aren't really a nigger-lover, then, are you?"

"I certainly am. I do my best to love everybody . . . I'm

hard put, sometimes—baby, it's never an insult to be called what somebody thinks is a bad name. It just shows you how poor that person is, it doesn't hurt you. So don't let Mrs. Dubose get you down. She has enough troubles of her own."

One afternoon a month later Jem was ploughing his way through Sir Walter Scout, as Jem called him, and Mrs. Dubose was correcting him at every turn, when there was a knock on the door. "Come in!" she screamed.

Atticus came in. He went to the bed and took Mrs. Dubose's hand. "I was coming from the office and didn't see the children," he said. "I thought they might still be here."

Mrs. Dubose smiled at him. For the life of me I could not figure out how she could bring herself to speak to him when she seemed to hate him so. "Do you know what time it is, Atticus?" she said. "Exactly fourteen minutes past five. The alarm clock's set for five-thirty. I want you to know that."

It suddenly came to me that each day we had been staying a little longer at Mrs. Dubose's, that the alarm clock went off a few minutes later every day, and that she was well into one of her fits by the time it sounded. Today she had antagonized Jem for nearly two hours with no intention of having a fit, and I felt hopelessly trapped. The alarm clock was the signal for our release; if one day it did not ring, what would we do?

"I have a feeling that Jem's reading days are numbered," said Atticus.

"Only a week longer, I think," she said, "just to make sure . . ."

Jem rose. "But—"

Atticus put out his hand and Jem was silent. On the way home, Jem said he had to do it just for a month and the month was up and it wasn't fair.

"Just one more week, son," said Atticus.

"No," said Jem.

"Yes," said Atticus.

The following week found us back at Mrs. Dubose's. The alarm clock had ceased sounding, but Mrs. Dubose would release us with, "That'll do," so late in the afternoon Atticus would be home reading the paper when we returned. Although her fits had passed off, she was in every other way her old self: when Sir Walter Scott became involved in lengthy descriptions of moats and castles, Mrs. Dubose would become bored and pick on us:

"Jeremy Finch, I told you you'd live to regret tearing up my camellias. You regret it now, don't you?"

Jem would say he certainly did.

"Thought you could kill my Snow-on-the-Mountain, did you? Well, Jessie says the top's growing back out. Next time you'll know how to do it right, won't you? You'll pull it up by the roots, won't you?"

Jem would say he certainly would.

"Don't you mutter at me, boy! You hold up your head and say yes ma'am. Don't guess you feel like holding it up, though, with your father what he is."

Jem's chin would come up, and he would gaze at Mrs. Dubose with a face devoid of resentment. Through the weeks he had cultivated an expression of polite and detached interest, which he would present to her in answer to her most blood-curdling inventions.

At last the day came. When Mrs. Dubose said, "That'll do," one afternoon, she added, "And that's all. Good-day to you."

It was over. We bounded down the sidewalk on a spree of sheer relief, leaping and howling.

That spring was a good one: the days grew longer and gave us more playing time. Jem's mind was occupied mostly with the vital statistics of every college football player in the nation. Every night Atticus would read us the sports pages of the newspapers. Alabama might go to the Rose Bowl again this year, judging from its prospects, not one of whose names we could pronounce. Atticus was in the middle of Windy Seaton's column one evening when the telephone rang.

He answered it, then went to the hat rack in the hall. "I'm

going down to Mrs. Dubose's for a while," he said. "I won't be long."

But Atticus stayed away until long past my bedtime. When he returned he was carrying a candy box. Atticus sat down in the livingroom and put the box on the floor beside his chair.

"What'd she want?" asked Jem.

We had not seen Mrs. Dubose for over a month. She was never on the porch any more when we passed.

"She's dead, son," said Atticus. "She died a few minutes ago."

"Oh," said Jem. "Well."

"Well is right," said Atticus. "She's not suffering any more. She was sick for a long time. Son, didn't you know what her fits were?"

Jem shook his head.

"Mrs. Dubose was a morphine addict," said Atticus. "She took it as a pain-killer for years. The doctor put her on it. She'd have spent the rest of her life on it and died without so much agony, but she was too contrary——"

"Sir?" said Jem.

Atticus said, "Just before your escapade she called me to make her will. Dr. Reynolds told her she had only a few months left. Her business affairs were in perfect order but she said, 'There's still one thing out of order.'"

"What was that?" Jem was perplexed.

"She said she was going to leave this world beholden to nothing and nobody. Jem, when you're sick as she was, it's all right to take anything to make it easier, but it wasn't all right for her. She said she meant to break herself of it before she died, and that's what she did."

Jem said, "You mean that's what her fits were?"

"Yes, that's what they were. Most of the time you were reading to her I doubt if she heard a word you said. Her whole mind and body were concentrated on that alarm clock. If you hadn't fallen into her hands, I'd have made you go read to her anyway. It may have been some distraction. There was another reason—"

"Did she die free?" asked Jem.

"As the mountain air," said Atticus. "She was conscious to the last, almost. Conscious," he smiled, "and cantankerous. She still disapproved heartily of my doings, and said I'd probably spend the rest of my life bailing you out of jail. She had Jessie fix you this box—"

Atticus reached down and picked up the candy box. He handed it to Jem.

Jem opened the box. Inside, surrounded by wads of damp cotton, was a white, waxy, perfect camellia. It was a Snow-on-the-Mountain.

Jem's eyes nearly popped out of his head. "Old hell-devil, old hell-devil!" he screamed, flinging it down. "Why can't she leave me alone?"

In a flash Atticus was up and standing over him. Jem buried his face in Atticus's shirt front. "Sh-h," he said. "I think that was her way of telling you—everything's all right now, Jem, everything's all right. You know, she was a great lady."

"A lady?" Jem raised his head. His face was scarlet. "After all those things she said about you, a lady?"

"She was. She had her own views about things, a lot different from mine, maybe . . . son, I told you that if you hadn't lost your head I'd have made you go read to her. I wanted you to see something about her—I wanted you to see what real courage is, instead of getting the idea that courage is a man with a gun in his hand. It's when you know you're licked before you begin but you begin anyway and you see it through no matter what. You rarely win, but sometimes you do. Mrs. Dubose won, all ninety-eight pounds of her. According to her views, she died beholden to nothing and nobody. She was the bravest person I ever knew."

Jem picked up the candy box and threw it in the fire. He picked up the camellia, and when I went off to bed I saw him fingering the wide petals. Atticus was reading the paper.

PART TWO

12

Jem was twelve. He was difficult to live with, inconsistent, moody. His appetite was appalling, and he told me so many times to stop pestering him I consulted Atticus: "Reckon he's got a tapeworm?" Atticus said no, Jem was growing. I must be patient with him and disturb him as little as possible.

This change in Jem had come about in a matter of weeks. Mrs. Dubose was not cold in her grave—Jem had seemed grateful enough for my company when he went to read to her. Overnight, it seemed, Jem had acquired an alien set of values and was trying to impose them on me: several times he went so far as to tell me what to do. After one altercation when Jem hollered, "It's time you started bein' a girl and acting right!" I burst into tears and fled to Calpurnia.

"Don't you fret too much over Mister Jem—" she began.

"Mis-ter Jem?"

"Yeah, he's just about Mister Jem now."

"He ain't that old," I said. "All he needs is somebody to beat him up, and I ain't big enough."

"Baby," said Calpurnia, "I just can't help it if Mister Jem's growin' up. He's gonna want to be off to himself a lot now, doin' whatever boys do, so you just come right on in the kitchen when you feel lonesome. We'll find lots of things to do in here."

The beginning of that summer boded well: Jem could do as he pleased; Calpurnia would do until Dill came. She seemed glad to see me when I appeared in the kitchen, and by watching her I began to think there was some skill involved in being a girl.

But summer came and Dill was not there. I received a letter and a snapshot from him. The letter said he had a new father whose picture was enclosed, and he would have to stay in Meridian because they planned to build a fishing boat. His father was a lawyer like Atticus, only much younger. Dill's new father had a pleasant face, which made me glad Dill had captured him, but I was crushed. Dill concluded by saying he would love me forever and not to worry, he would come get me and marry me as soon as he got enough money together, so please write.

The fact that I had a permanent fiancé was little compensation for his absence: I had never thought about it, but summer was Dill by the fishpool smoking string, Dill's eyes alive with complicated plans to make Boo Radley emerge; summer was the swiftness with which Dill would reach up and kiss me when Jem was not looking, the longings we sometimes felt each other feel. With him, life was routine; without him, life was unbearable. I stayed miserable for two days.

As if that were not enough, the state legislature was called into emergency session and Atticus left us for two weeks. The Governor was eager to scrape a few barnacles off the ship of state; there were sit-down strikes in Birmingham; bread lines in the cities grew longer, people in the country grew poorer. But these were events remote from the world of Jem and me.

We were surprised one morning to see a cartoon in the *Montgomery Advertiser* above the caption, "Maycomb's Finch." It showed Atticus barefooted and in short pants, chained to a desk: he was diligently writing on a slate while some frivolous-looking girls yelled, "Yoo-hoo!" at him.

"That's a compliment," explained Jem. "He spends his time doin' things that wouldn't get done if nobody did 'em."

"Huh?"

In addition to Jem's newly developed characteristics, he had acquired a maddening air of wisdom.

"Oh, Scout, it's like reorganizing the tax systems of the counties and things. That kind of thing's pretty dry to most men."

"How do you know?"

"Oh, go on and leave me alone. I'm readin' the paper."

Jem got his wish. I departed for the kitchen.

While she was shelling peas, Calpurnia suddenly said, "What am I gonna do about you all's church this Sunday?"

"Nothing, I reckon. Atticus left us collection."

Calpurnia's eyes narrowed and I could tell what was going through her mind. "Cal," I said, "you know we'll behave. We haven't done anything in church in years."

Calpurnia evidently remembered a rainy Sunday when we were both fatherless and teacherless. Left to its own devices, the class tied Eunice Ann Simpson to a chair and placed her in the furnace room. We forgot her, trooped upstairs to church, and were listening quietly to the sermon when a dreadful banging issued from the radiator pipes, persisting until someone investigated and brought forth Eunice Ann saying she didn't want to play Shadrach any more—Jem Finch said she wouldn't get burnt if she had enough faith, but it was hot down there.

"Besides, Cal, this isn't the first time Atticus has left us," I protested.

"Yeah, but he makes certain your teacher's gonna be there. I didn't hear him say this time—reckon he forgot it." Calpurnia scratched her head. Suddenly she smiled. "How'd you and Mister Jem like to come to church with me tomorrow?"

"Really?"

"How 'bout it?" grinned Calpurnia.

If Calpurnia had ever bathed me roughly before, it was nothing compared to her supervision of that Saturday night's routine. She made me soap all over twice, drew fresh water in the tub for each rinse; she stuck my head in the basin and washed it with Octagon soap and castile. She had trusted Jem for years, but that night she invaded his privacy and provoked an outburst: "Can't anybody take a bath in this house without the whole family lookin'?"

Next morning she began earlier than usual, to "go over our clothes." When Calpurnia stayed overnight with us she slept on a folding cot in the kitchen; that morning it was covered with our Sunday habiliments. She had put so much starch in my dress it came up like a tent when I sat down. She made me wear a petticoat and she wrapped a pink sash tightly around my waist. She went over my patent-leather shoes with a cold biscuit until she saw her face in them.

"It's like we were goin' to Mardi Gras," said Jem. "What's all this for, Cal?"

"I don't want anybody sayin' I don't look after my children," she muttered. "Mister Jem, you absolutely can't wear that tie with that suit. It's green."

"'smatter with that?"

"Suit's blue. Can't you tell?"

"Hee hee," I howled, "Jem's color blind."

His face flushed angrily, but Calpurnia said, "Now you all quit that. You're gonna go to First Purchase with smiles on your faces."

First Purchase African M.E. Church was in the Quarters outside the southern town limits, across the old sawmill tracks. It was an ancient paint-peeled frame building, the only church in Maycomb with a steeple and bell, called First Purchase because it was paid for from the first earnings of freed slaves. Negroes worshiped in it on Sundays and white men gambled in it on weekdays.

The churchyard was brick-hard clay, as was the cemetery beside it. If someone died during a dry spell, the body was covered with chunks of ice until rain softened the earth. A few graves in the cemetery were marked with crumbling tombstones; newer ones were outlined with brightly colored glass and broken Coca-Cola bottles. Lightning rods guarding some graves denoted dead who rested uneasily; stumps of burned-out candles stood at the heads of infant graves. It was a happy cemetery.

The warm bittersweet smell of clean Negro welcomed us as we entered the churchyard—Hearts of Love hairdressing mingled with asafoetida, snuff, Hoyt's Cologne, Brown's Mule, peppermint, and lilac talcum.

When they saw Jem and me with Calpurnia, the men stepped back and took off their hats; the women crossed their arms at their waists, weekday gestures of respectful attention. They parted and made a small pathway to the church door for us. Calpurnia walked between Jem and me, responding to the greetings of her brightly clad neighbors.

"What you up to, Miss Cal?" said a voice behind us.

Calpurnia's hands went to our shoulders and we stopped and looked around: standing in the path behind us was a tall Negro woman. Her weight was on one leg; she rested her left elbow in the curve of her hip, pointing at us with upturned palm. She was bullet-headed with strange almond-shaped eyes, straight nose, and an Indian-bow mouth. She seemed seven feet high.

I felt Calpurnia's hand dig into my shoulder. "What you want, Lula?" she asked, in tones I had never heard her use. She spoke quietly, contemptuously.

"I wants to know why you bringin' white chillun to nigger church."

"They's my comp'ny," said Calpurnia. Again I thought her voice strange: she was talking like the rest of them.

"Yeah, an' I reckon you's comp'ny at the Finch house durin' the week."

A murmur ran through the crowd. "Don't you fret," Calpurnia whispered to me, but the roses on her hat trembled indignantly.

When Lula came up the pathway toward us Calpurnia said, "Stop right there, nigger."

Lula stopped, but she said, "You ain't got no business bringin' white chillun here—they got their church, we got our'n. It is our church, ain't it, Miss Cal?"

Calpurnia said, "It's the same God, ain't it?"

Jem said, "Let's go home, Cal, they don't want us here—"

I agreed: they did not want us here. I sensed, rather than saw, that we were being advanced upon. They seemed to be drawing closer to us, but when I looked up at Calpurnia there was amusement in her eyes. When I looked down the pathway again, Lula was gone. In her place was a solid mass of colored people.

One of them stepped from the crowd. It was Zeebo, the garbage collector. "Mister Jem," he said, "we're mighty glad to have you all here. Don't pay no 'tention to Lula, she's contentious because Reverend Sykes threatened to church her. She's a troublemaker from way back, got fancy ideas an' haughty ways—we're mighty glad to have you all."

With that, Calpurnia led us to the church door where we were greeted by Reverend Sykes, who led us to the front pew.

First Purchase was unceiled and unpainted within. Along its walls unlighted kerosene lamps hung on brass brackets; pine benches served as pews. Behind the rough oak pulpit a faded pink silk banner proclaimed God Is Love, the church's only decoration except a rotogravure print of Hunt's *The Light of the World*. There was no sign of piano, organ, hymnbooks, church programs—the familiar ecclesiastical impedimenta we saw every Sunday. It was dim inside, with a damp coolness slowly dispelled by the gathering congregation. At each seat was a cheap cardboard fan bearing a garish Garden of Gethsemane, courtesy Tyndal's Hardware Co. (You-Name-It-We-Sell-It).

Calpurnia motioned Jem and me to the end of the row and placed herself between us. She fished in her purse, drew out her handkerchief, and untied the hard wad of change in its corner. She gave a dime to me and a dime to Jem. "We've got ours," he whispered. "You keep it," Calpurnia said, "you're my company." Jem's face showed brief indecision on the ethics of withholding his own dime, but his innate courtesy won and he shifted his dime to his pocket. I did likewise with no qualms.

"Cal," I whispered, "where are the hymn-books?"

"We don't have any," she said.

"Well how—?"

"Sh-h," she said. Reverend Sykes was standing behind the pulpit staring the congregation to silence. He was a short, stocky man in a black suit, black tie, white shirt, and a gold watch-chain that glinted in the light from the frosted windows.

He said, "Brethren and sisters, we are particularly glad to have company with us this morning. Mister and Miss Finch. You all know their father. Before I begin I will read some announcements."

Reverend Sykes shuffled some papers, chose one and held it at arm's length. "The Missionary Society meets in the home of Sister Annette Reeves next Tuesday. Bring your sewing."

He read from another paper. "You all know of Brother Tom Robinson's trouble. He has been a faithful member of First Purchase since he was a boy. The collection taken up today and for the next three Sundays will go to Helen—his wife, to help her out at home."

I punched Jem. "That's the Tom Atticus's de—"

"Sh-h!"

I turned to Calpurnia but was hushed before I opened my mouth. Subdued, I fixed my attention upon Reverend Sykes, who seemed to be waiting for me to settle down. "Will the music superintendent lead us in the first hymn," he said.

Zeebo rose from his pew and walked down the center aisle, stopping in front of us and facing the congregation. He was carrying a battered hymn-book. He opened it and said, "We'll sing number two seventy-three."

This was too much for me. "How're we gonna sing it if there ain't any hymn-books?"

Calpurnia smiled. "Hush baby," she whispered, "you'll see in a minute."

Zeebo cleared his throat and read in a voice like the rumble of distant artillery:

"There's a land beyond the river."

Miraculously on pitch, a hundred voices sang out Zeebo's words. The last syllable, held to a husky hum, was followed by Zeebo saying,

"That we call the sweet forever."

Music again swelled around us; the last note lingered and Zeebo met it with the next line: "And we only reach that shore by faith's decree."

The congregation hesitated, Zeebo repeated the line carefully, and it was sung. At the chorus Zeebo closed the book, a signal for the congregation to proceed without his help.

On the dying notes of "Jubilee," Zeebo said, "In that far-off sweet forever, just beyond the shining river."

Line for line, voices followed in simple harmony until the hymn ended in a melancholy murmur.

I looked at Jem, who was looking at Zeebo from the corners of his eyes. I didn't believe it either, but we had both heard it.

Reverend Sykes then called on the Lord to bless the sick and the suffering, a procedure no different from our church practice, except Reverend Sykes directed the Deity's attention to several specific cases.

His sermon was a forthright denunciation of sin, an austere declaration of the motto on the wall behind him: he warned his flock against the evils of heady brews, gambling, and strange women. Bootleggers caused enough trouble in the Quarters, but women were worse. Again, as I had often met it in my own church, I was confronted with the Impurity of Women doctrine that seemed to preoccupy all clergymen.

Jem and I had heard the same sermon Sunday after Sunday, with only one exception. Reverend Sykes used his pulpit more freely to express his views on individual lapses

138

from grace: Jim Hardy had been absent from church for five Sundays and he wasn't sick; Constance Jackson had better watch her ways—she was in grave danger for quarreling with her neighbors; she had erected the only spite fence in the history of the Quarters.

Reverend Sykes closed his sermon. He stood beside a table in front of the pulpit and requested the morning offering, a proceeding that was strange to Jem and me. One by one, the congregation came forward and dropped nickels and dimes into a black enameled coffee can. Jem and I followed suit, and received a soft, "Thank you, thank you," as our dimes clinked.

To our amazement, Reverend Sykes emptied the can onto the table and raked the coins into his hand. He straightened up and said, "This is not enough, we must have ten dollars."

The congregation stirred. "You all know what it's for— Helen can't leave those children to work while Tom's in jail. If everybody gives one more dime, we'll have it—" Reverend Sykes waved his hand and called to someone in the back of the church. "Alec, shut the doors. Nobody leaves here till we have ten dollars."

Calpurnia scratched in her handbag and brought forth a battered leather coin purse. "Naw Cal," Jem whispered, when she handed him a shiny quarter, "we can put ours in. Gimme your dime, Scout."

The church was becoming stuffy, and it occurred to me that Reverend Sykes intended to sweat the amount due out of his flock. Fans crackled, feet shuffled, tobacco-chewers were in agony.

Reverend Sykes startled me by saying sternly, "Carlow Richardson, I haven't seen you up this aisle yet."

A thin man in khaki pants came up the aisle and deposited a coin. The congregation murmured approval.

Reverend Sykes then said, "I want all of you with no children to make a sacrifice and give one more dime apiece. Then we'll have it."

Slowly, painfully, the ten dollars was collected. The door was opened, and the gust of warm air revived us. Zeebo lined *On Jordan's Stormy Banks,* and church was over.

I wanted to stay and explore, but Calpurnia propelled me up the aisle ahead of her. At the church door, while she paused to talk with Zeebo and his family, Jem and I chatted with Reverend Sykes. I was bursting with questions, but decided I would wait and let Calpurnia answer them.

"We were 'specially glad to have you all here," said Reverend Sykes. "This church has no better friend than your daddy."

My curiosity burst: "Why were you all takin' up collection for Tom Robinson's wife?"

"Didn't you hear why?" asked Reverend Sykes. "Helen's got three little'uns and she can't go out to work—"

"Why can't she take 'em with her, Reverend?" I asked. It was customary for field Negroes with tiny children to deposit them in whatever shade there was while their parents worked—usually the babies sat in the shade between two rows of cotton. Those unable to sit were strapped papoose-style on their mothers' backs, or resided in extra cotton bags.

Reverend Sykes hesitated. "To tell you the truth, Miss Jean Louise, Helen's finding it hard to get work these days . . . when it's picking time, I think Mr. Link Deas'll take her."

"Why not, Reverend?"

Before he could answer, I felt Calpurnia's hand on my shoulder. At its pressure I said, "We thank you for lettin' us come." Jem echoed me, and we made our way homeward.

"Cal, I know Tom Robinson's in jail an' he's done somethin' awful, but why won't folks hire Helen?" I asked.

Calpurnia, in her navy voile dress and tub of a hat, walked between Jem and me. "It's because of what folks say Tom's done," she said. "Folks aren't anxious to—to have anything to do with any of his family."

"Just what did he do, Cal?"

Calpurnia sighed. "Old Mr. Bob Ewell accused him of rapin' his girl an' had him arrested an' put in jail—"

"Mr. Ewell?" My memory stirred. "Does he have anything to do with those Ewells that come every first day of school an' then go home? Why, Atticus said they were absolute trash—I never heard Atticus talk about folks the way he talked about the Ewells. He said—"

"Yeah, those are the ones."

"Well, if everybody in Maycomb knows what kind of folks the Ewells are they'd be glad to hire Helen . . . what's rape, Cal?"

"It's somethin' you'll have to ask Mr. Finch about," she said. "He can explain it better than I can. You all hungry? The Reverend took a long time unwindin' this morning, he's not usually so tedious."

"He's just like our preacher," said Jem, "but why do you all sing hymns that way?"

"Linin'?" she asked.

"Is that what it is?"

"Yeah, it's called linin'. They've done it that way as long as I can remember."

Jem said it looked like they could save the collection money for a year and get some hymn-books.

Calpurnia laughed. "Wouldn't do any good," she said. "They can't read."

"Can't read?" I asked. "All those folks?"

"That's right," Calpurnia nodded. "Can't but about four folks in First Purchase read . . . I'm one of 'em."

"Where'd you go to school, Cal?" asked Jem.

"Nowhere. Let's see now, who taught me my letters? It was Miss Maudie Atkinson's aunt, old Miss Buford—"

"Are you *that* old?"

"I'm older than Mr. Finch, even." Calpurnia grinned. "Not sure how much, though. We started rememberin' one time, trying to figure out how old I was—I can remember back just a few years more'n he can, so I'm not much older, when you take off the fact that men can't remember as well as women."

"What's your birthday, Cal?"

"I just have it on Christmas, it's easier to remember that way—I don't have a real birthday."

"But Cal," Jem protested, "you don't look even near as old as Atticus."

"Colored folks don't show their ages so fast," she said.

"Maybe because they can't read. Cal, did you teach Zeebo?"

"Yeah, Mister Jem. There wasn't a school even when he was a boy. I made him learn, though."

Zeebo was Calpurnia's eldest son. If I had ever thought about it, I would have known that Calpurnia was of mature years—Zeebo had half-grown children—but then I had never thought about it.

"Did you teach him out of a primer, like us?" I asked.

"No, I made him get a page of the Bible every day, and there was a book Miss Buford taught me out of—bet you don't know where I got it," she said.

We didn't know.

Calpurnia said, "Your Grandaddy Finch gave it to me."

"Were you from the Landing?" Jem asked. "You never told us that."

"I certainly am, Mister Jem. Grew up down there between the Buford Place and the Landin'. I've spent all my days workin' for the Finches or the Bufords, an' I moved to Maycomb when your daddy and your mamma married."

"What was the book, Cal?" I asked.

"Blackstone's *Commentaries*."

Jem was thunderstruck. "You mean you taught Zeebo outa *that?*"

"Why yes sir, Mister Jem." Calpurnia timidly put her fingers to her mouth. "They were the only books I had. Your grandaddy said Mr. Blackstone wrote fine English—"

"That's why you don't talk like the rest of 'em," said Jem.

142

"The rest of who?"

"Rest of the colored folks. Cal, but you talked like they did in church. . . ."

That Calpurnia lead a modest double life never dawned on me. The idea that she had a separate existence outside our household was a novel one, to say nothing of her having command of two languages.

"Cal," I asked, "why do you talk nigger-talk to the—to your folks when you know it's not right?"

"Well, in the first place I'm black—"

"That doesn't mean you hafta talk that way when you know better," said Jem.

Calpurnia tilted her hat and scratched her head, then pressed her hat down carefully over her ears. "It's right hard to say," she said. "Suppose you and Scout talked colored-folks' talk at home—it'd be out of place, wouldn't it? Now what if I talked white-folks' talk at church, and with my neighbors? They'd think I was puttin' on airs to beat Moses."

"But Cal, you know better," I said.

"It's not necessary to tell all you know. It's not ladylike—in the second place, folks don't like to have somebody around knowin' more than they do. It aggravates 'em. You're not gonna change any of them by talkin' right, they've got to want to learn themselves, and when they don't want to learn there's nothing you can do but keep your mouth shut or talk their language."

"Cal, can I come to see you sometimes?"

She looked down at me. "See me, honey? You see me every day."

"Out to your house," I said. "Sometimes after work? Atticus can get me."

"Any time you want to," she said. "We'd be glad to have you."

We were on the sidewalk by the Radley Place.

"Look on the porch yonder," Jem said.

I looked over to the Radley Place, expecting to see its

phantom occupant sunning himself in the swing. The swing was empty.

"I mean our porch," said Jem.

I looked down the street. Enamored, upright, uncompromising, Aunt Alexandra was sitting in a rocking chair exactly as if she had sat there every day of her life.

13

Put my bag in the front bedroom, Calpurnia," was the first thing Aunt Alexandra said. "Jean Louise, stop scratching your head," was the second thing she said.

Calpurnia picked up Aunty's heavy suitcase and opened the door. "I'll take it," said Jem, and took it. I heard the suitcase hit the bedroom floor with a thump. The sound had a dull permanence about it.

"Have you come for a visit, Aunty?" I asked. Aunt Alexandra's visits from the Landing were rare, and she traveled in state. She owned a bright green square Buick and a black chauffeur, both kept in an unhealthy state of tidiness, but today they were nowhere to be seen.

"Didn't your father tell you?" she asked.

Jem and I shook our heads.

"Probably he forgot. He's not in yet, is he?"

"Nome, he doesn't usually get back till late afternoon," said Jem.

"Well, your father and I decided it was time I came to stay with you for a while."

"For a while" in Maycomb meant anything from three days to thirty years. Jem and I exchanged glances.

"Jem's growing up now and you are too," she said to me. "We decided that it would be best for you to have some feminine influence. It won't be many years, Jean Louise, before you become interested in clothes and boys—"

I could have made several answers to this: Cal's a girl, it would be many years before I would be interested in boys, I would never be interested in clothes . . . but I kept quiet.

"What about Uncle Jimmy?" asked Jem. "Is he comin', too?"

"Oh no, he's staying at the Landing. He'll keep the place going."

The moment I said, "Won't you miss him?" I realized that this was not a tactful question. Uncle Jimmy present or Uncle Jimmy absent made not much difference, he never said anything. Aunt Alexandra ignored my question.

I could think of nothing else to say to her. In fact I could never think of anything to say to her, and I sat thinking of past painful conversations between us: How are you, Jean Louise? Fine, thank you ma'am, how are you? Very well, thank you; what have you been doing with yourself? Nothin'. Don't you do anything? Nome. Certainly you have friends? Yessum. Well what do you all do? Nothin'.

It was plain that Aunty thought me dull in the extreme, because I once heard her tell Atticus that I was sluggish.

There was a story behind all this, but I had no desire to extract it from her then: today was Sunday, and Aunt Alexandra was positively irritable on the Lord's Day. I guess it was her Sunday corset. She was not fat, but solid, and she chose protective garments that drew up her bosom to giddy heights, pinched in her waist, flared out her rear, and managed to suggest that Aunt Alexandra's was once an hour-glass figure. From any angle, it was formidable.

The remainder of the afternoon went by in the gentle gloom that descends when relatives appear, but was dispelled when we heard a car turn in the driveway. It was Atticus, home from Montgomery. Jem, forgetting his dignity, ran with me to meet him. Jem seized his briefcase and bag, I jumped into his arms, felt his vague dry kiss and said, "'d you bring me a book? 'd you know Aunty's here?"

Atticus answered both questions in the affirmative. "How'd you like for her to come live with us?"

I said I would like it very much, which was a lie, but one

146

must lie under certain circumstances and at all times when one can't do anything about them.

"We felt it was time you children needed—well, it's like this, Scout," Atticus said. "Your aunt's doing me a favor as well as you all. I can't stay here all day with you, and the summer's going to be a hot one."

"Yes sir," I said, not understanding a word he said. I had an idea, however, that Aunt Alexandra's appearance on the scene was not so much Atticus's doing as hers. Aunty had a way of declaring What Is Best For The Family, and I suppose her coming to live with us was in that category.

Maycomb welcomed her. Miss Maudie Atkinson baked a Lane cake so loaded with shinny it made me tight; Miss Stephanie Crawford had long visits with Aunt Alexandra, consisting mostly of Miss Stephanie shaking her head and saying, "Uh,uh,uh." Miss Rachel next door had Aunty over for coffee in the afternoons, and Mr. Nathan Radley went so far as to come up in the front yard and say he was glad to see her.

When she settled in with us and life resumed its daily pace, Aunt Alexandra seemed as if she had always lived with us. Her Missionary Society refreshments added to her reputation as a hostess (she did not permit Calpurnia to make the delicacies required to sustain the Society through long reports on Rice Christians); she joined and became Secretary of the Maycomb Amanuensis Club. To all parties present and participating in the life of the county, Aunt Alexandra was one of the last of her kind: she had river-boat, boarding-school manners; let any moral come along and she would uphold it; she was born in the objective case; she was an incurable gossip. When Aunt Alexandra went to school, self-doubt could not be found in any textbook, so she knew not its meaning. She was never bored, and given the slightest chance she would exercise her royal prerogative: she would arrange, advise, caution, and warn.

She never let a chance escape her to point out the shortcomings of other tribal groups to the greater glory of our own, a habit that amused Jem rather than annoyed him: "Aunty better watch how she talks—scratch most folks in Maycomb and they're kin to us."

Aunt Alexandra, in underlining the moral of young Sam Merriweather's suicide, said it was caused by a morbid streak in the family. Let a sixteen-year-old girl giggle in the choir and Aunty would say, "It just goes to show you, all the Penfield women are flighty." Everybody in Maycomb, it seemed, had a Streak: a Drinking Streak, a Gambling Streak, a Mean Streak, a Funny Streak.

Once, when Aunty assured us that Miss Stephanie Crawford's tendency to mind other people's business was hereditary, Atticus said, "Sister, when you stop to think about it, our generation's practically the first in the Finch family not to marry its cousins. Would you say the Finches have an Incestuous Streak?"

Aunty said no, that's where we got our small hands and feet.

I never understood her preoccupation with heredity. Somewhere, I had received the impression that Fine Folks were people who did the best they could with the sense they had, but Aunt Alexandra was of the opinion, obliquely expressed, that the longer a family had been squatting on one patch of land the finer it was.

"That makes the Ewells fine folks, then," said Jem. The tribe of which Burris Ewell and his brethren consisted had lived on the same plot of earth behind the Maycomb dump, and had thrived on county welfare money for three generations.

Aunt Alexandra's theory had something behind it, though. Maycomb was an ancient town. It was twenty miles east of Finch's Landing, awkwardly inland for such an old town. But Maycomb would have been closer to the river had it not been for the nimble-wittedness of one Sinkfield, who in the dawn of history operated an inn where two pig-trails met, the only

tavern in the territory. Sinkfield, no patriot, served and supplied ammunition to Indians and settlers alike, neither knowing or caring whether he was a part of the Alabama Territory
or the Creek Nation so long as business was good. Business
was excellent when Governor William Wyatt Bibb, with a
view to promoting the newly created county's domestic tranquility, dispatched a team of surveyors to locate its exact center and there establish its seat of government. The surveyors,
Sinkfield's guests, told their host that he was in the territorial
confines of Maycomb County, and showed him the probable
spot where the county seat would be built. Had not Sinkfield
made a bold stroke to preserve his holdings, Maycomb would
have sat in the middle of Winston Swamp, a place totally
devoid of interest. Instead, Maycomb grew and sprawled out
from its hub, Sinkfield's Tavern, because Sinkfield reduced his
guests to myopic drunkenness one evening, induced them to
bring forward their maps and charts, lop off a little here, add
a bit there, and adjust the center of the county to meet his
requirements. He sent them packing next day armed with
their charts and five quarts of shinny in their saddlebags—
two apiece and one for the Governor.

Because its primary reason for existence was government,
Maycomb was spared the grubbiness that distinguished most
Alabama towns its size. In the beginning its buildings were
solid, its courthouse proud, its streets graciously wide.
Maycomb's proportion of professional people ran high: one
went there to have his teeth pulled, his wagon fixed, his heart
listened to, his money deposited, his soul saved, his mules vet-
ted. But the ultimate wisdom of Sinkfield's maneuver is open
to question. He placed the young town too far away from the
only kind of public transportation in those days—river-
boat—and it took a man from the north end of the county
two days to travel to Maycomb for store-bought goods. As a
result the town remained the same size for a hundred years,
an island in a patchwork sea of cottonfields and timberland.

Although Maycomb was ignored during the War Between

the States, Reconstruction rule and economic ruin forced the town to grow. It grew inward. New people so rarely settled there, the same families married the same families until the members of the community looked faintly alike. Occasionally someone would return from Montgomery or Mobile with an outsider, but the result caused only a ripple in the quiet stream of family resemblance. Things were more or less the same during my early years.

There was indeed a caste system in Maycomb, but to my mind it worked this way: the old citizens, the present generation of people who had lived side by side for years and years, were utterly predictable to one another: they took for granted attitudes, character shadings, even gestures, as having been repeated in each generation and refined by time. Thus the dicta No Crawford Minds His Own Business, Every Third Merriweather Is Morbid, The Truth Is Not in the Delafields, All the Bufords Walk Like That, were simply guides to daily living: never take a check from a Delafield without a discreet call to the bank; Miss Maudie Atkinson's shoulder stoops because she was a Buford; if Mrs. Grace Merriweather sips gin out of Lydia E. Pinkham bottles it's nothing unusual—her mother did the same.

Aunt Alexandra fitted into the world of Maycomb like a hand into a glove, but never into the world of Jem and me. I so often wondered how she could be Atticus's and Uncle Jack's sister that I revived half-remembered tales of changelings and mandrake roots that Jem had spun long ago.

These were abstract speculations for the first month of her stay, as she had little to say to Jem or me, and we saw her only at mealtimes and at night before we went to bed. It was summer and we were outdoors. Of course some afternoons when I would run inside for a drink of water, I would find the living-room overrun with Maycomb ladies, sipping, whispering, fanning, and I would be called: "Jean Louise, come speak to these ladies."

When I appeared in the doorway, Aunty would look as if

she regretted her request; I was usually mud-splashed or covered with sand.

"Speak to your Cousin Lily," she said one afternoon, when she had trapped me in the hall.

"Who?" I said.

"Your Cousin Lily Brooke," said Aunt Alexandra.

"She our cousin? I didn't know that."

Aunt Alexandra managed to smile in a way that conveyed a gentle apology to Cousin Lily and firm disapproval to me. When Cousin Lily Brooke left I knew I was in for it.

It was a sad thing that my father had neglected to tell me about the Finch Family, or to install any pride into his children. She summoned Jem, who sat warily on the sofa beside me. She left the room and returned with a purple-covered book on which *Meditations of Joshua S. St. Clair* was stamped in gold.

"Your cousin wrote this," said Aunt Alexandra. "He was a beautiful character."

Jem examined the small volume. "Is this the Cousin Joshua who was locked up for so long?"

Aunt Alexandra said, "How did you know that?"

"Why, Atticus said he went round the bend at the University. Said he tried to shoot the president. Said Cousin Joshua said he wasn't anything but a sewer-inspector and tried to shoot him with an old flintlock pistol, only it just blew up in his hand. Atticus said it cost the family five hundred dollars to get him out of that one—"

Aunt Alexandra was standing stiff as a stork. "That's all," she said. "We'll see about this."

Before bedtime I was in Jem's room trying to borrow a book, when Atticus knocked and entered. He sat on the side of Jem's bed, looked at us soberly, then he grinned.

"Er—h'rm," he said. He was beginning to preface some things he said with a throaty noise, and I thought he must at last be getting old, but he looked the same. "I don't exactly know how to say this," he began.

"Well, just say it," said Jem. "Have we done something?"

Our father was actually fidgeting. "No, I just want to explain to you that—your Aunt Alexandra asked me . . . son, you know you're a Finch, don't you?"

"That's what I've been told." Jem looked out of the corners of his eyes. His voice rose uncontrollably, "Atticus, what's the matter?"

Atticus crossed his knees and folded his arms. "I'm trying to tell you the facts of life."

Jem's disgust deepened. "I know all that stuff," he said.

Atticus suddenly grew serious. In his lawyer's voice, without a shade of inflection, he said: "Your aunt has asked me to try and impress upon you and Jean Louise that you are not from run-of-the-mill people, that you are the product of several generations' gentle breeding—" Atticus paused, watching me locate an elusive redbug on my leg.

"Gentle breeding," he continued, when I had found and scratched it, "and that you should try to live up to your name—" Atticus persevered in spite of us: "She asked me to tell you you must try to behave like the little lady and gentleman that you are. She wants to talk to you about the family and what it's meant to Maycomb County through the years, so you'll have some idea of who you are, so you might be moved to behave accordingly," he concluded at a gallop.

Stunned, Jem and I looked at each other, then at Atticus, whose collar seemed to worry him. We did not speak to him.

Presently I picked up a comb from Jem's dresser and ran its teeth along the edge.

"Stop that noise," Atticus said.

His curtness stung me. The comb was midway in its journey, and I banged it down. For no reason I felt myself beginning to cry, but I could not stop. This was not my father. My father never thought these thoughts. My father never spoke so. Aunt Alexandra had put him up to this, somehow. Through my tears I saw Jem standing in a similar pool of isolation, his head cocked to one side.

152

There was nowhere to go, but I turned to go and met Atticus's vest front. I buried my head in it and listened to the small internal noises that went on behind the light blue cloth: his watch ticking, the faint crackle of his starched shirt, the soft sound of his breathing.

"Your stomach's growling," I said.

"I know it," he said.

"You better take some soda."

"I will," he said.

"Atticus, is all this behavin' an' stuff gonna make things different? I mean are you——?"

I felt his hand on the back of my head. "Don't you worry about anything," he said. "It's not time to worry."

When I heard that, I knew he had come back to us. The blood in my legs began to flow again, and I raised my head. "You really want us to do all that? I can't remember everything Finches are supposed to do. . . ."

"I don't want you to remember it. Forget it."

He went to the door and out of the room, shutting the door behind him. He nearly slammed it, but caught himself at the last minute and closed it softly. As Jem and I stared, the door opened again and Atticus peered around. His eyebrows were raised, his glasses had slipped. "Get more like Cousin Joshua every day, don't I? Do you think I'll end up costing the family five hundred dollars?"

I know now what he was trying to do, but Atticus was only a man. It takes a woman to do that kind of work.

14

Although we heard no more about the Finch family from Aunt Alexandra, we heard plenty from the town. On Saturdays, armed with our nickels, when Jem permitted me to accompany him (he was now positively allergic to my presence when in public), we would squirm our way through sweating sidewalk crowds and sometimes hear, "There's his chillun," or, "Yonder's some Finches." Turning to face our accusers, we would see only a couple of farmers studying the enema bags in the Mayco Drugstore window. Or two dumpy countrywomen in straw hats sitting in a Hoover cart.

"They c'n go loose and rape up the countryside for all 'em who run this county care," was one obscure observation we met head on from a skinny gentleman when he passed us. Which reminded me that I had a question to ask Atticus.

"What's rape?" I asked him that night.

Atticus looked around from behind his paper. He was in his chair by the window. As we grew older, Jem and I thought it generous to allow Atticus thirty minutes to himself after supper.

He sighed, and said rape was carnal knowledge of a female by force and without consent.

"Well if that's all it is why did Calpurnia dry me up when I asked her what it was?"

Atticus looked pensive. "What's that again?"

"Well, I asked Calpurnia comin' from church that day what it was and she said ask you but I forgot to and now I'm askin' you."

His paper was now in his lap. "Again, please," he said.

I told him in detail about our trip to church with Calpurnia. Atticus seemed to enjoy it, but Aunt Alexandra, who was sitting in a corner quietly sewing, put down her embroidery and stared at us.

"You all were coming back from Calpurnia's church that Sunday?"

Jem said, "Yessum, she took us."

I remembered something. "Yessum, and she promised me I could come out to her house some afternoon. Atticus, I'll go next Sunday if it's all right, can I? Cal said she'd come get me if you were off in the car."

"You may *not*."

Aunt Alexandra said it. I wheeled around, startled, then turned back to Atticus in time to catch his swift glance at her, but it was too late. I said, "I didn't ask you!"

For a big man, Atticus could get up and down from a chair faster than anyone I ever knew. He was on his feet. "Apologize to your aunt," he said.

"I didn't ask her, I asked you—"

Atticus turned his head and pinned me to the wall with his good eye. His voice was deadly: "First, apologize to your aunt."

"I'm sorry, Aunty," I muttered.

"Now then," he said. "Let's get this clear: you do as Calpurnia tells you, you do as I tell you, and as long as your aunt's in this house, you will do as she tells you. Understand?"

I understood, pondered a while, and concluded that the only way I could retire with a shred of dignity was to go to the bathroom, where I stayed long enough to make them think I had to go. Returning, I lingered in the hall to hear a fierce discussion going on in the livingroom. Through the door I could see Jem on the sofa with a football magazine in front of his face, his head turning as if its pages contained a live tennis match.

". . . you've got to do something about her," Aunty was saying. "You've let things go on too long, Atticus, too long."

"I don't see any harm in letting her go out there. Cal'd look after her there as well as she does here."

Who was the "her" they were talking about? My heart sank: me. I felt the starched walls of a pink cotton penitentiary closing in on me, and for the second time in my life I thought of running away. Immediately.

"Atticus, it's all right to be soft-hearted, you're an easy man, but you have a daughter to think of. A daughter who's growing up."

"That's what I am thinking of."

"And don't try to get around it. You've got to face it sooner or later and it might as well be tonight. We don't need her now."

Atticus's voice was even: "Alexandra, Calpurnia's not leaving this house until she wants to. You may think otherwise, but I couldn't have got along without her all these years. She's a faithful member of this family and you'll simply have to accept things the way they are. Besides, sister, I don't want you working your head off for us—you've no reason to do that. We still need Cal as much as we ever did."

"But Atticus—"

"Besides, I don't think the children've suffered one bit from her having brought them up. If anything, she's been harder on them in some ways than a mother would have been . . . she's never let them get away with anything, she's never indulged them the way most colored nurses do. She tried to bring them up according to her lights, and Cal's lights are pretty good—and another thing, the children love her."

I breathed again. It wasn't me, it was only Calpurnia they were talking about. Revived, I entered the livingroom. Atticus had retreated behind his newspaper and Aunt Alexandra was worrying her embroidery. Punk, punk, punk, her needle broke the taut circle. She stopped, and pulled the cloth tighter: punk-punk-punk. She was furious.

Jem got up and padded across the rug. He motioned me to

follow. He led me to his room and closed the door. His face was grave.

"They've been fussing, Scout."

Jem and I fussed a great deal these days, but I had never heard of or seen anyone quarrel with Atticus. It was not a comfortable sight.

"Scout, try not to antagonize Aunty, hear?"

Atticus's remarks were still rankling, which made me miss the request in Jem's question. My feathers rose again. "You tryin' to tell me what to do?"

"Naw, it's—he's got a lot on his mind now, without us worrying him."

"Like what?" Atticus didn't appear to have anything especially on his mind.

"It's this Tom Robinson case that's worryin' him to death—"

I said Atticus didn't worry about anything. Besides, the case never bothered us except about once a week and then it didn't last.

"That's because you can't hold something in your mind but a little while," said Jem. "It's different with grown folks, we—"

His maddening superiority was unbearable these days. He didn't want to do anything but read and go off by himself. Still, everything he read he passed along to me, but with this difference: formerly because he thought I'd like it; now, for my edification and instruction.

"Jee crawling hova, Jem! Who do you think you are?"

"Now I mean it, Scout, you antagonize Aunty and I'll—I'll spank you."

With that, I was gone. "You damn morphodite, I'll kill you!" He was sitting on the bed, and it was easy to grab his front hair and land one on his mouth. He slapped me and I tried another left, but a punch in the stomach sent me sprawling on the floor. It nearly knocked the breath out of me, but it didn't matter because I knew he was fighting, he was fighting me back. We were still equals.

"Ain't so high and mighty now, are you!" I screamed, sailing in again. He was still on the bed and I couldn't get a firm stance, so I threw myself at him as hard as I could, hitting, pulling, pinching, gouging. What had begun as a fist-fight became a brawl. We were still struggling when Atticus separated us.

"That's all," he said. "Both of you go to bed right now."

"Taah!" I said at Jem. He was being sent to bed at my bed-time.

"Who started it?" asked Atticus, in resignation.

"Jem did. He was tryin' to tell me what to do. I don't have to mind *him* now, do I?"

Atticus smiled. "Let's leave it at this: you mind Jem when-ever he can make you. Fair enough?"

Aunt Alexandra was present but silent, and when she went down the hall with Atticus we heard her say, ". . . just one of the things I've been telling you about," a phrase that united us again.

Ours were adjoining rooms; as I shut the door between them Jem said, "Night, Scout."

"Night," I murmured, picking my way across the room to turn on the light. As I passed the bed I stepped on something warm, resilient, and rather smooth. It was not quite like hard rubber, and I had the sensation that it was alive. I also heard it move.

I switched on the light and looked at the floor by the bed. Whatever I had stepped on was gone. I tapped on Jem's door.

"What," he said.

"How does a snake feel?"

"Sort of rough. Cold. Dusty. Why?"

"I think there's one under my bed. Can you come look?"

"Are you bein' funny?" Jem opened the door. He was in his pajama bottoms. I noticed not without satisfaction that the mark of my knuckles was still on his mouth. When he saw I meant what I said, he said, "If you think I'm gonna put my face down to a snake you've got another think comin'. Hold on a minute."

158

He went to the kitchen and fetched the broom. "You better get up on the bed," he said.

"You reckon it's really one?" I asked. This was an occasion. Our houses had no cellars; they were built on stone blocks a few feet above the ground, and the entry of reptiles was not unknown but was not commonplace. Miss Rachel Haverford's excuse for a glass of neat whiskey every morning was that she never got over the fright of finding a rattler coiled in her bedroom closet, on her washing, when she went to hang up her negligee.

Jem made a tentative swipe under the bed. I looked over the foot to see if a snake would come out. None did. Jem made a deeper swipe.

"Do snakes grunt?"

"It ain't a snake," Jem said. "It's somebody."

Suddenly a filthy brown package shot from under the bed. Jem raised the broom and missed Dill's head by an inch when it appeared.

"God Almighty." Jem's voice was reverent.

We watched Dill emerge by degrees. He was a tight fit. He stood up and eased his shoulders, turned his feet in their ankle sockets, rubbed the back of his neck. His circulation restored, he said, "Hey."

Jem petitioned God again. I was speechless.

"I'm 'bout to perish," said Dill. "Got anything to eat?"

In a dream, I went to the kitchen. I brought him back some milk and half a pan of corn bread left over from supper. Dill devoured it, chewing with his front teeth, as was his custom.

I finally found my voice. "How'd you get here?"

By an involved route. Refreshed by food, Dill recited this narrative: having been bound in chains and left to die in the basement (there were basements in Meridian) by his new father, who disliked him, and secretly kept alive on raw field peas by a passing farmer who heard his cries for help (the good man poked a bushel pod by pod through the ventilator), Dill worked himself free by pulling the chains from the wall.

Still in wrist manacles, he wandered two miles out of Meridian where he discovered a small animal show and was immediately engaged to wash the camel. He traveled with the show all over Mississippi until his infallible sense of direction told him he was in Abbott County, Alabama, just across the river from Maycomb. He walked the rest of the way.

"How'd you get here?" asked Jem.

He had taken thirteen dollars from his mother's purse, caught the nine o'clock from Meridian and got off at Maycomb Junction. He had walked ten or eleven of the fourteen miles to Maycomb, off the highway in the scrub bushes lest the authorities be seeking him, and had ridden the remainder of the way clinging to the backboard of a cotton wagon. He had been under the bed for two hours, he thought; he had heard us in the diningroom, and the clink of forks on plates nearly drove him crazy. He thought Jem and I would never go to bed; he had considered emerging and helping me beat Jem, as Jem had grown far taller, but he knew Mr. Finch would break it up soon, so he thought it best to stay where he was. He was worn out, dirty beyond belief, and home.

"They must not know you're here," said Jem. "We'd know if they were lookin' for you. . . ."

"Think they're still searchin' all the picture shows in Meridian." Dill grinned.

"You oughta let your mother know where you are," said Jem. "You oughta let her know you're here. . . ."

Dill's eyes flickered at Jem, and Jem looked at the floor. Then he rose and broke the remaining code of our childhood. He went out of the room and down the hall. "Atticus," his voice was distant, "can you come here a minute, sir?"

Beneath its sweat-streaked dirt Dill's face went white. I felt sick. Atticus was in the doorway.

He came to the middle of the room and stood with his hands in his pockets, looking down at Dill.

I finally found my voice: "It's okay, Dill. When he wants you to know somethin', he tells you."

Dill looked at me. "I mean it's all right," I said. "You know he wouldn't bother you, you know you ain't scared of Atticus."

"I'm not scared . . ." Dill muttered.

"Just hungry, I'll bet." Atticus's voice had its usual pleasant dryness. "Scout, we can do better than a pan of cold corn bread, can't we? You fill this fellow up and when I get back we'll see what we can see."

"Mr. Finch, don't tell Aunt Rachel, don't make me go back, *please sir!* I'll run off again—!"

"Whoa, son," said Atticus. "Nobody's about to make you go anywhere but to bed pretty soon. I'm just going over to tell Miss Rachel you're here and ask her if you could spend the night with us—you'd like that, wouldn't you? And for goodness' sake put some of the county back where it belongs, the soil erosion's bad enough as it is."

Dill stared at my father's retreating figure.

"He's tryin' to be funny," I said. "He means take a bath. See there, I told you he wouldn't bother you."

Jem was standing in a corner of the room, looking like the traitor he was. "Dill, I had to tell him," he said. "You can't run three hundred miles off without your mother knowin'."

We left him without a word.

Dill ate, and ate, and ate. He hadn't eaten since last night. He used all his money for a ticket, boarded the train as he had done many times, coolly chatted with the conductor, to whom Dill was a familiar sight, but he had not the nerve to invoke the rule on small children traveling a distance alone: if you've lost your money the conductor will lend you enough for dinner and your father will pay him back at the end of the line.

Dill made his way through the leftovers and was reaching for a can of pork and beans in the pantry when Miss Rachel's Do-oo Je-sus went off in the hall. He shivered like a rabbit.

He bore with fortitude her Wait Till I Get You Home, Your Folks Are Out of Their Minds Worryin', was quite calm during That's All the Harris in You Coming Out, smiled at her Reckon You Can Stay One Night, and returned the hug at long last bestowed upon him.

Atticus pushed up his glasses and rubbed his face.

"Your father's tired," said Aunt Alexandra, her first words in hours, it seemed. She had been there, but I suppose struck dumb most of the time. "You children get to bed now."

We left them in the diningroom, Atticus still mopping his face. "From rape to riot to runaways," we heard him chuckle. "I wonder what the next two hours will bring."

Since things appeared to have worked out pretty well, Dill and I decided to be civil to Jem. Besides, Dill had to sleep with him so we might as well speak to him.

I put on my pajamas, read for a while and found myself suddenly unable to keep my eyes open. Dill and Jem were quiet; when I turned off my reading lamp there was no strip of light under the door to Jem's room.

I must have slept a long time, for when I was punched awake the room was dim with the light of the setting moon.

"Move over, Scout."

"He thought he had to," I mumbled. "Don't stay mad with him."

Dill got in bed beside me. "I ain't," he said. "I just wanted to sleep with you. Are you waked up?"

By this time I was, but lazily so. "Why'd you do it?"

No answer. "I said why'd you run off? Was he really hateful like you said?"

"Naw . . ."

"Didn't you all build that boat like you wrote you were gonna?"

"He just said we would. We never did."

I raised up on my elbow, facing Dill's outline. "It's no reason to run off. They don't get around to doin' what they say they're gonna do half the time. . . ."

"That wasn't it, he—they just wasn't interested in me."

This was the weirdest reason for flight I had ever heard. "How come?"

"Well, they stayed gone all the time, and when they were home, even, they'd get off in a room by themselves."

"What'd they do in there?"

"Nothin', just sittin' and readin'—but they didn't want me with 'em."

I pushed the pillow to the headboard and sat up. "You know something? I was fixin' to run off tonight because there they all were. You don't want 'em around you all the time, Dill—"

Dill breathed his patient breath, a half-sigh.

"—good night, Atticus's gone all day and sometimes half the night and off in the legislature and I don't know what—you don't want 'em around all the time, Dill, you couldn't do anything if they were."

"That's not it."

As Dill explained, I found myself wondering what life would be if Jem were different, even from what he was now; what I would do if Atticus did not feel the necessity of my presence, help and advice. Why, he couldn't get along a day without me. Even Calpurnia couldn't get along unless I was there. They needed me.

"Dill, you ain't telling me right—your folks couldn't do without you. They must be just mean to you. Tell you what to do about that—"

Dill's voice went on steadily in the darkness: "The thing is, what I'm tryin' to say is—they *do* get on a lot better without me, I can't help them any. They ain't mean. They buy me everything I want, but it's now-you've-got-it-go-play-with-it. You've got a roomful of things. I-got-you-that-book-so-go-read-it." Dill tried to deepen his voice. "You're not a boy. Boys get out and play baseball with other boys, they don't hang around the house worryin' their folks."

Dill's voice was his own again: "Oh, they ain't mean. They kiss you and hug you good night and good mornin' and good-bye and tell you they love you—Scout, let's get us a baby."

"Where?"

There was a man Dill had heard of who had a boat that he rowed across to a foggy island where all these babies were; you could order one—

"That's a lie. Aunty said God drops 'em down the chimney. At least that's what I think she said." For once, Aunty's diction had not been too clear.

"Well that ain't so. You get babies from each other. But there's this man, too—he has all these babies just waitin' to wake up, he breathes life into 'em. . . ."

Dill was off again. Beautiful things floated around in his dreamy head. He could read two books to my one, but he preferred the magic of his own inventions. He could add and subtract faster than lightning, but he preferred his own twilight world, a world where babies slept, waiting to be gathered like morning lilies. He was slowly talking himself to sleep and taking me with him, but in the quietness of his foggy island there rose the faded image of a gray house with sad brown doors.

"Dill?"

"Mm?"

"Why do you reckon Boo Radley's never run off?"

Dill sighed a long sigh and turned away from me.

"Maybe he doesn't have anywhere to run off to. . . ."

15

After many telephone calls, much pleading on behalf of the defendant, and a long forgiving letter from his mother, it was decided that Dill could stay. We had a week of peace together. After that, little, it seemed. A nightmare was upon us.

It began one evening after supper. Dill was over; Aunt Alexandra was in her chair in the corner, Atticus was in his; Jem and I were on the floor reading. It had been a placid week: I had minded Aunty; Jem had outgrown the treehouse, but helped Dill and me construct a new rope ladder for it; Dill had hit upon a foolproof plan to make Boo Radley come out at no cost to ourselves (place a trail of lemon drops from the back door to the front yard and he'd follow it, like an ant). There was a knock on the front door, Jem answered it and said it was Mr. Heck Tate.

"Well, ask him to come in," said Atticus.

"I already did. There's some men outside in the yard, they want you to come out."

In Maycomb, grown men stood outside in the front yard for only two reasons: death and politics. I wondered who had died. Jem and I went to the front door, but Atticus called, "Go back in the house."

Jem turned out the livingroom lights and pressed his nose to a window screen. Aunt Alexandra protested. "Just for a second, Aunty, let's see who it is," he said.

Dill and I took another window. A crowd of men was standing around Atticus. They all seemed to be talking at once.

". . . movin' him to the county jail tomorrow," Mr. Tate was saying, "I don't look for any trouble, but I can't guarantee there won't be any. . . ."

"Don't be foolish, Heck," Atticus said. "This is Maycomb."

". . . said I was just uneasy."

"Heck, we've gotten one postponement of this case just to make sure there's nothing to be uneasy about. This is Saturday," Atticus said. "Trial'll probably be Monday. You can keep him one night, can't you? I don't think anybody in Maycomb'll begrudge me a client, with times this hard."

There was a murmur of glee that died suddenly when Mr. Link Deas said, "Nobody around here's up to anything, it's that Old Sarum bunch I'm worried about . . . can't you get a—what is it, Heck?"

"Change of venue," said Mr. Tate. "Not much point in that, now is it?"

Atticus said something inaudible. I turned to Jem, who waved me to silence.

"—besides," Atticus was saying, "you're not scared of that crowd, are you?"

". . . know how they do when they get shinnied up."

"They don't usually drink on Sunday, they go to church most of the day . . ." Atticus said.

"This is a special occasion, though. . . ." someone said.

They murmured and buzzed until Aunty said if Jem didn't turn on the livingroom lights he would disgrace the family. Jem didn't hear her.

"—don't see why you touched it in the first place," Mr. Link Deas was saying. "You've got everything to lose from this, Atticus. I mean everything."

"Do you really think so?"

This was Atticus's dangerous question. "Do you really think you want to move there, Scout?" Bam, bam, bam, and the checkerboard was swept clean of my men. "Do you really think that, son? Then read this." Jem would struggle the rest of an evening through the speeches of Henry W. Grady.

166

"Link, that boy might go to the chair, but he's not going till the truth's told." Atticus's voice was even. "And you know what the truth is."

There was a murmur among the group of men, made more ominous when Atticus moved back to the bottom front step and the men drew nearer to him.

Suddenly Jem screamed, "Atticus, the telephone's ringing!"

The men jumped a little and scattered; they were people we saw every day: merchants, in-town farmers; Dr. Reynolds was there; so was Mr. Avery.

"Well, answer it, son," called Atticus.

Laughter broke them up. When Atticus switched on the overhead light in the livingroom he found Jem at the window, pale except for the vivid mark of the screen on his nose.

"Why on earth are you all sitting in the dark?" he asked.

Jem watched him go to his chair and pick up the evening paper. I sometimes think Atticus subjected every crisis of his life to tranquil evaluation behind *The Mobile Register, The Birmingham News* and *The Montgomery Advertiser.*

"They were after you, weren't they?" Jem went to him. "They wanted to get you, didn't they?"

Atticus lowered the paper and gazed at Jem. "What have you been reading?" he asked. Then he said gently, "No son, those were our friends."

"It wasn't a—a gang?" Jem was looking from the corners of his eyes.

Atticus tried to stifle a smile but didn't make it. "No, we don't have mobs and that nonsense in Maycomb. I've never heard of a gang in Maycomb."

"Ku Klux got after some Catholics one time."

"Never heard of any Catholics in Maycomb either," said Atticus, "you're confusing that with something else. Way back about nineteen-twenty there was a Klan, but it was a political organization more than anything. Besides, they couldn't find anybody to scare. They paraded by Mr. Sam Levy's house one night, but Sam just stood on his porch and told 'em things had come to a pretty pass, he'd sold 'em the very sheets on their backs. Sam made 'em so ashamed of themselves they went away."

The Levy family met all criteria for being Fine Folks: they did the best they could with the sense they had, and they had been living on the same plot of ground in Maycomb for five generations.

"The Ku Klux's gone," said Atticus. "It'll never come back."

I walked home with Dill and returned in time to overhear Atticus saying to Aunty, ". . . in favor of Southern womanhood as much as anybody, but not for preserving polite fiction at the expense of human life," a pronouncement that made me suspect they had been fussing again.

I sought Jem and found him in his room, on the bed deep in thought. "Have they been at it?" I asked.

"Sort of. She won't let him alone about Tom Robinson. She almost said Atticus was disgracin' the family. Scout . . . I'm scared."

"Scared'a what?"

"Scared about Atticus. Somebody might hurt him." Jem preferred to remain mysterious; all he would say to my questions was go on and leave him alone.

Next day was Sunday. In the interval between Sunday School and Church when the congregation stretched its legs, I saw Atticus standing in the yard with another knot of men. Mr. Heck Tate was present, and I wondered if he had seen the light. He never went to church. Even Mr. Underwood was there. Mr. Underwood had no use for any organization but *The Maycomb Tribune,* of which he was the sole owner, editor, and printer. His days were spent at his linotype, where he refreshed himself occasionally from an ever-present gallon jug of cherry wine. He rarely gathered news; people brought it to him. It was said that he made up every edition of *The Maycomb Tribune* out of his own head and wrote it down on the linotype. This was believable. Something must have been up to haul Mr. Underwood out.

168

I caught Atticus coming in the door, and he said that they'd moved Tom Robinson to the Maycomb jail. He also said, more to himself than to me, that if they'd kept him there in the first place there wouldn't have been any fuss. I watched him take his seat on the third row from the front, and I heard him rumble, "Nearer my God to thee," some notes behind the rest of us. He never sat with Aunty, Jem and me. He liked to be by himself in church.

The fake peace that prevailed on Sundays was made more irritating by Aunt Alexandra's presence. Atticus would flee to his office directly after dinner, where if we sometimes looked in on him, we would find him sitting back in his swivel chair reading. Aunt Alexandra composed herself for a two-hour nap and dared us to make any noise in the yard, the neighborhood was resting. Jem in his old age had taken to his room with a stack of football magazines. So Dill and I spent our Sundays creeping around in Deer's Pasture.

Shooting on Sundays was prohibited, so Dill and I kicked Jem's football around the pasture for a while, which was no fun. Dill asked if I'd like to have a poke at Boo Radley. I said I didn't think it'd be nice to bother him, and spent the rest of the afternoon filling Dill in on last winter's events. He was considerably impressed.

We parted at suppertime, and after our meal Jem and I were settling down to a routine evening, when Atticus did something that interested us: he came into the livingroom carrying a long electrical extension cord. There was a light bulb on the end.

"I'm going out for a while," he said. "You folks'll be in bed when I come back, so I'll say good night now."

With that, he put his hat on and went out the back door.

"He's takin' the car," said Jem.

Our father had a few peculiarities: one was, he never ate desserts; another was that he liked to walk. As far back as I could remember, there was always a Chevrolet in excellent condition in the carhouse, and Atticus put many miles on it in business trips, but in Maycomb he walked to and from his office four times a day, covering about two miles. He said his only exercise was walking. In Maycomb, if one went for a walk with no definite purpose in mind, it was correct to believe one's mind incapable of definite purpose.

Later on, I bade my aunt and brother good night and was well into a book when I heard Jem rattling around in his room. His go-to-bed noises were so familiar to me that I knocked on his door: "Why ain't you going to bed?"

"I'm goin' downtown for a while." He was changing his pants.

"Why? It's almost ten o'clock, Jem."

He knew it, but he was going anyway.

"Then I'm goin' with you. If you say no you're not, I'm goin' anyway, hear?"

Jem saw that he would have to fight me to keep me home, and I suppose he thought a fight would antagonize Aunty, so he gave in with little grace.

I dressed quickly. We waited until Aunty's light went out, and we walked quietly down the back steps. There was no moon tonight.

"Dill'll wanta come," I whispered.

"So he will," said Jem gloomily.

We leaped over the driveway wall, cut through Miss Rachel's side yard and went to Dill's window. Jem whistled bob-white. Dill's face appeared at the screen, disappeared, and five minutes later he unhooked the screen and crawled out. An old campaigner, he did not speak until we were on the sidewalk. "What's up?"

"Jem's got the look-arounds," an affliction Calpurnia said all boys caught at his age.

"I've just got this feeling," Jem said, "just this feeling."

We went by Mrs. Dubose's house, standing empty and shuttered, her camellias grown up in weeds and johnson grass. There were eight more houses to the post office corner.

The south side of the square was deserted. Giant monkey-puzzle bushes bristled on each corner, and between them an iron hitching rail glistened under the street lights. A light shone in the county toilet, otherwise that side of the courthouse was dark. A larger square of stores surrounded the courthouse square; dim lights burned from deep within them.

Atticus's office was in the courthouse when he began his law practice, but after several years of it he moved to quieter quarters in the Maycomb Bank building. When we rounded the corner of the square, we saw the car parked in front of the bank. "He's in there," said Jem.

But he wasn't. His office was reached by a long hallway. Looking down the hall, we should have seen *Atticus Finch, Attorney-at-Law* in small sober letters against the light from behind his door. It was dark.

Jem peered in the bank door to make sure. He turned the knob. The door was locked. "Let's go up the street. Maybe he's visitin' Mr. Underwood."

Mr. Underwood not only ran *The Maycomb Tribune* office, he lived in it. That is, above it. He covered the courthouse and jailhouse news simply by looking out his upstairs window. The office building was on the northwest corner of the square, and to reach it we had to pass the jail.

The Maycomb jail was the most venerable and hideous of the county's buildings. Atticus said it was like something Cousin Joshua St. Clair might have designed. It was certainly someone's dream. Starkly out of place in a town of square-faced stores and steep-roofed houses, the Maycomb jail was a miniature Gothic joke one cell wide and two cells high, complete with tiny battlements and flying buttresses. Its fantasy was heightened by its red brick facade and the thick steel bars at its ecclesiastical windows. It stood on no lonely hill, but was wedged between Tyndal's Hardware Store and *The Maycomb Tribune* office. The jail was Maycomb's only conversation piece: its detractors said it looked like a Victorian privy; its supporters said it gave the town a good solid respectable look, and no stranger would ever suspect that it was full of niggers.

As we walked up the sidewalk, we saw a solitary light burning in the distance. "That's funny," said Jem, "jail doesn't have an outside light."

"Looks like it's over the door," said Dill.

A long extension cord ran between the bars of a second-floor window and down the side of the building. In the light from its bare bulb, Atticus was sitting propped against the front door. He was sitting in one of his office chairs, and he was reading, oblivious of the nightbugs dancing over his head.

I made to run, but Jem caught me. "Don't go to him," he said, "he might not like it. He's all right, let's go home. I just wanted to see where he was."

We were taking a short cut across the square when four dusty cars came in from the Meridian highway, moving slowly in a line. They went around the square, passed the bank building, and stopped in front of the jail.

Nobody got out. We saw Atticus look up from his newspaper. He closed it, folded it deliberately, dropped it in his lap, and pushed his hat to the back of his head. He seemed to be expecting them.

"Come on," whispered Jem. We streaked across the square, across the street, until we were in the shelter of the Jitney Jungle door. Jem peeked up the sidewalk. "We can get closer," he said. We ran to Tyndal's Hardware door—near enough, at the same time discreet.

In ones and twos, men got out of the cars. Shadows became substance as light revealed solid shapes moving toward the jail door. Atticus remained where he was. The men hid him from view.

"He in there, Mr. Finch?" a man said.

"He is," we heard Atticus answer, "and he's asleep. Don't wake him up."

In obedience to my father, there followed what I later realized was a sickeningly comic aspect of an unfunny situation: the men talked in near-whispers.

"You know what we want," another man said. "Get aside from the door, Mr. Finch."

"You can turn around and go home again, Walter," Atticus said pleasantly. "Heck Tate's around somewhere."

"The hell he is," said another man. "Heck's bunch's so deep in the woods they won't get out till mornin'."

"Indeed? Why so?"

"Called 'em off on a snipe hunt," was the succinct answer. "Didn't you think a'that, Mr. Finch?"

"Thought about it, but didn't believe it. Well then," my father's voice was still the same, "that changes things, doesn't it?"

"It do," another deep voice said. Its owner was a shadow.

"Do you really think so?"

This was the second time I heard Atticus ask that question in two days, and it meant somebody's man would get jumped. This was too good to miss. I broke away from Jem and ran as fast as I could to Atticus.

Jem shrieked and tried to catch me, but I had a lead on him and Dill. I pushed my way through dark smelly bodies and burst into the circle of light.

"H-ey, Atticus!"

I thought he would have a fine surprise, but his face killed my joy. A flash of plain fear was going out of his eyes, but returned when Dill and Jem wriggled into the light.

There was a smell of stale whiskey and pigpen about, and when I glanced around I discovered that these men were strangers. They were not the people I saw last night. Hot embarrassment shot through me: I had leaped triumphantly into a ring of people I had never seen before.

Atticus got up from his chair, but he was moving slowly, like an old man. He put the newspaper down very carefully, adjusting its creases with lingering fingers. They were trembling a little.

"Go home, Jem," he said. "Take Scout and Dill home."

We were accustomed to prompt, if not always cheerful acquiescence to Atticus's instructions, but from the way he stood Jem was not thinking of budging.

"Go home, I said."

Jem shook his head. As Atticus's fists went to his hips, so did Jem's, and as they faced each other I could see little resemblance between them: Jem's soft brown hair and eyes, his oval face and snug-fitting ears were our mother's, contrasting oddly with Atticus's graying black hair and square-cut features, but they were somehow alike. Mutual defiance made them alike.

"Son, I said go home."

Jem shook his head.

"I'll send him home," a burly man said, and grabbed Jem roughly by the collar. He yanked Jem nearly off his feet.

"Don't you touch him!" I kicked the man swiftly. Barefooted, I was surprised to see him fall back in real pain. I intended to kick his shin, but aimed too high.

"That'll do, Scout." Atticus put his hand on my shoulder. "Don't kick folks. No—" he said, as I was pleading justification.

"Ain't nobody gonna do Jem that way," I said.

"All right, Mr. Finch, get 'em outa here," someone growled. "You got fifteen seconds to get 'em outa here."

In the midst of this strange assembly, Atticus stood trying to make Jem mind him. "I ain't going," was his steady answer to Atticus's threats, requests, and finally, "Please Jem, take them home."

I was getting a bit tired of that, but felt Jem had his own reasons for doing as he did, in view of his prospects once Atticus did get him home. I looked around the crowd. It was a summer's night, but the men were dressed, most of them, in overalls and denim shirts buttoned up to the collars. I thought they must be cold-natured, as their sleeves were unrolled and buttoned at the cuffs. Some wore hats pulled firmly down over their ears. They were sullen-looking, sleepy-eyed men who seemed unused to late hours. I sought once more for a familiar face, and at the center of the semi-circle I found one.

"Hey, Mr. Cunningham."

The man did not hear me, it seemed.

"Hey, Mr. Cunningham. How's your entailment gettin' along?"

Mr. Walter Cunningham's legal affairs were well known to me; Atticus had once described them at length. The big man blinked and hooked his thumbs in his overall straps. He seemed uncomfortable; he cleared his throat and looked away. My friendly overture had fallen flat.

Mr. Cunningham wore no hat, and the top half of his forehead was white in contrast to his sunscorched face, which led me to believe that he wore one most days. He shifted his feet, clad in heavy work shoes.

"Don't you remember me, Mr. Cunningham? I'm Jean Louise Finch. You brought us some hickory nuts one time, remember?" I began to sense the futility one feels when unacknowledged by a chance acquaintance.

"I go to school with Walter," I began again. "He's your boy, ain't he? Ain't he, sir?"

Mr. Cunningham was moved to a faint nod. He did know me, after all.

"He's in my grade," I said, "and he does right well. He's a good boy," I added, "a real nice boy. We brought him home for dinner one time. Maybe he told you about me, I beat him up one time but he was real nice about it. Tell him hey for me, won't you?"

Atticus had said it was the polite thing to talk to people about what they were interested in, not about what you were interested in. Mr. Cunningham displayed no interest in his son, so I tackled his entailment once more in a last-ditch effort to make him feel at home.

"Entailments are bad," I was advising him, when I slowly awoke to the fact that I was addressing the entire aggregation.

The men were all looking at me, some had their mouths half-open. Atticus had stopped poking at Jem: they were standing together beside Dill. Their attention amounted to fascination. Atticus's mouth, even, was half-open, an attitude he had once described as uncouth. Our eyes met and he shut it.

"Well, Atticus, I was just sayin' to Mr. Cunningham that entailments are bad an' all that, but you said not to worry, it takes a long time sometimes . . . that you all'd ride it out together . . ." I was slowly drying up, wondering what idiocy I had committed. Entailments seemed all right enough for livingroom talk.

I began to feel sweat gathering at the edges of my hair; I could stand anything but a bunch of people looking at me. They were quite still.

"What's the matter?" I asked.

Atticus said nothing. I looked around and up at Mr. Cunningham, whose face was equally impassive. Then he did a peculiar thing. He squatted down and took me by both shoulders.

"I'll tell him you said hey, little lady," he said.

Then he straightened up and waved a big paw. "Let's clear out," he called. "Let's get going, boys."

As they had come, in ones and twos the men shuffled back to their ramshackle cars. Doors slammed, engines coughed, and they were gone.

I turned to Atticus, but Atticus had gone to the jail and was leaning against it with his face to the wall. I went to him and pulled his sleeve. "Can we go home now?" He nodded, produced his handkerchief, gave his face a going-over and blew his nose violently.

"Mr. Finch?"

A soft husky voice came from the darkness above: "They gone?"

Atticus stepped back and looked up. "They've gone," he said. "Get some sleep, Tom. They won't bother you any more."

From a different direction, another voice cut crisply through the night: "You're damn tootin' they won't. Had you covered all the time, Atticus."

Mr. Underwood and a double-barreled shotgun were leaning out his window above *The Maycomb Tribune* office.

It was long past my bedtime and I was growing quite tired; it seemed that Atticus and Mr. Underwood would talk for the rest of the night, Mr. Underwood out the window and Atticus up at him. Finally Atticus returned, switched off the light above the jail door, and picked up his chair.

"Can I carry it for you, Mr. Finch?" asked Dill. He had not said a word the whole time.

"Why, thank you, son."

Walking toward the office, Dill and I fell into step behind Atticus and Jem. Dill was encumbered by the chair, and his pace was slower. Atticus and Jem were well ahead of us, and I assumed that Atticus was giving him hell for not going home, but I was wrong. As they passed under a streetlight, Atticus reached out and massaged Jem's hair, his one gesture of affection.

16

Jem heard me. He thrust his head around the connecting door. As he came to my bed Atticus's light flashed on. We stayed where we were until it went off; we heard him turn over, and we waited until he was still again.

Jem took me to his room and put me in bed beside him. "Try to go to sleep," he said. "It'll be all over after tomorrow, maybe."

We had come in quietly, so as not to wake Aunty. Atticus killed the engine in the driveway and coasted to the carhouse; we went in the back door and to our rooms without a word. I was very tired, and was drifting into sleep when the memory of Atticus calmly folding his newspaper and pushing back his hat became Atticus standing in the middle of an empty waiting street, pushing up his glasses. The full meaning of the night's events hit me and I began crying. Jem was awfully nice about it: for once he didn't remind me that people nearly nine years old didn't do things like that.

Everybody's appetite was delicate this morning, except Jem's: he ate his way through three eggs. Atticus watched in frank admiration; Aunt Alexandra sipped coffee and radiated waves of disapproval. Children who slipped out at night were a disgrace to the family. Atticus said he was right glad his disgraces had come along, but Aunty said, "Nonsense, Mr. Underwood was there all the time."

"You know, it's a funny thing about Braxton," said Atticus. "He despises Negroes, won't have one near him."

Local opinion held Mr. Underwood to be an intense, profane little man, whose father in a fey fit of humor christened Braxton Bragg, a name Mr. Underwood had done his best to live down. Atticus said naming people after Confederate generals made slow steady drinkers.

Calpurnia was serving Aunt Alexandra more coffee, and she shook her head at what I thought was a pleading winning look. "You're still too little," she said. "I'll tell you when you ain't." I said it might help my stomach. "All right," she said, and got a cup from the sideboard. She poured one table-spoonful of coffee into it and filled the cup to the brim with milk. I thanked her by sticking out my tongue at it, and looked up to catch Aunty's warning frown. But she was frowning at Atticus.

She waited until Calpurnia was in the kitchen, then she said, "Don't talk like that in front of them."

"Talk like what in front of whom?" he asked.

"Like that in front of Calpurnia. You said Braxton Underwood despises Negroes right in front of her."

"Well, I'm sure Cal knows it. Everybody in Maycomb knows it."

I was beginning to notice a subtle change in my father these days, that came out when he talked with Aunt Alexandra. It was a quiet digging in, never outright irritation. There was a faint starchiness in his voice when he said, "Anything fit to say at the table's fit to say in front of Calpurnia. She knows what she means to this family."

"I don't think it's a good habit, Atticus. It encourages them. You know how they talk among themselves. Everything that happens in this town's out to the Quarters before sundown."

My father put down his knife. "I don't know of any law that says they can't talk. Maybe if we didn't give them so much to talk about they'd be quiet. Why don't you drink your coffee, Scout?"

I was playing in it with the spoon. "I thought Mr. Cunningham was a friend of ours. You told me a long time ago he was."

"He still is."

"But last night he wanted to hurt you."

Atticus placed his fork beside his knife and pushed his plate aside. "Mr. Cunningham's basically a good man," he said, "he just has his blind spots along with the rest of us."

Jem spoke. "Don't call that a blind spot. He'da killed you last night when he first went there."

"He might have hurt me a little," Atticus conceded, "but son, you'll understand folks a little better when you're older. A mob's always made up of people, no matter what. Mr. Cunningham was part of a mob last night, but he was still a man. Every mob in every little Southern town is always made up of people you know—doesn't say much for them, does it?"

"I'll say not," said Jem.

"So it took an eight-year-old child to bring 'em to their senses, didn't it?" said Atticus. "That proves something—that a gang of wild animals *can* be stopped, simply because they're still human. Hmp, maybe we need a police force of children . . . you children last night made Walter Cunningham stand in my shoes for a minute. That was enough."

Well, I hoped Jem would understand folks a little better when he was older; I wouldn't. "First day Walter comes back to school'll be his last," I affirmed.

"You will not touch him," Atticus said flatly. "I don't want either of you bearing a grudge about this thing, no matter what happens."

"You see, don't you," said Aunt Alexandra, "what comes of things like this. Don't say I haven't told you."

Atticus said he'd never say that, pushed out his chair and got up. "There's a day ahead, so excuse me. Jem, I don't want you and Scout downtown today, please."

As Atticus departed, Dill came bounding down the hall into the diningroom. "It's all over town this morning," he announced, "all about how we held off a hundred folks with our bare hands. . . ."

Aunt Alexandra stared him to silence. "It was not a hundred folks," she said, "and nobody held anybody off. It was just a nest of those Cunninghams, drunk and disorderly."

"Aw, Aunty, that's just Dill's way," said Jem. He signaled us to follow him.

"You all stay in the yard today," she said, as we made our way to the front porch.

It was like Saturday. People from the south end of the county passed our house in a leisurely but steady stream.

Mr. Dolphus Raymond lurched by on his thoroughbred. "Don't see how he stays in the saddle," murmured Jem. "How c'n you stand to get drunk 'fore eight in the morning?"

A wagonload of ladies rattled past us. They wore cotton sunbonnets and dresses with long sleeves. A bearded man in a wool hat drove them. "Yonder's some Mennonites," Jem said to Dill. "They don't have buttons." They lived deep in the woods, did most of their trading across the river, and rarely came to Maycomb. Dill was interested. "They've all got blue eyes," Jem explained, "and the men can't shave after they marry. Their wives like for 'em to tickle 'em with their beards."

Mr. X Billups rode by on a mule and waved to us. "He's a funny man," said Jem. "X's his name, not his initial. He was in court one time and they asked him his name. He said X Billups. Clerk asked him to spell it and he said X. Asked him again and he said X. They kept at it till he wrote X on a sheet of paper and held it up for everybody to see. They asked him where he got his name and he said that's the way his folks signed him up when he was born."

As the county went by us, Jem gave Dill the histories and general attitudes of the more prominent figures: Mr. Tensaw Jones voted the straight Prohibition ticket; Miss Emily Davis dipped snuff in private; Mr. Byron Waller could play the violin; Mr. Jake Slade was cutting his third set of teeth.

A wagonload of unusually stern-faced citizens appeared. When they pointed to Miss Maudie Atkinson's yard, ablaze with summer flowers, Miss Maudie herself came out on the porch. There was an odd thing about Miss Maudie—on her porch she was too far away for us to see her features clearly, but we could always catch her mood by the way she stood. She was now standing arms akimbo, her shoulders dropping a little, her head cocked to one side, her glasses winking in the sunlight. We knew she wore a grin of the uttermost wickedness.

The driver of the wagon slowed down his mules, and a shrill-voiced woman called out: "He that cometh in vanity departeth in darkness!"

Miss Maudie answered: "A merry heart maketh a cheerful countenance!"

I guessed that the foot-washers thought that the Devil was quoting Scripture for his own purposes, as the driver speeded his mules. Why they objected to Miss Maudie's yard was a mystery, heightened in my mind because for someone who spent all the daylight hours outdoors, Miss Maudie's command of Scripture was formidable.

"You goin' to court this morning?" asked Jem. We had strolled over.

"I am not," she said. "I have no business with the court this morning."

"Aren't you goin' down to watch?" asked Dill.

"I am not. 't's morbid, watching a poor devil on trial for his life. Look at all those folks, it's like a Roman carnival."

"They hafta try him in public, Miss Maudie," I said. "Wouldn't be right if they didn't."

"I'm quite aware of that," she said. "Just because it's public, I don't have to go, do I?"

Miss Stephanie Crawford came by. She wore a hat and gloves. "Um, um, um," she said. "Look at all those folks— you'd think William Jennings Bryan was speakin'."

"And where are you going, Stephanie?" inquired Miss Maudie.

"To the Jitney Jungle."

Miss Maudie said she'd never seen Miss Stephanie go to the Jitney Jungle in a hat in her life.

182

"Well," said Miss Stephanie, "I thought I might just look in at the courthouse, to see what Atticus's up to."

"Better be careful he doesn't hand you a subpoena."

We asked Miss Maudie to elucidate: she said Miss Stephanie seemed to know so much about the case she might as well be called on to testify.

We held off until noon, when Atticus came home to dinner and said they'd spent the morning picking the jury. After dinner, we stopped by for Dill and went to town.

It was a gala occasion. There was no room at the public hitching rail for another animal, mules and wagons were parked under every available tree. The courthouse square was covered with picnic parties sitting on newspapers, washing down biscuit and syrup with warm milk from fruit jars. Some people were gnawing on cold chicken and cold fried pork chops. The more affluent chased their food with drugstore Coca-Cola in bulb-shaped soda glasses. Greasy-faced children popped-the-whip through the crowd, and babies lunched at their mothers' breasts.

In a far corner of the square, the Negroes sat quietly in the sun, dining on sardines, crackers, and the more vivid flavors of Nehi Cola. Mr. Dolphus Raymond sat with them.

"Jem," said Dill, "he's drinkin' out of a sack."

Mr. Dolphus Raymond seemed to be so doing: two yellow drugstore straws ran from his mouth to the depths of a brown paper bag.

"Ain't ever seen anybody do that," murmured Dill. "How does he keep what's in it in it?"

Jem giggled. "He's got a Co-Cola bottle full of whiskey in there. That's so's not to upset the ladies. You'll see him sip it all afternoon, he'll step out for a while and fill it back up."

"Why's he sittin' with the colored folks?"

"Always does. He likes 'em better'n he likes us, I reckon. Lives by himself way down near the county line. He's got a colored woman and all sorts of mixed chillun. Show you some of 'em if we see 'em."

"He doesn't look like trash," said Dill.

"He's not, he owns all one side of the riverbank down there, and he's from a real old family to boot."

"Then why does he do like that?"

"That's just his way," said Jem. "They say he never got over his weddin'. He was supposed to marry one of the—the Spender ladies, I think. They were gonna have a huge weddin', but they didn't—after the rehearsal the bride went upstairs and blew her head off. Shotgun. She pulled the trigger with her toes."

"Did they ever know why?"

"No," said Jem, "nobody ever knew quite why but Mr. Dolphus. They said it was because she found out about his colored woman, he reckoned he could keep her and get married too. He's been sorta drunk ever since. You know, though, he's real good to those chillun—"

"Jem," I asked, "what's a mixed child?"

"Half white, half colored. You've seen 'em, Scout. You know that red-kinky-headed one that delivers for the drugstore. He's half white. They're real sad."

"Sad, how come?"

"They don't belong anywhere. Colored folks won't have 'em because they're half white; white folks won't have 'em 'cause they're colored, so they're just in-betweens, don't belong anywhere. But Mr. Dolphus, now, they say he's shipped two of his up north. They don't mind 'em up north. Yonder's one of 'em."

A small boy clutching a Negro woman's hand walked toward us. He looked all Negro to me: he was rich chocolate with flaring nostrils and beautiful teeth. Sometimes he would skip happily, and the Negro woman tugged his hand to make him stop.

Jem waited until they passed us. "That's one of the little ones," he said.

"How can you tell?" asked Dill. "He looked black to me."

"You can't sometimes, not unless you know who they are. But he's half Raymond, all right."

184

"But how can you *tell?*" I asked.

"I told you, Scout, you just hafta know who they are."

"Well how do you know we ain't Negroes?"

"Uncle Jack Finch says we really don't know. He says as far as he can trace back the Finches we ain't, but for all he knows we mighta come straight out of Ethiopia durin' the Old Testament."

"Well if we came out durin' the Old Testament it's too long ago to matter."

"That's what I thought," said Jem, "but around here once you have a drop of Negro blood, that makes you all black. Hey, look—"

Some invisible signal had made the lunchers on the square rise and scatter bits of newspaper, cellophane, and wrapping paper. Children came to mothers, babies were cradled on hips as men in sweat-stained hats collected their families and herded them through the courthouse doors. In the far corner of the square the Negroes and Mr. Dolphus Raymond stood up and dusted their breeches. There were few women and children among them, which seemed to dispel the holiday mood. They waited patiently at the doors behind the white families.

"Let's go in," said Dill.

"Naw, we better wait till they get in, Atticus might not like it if he sees us," said Jem.

The Maycomb County courthouse was faintly reminiscent of Arlington in one respect: the concrete pillars supporting its south roof were too heavy for their light burden. The pillars were all that remained standing when the original courthouse burned in 1856. Another courthouse was built around them. It is better to say, built in spite of them. But for the south porch, the Maycomb County courthouse was early Victorian, presenting an unoffensive vista when seen from the north. From the other side, however, Greek revival columns clashed with a big nineteenth-century clock tower housing a rusty unreliable instrument, a view indicating a people determined to preserve every physical scrap of the past.

To reach the courtroom, on the second floor, one passed sundry sunless county cubbyholes: the tax assessor, the tax collector, the county clerk, the county solicitor, the circuit clerk, the judge of probate lived in cool dim hutches that smelled of decaying record books mingled with old damp cement and stale urine. It was necessary to turn on the lights in the daytime; there was always a film of dust on the rough floorboards. The inhabitants of these offices were creatures of their environment: little gray-faced men, they seemed untouched by wind or sun.

We knew there was a crowd, but we had not bargained for the multitudes in the first-floor hallway. I got separated from Jem and Dill, but made my way toward the wall by the stair-well, knowing Jem would come for me eventually. I found myself in the middle of the Idlers' Club and made myself as unobtrusive as possible. This was a group of white-shirted, khaki-trousered, suspendered old men who had spent their lives doing nothing and passed their twilight days doing same on pine benches under the live oaks on the square. Attentive critics of courthouse business, Atticus said they knew as much law as the Chief Justice, from long years of observation. Normally, they were the court's only spectators, and today they seemed resentful of the interruption of their comfortable routine. When they spoke, their voices sounded casually important. The conversation was about my father.

". . . thinks he knows what he's doing," one said.

"Oh-h now, I wouldn't say that," said another. "Atticus Finch's a deep reader, a mighty deep reader."

"He reads all right, that's all he does." The club snickered.

"Lemme tell you somethin' now, Billy," a third said, "you know the court appointed him to defend this nigger."

"Yeah, but Atticus aims to defend him. That's what I don't like about it."

This was news, news that put a different light on things: Atticus had to, whether he wanted to or not. I thought it odd that he hadn't said anything to us about it—we could have used it many times in defending him and ourselves. He had to, that's why he was doing it, equaled fewer fights and less fussing. But did that explain the town's attitude? The court appointed Atticus to defend him. Atticus aimed to defend him. That's what they didn't like about it. It was confusing.

The Negroes, having waited for the white people to go upstairs, began to come in. "Whoa now, just a minute," said a club member, holding up his walking stick. "Just don't start up them there stairs yet awhile."

The club began its stiff-jointed climb and ran into Dill and Jem on their way down looking for me. They squeezed past and Jem called, "Scout, come on, there ain't a seat left. We'll hafta stand up."

"Looka there, now," he said irritably, as the black people surged upstairs. The old men ahead of them would take most of the standing room. We were out of luck and it was all my fault, Jem informed me. We stood miserably by the wall.

"Can't you all get in?"

Reverend Sykes was looking down at us, black hat in hand.

"Hey, Reverend," said Jem. "Naw, Scout here messed us up."

"Well, let's see what we can do."

Reverend Sykes edged his way upstairs. In a few moments he was back. "There's not a seat downstairs. Do you all reckon it'll be all right if you all came to the balcony with me?"

"Gosh yes," said Jem. Happily, we sped ahead of Reverend Sykes to the courtroom floor. There, we went up a covered staircase and waited at the door. Reverend Sykes came puffing behind us, and steered us gently through the black people in the balcony. Four Negroes rose and gave us their front-row seats.

The Colored balcony ran along three walls of the courtroom like a second-story veranda, and from it we could see everything.

The jury sat to the left, under long windows. Sunburned,

lanky, they seemed to be all farmers, but this was natural: townsfolk rarely sat on juries, they were either struck or excused. One or two of the jury looked vaguely like dressed-up Cunninghams. At this stage they sat straight and alert.

The circuit solicitor and another man, Atticus and Tom Robinson sat at tables with their backs to us. There was a brown book and some yellow tablets on the solicitor's table; Atticus's was bare.

Just inside the railing that divided the spectators from the court, the witnesses sat on cowhide-bottomed chairs. Their backs were to us.

Judge Taylor was on the bench, looking like a sleepy old shark, his pilot fish writing rapidly below in front of him. Judge Taylor looked like most judges I had ever seen: amiable, white-haired, slightly ruddy-faced, he was a man who ran his court with an alarming informality—he sometimes propped his feet up, he often cleaned his fingernails with his pocket knife. In long equity hearings, especially after dinner, he gave the impression of dozing, an impression dispelled forever when a lawyer once deliberately pushed a pile of books to the floor in a desperate effort to wake him up. Without opening his eyes, Judge Taylor murmured, "Mr. Whitley, do that again and it'll cost you one hundred dollars."

He was a man learned in the law, and although he seemed to take his job casually, in reality he kept a firm grip on any proceedings that came before him. Only once was Judge Taylor ever seen at a dead standstill in open court, and the Cunninghams stopped him. Old Sarum, their stamping grounds, was populated by two families separate and apart in the beginning, but unfortunately bearing the same name. The Cunninghams married the Coninghams until the spelling of the names was academic—academic until a Cunningham disputed a Coningham over land titles and took to the law. During a controversy of this character, Jeems Cunningham testified that his mother spelled it Cunningham on deeds and things, but she was really a Coningham, she was an uncertain speller, a seldom reader, and was given to looking far away sometimes when she sat on the front gallery in the evening. After nine hours of listening to the eccentricities of Old Sarum's inhabitants, Judge Taylor threw the case out of court. When asked upon what grounds, Judge Taylor said, "Champertous connivance," and declared he hoped to God the litigants were satisfied by each having had their public say. They were. That was all they had wanted in the first place.

Judge Taylor had one interesting habit. He permitted smoking in his courtroom but did not himself indulge: sometimes, if one was lucky, one had the privilege of watching him put a long dry cigar into his mouth and munch it slowly up. Bit by bit the dead cigar would disappear, to reappear some hours later as a flat slick mess, its essence extracted and mingling with Judge Taylor's digestive juices. I once asked Atticus how Mrs. Taylor stood to kiss him, but Atticus said they didn't kiss much.

The witness stand was to the right of Judge Taylor, and when we got to our seats Mr. Heck Tate was already on it.

17

Jem," I said, "are those the Ewells sittin' down yonder?"

"Hush," said Jem, "Mr. Heck Tate's testifyin'."

Mr. Tate had dressed for the occasion. He wore an ordinary business suit, which made him look somehow like every other man: gone were his high boots, lumber jacket, and bullet-studded belt. From that moment he ceased to terrify me. He was sitting forward in the witness chair, his hands clasped between his knees, listening attentively to the circuit solicitor.

The solicitor, a Mr. Gilmer, was not well known to us. He was from Abbottsville; we saw him only when court convened, and that rarely, for court was of no special interest to Jem and me. A balding, smooth-faced man, he could have been anywhere between forty and sixty. Although his back was to us, we knew he had a slight cast in one of his eyes which he used to his advantage: he seemed to be looking at a person when he was actually doing nothing of the kind, thus he was hell on juries and witnesses. The jury, thinking themselves under close scrutiny, paid attention; so did the witnesses, thinking likewise.

". . . in your own words, Mr. Tate," Mr. Gilmer was saying.

"Well," said Mr. Tate, touching his glasses and speaking to his knees, "I was called—"

"Could you say it to the jury, Mr. Tate? Thank you. Who called you?"

Mr. Tate said, "I was fetched by Bob—by Mr. Bob Ewell yonder, one night—"

"What night, sir?"

Mr. Tate said, "It was the night of November twenty-first. I was just leaving my office to go home when B—Mr. Ewell came in, very excited he was, and said get out to his house quick, some nigger'd raped his girl."

"Did you go?"

"Certainly. Got in the car and went out as fast as I could."

"And what did you find?"

"Found her lying on the floor in the middle of the front room, one on the right as you go in. She was pretty well beat up, but I heaved her to her feet and she washed her face in a bucket in the corner and said she was all right. I asked her who hurt her and she said it was Tom Robinson—"

Judge Taylor, who had been concentrating on his finger-nails, looked up as if he were expecting an objection, but Atticus was quiet.

"—asked her if he beat her like that, she said yes he had. Asked her if he took advantage of her and she said yes he did. So I went down to Robinson's house and brought him back. She identified him as the one, so I took him in. That's all there was to it."

"Thank you," said Mr. Gilmer.

Judge Taylor said, "Any questions, Atticus?"

"Yes," said my father. He was sitting behind his table; his chair was skewed to one side, his legs were crossed and one arm was resting on the back of his chair.

"Did you call a doctor, Sheriff? Did anybody call a doctor?" asked Atticus.

"No sir," said Mr. Tate.

"Didn't call a doctor?"

"No sir," repeated Mr. Tate.

"Why not?" There was an edge to Atticus's voice.

"Well I can tell you why I didn't. It wasn't necessary, Mr. Finch. She was mighty banged up. Something sho' happened, it was obvious."

"But you didn't call a doctor? While you were there did anyone send for one, fetch one, carry her to one?"

"No sir—"

Judge Taylor broke in. "He's answered the question three times, Atticus. He didn't call a doctor."

Atticus said, "I just wanted to make sure, Judge," and the judge smiled.

Jem's hand, which was resting on the balcony rail, tightened around it. He drew in his breath suddenly. Glancing below, I saw no corresponding reaction, and wondered if Jem was trying to be dramatic. Dill was watching peacefully, and so was Reverend Sykes beside him. "What is it?" I whispered, and got a terse, "Sh-h!"

"Sheriff," Atticus was saying, "you say she was mighty banged up. In what way?"

"Well—"

"Just describe her injuries, Heck."

"Well, she was beaten around the head. There was already bruises comin' on her arms, and it happened about thirty minutes before—"

"How do you know?"

Mr. Tate grinned. "Sorry, that's what they said. Anyway, she was pretty bruised up when I got there, and she had a black eye comin'."

"Which eye?"

Mr. Tate blinked and ran his hands through his hair. "Let's see," he said softly, then he looked at Atticus as if he considered the question childish. "Can't you remember?" Atticus asked.

Mr. Tate pointed to an invisible person five inches in front of him and said, "Her left."

"Wait a minute, Sheriff," said Atticus. "Was it her left facing you or her left looking the same way you were?"

Mr. Tate said, "Oh yes, that'd make it her right. It was her right eye, Mr. Finch. I remember now, she was bunged up on that side of her face. . . ."

Mr. Tate blinked again, as if something had suddenly been made plain to him. Then he turned his head and looked

192

around at Tom Robinson. As if by instinct, Tom Robinson raised his head.

Something had been made plain to Atticus also, and it brought him to his feet. "Sheriff, please repeat what you said."

"It was her right eye, I said."

"No . . ." Atticus walked to the court reporter's desk and bent down to the furiously scribbling hand. It stopped, flipped back the shorthand pad, and the court reporter said, "'Mr. Finch. I remember now she was bunged up on that side of the face.'"

Atticus looked up at Mr. Tate. "Which side again, Heck?"

"The right side, Mr. Finch, but she had more bruises—you wanta hear about 'em?"

Atticus seemed to be bordering on another question, but he thought better of it and said, "Yes, what were her other injuries?" As Mr. Tate answered, Atticus turned and looked at Tom Robinson as if to say this was something they hadn't bargained for.

". . . her arms were bruised, and she showed me her neck. There were definite finger marks on her gullet—"

"All around her throat? At the back of her neck?"

"I'd say they were all around, Mr. Finch."

"You would?"

"Yes sir, she had a small throat, anybody could'a reached around it with—"

"Just answer the question yes or no, please, Sheriff," said Atticus dryly, and Mr. Tate fell silent.

Atticus sat down and nodded to the circuit solicitor, who shook his head at the judge, who nodded to Mr. Tate, who rose stiffly and stepped down from the witness stand.

Below us, heads turned, feet scraped the floor, babies were shifted to shoulders, and a few children scampered out of the courtroom. The Negroes behind us whispered softly among themselves; Dill was asking Reverend Sykes what it was all about, but Reverend Sykes said he didn't know. So far, things were utterly dull: nobody had thundered, there were no arguments between opposing counsel, there was no drama; a grave disappointment to all present, it seemed. Atticus was proceeding amiably, as if he were involved in a title dispute. With his infinite capacity for calming turbulent seas, he could make a rape case as dry as a sermon. Gone was the terror in my mind of stale whiskey and barnyard smells, of sleepy-eyed sullen men, of a husky voice calling in the night, "Mr. Finch? They gone?" Our nightmare had gone with daylight, everything would come out all right.

All the spectators were as relaxed as Judge Taylor, except Jem. His mouth was twisted into a purposeful half-grin, and his eyes happy about, and he said something about corroborating evidence, which made me sure he was showing off.

". . . Robert E. Lee Ewell!"

In answer to the clerk's booming voice, a little bantam cock of a man rose and strutted to the stand, the back of his neck reddening at the sound of his name. When he turned around to take the oath, we saw that his face was as red as his neck. We also saw no resemblance to his namesake. A shock of wispy new-washed hair stood up from his forehead; his nose was thin, pointed, and shiny; he had no chin to speak of—it seemed to be a part of his crepey neck.

"—so help me God," he crowed.

Every town the size of Maycomb had families like the Ewells. No economic fluctuations changed their status—people like the Ewells lived as guests of the county in prosperity as well as in the depths of a depression. No truant officers could keep their numerous offspring in school; no public health officer could free them from congenital defects, various worms, and the diseases indigenous to filthy surroundings.

Maycomb's Ewells lived behind the town garbage dump in what was once a Negro cabin. The cabin's plank walls were supplemented with sheets of corrugated iron, its roof shingled with tin cans hammered flat, so only its general shape suggested its original design: square, with four tiny rooms opening onto a shotgun hall, the cabin rested uneasily upon four irregular lumps of limestone. Its windows were merely open spaces in the walls, which in the summertime were covered with greasy strips of cheesecloth to keep out the varmints that feasted on Maycomb's refuse.

The varmints had a lean time of it, for the Ewells gave the dump a thorough gleaning every day, and the fruits of their industry (those that were not eaten) made the plot of ground around the cabin look like the playhouse of an insane child: what passed for a fence was bits of tree-limbs, broomsticks and tool shafts, all tipped with rusty hammer-heads, snaggle-toothed rake heads, shovels, axes and grubbing hoes, held on with pieces of barbed wire. Enclosed by this barricade was a dirty yard containing the remains of a Model-T Ford (on blocks), a discarded dentist's chair, an ancient icebox, plus lesser items: old shoes, worn-out table radios, picture frames, and fruit jars, under which scrawny orange chickens pecked hopefully.

One corner of the yard, though, bewildered Maycomb. Against the fence, in a line, were six chipped-enamel slop jars holding brilliant red geraniums, cared for as tenderly as if they belonged to Miss Maudie Atkinson, had Miss Maudie deigned to permit a geranium on her premises. People said they were Mayella Ewell's.

Nobody was quite sure how many children were on the place. Some people said six, others said nine; there were always several dirty-faced ones at the windows when anyone passed by. Nobody had occasion to pass by except at Christmas, when the churches delivered baskets, and when the mayor of Maycomb asked us to please help the garbage collector by dumping our own trees and trash.

Atticus took us with him last Christmas when he complied with the mayor's request. A dirt road ran from the highway past the dump, down to a small Negro settlement some five hundred yards beyond the Ewells'. It was necessary either to back out to the highway or go the full length of the road and turn around; most people turned around in the Negroes' front yards.

In the frosty December dusk, their cabins looked neat and snug with pale blue smoke rising from the chimneys and doorways glowing amber from the fires inside. There were delicious smells about: chicken, bacon frying crisp as the twilight air. Jem and I detected squirrel cooking, but it took an old countryman like Atticus to identify possum and rabbit, aromas that vanished when we rode back past the Ewell residence.

All the little man on the witness stand had that made him any better than his nearest neighbors was, that if scrubbed with lye soap in very hot water, his skin was white.

"Mr. Robert Ewell?" asked Mr. Gilmer.

"That's m'name, cap'n," said the witness.

Mr. Gilmer's back stiffened a little, and I felt sorry for him. Perhaps I'd better explain something now. I've heard that lawyers' children, on seeing their parents in court in the heat of argument, get the wrong idea: they think opposing counsel to be the personal enemies of their parents, they suffer agonies, and are surprised to see them often go out arm-in-arm with their tormenters during the first recess. This was not true of Jem and me. We acquired no traumas from watching our father win or lose. I'm sorry that I can't provide any drama in this respect; if I did, it would not be true. We could tell, however, when debate became more acrimonious than professional, but this was from watching lawyers other than our father. I never heard Atticus raise his voice in my life, except to a deaf witness. Mr. Gilmer was doing his job, as Atticus was doing his. Besides, Mr. Ewell was Mr. Gilmer's witness, and he had no business being rude to him of all people.

"Are you the father of Mayella Ewell?" was the next question.

"Well, if I ain't I can't do nothing about it now, her ma's dead," was the answer.

Judge Taylor stirred. He turned slowly in his swivel chair and looked benignly at the witness. "Are you the father of Mayella Ewell?" he asked, in a way that made the laughter below us stop suddenly.

196

"Yes sir," Mr. Ewell said meekly.

Judge Taylor went on in tones of good will: "This the first time you've ever been in court? I don't recall ever seeing you here." At the witness's affirmative nod he continued, "Well, let's get something straight. There will be no more audibly obscene speculations on any subject from anybody in this courtroom as long as I'm sitting here. Do you understand?"

Mr. Ewell nodded, but I don't think he did. Judge Taylor sighed and said, "All right, Mr. Gilmer?"

"Thank you, sir. Mr. Ewell, would you tell us in your own words what happened on the evening of November twenty-first, please?"

Jem grinned and pushed his hair back. Just-in-your-own words was Mr. Gilmer's trademark. We often wondered who else's words Mr. Gilmer was afraid his witness might employ.

"Well, the night of November twenty-one I was comin' in from the woods with a load o'kindlin' and just as I got to the fence I heard Mayella screamin' like a stuck hog inside the house—"

Here Judge Taylor glanced sharply at the witness and must have decided his speculations devoid of evil intent, for he subsided sleepily.

"What time was it, Mr. Ewell?"

"Just 'fore sundown. Well, I was sayin' Mayella was screamin' fit to beat Jesus—" another glance from the bench silenced Mr. Ewell.

"Yes? She was screaming?" said Mr. Gilmer.

Mr. Ewell looked confusedly at the judge. "Well, Mayella was raisin' this holy racket so I dropped m'load and run as fast as I could but I run into th' fence, but when I got distangled I run up to th' window and I seen—" Mr. Ewell's face grew scarlet. He stood up and pointed his finger at Tom Robinson. "—I seen that black nigger yonder ruttin' on my Mayella!"

So serene was Judge Taylor's court, that he had few occasions to use his gavel, but he hammered fully five minutes. Atticus was on his feet at the bench saying something to him,

Mr. Heck Tate as first officer of the county stood in the middle aisle quelling the packed courtroom. Behind us, there was an angry muffled groan from the colored people.

Reverend Sykes leaned across Dill and me, pulling at Jem's elbow. "Mr. Jem," he said, "you better take Miss Jean Louise home. Mr. Jem, you hear me?"

Jem turned his head. "Scout, go home. Dill, you'n'Scout go home."

"You gotta make me first," I said, remembering Atticus's blessed dictum.

Jem scowled furiously at me, then said to Reverend Sykes, "I think it's okay, Reverend, she doesn't understand it."

I was mortally offended. "I most certainly do, I c'n understand anything you can."

"Aw hush. She doesn't understand it, Reverend, she ain't nine yet."

Reverend Sykes's black eyes were anxious. "Mr. Finch know you all are here? This ain't fit for Miss Jean Louise or you boys either."

Jem shook his head. "He can't see us this far away. It's all right, Reverend."

I knew Jem would win, because I knew nothing could make him leave now. Dill and I were safe, for a while: Atticus could see us from where he was, if he looked.

As Judge Taylor banged his gavel, Mr. Ewell was sitting smugly in the witness chair, surveying his handiwork. With one phrase he had turned happy picknickers into a sulky, tense, murmuring crowd, being slowly hynotized by gavel taps lessening in intensity until the only sound in the courtroom was a dim pink-pink-pink: the judge might have been rapping the bench with a pencil.

In possession of his court once more, Judge Taylor leaned back in his chair. He looked suddenly weary; his age was showing, and I thought about what Atticus had said—he and Mrs. Taylor didn't kiss much—he must have been nearly seventy.

"There has been a request," Judge Taylor said, "that this

courtroom be cleared of spectators, or at least of women and children, a request that will be denied for the time being. People generally see what they look for, and hear what they listen for, and they have the right to subject their children to it, but I can assure you of one thing: you will receive what you see and hear in silence or you will leave this courtroom, but you won't leave it until the whole boiling of you come before me on contempt charges. Mr. Ewell, you will keep your testimony within the confines of Christian English usage, if that is possible. Proceed, Mr. Gilmer."

Mr. Ewell reminded me of a deaf-mute. I was sure he had never heard the words Judge Taylor directed at him—his mouth struggled silently with them—but their import registered on his face. Smugness faded from it, replaced by a dogged earnestness that fooled Judge Taylor not at all: as long as Mr. Ewell was on the stand, the judge kept his eyes on him, as if daring him to make a false move.

Mr. Gilmer and Atticus exchanged glances. Atticus was sitting down again, his fist rested on his cheek and we could not see his face. Mr. Gilmer looked rather desperate. A question from Judge Taylor made him relax: "Mr. Ewell, did you see the defendant having sexual intercourse with your daughter?"

"Yes, I did."

The spectators were quiet, but the defendant said something. Atticus whispered to him, and Tom Robinson was silent.

"You say you were at the window?" asked Mr. Gilmer.

"Yes sir."

"How far is it from the ground?"

" 'bout three foot."

"Did you have a clear view of the room?"

"Yes sir."

"How did the room look?"

"Well, it was all slung about, like there was a fight."

"What did you do when you saw the defendant?"

"Well, I run around the house to get in, but he run out the

front door just ahead of me. I sawed who he was, all right. I was too distracted about Mayella to run after'im. I run in the house and she was lyin' on the floor squallin'—"

"Then what did you do?"

"Why, I run for Tate quick as I could. I knowed who it was, all right, lived down yonder in that nigger-nest, passed the house every day. Jedge, I've asked this county for fifteen years to clean out that nest down yonder, they're dangerous to live around 'sides devaluin' my property—"

"Thank you, Mr. Ewell," said Mr. Gilmer hurriedly.

The witness made a hasty descent from the stand and ran smack into Atticus, who had risen to question him. Judge Taylor permitted the court to laugh.

"Just a minute, sir," said Atticus genially. "Could I ask you a question or two?"

Mr. Ewell backed up into the witness chair, settled himself, and regarded Atticus with haughty suspicion, an expression common to Maycomb County witnesses when confronted by opposing counsel.

"Mr. Ewell," Atticus began, "folks were doing a lot of running that night. Let's see, you say you ran into the house, you ran to the window, you ran inside, you ran to Mayella, you ran for Mr. Tate. Did you, during all this running, run for a doctor?"

"Wadn't no need to. I seen what happened."

"But there's one thing I don't understand," said Atticus. "Weren't you concerned with Mayella's condition?"

"I most positively was," said Mr. Ewell. "I seen who done it."

"No, I mean her physical condition. Did you not think the nature of her injuries warranted immediate medical attention?"

"What?"

"Didn't you think she should have had a doctor, immediately?"

The witness said he never thought of it, he had never called a doctor to any of his'n in his life, and if he had it would have cost him five dollars. "That all?" he asked.

"Not quite," said Atticus casually. "Mr. Ewell, you heard the sheriff's testimony, didn't you?"

"How's that?"

"You were in the courtroom when Mr. Heck Tate was on the stand, weren't you? You heard everything he said, didn't you?"

Mr. Ewell considered the matter carefully, and seemed to decide that the question was safe.

"Yes," he said.

"Do you agree with his description of Mayella's injuries?"

"How's that?"

Atticus looked around at Mr. Gilmer and smiled. Mr. Ewell seemed determined not to give the defense the time of day.

"Mr. Tate testified that her right eye was blackened, that she was beaten around the—"

"Oh yeah," said the witness. "I hold with everything Tate said."

"You do?" asked Atticus mildly. "I just want to make sure." He went to the court reporter, said something, and the reporter entertained us for some minutes by reading Mr. Tate's testimony as if it were stock-market quotations: ". . . which eye her left oh yes that'd make it her right it was her right eye Mr. Finch I remember now she was bunged." He flipped the page. "Up on that side of the face Sheriff please repeat what you said it was her right eye I said—"

"Thank you, Bert," said Atticus. "You heard it again, Mr. Ewell. Do you have anything to add to it? Do you agree with the sheriff?"

"I holds with Tate. Her eye was blacked and she was mighty beat up."

The little man seemed to have forgotten his previous humiliation from the bench. It was becoming evident that he thought Atticus an easy match. He seemed to grow ruddy again; his chest swelled, and once more he was a red little rooster. I thought he'd burst his shirt at Atticus's next question:

"Mr. Ewell, can you read and write?"

Mr. Gilmer interrupted. "Objection," he said. "Can't see what witness's literacy has to do with the case, irrelevant'n'immaterial."

Judge Taylor was about to speak but Atticus said, "Judge, if you'll allow the question plus another one you'll soon see."

"All right, let's see," said Judge Taylor, "but make sure we see, Atticus. Overruled."

Mr. Gilmer seemed as curious as the rest of us as to what bearing the state of Mr. Ewell's education had on the case.

"I'll repeat the question," said Atticus. "Can you read and write?"

"I most positively can."

"Will you write your name and show us?"

"I most positively will. How do you think I sign my relief checks?"

Mr. Ewell was endearing himself to his fellow citizens. The whispers and chuckles below us probably had to do with what a card he was.

I was becoming nervous. Atticus seemed to know what he was doing—but it seemed to me that he'd gone frog-sticking without a light. Never, never, never, on cross-examination ask a witness a question you don't already know the answer to, was a tenet I absorbed with my baby-food. Do it, and you'll often get an answer you don't want, an answer that might wreck your case.

Atticus was reaching into the inside pocket of his coat. He drew out an envelope, then reached into his vest pocket and unclipped his fountain pen. He moved leisurely, and had turned so that he was in full view of the jury. He unscrewed the fountain-pen cap and placed it gently on his table. He shook the pen a little, then handed it with the envelope to the witness. "Would you write your name for us?" he asked. "Clearly now, so the jury can see you do it."

Mr. Ewell wrote on the back of the envelope and looked up complacently to see Judge Taylor staring at him as if he were some fragrant gardenia in full bloom on the witness stand, to see Mr. Gilmer half-sitting, half-standing at his table. The jury was watching him, one man was leaning forward with his hands over the railing.

"What's so interestin'?" he asked.

"You're left-handed, Mr. Ewell," said Judge Taylor.

Mr. Ewell turned angrily to the judge and said he didn't see what his being left-handed had to do with it, that he was a Christ-fearing man and Atticus Finch was taking advantage of him. Tricking lawyers like Atticus Finch took advantage of him all the time with their tricking ways. He had told them what happened, he'd say it again and again—which he did. Nothing Atticus asked him after that shook his story, that he'd looked through the window, then ran the nigger off, then ran for the sheriff. Atticus finally dismissed him.

Mr. Gilmer asked him one more question. "About your writing with your left hand, are you ambidextrous, Mr. Ewell?"

"I most positively am not, I can use one hand good as the other. One hand good as the other," he added, glaring at the defense table.

Jem seemed to be having a quiet fit. He was pounding the balcony rail softly, and once he whispered, "We've got him."

I didn't think so: Atticus was trying to show, it seemed to me, that Mr. Ewell could have beaten up Mayella. That much I could follow. If her right eye was blacked and she was beaten mostly on the right side of the face, it would tend to show that a left-handed person did it. Sherlock Holmes and Jem Finch would agree. But Tom Robinson could easily be left-handed, too. Like Mr. Heck Tate, I imagined a person facing me, went through a swift mental pantomime, and concluded that he might have held her with his right hand and pounded her with his left. I looked down at him. His back was to us, but I could see his broad shoulders and bull-thick neck. He could easily have done it. I thought Jem was counting his chickens.

18

But someone was booming again.

"Mayella Violet Ewell—!"

A young girl walked to the witness stand. As she raised her hand and swore that the evidence she gave would be the truth, the whole truth, and nothing but the truth so help her God, she seemed somehow fragile-looking, but when she sat facing us in the witness chair she became what she was, a thick-bodied girl accustomed to strenuous labor.

In Maycomb County, it was easy to tell when someone bathed regularly, as opposed to yearly lavations: Mr. Ewell had a scalded look; as if an overnight soaking had deprived him of protective layers of dirt, his skin appeared to be sensitive to the elements. Mayella looked as if she tried to keep clean, and I was reminded of the row of red geraniums in the Ewell yard.

Mr. Gilmer asked Mayella to tell the jury in her own words what happened on the evening of November twenty-first of last year, just in her own words, please.

Mayella sat silently.

"Where were you at dusk on that evening?" began Mr. Gilmer patiently.

"On the porch."

"Which porch?"

"Ain't but one, the front porch."

"What were you doing on the porch?"

"Nothin'."

Judge Taylor said, "Just tell us what happened. You can do that, can't you?"

Mayella stared at him and burst into tears. She covered her mouth with her hands and sobbed. Judge Taylor let her cry for a while, then he said, "That's enough now. Don't be 'fraid of anybody here, as long as you tell the truth. All this is strange to you, I know, but you've nothing to be ashamed of and nothing to fear. What are you scared of?"

Mayella said something behind her hands. "What was that?" asked the judge.

"Him," she sobbed, pointing at Atticus.

"Mr. Finch?"

She nodded vigorously, saying, "Don't want him doin' me like he done Papa, tryin' to make him out left-handed . . ."

Judge Taylor scratched his thick white hair. It was plain that he had never been confronted with a problem of this kind. "How old are you?" he asked.

"Nineteen-and-a-half," Mayella said.

Judge Taylor cleared his throat and tried unsuccessfully to speak in soothing tones. "Mr. Finch has no idea of scaring you," he growled, "and if he did, I'm here to stop him. That's one thing I'm sitting up here for. Now you're a big girl, so you just sit up straight and tell the—tell us what happened to you. You can do that, can't you?"

I whispered to Jem, "Has she got good sense?"

Jem was squinting down at the witness stand. "Can't tell yet," he said. "She's got enough sense to get the judge sorry for her, but she might be just—oh, I don't know."

Mollified, Mayella gave Atticus a final terrified glance and said to Mr. Gilmer, "Well sir, I was on the porch and—and he came along and, you see, there was this old chiffarobe in the yard Papa'd brought in to chop up for kindlin'—Papa told me to do it while he was off in the woods but I wadn't feelin' strong enough then, so he came by—"

"Who is 'he'?"

Mayella pointed to Tom Robinson. "I'll have to ask you to be more specific, please," said Mr. Gilmer. "The reporter can't put down gestures very well."

"That'n yonder," she said. "Robinson."

"Then what happened?"

"I said come here, nigger, and bust up this chiffarobe for me, I gotta nickel for you. He coulda done it easy enough, he could. So he come in the yard an' I went in the house to get him the nickel and I turned around an 'fore I knew it he was on me. Just run up behind me, he did. He got me round the neck, cussin' me an' sayin' dirt—I fought'n'hollered, but he had me round the neck. He hit me agin an' agin—"

Mr. Gilmer waited for Mayella to collect herself: she had twisted her handkerchief into a sweaty rope; when she opened it to wipe her face it was a mass of creases from her hot hands. She waited for Mr. Gilmer to ask another question, but when he didn't she said, "—he chunked me on the floor an' choked me'n took advantage of me."

"Did you scream?" asked Mr. Gilmer. "Did you scream and fight back?"

"Reckon I did, hollered for all I was worth, kicked and hollered loud as I could."

"Then what happened?"

"I don't remember too good, but next thing I knew Papa was in the room a'standin' over me hollerin' who done it, who done it? Then I sorta fainted an' the next thing I knew Mr. Tate was pullin' me up offa the floor and leadin' me to the water bucket."

Apparently Mayella's recital had given her confidence, but it was not her father's brash kind: there was something stealthy about hers, like a steady-eyed cat with a twitchy tail.

"You say you fought him off as hard as you could? Fought him tooth and nail?" asked Mr. Gilmer.

"I positively did," Mayella echoed her father.

"You are positive that he took full advantage of you?"

Mayella's face contorted, and I was afraid that she would cry again. Instead, she said, "He done what he was after."

Mr. Gilmer called attention to the hot day by wiping his head with his hand. "That's all for the time being," he said pleasantly, "but you stay there. I expect big bad Mr. Finch has some questions to ask you."

"State will not prejudice the witness against counsel for the defense," murmured Judge Taylor primly, "at least not at this time."

Atticus got up grinning, but instead of walking to the witness stand, he opened his coat and hooked his thumbs in his vest, then he walked slowly across the room to the windows. He looked out, but didn't seem especially interested in what he saw, then he turned and strolled back to the witness stand. From long years of experience, I could tell he was trying to come to a decision about something.

"Miss Mayella," he said, smiling, "I won't try to scare you for a while, not yet. Let's just get acquainted. How old are you?"

"Said I was nineteen, said it to the judge yonder." Mayella jerked her head resentfully at the bench.

"So you did, so you did, ma'am. You'll have to bear with me, Miss Mayella, I'm getting along and can't remember as well as I used to. I might ask you things you've already said before, but you'll give me an answer, won't you? Good."

I could see nothing in Mayella's expression to justify Atticus's assumption that he had secured her wholehearted cooperation. She was looking at him furiously.

"Won't answer a word you say long as you keep on mockin' me," she said.

"Ma'am?" asked Atticus, startled.

"Long's you keep on makin' fun o'me."

Judge Taylor said, "Mr. Finch is not making fun of you. What's the matter with you?"

Mayella looked from under lowered eyelids at Atticus, but she said to the judge: "Long's he keeps on callin' me ma'am an sayin' Miss Mayella. I don't hafta take his sass, I ain't called upon to take it."

Atticus resumed his stroll to the windows and let Judge Taylor handle this one. Judge Taylor was not the kind of figure that ever evoked pity, but I did feel a pang for him as he tried to explain. "That's just Mr. Finch's way," he told Mayella. "We've done business in this court for years and years, and Mr. Finch is always courteous to everybody. He's not trying to mock you, he's trying to be polite. That's just his way."

The judge leaned back. "Atticus, let's get on with these proceedings, and let the record show that the witness has not been sassed, her views to the contrary."

I wondered if anybody had ever called her "ma'am" or "Miss Mayella" in her life; probably not, as she took offense to routine courtesy. What on earth was her life like? I soon found out.

"You say you're nineteen," Atticus resumed. "How many sisters and brothers have you?" He walked from the windows back to the stand.

"Seb'm," she said, and I wondered if they were all like the specimen I had seen the first day I started to school.

"You the eldest? The oldest?"

"Yes."

"How long has your mother been dead?"

"Don't know—long time."

"Did you ever go to school?"

"Read'n'write good as Papa yonder."

Mayella sounded like a Mr. Jingle in a book I had been reading.

"How long did you go to school?"

"Two year—three year—dunno."

Slowly but surely I began to see the pattern of Atticus's questions: from questions that Mr. Gilmer did not deem sufficiently irrelevant or immaterial to object to, Atticus was quietly building up before the jury a picture of the Ewells' home life. The jury learned the following things: their relief check was far from enough to feed the family, and there was strong suspicion that Papa drank it up anyway—he sometimes went off in the swamp for days and came home sick; the weather

208

was seldom cold enough to require shoes, but when it was, you could make dandy ones from strips of old tires; the family hauled its water in buckets from a spring that ran out at one end of the dump—they kept the surrounding area clear of trash—and it was everybody for himself as far as keeping clean went: if you wanted to wash you hauled your own water; the younger children had perpetual colds and suffered from chronic ground-itch; there was a lady who came around sometimes and asked Mayella why she didn't stay in school— she wrote down the answer; with two members of the family reading and writing, there was no need for the rest of them to learn—Papa needed them at home.

"Miss Mayella," said Atticus, in spite of himself, "a nine-teen-year-old girl like you must have friends. Who are your friends?"

The witness frowned as if puzzled. "Friends?"

"Yes, don't you know anyone near your age, or older, or younger? Boys and girls? Just ordinary friends?"

Mayella's hostility, which had subsided to grudging neutrality, flared again. "You makin' fun o'me agin, Mr. Finch?"

Atticus let her question answer his.

"Do you love your father, Miss Mayella?" was his next.

"Love him, whatcha mean?"

"I mean, is he good to you, is he easy to get along with?"

"He does tollable, 'cept when—"

"Except when?"

Mayella looked at her father, who was sitting with his chair tipped against the railing. He sat up straight and waited for her to answer.

"Except when nothin'," said Mayella. "I said he does tollable."

Mr. Ewell leaned back again.

"Except when he's drinking?" asked Atticus so gently that Mayella nodded.

"Does he ever go after you?"

"How you mean?"

"When he's—riled, has he ever beaten you?"

Mayella looked around, down at the court reporter, up at the judge. "Answer the question, Miss Mayella," said Judge Taylor.

"My paw's never touched a hair o' my head in my life," she declared firmly. "He never touched me."

Atticus's glasses had slipped a little, and he pushed them up on his nose. "We've had a good visit, Miss Mayella, and now I guess we'd better get to the case. You say you asked Tom Robinson to come chop up a—what was it?"

"A chiffarobe, a old dresser full of drawers on one side."

"Was Tom Robinson well known to you?"

"Whaddya mean?"

"I mean did you know who he was, where he lived?"

Mayella nodded. "I knowed who he was, he passed the house every day."

"Was this the first time you asked him to come inside the fence?"

Mayella jumped slightly at the question. Atticus was making his slow pilgrimage to the windows, as he had been doing: he would ask a question, then look out, waiting for an answer. He did not see her involuntary jump, but it seemed to me that he knew she had moved. He turned around and raised his eyebrows. "Was—" he began again.

"Yes it was."

"Didn't you ever ask him to come inside the fence before?"

She was prepared now. "I did not, I certainly did not."

"One did not's enough," said Atticus serenely. "You never asked him to do odd jobs for you before?"

"I mighta," conceded Mayella. "There was several niggers around."

"Can you remember any other occasions?"

"No."

"All right, now to what happened. You said Tom Robinson was behind you in the room when you turned around, that right?"

210

"Yes."

"You said he 'got you around the neck cussing and saying dirt'—is that right?"

"'t's right."

Atticus's memory had suddenly become accurate. "You say 'he caught me and choked me and took advantage of me'—is that right?"

"That's what I said."

"Do you remember him beating you about the face?"

The witness hesitated.

"You seem sure enough that he choked you. All this time you were fighting back, remember? You 'kicked and hollered as loud as you could.' Do you remember him beating you about the face?"

Mayella was silent. She seemed to be trying to get something clear to herself. I thought for a moment she was doing Mr. Heck Tate's and my trick of pretending there was a person in front of us. She glanced at Mr. Gilmer.

"It's an easy question, Miss Mayella, so I'll try again. Do you remember him beating you about the face?" Atticus's voice had lost its comfortableness; he was speaking in his arid, detached professional voice. "Do you remember him beating you about the face?"

"No, I don't recollect if he hit me. I mean yes I do, he hit me."

"Was your last sentence your answer?"

"Huh? Yes, he hit—I just don't remember, I just don't remember . . . it all happened so quick."

Judge Taylor looked sternly at Mayella. "Don't you cry, young woman—" he began, but Atticus said, "Let her cry if she wants to, Judge. We've got all the time in the world."

Mayella sniffed wrathfully and looked at Atticus. "I'll answer any question you got—get me up here an' mock me, will you? I'll answer any question you got—"

"That's fine," said Atticus. "There're only a few more. Miss Mayella, not to be tedious, you've testified that the defendant hit you, grabbed you around the neck, choked you, and took advantage of you. I want you to be sure you have the right man. Will you identify the man who raped you?"

"I will, that's him right yonder."

Atticus turned to the defendant. "Tom, stand up. Let Miss Mayella have a good long look at you. Is this the man, Miss Mayella?"

Tom Robinson's powerful shoulders rippled under his thin shirt. He rose to his feet and stood with his right hand on the back of his chair. He looked oddly off balance, but it was not from the way he was standing. His left arm was fully twelve inches shorter than his right, and hung dead at his side. It ended in a small shriveled hand, and from as far away as the balcony I could see that it was no use to him.

"Scout," breathed Jem. "Scout, look! Reverend, he's crippled!"

Reverend Sykes leaned across me and whispered to Jem. "He got it caught in a cotton gin, caught it in Mr. Dolphus Raymond's cotton gin when he was a boy . . . like to bled to death . . . tore all the muscles loose from his bones—"

Atticus said, "Is this the man who raped you?"

"It most certainly is."

Atticus's next question was one word long. "How?"

Mayella was raging. "I don't know how he done it, but he done it—I said it all happened so fast I—"

"Now let's consider this calmly—" began Atticus, but Mr. Gilmer interrupted with an objection: he was not irrelevant or immaterial, but Atticus was browbeating the witness.

Judge Taylor laughed outright. "Oh sit down, Horace, he's doing nothing of the sort. If anything, the witness's browbeating Atticus."

Judge Taylor was the only person in the courtroom who laughed. Even the babies were still, and I suddenly wondered if they had been smothered at their mothers' breasts.

"Now," said Atticus, "Miss Mayella, you've testified that the defendant choked and beat you—you didn't say that he sneaked up behind you and knocked you cold, but you turned around and there he was—" Atticus was back behind his table, and he emphasized his words by tapping his knuckles on it. "—do you wish to reconsider any of your testimony?"

"You want me to say something that didn't happen?"

"No ma'am, I want you to say something that did happen. Tell us once more, please, what happened?"

"I told'ja what happened."

"You testified that you turned around and there he was. He choked you then?"

"Yes."

"Then he released your throat and hit you?"

"I said he did."

"He blacked your left eye with his right fist?"

"I ducked and it—it glanced, that's what it did. I ducked and it glanced off." Mayella had finally seen the light.

"You're becoming suddenly clear on this point. A while ago you couldn't remember too well, could you?"

"I said he hit me."

"All right. He choked you, he hit you, then he raped you, that right?"

"It most certainly is."

"You're a strong girl, what were you doing all the time, just standing there?"

"I told'ja I hollered'n'kicked'n'fought—"

Atticus reached up and took off his glasses, turned his good right eye to the witness, and rained questions on her. Judge Taylor said, "One question at a time, Atticus. Give the witness a chance to answer."

"All right, why didn't you run?"

"I tried to . . ."

"Tried to? What kept you from it?"

"I—he slung me down. That's what he did, he slung me down'n got on top of me."

"You were screaming all this time?"

"I certainly was."

"Then why didn't the other children hear you? Where were they? At the dump?"

No answer.

"Where were they?"

"Why didn't your screams make them come running? The dump's closer than the woods, isn't it?"

No answer.

"Or didn't you scream until you saw your father in the window? You didn't think to scream until then, did you?"

No answer.

"Did you scream first at your father instead of at Tom Robinson? Was that it?"

No answer.

"Who beat you up? Tom Robinson or your father?"

No answer.

"What did your father see in the window, the crime of rape or the best defense to it? Why don't you tell the truth, child, didn't Bob Ewell beat you up?"

When Atticus turned away from Mayella he looked like his stomach hurt, but Mayella's face was a mixture of terror and fury. Atticus sat down wearily and polished his glasses with his handkerchief.

Suddenly Mayella became articulate. "I got somethin' to say," she said.

Atticus raised his head. "Do you want to tell us what happened?"

But she did not hear the compassion in his invitation. "I got somethin' to say an' then I ain't gonna say no more. That nigger yonder took advantage of me an' if you fine fancy gentlemen don't wanta do nothin' about it then you're all yellow stinkin' cowards, stinkin' cowards, the lot of you. Your fancy airs don't come to nothin'—your ma'amin' and Miss Mayellerin' don't come to nothin', Mr. Finch—"

Then she burst into real tears. Her shoulders shook with angry sobs. She was as good as her word. She answered no more questions, even when Mr. Gilmer tried to get her back on the track. I guess if she hadn't been so poor and ignorant, Judge Taylor would have put her under the jail for the contempt she had shown everybody in the courtroom. Somehow, Atticus had hit her hard in a way that was not clear to me, but it gave him no pleasure to do so. He sat with his head down, and I never saw anybody glare at anyone with the hatred Mayella showed when she left the stand and walked by Atticus's table.

When Mr. Gilmer told Judge Taylor that the state rested, Judge Taylor said, "It's time we all did. We'll take ten minutes."

Atticus and Mr. Gilmer met in front of the bench and whispered, then they left the courtroom by a door behind the witness stand, which was a signal for us all to stretch. I discovered that I had been sitting on the edge of the long bench, and I was somewhat numb. Jem got up and yawned, Dill did likewise, and Reverend Sykes wiped his face on his hat. The temperature was an easy ninety, he said.

Mr. Braxton Underwood, who had been sitting quietly in a chair reserved for the Press, soaking up testimony with his sponge of a brain, allowed his bitter eyes to rove over the Colored balcony, and they met mine. He gave a snort and looked away.

"Jem," I said, "Mr. Underwood's seen us."

"That's okay. He won't tell Atticus, he'll just put it on the social side of the *Tribune*." Jem turned back to Dill, explaining, I suppose, the finer points of the trial to him, but I wondered what they were. There had been no lengthy debates between Atticus and Mr. Gilmer on any points; Mr. Gilmer seemed to be prosecuting almost reluctantly; witnesses had been led by the nose as asses are, with few objections. But Atticus had once told us that in Judge Taylor's court any lawyer who was a strict constructionist on evidence usually wound up receiving strict instructions from the bench. He distilled this for me to mean that Judge Taylor might look lazy and operate in his sleep, but he was seldom reversed, and that was the proof of the pudding. Atticus said he was a good judge.

Presently Judge Taylor returned and climbed into his swivel chair. He took a cigar from his vest pocket and examined it thoughtfully. I punched Dill. Having passed the judge's inspection, the cigar suffered a vicious bite. "We come down sometimes to watch him," I explained. "It's gonna take him the rest of the afternoon, now. You watch." Unaware of public scrutiny from above, Judge Taylor disposed of the severed end by propelling it expertly to his lips and saying, "Fhluck!" He hit a spittoon so squarely we could hear it slosh. "Bet he was hell with a spitball," murmured Dill.

As a rule, a recess meant a general exodus, but today people weren't moving. Even the Idlers who had failed to shame younger men from their seats had remained standing along the walls. I guess Mr. Heck Tate had reserved the county toilet for court officials.

Atticus and Mr. Gilmer returned, and Judge Taylor looked at his watch. "It's gettin' on to four," he said, which was intriguing, as the courthouse clock must have struck the hour at least twice. I had not heard it or felt its vibrations.

"Shall we try to wind up this afternoon?" asked Judge Taylor. "How 'bout it, Atticus?"

"I think we can," said Atticus.

"How many witnesses you got?"

"One."

"Well, call him."

19

Thomas Robinson reached around, ran his fingers under his left arm and lifted it. He guided his arm to the Bible and his rubber-like left hand sought contact with the black binding. As he raised his right hand, the useless one slipped off the Bible and hit the clerk's table. He was trying again when Judge Taylor growled, "That'll do, Tom." Tom took the oath and stepped into the witness chair. Atticus very quickly induced him to tell us:

Tom was twenty-five years of age; he was married with three children; he had been in trouble with the law before: he once received thirty days for disorderly conduct.

"It must have been disorderly," said Atticus. "What did it consist of?"

"Got in a fight with another man, he tried to cut me."

"Did he succeed?"

"Yes suh, a little, not enough to hurt. You see, I—" Tom moved his left shoulder.

"Yes," said Atticus. "You were both convicted?"

"Yes suh, I had to serve 'cause I couldn't pay the fine. Other fellow paid his'n."

Dill leaned across me and asked Jem what Atticus was doing. Jem said Atticus was showing the jury that Tom had nothing to hide.

"Were you acquainted with Mayella Violet Ewell?" asked Atticus.

"Yes suh, I had to pass her place goin' to and from the field every day."

"Whose field?"

"I picks for Mr. Link Deas."

"Were you picking cotton in November?"

"No suh, I works in his yard fall an' wintertime. I works pretty steady for him all year round, he's got a lot of pecan trees'n things."

"You say you had to pass the Ewell place to get to and from work. Is there any other way to go?"

"No suh, none's I know of."

"Tom, did she ever speak to you?"

"Why, yes suh, I'd tip m'hat when I'd go by, and one day she asked me to come inside the fence and bust up a chiffarobe for her."

"When did she ask you to chop up the—the chiffarobe?"

"Mr. Finch, it was way last spring. I remember it because it was choppin' time and I had my hoe with me. I said I didn't have nothin' but this hoe, but she said she had a hatchet. She give me the hatchet and I broke up the chiffarobe. She said, 'I reckon I'll hafta give you a nickel, won't I?' an' I said, 'No ma'am, there ain't no charge.' Then I went home. Mr. Finch, that was way last spring, way over a year ago."

"Did you ever go on the place again?"

"Yes suh."

"When?"

"Well, I went lots of times."

Judge Taylor instinctively reached for his gavel, but let his hand fall. The murmur below us died without his help.

"Under what circumstances?"

"Please, suh?"

"Why did you go inside the fence lots of times?"

Tom Robinson's forehead relaxed. "She'd call me in, suh. Seemed like every time I passed by yonder she'd have some little somethin' for me to do—choppin' kindlin', totin' water for her. She watered them red flowers every day—"

"Were you paid for your services?"

"No suh, not after she offered me a nickel the first time. I was glad to do it, Mr. Ewell didn't seem to help her none, and neither did the chillun, and I knowed she didn't have no nickels to spare."

"Where were the other children?"

"They was always around, all over the place. They'd watch me work, some of 'em, some of 'em'd set in the window."

"Would Miss Mayella talk to you?"

"Yes sir, she talked to me."

As Tom Robinson gave his testimony, it came to me that Mayella Ewell must have been the loneliest person in the world. She was even lonelier than Boo Radley, who had not been out of the house in twenty-five years. When Atticus asked had she any friends, she seemed not to know what he meant, then she thought he was making fun of her. She was as sad, I thought, as what Jem called a mixed child: white people wouldn't have anything to do with her because she lived among pigs; Negroes wouldn't have anything to do with her because she was white. She couldn't live like Mr. Dolphus Raymond, who preferred the company of Negroes, because she didn't own a riverbank and she wasn't from a fine old family. Nobody said, "That's just their way," about the Ewells. Maycomb gave them Christmas baskets, welfare money, and the back of its hand. Tom Robinson was probably the only person who was ever decent to her. But she said he took advantage of her, and when she stood up she looked at him as if he were dirt beneath her feet.

"Did you ever," Atticus interrupted my meditations, "at any time, go on the Ewell property—did you ever set foot on the Ewell property without an express invitation from one of them?"

"No suh, Mr. Finch, I never did. I wouldn't do that, suh."

Atticus sometimes said that one way to tell whether a witness was lying or telling the truth was to listen rather than watch: I applied his test—Tom denied it three times in one breath, but quietly, with no hint of whining in his voice, and I found myself believing him in spite of his protesting too much. He seemed to be a respectable Negro, and a respectable Negro would never go up into somebody's yard of his own volition.

"Tom, what happened to you on the evening of November twenty-first of last year?"

Below us, the spectators drew a collective breath and leaned forward. Behind us, the Negroes did the same.

Tom was a black-velvet Negro, not shiny, but soft black velvet. The whites of his eyes shone in his face, and when he spoke we saw flashes of his teeth. If he had been whole, he would have been a fine specimen of a man.

"Mr. Finch," he said, "I was goin' home as usual that evenin', an' when I passed the Ewell place Miss Mayella were on the porch, like she said she were. It seemed real quiet like, an' I didn't quite know why. I was studyin' why, just passin' by, when she says for me to come there and help her a minute. Well, I went inside the fence an' looked around for some kindlin' to work on, but I didn't see none, and she says, 'Naw, I got somethin' for you to do in the house. Th' old door's off its hinges an' fall's comin' on pretty fast.' I said you got a screwdriver, Miss Mayella? She said she sho' had. Well, I went up the steps an' she motioned me to come inside, and I went in the front room an' looked at the door. I said Miss Mayella, this door look all right. I pulled it back'n forth and those hinges was all right. Then she shet the door in my face. Mr. Finch, I was wonderin' why it was so quiet like, an' it come to me that there weren't a chile on the place, not a one of 'em, and I said Miss Mayella, where the chillun?"

Tom's black velvet skin had begun to shine, and he ran his hand over his face.

"I say where the chillun?" he continued, "an' she says—she was laughin', sort of—she says they all gone to town to get ice creams. She says, 'Took me a slap year to save seb'm nickels, but I done it. They all gone to town.'"

Tom's discomfort was not from the humidity. "What did you say then, Tom?" asked Atticus.

"I said somethin' like, why Miss Mayella, that's right smart o'you to treat 'em. An' she said, 'You think so?' I don't think she understood what I was thinkin'—I meant it was smart of her to save like that, an' nice of her to treat 'em."

"I understand you, Tom. Go on," said Atticus.

"Well, I said I best be goin', I couldn't do nothin' for her, an' she says oh yes I could, an' I ask her what, and she says to just step on that chair yonder an' git that box down from on top of the chiffarobe."

"Not the same chiffarobe you busted up?" asked Atticus.

The witness smiled. "Naw suh, another one. Most as tall as the room. So I done what she told me, an' I was just reachin' when the next thing I knows she—she'd grabbed me round the legs, grabbed me round th' legs, Mr. Finch. She scared me so bad I hopped down an' turned the chair over—that was the only thing, only furniture, 'sturbed in that room, Mr. Finch, when I left it. I swear 'fore God."

"What happened after you turned the chair over?"

Tom Robinson had come to a dead stop. He glanced at Atticus, then at the jury, then at Mr. Underwood sitting across the room.

"Tom, you're sworn to tell the whole truth. Will you tell it?"

Tom ran his hand nervously over his mouth.

"What happened after that?"

"Answer the question," said Judge Taylor. One-third of his cigar had vanished.

"Mr. Finch, I got down offa that chair an' turned around an' she sorta jumped on me."

"Jumped on you? Violently?"

"No suh, she—she hugged me. She hugged me round the waist."

This time Judge Taylor's gavel came down with a bang, and as it did the overhead lights went on in the courtroom. Darkness had not come, but the afternoon sun had left the windows. Judge Taylor quickly restored order.

"Then what did she do?"

The witness swallowed hard. "She reached up an' kissed me 'side of th' face. She says she never kissed a grown man before an' she might as well kiss a nigger. She says what her papa do to her don't count. She says, 'Kiss me back, nigger.' I say Miss Mayella lemme outa here an' tried to run but she got her back to the door an' I'da had to push her. I didn't wanta harm her, Mr. Finch, an' I say lemme pass, but just when I say it Mr. Ewell yonder hollered through th' window."

"What did he say?"

Tom Robinson swallowed again, and his eyes widened. "Somethin' not fittin' to say—not fittin' for these folks'n chillun to hear—"

"What did he say, Tom? You *must* tell the jury what he said."

Tom Robinson shut his eyes tight. "He says you goddamn whore, I'll kill ya."

"Then what happened?"

"Mr. Finch, I was runnin' so fast I didn't know what happened."

"Tom, did you rape Mayella Ewell?"

"I did not, suh."

"Did you harm her in any way?"

"I did not, suh."

"Did you resist her advances?"

"Mr. Finch, I tried. I tried to 'thout bein' ugly to her. I didn't wanta be ugly, I didn't wanta push her or nothin'."

It occurred to me that in their own way, Tom Robinson's manners were as good as Atticus's. Until my father explained it to me later, I did not understand the subtlety of Tom's predicament: he would not have dared strike a white woman under any circumstances and expect to live long, so he took the first opportunity to run—a sure sign of guilt.

"Tom, go back once more to Mr. Ewell," said Atticus. "Did he say anything to you?"

"Not anything, suh. He mighta said somethin', but I weren't there—"

222

"That'll do," Atticus cut in sharply. "What you did hear, who was he talking to?"

"Mr. Finch, he were talkin' and lookin' at Miss Mayella."

"Then you ran?"

"I sho' did, suh."

"Why did you run?"

"I was scared, suh."

"Why were you scared?"

"Mr. Finch, if you was a nigger like me, you'd be scared, too."

Atticus sat down. Mr. Gilmer was making his way to the witness stand, but before he got there Mr. Link Deas rose from the audience and announced:

"I just want the whole lot of you to know one thing right now. That boy's worked for me eight years an' I ain't had a speck o'trouble outa him. Not a speck."

"*Shut your mouth, sir!*" Judge Taylor was wide awake and roaring. He was also pink in the face. His speech was miraculously unimpaired by his cigar. "Link Deas," he yelled, "if you have anything you want to say you can say it under oath and at the proper time, but until then you get out of this room, you hear me? Get out of this room, sir, you hear me? I'll be damned if I'll listen to this case again!"

Judge Taylor looked daggers at Atticus, as if daring him to speak, but Atticus had ducked his head and was laughing into his lap. I remembered something he had said about Judge Taylor's ex cathedra remarks sometimes exceeding his duty, but that few lawyers ever did anything about them. I looked at Jem, but Jem shook his head. "It ain't like one of the jurymen got up and started talking," he said. "I think it'd be different then. Mr. Link was just disturbin' the peace or something."

Judge Taylor told the reporter to expunge anything he happened to have written down after Mr. Finch if you were a nigger like me you'd be scared too, and told the jury to disregard the interruption. He looked suspiciously down the middle aisle and waited, I suppose, for Mr. Link Deas to effect total departure. Then he said, "Go ahead, Mr. Gilmer."

"You were given thirty days once for disorderly conduct, Robinson?" asked Mr. Gilmer.

"Yes suh."

"What'd the nigger look like when you got through with him?"

"He beat me, Mr. Gilmer."

"Yes, but you were convicted, weren't you?"

Atticus raised his head. "It was a misdemeanor and it's in the record, Judge." I thought he sounded tired.

"Witness'll answer, though," said Judge Taylor, just as wearily.

"Yes suh, I got thirty days."

I knew that Mr. Gilmer would sincerely tell the jury that anyone who was convicted of disorderly conduct could easily have had it in his heart to take advantage of Mayella Ewell, that was the only reason he cared. Reasons like that helped.

"Robinson, you're pretty good at busting up chiffarobes and kindling with one hand, aren't you?"

"Yes suh, I reckon so."

"Strong enough to choke the breath out of a woman and sling her to the floor?"

"I never done that, suh."

"But you are strong enough to?"

"I reckon so, suh."

"Had your eye on her a long time, hadn't you, boy?"

"No suh, I never looked at her."

"Then you were mighty polite to do all that chopping and hauling for her, weren't you, boy?"

"I was just tryin' to help her out, suh."

"That was mighty generous of you, you had chores at home after your regular work, didn't you?"

"Yes suh."

"Why didn't you do them instead of Miss Ewell's?"

"I done 'em both, suh."

"You must have been pretty busy. Why?"

"Why what, suh?"

"Why were you so anxious to do that woman's chores?"

Tom Robinson hesitated, searching for an answer. "Looked like she didn't have nobody to help her, like I says—"

"With Mr. Ewell and seven children on the place, boy?"

"Well, I says it looked like they never help her none—"

"You did all this chopping and work from sheer goodness, boy?"

"Tried to help her, I says."

Mr. Gilmer smiled grimly at the jury. "You're a mighty good fellow, it seems—did all this for not one penny?"

"Yes suh. I felt right sorry for her, she seemed to try more'n the rest of 'em—"

"*You* felt sorry for *her*, you felt *sorry* for her?" Mr. Gilmer seemed ready to rise to the ceiling.

The witness realized his mistake and shifted uncomfortably in the chair. But the damage was done. Below us, nobody liked Tom Robinson's answer. Mr. Gilmer paused a long time to let it sink in.

"Now you went by the house as usual, last November twenty-first," he said, "and she asked you to come in and bust up a chiffarobe?"

"No suh."

"Do you deny that you went by the house?"

"No suh—she said she had somethin' for me to do inside the house—"

"She says she asked you to bust up a chiffarobe, is that right?"

"No suh, it ain't."

"Then you say she's lying, boy?"

Atticus was on his feet, but Tom Robinson didn't need him. "I don't say she's lyin', Mr. Gilmer, I say she's mistaken in her mind."

To the next ten questions, as Mr. Gilmer reviewed Mayella's

version of events, the witness's steady answer was that she was mistaken in her mind.

"Didn't Mr. Ewell run you off the place, boy?"

"No suh, I don't think he did."

"Don't think, what do you mean?"

"I mean I didn't stay long enough for him to run me off."

"You're very candid about this, why did you run so fast?"

"I says I was scared, suh."

"If you had a clear conscience, why were you scared?"

"Like I says before, it weren't safe for any nigger to be in a—fix like that."

"But you weren't in a fix—you testified that you were resisting Miss Ewell. Were you so scared that she'd hurt you, you ran, a big buck like you?"

"No suh, I's scared I'd be in court, just like I am now."

"Scared of arrest, scared you'd have to face up to what you did?"

"No suh, scared I'd hafta face up to what I didn't do."

"Are you being impudent to me, boy?"

"No suh, I didn't go to be."

This was as much as I heard of Mr. Gilmer's cross-examination, because Jem made me take Dill out. For some reason Dill had started crying and couldn't stop; quietly at first, then his sobs were heard by several people in the balcony. Jem said if I didn't go with him he'd make me, and Reverend Sykes said I'd better go, so I went. Dill had seemed to be all right that day, nothing wrong with him, but I guessed he hadn't fully recovered from running away.

"Ain't you feeling good?" I asked, when we reached the bottom of the stairs.

Dill tried to pull himself together as we ran down the south steps. Mr. Link Deas was a lonely figure on the top step. "Anything happenin', Scout?" he asked as we went by. "No sir," I answered over my shoulder. "Dill here, he's sick."

"Come on out under the trees," I said. "Heat got you, I expect." We chose the fattest live oak and we sat under it.

226

"It was just him I couldn't stand," Dill said.

"Who, Tom?"

"That old Mr. Gilmer doin' him thataway, talking so hateful to him—"

"Dill, that's his job. Why, if we didn't have prosecutors—well, we couldn't have defense attorneys, I reckon."

Dill exhaled patiently. "I know all that, Scout. It was the way he said it made me sick, plain sick."

"He's supposed to act that way, Dill, he was cross—"

"He didn't act that way when—"

"Dill, those were his own witnesses."

"Well, Mr. Finch didn't act that way to Mayella and old man Ewell when he cross-examined them. The way that man called him 'boy' all the time and sneered at him, an' looked around at the jury every time he answered—"

"Well, Dill, after all he's just a Negro."

"I don't care one speck. It ain't right, somehow it ain't right to do 'em that way. Hasn't anybody got any business talkin' like that—it just makes me sick."

"That's just Mr. Gilmer's way, Dill, he does 'em all that way. You've never seen him get good'n down on one yet. Why, when—well, today Mr. Gilmer seemed to me like he wasn't half trying. They do 'em all that way, most lawyers, I mean."

"Mr. Finch doesn't."

"He's not an example, Dill, he's—" I was trying to grope in my memory for a sharp phrase of Miss Maudie Atkinson's. I had it: "He's the same in the courtroom as he is on the public streets."

"That's not what I mean," said Dill.

"I know what you mean, boy," said a voice behind us. We thought it came from the tree-trunk, but it belonged to Mr. Dolphus Raymond. He peered around the trunk at us. "You aren't thin-hided, it just makes you sick, doesn't it?"

20

Come on round here, son, I got something that'll settle your
stomach."

As Mr. Dolphus Raymond was an evil man I accepted his
invitation reluctantly, but I followed Dill. Somehow, I didn't
think Atticus would like it if we became friendly with Mr.
Raymond, and I knew Aunt Alexandra wouldn't.

"Here," he said, offering Dill his paper sack with straws in
it. "Take a good sip, it'll quieten you."

Dill sucked on the straws, smiled, and pulled at length.

"Hee hee," said Mr. Raymond, evidently taking delight in
corrupting a child.

"Dill, you watch out, now," I warned.

Dill released the straws and grinned. "Scout, it's nothing
but Coca-Cola."

Mr. Raymond sat up against the tree-trunk. He had been
lying on the grass. "You little folks won't tell on me now, will
you? It'd ruin my reputation if you did."

"You mean all you drink in that sack's Coca-Cola? Just
plain Coca-Cola?"

"Yes ma'am," Mr. Raymond nodded. I liked his smell: it
was of leather, horses, cottonseed. He wore the only English
riding boots I had ever seen. "That's all I drink, most of the
time."

"Then you just pretend you're half—? I beg your pardon,
sir," I caught myself. "I didn't mean to be—"

Mr. Raymond chuckled, not at all offended, and I tried to
frame a discreet question: "Why do you do like you do?"

"Wh—oh yes, you mean why do I pretend? Well, it's very simple," he said. "Some folks don't—like the way I live. Now I could say the hell with 'em, I don't care if they don't like it. I do say I don't care if they don't like it, right enough—but I don't say the hell with 'em, see?"

Dill and I said, "No sir."

"I try to give 'em a reason, you see. It helps folks if they can latch onto a reason. When I come to town, which is seldom, if I weave a little and drink out of this sack, folks can say Dolphus Raymond's in the clutches of whiskey—that's why he won't change his ways. He can't help himself, that's why he lives the way he does."

"That ain't honest, Mr. Raymond, making yourself out badder'n you are already—"

"It ain't honest but it's mighty helpful to folks. Secretly, Miss Finch, I'm not much of a drinker, but you see they could never, never understand that I live like I do because that's the way I want to live."

I had a feeling that I shouldn't be here listening to this sinful man who had mixed children and didn't care who knew it, but he was fascinating. I had never encountered a being who deliberately perpetrated fraud against himself. But why had he entrusted us with his deepest secret? I asked him why.

"Because you're children and you can understand it," he said, "and because I heard that one—"

He jerked his head at Dill: "Things haven't caught up with that one's instinct yet. Let him get a little older and he won't get sick and cry. Maybe things'll strike him as being—not quite right, say, but he won't cry, not when he gets a few years on him."

"Cry about what, Mr. Raymond?" Dill's maleness was beginning to assert itself.

"Cry about the simple hell people give other people—without even thinking. Cry about the hell white people give colored folks, without even stopping to think that they're people, too."

"Atticus says cheatin' a colored man is ten times worse than cheatin' a white man," I muttered. "Says it's the worst thing you can do."

Mr. Raymond said, "I don't reckon it's—Miss Jean Louise, you don't know your pa's not a run-of-the-mill man, it'll take a few years for that to sink in—you haven't seen enough of the world yet. You haven't even seen this town, but all you gotta do is step back inside the courthouse."

Which reminded me that we were missing nearly all of Mr. Gilmer's cross-examination. I looked at the sun, and it was dropping fast behind the store-tops on the west side of the square. Between two fires, I could not decide which I wanted to jump into: Mr. Raymond or the 5th Judicial Circuit Court. "C'mon, Dill," I said. "You all right, now?"

"Yeah. Glad to've metcha, Mr. Raymond, and thanks for the drink, it was mighty settlin'."

We raced back to the courthouse, up the steps, up two flights of stairs, and edged our way along the balcony rail. Reverend Sykes had saved our seats.

The courtroom was still, and again I wondered where the babies were. Judge Taylor's cigar was a brown speck in the center of his mouth; Mr. Gilmer was writing on one of the yellow pads on his table, trying to outdo the court reporter, whose hand was jerking rapidly. "Shoot," I muttered, "we missed it."

Atticus was halfway through his speech to the jury. He had evidently pulled some papers from his briefcase that rested beside his chair, because they were on his table. Tom Robinson was toying with them.

". . . absence of any corroborative evidence, this man was indicted on a capital charge and is now on trial for his life. . . ."

I punched Jem. "How long's he been at it?"

"He's just gone over the evidence," Jem whispered, "and we're gonna win, Scout. I don't see how we can't. He's been at it 'bout five minutes. He made it as plain and easy as—well, as I'da explained it to you. You could've understood it, even."

230

"Did Mr. Gilmer—?"

"Sh-h. Nothing new, just the usual. Hush now."

We looked down again. Atticus was speaking easily, with the kind of detachment he used when he dictated a letter. He walked slowly up and down in front of the jury, and the jury seemed to be attentive: their heads were up, and they followed Atticus's route with what seemed to be appreciation. I guess it was because Atticus wasn't a thunderer.

Atticus paused, then he did something he didn't ordinarily do. He unhitched his watch and chain and placed them on the table, saying, "With the court's permission—"

Judge Taylor nodded, and then Atticus did something I never saw him do before or since, in public or in private: he unbuttoned his vest, unbuttoned his collar, loosened his tie, and took off his coat. He never loosened a scrap of his clothing until he undressed at bedtime, and to Jem and me, this was the equivalent of him standing before us stark naked. We exchanged horrified glances.

Atticus put his hands in his pockets, and as he returned to the jury, I saw his gold collar button and the tips of his pen and pencil winking in the light.

"Gentlemen," he said. Jem and I again looked at each other: Atticus might have said, "Scout." His voice had lost its aridity, its detachment, and he was talking to the jury as if they were folks on the post office corner.

"Gentlemen," he was saying, "I shall be brief, but I would like to use my remaining time with you to remind you that this case is not a difficult one, it requires no minute sifting of complicated facts, but it does require you to be sure beyond all reasonable doubt as to the guilt of the defendant. To begin with, this case should never have come to trial. This case is as simple as black and white.

"The state has not produced one iota of medical evidence to the effect that the crime Tom Robinson is charged with ever took place. It has relied instead upon the testimony of two witnesses whose evidence has not only been called into serious question on cross-examination, but has been flatly contradicted by the defendant. The defendant is not guilty, but somebody in this courtroom is.

"I have nothing but pity in my heart for the chief witness for the state, but my pity does not extend so far as to her putting a man's life at stake, which she has done in an effort to get rid of her own guilt.

"I say guilt, gentlemen, because it was guilt that motivated her. She has committed no crime, she has merely broken a rigid and time-honored code of our society, a code so severe that whoever breaks it is hounded from our midst as unfit to live with. She is the victim of cruel poverty and ignorance, but I cannot pity her: she is white. She knew full well the enormity of her offense, but because her desires were stronger than the code she was breaking, she persisted in breaking it. She persisted, and her subsequent reaction is something that all of us have known at one time or another. She did something every child has done—she tried to put the evidence of her offense away from her. But in this case she was no child hiding stolen contraband: she struck out at her victim—of necessity she must put him away from her—he must be removed from her presence, from this world. She must destroy the evidence of her offense.

"What was the evidence of her offense? Tom Robinson, a human being. She must put Tom Robinson away from her. Tom Robinson was her daily reminder of what she did. What did she do? She tempted a Negro.

"She was white, and she tempted a Negro. She did something that in our society is unspeakable: she kissed a black man. Not an old Uncle, but a strong young Negro man. No code mattered to her before she broke it, but it came crashing down on her afterwards.

"Her father saw it, and the defendant has testified as to his remarks. What did her father do? We don't know, but there is circumstantial evidence to indicate that Mayella Ewell was beaten savagely by someone who led almost exclusively with his left. We do know in part what Mr. Ewell did: he did what any God-fearing, persevering, respectable white man would do under the circumstances—he swore out a warrant, no doubt signing it with his left hand, and Tom Robinson now sits before you, having taken the oath with the only good hand he possesses—his right hand.

"And so a quiet, respectable, humble Negro who had the unmitigated temerity to 'feel sorry' for a white woman has had to put his word against two white people's. I need not remind you of their appearance and conduct on the stand—you saw them for yourselves. The witnesses for the state, with the exception of the sheriff of Maycomb County, have presented themselves to you gentlemen, to this court, in the cynical confidence that their testimony would not be doubted, confident that you gentlemen would go along with them on the assumption—the evil assumption—that *all* Negroes lie, that *all* Negroes are basically immoral beings, that *all* Negro men are not to be trusted around our women, an assumption one associates with minds of their caliber.

"Which, gentlemen, we know is in itself a lie as black as Tom Robinson's skin, a lie I do not have to point out to you. You know the truth, and the truth is this: some Negroes lie, some Negroes are immoral, some Negro men are not to be trusted around women—black or white. But this is a truth that applies to the human race and to no particular race of men. There is not a person in this courtroom who has never told a lie, who has never done an immoral thing, and there is no man living who has never looked upon a woman without desire."

Atticus paused and took out his handkerchief. Then he took off his glasses and wiped them, and we saw another "first": we had never seen him sweat—he was one of those men whose faces never perspired, but now it was shining tan.

"One more thing, gentlemen, before I quit. Thomas Jefferson once said that all men are created equal, a phrase that the Yankees and the distaff side of the Executive branch in Washington are fond of hurling at us. There is a tendency in this year of grace, 1935, for certain people to use this phrase out of context, to satisfy all conditions. The most ridiculous example I can think of is that the people who run public education promote the stupid and idle along with the industrious—because all men are created equal, educators will gravely tell you, the children left behind suffer terrible feelings of inferiority. We know all men are not created equal in the sense some people would have us believe—some people are smarter than others, some people have more opportunity because they're born with it, some men make more money than others, some ladies make better cakes than others—some people are born gifted beyond the normal scope of most men.

"But there is one way in this country in which all men are created equal—there is one human institution that makes a pauper the equal of a Rockefeller, the stupid man the equal of an Einstein, and the ignorant man the equal of any college president. That institution, gentlemen, is a court. It can be the Supreme Court of the United States or the humblest J.P. court in the land, or this honorable court which you serve. Our courts have their faults, as does any human institution, but in this country our courts are the great levelers, and in our courts all men are created equal.

"I'm no idealist to believe firmly in the integrity of our courts and in the jury system—that is no ideal to me, it is a living, working reality. Gentlemen, a court is no better than each man of you sitting before me on this jury. A court is only as sound as its jury, and a jury is only as sound as the men who make it up. I am confident that you gentlemen will review without passion the evidence you have heard, come to a decision, and restore this defendant to his family. In the name of God, do your duty."

Atticus's voice had dropped, and as he turned away from the jury he said something I did not catch. He said it more to himself than to the court. I punched Jem. "What'd he say?"

"'In the name of God, believe him,' I think that's what he said."

234

Dill suddenly reached over me and tugged at Jem. "Looka yonder!"

We followed his finger with sinking hearts. Calpurnia was making her way up the middle aisle, walking straight toward Atticus.

21

She stopped shyly at the railing and waited to get Judge Taylor's attention. She was in a fresh apron and she carried an envelope in her hand.

Judge Taylor saw her and said, "It's Calpurnia, isn't it?"

"Yes sir," she said. "Could I just pass this note to Mr. Finch, please sir? It hasn't got anything to do with—with the trial."

Judge Taylor nodded and Atticus took the envelope from Calpurnia. He opened it, read its contents and said, "Judge, I—this note is from my sister. She says my children are missing, haven't turned up since noon . . . I . . . could you—"

"I know where they are, Atticus." Mr. Underwood spoke up. "They're right up yonder in the colored balcony—been there since precisely one-eighteen P.M."

Our father turned around and looked up. "Jem, come down from there," he called. Then he said something to the Judge we didn't hear. We climbed across Reverend Sykes and made our way to the staircase.

Atticus and Calpurnia met us downstairs. Calpurnia looked peeved, but Atticus looked exhausted.

Jem was jumping in excitement. "We've won, haven't we?"

"I've no idea," said Atticus shortly. "You've been here all afternoon? Go home with Calpurnia and get your supper—and stay home."

"Aw, Atticus, let us come back," pleaded Jem. "Please let us hear the verdict, *please* sir."

"The jury might be out and back in a minute, we don't

know—" but we could tell Atticus was relenting. "Well, you've heard it all, so you might as well hear the rest. Tell you what, you all can come back when you've eaten your supper—eat slowly, now, you won't miss anything important—and if the jury's still out, you can wait with us. But I expect it'll be over before you get back."

"You think they'll acquit him that fast?" asked Jem.

Atticus opened his mouth to answer, but shut it and left us.

I prayed that Reverend Sykes would save our seats for us, but stopped praying when I remembered that people got up and left in droves when the jury was out—tonight, they'd overrun the drugstore, the O.K. Café and the hotel, that is, unless they had brought their suppers too.

Calpurnia marched us home: "—skin every one of you alive, the very idea, you children listenin' to all that! Mister Jem, don't you know better'n to take your little sister to that trial? Miss Alexandra'll absolutely have a stroke of paralysis when she finds out! Ain't fittin' for children to hear. . . ."

The streetlights were on, and we glimpsed Calpurnia's indignant profile as we passed beneath them. "Mister Jem, I thought you was gettin' some kinda head on your shoulders—the very idea, she's your little sister! The very *idea*, sir! You oughta be perfectly ashamed of yourself—ain't you got any sense at all?"

I was exhilarated. So many things had happened so fast I felt it would take years to sort them out, and now here was Calpurnia giving her precious Jem down the country—what new marvels would the evening bring?

Jem was chuckling. "Don't you want to hear about it, Cal?"

"Hush your mouth, sir! When you oughta be hangin' your head in shame you go along laughin'—" Calpurnia revived a series of rusty threats that moved Jem to little remorse, and she sailed up the front steps with her classic, "If Mr. Finch don't wear you out, I will—get in that house, sir!"

Jem went in grinning, and Calpurnia nodded tacit consent

to having Dill in to supper. "You all call Miss Rachel right now and tell her where you are," she told him. "She's run distracted lookin' for you—you watch out she don't ship you back to Meridian first thing in the mornin'."

Aunt Alexandra met us and nearly fainted when Calpurnia told her where we were. I guess it hurt her when we told her Atticus said we could go back, because she didn't say a word during supper. She just rearranged food on her plate, looking at it sadly while Calpurnia served Jem, Dill and me with a vengeance. Calpurnia poured milk, dished out potato salad and ham, muttering, "'shamed of yourselves," in varying degrees of intensity. "Now you all eat slow," was her final command.

Reverend Sykes had saved our places. We were surprised to find that we had been gone nearly an hour, and were equally surprised to find the courtroom exactly as we had left it, with minor changes: the jury box was empty, the defendant was gone; Judge Taylor had been gone, but he reappeared as we were seating ourselves.

"Nobody's moved, hardly," said Jem.

"They moved around some when the jury went out," said Reverend Sykes. "The menfolk down there got the women-folk their suppers, and they fed their babies."

"How long have they been out?" asked Jem.

"'bout thirty minutes. Mr. Finch and Mr. Gilmer did some more talkin', and Judge Taylor charged the jury."

"How was he?" asked Jem.

"What say? Oh, he did right well. I ain't complainin' one bit—he was mighty fair-minded. He sorta said if you believe this, then you'll have to return one verdict, but if you believe this, you'll have to return another one. I thought he was leanin' a little to our side—" Reverend Sykes scratched his head.

Jem smiled. "He's not supposed to lean, Reverend, but don't fret, we've won it," he said wisely. "Don't see how any jury could convict on what we heard—"

238

"Now don't you be so confident, Mr. Jem, I ain't ever seen any jury decide in favor of a colored man over a white man. . . ." But Jem took exception to Reverend Sykes, and we were subjected to a lengthy review of the evidence with Jem's ideas on the law regarding rape: it wasn't rape if she let you, but she had to be eighteen—in Alabama, that is—and Mayella was nineteen. Apparently you had to kick and holler, you had to be overpowered and stomped on, preferably knocked stone cold. If you were under eighteen, you didn't have to go through all this.

"Mr. Jem," Reverend Sykes demurred, "this ain't a polite thing for little ladies to hear . . ."

"Aw, she doesn't know what we're talkin' about," said Jem. "Scout, this is too old for you, ain't it?"

"It most certainly is not, I know every word you're saying." Perhaps I was too convincing, because Jem hushed and never discussed the subject again.

"What time is it, Reverend?" he asked.

"Gettin' on toward eight."

I looked down and saw Atticus strolling around with his hands in his pockets: he made a tour of the windows, then walked by the railing over to the jury box. He looked in it, inspected Judge Taylor on his throne, then went back to where he started. I caught his eye and waved to him. He acknowledged my salute with a nod, and resumed his tour.

Mr. Gilmer was standing at the windows talking to Mr. Underwood. Bert, the court reporter, was chain-smoking: he sat back with his feet on the table.

But the officers of the court, the ones present—Atticus, Mr. Gilmer, Judge Taylor sound asleep, and Bert, were the only ones whose behavior seemed normal. I had never seen a packed courtroom so still. Sometimes a baby would cry out fretfully, and a child would scurry out, but the grown people sat as if they were in church. In the balcony, the Negroes sat and stood around us with biblical patience.

The old courthouse clock suffered its preliminary strain

and struck the hour, eight deafening bongs that shook our bones.

When it bonged eleven times I was past feeling: tired from fighting sleep, I allowed myself a short nap against Reverend Sykes's comfortable arm and shoulder. I jerked awake and made an honest effort to remain so, by looking down and concentrating on the heads below: there were sixteen bald ones, fourteen men that could pass for redheads, forty heads varying between brown and black, and—I remembered something Jem had once explained to me when he went through a brief period of psychical research: he said if enough people—a stadium full, maybe—were to concentrate on one thing, such as setting a tree afire in the woods, that the tree would ignite of its own accord. I toyed with the idea of asking everyone below to concentrate on setting Tom Robinson free, but thought if they were as tired as I, it wouldn't work.

Dill was sound asleep, his head on Jem's shoulder, and Jem was quiet.

"Ain't it a long time?" I asked him.

"Sure is, Scout," he said happily.

"Well, from the way you put it, it'd just take five minutes."

Jem raised his eyebrows. "There are things you don't understand," he said, and I was too weary to argue.

But I must have been reasonably awake, or I would not have received the impression that was creeping into me. It was not unlike one I had last winter, and I shivered, though the night was hot. The feeling grew until the atmosphere in the courtroom was exactly the same as a cold February morning, when the mockingbirds were still, and the carpenters had stopped hammering on Miss Maudie's new house, and every wood door in the neighborhood was shut as tight as the doors of the Radley Place. A deserted, waiting, empty street, and the courtroom was packed with people. A steaming summer night was no different from a winter morning. Mr. Heck Tate, who had entered the courtroom and was talking to Atticus, might have been wearing his high boots and lumber

240

jacket. Atticus had stopped his tranquil journey and had put his foot onto the bottom rung of a chair; as he listened to what Mr. Tate was saying, he ran his hand slowly up and down his thigh. I expected Mr. Tate to say any minute, "Take him, Mr. Finch. . . ."

But Mr. Tate said, "This court will come to order," in a voice that rang with authority, and the heads below us jerked up. Mr. Tate left the room and returned with Tom Robinson. He steered Tom to his place beside Atticus, and stood there. Judge Taylor had roused himself to sudden alertness and was sitting up straight, looking at the empty jury box.

What happened after that had a dreamlike quality: in a dream I saw the jury return, moving like underwater swimmers, and Judge Taylor's voice came from far away, and was tiny. I saw something only a lawyer's child could be expected to see, could be expected to watch for, and it was like watching Atticus walk into the street, raise a rifle to his shoulder and pull the trigger, but watching all the time knowing that the gun was empty.

A jury never looks at a defendant it has convicted, and when this jury came in, not one of them looked at Tom Robinson. The foreman handed a piece of paper to Mr. Tate who handed it to the clerk who handed it to the judge. . . .

I shut my eyes. Judge Taylor was polling the jury: "Guilty . . . guilty . . . guilty . . . guilty . . ." I peeked at Jem: his hands were white from gripping the balcony rail, and his shoulders jerked as if each "guilty" was a separate stab between them.

Judge Taylor was saying something. His gavel was in his fist, but he wasn't using it. Dimly, I saw Atticus pushing papers from the table into his briefcase. He snapped it shut, went to the court reporter and said something, nodded to Mr. Gilmer, and then went to Tom Robinson and whispered something to him. Atticus put his hand on Tom's shoulder as he whispered. Atticus took his coat off the back of his chair and pulled it over his shoulder. Then he left the courtroom, but not by his usual exit. He must have wanted to go home the short way, because he walked quickly down the middle aisle toward the south exit. I followed the top of his head as he made his way to the door. He did not look up.

Someone was punching me, but I was reluctant to take my eyes from the people below us, and from the image of Atticus's lonely walk down the aisle.

"Miss Jean Louise?"

I looked around. They were standing. All around us and in the balcony on the opposite wall, the Negroes were getting to their feet. Reverend Sykes's voice was as distant as Judge Taylor's:

"Miss Jean Louise, stand up. Your father's passin'."

22

It was Jem's turn to cry. His face was streaked with angry tears as we made our way through the cheerful crowd. "It ain't right," he muttered, all the way to the corner of the square where we found Atticus waiting. Atticus was standing under the street light looking as though nothing had happened: his vest was buttoned, his collar and tie were neatly in place, his watch-chain glistened, he was his impassive self again.

"It ain't right, Atticus," said Jem.

"No son, it's not right."

We walked home.

Aunt Alexandra was waiting up. She was in her dressing gown, and I could have sworn she had on her corset underneath it. "I'm sorry, brother," she murmured. Having never heard her call Atticus "brother" before, I stole a glance at Jem, but he was not listening. He would look up at Atticus, then down at the floor, and I wondered if he thought Atticus somehow responsible for Tom Robinson's conviction.

"Is he all right?" Aunty asked, indicating Jem.

"He'll be so presently," said Atticus. "It was a little too strong for him." Our father sighed. "I'm going to bed," he said. "If I don't wake up in the morning, don't call me."

"I didn't think it wise in the first place to let them—"

"This is their home, sister," said Atticus. "We've made it this way for them, they might as well learn to cope with it."

"But they don't have to go to the courthouse and wallow in it—"

"It's just as much Maycomb County as missionary teas."

"Atticus—" Aunt Alexandra's eyes were anxious. "You are the last person I thought would turn bitter over this."

"I'm not bitter, just tired. I'm going to bed."

"Atticus—" said Jem bleakly.

He turned in the doorway. "What, son?"

"How could they do it, how could they?"

"I don't know, but they did it. They've done it before and they did it tonight and they'll do it again and when they do it—seems that only children weep. Good night."

But things are always better in the morning. Atticus rose at his usual ungodly hour and was in the livingroom behind *The Mobile Register* when we stumbled in. Jem's morning face posed the question his sleepy lips struggled to ask.

"It's not time to worry yet," Atticus reassured him, as we went to the diningroom. "We're not through yet. There'll be an appeal, you can count on that. Gracious alive, Cal, what's all this?" He was staring at his breakfast plate.

Calpurnia said, "Tom Robinson's daddy sent you along this chicken this morning. I fixed it."

"You tell him I'm proud to get it—bet they don't have chicken for breakfast at the White House. What are these?"

"Rolls," said Calpurnia. "Estelle down at the hotel sent 'em."

Atticus looked up at her, puzzled, and she said, "You better step out here and see what's in the kitchen, Mr. Finch."

We followed him. The kitchen table was loaded with enough food to bury the family: hunks of salt pork, tomatoes, beans, even scuppernongs. Atticus grinned when he found a jar of pickled pigs' knuckles. "Reckon Aunty'll let me eat these in the diningroom?"

Calpurnia said, "This was all 'round the back steps when I got here this morning. They—they 'preciate what you did, Mr. Finch. They—they aren't oversteppin' themselves, are they?"

Atticus's eyes filled with tears. He did not speak for a moment. "Tell them I'm very grateful," he said. "Tell them—tell them they must never do this again. Times are too hard. . . ."

244

He left the kitchen, went in the diningroom and excused himself to Aunt Alexandra, put on his hat and went to town.

We heard Dill's step in the hall, so Calpurnia left Atticus's uneaten breakfast on the table. Between rabbit-bites Dill told us of Miss Rachel's reaction to last night, which was: if a man like Atticus Finch wants to butt his head against a stone wall it's his head.

"I'da got her told," growled Dill, gnawing a chicken leg, "but she didn't look much like tellin' this morning. Said she was up half the night wonderin' where I was, said she'da had the sheriff after me but he was at the hearing."

"Dill, you've got to stop goin' off without tellin' her," said Jem. "It just aggravates her."

Dill sighed patiently. "I told her till I was blue in the face where I was goin'—she's just seein' too many snakes in the closet. Bet that woman drinks a pint for breakfast every morning—know she drinks two glasses full. Seen her."

"Don't talk like that, Dill," said Aunt Alexandra. "It's not becoming to a child. It's—cynical."

"I ain't cynical, Miss Alexandra. Tellin' the truth's not cynical, is it?"

"The way you tell it, it is."

Jem's eyes flashed at her, but he said to Dill, "Let's go. You can take that runner with you."

When we went to the front porch, Miss Stephanie Crawford was busy telling it to Miss Maudie Atkinson and Mr. Avery. They looked around at us and went on talking. Jem made a feral noise in his throat. I wished for a weapon.

"I hate grown folks lookin' at you," said Dill. "Makes you feel like you've done something."

Miss Maudie yelled for Jem Finch to come there.

Jem groaned and heaved himself up from the swing. "We'll go with you," Dill said.

Miss Stephanie's nose quivered with curiosity. She wanted to know who all gave us permission to go to court—she didn't see us but it was all over town this morning that we were in the Colored balcony. Did Atticus put us up there as a sort of—? Wasn't it right close up there with all those—? Did Scout understand all the—? Didn't it make us mad to see our daddy beat?

"Hush, Stephanie." Miss Maudie's diction was deadly. "I've not got all the morning to pass on the porch—Jem Finch, I called to find out if you and your colleagues can eat some cake. Got up at five to make it, so you better say yes. Excuse us, Stephanie. Good morning, Mr. Avery."

There was a big cake and two little ones on Miss Maudie's kitchen table. There should have been three little ones. It was not like Miss Maudie to forget Dill, and we must have shown it. But we understood when she cut from the big cake and gave the slice to Jem.

As we ate, we sensed that this was Miss Maudie's way of saying that as far as she was concerned, nothing had changed. She sat quietly in a kitchen chair, watching us.

Suddenly she spoke: "Don't fret, Jem. Things are never as bad as they seem."

Indoors, when Miss Maudie wanted to say something lengthy she spread her fingers on her knees and settled her bridgework. This she did, and we waited.

"I simply want to tell you that there are some men in this world who were born to do our unpleasant jobs for us. Your father's one of them."

"Oh," said Jem. "Well."

"Don't you oh well me, sir," Miss Maudie replied, recognizing Jem's fatalistic noises, "you are not old enough to appreciate what I said."

Jem was staring at his half-eaten cake. "It's like bein' a caterpillar in a cocoon, that's what it is," he said. "Like somethin' asleep wrapped up in a warm place. I always thought Maycomb folks were the best folks in the world, least that's what they seemed like."

"We're the safest folks in the world," said Miss Maudie.

"We're so rarely called on to be Christians, but when we are, we've got men like Atticus to go for us."

Jem grinned ruefully. "Wish the rest of the county thought that."

"You'd be surprised how many of us do."

"Who?" Jem's voice rose. "Who in this town did one thing to help Tom Robinson, just who?"

"His colored friends for one thing, and people like us. People like Judge Taylor. People like Mr. Heck Tate. Stop eating and start thinking, Jem. Did it ever strike you that Judge Taylor naming Atticus to defend that boy was no accident? That Judge Taylor might have had his reasons for naming him?"

This was a thought. Court-appointed defenses were usually given to Maxwell Green, Maycomb's latest addition to the bar, who needed the experience. Maxwell Green should have had Tom Robinson's case.

"You think about that," Miss Maudie was saying. "It was no accident. I was sittin' there on the porch last night, waiting. I waited and waited to see you all come down the sidewalk, and as I waited I thought, Atticus Finch won't win, he can't win, but he's the only man in these parts who can keep a jury out so long in a case like that. And I thought to myself, well, we're making a step—it's just a baby-step, but it's a step."

"'t's all right to talk like that—can't any Christian judges an' lawyers make up for heathen juries," Jem muttered. "Soon's I get grown—"

"That's something you'll have to take up with your father," Miss Maudie said.

We went down Miss Maudie's cool new steps into the sunshine and found Mr. Avery and Miss Stephanie Crawford still at it. They had moved down the sidewalk and were standing in front of Miss Stephanie's house. Miss Rachel was walking toward them.

"I think I'll be a clown when I get grown," said Dill.

Jem and I stopped in our tracks.

"Yes sir, a clown," he said. "There ain't one thing in this world I can do about folks except laugh, so I'm gonna join the circus and laugh my head off."

"You got it backwards, Dill," said Jem. "Clowns are sad, it's folks that laugh at them."

"Well I'm gonna be a new kind of clown. I'm gonna stand in the middle of the ring and laugh at the folks. Just looka yonder," he pointed. "Every one of 'em oughta be ridin' broomsticks. Aunt Rachel already does."

Miss Stephanie and Miss Rachel were waving wildly at us, in a way that did not give the lie to Dill's observation.

"Oh gosh," breathed Jem. "I reckon it'd be ugly not to see 'em."

Something was wrong. Mr. Avery was red in the face from a sneezing spell and nearly blew us off the sidewalk when we came up. Miss Stephanie was trembling with excitement, and Miss Rachel caught Dill's shoulder. "You get on in the back yard and stay there," she said. "There's danger a'comin'."

"'s matter?" I asked.

"Ain't you heard yet? It's all over town—"

At that moment Aunt Alexandra came to the door and called us, but she was too late. It was Miss Stephanie's pleasure to tell us: this morning Mr. Bob Ewell stopped Atticus on the post office corner, spat in his face, and told him he'd get him if it took the rest of his life.

23

I wish Bob Ewell wouldn't chew tobacco," was all Atticus said about it.

According to Miss Stephanie Crawford, however, Atticus was leaving the post office when Mr. Ewell approached him, cursed him, spat on him, and threatened to kill him. Miss Stephanie (who, by the time she had told it twice was there and had seen it all—passing by from the Jitney Jungle, she was)—Miss Stephanie said Atticus didn't bat an eye, just took out his handkerchief and wiped his face and stood there and let Mr. Ewell call him names wild horses could not bring her to repeat. Mr. Ewell was a veteran of an obscure war; that plus Atticus's peaceful reaction probably prompted him to inquire, "Too proud to fight, you nigger-lovin' bastard?" Miss Stephanie said Atticus said, "No, too old," put his hands in his pockets and strolled on. Miss Stephanie said you had to hand it to Atticus Finch, he could be right dry sometimes.

Jem and I didn't think it entertaining.

"After all, though," I said, "he was the deadest shot in the county one time. He could—"

"You know he wouldn't carry a gun, Scout. He ain't even got one—" said Jem. "You know he didn't even have one down at the jail that night. He told me havin' a gun around's an invitation to somebody to shoot you."

"This is different," I said. "We can ask him to borrow one."

We did, and he said, "Nonsense."

Dill was of the opinion that an appeal to Atticus's better nature might work: after all, we would starve if Mr. Ewell killed him, besides be raised exclusively by Aunt Alexandra, and we all knew the first thing she'd do before Atticus was under the ground good would be to fire Calpurnia. Jem said it might work if I cried and flung a fit, being young and a girl. That didn't work either.

But when he noticed us dragging around the neighborhood, not eating, taking little interest in our normal pursuits, Atticus discovered how deeply frightened we were. He tempted Jem with a new football magazine one night; when he saw Jem flip the pages and toss it aside, he said, "What's bothering you, son?"

Jem came to the point: "Mr. Ewell."

"What has happened?"

"Nothing's happened. We're scared for you, and we think you oughta do something about him."

Atticus smiled wryly. "Do what? Put him under a peace bond?"

"When a man says he's gonna get you, looks like he means it."

"He meant it when he said it," said Atticus. "Jem, see if you can stand in Bob Ewell's shoes a minute. I destroyed his last shred of credibility at that trial, if he had any to begin with. The man had to have some kind of comeback, his kind always does. So if spitting in my face and threatening me saved Mayella Ewell one extra beating, that's something I'll gladly take. He had to take it out on somebody and I'd rather it be me than that houseful of children out there. You understand?"

Jem nodded.

Aunt Alexandra entered the room as Atticus was saying, "We don't have anything to fear from Bob Ewell, he got it all out of his system that morning."

"I wouldn't be so sure of that, Atticus," she said. "His kind'd do anything to pay off a grudge. You know how those people are."

"What on earth could Ewell do to me, sister?"

"Something furtive," Aunt Alexandra said. "You may count on that."

"Nobody has much chance to be furtive in Maycomb," Atticus answered.

After that, we were not afraid. Summer was melting away, and we made the most of it. Atticus assured us that nothing would happen to Tom Robinson until the higher court reviewed his case, and that Tom had a good chance of going free, or at least of having a new trial. He was at Enfield Prison Farm, seventy miles away in Chester County. I asked Atticus if Tom's wife and children were allowed to visit him, but Atticus said no.

"If he loses his appeal," I asked one evening, "what'll happen to him?"

"He'll go to the chair," said Atticus, "unless the Governor commutes his sentence. Not time to worry yet, Scout. We've got a good chance."

Jem was sprawled on the sofa reading *Popular Mechanics*. He looked up. "It ain't right. He didn't kill anybody even if he was guilty. He didn't take anybody's life."

"You know rape's a capital offense in Alabama," said Atticus.

"Yessir, but the jury didn't have to give him death—if they wanted to they could've gave him twenty years."

"Given," said Atticus. "Tom Robinson's a colored man, Jem. No jury in this part of the world's going to say, 'We think you're guilty, but not very,' on a charge like that. It was either a straight acquittal or nothing."

Jem was shaking his head. "I know it's not right, but I can't figure out what's wrong—maybe rape shouldn't be a capital offense. . . ."

Atticus dropped his newspaper beside his chair. He said he didn't have any quarrel with the rape statute, none whatever, but he did have deep misgivings when the state asked for and the jury gave a death penalty on purely circumstantial evidence. He glanced at me, saw I was listening, and made it easier. "—I mean, before a man is sentenced to death for murder, say, there should be one or two eye-witnesses. Someone should be able to say, 'Yes, I was there and saw him pull the trigger.'"

"But lots of folks have been hung—hanged—on circumstantial evidence," said Jem.

"I know, and lots of 'em probably deserved it, too—but in the absence of eyewitnesses there's always a doubt, sometimes only the shadow of a doubt. The law says 'reasonable doubt,' but I think a defendant's entitled to the shadow of a doubt. There's always the possibility, no matter how improbable, that he's innocent."

"Then it all goes back to the jury, then. We oughta do away with juries." Jem was adamant.

Atticus tried hard not to smile but couldn't help it. "You're rather hard on us, son. I think maybe there might be a better way. Change the law. Change it so that only judges have the power of fixing the penalty in capital cases."

"Then go up to Montgomery and change the law."

"You'd be surprised how hard that'd be. I won't live to see the law changed, and if you live to see it you'll be an old man."

This was not good enough for Jem. "No sir, they oughta do away with juries. He wasn't guilty in the first place and they said he was."

"If you had been on that jury, son, and eleven other boys like you, Tom would be a free man," said Atticus. "So far nothing in your life has interfered with your reasoning process. Those are twelve reasonable men in everyday life, Tom's jury, but you saw something come between them and reason. You saw the same thing that night in front of the jail. When that crew went away, they didn't go as reasonable men, they went because we were there. There's something in our world that makes men lose their heads—they couldn't be fair if they tried. In our courts, when it's a white man's word against a black man's, the white man always wins. They're ugly, but those are the facts of life."

"Doesn't make it right," said Jem stolidly. He beat his fist softly on his knee. "You just can't convict a man on evidence like that—you can't."

"You couldn't, but they could and did. The older you grow the more of it you'll see. The one place where a man ought to get a square deal is in a courtroom, be he any color of the rainbow, but people have a way of carrying their resentments right into a jury box. As you grow older, you'll see white men cheat black men every day of your life, but let me tell you something and don't you forget it—whenever a white man does that to a black man, no matter who he is, how rich he is, or how fine a family he comes from, that white man is trash."

Atticus was speaking so quietly his last word crashed on our ears. I looked up, and his face was vehement. "There's nothing more sickening to me than a low-grade white man who'll take advantage of a Negro's ignorance. Don't fool yourselves—it's all adding up and one of these days we're going to pay the bill for it. I hope it's not in you children's time."

Jem was scratching his head. Suddenly his eyes widened. "Atticus," he said, "why don't people like us and Miss Maudie ever sit on juries? You never see anybody from Maycomb on a jury—they all come from out in the woods."

Atticus leaned back in his rocking-chair. For some reason he looked pleased with Jem. "I was wondering when that'd occur to you," he said. "There are lots of reasons. For one thing, Miss Maudie can't serve on a jury because she's a woman—"

"You mean women in Alabama can't—?" I was indignant.

"I do. I guess it's to protect our frail ladies from sordid cases like Tom's. Besides," Atticus grinned, "I doubt if we'd ever get a complete case tried—the ladies'd be interrupting to ask questions."

Jem and I laughed. Miss Maudie on a jury would be impressive. I thought of old Mrs. Dubose in her wheelchair— "Stop that rapping, John Taylor, I want to ask this man something." Perhaps our forefathers were wise.

Atticus was saying, "With people like us—that's our share

of the bill. We generally get the juries we deserve. Our stout Maycomb citizens aren't interested, in the first place. In the second place, they're afraid. Then, they're—"

"Afraid, why?" asked Jem.

"Well, what if—say, Mr. Link Deas had to decide the amount of damages to award, say, Miss Maudie, when Miss Rachel ran over her with a car. Link wouldn't like the thought of losing either lady's business at his store, would he? So he tells Judge Taylor that he can't serve on the jury because he doesn't have anybody to keep store for him while he's gone. So Judge Taylor excuses him. Sometimes he excuses him wrathfully."

"What'd make him think either one of 'em'd stop trading with him?" I asked.

Jem said, "Miss Rachel would, Miss Maudie wouldn't. But a jury's vote's secret, Atticus."

Our father chuckled. "You've many more miles to go, son. A jury's vote's supposed to be secret. Serving on a jury forces a man to make up his mind and declare himself about some-thing. Men don't like to do that. Sometimes it's unpleasant."

"Tom's jury sho' made up its mind in a hurry," Jem mut-tered.

Atticus's fingers went to his watchpocket. "No it didn't," he said, more to himself than to us. "That was the one thing that made me think, well, this may be the shadow of a beginning. That jury took a few hours. An inevitable verdict, maybe, but usually it takes 'em just a few minutes. This time—" he broke off and looked at us. "You might like to know that there was one fellow who took considerable wearing down—in the beginning he was rarin' for an outright acquittal."

"Who?" Jem was astonished.

Atticus's eyes twinkled. "It's not for me to say, but I'll tell you this much. He was one of your Old Sarum friends . . ."

"One of the Cunninghams?" Jem yelped. "One of—I didn't recognize any of 'em . . . you're jokin'." He looked at Atticus from the corners of his eyes.

254

"One of their connections. On a hunch, I didn't strike him. Just on a hunch. Could've, but I didn't."

"Golly Moses," Jem said reverently. "One minute they're tryin' to kill him and the next they're tryin' to turn him loose . . . I'll never understand those folks as long as I live."

Atticus said you just had to know 'em. He said the Cunninghams hadn't taken anything from or off of anybody since they migrated to the New World. He said the other thing about them was, once you earned their respect they were for you tooth and nail. Atticus said he had a feeling, nothing more than a suspicion, that they left the jail that night with considerable respect for the Finches. Then too, he said, it took a thunderbolt plus another Cunningham to make one of them change his mind. "If we'd had two of that crowd, we'd've had a hung jury."

Jem said slowly, "You mean you actually put on the jury a man who wanted to kill you the night before? How could you take such a risk, Atticus, how could you?"

"When you analyze it, there was little risk. There's no difference between one man who's going to convict and another man who's going to convict, is there? There's a faint difference between a man who's going to convict and a man who's a little disturbed in his mind, isn't there? He was the only uncertainty on the whole list."

"What kin was that man to Mr. Walter Cunningham?" I asked.

Atticus rose, stretched and yawned. It was not even our bedtime, but we knew he wanted a chance to read his newspaper. He picked it up, folded it, and tapped my head. "Let's see now," he droned to himself. "I've got it. Double first cousin."

"How can that be?"

"Two sisters married two brothers. That's all I'll tell you—you figure it out."

I tortured myself and decided that if I married Jem and Dill had a sister whom he married our children would be double first cousins. "Gee minetti, Jem," I said, when Atticus had gone, "they're funny folks. 'd you hear that, Aunty?"

Aunt Alexandra was hooking a rug and not watching us, but she was listening. She sat in her chair with her workbasket beside it, her rug spread across her lap. Why ladies hooked woolen rugs on boiling nights never became clear to me.

"I heard it," she said.

I remembered the distant disastrous occasion when I rushed to young Walter Cunningham's defense. Now, I was glad I'd done it. "Soon's school starts I'm gonna ask Walter home to dinner," I planned, having forgotten my private resolve to beat him up the next time I saw him. "He can stay over sometimes after school, too. Atticus could drive him back to Old Sarum. Maybe he could spend the night with us sometime, okay, Jem?"

"We'll see about that," Aunt Alexandra said, a declaration that with her was always a threat, never a promise. Surprised, I turned to her. "Why not, Aunty? They're good folks."

She looked at me over her sewing glasses. "Jean Louise, there is no doubt in my mind that they're good folks. But they're not our kind of folks."

Jem says, "She means they're yappy, Scout."

"What's a yap?"

"Aw, tacky. They like fiddlin' and things like that."

"Well I do too—"

"Don't be silly, Jean Louise," said Aunt Alexandra. "The thing is, you can scrub Walter Cunningham till he shines, you can put him in shoes and a new suit, but he'll never be like Jem. Besides, there's a drinking streak in that family a mile wide. Finch women aren't interested in that sort of people."

"Aun-ty," said Jem, "she ain't nine yet."

"She may as well learn it now."

Aunt Alexandra had spoken. I was reminded vividly of the last time she had put her foot down. I never knew why. It was when I was absorbed with plans to visit Calpurnia's house—I was curious, interested; I wanted to be her "company," to see

256

how she lived, who her friends were. I might as well have wanted to see the other side of the moon. This time the tactics were different, but Aunt Alexandra's aim was the same. Perhaps this was why she had come to live with us—to help us choose our friends. I would hold her off as long as I could: "If they're good folks, then why can't I be nice to Walter?"

"I didn't say not to be nice to him. You should be friendly and polite to him, you should be gracious to everybody, dear. But you don't have to invite him home."

"What if he was kin to us, Aunty?"

"The fact is that he is not kin to us, but if he were, my answer would be the same."

"Aunty," Jem spoke up, "Atticus says you can choose your friends but you sho' can't choose your family, an' they're still kin to you no matter whether you acknowledge 'em or not, and it makes you look right silly when you don't."

"That's your father all over again," said Aunt Alexandra, "and I still say that Jean Louise will not invite Walter Cunningham to this house. If he were her double first cousin once removed he would still not be received in this house unless he comes to see Atticus on business. Now that is that."

She had said Indeed Not, but this time she would give her reasons: "But I want to play with Walter, Aunty, why can't I?"

She took off her glasses and stared at me. "I'll tell you why," she said. "Because—he—is—trash, that's why you can't play with him. I'll not have you around him, picking up his habits and learning Lord-knows-what. You're enough of a problem to your father as it is."

I don't know what I would have done, but Jem stopped me. He caught me by the shoulders, put his arm around me, and led me sobbing in fury to his bedroom. Atticus heard us and poked his head around the door. "'s all right, sir," Jem said gruffly, "'s not anything." Atticus went away.

"Have a chew, Scout." Jem dug into his pocket and extracted a Tootsie Roll. It took a few minutes to work the candy into a comfortable wad inside my jaw.

257

Jem was rearranging the objects on his dresser. His hair stuck up behind and down in front, and I wondered if it would ever look like a man's—maybe if he shaved it off and started over, his hair would grow back neatly in place. His eyebrows were becoming heavier, and I noticed a new slimness about his body. He was growing taller.

When he looked around, he must have thought I would start crying again, for he said, "Show you something if you won't tell anybody." I said what. He unbuttoned his shirt, grinning shyly.

"Well what?"

"Well can't you see it?"

"Well no."

"Well it's hair."

"Where?"

"There. Right there."

He had been a comfort to me, so I said it looked lovely, but I didn't see anything. "It's real nice, Jem."

"Under my arms, too," he said. "Goin' out for football next year. Scout, don't let Aunty aggravate you."

It seemed only yesterday that he was telling me not to aggravate Aunty.

"You know she's not used to girls," said Jem, "leastways, not girls like you. She's trying to make you a lady. Can't you take up sewin' or somethin'?"

"Hell no. She doesn't like me, that's all there is to it, and I don't care. It was her callin' Walter Cunningham trash that got me goin', Jem, not what she said about me being a problem to Atticus. We got that all straight one time, I asked him if I was a problem and he said not much of one, at most one that he could always figure out, and not to worry my head a second about botherin' him. Naw, it was Walter—that boy's not trash, Jem. He ain't like the Ewells."

Jem kicked off his shoes and swung his feet to the bed. He propped himself against a pillow and switched on the reading light. "You know something, Scout? I've got it all figured out,

258

now. I've thought about it a lot lately and I've got it figured out. There's four kinds of folks in the world. There's the ordinary kind like us and the neighbors, there's the kind like the Cunninghams out in the woods, the kind like the Ewells down at the dump, and the Negroes."

"What about the Chinese, and the Cajuns down yonder in Baldwin County?"

"I mean in Maycomb County. The thing about it is, our kind of folks don't like the Cunninghams, the Cunninghams don't like the Ewells, and the Ewells hate and despise the colored folks."

I told Jem if that was so, then why didn't Tom's jury, made up of folks like the Cunninghams, acquit Tom to spite the Ewells?

Jem waved my question away as being infantile.

"You know," he said, "I've seen Atticus pat his foot when there's fiddlin' on the radio, and he loves pot liquor better'n any man I ever saw—"

"Then that makes us like the Cunninghams," I said. "I can't see why Aunty—"

"No, lemme finish—it does, but we're still different somehow. Atticus said one time the reason Aunty's so hipped on the family is because all we've got's background and not a dime to our names."

"Well Jem, I don't know—Atticus told me one time that most of this Old Family stuff's foolishness because everybody's family's just as old as everybody else's. I said did that include the colored folks and Englishmen and he said yes."

"Background doesn't mean Old Family," said Jem. "I think it's how long your family's been readin' and writin'. Scout, I've studied this real hard and that's the only reason I can think of. Somewhere along when the Finches were in Egypt one of 'em must have learned a hieroglyphic or two and he taught his boy." Jem laughed. "Imagine Aunty being proud her great-grandaddy could read an' write—ladies pick funny things to be proud of."

"Well I'm glad he could, or who'da taught Atticus and them, and if Atticus couldn't read, you and me'd be in a fix. I don't think that's what background is, Jem."

"Well then, how do you explain why the Cunninghams are different? Mr. Walter can hardly sign his name, I've seen him. We've just been readin' and writin' longer'n they have."

"No, everybody's gotta learn, nobody's born knowin'. That Walter's as smart as he can be, he just gets held back sometimes because he has to stay out and help his daddy. Nothin's wrong with him. Naw, Jem, I think there's just one kind of folks. Folks."

Jem turned around and punched his pillow. When he settled back his face was cloudy. He was going into one of his declines, and I grew wary. His brows came together; his mouth became a thin line. He was silent for a while.

"That's what I thought, too," he said at last, "when I was your age. If there's just one kind of folks, why can't they get along with each other? If they're all alike, why do they go out of their way to despise each other? Scout, I think I'm beginning to understand something. I think I'm beginning to understand why Boo Radley's stayed shut up in the house all this time . . . it's because he *wants* to stay inside."

24

Calpurnia wore her stiffest starched apron. She carried a tray of charlotte. She backed up to the swinging door and pressed gently. I admired the ease and grace with which she handled heavy loads of dainty things. So did Aunt Alexandra, I guess, because she had let Calpurnia serve today.

August was on the brink of September. Dill would be leaving for Meridian tomorrow; today he was off with Jem at Barker's Eddy. Jem had discovered with angry amazement that nobody had ever bothered to teach Dill how to swim, a skill Jem considered necessary as walking. They had spent two afternoons at the creek, they said they were going in naked and I couldn't come, so I divided the lonely hours between Calpurnia and Miss Maudie.

Today Aunt Alexandra and her missionary circle were fighting the good fight all over the house. From the kitchen, I heard Mrs. Grace Merriweather giving a report in the living-room on the squalid lives of the Mrunas, it sounded like to me. They put the women out in huts when their time came, whatever that was; they had no sense of family—I knew that'd distress Aunty—they subjected children to terrible ordeals when they were thirteen; they were crawling with yaws and earworms, they chewed up and spat out the bark of a tree into a communal pot and then got drunk on it.

Immediately thereafter, the ladies adjourned for refreshments.

I didn't know whether to go into the diningroom or stay out. Aunt Alexandra told me to join them for refreshments; it was not necessary that I attend the business part of the meeting, she said it'd bore me. I was wearing my pink Sunday dress, shoes, and a petticoat, and reflected that if I spilled anything Calpurnia would have to wash my dress again for tomorrow. This had been a busy day for her. I decided to stay out.

"Can I help you, Cal?" I asked, wishing to be of some service.

Calpurnia paused in the doorway. "You be still as a mouse in that corner," she said, "an' you can help me load up the trays when I come back."

The gentle hum of ladies' voices grew louder as she opened the door: "Why, Alexandra, I never saw such charlotte . . . just lovely . . . I never can get my crust like this, never can . . . who'd've thought of little dewberry tarts . . . Calpurnia? . . . who'da thought it . . . anybody tell you that the preacher's wife's . . . no-oo, well she is, and that other one not walkin' yet. . . ."

They became quiet, and I knew they had all been served. Calpurnia returned and put my mother's heavy silver pitcher on a tray. "This coffee pitcher's a curiosity," she murmured, "they don't make 'em these days."

"Can I carry it in?"

"If you be careful and don't drop it. Set it down at the end of the table by Miss Alexandra. Down there by the cups'n things. She's gonna pour."

I tried pressing my behind against the door as Calpurnia had done, but the door didn't budge. Grinning, she held it open for me. "Careful now, it's heavy. Don't look at it and you won't spill it."

My journey was successful: Aunt Alexandra smiled brilliantly. "Stay with us, Jean Louise," she said. This was a part of her campaign to teach me to be a lady.

It was customary for every circle hostess to invite her neighbors in for refreshments, be they Baptists or Presbyterians, which accounted for the presence of Miss Rachel (sober as a

262

judge), Miss Maudie and Miss Stephanie Crawford. Rather nervous, I took a seat beside Miss Maudie and wondered why ladies put on their hats to go across the street. Ladies in bunches always filled me with vague apprehension and a firm desire to be elsewhere, but this feeling was what Aunt Alexandra called being "spoiled."

The ladies were cool in fragile pastel prints: most of them were heavily powdered but unrouged; the only lipstick in the room was Tangee Natural. Cutex Natural sparkled on their fingernails, but some of the younger ladies wore Rose. They smelled heavenly. I sat quietly, having conquered my hands by tightly gripping the arms of the chair, and waited for someone to speak to me.

Miss Maudie's gold bridgework twinkled. "You're mighty dressed up, Miss Jean Louise," she said. "Where are your britches today?"

"Under my dress."

I hadn't meant to be funny, but the ladies laughed. My cheeks grew hot as I realized my mistake, but Miss Maudie looked gravely down at me. She never laughed at me unless I meant to be funny.

In the sudden silence that followed, Miss Stephanie Crawford called from across the room, "Whatcha going to be when you grow up, Jean Louise? A lawyer?"

"Nome, I hadn't thought about it . . ." I answered, grateful that Miss Stephanie was kind enough to change the subject. Hurriedly I began choosing my vocation. Nurse? Aviator? "Well . . ."

"Why shoot, I thought you wanted to be a lawyer, you've already commenced going to court."

The ladies laughed again. "That Stephanie's a card," somebody said. Miss Stephanie was encouraged to pursue the subject: "Don't you want to grow up to be a lawyer?"

Miss Maudie's hand touched mine and I answered mildly enough, "Nome, just a lady."

Miss Stephanie eyed me suspiciously, decided that I meant

no impertinence, and contented herself with, "Well, you won't get very far until you start wearing dresses more often."

Miss Maudie's hand closed tightly on mine, and I said nothing. Its warmth was enough.

Mrs. Grace Merriweather sat on my left, and I felt it would be polite to talk to her. Mr. Merriweather, a faithful Methodist under duress, apparently saw nothing personal in singing, "Amazing Grace, how sweet the sound, that saved a wretch like me . . ." It was the general opinion of Maycomb, however, that Mrs. Merriweather had sobered him up and made a reasonably useful citizen of him. For certainly Mrs. Merriweather was the most devout lady in Maycomb. I searched for a topic of interest to her. "What did you all study this afternoon?" I asked.

"Oh child, those poor Mrunas," she said, and was off. Few other questions would be necessary.

Mrs. Merriweather's large brown eyes always filled with tears when she considered the oppressed. "Living in that jungle with nobody but J. Grimes Everett," she said. "Not a white person'll go near 'em but that saintly J. Grimes Everett."

Mrs. Merriweather played her voice like an organ; every word she said received its full measure: "The poverty . . . the darkness . . . the immorality—nobody but J. Grimes Everett knows. You know, when the church gave me that trip to the camp grounds J. Grimes Everett said to me—"

"Was he there, ma'am? I thought—"

"Home on leave. J. Grimes Everett said to me, he said, 'Mrs. Merriweather, you have no conception, no conception of what we are fighting over there.' That's what he said to me."

"Yes ma'am."

"I said to him, 'Mr. Everett,' I said, 'the ladies of the Maycomb Alabama Methodist Episcopal Church South are behind you one hundred per cent.' That's what I said to him. And you know, right then and there I made a pledge in my heart. I said to myself, when I go home I'm going to give a

264

course on the Mrunas and bring J. Grimes Everett's message to Maycomb and that's just what I'm doing."

"Yes ma'am."

When Mrs. Merriweather shook her head, her black curls jiggled. "Jean Louise," she said, "you are a fortunate girl. You live in a Christian home with Christian folks in a Christian town. Out there in J. Grimes Everett's land there's nothing but sin and squalor."

"Yes ma'am."

"Sin and squalor—what was that, Gertrude?" Mrs. Merriweather turned on her chimes for the lady sitting beside her. "Oh that. Well, I always say forgive and forget, forgive and forget. Thing that church ought to do is help her lead a Christian life for those children from here on out. Some of the men ought to go out there and tell that preacher to encourage her."

"Excuse me, Mrs. Merriweather," I interrupted, "are you all talking about Mayella Ewell?"

"May—? No, child. That darky's wife. Tom's wife, Tom—"

"Robinson, ma'am."

Mrs. Merriweather turned back to her neighbor. "There's one thing I truly believe, Gertrude," she continued, "but some people just don't see it my way. If we just let them know we forgive 'em, that we've forgotten it, then this whole thing'll blow over."

"Ah—Mrs. Merriweather," I interrupted once more, "what'll blow over?"

Again, she turned to me. Mrs. Merriweather was one of those childless adults who find it necessary to assume a different tone of voice when speaking to children. "Nothing, Jean Louise," she said, in stately largo, "the cooks and field hands are just dissatisfied, but they're settling down now—they grumbled all next day after that trial."

Mrs. Merriweather faced Mrs. Farrow: "Gertrude, I tell you there's nothing more distracting than a sulky darky. Their mouths go down to here. Just ruins your day to have one of 'em in the kitchen. You know what I said to my Sophy, Gertrude? I said, 'Sophy,' I said, 'you simply are not being a Christian today. Jesus Christ never went around grumbling and complaining,' and you know, it did her good. She took her eyes off that floor and said, 'Nome, Miz Merriweather, Jesus never went around grumblin'.' I tell you, Gertrude, you never ought to let an opportunity go by to witness for the Lord."

I was reminded of the ancient little organ in the chapel at Finch's Landing. When I was very small, and if I had been very good during the day, Atticus would let me pump its bellows while he picked out a tune with one finger. The last note would linger as long as there was air to sustain it. Mrs. Merriweather had run out of air, I judged, and was replenishing her supply while Mrs. Farrow composed herself to speak.

Mrs. Farrow was a splendidly built woman with pale eyes and narrow feet. She had a fresh permanent wave, and her hair was a mass of tight gray ringlets. She was the second most devout lady in Maycomb. She had a curious habit of prefacing everything she said with a soft sibilant sound.

"S-s-s Grace," she said, "it's just like I was telling Brother Hutson the other day. 'S-s-s Brother Hutson,' I said, 'looks like we're fighting a losing battle, a losing battle.' I said, 'S-s-s it doesn't matter to 'em one bit. We can educate 'em till we're blue in the face, we can try till we drop to make Christians out of 'em, but there's no lady safe in her bed these nights.' He said to me, 'Mrs. Farrow, I don't know what we're coming to down here.' S-s-s I told him that was certainly a fact."

Mrs. Merriweather nodded wisely. Her voice soared over the clink of coffee cups and the soft bovine sounds of the ladies munching their dainties. "Gertrude," she said, "I tell you there are some good but misguided people in this town. Good, but misguided. Folks in this town who think they're doing right, I mean. Now far be it from me to say who, but some of 'em in this town thought they were doing the right thing a while back, but all they did was stir 'em up. That's all they did.

266

Might've looked like the right thing to do at the time, I'm sure I don't know, I'm not read in that field, but sulky . . . dissatisfied . . . I tell you if my Sophy'd kept it up another day I'd have let her go. It's never entered that wool of hers that the only reason I keep her is because this depression's on and she needs her dollar and a quarter every week she can get it."

"His food doesn't stick going down, does it?"

Miss Maudie said it. Two tight lines had appeared at the corners of her mouth. She had been sitting silently beside me, her coffee cup balanced on one knee. I had lost the thread of conversation long ago, when they quit talking about Tom Robinson's wife, and had contented myself with thinking of Finch's Landing and the river. Aunt Alexandra had got it backwards: the business part of the meeting was blood-curdling, the social hour was dreary.

"Maudie, I'm sure I don't know what you mean," said Mrs. Merriweather.

"I'm sure you do," Miss Maudie said shortly.

She said no more. When Miss Maudie was angry her brevity was icy. Something had made her deeply angry, and her gray eyes were as cold as her voice. Mrs. Merriweather reddened, glanced at me, and looked away. I could not see Mrs. Farrow.

Aunt Alexandra got up from the table and swiftly passed more refreshments, neatly engaging Mrs. Merriweather and Mrs. Gates in brisk conversation. When she had them well on the road with Mrs. Perkins, Aunt Alexandra stepped back. She gave Miss Maudie a look of pure gratitude, and I wondered at the world of women. Miss Maudie and Aunt Alexandra had never been especially close, and here was Aunty silently thanking her for something. For what, I knew not. I was content to learn that Aunt Alexandra could be pierced sufficiently to feel gratitude for help given. There was no doubt about it, I must soon enter this world, where on its surface fragrant ladies rocked slowly, fanned gently, and drank cool water.

But I was more at home in my father's world. People like Mr. Heck Tate did not trap you with innocent questions to make fun of you; even Jem was not highly critical unless you said something stupid. Ladies seemed to live in faint horror of men, seemed unwilling to approve wholeheartedly of them. But I liked them. There was something about them, no matter how much they cussed and drank and gambled and chewed; no matter how undelectable they were, there was something about them that I instinctively liked ... they weren't—

"Hypocrites, Mrs. Perkins, born hypocrites," Mrs. Merriweather was saying. "At least we don't have that sin on our shoulders down here. People up there set 'em free, but you don't see 'em settin' at the table with 'em. At least we don't have the deceit to say to 'em yes you're as good as we are but stay away from us. Down here we just say you live your way and we'll live ours. I think that woman, that Mrs. Roosevelt's lost her mind—just plain lost her mind coming down to Birmingham and tryin' to sit with 'em. If I was the Mayor of Birmingham I'd—"

Well, neither of us was the Mayor of Birmingham, but I wished I was the Governor of Alabama for one day: I'd let Tom Robinson go so quick the Missionary Society wouldn't have time to catch its breath. Calpurnia was telling Miss Rachel's cook the other day how bad Tom was taking things and she didn't stop talking when I came into the kitchen. She said there wasn't a thing Atticus could do to make being shut up easier for him, that the last thing he said to Atticus before they took him down to the prison camp was, "Good-bye, Mr. Finch, there ain't nothin' you can do now, so there ain't no use tryin'." Calpurnia said Atticus told her that the day they took Tom to prison he just gave up hope. She said Atticus tried to explain things to him, and that he must do his best not to lose hope because Atticus was doing his best to get him free. Miss Rachel's cook asked Calpurnia why didn't Atticus just say yes, you'll go free, and leave it at that—seemed like that'd be a big comfort to Tom. Calpurnia said, "Because you ain't familiar with the law. First thing you learn when you're in a lawin' family is that there ain't any definite answers to anything. Mr. Finch couldn't say somethin's so when he doesn't know for sure it's so."

The front door slammed and I heard Atticus's footsteps in the hall. Automatically I wondered what time it was. Not nearly time for him to be home, and on Missionary Society days he usually stayed downtown until black dark.

He stopped in the doorway. His hat was in his hand, and his face was white.

"Excuse me, ladies," he said. "Go right ahead with your meeting, don't let me disturb you. Alexandra, could you come to the kitchen a minute? I want to borrow Calpurnia for a while."

He didn't go through the diningroom, but went down the back hallway and entered the kitchen from the rear door. Aunt Alexandra and I met him. The diningroom door opened again and Miss Maudie joined us. Calpurnia had half risen from her chair.

"Cal," Atticus said, "I want you to go with me out to Helen Robinson's house—"

"What's the matter?" Aunt Alexandra asked, alarmed by the look on my father's face.

"Tom's dead."

Aunt Alexandra put her hands to her mouth.

"They shot him," said Atticus. "He was running. It was during their exercise period. They said he just broke into a blind raving charge at the fence and started climbing over. Right in front of them—"

"Didn't they try to stop him? Didn't they give him any warning?" Aunt Alexandra's voice shook.

"Oh yes, the guards called to him to stop. They fired a few shots in the air, then to kill. They got him just as he went over the fence. They said if he'd had two good arms he'd have made it, he was moving that fast. Seventeen bullet holes in him. They didn't have to shoot him that much. Cal, I want you to come out with me and help me tell Helen."

"Yes sir," she murmured, fumbling at her apron. Miss Maudie went to Calpurnia and untied it.

"This is the last straw, Atticus," Aunt Alexandra said.

"Depends on how you look at it," he said. "What was one Negro, more or less, among two hundred of 'em? He wasn't Tom to them, he was an escaping prisoner."

Atticus leaned against the refrigerator, pushed up his glasses, and rubbed his eyes. "We had such a good chance," he said. "I told him what I thought, but I couldn't in truth say that we had more than a good chance. I guess Tom was tired of white men's chances and preferred to take his own. Ready, Cal?"

"Yessir, Mr. Finch."

"Then let's go."

Aunt Alexandra sat down in Calpurnia's chair and put her hands to her face. She sat quite still; she was so quiet I wondered if she would faint. I heard Miss Maudie breathing as if she had just climbed the steps, and in the diningroom the ladies chattered happily.

I thought Aunt Alexandra was crying, but when she took her hands away from her face, she was not. She looked weary. She spoke, and her voice was flat.

"I can't say I approve of everything he does, Maudie, but he's my brother, and I just want to know when this will ever end." Her voice rose: "It tears him to pieces. He doesn't show it much, but it tears him to pieces. I've seen him when—what else do they want from him, Maudie, what else?"

"What does who want, Alexandra?" Miss Maudie asked.

"I mean this town. They're perfectly willing to let him do what they're too afraid to do themselves—it might lose 'em a nickel. They're perfectly willing to let him wreck his health doing what they're afraid to do, they're—"

"Be quiet, they'll hear you," said Miss Maudie. "Have you ever thought of it this way, Alexandra? Whether Maycomb

270

knows it or not, we're paying the highest tribute we can pay a man. We trust him to do right. It's that simple."

"Who?" Aunt Alexandra never knew she was echoing her twelve-year-old nephew.

"The handful of people in this town who say that fair play is not marked White Only; the handful of people who say a fair trial is for everybody, not just us; the handful of people with enough humility to think, when they look at a Negro, there but for the Lord's kindness am I." Miss Maudie's old crispness was returning: "The handful of people in this town with background, that's who they are."

Had I been attentive, I would have had another scrap to add to Jem's definition of background, but I found myself shaking and couldn't stop. I had seen Enfield Prison Farm, and Atticus had pointed out the exercise yard to me. It was the size of a football field.

"Stop that shaking," commanded Miss Maudie, and I stopped. "Get up, Alexandra, we've left 'em long enough."

Aunt Alexandra rose and smoothed the various whalebone ridges along her hips. She took her handkerchief from her belt and wiped her nose. She patted her hair and said, "Do I show it?"

"Not a sign," said Miss Maudie. "Are you together again, Jean Louise?"

"Yes ma'am."

"Then let's join the ladies," she said grimly.

Their voices swelled when Miss Maudie opened the door to the diningroom. Aunt Alexandra was ahead of me, and I saw her head go up as she went through the door.

"Oh, Mrs. Perkins," she said, "you need some more coffee. Let me get it."

"Calpurnia's on an errand for a few minutes, Grace," said Miss Maudie. "Let me pass you some more of these dewberry tarts. 'dyou hear what that cousin of mine did the other day, the one who likes to go fishing? . . ."

And so they went, down the row of laughing women,

around the diningroom, refilling coffee cups, dishing out goodies as though their only regret was the temporary domestic disaster of losing Calpurnia.

The gentle hum began again: "Yes sir, Mrs. Perkins, that J. Grimes Everett is a martyred saint, he . . . needed to get married so they ran . . . to the beauty parlor every Saturday afternoon . . . soon as the sun goes down. He goes to bed with the . . . chickens, a crate full of sick chickens, Fred says that's what started it all. Fred says . . ."

Aunt Alexandra looked across the room at me and smiled. She looked at a tray of cookies on the table and nodded at them. I carefully picked up the tray and watched myself walk to Mrs. Merriweather. With my very best company manners, I asked her if she would have some. After all, if Aunty could be a lady at a time like this, so could I.

25

Don't do that, Scout. Set him out on the back steps."

"Jem, are you crazy? . . ."

"I said set him out on the back steps."

Sighing, I scooped up the small creature, placed him on the bottom step and went back to my cot. September had come, but not a trace of cool weather with it, and we were still sleeping on the back screen porch. Lightning bugs were still about, the night crawlers and flying insects that beat against the screen the summer long had not gone wherever they go when autumn comes.

A roly-poly had found his way inside the house; I reasoned that the tiny varmint had crawled up the steps and under the door. I was putting my book on the floor beside my cot when I saw him. The creatures are no more than an inch long, and when you touch them they roll themselves into a tight gray ball.

I lay on my stomach, reached down and poked him. He rolled up. Then, feeling safe, I suppose, he slowly unrolled. He traveled a few inches on his hundred legs and I touched him again. He rolled up. Feeling sleepy, I decided to end things. My hand was going down on him when Jem spoke.

Jem was scowling. It was probably a part of the stage he was going through, and I wished he would hurry up and get through it. He was certainly never cruel to animals, but I had never known his charity to embrace the insect world.

"Why couldn't I mash him?" I asked.

"Because they don't bother you," Jem answered in the darkness. He had turned out his reading light.

"Reckon you're at the stage now where you don't kill flies and mosquitoes now, I reckon," I said. "Lemme know when you change your mind. Tell you one thing, though, I ain't gonna sit around and not scratch a redbug."

"Aw dry up," he answered drowsily.

Jem was the one who was getting more like a girl every day, not I. Comfortable, I lay on my back and waited for sleep, and while waiting I thought of Dill. He had left us the first of the month with firm assurances that he would return the minute school was out—he guessed his folks had got the general idea that he liked to spend his summers in Maycomb. Miss Rachel took us with them in the taxi to Maycomb Junction, and Dill waved to us from the train window until he was out of sight. He was not out of mind: I missed him. The last two days of his time with us, Jem had taught him to swim—

Taught him to swim. I was wide awake, remembering what Dill had told me.

Barker's Eddy is at the end of a dirt road off the Meridian highway about a mile from town. It is easy to catch a ride down the highway on a cotton wagon or from a passing motorist, and the short walk to the creek is easy, but the prospect of walking all the way back home at dusk, when the traffic is light, is tiresome, and swimmers are careful not to stay too late.

According to Dill, he and Jem had just come to the highway when they saw Atticus driving toward them. He looked like he had not seen them, so they both waved. Atticus finally slowed down; when they caught up with him he said, "You'd better catch a ride back. I won't be going home for a while." Calpurnia was in the back seat.

Jem protested, then pleaded, and Atticus said, "All right, you can come with us if you stay in the car."

On the way to Tom Robinson's, Atticus told them what had happened.

They turned off the highway, rode slowly by the dump and

past the Ewell residence, down the narrow lane to the Negro cabins. Dill said a crowd of black children were playing marbles in Tom's front yard. Atticus parked the car and got out. Calpurnia followed him through the front gate.

Dill heard him ask one of the children, "Where's your mother, Sam?" and heard Sam say, "She down at Sis Stevens's, Mr. Finch. Want me run fetch her?"

Dill said Atticus looked uncertain, then he said yes, and Sam scampered off. "Go on with your game, boys," Atticus said to the children.

A little girl came to the cabin door and stood looking at Atticus. Dill said her hair was a wad of tiny stiff pigtails, each ending in a bright bow. She grinned from ear to ear and walked toward our father, but she was too small to navigate the steps. Dill said Atticus went to her, took off his hat, and offered her his finger. She grabbed it and he eased her down the steps. Then he gave her to Calpurnia.

Sam was trotting behind his mother when they came up. Dill said Helen said, "'evenin', Mr. Finch, won't you have a seat?" But she didn't say any more. Neither did Atticus.

"Scout," said Dill, "she just fell down in the dirt. Just fell down in the dirt, like a giant with a big foot just came along and stepped on her. Just ump—" Dill's fat foot hit the ground. "Like you'd step on an ant."

Dill said Calpurnia and Atticus lifted Helen to her feet and half carried, half walked her to the cabin. They stayed inside a long time, and Atticus came out alone. When they drove back by the dump, some of the Ewells hollered at them, but Dill didn't catch what they said.

Maycomb was interested by the news of Tom's death for perhaps two days; two days was enough for the information to spread through the county. "Did you hear about? . . . No? Well, they say he was runnin' fit to beat lightnin' . . ." To Maycomb, Tom's death was Typical. Typical of a nigger to cut and run. Typical of a nigger's mentality to have no plan, no thought for the future, just run blind first chance he saw.

Funny thing, Atticus Finch might've got him off scot free, but wait—? Hell no. You know how they are. Easy come, easy go. Just shows you, that Robinson boy was legally married, they say he kept himself clean, went to church and all that, but when it comes down to the line the veneer's mighty thin. Nigger always comes out in 'em.

A few more details, enabling the listener to repeat his version in turn, then nothing to talk about until *The Maycomb Tribune* appeared the following Thursday. There was a brief obituary in the Colored News, but there was also an editorial.

Mr. B. B. Underwood was at his most bitter, and he couldn't have cared less who canceled advertising and subscriptions. (But Maycomb didn't play that way: Mr. Underwood could holler till he sweated and write whatever he wanted to, he'd still get his advertising and subscriptions. If he wanted to make a fool of himself in his paper that was his business.) Mr. Underwood didn't talk about miscarriages of justice, he was writing so children could understand. Mr. Underwood simply figured it was a sin to kill cripples, be they standing, sitting, or escaping. He likened Tom's death to the senseless slaughter of songbirds by hunters and children, and Maycomb thought he was trying to write an editorial poetical enough to be reprinted in *The Montgomery Advertiser.*

How could this be so, I wondered, as I read Mr. Underwood's editorial. Senseless killing—Tom had been given due process of law to the day of his death; he had been tried openly and convicted by twelve good men and true; my father had fought for him all the way. Then Mr. Underwood's meaning became clear: Atticus had used every tool available to free men to save Tom Robinson, but in the secret courts of men's hearts Atticus had no case. Tom was a dead man the minute Mayella Ewell opened her mouth and screamed.

The name Ewell gave me a queasy feeling. Maycomb had lost no time in getting Mr. Ewell's views on Tom's demise and passing them along through that English Channel of gossip, Miss Stephanie Crawford. Miss Stephanie told Aunt Alexandra in Jem's presence ("Oh foot, he's old enough to listen") that Mr. Ewell said it made one down and about two more to go. Jem told me not to be afraid, Mr. Ewell was more hot gas than anything. Jem also told me that if I breathed a word to Atticus, if in any way I let Atticus know I knew, Jem would personally never speak to me again.

26

School started, and so did our daily trips past the Radley Place. Jem was in the seventh grade and went to high school, beyond the grammar-school building; I was now in the third grade, and our routines were so different I only walked to school with Jem in the mornings and saw him at mealtimes. He went out for football, but was too slender and too young yet to do anything but carry the team water buckets. This he did with enthusiasm; most afternoons he was seldom home before dark.

The Radley Place had ceased to terrify me, but it was no less gloomy, no less chilly under its great oaks, and no less uninviting. Mr. Nathan Radley could still be seen on a clear day, walking to and from town; we knew Boo was there, for the same old reason—nobody'd seen him carried out yet. I sometimes felt a twinge of remorse, when passing by the old place, at ever having taken part in what must have been sheer torment to Arthur Radley—what reasonable recluse wants children peeping through his shutters, delivering greetings on the end of a fishing-pole, wandering in his collards at night?

And yet I remembered. Two Indian-head pennies, chewing gum, soap dolls, a rusty medal, a broken watch and chain. Jem must have put them away somewhere. I stopped and looked at the tree one afternoon: the trunk was swelling around its cement patch. The patch itself was turning yellow.

We had almost seen him a couple of times, a good enough score for anybody.

But I still looked for him each time I went by. Maybe

someday we would see him. I imagined how it would be: when it happened, he'd just be sitting in the swing when I came along. "Hidy do, Mr. Arthur," I would say, as if I had said it every afternoon of my life. "Evening, Jean Louise," he would say, as if he had said it every afternoon of my life, "right pretty spell we're having, isn't it?" "Yes sir, right pretty," I would say, and go on.

It was only a fantasy. We would never see him. He probably did go out when the moon was down and gaze upon Miss Stephanie Crawford. I'd have picked somebody else to look at, but that was his business. He would never gaze at us.

"You aren't starting that again, are you?" said Atticus one night, when I expressed a stray desire just to have one good look at Boo Radley before I died. "If you are, I'll tell you right now: stop it. I'm too old to go chasing you off the Radley property. Besides, it's dangerous. You might get shot. You know Mr. Nathan shoots at every shadow he sees, even shadows that leave size-four bare footprints. You were lucky not to be killed."

I hushed then and there. At the same time I marveled at Atticus. This was the first he had let us know he knew a lot more about something than we thought he knew. And it had happened years ago. No, only last summer—no, summer before last, when . . . time was playing tricks on me. I must remember to ask Jem.

So many things had happened to us, Boo Radley was the least of our fears. Atticus said he didn't see how anything else could happen, that things had a way of settling down, and after enough time passed people would forget that Tom Robinson's existence was ever brought to their attention.

Perhaps Atticus was right, but the events of the summer hung over us like smoke in a closed room. The adults in Maycomb never discussed the case with Jem and me; it seemed that they discussed it with their children, and their attitude must have been that neither of us could help having Atticus for a parent, so their children must be nice to us in spite of him. The children would never have thought that up for themselves: had our classmates been left to their own devices, Jem and I would have had several swift, satisfying fistfights apiece and ended the matter for good. As it was, we were compelled to hold our heads high and be, respectively, a gentleman and a lady. In a way, it was like the era of Mrs. Henry Lafayette Dubose, without all her yelling. There was one odd thing, though, that I never understood: in spite of Atticus's shortcomings as a parent, people were content to re-elect him to the state legislature that year, as usual, without opposition. I came to the conclusion that people were just peculiar, I withdrew from them, and never thought about them until I was forced to.

I was forced to one day in school. Once a week, we had a Current Events period. Each child was supposed to clip an item from a newspaper, absorb its contents, and reveal them to the class. This practice allegedly overcame a variety of evils: standing in front of his fellows encouraged good posture and gave a child poise; delivering a short talk made him word-conscious; learning his current event strengthened his memory; being singled out made him more than ever anxious to return to the Group.

The idea was profound, but as usual, in Maycomb it didn't work very well. In the first place, few rural children had access to newspapers, so the burden of Current Events was borne by the town children, convincing the bus children more deeply that the town children got all the attention anyway. The rural children who could, usually brought clippings from what they called The Grit Paper, a publication spurious in the eyes of Miss Gates, our teacher. Why she frowned when a child recited from The Grit Paper I never knew, but in some way it was associated with liking fiddling, eating syrupy biscuits for lunch, being a holy-roller, singing *Sweetly Sings the Donkey* and pronouncing it dunkey, all of which the state paid teachers to discourage.

Even so, not many of the children knew what a Current

Event was. Little Chuck Little, a hundred years old in his knowledge of cows and their habits, was halfway through an Uncle Natchell story when Miss Gates stopped him: "Charles, that is not a current event. That is an advertisement."

Cecil Jacobs knew what one was, though. When his turn came, he went to the front of the room and began, "Old Hitler—"

"Adolf Hitler, Cecil," said Miss Gates. "One never begins with Old anybody."

"Yes ma'am," he said. "Old Adolf Hitler has been prosecutin' the—"

"Persecuting, Cecil . . ."

"Nome, Miss Gates, it says here—well anyway, old Adolf Hitler has been after the Jews and he's puttin' 'em in prisons and he's taking away all their property and he won't let any of 'em out of the country and he's washin' all the feeble-minded and—"

"Washing the feeble-minded?"

"Yes ma'am, Miss Gates, I reckon they don't have sense enough to wash themselves, I don't reckon an idiot could keep hisself clean. Well anyway, Hitler's started a program to round up all the half-Jews too and he wants to register 'em in case they might wanta cause him any trouble and I think this is a bad thing and that's my current event."

"Very good, Cecil," said Miss Gates. Puffing, Cecil returned to his seat.

A hand went up in the back of the room. "How can he do that?"

"Who do what?" asked Miss Gates patiently.

"I mean how can Hitler just put a lot of folks in a pen like that, looks like the govamint'd stop him," said the owner of the hand.

"Hitler is the government," said Miss Gates, and seizing an opportunity to make education dynamic, she went to the blackboard. She printed DEMOCRACY in large letters. "Democracy," she said. "Does anybody have a definition?"

"Us," somebody said.

I raised my hand, remembering an old campaign slogan Atticus had once told me about.

"What do you think it means, Jean Louise?"

"'Equal rights for all, special privileges for none,'" I quoted.

"Very good, Jean Louise, very good," Miss Gates smiled. In front of DEMOCRACY, she printed WE ARE A. "Now class, say it all together, 'We are a democracy.'"

We said it. Then Miss Gates said, "That's the difference between America and Germany. We are a democracy and Germany is a dictatorship. Dictator-ship," she said. "Over here we don't believe in persecuting anybody. Persecution comes from people who are prejudiced. Pre-ju-dice," she enunciated carefully. "There are no better people in the world than the Jews, and why Hitler doesn't think so is a mystery to me."

An inquiring soul in the middle of the room said, "Why don't they like the Jews, you reckon, Miss Gates?"

"I don't know, Henry. They contribute to every society they live in, and most of all, they are a deeply religious people. Hitler's trying to do away with religion, so maybe he doesn't like them for that reason."

Cecil spoke up. "Well I don't know for certain," he said, "they're supposed to change money or somethin', but that ain't no cause to persecute 'em. They're white, ain't they?"

Miss Gates said, "When you get to high school, Cecil, you'll learn that the Jews have been persecuted since the beginning of history, even driven out of their own country. It's one of the most terrible stories in history. Time for arithmetic, children."

As I had never liked arithmetic, I spent the period looking out the window. The only time I ever saw Atticus scowl was when Elmer Davis would give us the latest on Hitler. Atticus would snap off the radio and say, "Hmp!" I asked him once why he was impatient with Hitler and Atticus said, "Because he's a maniac."

This would not do, I mused, as the class proceeded with its sums. One maniac and millions of German folks. Looked to me like they'd shut Hitler in a pen instead of letting him shut them up. There was something else wrong—I would ask my father about it.

I did, and he said he could not possibly answer my question because he didn't know the answer.

"But it's okay to hate Hitler?"

"It is not," he said. "It's not okay to hate anybody."

"Atticus," I said, "there's somethin' I don't understand. Miss Gates said it was awful, Hitler doin' like he does, she got real red in the face about it—"

"I should think she would."

"But—"

"Yes?"

"Nothing, sir." I went away, not sure that I could explain to Atticus what was on my mind, not sure that I could clarify what was only a feeling. Perhaps Jem could provide the answer. Jem understood school things better than Atticus.

Jem was worn out from a day's water-carrying. There were at least twelve banana peels on the floor by his bed, surrounding an empty milk bottle. "Whatcha stuffin' for?" I asked.

"Coach says if I can gain twenty-five pounds by year after next I can play," he said. "This is the quickest way."

"If you don't throw it all up. Jem," I said, "I wanta ask you somethin'."

"Shoot." He put down his book and stretched his legs.

"Miss Gates is a nice lady, ain't she?"

"Why sure," said Jem. "I liked her when I was in her room."

"She hates Hitler a lot . . ."

"What's wrong with that?"

"Well, she went on today about how bad it was him treatin' the Jews like that. Jem, it's not right to persecute anybody, is it? I mean have mean thoughts about anybody, even, is it?"

"Gracious no, Scout. What's eatin' you?"

"Well, coming out of the courthouse that night Miss Gates was—she was goin' down the steps in front of us, you musta not seen her—she was talking with Miss Stephanie Crawford. I heard her say it's time somebody taught 'em a lesson, they were gettin' way above themselves, an' the next thing they think they can do is marry us. Jem, how can you hate Hitler so bad an' then turn around and be ugly about folks right at home—"

Jem was suddenly furious. He leaped off the bed, grabbed me by the collar and shook me. "I never wanta hear about that courthouse again, ever, ever, you hear me? You hear me? Don't you ever say one word to me about it again, you hear? Now go on!"

I was too surprised to cry. I crept from Jem's room and shut the door softly, lest undue noise set him off again. Suddenly tired, I wanted Atticus. He was in the livingroom, and I went to him and tried to get in his lap.

Atticus smiled. "You're getting so big now, I'll just have to hold a part of you." He held me close. "Scout," he said softly, "don't let Jem get you down. He's having a rough time these days. I heard you back there."

Atticus said that Jem was trying hard to forget something, but what he was really doing was storing it away for a while, until enough time passed. Then he would be able to think about it and sort things out. When he was able to think about it, Jem would be himself again.

27

Things did settle down, after a fashion, as Atticus said they would. By the middle of October, only two small things out of the ordinary happened to two Maycomb citizens. No, there were three things, and they did not directly concern us—the Finches—but in a way they did.

The first thing was that Mr. Bob Ewell acquired and lost a job in a matter of days and probably made himself unique in the annals of the nineteen-thirties: he was the only man I ever heard of who was fired from the WPA for laziness. I suppose his brief burst of fame brought on a briefer burst of industry, but his job lasted only as long as his notoriety: Mr. Ewell found himself as forgotten as Tom Robinson. Thereafter, he resumed his regular weekly appearances at the welfare office for his check, and received it with no grace amid obscure mutterings that the bastards who thought they ran this town wouldn't permit an honest man to make a living. Ruth Jones, the welfare lady, said Mr. Ewell openly accused Atticus of getting his job. She was upset enough to walk down to Atticus's office and tell him about it. Atticus told Miss Ruth not to fret, that if Bob Ewell wanted to discuss Atticus's "getting" his job, he knew the way to the office.

The second thing happened to Judge Taylor. Judge Taylor was not a Sunday-night churchgoer; Mrs. Taylor was. Judge Taylor savored his Sunday night hour alone in his big house, and church-time found him holed up in his study reading the writings of Bob Taylor (no kin, but the judge would have been proud to claim it). One Sunday night, lost in fruity metaphors and florid diction, Judge Taylor's attention was wrenched from the page by an irritating scratching noise. "Hush," he said to Ann Taylor, his fat nondescript dog. Then he realized he was speaking to an empty room; the scratching noise was coming from the rear of the house. Judge Taylor clumped to the back porch to let Ann out and found the screen door swinging open. A shadow on the corner of the house caught his eye, and that was all he saw of his visitor. Mrs. Taylor came home from church to find her husband in his chair, lost in the writings of Bob Taylor, with a shotgun across his lap.

The third thing happened to Helen Robinson, Tom's widow. If Mr. Ewell was as forgotten as Tom Robinson, Tom Robinson was as forgotten as Boo Radley. But Tom was not forgotten by his employer, Mr. Link Deas. Mr. Link Deas made a job for Helen. He didn't really need her, but he said he felt right bad about the way things turned out. I never knew who took care of her children while Helen was away. Calpurnia said it was hard on Helen, because she had to walk nearly a mile out of her way to avoid the Ewells, who, according to Helen, "chunked at her" the first time she tried to use the public road. Mr. Link Deas eventually received the impression that Helen was coming to work each morning from the wrong direction, and dragged the reason out of her. "Just let it be, Mr. Link, please suh," Helen begged. "The hell I will," said Mr. Link. He told her to come by his store that afternoon before she left. She did, and Mr. Link closed his store, put his hat firmly on his head, and walked Helen home. He walked her the short way, by the Ewells'. On his way back, Mr. Link stopped at the crazy gate.

"Ewell?" he called. "I say Ewell!"

The windows, normally packed with children, were empty.

"I know every last one of you's in there a-layin' on the floor! Now hear me, Bob Ewell: if I hear one more peep outa my girl Helen about not bein' able to walk this road I'll have you in jail before sundown!" Mr. Link spat in the dust and walked home.

Helen went to work next morning and used the public

road. Nobody chunked at her, but when she was a few yards beyond the Ewell house, she looked around and saw Mr. Ewell walking behind her. She turned and walked on, and Mr. Ewell kept the same distance behind her until she reached Mr. Link Deas's house. All the way to the house, Helen said, she heard a soft voice behind her, crooning foul words. Thoroughly frightened, she telephoned Mr. Link at his store, which was not too far from his house. As Mr. Link came out of his store he saw Mr. Ewell leaning on the fence. Mr. Ewell said, "Don't you look at me, Link Deas, like I was dirt. I ain't jumped your—"

"First thing you can do, Ewell, is get your stinkin' carcass off my property. You're leanin' on it an' I can't afford fresh paint for it. Second thing you can do is stay away from my cook or I'll have you up for assault—"

"I ain't touched her, Link Deas, and ain't about to go with no nigger!"

"You don't have to touch her, all you have to do is make her afraid, an' if assault ain't enough to keep you locked up a while, I'll get you in on the Ladies' Law, so get outa my sight! If you don't think I mean it, just bother that girl again!"

Mr. Ewell evidently thought he meant it, for Helen reported no further trouble.

"I don't like it, Atticus, I don't like it at all," was Aunt Alexandra's assessment of these events. "That man seems to have a permanent running grudge against everybody connected with that case. I know how that kind are about paying off grudges, but I don't understand why he should harbor one—he had his way in court, didn't he?"

"I think I understand," said Atticus. "It might be because he knows in his heart that very few people in Maycomb really believed his and Mayella's yarns. He thought he'd be a hero, but all he got for his pain was . . . was, okay, we'll convict this Negro but get back to your dump. He's had his fling with about everybody now, so he ought to be satisfied. He'll settle down when the weather changes."

"But why should he try to burgle John Taylor's house? He obviously didn't know John was home or he wouldn't've tried. Only lights John shows on Sunday nights are on the front porch and back in his den . . ."

"You don't know if Bob Ewell cut that screen, you don't know who did it," said Atticus. "But I can guess. I proved him a liar but John made him look like a fool. All the time Ewell was on the stand I couldn't dare look at John and keep a straight face. John looked at him as if he were a three-legged chicken or a square egg. Don't tell me judges don't try to prejudice juries," Atticus chuckled.

By the end of October, our lives had become the familiar routine of school, play, study. Jem seemed to have put out of his mind whatever it was he wanted to forget, and our classmates mercifully let us forget our father's eccentricities. Cecil Jacobs asked me one time if Atticus was a Radical. When I asked Atticus, Atticus was so amused I was rather annoyed, but he said he wasn't laughing at me. He said, "You tell Cecil I'm about as radical as Cotton Tom Heflin."

Aunt Alexandra was thriving. Miss Maudie must have silenced the whole missionary society at one blow, for Aunty again ruled that roost. Her refreshments grew even more delicious. I learned more about the poor Mrunas' social life from listening to Mrs. Merriweather: they had so little sense of family that the whole tribe was one big family. A child had as many fathers as there were men in the community, as many mothers as there were women. J. Grimes Everett was doing his utmost to change this state of affairs, and desperately needed our prayers.

Maycomb was itself again. Precisely the same as last year and the year before that, with only two minor changes. Firstly, people had removed from their store windows and automobiles the stickers that said NRA—WE DO OUR PART. I asked Atticus why, and he said it was because the National Recovery Act was dead. I asked who killed it; he said nine old men.

The second change in Maycomb since last year was not one of national significance. Until then, Halloween in Maycomb was a completely unorganized affair. Each child did what he wanted to do, with assistance from other children if there was anything to be moved, such as placing a light buggy on top of the livery stable. But parents thought things went too far last year, when the peace of Miss Tutti and Miss Frutti was shattered.

Misses Tutti and Frutti Barber were maiden ladies, sisters, who lived together in the only Maycomb residence boasting a cellar. The Barber ladies were rumored to be Republicans, having migrated from Clanton, Alabama, in 1911. Their ways were strange to us, and why they wanted a cellar nobody knew, but they wanted one, and they dug one, and they spent the rest of their lives chasing generations of children out of it.

Misses Tutti and Frutti (their names were Sarah and Frances), aside from their Yankee ways, were both deaf. Miss Tutti denied it and lived in a world of silence, but Miss Frutti, not about to miss anything, employed an ear trumpet so enormous that Jem declared it was a loudspeaker from one of those dog Victrolas.

With these facts in mind and Halloween at hand, some wicked children had waited until the Misses Barber were thoroughly asleep, slipped into their livingroom (nobody but the Radleys locked up at night), stealthily made away with every stick of furniture therein, and hid it in the cellar. I deny having taken part in such a thing.

"I heard 'em!" was the cry that awoke the Misses Barber's neighbors at dawn next morning. "Heard 'em drive a truck up to the door! Stomped around like horses. They're in New Orleans by now!"

Miss Tutti was sure those traveling fur sellers who came through town two days ago had purloined their furniture. "Da-rk they were," she said. "Syrians."

Mr. Heck Tate was summoned. He surveyed the area and said he thought it was a local job. Miss Frutti said she'd know a Maycomb voice anywhere, and there were no Maycomb voices in that parlor last night—rolling their r's all over her premises, they were. Nothing less than the bloodhounds must be used to locate their furniture, Miss Tutti insisted, so Mr. Tate was obliged to go ten miles out the road, round up the county hounds, and put them on the trail.

Mr. Tate started them off at the Misses Barber's front steps, but all they did was run around to the back of the house and howl at the cellar door. When Mr. Tate set them in motion three times, he finally guessed the truth. By noontime that day, there was not a barefooted child to be seen in Maycomb, and nobody took off his shoes until the hounds were returned.

So the Maycomb ladies said things would be different this year. The high-school auditorium would be open, there would be a pageant for the grown-ups; apple-bobbing, taffy-pulling, pinning the tail on the donkey for the children. There would also be a prize of twenty-five cents for the best Halloween costume, created by the wearer.

Jem and I both groaned. Not that we'd ever done anything, it was the principle of the thing. Jem considered himself too old for Halloween anyway; he said he wouldn't be caught anywhere near the high school at something like that. Oh well, I thought, Atticus would take me.

I soon learned, however, that my services would be required on stage that evening. Mrs. Grace Merriweather had composed an original pageant entitled *Maycomb County: Ad Astra Per Aspera,* and I was to be a ham. She thought it would be adorable if some of the children were costumed to represent the county's agricultural products: Cecil Jacobs would be dressed up to look like a cow; Agnes Boone would make a lovely butterbean, another child would be a peanut, and on down the line until Mrs. Merriweather's imagination and the supply of children were exhausted.

Our only duties, as far as I could gather from our two rehearsals, were to enter from stage left as Mrs. Merriweather (not only the author, but the narrator) identified us. When she called out, "Pork," that was my cue. Then the assembled company would sing, "Maycomb County, Maycomb County, we will aye be true to thee," as the grand finale, and Mrs. Merriweather would mount the stage with the state flag.

My costume was not much of a problem. Mrs. Crenshaw, the local seamstress, had as much imagination as Mrs. Merriweather. Mrs. Crenshaw took some chicken wire and bent it into the shape of a cured ham. This she covered with brown cloth, and painted it to resemble the original. I could duck under and someone would pull the contraption down over my head. It came almost to my knees. Mrs. Crenshaw thoughtfully left two peepholes for me. She did a fine job; Jem said I looked exactly like a ham with legs. There were several discomforts, though: it was hot, it was a close fit; if my nose itched I couldn't scratch, and once inside I could not get out of it alone.

When Halloween came, I assumed that the whole family would be present to watch me perform, but I was disappointed. Atticus said as tactfully as he could that he just didn't think he could stand a pageant tonight, he was all in. He had been in Montgomery for a week and had come home late that afternoon. He thought Jem might escort me if I asked him.

Aunt Alexandra said she just had to get to bed early, she'd been decorating the stage all afternoon and was worn out— she stopped short in the middle of her sentence. She closed her mouth, then opened it to say something, but no words came.

"'s matter, Aunty?" I asked.

"Oh nothing, nothing," she said, "somebody just walked over my grave." She put away from her whatever it was that gave her a pinprick of apprehension, and suggested that I give the family a preview in the livingroom. So Jem squeezed me into my costume, stood at the livingroom door, called out "Po-ork," exactly as Mrs. Merriweather would have done, and I marched in. Atticus and Aunt Alexandra were delighted.

I repeated my part for Calpurnia in the kitchen and she said I was wonderful. I wanted to go across the street to show Miss Maudie, but Jem said she'd probably be at the pageant anyway.

After that, it didn't matter whether they went or not. Jem said he would take me. Thus began our longest journey together.

28

The weather was unusually warm for the last day of October. We didn't even need jackets. The wind was growing stronger, and Jem said it might be raining before we got home. There was no moon.

The street light on the corner cast sharp shadows on the Radley house. I heard Jem laugh softly. "Bet nobody bothers them tonight," he said. Jem was carrying my ham costume, rather awkwardly, as it was hard to hold. I thought it gallant of him to do so.

"It is a scary place though, ain't it?" I said. "Boo doesn't mean anybody any harm, but I'm right glad you're along."

"You know Atticus wouldn't let you go to the schoolhouse by yourself," Jem said.

"Don't see why, it's just around the corner and across the yard."

"That yard's a mighty long place for little girls to cross at night," Jem teased. "Ain't you scared of haints?"

We laughed. Haints, Hot Steams, incantations, secret signs, had vanished with our years as mist with sunrise. "What was that old thing," Jem said, "Angel bright, life-in-death; get off the road, don't suck my breath."

"Cut it out, now," I said. We were in front of the Radley Place.

Jem said, "Boo must not be at home. Listen."

High above us in the darkness a solitary mocker poured out his repertoire in blissful unawareness of whose tree he sat in, plunging from the shrill kee, kee of the sunflower bird to the irascible qua-ack of a bluejay, to the sad lament of Poor Will, Poor Will, Poor Will.

We turned the corner and I tripped on a root growing in the road. Jem tried to help me, but all he did was drop my costume in the dust. I didn't fall, though, and soon we were on our way again.

We turned off the road and entered the schoolyard. It was pitch black.

"How do you know where we're at, Jem?" I asked, when we had gone a few steps.

"I can tell we're under the big oak because we're passin' through a cool spot. Careful now, and don't fall again."

We had slowed to a cautious gait, and were feeling our way forward so as not to bump into the tree. The tree was a single and ancient oak; two children could not reach around its trunk and touch hands. It was far away from teachers, their spies, and curious neighbors: it was near the Radley lot, but the Radleys were not curious. A small patch of earth beneath its branches was packed hard from many fights and furtive crap games.

The lights in the high school auditorium were blazing in the distance, but they blinded us, if anything. "Don't look ahead, Scout," Jem said. "Look at the ground and you won't fall."

"You should have brought the flashlight, Jem."

"Didn't know it was this dark. Didn't look like it'd be this dark earlier in the evening. So cloudy, that's why. It'll hold off a while, though."

Someone leaped at us.

"God amighty!" Jem yelled.

A circle of light burst in our faces, and Cecil Jacobs jumped in glee behind it. "Ha-a-a, gotcha!" he shrieked. "Thought you'd be comin' along this way!"

"What are you doin' way out here by yourself, boy? Ain't you scared of Boo Radley?"

Cecil had ridden safely to the auditorium with his parents,

hadn't seen us, then had ventured down this far because he knew good and well we'd be coming along. He thought Mr. Finch'd be with us, though.

"Shucks, ain't much but around the corner," said Jem. "Who's scared to go around the corner?" We had to admit that Cecil was pretty good, though. He *had* given us a fright, and he could tell it all over the schoolhouse, that was his privilege.

"Say," I said, "ain't you a cow tonight? Where's your costume?"

"It's up behind the stage," he said. "Mrs. Merriweather says the pageant ain't comin' on for a while. You can put yours back of the stage by mine, Scout, and we can go with the rest of 'em."

This was an excellent idea, Jem thought. He also thought it a good thing that Cecil and I would be together. This way, Jem would be left to go with people his own age.

When we reached the auditorium, the whole town was there except Atticus and the ladies worn out from decorating, and the usual outcasts and shut-ins. Most of the county, it seemed, was there: the hall was teeming with slicked-up country people. The high school building had a wide downstairs hallway; people milled around booths that had been installed along each side.

"Oh Jem, I forgot my money," I sighed, when I saw them.

"Atticus didn't," Jem said. "Here's thirty cents, you can do six things. See you later on."

"Okay," I said, quite content with thirty cents and Cecil. I went with Cecil down to the front of the auditorium, through a door on one side, and backstage. I got rid of my ham costume and departed in a hurry, for Mrs. Merriweather was standing at a lectern in front of the first row of seats making last-minute, frenzied changes in the script.

"How much money you got?" I asked Cecil. Cecil had thirty cents, too, which made us even. We squandered our first nickels on the House of Horrors, which scared us not at all; we entered the black seventh-grade room and were led around by the temporary ghoul in residence and were made to touch several objects alleged to be the component parts of a human being. "Here's his eyes," we were told when we touched two peeled grapes on a saucer. "Here's his heart," which felt like raw liver. "These are his innards," and our hands were thrust into a plate of cold spaghetti.

Cecil and I visited several booths. We each bought a sack of Mrs. Judge Taylor's homemade divinity. I wanted to bob for apples, but Cecil said it wasn't sanitary. His mother said he might catch something from everybody's heads having been in the same tub. "Ain't anything around town now to catch," I protested. But Cecil said his mother said it was unsanitary to eat after folks. I later asked Aunt Alexandra about this, and she said people who held such views were usually climbers.

We were about to purchase a blob of taffy when Mrs. Merriweather's runners appeared and told us to go backstage, it was time to get ready. The auditorium was filling with people; the Maycomb County High School band had assembled in front below the stage; the stage footlights were on and the red velvet curtain rippled and billowed from the scurrying going on behind it.

Backstage, Cecil and I found the narrow hallway teeming with people: adults in homemade three-corner hats, Confederate caps, Spanish-American War hats, and World War helmets. Children dressed as various agricultural enterprises crowded around the one small window.

"Somebody's mashed my costume," I wailed in dismay. Mrs. Merriweather galloped to me, reshaped the chicken wire, and thrust me inside.

"You all right in there, Scout?" asked Cecil. "You sound so far off, like you was on the other side of a hill."

"You don't sound any nearer," I said.

The band played the national anthem, and we heard the audience rise. Then the bass drum sounded. Mrs. Merriweather, stationed behind her lectern beside the band, said: "Maycomb

County: Ad Astra Per Aspera." The bass drum boomed again. "That means," said Mrs. Merriweather, translating for the rustic elements, "from the mud to the stars." She added, unnecessarily, it seemed to me, "A pageant."

"Reckon they wouldn't know what it was if she didn't tell 'em," whispered Cecil, who was immediately shushed.

"The whole town knows it," I breathed.

"But the country folks've come in," Cecil said.

"Be quiet back there," a man's voice ordered, and we were silent.

The bass drum went boom with every sentence Mrs. Merriweather uttered. She chanted mournfully about Maycomb County being older than the state, that it was a part of the Mississippi and Alabama Territories, that the first white man to set foot in the virgin forests was the Probate Judge's great-grandfather five times removed, who was never heard of again. Then came the fearless Colonel Maycomb, for whom the county was named.

Andrew Jackson appointed him to a position of authority, and Colonel Maycomb's misplaced self-confidence and slender sense of direction brought disaster to all who rode with him in the Creek Indian Wars. Colonel Maycomb persevered in his efforts to make the region safe for democracy, but his first campaign was his last. His orders, relayed to him by a friendly Indian runner, were to move south. After consulting a tree to ascertain from its lichen which way was south, and taking no lip from the subordinates who ventured to correct him, Colonel Maycomb set out on a purposeful journey to rout the enemy and entangled his troops so far northwest in the forest primeval that they were eventually rescued by settlers moving inland.

Mrs. Merriweather gave a thirty-minute description of Colonel Maycomb's exploits. I discovered that if I bent my knees I could tuck them under my costume and more or less sit. I sat down, listened to Mrs. Merriweather's drone and the bass drum's boom and was soon fast asleep.

They said later that Mrs. Merriweather was putting her all into the grand finale, that she had crooned, "Po-ork," with a confidence born of pine trees and butterbeans entering on cue. She waited a few seconds, then called, "Po-ork?" When nothing materialized, she yelled, "Pork!"

I must have heard her in my sleep, or the band playing *Dixie* woke me, but it was when Mrs. Merriweather triumphantly mounted the stage with the state flag that I chose to make my entrance. Chose is incorrect: I thought I'd better catch up with the rest of them.

They told me later that Judge Taylor went out behind the auditorium and stood there slapping his knees so hard Mrs. Taylor brought him a glass of water and one of his pills.

Mrs. Merriweather seemed to have a hit, everybody was cheering so, but she caught me backstage and told me I had ruined her pageant. She made me feel awful, but when Jem came to fetch me he was sympathetic. He said he couldn't see my costume much from where he was sitting. How he could tell I was feeling bad under my costume I don't know, but he said I did all right, I just came in a little late, that was all. Jem was becoming almost as good as Atticus at making you feel right when things went wrong. Almost—not even Jem could make me go through that crowd, and he consented to wait backstage with me until the audience left.

"You wanta take it off, Scout?" he asked.

"Naw, I'll just keep it on," I said. I could hide my mortification under it.

"You all want a ride home?" someone asked.

"No sir, thank you," I heard Jem say. "It's just a little walk."

"Be careful of haints," the voice said. "Better still, tell the haints to be careful of Scout."

"There aren't many folks left now," Jem told me. "Let's go."

We went through the auditorium to the hallway, then down the steps. It was still black dark. The remaining cars were parked on the other side of the building, and their headlights were little help. "If some of 'em were goin' in our direction we could see better," said Jem. "Here Scout, let me hold onto your—hock. You might lose your balance."

"I can see all right."

"Yeah, but you might lose your balance." I felt a slight pressure on my head, and assumed that Jem had grabbed that end of the ham. "You got me?"

"Uh huh."

We began crossing the black schoolyard, straining to see our feet. "Jem," I said, "I forgot my shoes, they're back behind the stage."

"Well let's go get 'em." But as we turned around, the auditorium lights went off. "You can get 'em tomorrow," he said.

"But tomorrow's Sunday," I protested, as Jem turned me homeward.

"You can get the janitor to let you in . . . Scout?"

"Hm?"

"Nothing."

Jem hadn't started that in a long time. I wondered what he was thinking. He'd tell me when he wanted to, probably when we got home. I felt his fingers press the top of my costume, too hard, it seemed. I shook my head. "Jem, you don't hafta—"

"Hush a minute, Scout," he said, pinching me.

We walked along silently. "Minute's up," I said. "Whatcha thinkin' about?" I turned to look at him, but his outline was barely visible.

"Thought I heard something," he said. "Stop a minute."

We stopped.

"Hear anything?" he asked.

"No."

We had not gone five paces before he made me stop again.

"Jem, are you tryin' to scare me? You know I'm too old—"

"Be quiet," he said, and I knew he was not joking.

The night was still. I could hear his breath coming easily beside me. Occasionally there was a sudden breeze that hit my bare legs, but it was all that remained of a promised windy night. This was the stillness before a thunderstorm. We listened.

"Heard an old dog just then," I said.

"It's not that," Jem answered. "I hear it when we're walkin' along, but when we stop I don't hear it."

"You hear my costume rustlin'. Aw, it's just Halloween got you. . . ."

I said it more to convince myself than Jem, for sure enough, as we began walking, I heard what he was talking about. It was not my costume.

"It's just old Cecil," said Jem presently. "He won't get us again. Let's don't let him think we're hurrying."

We slowed to a crawl. I asked Jem how Cecil could follow us in this dark, looked to me like he'd bump into us from behind.

"I can see you, Scout," Jem said.

"How? I can't see you."

"Your fat streaks are showin'. Mrs. Crenshaw painted 'em with some of that shiny stuff so they'd show up under the footlights. I can see you pretty well, an' I expect Cecil can see you well enough to keep his distance."

I would show Cecil that we knew he was behind us and we were ready for him. "Cecil Jacobs is a big wet he-en!" I yelled suddenly, turning around.

We stopped. There was no acknowledgement save he-en bouncing off the distant schoolhouse wall.

"I'll get him," said Jem. *"He-y!"*

Hay-e-hay-e-hay-e, answered the schoolhouse wall.

It was unlike Cecil to hold out for so long; once he pulled a joke he'd repeat it time and again. We should have been leapt at already. Jem signaled for me to stop again.

He said softly, "Scout, can you take that thing off?"

"I think so, but I ain't got anything on under it much."

"I've got your dress here."

"I can't get it on in the dark."

"Okay," he said, "never mind."

"Jem, are you afraid?"

"No. Think we're almost to the tree now. Few yards from

that, an' we'll be to the road. We can see the street light then."
Jem was talking in an unhurried, flat toneless voice. I wondered how long he would try to keep the Cecil myth going.

"You reckon we oughta sing, Jem?"

"No. Be real quiet again, Scout."

We had not increased our pace. Jem knew as well as I that
it was difficult to walk fast without stumping a toe, tripping
on stones, and other inconveniences, and I was barefooted.
Maybe it was the wind rustling the trees. But there wasn't any
wind and there weren't any trees except the big oak.

Our company shuffled and dragged his feet, as if wearing
heavy shoes. Whoever it was wore thick cotton pants; what I
thought were trees rustling was the soft swish of cotton on
cotton, wheek, wheek, with every step.

I felt the sand go cold under my feet and I knew we were
near the big oak. Jem pressed my head. We stopped and listened.

Shuffle-foot had not stopped with us this time. His
trousers swished softly and steadily. Then they stopped. He
was running, running toward us with no child's steps.

"Run, Scout! Run! Run!" Jem screamed.

I took one giant step and found myself reeling: my arms
useless, in the dark, I could not keep my balance.

"Jem, Jem, help me, Jem!"

Something crushed the chicken wire around me. Metal
ripped on metal and I fell to the ground and rolled as far as I
could, floundering to escape my wire prison. From somewhere near by came scuffling, kicking sounds, sounds of shoes
and flesh scraping dirt and roots. Someone rolled against me
and I felt Jem. He was up like lightning and pulling me with
him but, though my head and shoulders were free, I was so
entangled we didn't get very far.

We were nearly to the road when I felt Jem's hand leave
me, felt him jerk backwards to the ground. More scuffling,
and there came a dull crunching sound and Jem screamed.

I ran in the direction of Jem's scream and sank into a

flabby male stomach. Its owner said, "Uff!" and tried to catch my arms, but they were tightly pinioned. His stomach was soft but his arms were like steel. He slowly squeezed the breath out of me. I could not move. Suddenly he was jerked backwards and flung on the ground, almost carrying me with him. I thought, Jem's up.

One's mind works very slowly at times. Stunned, I stood there dumbly. The scuffling noises were dying; someone wheezed and the night was still again.

Still but for a man breathing heavily, breathing heavily and staggering. I thought he went to the tree and leaned against it. He coughed violently, a sobbing, bone-shaking cough.

"Jem?"

There was no answer but the man's heavy breathing.

"Jem?"

Jem didn't answer.

The man began moving around, as if searching for something. I heard him groan and pull something heavy along the ground. It was slowly coming to me that there were now four people under the tree.

"Atticus . . . ?"

The man was walking heavily and unsteadily toward the road.

I went to where I thought he had been and felt frantically along the ground, reaching out with my toes. Presently I touched someone.

"Jem?"

My toes touched trousers, a belt buckle, buttons, something I could not identify, a collar, and a face. A prickly stubble on the face told me it was not Jem's. I smelled stale whiskey.

I made my way along in what I thought was the direction of the road. I was not sure, because I had been turned around so many times. But I found it and looked down to the street light. A man was passing under it. The man was walking with the staccato steps of someone carrying a load too heavy for him. He was going around the corner. He was carrying Jem. Jem's arm was dangling crazily in front of him.

By the time I reached the corner the man was crossing our front yard. Light from our front door framed Atticus for an instant; he ran down the steps, and together, he and the man took Jem inside.

I was at the front door when they were going down the hall. Aunt Alexandra was running to meet me. "Call Dr. Reynolds!" Atticus's voice came sharply from Jem's room. "Where's Scout?"

"Here she is," Aunt Alexandra called, pulling me along with her to the telephone. She tugged at me anxiously. "I'm all right, Aunty," I said, "you better call."

She pulled the receiver from the hook and said, "Eula May, get Dr. Reynolds, quick!"

"Agnes, is your father home? Oh God, where is he? Please tell him to come over here as soon as he comes in. Please, it's urgent!"

There was no need for Aunt Alexandra to identify herself; people in Maycomb knew each other's voices.

Atticus came out of Jem's room. The moment Aunt Alexandra broke the connection, Atticus took the receiver from her. He rattled the hook, then said, "Eula May, get me the sheriff, please."

"Heck? Atticus Finch. Someone's been after my children. Jem's hurt. Between here and the schoolhouse. I can't leave my boy. Run out there for me, please, and see if he's still around. Doubt if you'll find him now, but I'd like to see him if you do. Got to go now. Thanks, Heck."

"Atticus, is Jem dead?"

"No, Scout. Look after her, sister," he called, as he went down the hall.

Aunt Alexandra's fingers trembled as she unwound the crushed fabric and wire from around me. "Are you all right, darling?" she asked over and over as she worked me free.

It was a relief to be out. My arms were beginning to tingle, and they were red with small hexagonal marks. I rubbed them, and they felt better.

"Aunty, is Jem dead?"

"No—no, darling, he's unconscious. We won't know how badly he's hurt until Dr. Reynolds gets here. Jean Louise, what happened?"

"I don't know."

She left it at that. She brought me something to put on, and had I thought about it then, I would have never let her forget it: in her distraction, Aunty brought me my overalls. "Put these on, darling," she said, handing me the garments she most despised.

She rushed back to Jem's room, then came to me in the hall. She patted me vaguely, and went back to Jem's room.

A car stopped in front of the house. I knew Dr. Reynolds's step almost as well as my father's. He had brought Jem and me into the world, had led us through every childhood disease known to man including the time Jem fell out of the treehouse, and he had never lost our friendship. Dr. Reynolds said if we had been boil-prone things would have been different, but we doubted it.

He came in the door and said, "Good Lord." He walked toward me, said, "You're still standing," and changed his course. He knew every room in the house. He also knew that if I was in bad shape, so was Jem.

After ten forevers Dr. Reynolds returned. "Is Jem dead?" I asked.

"Far from it," he said, squatting down to me. "He's got a bump on the head just like yours, and a broken arm. Scout, look that way—no, don't turn your head, roll your eyes. Now look over yonder. He's got a bad break, so far as I can tell now it's in the elbow. Like somebody tried to wring his arm off . . . now look at me."

"Then he's not dead?"

"No-o!" Dr. Reynolds got to his feet. "We can't do much tonight," he said, "except try to make him as comfortable as

304

we can. We'll have to X-ray his arm—looks like he'll be wearing his arm 'way out by his side for a while. Don't worry, though, he'll be as good as new. Boys his age bounce."

While he was talking, Dr. Reynolds had been looking keenly at me, lightly fingering the bump that was coming on my forehead. "You don't feel broke anywhere, do you?"

Dr. Reynolds's small joke made me smile. "Then you don't think he's dead, then?"

He put on his hat. "Now I may be wrong, of course, but I think he's very alive. Shows all the symptoms of it. Go have a look at him, and when I come back we'll get together and decide."

Dr. Reynolds's step was young and brisk. Mr. Heck Tate's was not. His heavy boots punished the porch and he opened the door awkwardly, but he said the same thing Dr. Reynolds said when he came in. "You all right, Scout?" he added.

"Yes sir, I'm goin' in to see Jem. Atticus'n'them's in there."

"I'll go with you," said Mr. Tate.

Aunt Alexandra had shaded Jem's reading light with a towel, and his room was dim. Jem was lying on his back. There was an ugly mark along one side of his face. His left arm lay out from his body; his elbow was bent slightly, but in the wrong direction. Jem was frowning.

"Jem . . . ?"

Atticus spoke. "He can't hear you, Scout, he's out like a light. He was coming around, but Dr. Reynolds put him out again."

"Yes sir." I retreated. Jem's room was large and square. Aunt Alexandra was sitting in a rocking-chair by the fireplace. The man who brought Jem in was standing in a corner, leaning against the wall. He was some countryman I did not know. He had probably been at the pageant, and was in the vicinity when it happened. He must have heard our screams and come running.

Atticus was standing by Jem's bed.

Mr. Heck Tate stood in the doorway. His hat was in his

hand, and a flashlight bulged from his pants pocket. He was in his working clothes.

"Come in, Heck," said Atticus. "Did you find anything? I can't conceive of anyone low-down enough to do a thing like this, but I hope you found him."

Mr. Tate sniffed. He glanced sharply at the man in the corner, nodded to him, then looked around the room—at Jem, at Aunt Alexandra, then at Atticus.

"Sit down, Mr. Finch," he said pleasantly.

Atticus said, "Let's all sit down. Have that chair, Heck. I'll get another one from the livingroom."

Mr. Tate sat in Jem's desk chair. He waited until Atticus returned and settled himself. I wondered why Atticus had not brought a chair for the man in the corner, but Atticus knew the ways of country people far better than I. Some of his rural clients would park their long-eared steeds under the china-berry trees in the back yard, and Atticus would often keep appointments on the back steps. This one was probably more comfortable where he was.

"Mr. Finch," said Mr. Tate, "tell you what I found. I found a little girl's dress—it's out there in my car. That your dress, Scout?"

"Yes sir, if it's a pink one with smockin'," I said. Mr. Tate was behaving as if he were on the witness stand. He liked to tell things his own way, untrammeled by state or defense, and sometimes it took him a while.

"I found some funny-looking pieces of muddy-colored cloth—"

"That's m'costume, Mr. Tate."

Mr. Tate ran his hands down his thighs. He rubbed his left arm and investigated Jem's mantelpiece, then he seemed to be interested in the fireplace. His fingers sought his long nose.

"What is it, Heck?" said Atticus.

Mr. Tate found his neck and rubbed it. "Bob Ewell's lyin' on the ground under that tree down yonder with a kitchen knife stuck up under his ribs. He's dead, Mr. Finch."

29

Aunt Alexandra got up and reached for the mantelpiece. Mr. Tate rose, but she declined assistance. For once in his life, Atticus's instinctive courtesy failed him: he sat where he was.

Somehow, I could think of nothing but Mr. Bob Ewell saying he'd get Atticus if it took him the rest of his life. Mr. Ewell almost got him, and it was the last thing he did.

"Are you sure?" Atticus said bleakly.

"He's dead all right," said Mr. Tate. "He's good and dead. He won't hurt these children again."

"I didn't mean that." Atticus seemed to be talking in his sleep. His age was beginning to show, his one sign of inner turmoil: the strong line of his jaw melted a little, one became aware of telltale creases forming under his ears, one noticed not his jet-black hair but the gray patches growing at his temples.

"Hadn't we better go to the livingroom?" Aunt Alexandra said at last.

"If you don't mind," said Mr. Tate, "I'd rather us stay in here if it won't hurt Jem any. I want to have a look at his injuries while Scout . . . tells us about it."

"Is it all right if I leave?" she asked. "I'm just one person too many in here. I'll be in my room if you want me, Atticus." Aunt Alexandra went to the door, but she stopped and turned. "Atticus, I had a feeling about this tonight—I—this is my fault," she began. "I should have—"

Mr. Tate held up his hand. "You go ahead, Miss Alexandra, I know it's been a shock to you. And don't you fret yourself about anything—why, if we followed our feelings all the time we'd be like cats chasin' their tails. Miss Scout, see if you can tell us what happened, while it's still fresh in your mind. You think you can? Did you see him following you?"

I went to Atticus and felt his arms go around me. I buried my head in his lap. "We started home. I said Jem, I've forgot m'shoes. Soon's we started back for 'em the lights went out. Jem said I could get 'em tomorrow. . . ."

"Scout, raise up so Mr. Tate can hear you," Atticus said. I crawled into his lap.

"Then Jem said hush a minute. I thought he was thinkin'—he always wants you to hush so he can think—then he said he heard somethin'. We thought it was Cecil."

"Cecil?"

"Cecil Jacobs. He scared us once tonight, an' we thought it was him again. He had on a sheet. They gave a quarter for the best costume, I don't know who won it—"

"Where were you when you thought it was Cecil?"

"Just a little piece from the schoolhouse. I yelled somethin' at him—"

"You yelled, what?"

"Cecil Jacobs is a big fat hen, I think. We didn't hear nothin'—then Jem yelled hello or somethin' loud enough to wake the dead—"

"Just a minute, Scout," said Mr. Tate. "Mr. Finch, did you hear them?"

Atticus said he didn't. He had the radio on. Aunt Alexandra had hers going in her bedroom. He remembered because she told him to turn his down a bit so she could hear hers. Atticus smiled. "I always play a radio too loud."

"I wonder if the neighbors heard anything. . . ." said Mr. Tate.

"I doubt it, Heck. Most of them listen to their radios or go to bed with the chickens. Maudie Atkinson may have been up, but I doubt it."

"Go ahead, Scout," Mr. Tate said.

"Well, after Jem yelled we walked on. Mr. Tate, I was shut

308

up in my costume but I could hear it myself, then. Footsteps, I mean. They walked when we walked and stopped when we stopped. Jem said he could see me because Mrs. Crenshaw put some kind of shiny paint on my costume. I was a ham."

"How's that?" asked Mr. Tate, startled.

Atticus described my role to Mr. Tate, plus the construction of my garment. "You should have seen her when she came in," he said, "it was crushed to a pulp."

Mr. Tate rubbed his chin. "I wondered why he had those marks on him. His sleeves were perforated with little holes. There were one or two little puncture marks on his arms to match the holes. Let me see that thing if you will, sir."

Atticus fetched the remains of my costume. Mr. Tate turned it over and bent it around to get an idea of its former shape. "This thing probably saved her life," he said. "Look."

He pointed with a long forefinger. A shiny clean line stood out on the dull wire. "Bob Ewell meant business," Mr. Tate muttered.

"He was out of his mind," said Atticus.

"Don't like to contradict you, Mr. Finch—wasn't crazy, mean as hell. Low-down skunk with enough liquor in him to make him brave enough to kill children. He'd never have met you face to face."

Atticus shook his head. "I can't conceive of a man who'd—"

"Mr. Finch, there's just some kind of men you have to shoot before you can say hidy to 'em. Even then, they ain't worth the bullet it takes to shoot 'em. Ewell 'as one of 'em."

Atticus said, "I thought he got it all out of him the day he threatened me. Even if he hadn't, I thought he'd come after me."

"He had guts enough to pester a poor colored woman, he had guts enough to pester Judge Taylor when he thought the house was empty, so do you think he'da met you to your face in daylight?" Mr. Tate sighed. "We'd better get on. Scout, you heard him behind you—"

"Yes sir. When we got under the tree—"

"How'd you know you were under the tree, you couldn't see thunder out there."

"I was barefooted, and Jem says the ground's always cooler under a tree."

"We'll have to make him a deputy, go ahead."

"Then all of a sudden somethin' grabbed me an' mashed my costume . . . think I ducked on the ground . . . heard a tusslin' under the tree sort of . . . they were bammin' against the trunk, sounded like. Jem found me and started pullin' me toward the road. Some—Mr. Ewell yanked him down, I reckon. They tussled some more and then there was this funny noise—Jem hollered . . ." I stopped. That was Jem's arm.

"Anyway, Jem hollered and I didn't hear him any more an' the next thing—Mr. Ewell was tryin' to squeeze me to death, I reckon . . . then somebody yanked Mr. Ewell down. Jem must have got up, I guess. That's all I know . . ."

"And then?" Mr. Tate was looking at me sharply.

"Somebody was staggerin' around and pantin' and—coughing fit to die. I thought it was Jem at first, but it didn't sound like him, so I went lookin' for Jem on the ground. I thought Atticus had come to help us and had got wore out—"

"Who was it?"

"Why there he is, Mr. Tate, he can tell you his name."

As I said it, I half pointed to the man in the corner, but brought my arm down quickly lest Atticus reprimand me for pointing. It was impolite to point.

He was still leaning against the wall. He had been leaning against the wall when I came into the room, his arms folded across his chest. As I pointed he brought his arms down and pressed the palms of his hands against the wall. They were white hands, sickly white hands that had never seen the sun, so white they stood out garishly against the dull cream wall in the dim light of Jem's room.

I looked from his hands to his sand-stained khaki pants; my eyes traveled up his thin frame to his torn denim shirt.

310

His face was as white as his hands, but for a shadow on his jutting chin. His cheeks were thin to hollowness; his mouth was wide; there were shallow, almost delicate indentations at his temples, and his gray eyes were so colorless I thought he was blind. His hair was dead and thin, almost feathery on top of his head.

When I pointed to him his palms slipped slightly, leaving greasy sweat streaks on the wall, and he hooked his thumbs in his belt. A strange small spasm shook him, as if he heard fingernails scrape slate, but as I gazed at him in wonder the tension slowly drained from his face. His lips parted into a timid smile, and our neighbor's image blurred with my sudden tears.

"Hey, Boo," I said.

.

30

Mr. Arthur, honey," said Atticus, gently correcting me. "Jean Louise, this is Mr. Arthur Radley. I believe he already knows you."

If Atticus could blandly introduce me to Boo Radley at a time like this, well—that was Atticus.

Boo saw me run instinctively to the bed where Jem was sleeping, for the same shy smile crept across his face. Hot with embarrassment, I tried to cover up by covering Jem up.

"Ah-ah, don't touch him," Atticus said.

Mr. Heck Tate sat looking intently at Boo through his horn-rimmed glasses. He was about to speak when Dr. Reynolds came down the hall.

"Everybody out," he said, as he came in the door. "Evenin', Arthur, didn't notice you the first time I was here."

Dr. Reynolds's voice was as breezy as his step, as though he had said it every evening of his life, an announcement that astounded me even more than being in the same room with Boo Radley. Of course . . . even Boo Radley got sick sometimes, I thought. But on the other hand I wasn't sure.

Dr. Reynolds was carrying a big package wrapped in newspaper. He put it down on Jem's desk and took off his coat. "You're quite satisfied he's alive, now? Tell you how I knew. When I tried to examine him he kicked me. Had to put him out good and proper to touch him. So scat," he said to me.

"Er—" said Atticus, glancing at Boo. "Heck, let's go out on the front porch. There are plenty of chairs out there, and it's still warm enough."

I wondered why Atticus was inviting us to the front porch instead of the livingroom, then I understood. The livingroom lights were awfully strong.

We filed out, first Mr. Tate—Atticus was waiting at the door for him to go ahead of him. Then he changed his mind and followed Mr. Tate.

People have a habit of doing everyday things even under the oddest conditions. I was no exception: "Come along, Mr. Arthur," I heard myself saying, "you don't know the house real well. I'll just take you to the porch, sir."

He looked down at me and nodded.

I led him through the hall and past the livingroom.

"Won't you have a seat, Mr. Arthur? This rocking-chair's nice and comfortable."

My small fantasy about him was alive again: he would be sitting on the porch . . . right pretty spell we're having, isn't it, Mr. Arthur?

Yes, a right pretty spell. Feeling slightly unreal, I led him to the chair farthest from Atticus and Mr. Tate. It was in deep shadow. Boo would feel more comfortable in the dark.

Atticus was sitting in the swing, and Mr. Tate was in a chair next to him. The light from the livingroom windows was strong on them. I sat beside Boo.

"Well, Heck," Atticus was saying, "I guess the thing to do—good Lord, I'm losing my memory . . ." Atticus pushed up his glasses and pressed his fingers to his eyes. "Jem's not quite thirteen . . . no, he's already thirteen—I can't remember. Anyway, it'll come before county court—"

"What will, Mr. Finch?" Mr. Tate uncrossed his legs and leaned forward.

"Of course it was clear-cut self-defense, but I'll have to go to the office and hunt up—"

"Mr. Finch, do you think Jem killed Bob Ewell? Do you think that?"

"You heard what Scout said, there's no doubt about it. She said Jem got up and yanked him off her—he probably got hold of Ewell's knife somehow in the dark . . . we'll find out tomorrow."

"Mis-ter Finch, hold on," said Mr. Tate. "Jem never stabbed Bob Ewell."

Atticus was silent for a moment. He looked at Mr. Tate as if he appreciated what he said. But Atticus shook his head.

"Heck, it's mighty kind of you and I know you're doing it from that good heart of yours, but don't start anything like that."

Mr. Tate got up and went to the edge of the porch. He spat into the shrubbery, then thrust his hands into his hip pockets and faced Atticus. "Like what?" he said.

"I'm sorry if I spoke sharply, Heck," Atticus said simply, "but nobody's hushing this up. I don't live that way."

"Nobody's gonna hush anything up, Mr. Finch."

Mr. Tate's voice was quiet, but his boots were planted so solidly on the porch floorboards it seemed that they grew there. A curious contest, the nature of which eluded me, was developing between my father and the sheriff.

It was Atticus's turn to get up and go to the edge of the porch. He said, "H'rm," and spat dryly into the yard. He put his hands in his pockets and faced Mr. Tate.

"Heck, you haven't said it, but I know what you're thinking. Thank you for it. Jean Louise—" he turned to me. "You said Jem yanked Mr. Ewell off you?"

"Yes sir, that's what I thought . . . I—"

"See there, Heck? Thank you from the bottom of my heart, but I don't want my boy starting out with something like this over his head. Best way to clear the air is to have it all out in the open. Let the county come and bring sandwiches. I don't want him growing up with a whisper about him, I don't want anybody saying, 'Jem Finch . . . his daddy paid a mint to get him out of that.' Sooner we get this over with the better."

"Mr. Finch," Mr. Tate said stolidly, "Bob Ewell fell on his knife. He killed himself."

Atticus walked to the corner of the porch. He looked at

the wisteria vine. In his own way, I thought, each was as stubborn as the other. I wondered who would give in first. Atticus's stubbornness was quiet and rarely evident, but in some ways he was as set as the Cunninghams. Mr. Tate's was unschooled and blunt, but it was equal to my father's.

"Heck," Atticus's back was turned. "If this thing's hushed up it'll be a simple denial to Jem of the way I've tried to raise him. Sometimes I think I'm a total failure as a parent, but I'm all they've got. Before Jem looks at anyone else he looks at me, and I've tried to live so I can look squarely back at him . . . if I connived at something like this, frankly I couldn't meet his eye, and the day I can't do that I'll know I've lost him. I don't want to lose him and Scout, because they're all I've got."

"Mr. Finch." Mr. Tate was still planted to the floorboards. "Bob Ewell fell on his knife. I can prove it."

Atticus wheeled around. His hands dug into his pockets. "Heck, can't you even try to see it my way? You've got children of your own, but I'm older than you. When mine are grown I'll be an old man if I'm still around, but right now I'm—if they don't trust me they won't trust anybody. Jem and Scout know what happened. If they hear of me saying downtown something different happened—Heck, I won't have them any more. I can't live one way in town and another way in my home."

Mr. Tate rocked on his heels and said patiently, "He'd flung Jem down, he stumbled over a root under that tree and—look, I can show you."

Mr. Tate reached in his side pocket and withdrew a long switch-blade knife. As he did so, Dr. Reynolds came to the door. "The son—deceased's under that tree, doctor, just inside the schoolyard. Got a flashlight? Better have this one."

"I can ease around and turn my car lights on," said Dr. Reynolds, but he took Mr. Tate's flashlight. "Jem's all right. He won't wake up tonight, I hope, so don't worry. That the knife that killed him, Heck?"

"No sir, still in him. Looked like a kitchen knife from the handle. Ken oughta be there with the hearse by now, doctor. 'night."

Mr. Tate flicked open the knife. "It was like this," he said. He held the knife and pretended to stumble; as he leaned forward his left arm went down in front of him. "See there? Stabbed himself through that soft stuff between his ribs. His whole weight drove it in."

Mr. Tate closed the knife and jammed it back in his pocket. "Scout is eight years old," he said. "She was too scared to know exactly what went on."

"You'd be surprised," Atticus said grimly.

"I'm not sayin' she made it up, I'm sayin' she was too scared to know exactly what happened. It was mighty dark out there, black as ink. 'd take somebody mighty used to the dark to make a competent witness . . ."

"I won't have it," Atticus said softly.

"God damn it, I'm not thinking of Jem!"

Mr. Tate's boot hit the floorboards so hard the lights in Miss Maudie's bedroom went on. Miss Stephanie Crawford's lights went on. Atticus and Mr. Tate looked across the street, then at each other. They waited.

When Mr. Tate spoke again his voice was barely audible. "Mr. Finch, I hate to fight you when you're like this. You've been under a strain tonight no man should ever have to go through. Why you ain't in the bed from it I don't know, but I do know that for once you haven't been able to put two and two together, and we've got to settle this tonight because tomorrow'll be too late. Bob Ewell's got a kitchen knife in his craw."

Mr. Tate added that Atticus wasn't going to stand there and maintain that any boy Jem's size with a busted arm had fight enough left in him to tackle and kill a grown man in the pitch dark.

"Heck," said Atticus abruptly, "that was a switchblade you were waving. Where'd you get it?"

316

"Took it off a drunk man," Mr. Tate answered coolly.

I was trying to remember. Mr. Ewell was on me . . . then he went down. . . . Jem must have gotten up. At least I thought . . .

"Heck?"

"I said I took it off a drunk man downtown tonight. Ewell probably found that kitchen knife in the dump somewhere. Honed it down and bided his time . . . just bided his time."

Atticus made his way to the swing and sat down. His hands dangled limply between his knees. He was looking at the floor. He had moved with the same slowness that night in front of the jail, when I thought it took him forever to fold his newspaper and toss it in his chair.

Mr. Tate clumped softly around the porch. "It ain't your decision, Mr. Finch, it's all mine. It's my decision and my responsibility. For once, if you don't see it my way, there's not much you can do about it. If you wanta try, I'll call you a liar to your face. Your boy never stabbed Bob Ewell," he said slowly, "didn't come near a mile of it and now you know it. All he wanted to do was get him and his sister safely home."

Mr. Tate stopped pacing. He stopped in front of Atticus, and his back was to us. "I'm not a very good man, sir, but I am sheriff of Maycomb County. Lived in this town all my life an' I'm goin' on forty-three years old. Know everything that's happened here since before I was born. There's a black boy dead for no reason, and the man responsible for it's dead. Let the dead bury the dead this time, Mr. Finch. Let the dead bury the dead."

Mr. Tate went to the swing and picked up his hat. It was lying beside Atticus. Mr. Tate pushed back his hair and put his hat on.

"I never heard tell that it's against the law for a citizen to do his utmost to prevent a crime from being committed, which is exactly what he did, but maybe you'll say it's my duty to tell the town all about it and not hush it up. Know what'd happen then? All the ladies in Maycomb includin' my wife'd be knocking on his door bringing angel food cakes. To my way of thinkin', Mr. Finch, taking the one man who's done you and this town a great service an' draggin' him with his shy ways into the limelight—to me, that's a sin. It's a sin and I'm not about to have it on my head. If it was any other man it'd be different. But not this man, Mr. Finch."

Mr. Tate was trying to dig a hole in the floor with the toe of his boot. He pulled his nose, then he massaged his left arm. "I may not be much, Mr. Finch, but I'm still sheriff of Maycomb County and Bob Ewell fell on his knife. Good night, sir."

Mr. Tate stamped off the porch and strode across the front yard. His car door slammed and he drove away.

Atticus sat looking at the floor for a long time. Finally he raised his head. "Scout," he said, "Mr. Ewell fell on his knife. Can you possibly understand?"

Atticus looked like he needed cheering up. I ran to him and hugged him and kissed him with all my might. "Yes sir, I understand," I reassured him. "Mr. Tate was right."

Atticus disengaged himself and looked at me. "What do you mean?"

"Well, it'd be sort of like shootin' a mockingbird, wouldn't it?"

Atticus put his face in my hair and rubbed it. When he got up and walked across the porch into the shadows, his youthful step had returned. Before he went inside the house, he stopped in front of Boo Radley. "Thank you for my children, Arthur," he said.

31

When Boo Radley shuffled to his feet, light from the living-room windows glistened on his forehead. Every move he made was uncertain, as if he were not sure his hands and feet could make proper contact with the things he touched. He coughed his dreadful raling cough, and was so shaken he had to sit down again. His hand searched for his hip pocket, and he pulled out a handkerchief. He coughed into it, then he wiped his forehead.

Having been so accustomed to his absence, I found it incredible that he had been sitting beside me all this time, present. He had not made a sound.

Once more, he got to his feet. He turned to me and nodded toward the front door.

"You'd like to say good night to Jem, wouldn't you, Mr. Arthur? Come right in."

I led him down the hall. Aunt Alexandra was sitting by Jem's bed. "Come in, Arthur," she said. "He's still asleep. Dr. Reynolds gave him a heavy sedative. Jean Louise, is your father in the livingroom?"

"Yes ma'am, I think so."

"I'll just go speak to him a minute. Dr. Reynolds left some . . ." her voice trailed away.

Boo had drifted to a corner of the room, where he stood with his chin up, peering from a distance at Jem. I took him by the hand, a hand surprisingly warm for its whiteness. I tugged him a little, and he allowed me to lead him to Jem's bed.

Dr. Reynolds had made a tent-like arrangement over Jem's

arm, to keep the cover off, I guess, and Boo leaned forward and looked over it. An expression of timid curiosity was on his face, as though he had never seen a boy before. His mouth was slightly open, and he looked at Jem from head to foot. Boo's hand came up, but he let it drop to his side.

"You can pet him, Mr. Arthur, he's asleep. You couldn't if he was awake, though, he wouldn't let you . . ." I found myself explaining. "Go ahead."

Boo's hand hovered over Jem's head.

"Go on, sir, he's asleep."

His hand came down lightly on Jem's hair.

I was beginning to learn his body English. His hand tightened on mine and he indicated that he wanted to leave.

I led him to the front porch, where his uneasy steps halted. He was still holding my hand and he gave no sign of letting me go.

"Will you take me home?"

He almost whispered it, in the voice of a child afraid of the dark.

I put my foot on the top step and stopped. I would lead him through our house, but I would never lead him home.

"Mr. Arthur, bend your arm down here, like that. That's right, sir."

I slipped my hand into the crook of his arm.

He had to stoop a little to accommodate me, but if Miss Stephanie Crawford was watching from her upstairs window, she would see Arthur Radley escorting me down the sidewalk, as any gentleman would do.

We came to the street light on the corner, and I wondered how many times Dill had stood there hugging the fat pole, watching, waiting, hoping. I wondered how many times Jem and I had made this journey, but I entered the Radley front gate for the second time in my life. Boo and I walked up the steps to the porch. His fingers found the front doorknob. He gently released my hand, opened the door, went inside, and shut the door behind him. I never saw him again.

Neighbors bring food with death and flowers with sickness and little things in between. Boo was our neighbor. He gave us two soap dolls, a broken watch and chain, a pair of good-luck pennies, and our lives. But neighbors give in return. We never put back into the tree what we took out of it: we had given him nothing, and it made me sad.

I turned to go home. Street lights winked down the street all the way to town. I had never seen our neighborhood from this angle. There were Miss Maudie's, Miss Stephanie's— there was our house, I could see the porch swing—Miss Rachel's house was beyond us, plainly visible. I could even see Mrs. Dubose's.

I looked behind me. To the left of the brown door was a long shuttered window. I walked to it, stood in front of it, and turned around. In daylight, I thought, you could see to the postoffice corner.

Daylight . . . in my mind, the night faded. It was daytime and the neighborhood was busy. Miss Stephanie Crawford crossed the street to tell the latest to Miss Rachel. Miss Maudie bent over her azaleas. It was summertime, and two children scampered down the sidewalk toward a man approaching in the distance. The man waved, and the children raced each other to him.

It was still summertime, and the children came closer. A boy trudged down the sidewalk dragging a fishing-pole behind him. A man stood waiting with his hands on his hips. Summertime, and his children played in the front yard with their friend, enacting a strange little drama of their own invention.

It was fall, and his children fought on the sidewalk in front of Mrs. Dubose's. The boy helped his sister to her feet, and they made their way home. Fall, and his children trotted to and fro around the corner, the day's woes and triumphs on their faces. They stopped at an oak tree, delighted, puzzled, apprehensive.

Winter, and his children shivered at the front gate, silhouetted against a blazing house. Winter, and a man walked into the street, dropped his glasses, and shot a dog.

Summer, and he watched his children's heart break. Autumn again, and Boo's children needed him.

Atticus was right. One time he said you never really know a man until you stand in his shoes and walk around in them. Just standing on the Radley porch was enough.

The street lights were fuzzy from the fine rain that was falling. As I made my way home, I felt very old, but when I looked at the tip of my nose I could see fine misty beads, but looking cross-eyed made me dizzy so I quit. As I made my way home, I thought what a thing to tell Jem tomorrow. He'd be so mad he missed it he wouldn't speak to me for days. As I made my way home, I thought Jem and I would get grown but there wasn't much else left for us to learn, except possibly algebra.

I ran up the steps and into the house. Aunt Alexandra had gone to bed, and Atticus's room was dark. I would see if Jem might be reviving. Atticus was in Jem's room, sitting by his bed. He was reading a book.

"Is Jem awake yet?"

"Sleeping peacefully. He won't be awake until morning."

"Oh. Are you sittin' up with him?"

"Just for an hour or so. Go to bed, Scout. You've had a long day."

"Well, I think I'll stay with you for a while."

"Suit yourself," said Atticus. It must have been after midnight, and I was puzzled by his amiable acquiescence. He was shrewder than I, however: the moment I sat down I began to feel sleepy.

"Whatcha readin'?" I asked.

Atticus turned the book over. "Something of Jem's. Called *The Gray Ghost*."

I was suddenly awake. "Why'd you get that one?"

"Honey, I don't know. Just picked it up. One of the few things I haven't read," he said pointedly.

"Read it out loud, please, Atticus. It's real scary."

"No," he said. "You've had enough scaring for a while. This is too—"

"Atticus, I wasn't scared."

He raised his eyebrows, and I protested: "Leastways not till I started telling Mr. Tate about it. Jem wasn't scared. Asked him and he said he wasn't. Besides, nothin's real scary except in books."

Atticus opened his mouth to say something, but shut it again. He took his thumb from the middle of the book and turned back to the first page. I moved over and leaned my head against his knee. "H'rm," he said. "*The Gray Ghost*, by Seckatary Hawkins. Chapter One . . ."

I willed myself to stay awake, but the rain was so soft and the room was so warm and his voice was so deep and his knee was so snug that I slept.

Seconds later, it seemed, his shoe was gently nudging my ribs. He lifted me to my feet and walked me to my room. "Heard every word you said," I muttered. ". . . wasn't sleep at all, 's about a ship an' Three-Fingered Fred 'n' Stoner's Boy. . . ."

He unhooked my overalls, leaned me against him, and pulled them off. He held me up with one hand and reached for my pajamas with the other.

"Yeah, an' they all thought it was Stoner's Boy messin' up their clubhouse an' throwin' ink all over it an' . . ."

He guided me to the bed and sat me down. He lifted my legs and put me under the cover.

"An' they chased him 'n' never could catch him 'cause they didn't know what he looked like, an' Atticus, when they finally saw him, why he hadn't done any of those things . . . Atticus, he was real nice. . . ."

His hands were under my chin, pulling up the cover, tucking it around me.

"Most people are, Scout, when you finally see them."

He turned out the light and went into Jem's room. He would be there all night, and he would be there when Jem waked up in the morning.

323

About the Author

HARPER LEE was born in 1926 in Monroeville, Alabama. She is also the author of *Go Set a Watchman*, and has been awarded the Pulitzer Prize, the Presidential Medal of Freedom, and numerous other literary awards and honors.